GRAVE REFRAIN

A LOVE STORY

SARAH M. GLOVER

OMNIFIC PUBLISHING

DALLAS

Omnific Publishing
P.O. Box 793871, Dallas, TX 75379
www.omnificpublishing.com

First Omnific eBook edition, February 2012
First Omnific trade paperback edition, February 2012

The characters and events in this book are fictitious.
Any similarity to real persons, living or dead,
is coincidental and not intended by the author.

Library of Congress Cataloguing-in-Publication Data

Glover, Sarah M.
    Grave Refrain, A ~~Love~~ Ghost Story / Sarah M. Glover — 1st ed.
    ISBN 978-1-936305-90-2
    1. Love — Fiction. 2. Paranormal Romance — Fiction.
    3. San Francisco — Fiction. 4. Ghost — Fiction.
    I. Title

10 9 8 7 6 5 4 3 2 1

Cover Design by Micha Stone and Stephanie Swartz
Interior Book Design by Coreen Montagna

Printed in the United States of America

To Peter and Natalie, for their belief in ghosts.

Neil St. John wanted the young man to kill. He had killed the last two nights—brutally according to certain rumors, beautifully according to others. Unfortunately, Neil had not been there to witness it.

The mob pressed him on all sides as he battled his way to the last remaining table near the stage of the dark, subterranean club. The air reeked of pot, of hot, close bodies covered in sweat and anticipation. These were the scents he remembered from his youth, when the buzzing energy of bands drugged and seduced him with their violence and sound. And although this time he had come to London for other reasons, he inevitably found himself drawn back into the clubs, to where his life had begun so many years ago.

At about nine-thirty the opening act, an accordionist trying his best to channel They Might be Giants but without the requisite wit, abandoned the stage to two guitarists and a drummer. They hustled into position to raucous applause, waving briefly at the audience who appeared to know them well. They were clothed in the nameless rugby shirts and torn jeans that were the uniform of every other indie, pseudo-intellectual band Neil had encountered over the last decade, fresh from college, with little representation and even less money. A chosen few he had gone on to manage—to guide them to success, broker their recording deals, oversee the production of their albums, and stand behind them as they collected their fame—but most he had dismissed after hearing their first set.

Neil knew the sound he expected to expect tonight. There was little new under the sun, and all bands these days stole their styles from somewhere or someone else. "They're X, with some Y, reminiscent of Z," he had been quoted as saying recently in one of his rare interviews. For him, the variables and the math might change, but the songs remained the same. He had spent the last twenty years of his life searching for it to be otherwise, to find a group that gutted reason, battered his senses, and made him want to want. He sat straight in his chair, readying himself, each time expecting that miracle to happen.

His attention, as well as the rest of the room's, quickly focused on the lead guitarist, a young man who stood under the lights and stared out at the crowd. He wore the defiant awkwardness that most young rockers strived for, although the boy's face held something more. An impatience, perhaps? Whatever it was, it only intensified as he adjusted his guitar, checked his pedals, and tossed the ratty red scarf he wore about his neck. Closing his eyes, he whispered bitingly, "One, two — one, two, three, four…"

Sound exploded against the walls. Sound so raw and vibrant and — there were no other words for it — fucking joyous. The crowd screamed while young girls rocketed from their seats below the stage and gripped the edge of the small tables, their flame-colored nails impaling the bar napkins against the wood. Within minutes, those young men owned the universe, and all around them gathered there, in from the frozen London streets, a crowd lucky to be alive at that moment, to be in their orbit, to hear their words.

They played two more songs, each one ratcheting up the already eardrum-splitting cheering in the club. By the fourth number, people were on their feet, bodies slamming, arms over their heads. Ecstasy shone on the young man's face as he saw the crowd going wild. He closed his eyes and let loose a string of profanities so sharp, so wry and vicious, that Neil gripped the table himself.

The song ended in a blistering solo from the drummer, nothing but elbows and angles, his face a younger version of an older John Lennon — complete with round glasses — his coiled arms given license to bash and thrash. Next to him, the bass guitarist swayed on with his head down, all handsome dreadlocks, brown skin, wide open face, and bliss. He nodded to the lead guitarist, sharing the inside joke that lived in each band, the one you'd kill to know.

As the applause died down, the lead guitarist approached the microphone with a tense smile and leaned forward. "Thanks, thanks truly." In the harsh focus of the lights, sweat glistened on the converging angles of his face; a flush of red swept from his temple to his jaw, mirroring the scarf around his neck. His skin, a ruddy golden hue, was only slightly lighter than the disarray of his brown hair. Everything about him seemed alert — manic, even — from his eyes to his shoulders and forearms, down to his fingers that twisted continuously about the neck of his guitar. No part of him could stand still.

He shook the hair from his eyes, and in a fit of apparent frustration, blew the strands away with a loud raspberry followed by a muttered, "Christ."

Neil's breath stopped short; a ghost passed through his heart. He remembered the woman who had long ago done the same thing: over books, over a pint of bitter, over him.

"Evening. Thanks for coming out in this god-awful shit, yes? Snow? Ludicrous stuff, makes you want a drink, doesn't it?" He took a swig of a Guinness and toasted the shouting crowd, waiting until only a few hoots and cat calls remained. "Just finished our first album today. Thought it might be wise since we've left university a tad prematurely."

More shouts erupted as the bassist strummed the classic Pink Floyd riff dissing the need for education, which made the young man laugh. Neil was aware that everyone around him laughed — they had to, the young man had laughed.

"That's Christian Wood on bass, by the way — for your listening pleasure. And the incomparable Simon Godden on drums." He offered up another smile, but this one was filled with self-conscious gratitude. "And I'm Andrew Hayes. We are The Lost Boys."

In Neil's mind, the memory of the woman smiled. Yes, as if he could ever forget any detail about her. He'd heard she had a son. This boy couldn't be more than twenty-two, twenty-three at most, old enough to be her first born, perhaps.

Before Neil could orchestrate his thoughts any further, Andrew unplugged his guitar and set it on its stand. "This has been coming to me for a while now. Mostly in my dreams. Hope you like it. Okay, right…yes, right."

Neil watched Andrew's band mates watch Andrew. It was an ingrained response he had developed over years of practice. He learned more that way, studying a band's dynamic, searching for holes in their fabric, uncovering any potential warning signs. In this case, it distracted him from the dangerous path where his thoughts were heading. He saw concern battle curiosity as the boys stared at Andrew while he tightened a tuner and plucked the harmonics on the strings. Especially the drummer, who raised his chin, his eyes fixed on the guitarist's back.

The beginning chords were haunting, the words oddly poetic in their way, and Neil could understand the band mates' unease. Andrew had deviated from the set list, and by the looks of things, this was evidently a common occurrence. Not good.

It marked the young man's first mistake; it was too pretentious a choice for this crowd — a beginner's muck up, understandable but second-rate. He was too cheeky, too manic, and although his voice was poignant when stripped of everything else, he didn't have the gravitas to carry off this piece and not appear the sincere young man with his sincere guitar, busking on a street corner. This was the last thing this fired-up horde wanted to hear. Coughs would come next, followed by averted eyes, laughter, and then the cringing descent into heckling and boos. He felt sorry for this Andrew Hayes, but it was a necessary evil; every performer had to learn to read one's audience and recognize one's limitations. It also made Neil feel infinitely better. He could return to his accustomed sense of superiority, as the previous minutes had left him badly shaken. No, it was good to know the way the world turned.

Except the world had tilted. For everyone there, every man, every woman, responded to this young man. His music uncoiled, recalling memories of loss and longing and of words uttered too late. But it also offered hope — didn't swear it — just gave it away. And because of that, eyes teared up, couples grasped hands more tightly, and Neil knew without a shadow of a doubt that a great deal of people were going to get laid that night.

All too quickly the song ended. Then silence.

No one clapped. The young man sat there stoically, his hand muffling the strings as though they would give him the answer he was looking for. Then his painfully familiar face rose from the guitar, and the house came down.

Surprise overtook Andrew Hayes, or it might have been embarrassment. In response, he grabbed his Stratocaster like armor, and the three of them, these Lost Boys, ignited the stage in the same frenzied style as before.

Neil had to meet him.

"Well, I'd say that definitely didn't suck," Simon announced as he snapped shut the last of the equipment cases and shoved his drum sticks in the back pocket of his jeans.

The club had cleared out; only the bartender and a few waitresses remained. Andrew hadn't realized he'd been staring at one of them until she tilted her head in invitation. Immediately his gaze shot to the floor, an embarrassing blush heating his face. Ridiculous, he knew, given his stellar performance, not to mention his age. All he would have to do was smile in return; she would approach, he would crack a few jokes, and good night to all. Except he was too restless for sex, too restless to concentrate on pleasing someone. What he wanted was a cigarette, but he reminded himself he had quit, or tried to, or had at least hidden them in the glove box of the truck. *Christ.* Why wasn't she here tonight? He swore she would be here tonight. And that too was ridiculous.

"Yeah, if they all could suck like that, man," Christian crooned, his New Orleans' patois ever the perfect counterpoint to Simon's staccato Irish brogue. The beads on his dreadlocks clacked their approval, and he looked up at Andrew with a dazzling grin. "Though I got to say, that was a fine piece of music you played tonight. When did you write it?"

"That? That's nothing."

Andrew did not want to get into the details. They would only razz him, and he was too keyed up from coming off the high of performing for such an appreciative crowd. He needed sleep, yet he knew he wouldn't get more than his usual four hours. Plus, he was wallowing in self-pity again. She was not here tonight. Why did he feel like she would be? Romantic tosh, he knew it was, all of it. He shook his head hoping to toss away the thought.

"You're getting that look again, my friend," said Simon. "We need to ditch the equipment and get you some fine—What's the name of the place across the street?"

"The Rat Hole," Andrew answered archly and slung his gig bag over his shoulder.

"Hmmm. Well then, some fine Rat Hole grub 'tis. Just bat those Byronic eyelashes of yours in the closest serving wench's direction."

"Will you let it lie, already? I do not have Byronic shit, understand?"

"He doth crap and the poets weep," Simon intoned, his hand over his heart.

"Sod off."

Simon took endless delight in quoting the most recent write-up the band had received. It had appeared in the local newspaper a few weeks earlier, and the writer, who could not control being twenty, pert, and blond, evidently could not control her painful vocabulary either and opted to gush nauseatingly about the band, Andrew in particular. *A coiled spring of Byronic sex*, was the most ghastly of the epithets she had burdened him with. But the gibe stuck.

"Come on, Paulie boy. I'm going to gnaw Christian's arm off if I don't get some food soon, so let's be off."

"If you stopped wearing those hideous glasses, you could be Paul instead."

"I'll never be Paul. No need."

Simon pushed his glasses up his long, thin nose with a pronounced shove of his middle finger, exactly as he had when Andrew had met him in their first year at school. He'd been a boy, all skin and bones, a veritable eleven-year-old Iggy Pop, wearing those same wire-rimmed, round glasses and a Chairman Mao jacket, forever searching for a fight or a rehearsal room.

The Rat Hole proved to be a postage stamp-sized restaurant that, from the chalkboard menu and the sticky Naugahyde booths, seemed to specialize in grease. A waitress stalked over to their table wearing an untied apron and a closing-time scowl. The few patrons remaining, pale and hunkered down over their drinks, appeared too intimidated by her to ask for another as she passed, but the moment she laid eyes on Andrew, Simon, and Christian, her pen and her smile clicked to attention.

Simon peered over his glasses at her waxy fuchsia lips. "What's your name, love?"

"Gloria."

He carefully spelled out her name as though gaining enlightenment. Before anyone knew what was happening, a grin burst across his face and he began to wail the chorus of the iconic song, causing the stricken waitress to drop her pad with a cry. Confusion reigned as Simon kept on, pausing only to order, while the other customers around them hunkered down further in their seats.

"Hit me," Christian shouted to Andrew over the din.

"You or him?"

"Him, actually, but hit me with it."

"'Gloria' by Van the Man, with his band at the time, Them. Recorded it in sixty-four on the B-side of 'Baby, Please Don't Go.' And Shadows of Knight released it in sixty-five and got it all the way to number ten."

"Covers?"

"Covered by every damn man alive, although I'm digging Simon's take on it. It's almost religious — makes you wish for death."

It was their thing. Christian or Simon would name an obscure lyric and see if Andrew could place it. He could — always — as well as the original recording and any subsequent covers. It drove them insane.

A few minutes later, the waitress returned and crammed a pyramid-like pile of burgers, onion rings, and pints of Guinness around them before swiftly departing.

"I've been in touch with some people in Amsterdam," Andrew announced midway through the meal, gauging his band mates' reaction on whether they paused in their gorging or not. "We can line up a decent string of gigs there after we finish our rounds here, then start up in Prague again before Berlin."

Simon swallowed hard in response, but his protests were interrupted when the door of the restaurant opened and a tall gentleman entered. Andrew hadn't fully appreciated the true squalor of the restaurant until it served as the backdrop for the man's Savile Row coat. Together with his tailored clothes and silk tie, Andrew reckoned his outfit probably cost more than their van *and* their equipment *and* their last two nights' draws, all combined. As the man approached, the anemic overhead lights accented the highlights in his dark blond hair and the laugh lines near the edges of his eyes that had left white quotation marks against his tanned skin.

"Cleaned favored and imperially slim," Andrew whispered to himself, quoting *Richard Cory*. It was the curse of his *almost* poetry major to see everything in stanzas, second only in uselessness to his *almost* music major. The man must either have been lost or needed to take a piss.

"Andrew Hayes?"

The fact that he knew Andrew's name didn't bode well. Andrew stood and extended his hand; good manners had been drilled into him since he had been old enough to slouch, and he reasoned whatever was coming, it would be better to just get it over with.

"The same," said Andrew cautiously.

The man removed his glove and offered his hand, his grip hard and immediate, like a polite arm wrestle. "May I?" He nodded to the booth where Simon and Christian sat.

"If we owe anything, we can't pay it. At least not until the last check clears. But we're good for it, or at least he is," Simon stated, pointing his finger at Andrew.

The man smiled and took a seat before motioning to the bartender to replenish the empty glasses on the table. Curious silence held them together, as though they were watching each other through a zoo enclosure. Andrew especially felt the man's scrutiny. Had they damaged something at the club? Was he some girl's father? Was he a dealer? He knew Simon had been clean for years, so he couldn't be a dealer. *Christ, please let him not be a dealer.*

The tension finally got the better of Simon, and he asked, "And you would be?"

"Neil St. John."

Andrew fell into his seat, not realizing he was still standing. His mind shot into overdrive. The name…he knew the name, but from where? Images flooded his consciousness first, as they always did, and then came the torrent of words and sounds: his favorite band, a television reporter, a face responding to questions. *How do you account for The Fractures' meteoric rise to success, when a few short months ago they were playing dive bars?* Then the screen cut to a face that held a curt smile and feigned interest. *They needed the proper help.* The caption read Neil St. John. *The* Neil St. John. But he had retired after helping to produce The Compositions' last album and was currently living in — oh, where the hell was it…San Francisco.

No, it couldn't be, Andrew thought. *Bloody Christ.* Evidently, Simon and Christian hadn't put two and two together yet, or weren't nearly as fazed as Andrew was by the fact that one of the world's greatest managers now sat a few feet away from them.

Perhaps that was for the best. The last thing Andrew wanted was for them to appear desperate, and Christian would never be able to control his excitement if he knew who this man truly was. Being in a band had never lost its initial thrill for him despite the sleepless nights, the rotten food, and the endless headaches. Getting someone like Neil St. John to back them would be huge. Beyond huge. Andrew felt his mouth go dry and his ADD make its way out of his hands as they began to play the underside of the table, fast and faster until he forced them flat in his lap.

"I was impressed by what I heard tonight. It's raw and needs work, a lot of work actually, but it's got something, something that could be incredible if you do the right things. You recorded an album. On what label?"

Andrew blinked, and his mind raced to comprehend the situation before him. "We don't have one. It's self-financed." He was not sure this was what Neil wanted to hear, yet the man's face gave nothing away. Christ, he had to stop his hands from shaking. Neil St. John. *The* Neil St. John.

"No manager, no agent?"

"Nothing."

"How do you do it?"

"Well…" Andrew took a deep breath. How did they do it? In the beginning, they had hired one Mr. Lou Fratteni, a squat, paunchy chartered-accountant type from Liverpool who claimed he knew the business inside and out. He ended up disappearing one night with most of their money and Andrew's best Cherryburst Les Paul. After that, they swore off the idea, deciding to manage the band on their own. It worked, or had worked for a while. Andrew knew they couldn't go on like this forever though; they needed help. It was too much — too much work, too much tension, too much everything.

"We manage pretty well. We exploit every form of social media we can get our hands on, and we're obsessively fan driven. Arrange our shows where we can gather the most bodies. Like tonight, we knew a ton of our fans would show up if we could book that particular site. See, we can usually fill up houses that way, that and by word-of-mouth. There isn't much left over for marketing   a little radio, flyers, and whatever the venue is willing to front." Andrew wanted to sound intelligent or at least intelligible, but his excitement left him rocking back and forth like his seat was on fire.

"We're the rock geek darlings of the Internet," Simon added, peering briefly over his glasses at his band mate. "We give our knickers away for free online, let 'em listen to our music, get them hooked, but make them pay at the door to hear it live." His hand curled around the handle of his glass, the letters I-R-O-N tattooed on the back of his fingers. Simon wiggled his pinky, emblazoned with a Y.

Over the next Guinness, Andrew could feel the anticipation hum around them much like the bristling nervous edge of walking onstage. It was apparent that Neil was interested; he seemed full of questions and noted their answers in errant scribbles on the paper placemats. How interested, who knew, but the communal sense of unease of a few minutes ago had given way to fast conversation, people talking over people, and in the back of Andrew's mind the future was quickly being reduced to this booth on Saturday, December 27, 2009. Their first conversation, the anthologies would say. He could see the article in *Spin*, with a black and white picture of the four of them leaning against the tattered booth.

"Wait, you've been touring for how long?" Neil asked, bringing Andrew back down to earth.

"Two straight years with no breaks," Christian answered, a hint of pride mingled with disbelief in his tone. "Unless you account for the time we took to record the album and the two weeks off for Christmas so my parents could scream at me for squandering my Cambridge scholarship. I told them I just couldn't get enough of living in a van with Euro-trash degenerates and using travel-sized mini-soaps."

Neil laughed out loud at that, which allowed the rest of them to join along.

"Christian was playing jazz downtown when we saved him from wasting his fine talents on decent pay," Simon interrupted, wanting to set the record straight. "We had left university and thought it would be a healthy career choice for him as well."

"Proving that slavery never died," added Christian.

"And you two? How did you meet?" Neil looked between Andrew and Simon.

"Go ahead," Simon offered with a wave of his glass, R-O-N-Y stretching wide. It was a story they had recited countless times, never tiring in the retelling, as it always gave them the opportunity to get a rise out of the other. "I'll correct it anyway. You always fuck it up, trying to make yourself look superior with that Byronic sex appeal."

"Christ." Andrew blew the long hair out of his eyes and shook his head, to which Neil took a measured swig of his drink.

"Simon ruined my otherwise exemplary boarding school experience. He got me thrown into detention more times than I can remember, the git. For the first two years of school we tortured each other—tor-tured each other," Andrew said, grinning and slapping his hand against the table as he dragged out the syllables.

"Then one day a music professor, who was either mental or more likely bloody sick of us, set us to compose our first piece of music together. He locked us in a rehearsal room—I mean literally locked us in with a few bottles of water and a tin of stale biscuits. We didn't leave that godforsaken place for fifteen hours, despite the kicking and the screaming."

"And the begging," interjected Simon.

"You begged. I never begged."

"Paulie boy here had to get taken down a notch or two. He needed to realize that there was a greater talent other than his out there under the sun. Everyone thought he could walk on water."

"Paulie?" Neil asked, smirking at Andrew.

"Simon is convinced he's John Lennon's love child. Long story," Andrew explained with a dismissive wave at Simon. "So by default, I'm Paul. Or I should say, he requires a Paul."

"And I, of course, look exactly like George," remarked Christian with a jangle of his dreads. "Not to mention that I've met Simon's mom, and I know for a fact she has a major problem with the whole love child thing. She knows exactly who the fathers are of all her children."

"And I'm her best hope. The rest of her family are out driving trolleys or doing construction if they're not drinking themselves shit-faced, while I'm off on scholarship to boarding school and university. No, I am firmly entrenched in the warm bosom of me mum, though she's not talking to me at the present. Hates the band as much as Christian's lot does. Thank God for Claudia. Now there's a peach of a woman, putting up with all our shit. I'd bloody marry the woman if she'd have me, but then I'd be related to this twat and I'd be forced to shoot myself."

"Claudia?" Neil repeated, his glass halfway to his lips.

"Andrew's mum. Thank God for her. She's our benefactor. Meal ticket. When we find ourselves in times of trouble, you get the picture."

"She lives nearby?" Neil asked, more insistent now.

Full of the swell of goodwill rising up inside of him, not to mention the continued flow of stout, Andrew formulated the idea on the spot. "Listen, we're heading over there next. She's having a small get together for us before we push off again, and it's loads more comfortable. Would you care to join us?"

Neil appeared aghast; in Andrew's dimming focus, it took him a minute to realize that it was already nearing midnight, and the thought of crashing some unknown lady's flat, no matter how posh, certainly wouldn't be his cup of tea. But instead of politely backing out, Neil's eyes focused directly on Andrew's.

"When are you going out on the road? Where?"

Andrew tried to look away but couldn't; Neil's gaze was too severe. "Well…we've got three shows set up in Glasgow first, and from there we'll head over to Edinburgh, then south to—"

"Andrew likes to keep moving. Thinks he'll find her if he visits every city on the globe," said Simon dryly.

"Who?" Neil asked.

"His muse."

"Excuse me?"

"Shut it, Simon," Andrew warned. The silence stretched thin between the two men. Simon downed the rest of his pint.

A string of idle small talk unraveled itself about the table before Neil hesitated and eyed his watch. "I must apologize, but I have another engagement, and I'm late, in fact."

All three men got up when Neil stood. The abruptness of his departure made Andrew want to pound the wall. Why the hell couldn't Simon keep his mouth shut? Why bring it up now when Neil would think he was certifiable? Fuck! But then Neil said the miraculous, causing all three musicians to stare at him in shock.

"You know, I'm remodeling a house in San Francisco and converting it into flats. It's a nasty business, headache and all. Can't really rent it in its current shape, but if you ever need a place to crash, I mean, if you find yourself in the city, it's yours. I could line up some gigs for you as well, keep you busy for some time."

"That's an incredibly generous offer."

As if sensing the incredulity in Simon's voice, Neil went on. "No really, you haven't seen the house. It's falling down around one's ears at the present. Rather difficult to retain a crew, you see. It's haunted. Charming, really." He added this last part as more of an excuse than explanation.

"Haunted?" Andrew blinked at Neil, wondering if he had heard him correctly. "As in a ghost?"

"No."

"Thank God, for a minute there I thought you said—"

"As in ghosts. Plural. Lovers, I suppose. They can't seem to locate one another other as they've never been seen in the same room at the same time. I gather it frustrates them, from the wailings going on. My wife even named them — Nick and Nora," he concluded as though he had no desire to discuss it further.

And with that, all of Andrew's hopes and dreams of the last few minutes came crashing down like an armful of cymbals. The man was mental. He believed in ghosts, literary ghosts perhaps, but ghosts nonetheless. Andrew glanced over to Simon and Christian to see if this revelation had the same effect on them but saw they were still slack jawed with wonder.

"Here's my card." They all stared down at the crisp, expensive-looking business card Neil placed on the table, ending for Andrew any chance of further clarification on the subject of the supernatural. "Like I said, look me up. I still have some pull in the industry, and there are plenty of first-rate venues to show off your talent properly, and we could chat more about your future. There's only so long you can continue to do this on your own, you know. You really need to take the next step."

With that, he tossed a sizable wad of cash on the table to cover the drinks and then some, shook their hands, and departed.

"Holy…fucking…hell." Simon grabbed the card as they all sat back down, but Christian pushed him aside, wrestling it from his hands.

Andrew's fingers began their incessant drumming again.

"Neil St. John. Neil fucking St. John." Simon whistled, his back slamming against the booth. "Neil St. John. Andrew, do you believe this? Lord Almighty. Here's what we're going to do. We go to San Francisco, play his gigs, and stay there as long as it takes to drag the bloke out of retirement. We'll offer to remodel the place on our own, if that's what's necessary."

Andrew didn't respond but sat staring at the door.

"Andrew…"

"No, I understand. This is bloody amazing…"

"But what?"

"But ghosts? The man sees ghosts. Multiple ghosts. He's named them."

"Who the hell cares?"

"You don't think it's a little strange that the man actually admits to seeing ghosts?"

"And you don't?"

"It's not the same."

"Oh, hell yes, it is. And the only difference is that he's met his ghosts and you never will."

"We should play the gigs we've lined up, finish out here before we—"

"Oh no. Oh no, no, no. Stop it. Stop it now. You can't be at all serious? You're not turning down this opportunity because the guy sees a few dead people. He could be blowing Elvis for all I care. When are you going to realize she's not out there? Even if we play every shithole from here to Bucharest, you're not going to find her. She's in your head. In your head, man—but I sure as hell wish she were flesh and blood so I could strangle her with my bare hands."

"I beg to differ," Christian offered, trying to diffuse the situation. "Personally, I'm cool with her living up in his head, or Graceland for that matter, as long as she keeps paying him a visit in his dreams every now and then. Makes for some incredible music. It's best not to mess with one's muse. Riles up the ghost world."

Simon rolled his eyes. "Cut the voodoo hoodoo shit."

"Hey, I learned that shit on my *tante's* knee. Our boy's haunted too. You got to respect that."

"No he's not! That muse of his isn't some ghost. She never was real and never will be real. He's got to give it up—it's not healthy." Simon turned to Andrew, trying to reason with him. "Listen, okay, listen…independent of this muse obsession of yours, or Christian's ghost world, or this bloody Nick and Nora, I think we all need some time to get our heads screwed on straight after the last two years. We've been on the road constantly. You especially—you've been going at it like a madman, writing all hours of the night, never sleeping, pushing yourself to do everything to fucking perfection. You drive yourself to the brink during every performance. And don't tell me you rested over Christmas. I know you didn't. Your mum told us you were haunting the pubs. You're going burn out or break down. Do you want to go through all that shit again?"

Andrew didn't answer.

"I think we need to stay in one place for a while. And not for just a few days, either. Let's relax for once before we head out again. This is a good thing. We play the gigs he lines up, he's stoked, he—"

"He what, Simon? Comes out of retirement and manages us?" Andrew caught himself. It was what he wanted, what he had fantasized about only minutes ago before Neil went delusional. But to stop moving, to drop anchor in one place?

"I don't know. But it sure as hell beats chasing after a woman that doesn't exist. You have to live in the real world. I'm not going back to Dublin with nothing to show for it, and I'm not playing studio back up for the rest of whatever. This is our chance."

The two men stared at each other; neither one moved. The few late night patrons had gone silent, and even Christian sat forward, convinced that this time Simon might actually haul off and punch his best friend.

"Because you know what, Paulie?" Simon slowly reached over and took hold of the malt vinegar bottle, IRONY tightening around the neck. Andrew didn't blink. Simon clenched it tighter. *This is it*, Christian's face read. *He's going to beat the living shit out of him*. Simon moved the bottle to his mouth as though he might rip the top off with his teeth, but instead he held it to his lips like a microphone. A second later he began to belt to all who would listen about pictures fading to black and white and time standing still.

A loud groan rose from the customers as they hunkered down under the new vocal onslaught. Andrew sat back, shaking his head and scrubbing his face with his hands while Simon carried on.

Christian pointed his finger at Andrew.

"Elton John," he shouted over the caterwauling. "Off of *Caribou*, nineteen seventy-four. Covers, again tons, but Maynard Ferguson did a wicked jazz rendition of it."

"You frighten me, Andrew, you really do. Hey, but seriously, have you had any other visitations from your muse? Any dreams?"

Andrew swallowed at Christian's question and dropped his glance into the bottom of his Guinness. "No."

Christian had always been completely accepting of Andrew's muse, which made Andrew feel a little less crazy, but he had searched for her all his life and he knew Christian was right. He was haunted in ways he could never explain and barely understood himself.

At some point during the last refrain, the cook trudged out of the kitchen brandishing a spatula, and Simon reluctantly sat back down. He grabbed another onion ring and waved it at Andrew.

"Forget her, my friend. Long term women, fantasy or otherwise, are not in the cards right now. And who needs them? Look at us, I mean, who would've thought we'd be sitting in this most fashionable dining establishment, feasting on these most succulent grease delivery vehicles when only a few years ago we were starving uni students?"

"I've got news for you, Simon. We're still starving."

"Ah, yes, but now we're starving and about to be dead famous," he said and popped the onion ring into his mouth.

"He's got a point," Christian said, nodding.

"I haven't said yes yet."

"But you will."

2

.

The flyer hung in the window of Vintage on the Haight. Emily Thomas had seen the same one a few blocks down at Amoeba Records and another one at The Red Vic. It was difficult to ignore with its blaring neon-yellow paper and jarring font. It had been equally difficult to ignore when her roommate, Zoey, had smacked it down on their kitchen counter that morning with a cry that she knew the bass guitarist and they had, had, *had* to go.

"Heartrending?" Emily repeated aloud. Frost was heartrending, Dickinson, Browning even. But a band? Somewhere a publicist needed to be shot.

With a shudder, she pushed open the shop's door. The romantic strains of Frank Sinatra greeted her as they did every Monday, Wednesday, and Friday evening, as did the musty scent of memories. She knew every item on each of the endless clothes racks and dilapidated mannequins long before her eyes adjusted to the glow of the shop's lights. The display and bookcases that she had helped stock full to the bursting point with everything from chipped Wedgewood tea sets to mismatched champagne flutes heaved a sigh of welcome. It was too much for such a small space, but there was nothing Emily would change; she would only add more and make it worse, yet better at the same time. Her sights settled on the old, Bantam rooster of a woman behind the counter who was busy sorting a tray of jewelry.

"Heartrending, Myra?" Emily announced while navigating around two hat racks and a Victorian fainting couch to make it to the white-haired woman's side. "Did you know the flyer in the window actually says 'heartrending'?"

"You're late."

"I'll tell you what heartrending is. Having your landlord announce you have one month to vacate the premises. That's heartrending. Facing life on a sewer grate and picking through the trash for breakfast. That's heartrending. Graduating with no hope of a job, that's—"

"I heard you." Myra paused in the examination of a brooch and tilted her cheek to receive Emily's kiss. "But you should have seen the young gentleman that handed that flyer to me. He looked like he should be in some old black and white movie, you know what I'm saying to you?" Her birdlike hands fluttered along a row of rings, and she plucked a few out for further inspection.

Emily waited. Who would it be today? Tyrone Power? Laurence Olivier? Last week, Emily had unwrapped a complete twelve-piece place setting of Havilland china listening to how Myra's unmarried podiatrist was the spitting image of a young Jimmy Stewart in *Mr. Smith Goes to Washington*. Evidently, Emily's imminent homelessness did not matter when eligible men were afoot.

"So, how are you today?"

"Biding my time until death claims me, what do you think? Now that boy who came in, he had the most gorgeous caramel brown skin, he did.

And his hair — like coffee with these honey streaks running through it, and you know what? He blushed when he asked me if I would hang the flyer in the window. My right hand to God. Blushed! How many young men blush any more, a deep cherry red even. Like a borscht."

"Sounds edible," Emily remarked dryly.

"Yes! Exactly. And he spoke like on *Masterpiece Theatre*, which slayed me. Stayed here quite a while, fascinated with the old records especially. And the books. The poetry, too." She paused for a moment, looking down at the tray of rings. "Did I mention the poetry?"

Emily continued to sort the remaining jewelry. For months she had listened to Myra go on about the same thing, feverishly trying to set her up with everyone from the delivery man to her accountant, as if Emily was reaching her expiration date and would suddenly begin to emit a foul odor or sprout a tail. For Myra, any young woman of procreative age needed to start acting responsibly — or at least cinematically, like Maureen O'Hara in *The Quiet Man* — and begin kissing the first available bachelor, even if it was during a deluge in a graveyard.

"It'd do you good to get out for a change instead of hiding out here on a Friday night."

"I do not hide out."

"Yes, you do."

"You pay me to come here, Myra — it's my job."

"Emily…" Myra took Emily's chin in a firm grip and twisted it down so that her shrewd little eyes could inventory the young woman's face. "A lovely thing, like Gene Tierney in *The Ghost and Mrs. Muir*, except for those curls and that wide mouth which God must have given you to smile more 'cause otherwise it's just a waste of lips and teeth." She released her, but not before she pinched Emily's cheek for good measure, leaving behind the comforting scent of cinnamon and liniment.

"And you know how to put yourself together, even if you tend to camouflage it with those men's jackets and boots. In my day we showed off our curves. It wouldn't kill you to do the same, you know what I'm telling you? You take off that Friday night, wear a dress, and go to hear that band — have fun with your friends instead of pawing through old things with an old thing."

"You're not old."

"I'm old enough to know that you're hiding out. Hiding out at that college and hiding out here with more books and hundred-year-old hats.

Not that I don't love having you about, honey pie, but you need to live. Get your roommates, go out with those nice girls."

"I can't. I have work I need to finish for Dr. Vandin."

"Doctor? He ain't no doctor. Not the kind that counts."

"He's got his PhD from Harvard, Myra, and that's all that counts."

Myra did not look convinced. "Well, typing up some papers for some skirt-chasing Ruskie professor who ought to know better isn't the kind of Friday night any self-respecting young woman should be having. Going at you the way he does, and you a student. It's not right."

Emily wanted to explain to her that she needed his class to graduate. Between the income she scraped together from Vandin's job, this shop, and her scholarship, she had barely enough left to make it to the end of the semester. The last thing she needed to be doing was paying an outrageous cover charge to sit in some seedy bar and drink ten dollar beers and listen to a bunch of — she pointed to the flyer in a fit of disgust and read, "Nervy, explosive men that can power a small country. *Really.*"

Completely ignoring her, Myra held out a ring from the box she had been sorting, placed it in Emily's palm, and gave her one long, calculating look.

The ring was beautiful. A platinum band encircled by a vine of tiny diamonds, Emily took it in her fingers, overcome with the urge to hold it, to feel its history in her hand as she did with so many things in this shop. "This is lovely. Where did you get it?"

Undeterred, the old woman strode over to the front of the shop, ripped the flyer off the window, and smacked it down on the counter, much as Emily's roommate had done that morning. "See that? When is the last time you've been stunned, had the hair on your neck electrified? When?"

Emily continued to stare at the ring. She knew Myra was being discreet but no less brutal in her analysis of her sex life. In truth, Emily had remained "unelectrified" by most men during her years at college; as a writer, she preferred to couch it in more poetic terms, such as detachment. She preferred detachment. Detachment kept her from partaking in the endless hook-ups and one night stands of college life. And it also kept her from becoming special to someone else. The most special. The kind of special that would involve a ring like this. Yet, if she was being honest with herself, which she wasn't, she would have liked to have been someone's only — not be shared, but be the one, the reason, the most coveted above all, even if it hurt. She wanted to feel the moment of knowing it was she who could cause a face to turn, eyes to widen in happiness with a look that couldn't be faked. It would happen too suddenly to be anything other than sincere, the joy passing from face to heart and hammered there with the words: *It's you.*

But that was one tall order in twenty-first-century San Francisco where relationships lasted about as long as a latte. And the Skellar, where those Lost Boys were playing? She hated the punk-jazz-grunge-goth bar. It was dirty and loud and filled with the heroin-chic students that were so popular at college. No, she would come here and burrow into her favorite overstuffed club chair in the back with a copy of Browning and the glass of wine Myra always gave her every Friday night. *Every* Friday night.

Nervy. Heartrending. Explosive. The words taunted her. In the end she rationalized it was because they were so poorly written. So dramatic. So challenging.

"You go to that show, and I'll put that ring on layaway for you. Wholesale."

Emily glanced down at the vine of tiny diamonds. Her closet at home was filled with so-called layaway clothes Myra had claimed she couldn't sell, when in actuality she had seen Emily caress a sleeve or hold up a dress to see if it fit. But that ring was much more costly than a beaded purse or a pillbox hat; she would be lucky if she could ever pay it off. Still, it called to her and made her heart ache with the fear that someone might snatch it up, some tourist who couldn't understand the workmanship that went into such a striking band. She had to have it. It made no sense, especially with the probability of a staggering rent increase looming on the horizon, but she simply had to have it. It was old and odd, like everything in the store. Old and odd, like everything she loved. She would work it off slowly.

"I'll go," she decided and pushed the flyer away for the last time. "If nothing else, I'll tell them to change their copy. Heartrending? *God.*"

Myra smiled and put aside the ring. "Moonlight Serenade" began to play.

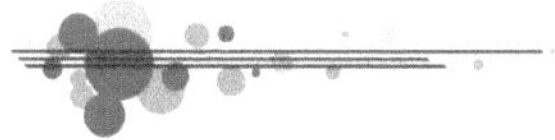

After closing up the shop with Myra, Emily gathered her thick wool jacket about her and headed down Haight Street. Most of the lining and all of the pockets had worn out, leaving her no place to keep her hands warm, so she opted to grab a cup of tea before catching the bus. She had the extra bonus of having a decent book in her messenger bag.

With her Earl Grey in hand she found a bench near the park, opened her book, and started to read. Across the lawn, the Friday night gathering of t-shirt and shorts-clad pothead bongo drummers had started up, oblivious to the cooling fog making its way from the ocean. Their tie-dyed, peasant-skirted groupies twirled barefoot to the music, arms raised in some sort of farewell rite to the disappearing sun. Emily tried to ignore them, but the sound of nearby chuckling made her glance up from her book.

On a low stone wall several yards away sat a homeless man who was only slightly less shabby than the hippies. He stared at them, laughed, and strummed his guitar idly, his case open for donations at his feet. Clearly he wasn't bothered by too much competition for one corner, as this end of the park was notorious for its stoner population who liked to camp under the trees, defecate in the bushes, and frequent the McDonald's across the street. Emily turned the page and took a sip of her tea, hoping to God that she and her roommates would not be reduced to this if worst came to worst. The guitarist began to play in a more complicated way than befitted the average drug addict. Emily had read the same paragraph three times before she gave up and peered over the top of her book at him.

He wore a thick fisherman's sweater, a shabby red scarf, and equally disreputable jeans, although his shoes looked new, but those could have been part of some shelter's outreach program for all she knew. Though the black cabbie cap pulled down over his forehead was intriguing, it also shielded his eyes. Why she wanted to see them, she couldn't say.

The damp wind made her huddle into her coat and wrap her fingers around her tea. As always, she felt the cold clear through to her bones and shivered. She had been raised in New York City, a place with four vocal seasons, not this interminable wet fall. The chill moved through the trees, and the bongos became a distant heartbeat. Even the guitar was muffled, for he had turned to the side, his leg hitched on the low wall. He began to sing.

There was a guitar and there were hands — beautiful hands strummed those chords. Emily understood this; she could see this. She could smell pot and the grease from McDonald's and the dregs of her tea. Other people had gathered to listen now; she did not know what they could see or smell or feel, but a hush fell over them, and they stopped and waited. It reminded Emily of the feeling she had when she was very young, sitting in the dark in her living room, waiting for her parents to turn on the Christmas tree lights for the first time…the very air around her changed. Everything changed. She was bewitched.

She watched him until it grew late. She did not move a muscle, only held her tea between her frozen fingers. He finally packed up and left, oblivious to her still huddled on the bench. When she was sure he had gone, when she was sure everyone had gone, when she was sure she was alone, she whispered to the night, to the empty space on the wall.

"It's you."

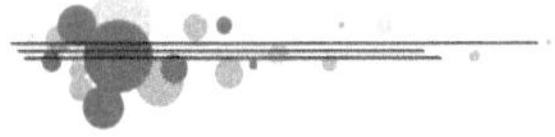

For the next several nights Emily went to listen to the homeless man with the red scarf play his guitar. He had shown up like clockwork, each evening from five till seven, and Emily sat close enough to hear him but far enough away to allow the crowd of people that invariably formed around him to block her from view. Sometimes he played nothing but classical music, other times nothing but jazz, and one night he spent an hour jamming out with a shopping cart guy who wailed away on the harmonica to their mutual delight.

On the eighth night Emily made the decision that she would leave a dollar in his case, or a sandwich, something, anything, to allow her to speak to him, to thank him. She had been too daunted to approach him before and hadn't wanted him to know she came every day. She feared he might think she was crazy, stalking him as she was. That, or desperate. Either way, she didn't want the surreal situation to change, but she knew she had to say something to him, and she fretted the whole afternoon, even wearing her favorite Chanel jacket and scarf. Lipstick, too.

He did not show.

He did not show the next night, or the one after that. Emily tried to act as if it didn't bother her, and gathered her famous air of detachment about her, but it didn't work. She found herself walking through the park between classes, hoping to spot the red scarf. Her roommates thought her distracted behavior was due either to the fact that they hadn't found a new rental yet, or that Dr. Vandin was continuing to give her an exceptionally difficult time in class or at work. In response, they'd arranged for more and more apartment viewings.

By the following Friday night, Emily stood in front of the Skellar as she had promised Myra. She didn't want to be there; she wanted to be back at the park searching for the guitarist, though at this late hour he would certainly be long gone. With one last look toward the park, she shoved her way through the scrum of students into the club.

"Emmmiiiiieeee!" she heard her one roommate, Zoey, shout like Stanley Kowalski. "Emmmiiieee!" A pair of sturdy arms parted the crowd and grabbed Emily in a fierce hug. She surrendered to its warmth and heft. Clearly straight from her latest tiling job in Pacific Heights, Zoey had coupled her grout covered overalls with gargantuan chandelier earrings and so many silver African fertility bracelets Emily feared her muscular wrists might just snap off under the strain. Despite her recent degree, she wore the moniker of "itinerant laborer and starving artist" proudly like one of the many tattoos blazing up from the collar of her T-shirt. "You came, you actually came. Good for you!" she said and dragged her to their table in the murky back corner that stunk from its proximity to the bathrooms.

Margot, her other roommate, uncurled herself from her seat and gave Emily a peck on the cheek. A waiter materialized from out of nowhere, and Margot placed a firm hand on his arm. Her blunt black hair guillotined the collar of her blouse as she turned to look up into his eyes, her leather skirt inching its way along the unending length of her legs. "Another margarita, please. With a sigh, and I mean a sigh of salt. Don't slather it on this time—dip it lightly. A sigh, you understand, just coat the rim like you were kissing it. And please, for all that is holy, keep them coming. It's been an abysmal day."

"Midterms?" Emily ventured. This was Margot's first year working as an assistant professor at the same college Emily attended, and by the looks of her two drained glasses, things hadn't gone well.

"I hate all undergraduates," Margot replied. "Both classes retained nothing. Mouth breathers all."

"So where the hell were you today?"

Emily's mind raced, trying to decipher the look of consternation on Zoey's face. "Oh God, I'm so sorry. I totally forgot you had the appointments to look at those listings. I was in Vandin's office till the afternoon, and then I went to look—well…you know how it is." Unable to tell them she had wandered the pathways around the Academy of Science most of the afternoon searching for a homeless musician she had never spoken to, Emily felt her roommates' stress radiating off their bodies like sweat.

"No, I don't know how it is," Zoey said. "Do you know how many cultures enslave their women with that kind of bullshit? That man's a troglodyte."

"Did you find an apartment?"

"We saw five places, and the best one had a drunk asleep in his own vomit in the lobby."

"Evidently, that is what was meant by 'doorman,'" Margot qualified.

"What about the other four?"

"One had been recently vacated by an old man with ferrets, and the other one was over a medical marijuana shop, which wouldn't have been so bad, but there was a LaRouche headquarters next to it, and even I have standards. The last two didn't have nearly enough natural light, and I can't paint without good light. Ain't gonna happen," Zoey declared.

Emily looked to Margot since she provided the only reliable income of the three.

"Personally, I don't give a rat's ass," Margot offered while she scanned the bar for their errant waiter. "Although I do have a fundamental problem with residual ferret shit. But resistance is futile, Emily, you have to know that. Once Zoey sets what she wants in her mind…" She held up her hands as though offering them up to God.

Before Emily could respond, the lights dimmed and an excessively pierced girl came onto the stage to announce the evening's act. Zoey shoved her fingers in her mouth to whistle, and then started spitting on the table, which earned her a questionable glance from Margot.

"Grout." Zoey gagged. "The Andersens' bathroom on Waller. My plastic gloves broke."

The metal-enhanced girl exited the stage and nodded at two men as they strode past her. One stopped to pick up his bass off of a stand, and the other slung his guitar across his chest. The sight of it tightened Emily's throat.

It isn't him. Her breathing returned to normal. *It isn't him,* she repeated to herself. *Stop this now. This is bordering on delusional. First, he is probably sleeping in the park right now; second, you will probably never see him again. Learn to live with it. Move on.*

But it could have been him. From the back, the height wasn't far off, although when the man turned around his hair was shaggy. He wore tiny, round, tinted glasses, and his arms weren't the arms she remembered. He mumbled a greeting in an Irish accent, which jump-started her heart. A handsome, dreadlocked man joined him a few feet away on stage.

"That's him, that's Christian!" Zoey cried and whistled again wildly, although there wasn't a chance in hell he could hear her with the shouting around them.

"Excuse us, folks," Christian announced to the audience. "We're fairly new in town, this being our first time in San Francisco, so we felt that we couldn't go wrong with a little grass."

The crowd erupted in hoots and cheers. The shaggy, bespectacled man cracked up as he turned to Christian. "Or bluegrass, man. Though whatever makes you happy out there is completely fine with me." He shot a shy grin to the crowd. "I'm Simon, by the way. And we are" — he pointed his finger like a gun between himself and the still grinning Christian — "anything you desire us to be. Though seriously," Simon added, his accent more pronounced, "we're The Lost Boys, and thanks much for coming out on this fine evening."

Seconds later the club erupted in wild, blistering music, so raucous that even the most cynical urbanite students were lost in the clear elation of the duo on stage. Despite the music, despite their obvious rapport, despite the insane brilliance of their lyrics, something was missing. Midway through the third song, she noticed Christian glance over at the bar, his smile even more radioactive than before. He nodded his head to the side as if to say, *come on up,* which Emily thought was odd, but maybe they were into audience participation. If so, wild horses wouldn't keep Zoey in her seat tonight, she thought.

The music toned down to background strumming, and Christian spoke into the microphone. "I love San Francisco." The crowd cheered in return and he laughed. "But your public transportation sucks and so do your taxis." More cheers erupted, as well as a few good natured boos. "Sorry, don't mean to piss anybody off, but how the hell do you people get anywhere?"

Simon rolled his eyes and muttered something under his breath, like, *move on, laddie,* to which Christian chuckled.

"I don't know if any of you have noticed, but we've been one short all night. And I can tell you ladies out there that I'm not used to faking it."

More hysterical yelling and clapping ensued. Just then a bra shot onto the stage and hit Simon on the shoulder. He was caught off guard for a split second before he recognized what he was holding in his hands. He made a show of draping it around the microphone stand. Christian was nearly bent over in laughter and hooted, "Oh God, not again."

"Hey, it's red lace." Simon smirked at Christian. "Last time it was black." He returned his attention to the crowd. "I confess, I don't like faking it either." He fingered the lace affectionately. "Truthfully, we've been one short. But I don't think we've been that poor. And what do you know — he's finally here. Get your boney ass up here, Paulie boy."

Emily swung around to the direction of the bar that Simon had been addressing, but she couldn't see anyone. The whole audience was going crazy, shouting and clapping louder and louder. The lights dimmed a little bit more, and a man climbed up the stage, his head slightly ducked down, a tight smile on his face.

Everything disappeared at that moment: the crowded tables, the smoke, the music. Only one thing remained. His face. All of his face. His intense blue eyes, buzzing and alive. The sharp cheekbones. The determined mouth. He sidled up to the microphone as he slipped on his guitar, plugged it in, and tossed his red scarf over his shoulder. He spoke in a clipped accent — a voice she would remember anywhere.

"Hello, all. I'm Andrew. Andrew Hayes. Terribly sorry for being late."

After the show, Andrew sat on the running board of their truck, a beer in his hands and his head on fire. They were parked in a lot near the Skellar, Golden Gate Park a block away. Andrew could almost see the wall where he had busked for the past week, but he was too tired to turn his head. Late for a show—for the first time in his life he was late for a goddamn show. How had he let that happen?

"Where's Christian?" Andrew asked Simon.

"He got lucky, the bastard. Texted, said not to wait up. I told you we should have stayed behind and signed autographs, but nooo, you were hell bent to get out of there so we could—oh, sit in some car park and get pissed," Simon muttered from the driver's side. He was wrapped in his army surplus jacket, his hair pulled back in the standard post-show ponytail. He had tilted the seat back and was nursing the remains of a beer. "So, are you going to share with the class as to where the hell you were, oh, for the first three bleeding songs?"

"You don't want to know, mate, trust me."

"Oh, trust me, I do. I can't play guitar for shit, and you left me up there defenseless with bras being thrown at me head. You've never been late for a show in your pathetic excuse of a life, so I reckon this better be good. I had you dead and bleeding, or kidnapped by one of those psychotic fans of yours and stuffed in some boot with that stupid red scarf strangling your neck. All I'm saying is it's a damn good thing Neil wasn't there tonight, or he'd have your balls for bacon."

"But he wasn't there."

They had been in San Francisco for one month and nothing had happened at all on that front. Yes, Simon and Christian were content to bask in the adulation of their newfound popularity, but they were equally content to believe the pipe dream that Neil St. John would swoop down and take them under his wing. In actuality, all he had done was arrange a handful of gigs and provide the nightmare of a house where they now lived. But Andrew didn't want to think about Neil; he'd deal with that headache later. Now he had to figure out how to explain his whereabouts to Simon, whose sly eyes saw through the most suave serving of bullshit. He opted for the truth.

"I fell asleep in the park. On a bench…listening to a concert."

"Are you high?"

"What do you want me to say?"

"That you were banging some girl, or that you got stuck in traffic—something normal. You sounded shitfaced on the phone. At least tell me you were drinking."

"I wasn't drinking. Too early."

"Then what?"

Honestly? You honestly want to know what I did today? I wandered San Francisco, that's what I did today, like I've done nearly every day since we got here. I wandered San Francisco searching for a woman I've never seen and I'm not sure exists anymore. And you know what else? She wasn't there. She's never there—in all the godforsaken cities we've toured, she's never, ever there. And I thought this town would be different, this bloody damp city with fucking palm trees and no sun, because it felt different. Everywhere I turned, something felt different. The shops, the streets, even that disgusting piss-soaked corner of the park up there where I've been playing, hoping that one of the faces that passes by might be hers. My muse. The woman you despise. Remember her?

This was what Andrew wanted to say, he wanted to scream it actually, but instead he dragged himself up from the seat and threw his bottle in the trash.

He had eventually fallen asleep on a bench—that part of the story was true. And he had spent the afternoon walking the park, anxious and on edge for no reason, repeatedly opening and closing the same pack of cigarettes that he never smoked, then tired and sick of himself, he collapsed in front of the bandshell to hear some lame student orchestra or some such shit.

And when the first strains of Brahms squealed from those wretched violins, he could do nothing but sit uselessly, knees to chin, on that stone bench. Only when he awoke several hours later, frozen to the bone like some pissed sot, was he shocked to realize he was late for the show. For the first time in his life, he was late for a goddamn show — all because he couldn't find her.

"Please tell me you're pulling my chain and it was actually some girl's fault," Simon begged as he started up the truck.

"It's always a girl's fault with me, isn't it?" Andrew muttered in reply.

"That's what I'm afraid of, but how about a real one this time, the kind that leaves marks."

"Trust me. She leaves marks."

They drove home in silence. All the while Andrew fell further and further into a black mood. He was trapped here like Odysseus in some lotus land, and every day he waited was too long. No matter what Simon called it, a madman's dream or a doomed quest, they had to leave San Francisco and get back on the road. Nothing was going to happen with Neil. They couldn't stay here; they needed to tour. The man was wasting their time.

The light on Franklin flashed to red, and the truck hummed to a stop, waiting. Simon's fingers drummed the steering wheel, and he stared straight ahead wearing that same inscrutable expression, not quite smiling, not quite frowning, a look that always drove Andrew mad. They had bought the truck their first day in San Francisco, fully loaded because Simon was sure of their soon-to-be fame, and its cost had depleted their coffers substantially. The cab was large enough to hold their equipment, and they could sleep in it if need be, which Andrew supposed they might end up doing after tonight's show.

"Do you really trust Neil?" Andrew asked.

The light changed, and the truck accelerated up a narrow slip of a street, past manicured homes hidden by equally manicured shrubs glistening blue-black from the fog in the light of the streetlamps.

"He fakes sincerity well, if that's what you mean. But he's better than Lou — you've still got your guitar."

"Can you be serious for a moment? Then why has he offered the house and these gigs and made no move to rep us? He's had time enough to know if he likes what he's heard. Or was it all some sort of test to see if we're worthy enough of his time? And what is it with all this dropping in and out whenever he wants and staying as long as he likes? Like he's really managing that clusterfuck of a remodel as a hobby? He could pay a boatload of general contractors and architects to do it for him. It's mad."

"He lived there when his wife was sick," Simon replied quietly. "It was near the hospital where she was getting treatment before she died. He just didn't want to sell it. Memories, I reckon."

"When did he tell you that?" Andrew asked, surprised by the frustration he felt.

"The other day when you were playing for tourists in the park."

"Shit…how did you know?"

"You ought to think about that—giving it away for free—we're too well known now. Your voice is recognizable no matter how you try to disguise that mug of yours—and that's becoming even more recognizable by the day. You need to be careful. That's what Neil says."

"Neil knows?"

"When are you gonna realize that man knows everything?"

Simon cut the engine; they had reached the house. "Home sweet home," he announced with a distinct air of finality.

Barely visible in the darkness, the Victorian loomed large across the street. It sat at the forgotten edge of a city playground, its wrought iron fence standing between the gnarled, construction-stricken front garden and the sidewalk. Omnipresent fog hung around the monstrosity like a moat. A weed-rioted path led to a grand door that would do Jacob Marley's disembodied head proud.

Lights glowed through the mullioned windows on the lower floor where they lived. Evidently Christian's plans had not been successful. The windows of the vacant upper floor remained dark, and those of the glass attic conservatory that topped the mansion like a wrought iron tiara were darker still. The truck creaked and settled into gear. Simon made no move to exit.

"It'd be a shame to pack up since we've done so much work to the thing, don't you think?" Simon responded dryly. "Although I would have liked to have run into Nick at least once before you dragged us back on the road again. I feel somehow denied."

"The crew swears they've seen him."

"Yeah, 'Shit, martini, ghost,' all sound about the same in Spanish, as does the screaming," he said with a laugh. After a long moment, he turned to face Andrew, all good humor gone. "You're not seriously thinking of packing up. We just got here, and things are really starting to come together. Look at tonight—three encores, and we've got the show tomorrow night and two the following week. It's brilliant."

"But what about Neil?"

"What about him? He's crackers, absolutely. God bless 'em for it. He's testing out the wares is what he's doing, and it makes sense. Would you really want him to fuck on the first date? Come on, he's a conservative wanker, you have to respect that in the man, but look at all he's done for us. I mean, where else can you live in such high style outside of Calcutta? No heat, little electricity, hoards of people underfoot. It's like being back at home with me mum. I'm serious, Paulie, I don't want to pull out yet. We're so close. You've got to have a little more faith."

"Spoken like a true atheist."

"Hey, I'd kneel down in front of the altar of Neil St. John any day if he can keep doing what he's doing. You want things too fast. It's always been that way with you. You never wanted for anything. Your da was loaded, but mine sure as hell wasn't. You've still got a trust fund to fall back on and a mum who'll wipe your arse if asked."

"Fuck you."

"But that's not it, is it? Aw, you're not going there are you? Tell me it's not about her again."

"No."

"No, you won't tell me, or no, it's not about her? Because I'm telling you, if this is about her — you're touring by yourself, is what you're doing. I'm sick of having this argument with you. First it was bloody eccentric, but then after what happened in New Orleans — you have got to get help. Don't you see it? There's no shame in it. You need help."

Simon's glasses reflected the streetlamp as he stared straight at him. Andrew had known Simon long enough to understand when he was being serious. Like when he punched him in the face the first time, or when he wrote his first legit song, or when he'd sat curled up in the corner of a hotel room, knowing he had to stop using. And he had, for himself and for the band. Suddenly the truck felt claustrophobic.

"You don't understand, all right? Leave it at that."

"Then make me understand."

Andrew threw open the door and headed to the house, Simon not far behind.

"Are you going to answer me, or are you going to run away again?"

"I'm not running."

"You're not living, is what you're not doing. When is it going to be enough? We're finally getting some serious traction, you heard that crowd tonight? This is what you want. This is the real world. Get help, Andrew, talk to someone, get them to give you something at least. This thing is going to kill you. And you can't let it, you understand? You can't."

The shock of seeing the preternaturally cool Simon so shaken stopped Andrew in his tracks. "Can we talk about this another time? I'm exhausted, and I don't want to fight."

A swath of red had risen up Simon's throat, and he was breathing like he did after a show when he would throw his sticks to the floor and fall forward over his drums. "Fine." He wiped the back of his wrist across his mouth. "I'd whip your boney arse anyway."

Andrew knew Simon wanted him to be strong. To him, Andrew would always be the one who saw him through detox, the one who didn't flinch a muscle when he vomited and convulsed in cold sweats. The one that was always there. Period. But right now he felt like his head might explode at any moment—he couldn't think—he needed to sleep. He trudged up to the house, intending to disappear into his room and collapse.

A dusty chandelier hung from the high ceiling of the foyer, the light of which reflected off the brass number one on their door. Simon wrestled with the key as Andrew glanced up the stairs at the dark landing. "Hullo," he said. Simon paused and peered up at the stack of boxes there. It wasn't the first time that Andrew had sworn he had seen someone standing behind them, waiting. It set the hairs on his arms on end. "Hullo," he said again.

"What is it?" Simon asked.

"Forget it," he replied in frustration. There was nothing there.

Whatever unearthly feeling Andrew may have experienced disappeared when he stepped over the threshold into their flat. Bedlam reigned inside, complete anarchy for sale. Blueprints and buckets of tools filled the front parlor, and a new set of wires dangled from the ceiling. Its walls (what little remained of them) stood in various stages of being re-plastered, and the floors were covered in tarps, which in turn were covered in sawdust and paint.

The air continually reeked with the odor of turpentine and something that smelled remarkably like burned pizza. The sight made Andrew want to smash a hole in the wall, not that anyone would notice.

"This old fucking house," Simon muttered.

Suddenly they heard laughter come from the kitchen, the only room in the house that remained untouched, although it didn't matter since most of the appliances rarely worked. Andrew pulled apart the pocket doors that led to the dining room and onto the kitchen when he ran straight into Neil St. John, who was busy barking orders into a cell phone. Simon merely whistled and walked past, leaving Andrew to his mercy.

"This is the third one this week," Neil yelled. "How the hell are we ever going to get the bathroom completed if every goddamn worker runs screaming from the place? I don't care how you do it, Sid, find a plumber—hire a blind one if that's what is necessary. And remind me why I signed on for this debacle. A man in my position shouldn't be subjected to this incompetence."

Andrew could picture the man cowering on the other end of the line: Sid, the short, crew-cutted, and beleaguered foreman on the job, whose main goal in life was to try to explain to his ashen-faced crew why the temperature in the house could drop ten degrees while the radiator banged away. Why plaster buckets were turned over and tarps went missing. Why a tin-pan piano sounded from the empty attic early in the morning and at dusk.

Neil ended the call and stared straight at Andrew. "I received a call from a rather irate promoter who wanted to know where the lost Lost Boy was."

"Apologies. It won't happen again."

Neil, clad in a well-pressed oxford shirt and trousers, looked over Andrew in his threadbare t-shirt and jeans, the red scarf hanging limp around his neck. "Please understand, I've pulled a lot of strings to get you these gigs, and I don't want to be made to look like an idiot. It isn't much to ask for you to show up on time. Either you're going to act professionally or you're not. It's your decision."

The tone in Neil's voice only served to drive the point home. Andrew had had it; he had to get the band out of here. He was done being on probation like a schoolboy.

"Have we let you down in any particular way? If I'm not mistaken, we've sold out every one of our shows, with multiple encores each night. It was my fault I was late tonight, for which I'm sorry. Like I said, it won't happen again." He took a deep breath. "We have to think about getting back on the road, anyway. We have a list of places in Boston and New York that are interested, and I'm sure you'd like us out from underfoot."

Neil stopped short. "What? You have the shows in Sacramento next week, I've already confirmed them."

Just then Christian emerged from the kitchen, accompanied by a zaftig woman dressed in overalls. She was coiled around him in a fervent embrace, her fright of shoulder-length tortoiseshell hair caught up with his dreads as he hugged her in earnest, babbling something in French. Her handsome face widened in laughter as she stepped back to examine him, her wrists jangling with silver jewelry as she did so.

"Fucking-A, Christian. Shit, I can't believe it! Look at your bad self," she gushed.

Andrew leveled a glance at Simon, who had just entered the room and stood against the wall with his arms crossed over his chest. Groupies. Hell. The last thing he needed tonight. He peered into the kitchen for her likely friends.

Without a moment's hesitation, Christian slung his arm around her large shoulders and squeezed her until the woman cackled in glee. Christian beamed. "Everyone, this is Zoey Cohen. Zoey and I went to summer camp together for—what was it—for six years?"

What kind of camp would cater to the likes of two such disparate people, Andrew had no idea, but by the way they were grinning, there must have been a good reason why they kept returning, and it had nothing to do with s'mores. Fatigue, however, had overcome him. Plus, he wasn't feeling the least bit social after his arguments with Simon and Neil.

Before he could excuse himself, the group had plowed back into the kitchen, and Christian's exuberant old girlfriend began to pull food from grocery bags that littered the kitchen floor. Food. They hadn't seen unboxed food in a long time. If that wasn't shocking enough, she performed her first miracle and actually got the stove to light. Then she began to cook. And cook. Like some punked out Snow White, she produced a bottle of Jack from another bag, found clean drinking glasses in the sagging cupboards, and placed them on a makeshift table she had created out of a stray piece of plywood and two sawhorses and placed in the middle of the kitchen, all the while directing Christian on how to grill the steaks. She poured, toasted, and downed hers in one shot, gushing how she loved the room's high ceilings and long casement windows…and was that a garden out back? She sipped away at her second like it should have an umbrella in it as she sautéed mushrooms and apologized that her roommates had to leave early. All the while the men gazed at her in awe, wondering if her roommates too, came with their own grocery bags.

Christian, in his typical fashion, jumped in and invited them to the show tomorrow night, even throwing in drinks with the offer.

Zoey's face instantly fell. "Can't do it. Crap, you know I'd love to, but we're looking at apartments on Saturday, otherwise I'd be there with bells on. God, I can't believe how amazing you all were. My roommates—they were totally in shock. I've never seen them look like that. It was like when Emily ate a peanut and had one of her allergic reactions, she was so pale and shook up. I thought for sure we'd be doing that whole *Pulp Fiction* needle in the heart thing before the end of your first set."

"And that's a good thing?" Andrew asked, torn between the desire to flee to his room or devour a plate of piping hot garlic bread.

But she didn't respond. "Fucking awesome tattoo." She gawked at the letters on Simon's fingers, fingers that were wrapped around the neck of a beer bottle, the only item not to come from her grocery bags. "Do you want to see my latest? I just got it done down at Santa Cruz. Here…it's a little lower on my hip."

Simon's eyes had flashed wide open at the speed with which Zoey had unbuckled her overalls and was yanking aside the strap of her thong.

"Whoa! That's cool, Zoey. But we don't want to be slamming that hypodermic into Simon," Christian cried and helped her refasten herself.

The conversation and drinks continued. Each time Andrew attempted to get away, Zoey grabbed his arm as she regaled them with another story of the horror of apartments they had checked out, or the plight of being reduced to producing her huge canvases in the loo because it was the only room in their flat with natural light, much to her roommates' constant vexation.

By the end of the night, Andrew was wound tight and drinking heavily. As for Zoey, everyone loved the woman, as her nature demanded it. Even Neil had stayed, his keen eyes taking it all in: Andrew's never empty glass, Simon's ever growing look of concern, and how Christian stared at the artist's ample breasts which jiggled seismically beneath her overalls whenever she laughed.

Sometime around one-thirty Neil finished his drink and put down his glass with a resounding thud. His sat back on the wooden chair. "I have a solution to your problem," he told her.

Zoey's thick eyebrows scrunched together like caterpillars, probably wondering which problem he was addressing; the woman seemed to collect them.

"I have a flat for rent."

Her eyes mimicked Simon's, the caterpillars now residents in her bleached bangs.

"Yer jokin'," Simon remarked, clearly buzzed. "Why the hell aren't *we* livin' there?"

"Because it happens to be above yours."

Andrew leaned forward to make sure he heard him correctly, his brain slamming against the inside of his skull as he did so.

"Would you like to see it? It's got wonderful light," Neil continued to a smitten Zoey.

"Yeah, 'cause it hasn't a roouuf," Andrew slurred, taken aback. What was Neil thinking? The flat was a disaster; Andrew had seen it. No one in their right mind would live there. The man was either incredibly generous or a sadist. Or he was entirely nutters, as Andrew had always suspected.

It didn't matter. Zoey had been lured in, hook, line and sinker. She was already getting out of her seat to take a tour. As for Christian, there was only one word to describe him. Smitten. For Simon. Intrigued. For Neil. Pleased.

Shit, Andrew thought. How was he ever going to get them to leave now? He laid his head down on the table and groaned. The room began to spin, in that Tilt-a-Whirl-amusement-park-ride way, the precursor to what was sure to be a killer hangover. But before he cast off into inebriated sleep, he swore he heard something coming from the floor above. It sent ice water through his veins and stood the hairs on his neck on end. With a shudder, he placed his arm over his other ear to block out the sound. A sound he had heard before. It was unmistakable—a man's eerie laughter and the tinkling of a piano.

The following night, students crammed through the front doors of the Skellar, yelling over one another, impatient to reach the seats below. Emily fought her way through the mob as well but could barely make any progress, the crowd was so great.

The Lost Boys were already playing; she could hear the crescendo of the guitars, but the harder she fought to reach the floor, the stronger the bodies buffeted her back. She twisted this way and that on tip-toe in an attempt to locate Zoey or Margot, but she could see nothing except backs and shoulders and the glare of angry half-turned faces that stood between her and the stage. Suddenly cheers and applause broke out around her, and over the din she heard a clipped London accent thanking everyone for coming.

The crowd began to drift apart, and for the first time Emily noticed that the men were dressed in suits, not jeans and T-shirts or hooded sweats as she would have expected, but suits that were broad in the shoulders, with peaked lapels, some with wide stripes, others with bolder plaids, and a few in the surreal colors of emerald green or electric blue. They wore their hair slicked back and slinked their arms around women whom seemed to have stepped out of Myra's shop, women with lips of cherry red and bodies wrapped in wasp-waisted dresses with netted hats obscuring their pale faces.

Was it a party? A costume party that she hadn't known about? She looked down at her own clothes but was mortified to see that she wore only a nightshirt and her feet were bare. Immediately self-conscious, she spun around, searching the crowd to see if anyone noticed, but they hadn't. They didn't see her at all.

Cigarettes glowed and ashed between nearly everyone's fingers now. A blonde, her hair slinked over one eye, blew a puff of smoke from the side of her mouth where it joined the dense fog under the club's dim lights.

"They were fabulous, darling," she cried to her date. "Fabulous."

The voice from the stage continued, "Thank you, yes, thank you. You've been grand. Good night." It was followed by the finality of footsteps thundering across wood.

No! How could she have been this late? How could she have missed the entire show?

"I thought she'd be here," the woman said to her date and threw the cigarette to the floor, grinding it under her heel before she turned to leave.

"I'm here!" Emily shouted back, but her words sounded like they came up from underwater. The gang of people maddening to depart crashed about her in waves, their faces twisted and distorted and ghostly white. With all her might, she flung herself forward and broke through the horde, sending chairs clattering to the floor.

"I'm here!" she cried at the top of her lungs, but the doors to the back stage had slammed shut, leaving only a drum set behind. Frantic, she turned back to the crowd, ready to force her way through them, but what she saw made her freeze in place. The room was entirely deserted—no one remained, not a table, not a chair—every suit and gold lamé dress had vanished. Only shadows and the echo of a ticking clock filled the vacant space.

A cool hand of dread clutched at her shoulder, and she knew she had to get out of there, she had to run. As fast as she could she bolted for the door, the same door where the band had exited. It was cast iron, indescribably heavy, and required all her strength to budge, but finally she managed to shove her shoulder against it hard enough to force it to open a crack.

She slipped through and reached the other side, letting the door slam behind her. Relieved to have escaped, she plastered her back against the door, but when she turned to run, there was no hallway, no dressing area as she had thought. Instead she stood in a high-ceilinged Victorian room.

Sunlight streamed through a pair of tall casement windows that hung opposite her. A breeze ruffled their sheer curtains and brought with it the distant scent of lilac and the sounds of birds and spring. The sun's rays reflected in the crystals of a chandelier hanging from the ceiling and then stippled their way down the lime-washed walls, catching the glitter of swirling dust motes. In the center of the room sat a brass bed covered in rumpled sheets.

The tension and fear in her body evaporated, and joy rushed through her veins. She knew this bed, she knew the sounds it made and the softness of its mattress, but more importantly, she knew the man who lay on top of it. He took a sip from his wine glass, stared up at her, smiled, and said nothing. A thrill lighted her blood at the sight of his face, the white, starched shirt unbuttoned at his throat, and the baggy trousers that he wore. All familiar, all known.

"What took you so long?" He stood, placed the glass on the floor, and walked toward her, his eyes never leaving hers.

"I don't know." Her voice broke; she felt weightless and hopeful and fragile and wanted nothing more than for him to hold her to the earth.

She knew what would come next. He would kiss her, not now, but soon. He would falter at first and knock his nose against hers, and then they would laugh before she cried, a strangled sound into which they both would fall. Later, naked and entwined, her hair would drape his face, shield it from the setting sun that would steal over the wood floor and across their empty glasses until it gilded the magnificent gramophone that sat in the corner. He would wait, wait until the record he had placed there began to play, wait until his hands had finished caressing her, wait for his body to settle into hers, to inhale and exhale, to be alive. Tremulously, his mouth would cover her mouth, and he would kiss her with a word, always the same word.

"Wait."

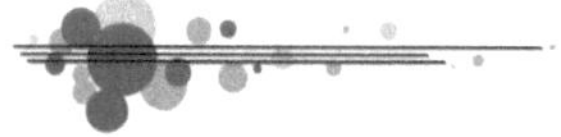

Emily sat bolt upright in her bed. The dream rushed past her eyes like the snap of an old film being ripped from a projector. She fought to grasp hold of a frame, to snatch an image before it receded into oblivion. But she failed. In its place stood the stark backdrop of her room, dark, spare, and jammed with stacks of books and moving boxes, all too silent and real.

"Oh God, oh God, oh God," she said and lowered her face into her hands, her words creating a perfect descant to her pounding heart. "Oh God." Despite the chill in the air, sweat covered her. "It was just a dream, just a dream," she repeated to herself. That's all it was—a dream.

They had studied dreams in her psychology class. Dr. Vandin had spent half a semester on them alone. This one would be, oh, what would it be? An illustration of some deep-seated fear, or a failure to cope with the past, triggered by some conflict in the present. Undoubtedly, Vandin would know and would lecture her about some urgent message brewing in her subconscious that was demanding to be understood and would plague her until she dealt with it. Yes, that was what he would say, and then berate her for not knowing the fact to begin with. Yet if it was a dream, why could she still feel the pressure of her lover's hips and the heat of his fingertips as he played her? Why could she remember every detail of his face?

The same face as that of her guitar player. Her guitar player who wasn't homeless or destitute or drug-addled after all. Who was the lead guitarist of a band, but not just any band, a band that "stunned crowds whenever they performed." A "heartrending" band to be sure, if the women around her last night were any indication, screaming like their tongues were on fire.

Seeking refuge in the bathroom, she was thankful only cold water rushed from the faucets, as the apartment was too old to produce anything warmer. She splashed her face, then bracing her hands on the basin, stared at herself in the mirror.

"But I found him first."

That was her first reaction upon seeing him surrounded by those other women last night. A reaction that was as instinctual as it was selfish, one she hadn't felt since she was a child, one that should be accompanied by a stamp of the foot or a slam of a door. She had found Andrew first.

Andrew Hayes. That was his name. The man who haunted her dreams and so many of her waking moments; the man she knew nothing about, who knew nothing about her. How had she let herself fall into such a hopeless obsession?

Oh God, oh God, oh God.

She wasn't proud of this fact; the whole episode, no matter how one tried to explain it, made her feel desperate and not the least bit sane. In fact, it made her feel ridiculous and ashamed. Fantasizing about him like some crazed groupie — *God*. His face. His body. His hands. As though once they met, some fantasy would explode to life. But above everything else, this fascination scared her. She had no idea how it had taken such a hold of her or how, for the first time in her life, she could not control any of her thoughts or feelings when it came to a man. How had she become so consumed by an illusion? And because of this, she had made the decision not to let her roommates know anything about the whole sordid mess. If nothing else, she had her pride; it had taken her far too long to stand on her own two feet. Dream or no, she wasn't the type of woman to drop everything for a man—her mother had drilled that into her head from the time she could nod back in agreement.

It was all for naught, anyway, she told herself; he'd soon be long gone. He was a in a band. Bands toured. They also engaged in clawing, disease-ridden sex with women like the ones at the Skellar, but that was when they weren't busy destroying their hotel rooms or crashing their Maseratis off cliffs. She had watched too many documentaries to think otherwise. If the car crashes didn't kill them, then the overdoses, the suicides, or the auto-erotic asphyxiation most certainly would. Margot had been more than willing to recite an impressive list of dead rockers last night on the ride home.

But Andrew was here now. In San Francisco. The Lost Boys would be playing at the Skellar again tonight. What would it hurt to see him one more time? To see him standing there, to see those clear, maddening blue eyes that she hadn't seen before. To see his hands.

"Emily?" Margot asked, grounding her back into the reality of the freezing four-by-four bathroom. "Are you going to be in there long? I need to shower."

Emily opened the door. Margot stood there, the picture of composure, back from her morning run without a drop of sweat upon her. Not even a wisp of her blue-black hair that framed her pointed chin and strict cheekbones dared to disobey her.

Margot had once explained that she was a perfect genetic combination of a painfully beautiful Filipino mother and a never-to-retire Marine captain father. The resulting agile mind for figures, coupled with such an agile figure, continued to discombobulate the most seasoned of her physics professors, long after she had finished her PhD.

"So has she returned yet, or is she officially declared a spoil of war?" Margot asked, meaning Zoey, of course, who, as of two a.m., had not surfaced.

However, there was no judgment in her voice as to their roommate's whereabouts. The creak of Margot's bedroom door opening in the early morning hours was not an unfamiliar sound in the apartment, although not a common one. It was inevitably followed by the fumble of heavy shoes and the curses of a man stumbling and trying to dress while being led to the front door. For as long as Emily had known Margot, none of her men had ever been invited to stay for breakfast. They had, according to Margot, never earned the right.

"No sign of her. You remember she knew one of the musicians? She could be in L.A. by now for all we know."

Margot looked askance at her as she shut the door behind her. Emily padded across to the kitchen, the walls of their soon-to-be-vacated apartment looking depressing and worn now stripped of Zoey's vibrant canvases. At first, the apartment had belonged to Margot and Zoey, but Zoey's tiling work often took a back seat to the creation of those canvases and other forms of her "art," and Margot felt that the third bedroom/closet should be put to better use. Whether Emily was the first to respond to their ad, or the only one, didn't matter; their friendship was instantaneous. Even Margot's incongruous shrine to every Catholic saint imaginable (courtesy of her mother, who never stopped trying to lure her back to the church), with its prayer cards and little plastic figurines which sat peering out from the mantle, did not dissuade her.

Emily had finished her first cup of coffee when Margot reappeared wearing a black turtleneck and obedient slacks, waving her phone over her head. "She has good news and bad news—which do you want first?"

"The good."

"Oh, ever my little optimist. All right, please bear in mind this is highly subjective, but the 'good' news is that she has a line on a 'killer' apartment—her words, not mine. But that she has to—" she paused to scroll down the message and read further "'—experience it in natural light. Dirt cheap, available right away. Tell Em it's near her work and has charm out the wazoo.'"

"And the bad news?"

"It seems we're all going to the ball, Cinderella. She got us reserved seating at The Lost Boys' show tonight, compliments of this Christian of hers. And it seems they also want to take us out for drinks afterward."

"No."

"I'll give her this, she works fast." Margot poured herself a mug of coffee.

"No…no, no, no."

"Listen, if I have to go, you have to go."

"No, you don't understand. I can't go. I can't—I don't have anything to wear. And I have to—I have—Vandin has a paper that he's submitting and I have to finish editing the bibliography. Drinks? Where?"

Margot's mug stopped midway to her lips. "What's the matter with you?"

"Nothing. It's just that it's so sudden. To invite us, and he doesn't even know who we are, what happens if he, if they —"

"Yes?"

"I mean, it's one thing to look up there and watch them play, but to have to talk? I don't think I'm ready for that — I mean, what would we say? We have nothing in common."

"We're going out for drinks, not giving them a kidney. And seriously, we've suffered through worse for her before. All we have to do is endure a few hours of noise and the obligatory first drink and then we leave. That's it, just drinks. It's probably a good thing that we meet her little musician and his friends and make sure she hasn't made a complete fool of herself yet."

"There's nothing little about him."

"Excuse me?"

Emily floundered. "The drummer — the drummer's tall," she blurted out in the vain hope that Margot's guarded intrigue in the Irish drummer, with his battering arms and sly banter, would effectively detour the direction of the conversation and put an end to her increasingly critical stare.

"Statistically, I'd say he falls onto the far end of the bell curve, yes," Margot offered into her coffee mug. "At least when it comes to talent, that is. But he looks unwashed."

"True. But didn't Newton or somebody say something about opposites attracting?"

"Attractive? Well…I suppose he might be in a James Joyce, John Lennon, rebel-as-artist sort of way, if you like that sort of thing. But I need a mind functioning within all that…noise. And somehow, that man couldn't have both — it's not statistically possible."

"What? Look at you. Why can't that happen with a Y-chromosome?"

"Because it can't, and even if it could, it ultimately comes to down to someone sacrificing to make it work. And women are engineered to sacrifice, it's in our DNA. Whereas the best of men, no matter how talented or intelligent or attractive, will suck you dry and then complain to you about the aftertaste. Trust me. Men aren't engineered to sacrifice or to stay around, especially men in bands, so it's better to leave first before you end up making a huge mistake."

"But we're just talking about drinks here."

"My point, exactly. So I suggest you be ready to go by seven."

Emily sometimes hated having a genius for a roommate.

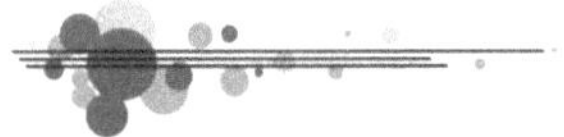

As Emily entered the Skellar, she pinched herself to verify she was indeed awake, and as an extra precaution, scanned the club to make sure the audience looked firmly of this century. At her side, Margot took no notice, or if she did she didn't say a word. She hadn't said a word about Emily's attire of a blue-black velvet jacket and treacherously high pumps donated with relish by Myra for the occasion who claimed they made Emily look exactly like a feminist fairy tale princess. Margot was used to her friend's bohemian style of dress, herself opting for a leather jacket and appropriately frayed jeans as did the rest of the crowd. Her black, tight-fitting T-shirt, however, bore a bright yellow radioactive symbol on it in apparent warning.

The same as the previous evening, the dark room was packed. Within seconds of reaching the tables they were whisked along by Zoey, who nabbed them each by the arm and escorted them to one that bore a reserved VIP sign. She must have come home at some point during the day, thought Emily, because she was done up in a macraméd peasant dress and white go-go boots. No sooner had they taken their seats than she launched into the description of their new apartment.

"But a house?" Emily said after finding out the details. "We barely make enough between us to afford our current place. How much is the rent?"

"It's cheaper than our place," said Zoey, "that's the beauty of it. And it's a Victorian. And it's an apartment, not the whole house, so don't start worrying about cleaning and all that because there's no need. It's getting some work done."

Margot barked a laugh. "Sounds like it's getting Botox. What do you mean exactly when you say 'work'?"

"Nothing that we can't live in," answered Zoey a bit too quickly. "Wait till you see her — the wainscoting, the fireplaces, the light, and there's even this little garden, and we share a conservatory in the attic." She began to sketch the layout on a nearby napkin and continued on in an orgasmic *Architectural Digest* fashion about the vintage Chambers stove and the window seats, but all Emily could hear was one word: share.

"Whoa, whoa…share?" Margot interrupted before Emily could open her mouth. "You mean to tell me we'll be living in a apartment with God knows who traipsing through it every day to make sure it doesn't collapse on our heads, plus we have to live with other people?"

Just then a body walked onto the stage, and Emily's heart skipped a beat. She nearly snapped the stem of her wine glass between her fingers. But he was only there to check equipment and quickly left.

Why was she so nervous? She had until midnight. Wasn't that true of all fairy tales? Then this fantasy of hers would return to just that. She didn't want to think about it anymore, the reality of expected disappointment. All she wanted were beginnings and hope and happiness, not what she knew would come once the last encore was done and the lights came up and they said hello. But what happened if they did hit it off? If he found her beautiful and charming and intelligent? Was that so farfetched?

Suddenly the lights dimmed, and Emily's heart began to make its way to her throat via her lungs. Her hands were sweating and freezing all at the same time. The room was beyond capacity at this point. Bodies were everywhere, all holding their collective breath.

Again, the metal-studded girl scurried on stage to announce the band. The door opened up from the side of the stage, and The Lost Boys entered. Wild applause rang out.

Christian was the first to take his place. He grabbed his bass from its stand and fiddled with it, while Simon followed and snatched up his sticks, getting comfortable behind his barricade of drums. Both were wearing low slung jeans and dark t-shirts. They grinned as the crowd cheered and raised their hands in greeting.

Andrew was the last to come on stage, not because he wanted to make an entrance, but because he was speaking quickly to the girl who had introduced them. He made a motion with his hand to the audience, nodded in understanding, then jumped up onto the stage. The applause was deafening.

His fans were back in droves. He seemed a bit puzzled by the number of shrieking women but just shrugged his shoulders and welcomed the crowd.

"Thank you. Thank you very much. It's a pleasure to be back here at the Skellar tonight. You have a charming city here. I've been told that the natives are quite friendly."

The natives erupted in screams. He grinned back. It still disconcerted her to hear his clipped British accent from the Mediterranean combination of blue eyes, tan skin, and dark hair.

"The first song we'd like to perform for you tonight is from our forthcoming album. We finished recording it back home over the holidays. Hope you enjoy it."

Christian smiled back at Andrew's nod, and Simon set the beat on the drums. Zoey let out a whistle of delight, while Margot sat perfectly still.

By the middle of the third song, the audience was feverishly pressing in around the stage. Zoey hauled them closer, not satisfied to have to stand on the chairs to see the band like so many others were forced to.

After the song ended, Andrew put aside his electric guitar and took up his acoustic. The mood of the room shifted with the dimming lights. He stood before the microphone, all riled up from the previous set, his legs still rocking through his tattered jeans. His Doc Martens were tapping a beat, slow and steady. He strummed a few chords and hummed to himself, tuning his guitar.

He seemed ready now. Emily stood straighter, high on her toes, willing his eyes so filled with fire to find hers in the darkness. *Please see me out here. I'm here. I've always been here.*

At that precise moment his eyes meet hers. His strumming faltered. Emily immediately pulled herself into the shadows, unable to breathe, unable to move any further. Then he blinked as though shaking himself out of a stupor.

"Forgive me," he said, his voice a bit strained, "thought I might be losing my mind there for a moment. But just in case I'm not mad, this next song is about a girl. It's always about a girl, isn't it?" He sighed and glanced at the floor. "Well, this one is, because it has always been about her."

He began to play.

When the heart breaks there is no sound. There is only the sensation of threads of hope held taut and cut. Then the ghost pain comes, pain that exists in their absence.

She couldn't stay. She couldn't stand here and watch him sing of his love for another woman; it was too painful, too humiliating. What had she been thinking? What fantasies had she spun to get her to this point? How ridiculous had she become?

Blindly, she reached for her coat. She had retreated only two steps when she accidently knocked into a group of startled students. One of them, angered at being nearly pushed into a table, shoved back into Emily, sending her flying into a nearby waitress who bore a large tray of drinks. The impact knocked the tray from the waitress's hands and catapulted its contents clear across the stage. In the uproar, glasses shattered and ice scuttled everywhere. Andrew barely escaped being hit by a beer bottle that crashed near his feet.

Frantic, Emily tried to help the waitress up but was pulled off balance, causing them both to tumble to the floor at the edge of the stage. Skinning her elbow across the cement, she cursed loudly.

Despite the mayhem, Andrew's eyes narrowed as he scoured the darkness. He muttered something unrecognizable, then his eyes met Emily's. He froze and his face blanched, "You? No. Christ, it is you! Bloody hell."

The sharpness of his voice sent a shock down her spine. "What?" she managed to get out, struggling to retrieve her coat from the floor.

"You're here. How did you find me?" he demanded more loudly now, ignoring the crew attempting to clean up the debris around him. "How?"

She took a step backward. She felt all the eyes in that room glued to the specter she must have made standing there, mortified, holding that blackest of blue coats. She felt his glare most of all, demanding an explanation.

"I didn't…I'm sorry."

"But it's you," he insisted, beyond vehement now, pushing aside the microphone stand. "It can't be you."

Panicked, the memory of her own words haunted her — the words she had spoken on that damp park bench the first night she saw him. He had recognized her after all. His personal stalker had crashed his show. How the hell had she descended to these depths?

Suddenly it all became too much. The riot of her emotions and the crush of the walls closed in on her and choked the air from her lungs. Gasping for breath and desperate for escape, she shoved the onlookers aside and escaped toward the exit. Zoey and Margot shouted her name in confusion.

She did the only thing she could do — she ran. She had to get out of there. Humiliated, she ran into the black, cold, foggy street. She ran until she couldn't move anymore, couldn't drag herself another foot. Ten blocks she ran, fighting back tears. She ran until she collapsed against a vacant alley, her lungs on fire, her body bent over and panting.

And there, under the fog and a fizzling street lamp, clutching her coat about her shoulders, she realized: she had lost one shoe. She slumped down the wall and stared up into the night sky, feeling the trail of a hot tear down her cheek. To hell with those stupid fairy tales.

5

Blood pounded in his ears as the world spiraled down into a pinprick of soundlessness. *She was here. I am here. She was here. I am here. Here.* Andrew could feel the words echo in the reverb of his guitar and pulsate under his fingertips. He was either hallucinating or truly going mad this time; both were valid options. But he knew, without any doubt, that she—his muse—had stood before him, close enough to touch, and that was the only reality that mattered anymore.

Then she had vanished and left him speechless, holding his guitar and what little remained of his sanity. The empty place that she had filled narrowed to a kaleidoscopic lens with each frame holding her image, the backdrop ever changing, her clothes different in each view, but always with the same expression on her face—as if she were staring at an old photograph, the kind you would hold to your heart long after you had finished gazing at it.

Without thinking, Andrew threw his guitar to the ground and leaped off the stage. The shocked audience stumbled apart to make way for him, then surged back in a wave, not wanting to miss any part of the excitement. Shoulders smashed into his and long nails tore at his hair as he struggled to pass. The last thing Andrew heard as he made it to the exit was Christian's voice announcing, "Going to take a break, folks!"

At the door, the bouncer gaped in confusion at the sight of the wild guitarist, but Andrew ignored him and pushed past the velvet ropes and out into the night. Immediately, the chill and fog hit him square in the face, and his eyes teared and fought to adjust to the darkness. All he could see before him was a street littered with the dregs of people out on a Saturday night, almost translucent under the streetlamps.

Scrambling for what to do next, he felt his legs begin to pump. He ran. Harder and harder. But to where? Up two blocks, back down three. *Where are you? Where are you?* Was he shouting the words, or was he thinking them? He couldn't tell.

Like a madman he scoured the streets for her, for that black coat, that delicate face. She couldn't have gotten very far; she had to be near some storefront or trying to flag down a taxi, something. But all he could see were the ghosts of Haight Street, hands shoved in their pockets, as though each was wanting to be somewhere else.

After several more futile minutes spent searching for her, he slammed his foot against a nearby newspaper stand, then cursed and collapsed down on the curb, listening to his heart pound out in three quarter time: *she — was — here, she — was — here, she — was — here*. A lifetime of searching and he had finally seen her. The realization should have instilled in him some sense of vindication, should have made him want to climb up to some rooftop and proclaim it to the world. *See, I'm not mad. I've been right all along. Screw you all!* But having the contents of his mind made manifest before his very eyes only kept him cemented to the curb. It was one thing to deal with the desires of one's subconscious, but quite another to have to handle a living, breathing girl. How was he going to approach her? How was he even to say hello? What happened if she wanted nothing to do with him and kicked him to the curb where he sat huddled now? Hell, how was he even going to find her?

The fog clamped down around him, and he felt colder now than he ever had in this beastly town. It had never occurred to him that she would run from him, or worse yet, refuse him. In all his plans, he always believed that once he had found her, everything was going to be brilliant.

"Where is she? How am I going to find her?" he muttered to himself. "How?"

Suddenly he was startled by a sound from a few yards in front of him. A homeless man stood picking through the contents of his grocery cart. His hair and mustache were matted and plastered onto his head in patches of brown and gold. Fingerless gloves covered his hands, and it appeared as though he wore two or three threadbare coats. His sneakers were tied onto his feet with twine.

Moved by the sight, Andrew reached into his pocket and tucked a few dollars in the paper cup by his cart. The man grunted something in response and continued rummaging through old newspapers and layers of orange tarp.

Just as Andrew was about to turn away, a hand reached out to grab his arm but missed. The eyes that had been shielded by the brim of his cap peered at Andrew from behind grimy spectacles. They were white, entirely white, and made the hair on the back of Andrew's neck stand straight on end. The blind man leaned forward and whispered, "You're making it way harder than it has to be, kid. Dames ain't that hard to understand. Every one of them wants to be pursued, to be wooed. Don't matter what they say, they want you to work for it. All romance requires a level of suffering, just don't step on your crank too much while you're going about it 'cause you'll end up looking like a schmuck and make me look bad. And trust me, you don't have time for that."

Andrew stared at him, not knowing what to say, but then spoke somberly, guessing the man was either completely mental or a mind reader. Still, his eyes were so unsettling, but it could be a trick of the light. "Do I know you?"

"No, you don't, but you will eventually." He chuckled dryly. "You're so damn young — still believe all your choices are up to you, don't you? Well, keep believing that as long as you can, kid, that's my advice to you."

"I don't need advice, thank you."

"Oh, I think you do. But don't worry, I won't let you screw up too badly."

The honk of a passing car caught his attention, and when Andrew looked back the homeless man, his grocery cart, the orange tarp — every thing was gone. A wave of shocked dizziness overtook him, and he spun around in a vain attempt to locate the panhandler. Hands to knees, he took several deep breaths, willing his clouded vision to clear. A panic attack. He knew the symptoms. That, or someone had slipped something in his water bottle at the show. Was he tripping out after all? He pinched his arm hard until it hurt. No, he was here, now.

Before he could worry any further, other images began to flash into his mind: an abandoned room full of paying customers who were probably demanding their money back, not to mention the *what the fuck?* glares of Simon and Christian. Those were real — nothing eerie or supernatural about them unless a vision of his own imminent murder classified as one. He took one last look around the street for a sign of the homeless man and began his return to the Skellar.

Think, he told himself, he had to think rationally. Whatever delusions he might be suffering, he knew someone at the club must know her. Maybe she had come with friends? After the show he would ask, ask anyone he could get his hands on. The bartender, the bouncer, someone had to have talked with her. The whole way back he plotted. *Because she was here. Here.*

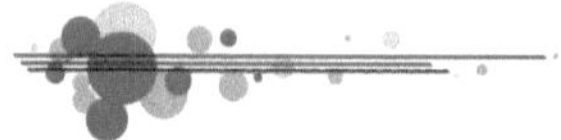

Despite the lead guitarist's aberrant behavior, The Lost Boys still managed two encores. When the cheering eventually died down, Andrew, as planned, immersed himself in the crowd and began to interrogate the fans who remained. Unfortunately, no one knew her, this woman who had knocked over the chair and ran. The girl in the black coat and the high-heeled shoes may as well have been a ghost.

"Oh, that chick who pissed you off? No idea," the bartender told Andrew. "Remind me never to get on your bad side, man. There's gotta be an easier way to deal with hecklers, is all I'm saying."

Christ, Andrew thought, now on top of finding her, he had the extra bonus of convincing her he wasn't deranged. Back on stage, Simon, Christian, and some weary looking staff from the Skellar were busy packing up the rest of the equipment. Simon, his face drawn as tight as a wire, shook his head in silent disgust and took great pains to avoid even glancing in Andrew's direction, but Andrew could feel the heap of curses being psychically hurled in his direction. Christian, on the other hand, ignored everyone completely and stared at his phone as though it had just bit him. Apparently Zoey had texted him immediately after the show and called off drinks. Andrew couldn't blame her; he had tried to attack a patron. Who'd want to party with that?

Given the emotional rollercoaster of the night, Andrew couldn't envision how things could get much worse, but they did. As the exhausted trio were finally ready to leave, having issued their last apologies to the still fuming club manager, Neil St. John stepped up to the empty stage causing Andrew to nearly drop his guitar case on his foot.

"Shit," muttered Simon, reaching into his Mao jacket for a cigarette despite the fact that smoking was verboten in the club.

Andrew wished he would offer him one, but Simon didn't seem in any mood to share. Neil's face was, as always, unreadable, but the tone of his voice was both biting and truthful. "Great show."

"About what happened—" Andrew began.

"I don't want to know. All I want to hear is that you plan to play those shows in Sacramento next week, minus the theatrics."

"Sacramento?" Andrew had entirely forgotten about the dates Neil had arranged for them. No, no they couldn't possibly go now—it was out of the question.

Neil crossed his arms over his leather jacket, and every inch of him, from the distress of his jeans to the appropriate black t-shirt, seemed controlled. Only a slight twitch at the side of his mouth gave any indication of his mounting frustration.

"But—we can't, you don't understand, I just saw…" But Andrew couldn't finish the sentence. How could he? Between the glares being leveled at him from all sides and his own guilt, there was no way he could explain without coming across as even more unbalanced than he already appeared. Neil waited for him to finish.

"Fair enough," Andrew surrendered as he bit his lip and shook his head. "And no, no theatrics."

Whether Neil was surprised by Andrew's response, he didn't say. What he did do surprised all present. He placed his hand on Andrew's shoulder. "Tonight was the best you've done. I keep thinking it can't get any better. I'm still trying to figure out how you put such age into it. It shouldn't work, but it does. It's poetic, as much as I loathe that word. It's poetic without trying—there's no trying, in fact. It's effortless."

The words descended over them, better than any applause. Simon cleared his throat. "Thank you."

Neil stepped back and nodded, heading for the door with a final wave goodnight.

"If I set me drums on fire maybe he'll take us on, you think?" Simon mused when they later loaded their equipment into the truck.

"Maybe," Andrew replied, but only gave it half his mind as he stared down the vacant street.

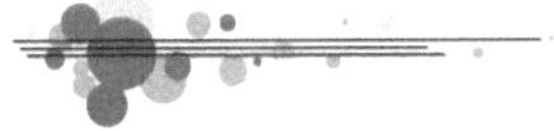

On Tuesday morning as The Lost Boys were driving to Sacramento, Emily parked her aged Citroën under the boughs of a magnolia tree on a secluded corner of Asbury Heights. The contents of her life were crammed behind her, tied to her roof, or shoved in Margot's car, which was parked across the street.

The days leading up to moving were filled with the grunt labor of packing and managed to keep her spirits from sinking any lower. There was a saving grace in moving forward fast enough to leave your emotions behind, but when she stepped out and breathed in the perfume of the flowers, she felt her heart yearn again, and she hated it. She turned her face from the sun and took a deep breath. Life would go on, yes. She imagined herself as Ilsa in *Casablanca*, wearing a to-die-for hat, standing on that foggy runway. She would go to graduate school like her parents wanted, become a professor, and meet her own Victor Laszlow, a man she could admire. They would grow to love each other and one day live in a fine house like the ones on this block. She would teach, and if she were lucky, she would become a dean. It would be so very respectable. So very dependable. So very miserable.

Shaking herself out of her future, she walked up the cracked walkway to her new home. It was a testament to her mental state that she had allowed Zoey to talk her into renting this house sight unseen. She could only imagine what the house looked like in the dark with its turrets and wrought iron. Yet there was a grand desolation to the place that she instantly loved—a great Miss Havisham of a house. All it needed was some "speckle-legged spiders with blotchy bodies" around a wedding cake.

Knowing that their unit was the one on the top floor, Emily wearily hoisted her bag over her shoulder, entered the house, and made the first of what she guessed to be many slogs up the steep staircase. Zoey had explained the house in such painstaking detail that Emily felt she knew what lay on the other side of the door. Her fingers twitched while handling the keys, and she imagined the dining room's original wainscoting, the large, sunny kitchen, the back garden, and the much raved about conservatory on the third floor.

When she entered the apartment, she knew Zoey had been right. A large window seat would be perfect in the front room—because it would block the gutted holes in the wall. The sunlight was indeed lovely and swirled in through the trees, all the better to bathe the exposed joist planks on the floor in rainbows of light. And the ceilings were high, but she was sure she was probably looking at the underside of the floor above her.

Zoey and Margot shouted to her from what turned out to be the kitchen that she eventually reached after running the gauntlet of ladders, toolboxes, PVC pipe, and several men in white overalls who sat on the floor drinking coffee. There she found her roommates unloading boxes that rested on the top of a newly-installed island in the middle of the room. Its presence was a blessing given that Emily could see no other visible horizontal surface to eat upon in the place.

Zoey beamed, white dust covering her UC Banana Slug sweatshirt, her hair held back like an old Russian woman's in a patchwork kerchief. "So you like it? Was I right about the light? And no more art in the bathroom, although there isn't much of a bathroom yet. But Sid—he's around here somewhere—said he'd have the toilet working by this afternoon, and the shower works if you force the hot water on all the way first."

"Or say a novena to St. Jude, patron saint of lost causes," added Margot, whose black leggings and sweater were approaching mottled from all the dust. "Speaking of which, in ten minutes I'll be laying out my shrine over the fireplace. You presence is requested. New apartment, new shrine. I'm adding my Joan of Arc action figure to this one—she comes with her own matches." She waggled her eyebrows in anticipatory delight.

Emily smiled, left her friends behind, and wandered down the hall. Old gas sconces lined the walls; she let her fingers trail along the rough plaster as she passed several rooms which already housed her friends' moving boxes. A door at the far end was closed. Her bedroom, she supposed. If not, she was going to claim it. The room was set off from the others, and the thought of such privacy made her lightheaded.

The door opened softly. A blush of light fell over the hardwood floor from a large sun-spattered arched window. One wall was nothing but floor-to-ceiling bookcases while the other held an old desk with wrought iron legs and a flip top of some dark wood. She stepped toward it and ran her fingers along the top, finding the old-fashioned inkwell. She peeked into the closet and nearly sighed. It was huge. No more plastic bins filled with Myra's treasures, no more rope tied up between windows to hang clothes on.

In spite of the sun, the air in the room was chilly, and she approached the radiator in hopes that it was one of the things in the apartment still functioning. Funny, it felt warm. After she turned the nozzle all the way, she pulled her cardigan across her tank top and, in hushed silence, took one last loving look at the room before shutting the door behind her.

"Zoey!" she yelled. She found her on a ladder measuring a beam between the kitchen and the dining room.

Margot looked up from sorting her holy cards.

"There's furniture in my bedroom," Emily said, helping Zoey down. "Do we need to return it?"

"Don't worry about that. It's probably Neil's, the guy who owns the house. He said he'd leave a few things to make us comfortable. Texted me last night and said he'd drop by to say hello. Really nice guy, you'll love him. A little old for me, but Christian says he's cool."

"Christian? Christian knows him?"

"They're both in the music business."

Emily wanted to inquire further but knew it would bring up a conversation she had avoided up to this point. But apparently Zoey was still talking with Christian. Christian lived with Andrew. The dots were easy to connect.

"Are you two going to stand there," Margot asked, "or are you going to help me sort out the Fourteen Holy Helpers for my shrine? I think I'm missing St. Margaret of Antioch, virgin and martyr. Must have left her at work."

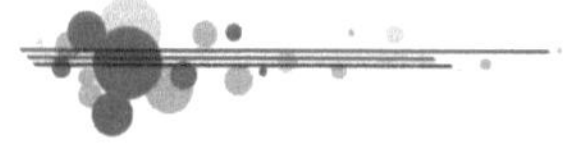

By midweek, the women had settled in as much as possible, given the chaotic nature of the place. Do-it-yourself tables were created so Margot could grade papers, the small fourth bedroom had been transformed into Zoey's studio, and Emily attempted to study, unpack, and convince herself she couldn't possibly have a broken heart.

And even more, she tried to tell herself that she had gratefully escaped the clutches of a lunatic who had, according to her roommates, bounded off the stage after her as if he hadn't shouted at her enough. But Emily could tell that while they bought the story that her allergic reaction to peanuts forced her to flee the club, they weren't sold on his reaction. They might believe that his aberrant behavior had hastened her departure, but they questioned her protests that she knew nothing about him. Thankfully, though, they didn't pry further.

On Thursday morning coffee was successfully brewed, a minor miracle given the bleak prospect of finding a working outlet and a plumbed faucet in the house. Emily wandered into the kitchen in her pajamas and grunted her thanks to Margot, who was still in a robe at the kitchen island hunkered over the *Times'* crossword puzzle. Zoey was chatting up someone in the dining room, from the sounds of it.

"No one should be that happy before the day is warm," Margot mumbled. "I need a three letter word for lecher."

On cue, a stout man in white overalls appeared in the entrance to the kitchen.

"Ah, Sid," murmured Margot, filling in her puzzle. "Sid, say hello to Emily."

"Hello, Sid." Emily was greeted with an electric leer. "You're the foreman here, right?"

"Yep, and me and the men were just helping Zoey move some things. Gotta say, it's the first time I've ever lugged a six-foot paper-mache penis up a flight of stairs."

"Really? Well, thank you." Emily shot her roommate a look as if to say, *where the hell is it now?* but Margot just scratched in another entry and yawned.

"Don't mention it. Anything you need help with, just give a holler. If we're not here, we'll be downstairs most days, working on that place. You three beautiful girls shouldn't be lifting this heavy stuff. You'll pull a muscle somewhere." By the tone of his voice, Emily didn't know whether Sid wanted to be her father or her boyfriend, but she didn't care for either. And she wasn't thrilled with the fact that his gaze had drifted down to her breasts. "Just stop on down anytime. Especially if you get spooked. Not that I'm saying that you're gonna, but it's bound to happen sooner or later. Things seem to be getting worse lately."

"Spooked about what?" Emily asked, confused by his odd choice of words.

"It's just that, you know, things here get kind of creepy sometimes. Weird sounds and all, like from the attic. They say it gets worse at night, not that I can keep anybody here past five, anyways, but don't let it bother you. It's not like anybody's *seen* anything."

"What do you mean 'seen anything'?"

"Aw, nothIng. The crew hears stuff, voices, sometimes crying. But I told 'em it's probably just Nick and Nora. It ain't like we need to call a priest or something. But the stuff on your mantle couldn't hurt."

"Nick and Nora. Is that who lives downstairs?" Margot asked, her crossword puzzle discarded by her coffee cup. "Are they sane?"

"Sane? Well, I'd say that's kind of up for grabs. It's not good to speak ill of those that have, you know —"

A knock at the door interrupted them. By the time they arrived in the living room they only found Zoey, vivid in her chartreuse yoga pants and Zombie Survival Squad T-shirt. She was greeting a handsome man who stood in the entrance way. He held a basket of what appeared to be muffins and scones and proceeded to hand it to her with a smile.

"Welcome." His accent caught hold of Emily's heart.

"Oh, wow, Neil, thank you. Come on in! Hey guys!" Zoey turned. "Oh, there you are," she said, surprised by their close proximity. "Neil's here!" She announced this like he stopped in every morning for tea.

He smiled back at her exuberance. Introductions were made all around, with Sid bowing out, clearly uncomfortable around the house's owner for some reason. Emily noticed that Neil's gaze returned to her repeatedly as he explained to them about walls in the dining room that needed to be opened up and the planned alterations to the bathroom and kitchen.

"Is there any chance you might be able to introduce us to our neighbors?" Emily asked. "Sid was just telling us about them."

"No rush there," Zoey interjected. "Honestly."

"Of course, I'd be delighted. They just got in, in fact. I'll see if they're available. If you'd excuse me for a moment."

They watched him trot down the stairs. Zoey summarily disappeared without a trace and left Margot and Emily to eat their newly delivered breakfast in peace. But after they dressed, Emily could no longer keep her curiosity from getting the better of her. What had Sid meant about strange sounds, and what about the attic? It had been locked since they arrived, and they had been unable to see it. She remembered Zoey saying something about it being unsafe to enter. Maybe she could charm a key from Sid and check it out herself?

It didn't look like Neil was going to return with this Nick and Nora from downstairs any time soon, so unable to resist any longer, Emily announced to Margot that she was going to bring up a bunch of boxes from the foyer. After she slipped out the front, she padded toward the small door at the end of the hall that led to the attic. She gave a turn of the knob; it was still locked. Not to be thwarted, she headed down the stairs in search of Sid but instead found a workman at the foot of the steps. "You mind moving a few of these, miss?" he said, pointing to the stacks of small boxes on the steps. "We gotta bring up some equipment."

Begrudgingly, she stacked as many boxes as she could handle in her arms, all the way up to her chin before she cast a last look at the door to the downstairs apartment and turned to trudge back up the stairs, intent on returning for the key soon. Midway she felt an icy chill blow across her neck, like a gust from an open window, and she shivered so violently that the boxes fell from her arms in a tumble.

Hell.

She knelt down to stack the boxes again when she spotted it. Her one shoe left from the night of the show. Alone, by itself. Small and stylish, a little poetry for no one to see again.

That night came back to her in all its hope and disappointment. What remained was one old shoe, an odd, forgotten thing. Suddenly overcome with the emotion she had fought so hard against, she grabbed the boxes roughly in her arms, and clumped back up the stairs, angry at herself for being so weak.

When she reached the top, a shattering bang from below frightened the wits out of her, and she cried out loud. The boxes wobbled, and she lost her grip. One after another they careened out of her hands, shoes falling everywhere.

Hell, hell, hell!

She spun around and looked down to the foot of the steps. In shock, her body fought to understand what her eyes were telling her mind. No. It was impossible. He was here. He was standing in her foyer — her foyer — wearing a torn T-shirt and jeans and looking like he just stepped off a stage. *Andrew Hayes was standing in her foyer.*

Now he was kneeling down. Before she could ask herself why, he picked up her lone shoe out of the mess. "I believe this is yours," was all he said, looking at her in amazement.

She didn't know how long she stood there, frozen in time. All she knew was that his incredulity had begun to ebb, and caution overcame his sharp features as if he was afraid she might start screaming.

"Th-Th-Th…" She tried to thank him but words failed her. Plus, in the dim recesses of her mind, she knew that it was impossible to make a *th* sound with your mouth open wide. Before she could shut it and stutter another syllable, Zoey came marching down the stairs, passed her, and grabbed the shoe from his hand.

"Was that your sick idea of fan appreciation the other night? Freaking my friend out like that? It was an accident. Get over it," Zoey shouted. In utter shock, Emily watched as her roommate swatted his arm with the missing shoe to punctuate her words. "What — the — hell — were — you — thinking?"

Zoey spun around, dropped the shoe, grabbed Emily's hand, and dragged her back up the stairs. The last thing Emily saw as their door slammed shut behind her was the half-enchanted, half-stricken face of Andrew Hayes rubbing his arm as he stared at her shoe.

What was Andrew Hayes doing here? Here? In *her* house? Thoughts raced in Emily's mind at the possibilities. One, he had tracked her down to finish berating her. Or two, he had come to apologize. No, that was never going to happen. How would he ever find her? Plus, what kind of madman would track down a woman he had only seen once? The kind who had chased her clear out of the club — that kind of madman. The rational side of her mind was screaming at her to barricade herself in her room, but her heart and her body were pumping with so much adrenaline they overtook all reason.

"You — you hit him in the arm with my shoe!" Emily gasped as Zoey dragged her back into the living room and threw her onto the couch.

At the sound of all the commotion, Margot walked in from the kitchen, coffee in hand and paper under her arm. She plopped down next to Emily on the neighboring couch, whispering, "What did I miss?"

"Not a word from you," Zoey reprimanded her, and she scooped up a few prayer cards that had blown off the mantle from her arrival. "And as for you…" She threw a look at Emily. "What the hell gives? What's going on between the two of you? You haven't said a word all week about what happened at the Skellar and we didn't force it. So out with it."

"Out with what?"

"So you're going to stand there and tell me that he stopped a show and stormed out the door because you had some allergic reaction and couldn't breathe and made a waitress spill a tray of drinks?"

Emily's face struggled to maintain a pretense of control.

"Well, in that case, it's a good thing I hit the bastard. Jesus, the man has issues."

"But you hit him with my shoe. He might be hurt. He might be bleeding."

"He might want to sue," Margot added with a nod.

"Christian should have warned me about him if we were going to be living here. What a piece of work — just like that asshole professor of yours," Zoey muttered. "You're always making excuses for people's bad behavior."

"We're not talking about Vandin, now," Emily snapped. "Wait. What did you mean 'Christian should have warned you'? Why does Christian have anything to do with it?"

She hesitated. "He lives here."

Emily looked stunned. Even Margot put down the newspaper.

"They all live here, the whole band, all right? It's out now. Okay? I was sure you'd never agree to rent the place if you knew, that's why I didn't mention it in the first place. But I knew you'd love it once you saw it. The house was too good to pass up. I mean, look at it."

"Yes, look at it." Margot retorted wryly, waving her hand in the air.

"And as for this Andrew, listen, it's a pretty simple process to get a restraining order. I've done it a dozen times. You slam that on his ass, and you can kiss your problems goodbye."

"Zoey!"

Suddenly another knock came from the front door, and three heads wrenched toward it. Zoey strode over and whipped it open. "Listen, dickhead, you better have a good explanation for the horrible way you —"

"Sorry to interrupt," an English voice soothed from the landing, spiking Emily's heart rate until she quickly realized that it was that of her recently acquired landlord. "I was wondering if I might introduce the downstairs tenants to your friends? We were heading up for a tour of the conservatory. It's just been finished, or let's say, it's safe enough to inhabit now. Or we could come back if this is a bad time."

The sounds of people shuffling outside the door hit Emily full force. If The Lost Boys were going to be their downstairs neighbors, that meant only one thing: Andrew Hayes would be living, breathing, and…showering under her feet.

"How ya doing, Zoey girl?" another voice cried from the landing.

"Christian. This is kind of a bad time."

"Excuse me." Margot jammed her head through the entryway. "We'll meet you upstairs in a few minutes, if that's all right with you. Thank you." Then she slammed the door shut in their shocked faces.

Now it was Zoey's turn to appear stunned. "Why did you do that?"

"To keep both of you from losing what little you had left of your dignity. Jesus, Mary, and Joseph. Zoey, I could tolerate living in a complete dump, I could tolerate the leers from the workmen and possibly even the complete lack of indoor plumbing, but do you seriously understand what life is going to be like living over a band?"

"See? This is why I couldn't tell you—you always see the negative in everything. And seriously, I don't think it's going to be that big of a deal," Zoey argued. "They'll be on the road most of the time, anyway. That's what they do. They probably never live in one place long enough to buy furniture."

"But they're here now. How are we ever going to sleep with all that racket, study and grade papers, much less put up with whatever the hell they decide to drag home? You never think anything through. You lied to us to get what you wanted, and now I've just sunk all the rest of my money to pay to move all our furniture to this construction site with crazed, stoned, and drunk idiots partying all night under my feet."

"So you haven't met them and you've already decided exactly who they are, is that it? It must be great to be right about everyone all the time. Maybe you can give a seminar on that. So I lied, I'm sorry, but at least I put myself out there."

"Yeah, we're so far out there that we have to defend ourselves from our new neighbors with footwear."

The resulting showdown was one of the loudest and most colorful that Emily had ever witnessed between her two friends. In the end, two things were decided. First, Margot would agree to stay in the apartment. Second, she maintained full rights to call the cops if their neighbors got too loud. With their friendship still intact, Zoey and Margot headed up to the attic while Emily made a promise to meet them momentarily.

Frantic, Emily paced the length of the living room, trying to figure out what to do. Stay or go? Her situation was very different than Zoey and Margot's. It wasn't as simple as dealing with loud neighbors. If she was going to live here she had to come to terms with this strange attraction she felt for this Andrew Hayes. An attraction that troubled her and left her questioning her normally sound judgment, even as it seemed to intensify with each passing day. There would eventually come a day when they would have to talk. Or she could avoid him; he wouldn't be there much. Zoey was right about that. He'd be on the road most of the time.

Why she thought of Myra at that moment, she couldn't say. But in her mind's eye she could picture the old woman's finger wagging at her, demanding she channel Tracy Lord. "Bring it on, C.K. Dexter Haven," she could almost hear her whisper. "What's the worst he can do?"

That was it. Let him bring on his worst; she would remain calm, cool and unruffled, which wasn't difficult since the heat seemed to have gone out yet again, a particularly chill blast hitting her as she reached the door. She turned about on instinct but saw only the empty apartment. There was no one there. Yet at that instant she swore she felt a cold pressure on her arm like those of fingers, icy and singular, pushing her forward.

Shaking it off, she reached the attic door and hurried up a dark, narrow staircase to the conservatory. Another door waited for her at the top of the stairs. She swallowed hard and pushed it open.

Immediately bright sunlight flooded down upon her, forcing her to squint and raise her hands to her eyes. A ceiling of glass seemed the only thing between her and the endless blue sky. Before her lay a long room, the entire structure made of glass and wrought iron like a hothouse except it was perfectly pleasant. Dozens of half-dead orchids lined the shelves on the perimeter, and planters full of the remains of mottled geraniums and spidery ferns sat next to the assortment of abused wicker furniture that dotted the tile floor. At the other end, a landing exited to what Emily could only assume was a roof garden.

But Emily saw nothing beyond that. For there, set off near the corner, Andrew Hayes stood, his back turned away from all of them, silhouetted in sunlight like some formidable saint from Margot's holy card collection.

Her first instinct was to laugh. It was all so ridiculous — a fantasy at best, a sickness at worst. But whatever it was, whatever emotion was wreaking havoc with both her mind and her body, would end the moment they exchanged words. It had to. It couldn't survive past the first hello. If it did, she wasn't sure she would.

As for her friends, she was relieved to see that they hadn't abandoned their protective stance. Zoey had joined Christian, and although she had reignited her nonstop praise of the house, she kept her sights fixed on

Andrew. Margot had gone so far as to pick up a particularly heavy potted orchid for examination, as if to test how far she could throw it if necessary.

"Zoey you've met. Margot and Emily," Neil said, "I'd like you to meet your neighbors, Christian, Simon and, oh, there you are, Andrew. Ladies, may I introduce Christian Wood, Simon Godden, and Andrew Hayes. Gentlemen, Margot Larson and Emily Thomas."

Emily watched Andrew shake hands with everyone until he came to her. "Emily," he said oddly, and it sounded to her as though he were confirming her name. "Emily Thomas."

His hand covered hers in greeting. One hand over the other, equally cool, equally tentative, but his touch seemed to draw from her a stream of memories that were in no way cool or tentative. The rest of the room seemed to watch them with varying levels of wariness, unsure if another blowout might ensue. No one ventured to mention the bizarre episode at the club and risk breaking the apparent peace.

"It's Andrew, right?" she heard herself say through the maelstrom, and in the dim recesses of her mind she knew she should be trying to channel Katherine Hepburn, as she intended. *Composure, Emily. Composure. Don't let on that you know him. You're going to ruin everything.* Yet how did she know him? She could not even answer that herself.

He cocked his head to one side and studied her. He was almost too alive to look at. It was too much to take in. The precise structure of his face coupled with the strokes of red that ran along the lines of his cheekbones etched themselves into her mind like an overexposed photograph.

"Yes. My name is Andrew Hayes. We're the—"

"We're the eejits downstairs," Simon cut in. "You might as well get used to referring to us that way. If we get too loud, an easy fix is to pound on the floor. We probably won't hear you, but hell, it's worth a try—Emily, it's Emily, yeah?"

The way he stared at her caused Andrew to stare at him.

"Oh, you're a drummer, right?" Margot asked as if she had never seen him before. She put down the planter, and her heels clipped along the tiles as she made her way to Simon's side. "Feel free to do the same, bang on the ceiling that is, if we get too loud. I've been told I often do." Margot tossed her hair in an uncharacteristic flounce, all black sheen and menace.

"Oh, well have a go at it then, there'll be plenty of bangin' with all this remodeling going on," Simon countered, not to be outdone, his brogue thickening by the minute. "It's the endless screwin' and that drillin' that makes the most racket, don't you think, girlie?"

"Girlie?"

"Or the wailing from the ghosts—that's what's really going kill you," said Christian with a nonchalance that no one else seemed to embrace.

"Ghosts?" Zoey asked, and Emily noticed Andrew shoot a flat look at Christian, who went on undeterred. "Haven't you heard yours yet?"

"Wonderful. First a band and now the undead. We should have a dinner and see what else shows up," said Margot stiffly. "Zombies? Witches? Really." Her words, however, had the opposite effect on Zoey and Christian, who decided that a dinner would be just the ticket for all of them. The next fifteen minutes were spent on who was going to bring what, with people drifting here and there, trying to position themselves closer to or farther from each other, depending on the individual.

During this time, Emily watched Andrew and Simon stroll over to the glass door that exited to the roof gardens. Andrew was gesturing riotously with his hands, something Emily had seen him do on stage when he got agitated. Suddenly his eyes narrowed infinitesimally, and his fingers paused in mid-air like they were changing chords. He knew she was watching him.

Her eyes raced back down to the shelf of flowers, willing herself to appear aloof and disinterested. Some discarded construction blueprints allowed her to look busy, and she folded over page after page until she noticed her watch. She would have to leave soon if she didn't want to be late for Vandin's lecture. It was her escape.

"Emily," a voice said from behind her shoulder.

Startled, she swallowed and drew on an untapped sense of courage before she slowly turned. The first thing she saw were his eyes. They were blue like…like nothing and everything and filled with such earnestness that her heart nearly melted at the sight. Yet she was far too wary to trust him—or herself for that matter—with anything more than a hello.

The blue eyes widened in amusement. "You're actually here. You live here. In this house."

How should she respond? Did he still think she was a crazed fan who had hunted him down from the park to the show to his home? Though the look on his face seemed to contradict any ill will, she couldn't be sure. Perhaps he hadn't recognized her from the park at all. Perhaps he merely recognized her from the club, though that might prove bad enough in its own right.

"I had no idea you lived here too," she offered in hasty explanation. "I mean, that anyone lived here too. Well, not really, but we only moved in a week ago and we were told our neighbors were named Nick and Nora. Old people—who weren't sane."

His mouth quirked and she could tell he fought not to laugh. "They are, unfortunately. Old, that is. Dead actually."

"Ghosts? Really? And you live here too," she whispered, staring at him before she caught herself. "Sorry, how long have you been here?"

"Only a month or so. Did you like the show? You ran off rather suddenly."

"Yeah, yes. About that—I'd like to say, that is, I'm sorry. I never meant to crash your show in any way. I was sick. There were peanuts. I had some bad peanuts—they'll kill you if you're not careful. You weren't hurt were you?"

"From the peanuts?"

"No." She shook her head emphatically. "There was glass everywhere."

"I didn't notice."

"Oh…Oh! Then why did you—"

"Run after you? You looked like—well actually I swore you were someone I hadn't seen for a long time. A very long time. Trust me, I usually don't accost patrons—bad for business you know. I'm horribly sorry."

They both stood silent, struggling for something to say in light of the current revelations.

Unable to bear the awkwardness, Emily finally asked, "We have ghosts then. You haven't *seen* anything, have you?"

"No, we haven't had any actual sightings," he replied quickly, in evident relief. "I was a sworn nonbeliever at first, never put much store in any of this, though I'm done second guessing anything at this rate…Nick tends to be rather opinionated in his tastes. He doesn't care for my guitar playing late at night, and I don't think he fancies people ripping his home apart either. But I can't blame him for that first one. So, ah, welcome to the neighborhood, then. It's amazing…you're here." If possible his expression became more enrapt. "You're truly here."

"Excuse me?"

"No, it's only that you're—you're actually living in that flat upstairs. It's abysmal from what I've seen, that anyone could live there, that is." His words tumbled out faster than she thought possible.

"It beats living in the park." At the mention of the park his eyes fixed on hers, and she felt the blood race to her cheeks. Did he recognize her from there? She was mortified he might. If so, he had the good grace not to say a word.

"Hey, Andrew, hit me, man," Christian asked, trotting toward them from across the room.

"Pardon?" replied Andrew, not taking his eyes from Emily.

"We had an argument about the song I heard Nick playing on the piano the other night," Christian explained and smiled at Emily. "It's a game we play, actually."

A second later Neil joined them, intrigued.

"Andrew can name the song, when it was recorded, the album it originated on, and any notable covers. It's kinda creepy, but hey, the man's a genius."

"Is that right?" said Margot.

"Christian, I'd rather not."

"Okay, so here's the lyric."

"You're telling me this ghost Nick was singing?" asked Margot.

"Yeah. Something about needing someone to love him and take him back to San Francisco and bury him there."

Andrew hesitated.

"Ah, hah! See, I knew I could stump him. Yes! Finally."

"'Hong Kong Blues,' recorded in thirty-eight by Hoagy Carmichael. I can't place the album, but George Harrison covered it in eighty-one."

"Oh, that's nothing," Margot scoffed. "Give Emily a line of poetry and she can recite the entire poem, not just some useless stats."

Emily glared at Margot and suddenly felt a strange kinship to Andrew, as though they were two talking parrots in the room brought out for entertainment. She might as well have been seven years old again at a holiday dinner, her father coaxing her to impress some distant relatives who adored how she knew "those Keats and Yeats" fellows.

But it was Andrew who spoke first. "Escape me? Never."

Emily knew this poem. It was Browning, and Browning was her Achilles' heel. Yet why would he know it? More importantly, how could she recite those words and keep her emotions from seeping into them? Her voice drifted into a whisper.

"Beloved!
While I am I, and you are you,
So long as the world contains us both,
Me the loving and you the loth,
While the one eludes, must the other pursue.
My life is a fault at last, I fear:
It seems too much like a fate, indeed!
Though I do my best I shall scarce succeed.
But what if I fail of my purpose here?"

Emily closed her eyes, unable to finish, as Zoey began to clap, and soon everyone joined in. When Emily lifted her eyes, she found Andrew. He stood completely still.

"She could give your muse a run for her money, couldn't she," Simon remarked.

"Don't mess with Andrew's girl. We owe her big time," Christian jumped in, smiling good naturedly at Andrew. "But like you said, maybe it's better if she actually lived here and not—"

"Christian, stop!" Andrew ordered, his hands in the pockets of his jeans and his shoulders stiff. The look said it all for Emily. She had almost forgotten. *It's always about a girl. The mystery girl back home.* It was then that everything became clear. He was a man in love. And not the nonchalant kind—the messy, heartbreaking kind. The kind that made everyone outside that rarified air squirm. Timing was everything, wasn't it?

"Emily."

"No, it's wonderful that you have such inspiration, being a musician and all. She must be a huge help to you."

She immediately found Margot's eyes in the group. Margot knew exactly what was going on; she was far too observant and cynical to pretend otherwise.

"Sorry everybody, but I've got classes this morning, and I'm really running late."

"Watch out for yourself with Vandin," Zoey said softly, interpreting the pain in her voice for other reasons.

"I'll try. See you girls later. Goodbye guys, nice meeting you."

"Make sure he at least chills the wine this time," Emily heard Margot shout as she headed to the door.

Andrew hurried toward her. "Emily, wait." He reached her side. "It was—it was—a joy—meeting you." He waited for her to reply.

"Yes, yes it was," Emily whispered back at last and reached out to offer her hand in farewell but instead headed down the stairs.

"It was a joy meeting you."

A joy. When had any man ever said that to her? Never. *It was nice, Emily. Great seeing you. Later.*

But a joy?

With that, she seized a tattered *Norton Anthology* from her bedroom desk and with untold rage hurled it across the room and screamed. It crashed against her closet door and fell to the floor in page-fluttering finality. The rest of the apartment went silent. The momentary satisfaction of violence gave way to the shame of losing her shit so spectacularly, and she slumped against the wall and slid down onto a pile of recently unpacked clothes.

A chiffon bowler blouse, a lindy-hop pinup dress, and her cherished black Chanel jacket surrounded her, clothes she had bought believing they would transform her into the type of woman immune to such outbursts. She smoothed the edge of one of the jacket's mother of pearl buttons with her fingertip — 1930s, French, ghostly iridescent shells, and still beautiful after so much time.

Hearing those words had been a joy for her too. And suddenly all the poets' jangled words of love had twisted and raced within her mind when he had looked at her: the earth spun beneath her feet as they said it would, and suddenly there was nothing holding her to this world, only joy. But it had all collapsed under the weight of understanding that he loved a girl so dearly that she was nothing short of his muse. Muse. A word that bespoke a creature too mysterious and too ethereal—too perfect. A woman Emily would never be.

Not that she had ever aspired to be such a woman. No. She was confident enough to know she was attractive, lovely even when she put forth the effort, but she was no goddess. Her mouth was too wide, her laugh was too loud, and her eyes—no, her eyes were sly and inquisitive, Thomas eyes, and she was exceedingly proud of them. But it wasn't about beauty. Surprisingly, it wasn't about beauty at all, she thought and wiped at those eyes with the back of her hand. She had wanted something else from him, something far more fundamental. For once she had wanted to inspire. Haunt all his songs. Only her.

"But he's in love with someone else…"

The words settled around her. Somehow she had to force her wretched yearning to stop; it was madness. She had barely spoken to the man, barely knew anything about him. It was a crush, perhaps a particularly potent one, but a crush nonetheless, brought on, no doubt, by the combination of a staggering sexual drought and a dangerously romantic imagination. This was the real world, and the rest was merely one old black-and-white movie—like a fairy tale with better clothes. And that being said, she was no princess, nor was she about to shed the rest of her self-esteem for a man. There was precious little left.

With a renewed sense of purpose, she donned her Chanel jacket and reached for her keys, determined not to be late for her class yet again. But they were nowhere to be found. She distinctly remembered leaving them on the dresser, next to her *Collection of Essential de la Mare*. With growing frustration she continued to hunt, checking the pockets of unwashed jeans and her old wool coat, but only found her MUNI pass and a crumpled twenty.

Strangely, the room seemed to become colder the longer she searched, despite the brilliant sun outside. Goosebumps crept up her skin; she swore she saw her breath wisp in white puffs before her. Muttering to herself, she crouched down to check that the heat register on the floor was still functioning.

"I swear to God, if this is broken too…" she groaned. Suddenly, an icy breeze blew across the back of her neck. She drew her sweater closer around her shoulders.

"Take the bus," a soft voice spoke behind her ear. "Take the bussss, Emily, my dear. The buuuuussss."

She whipped around. There was no one — the room was vacant; she was completely alone. Only the image of de la Mare stared back at her from the cover of the book, his fingers curled in thought about his shrewd face.

"A host of phantom listeners. Is that it?" she spoke sharply to the emptiness.

There was no response — not from the poet, not from anyone. Birds chirped in the nearby magnolia tree, and the sound of sawing came from somewhere below. Convinced that what she had heard were the workmen outside on the front porch on one of their endless breaks, she recommenced her search and headed for the closet to pilfer her coats.

"Ah, *The Listeners*," an unearthly voice breathed behind her. "I adore a good ghostly poem, don't you?"

With a cry, Emily twisted around. "Zoey, Margot, is that you? Cut it out, this isn't funny."

But before she could say another word, the closet door creaked open an inch on its own. Icy fear shot down Emily's back. Every instinct told her to run, to scream. Instead, she closed her eyes and took a measured breath.

No, no, no, no. There were no such things as ghosts. She had specifically taken Dr. Vandin's class to rid herself of her unhealthy fascination with them, to anchor herself to the real world — to grow up. Ghosts were nothing but electrical disturbances and hallucinations triggered by stress, not discontented, disembodied spirits. Garnering her courage, she stepped toward the closet door and placed her hand on the knob, ready to chew out Zoey or Margot for trying to frighten her to death.

The metal was cold to the touch, and she could feel her pulse pounding in her fingertips. With a lurch, she threw open the door. The closet was empty. Nothing, no one inside. Just her clothes.

"There is no such thing as ghosts," she told herself and the shadows inside.

"There *are* no such *things* as ghosts," a silky woman's voice replied. "And by the way, I adore this coat."

From within the closet, the hanger holding Emily's velvet coat rose off the rod. The hanger hovered there, hung in mid-air, swishing the coat as though someone or something was admiring it.

That was all it took. Emily staggered to the bed, grabbed her backpack, and bolted for the door.

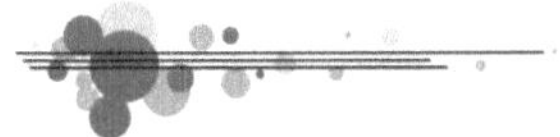

Glued to the spot where Emily had left him, Andrew tried to figure out what the hell he was going to do next. Her presence had shaken him to the core and left him feeling like he was victim to some sort of surreal dream, the kind where he knew the harder he struggled to manipulate the ending, the sooner he would awaken. Then, just like Cinderella, she had vanished. Again. Fairy tales were beginning to piss him off royally.

He was dimly aware of Neil bidding them adieu and telling them he would stop by to talk soon. The severe looking Asian professor, however, was glaring at him from where she stood near the windows. Seconds later she stalked over to Andrew's side.

He recalled saying something akin to hello but was cut off from making any further utterances.

"Stop," she said so that no one else could hear her knife-edged voice. She dragged him out the attic door and back to the farthest corner of the roof gardens until he feared she might heave him off the side. Instead, she shoved him down onto one of the many shabby benches strewn about a derelict collection of raised wood flower beds and planters. Most of the few remaining plants had long ago gone to seed, now yellow-brown in neglect.

"It's Margot, right?"

The wind whipped her black hair across her stern face, and she struck it away. She was either taller than she first appeared or she just bristled well, like some sort of Siamese cat. "I don't understand what's going on between you and my friend, but I don't like it. Every time she sees you she ends up running out of the room, which, among other things, is going to make our days and nights here highly annoying if we are all living under the same roof. So if you have someone—"

Her dark eyes narrowed and zeroed in on Simon who had chosen that moment to wander outside. He lit up a cigarette and began drumming against a wooden bench with his free hand. She lowered her tone.

"If you have someone you're with, fine. More power to you. But no playing games with Emily. Her heart's been broken too many times. So if you decide that a warm bed on each side of the pond is your cup of tea"—she mimicked Andrew's accent perfectly—"I'll rip off your balls and fry them up for breakfast."

Simon must have heard the last bit, for his eyes flashed to Andrew's and he raised an eyebrow provocatively. Andrew shook his head, and Simon paused and took a long drag before returning to his drumming.

Now while Andrew admired this Margot's loyalty, he did not like being proven guilty before having been assumed innocent, and he sure as hell didn't care for her championing another man. She had insinuated something about Emily's professor right before she had left the attic. He needed to know what he was up against.

"This professor bloke. Is she dating him?" he asked her, careful to keep his tone even.

She cast him a stare so critical he sat straighter on instinct. "This muse of yours. Are you dating her?"

How could he possibly confess to her that Emily was his muse, that he had traveled halfway across the globe searching for her? She'd fancy him a right stalker and not let him within a foot of her.

"She—we didn't get on. We parted amicably." Andrew let the lie slip from his mouth, instantly wishing he could take it back. He knew it would come back to haunt him.

Margot cross-examined his face, looking for lies, he was sure. He held her gaze. Whatever she saw in his eyes thawed the corners of her mouth.

"Dr. Pavel Vandin. You must have heard of him—*New York Times* bestsellers, constantly on the lecture circuit when he's not chasing skirts or drinking. He is brilliant, I'll give him that. He's a visiting professor and apparently he's slumming in our college this year. He made a move on Emily at the beginning of the semester, and she shot him down. Seems he doesn't deal well with rejection."

"How so?"

"He humiliates his students for the fun of it, women in particular. She used to talk about it, but she won't anymore. I can't get her to say a word. With Emily, he skates a fine line claiming he's criticizing her academic performance. He does it to other students too. He's notorious for it, really, but he seems to delight in attacking her. Someone needs to…well, I don't condone the use of violence, but someone needs to adjust his—"

"Philosophy?" Simon said, tossing his butt away and taking a place at Andrew's side. He had made his way over to join them without either of them noticing.

"Maybe," Margot answered dryly.

"Then why does she—"

"Put up with it?" She laughed bitterly. "And you mean to tell me neither of you gentlemen has ever taken advantage of your status for your benefit?"

"Sounds like you're defending him," Simon replied, lighting another cigarette.

"I'm sure you play your rock star persona with all the doe-eyed, underage—"

"Oh course, what do you think, we're mad?"

"Simon…" Andrew was in no mood for this. "There has to be something one can do, register a complaint, speak to the Vice Chancellor? Perhaps I could help?" He knew Margot and Simon could hear the fervor in his voice, and he tried to tamp it down with a cough.

Margot stood there, her red lips thinning, weighing the options and the risk. "I suggest you ask Emily first," she said, and as though making a decision, she walked over to a small table, scribbled something on a piece of paper and handed it to him. "Room 166, Payne Hall. Her classes end at one. A good time for lunch."

Simon whistled to himself and strode back into the conservatory. Andrew did his best to ignore him.

"Why are you telling me this?"

Margot didn't answer at first. Perhaps she didn't know or perhaps she didn't want to tell. "Because I've never seen a person look at another like that."

"Like I look at her?"

"No. Like Emily looks at you."

"Parapsychology, parapsychology, parapsychology. A word that conjures up a great deal of images, does it not? Now parapsychologists, people who study parapsychology, study a number of alleged paranormal phenomena. Is there anyone here with a brain in their head who can name one?"

Emily had chosen this moment to enter the crowded lecture hall. The heavy metal door slammed shut behind her with a huge echo, causing all eyes to lock on hers. She began her silent descent into the huge dungeon pit of a room, passing row upon row of ancient desks and chairs: torturous one-piece rack-like devices that made sitting for any length of time sheer agony. The absence of windows and the dank smell of mildew completed the veritable prison.

Contemporary Psychology was a huge haul from the bus stop clear across campus. Out of breath from the run and with her nerves still on edge from her ghostly encounter, she nearly tripped down the steep steps, eliciting her fair share of sniggers from the surrounding students. Unfortunately, the lone available seat was directly in front of where the hulk of Dr. Vandin loomed.

His hand ceased its theory-espousing conducting and remained poised in the air when he saw her, as if he were holding one of his trademark cigars. The rumple of his black turtleneck, the reddish shine of his forehead, and the sloop of his uncombed hair bore testament to another night of his notorious drinking.

"Miss Thomas?" He raised his cunning, albeit bloodshot, eyes to her, visible even behind his reading glasses, and rolled up the sleeves of his sweater. "Miss Thomas, you are always so ready to offer your opinion. Go ahead, amaze us. It is a Monday afternoon. What else do we live for but to hear your, what is the word in English…oh, ah, that's it — perspective."

Apparently he was sober today.

"I'm sorry, I didn't hear the question."

"Well, if someone had their head in the game and could tell time, we would have enlightenment, would we not, class? I suppose I'm going to have to tell you then. Take good notes, everyone. Oh, and Miss Thomas, you might want to take a seat. Make yourself comfortable, by all means."

Emily tripped over a sorority sister's hot pink toes and nearly upended three laptops in an attempt to get to her chair. Dr. Vandin cleared his throat and positioned his papers, peering at her from over his black-rimmed reading glasses.

"First, telepathy, the transfer of information or emotions between individuals by some means other than sensory perception.

"Miss Thomas, you will be a good sport, won't you, and serve as an illustration, since you missed half the class. Good. Now, one would say she appears anxious, fidgeting with her bag like she does as she retrieves her notes." Here he shook his notes for effect, a lock of his black hair tumbling across his forehead. "See how she doodles in her book and drums her fingers?" Emily's eyes flashed to his; he took no notice but chose to begin pacing back and forth in front of her row. "I mean no offense to Miss Thomas, I'm merely trying to illustrate how she is perhaps able to communicate with me telepathically. Perhaps she is telling me how attractive the female student body finds me? How much she—how much they—long for the presence of the university's sexiest professor?" Snorts and guffaws peppered the class. "Or perhaps not?" He pushed his glasses up his nose and turned the pages of his notes with an attempt at a smile.

"Ah, but if she wasn't telepathic, I could use my clairvoyance, that's right, clair-voy-ance, scribble that word down. You too, Miss Thomas, right next to the doodles of Prince Charming or whatever secrets you have adorning your notebook."

His eyes found hers this time, and she flattened her hand over her notes. A sketch she didn't remember making of Andrew lay hidden underneath her palm.

"Clairvoyance: a supernatural ability to retrieve information about people or places or even events. But that is not good enough. Miss Thomas doesn't want anything to do with me. See how she sits, straight-backed and rigid? No slamming her books shut and storming out the door, no such drama for her. How do I know that? I have precognition—scribble again you monkeys—an understanding of information about future places or events before they occur through extrasensory means.

"I see she will not slam her book shut and storm out the door, but wait instead until after class to upbraid me. So I apply psychokinesis, another phenomena, class—no, not just the mind's ability to twist and turn spoons, but the ability of the mind to affect time or energy by means unknown, and so I have her fall madly in love with me."

He stood directly in front of Emily now, as if awaiting her reply. She met his stare and said nothing. "Ah, but I tire of her," he said and dismissed her with a smile and a flip of his hand. "She grows clingy. Unable to bear the pain of being separated from me, she, of course, ends her life, hoping for reincarnation, that's right, another phenomena, the rebirth of a soul in a new physical body after death. Perhaps one who could tell time?

"But alas, she merely becomes a ghost. Which brings us to our last phenomena, haunting. My area of expertise, as you well know, wherein the deceased individual frequents his former home or, pardon the pun, haunts."

Several of the girls in the class had ceased taking notes, enamored by Vandin's commanding stage presence. Like any performer, he used his physical prowess and resounding voice to his benefit, and Emily could remember how easily it was to fall under Vandin's spell. The sexuality of the intellect, Margot had branded it. The brilliant, Russian bear of a man. Emily had almost fallen for it. Almost. The reality of the man had won out. Even his accent was an affectation, practiced to complete the image of "the hard biting, worldly professor," but in the end it proved yet another demonstration of his boorishness and arrogance. He could fake a Boston Brahmin just as well. Who knew if even his last name was authentic or just manufactured for a dustjacket?

"There is a whole mythology surrounding ghosts," Vandin continued, "encompassing how a ghost can communicate with the physical world, what they are forbidden to say or do, to even the ridiculous notion of what can and cannot destroy them. Say what you want of the rest of this questionable science, but as you know from my research, I have spent the greater part of twenty years repudiating this particular fallacy. I have, in all of my cases, been able to prove that what was first purported as a haunted house is nothing more than a—"

"I saw a ghost," Emily said. Why the words left her mouth, she was unsure. Perhaps a semester of being Vandin's favorite whipping girl had finally taken its toll and she had reached a breaking point. Perhaps she wanted to see him proven wrong, discredited, embarrassed.

"Miss Thomas?"

"The old Victorian I just moved in to. My closet—it's haunted by a woman. I've heard her."

The announcement created quite a stir in the classroom as expected. Heads twisted between Emily and Vandin as they waited for his response.

"There has never been any reproducible scientific evidence to support—"

"She spoke to me. She knew Walter de la Mare—and she liked my clothes."

"You can't be serious."

"I am. A hanger in my closet…it levitated, and I distinctly heard a woman's voice." The more she spoke, the greater her conviction grew.

"Miss Thomas, do you usually drink this early in the day?"

"No. I'm not a professor yet."

The class laughed, but Dr. Vandin did not.

"And nor will you ever be at this rate."

"Thank God for that. I'd hate to aspire to ghost-busting as my academic career."

A susurrus of shock filled the room. Emily didn't realize she was standing, her hands balled into fists.

"Please see me after class."

She slammed her books, grabbed her satchel, and stormed toward the aisle.

"Going so soon?" Vandin remarked offhandedly.

That's when she heard them. Footsteps. The sound rifled down the lecture hall and stopped halfway. An eerie quiet descended on the class as Dr. Vandin looked up from his notes; his smirk soured to an irritated stare. Emily heard a few girls next to her gasp, and she turned.

"Might I suggest you change the style of your lecturing method?" Andrew said, his voice deathly cool as he stood there with his arms at the sides of his black leather jacket. "I believe you have heard of the term sexual harassment? You seem to possess a passing intelligence. I suggest you look it up."

By now the class had leaned forward like spectators at a boxing match. A few began to whisper among themselves, evidently aware of who Andrew was.

"Miss Thomas, class isn't over. Given your poor grades, I suggest you ask your boyfriend here to leave."

"You're all right, yes?" Andrew asked her, ignoring the hisses around him. She raised her face to his and nodded. "Let's get you out of here, then."

"Miss Thomas," Vandin warned.

But Andrew had offered his hand, and she took it, and together they walked up the steep stairs and back out into the day.

They stood outside in the quad. The sunlight danced off Emily's face as she smiled demurely at Andrew. All of his courage from a few minutes before had vanished. Storming the castle was one thing — but now…

"I was about to leave, you know. He was a — "

"A shite?" Andrew couldn't stop himself.

"That's the word I was looking for." They laughed together, their prior awkwardness slowly dissipating like bubbles rising from champagne. "Thank you. He was just being particularly brutal today. It's part of the persona — he likes to get a rise out of…he likes to see his students squirm. It must be a Russian thing, I guess. But what brings you here? I mean why were you — I mean, you aren't taking a class, are you?"

"I was on campus looking for a place to rehearse, actually. Didn't think you'd care for that kind of late night entertainment. Good neighbors and all…Margot had mentioned you had a class here. Thought maybe you might need a ride back home."

"How did you know I didn't drive?"

"I took a chance." Christ, he thought, how easily the lies came when he needed them.

She tilted her head to look up at him and a wrinkle formed between her eyes, and something melancholy passed through them. Her auburn curls danced about her face, a few strands getting caught in her old fashioned sweater, twining about the top button.

"Actually, I took the MUNI. I better be going if I'm going to catch the next one though."

"Have you had lunch?" he said a bit too quickly. "Would you care to join me? That is, if you don't have any other plans."

Her hands slid into the pockets of her jeans and she rocked on her toes. She smiled now, more settled. "I'd like that. There's this little place not far from here. They serve tea the proper way."

His grin ignited hers. She almost sounded British.

In retrospect, Andrew couldn't have remembered the way to the shop if someone had put a gun to his head. He was too busy listening to her, gazing at her as she pointed out the shops and the restaurants.

"And that's where the witches are." She nodded to an alley between stores at the corner.

"Witches?"

"It's one of my favorite shops. You can have your palm read and collect all your coven related material inside. It looks like something out of Hawthorne. Do you want to see it?"

They wandered down the alley, where bougainvillea and jasmine ran wild along the surrounding brick walls. A small fountain sat sentinel in the courtyard, and the top of a Dutch door hung open at the far end. A sign bearing the words *The Bell and the Candle* hung overhead. Andrew almost expected to see a grizzled-haired witch poke her head through the opening and cackle.

Instead, a heavily hennaed man with a preponderance of facial hair nodded in their direction as they entered: part surfer dude, part Black Sabbath cover band drummer, by Andrew's guess. Emily made quick work of looking over the antique display counters, scrunching her nose up at the odd selection of jewelry, then turning her attention to a collection of old leather-bound books.

"I found a first edition Poe in here, believe it or not. They carry the oddest treasures. Odd and old, my favorite things."

"Odd and old?"

"Um-hmm. I like the feel of memories. Antique brooches, vintage jackets—who wore them, what lives did they live? What secrets did they hold? I've traveled so little that I love finding things from far, far away. Like this old ring I found at the vintage shop where I work. I'm saving up for it. Can't afford it, but I've got a childish fascination with it. Or this old hat." She took a stylish fedora off a stand and playfully placed it on her head before turning to a mirror.

"Definitely not Garbo. With this hair, more like Harpo," she mused, then returned it to its stand and shook her curls loose.

Like no woman in the world, Andrew wanted to say. She was of a different time, as if she had stepped out of an old photograph. Her quirkiness, her energy, her sadness. Odd and old. But in a good way. A good, good way.

He thought about the coat she had worn that night at the Skellar and pictured her in Paris. He pictured them together in the night, and what it would feel like to kiss her.

The man had taken his seat in the corner at a fringed table near a small wood burning stove and asked, "Honeymooners?"

They both stared at each other, and after a very heated pause blurted out, "No!"

"Yo, dude and dudess, that's not the vibe I'm getting. Old souls. You've been together in at least one past life for sure. Here, come on over by the fire and let me take a look. Name's Dwayne, by the way."

Emily and Andrew both looked at the other, the deck of tarot cards, and a crystal ball on the table, with a combination of alarm and hysterics, each daring the other to go first. Finally they gave in. Andrew extended his hand in greeting, about to introduce himself, when Dwayne admonished, "No names, please. It damages my visions. Just sit on down. Her next to you. I need both your hands."

Two small chairs sat empty next to Dwayne. Andrew pulled out one for Emily and sat down himself. Dwayne grasped Emily's hand in his and pressed Andrew's next to it.

"Oh man. You see these lines, these lines here?"

Their heads nestled together, Andrew felt her hair fall onto his shoulder and her breath warm his face. He swallowed hard. Emily's heart was beating a mile a minute.

"That's your life lines. See how they match, how they overlap in the same exact pattern? I've never seen anything like that."

"What does it mean?" Emily asked.

"Well, it's pretty flippin' unbelievable."

Andrew envisioned the worst. Ages of being brother and sister. Father, daughter…mother, son. *Christ.*

"Look at the love lines. Just look at 'em — it's the love lines that tell you everything, everything you'll ever need. You mind if I call my friend? He's never going to believe this shit."

"Do you mind," Andrew said, trying to hide his irritation. "We're catching lunch and — "

"Yeah, yeah, I hear you, man. Bummer though. Egan, my friend, he's one major palmist, and I'd bet you this shop he's never seen anything like this."

Andrew glanced down at Emily; she was pale.

"You belong to him." The words froze them, inches from each other. They blinked their eyes at the same time and stared at him. Dwayne beamed at Emily. "You can't diss this kind of fate. No how, no way. No matter how hard you try and fight it, no matter how far apart you are, it'll always find you and bring you two together. I mean it's seriously big-time karmic. You're his. Always have been. Always will be. There's never been a lifetime you haven't been completely and totally his. I mean, like in the core of your being. See here? Slave, concubine, mistress, mistress, lover…goes on and on."

He turned and laid his all-knowing gaze on Andrew. "Yo, man, this here lady's your muse! Righteous."

Emily's eyes widened in utter disbelief. "What?"

Righteous indeed.

"Was I ever even legal?"

Emily stared at Dwayne as though he had just spoken to her in tongues. Her head shook in confusion, and if Andrew wasn't mistaken, with no small amount of anger.

"You see that chain line?" His black enameled fingernail traced a basket weave pattern on her palm. "That's oh, ten, twenty, thirty lifetimes right there. I don't think you're grasping the significance of this. You're his inspiration, his drive—his reason for being, lady. Don't matter if it's legal or not."

"But a concubine?" she challenged him under her breath. "How can you see that in a bunch of wrinkles?"

She was ticked off, that much Andrew could tell, and she didn't appear to believe a bloody word. He also thought that if he didn't move her quickly she might pick up the crystal ball from the table and smash the palmist's head in with it.

She stared deeply into her palm and swallowed. "If he loved me so much, you think he'd find the decency to marry me, right? Anyway," she said bracingly, "he already has a muse."

Dwayne frowned at her in disagreement. "The lines don't lie, lady. See your mound of Venus, here by your thumb…" His fingernails continued to poke at her hand, and Andrew saw Emily's shoulders curl around herself in defiance. She was shutting down.

"Why don't we head over to lunch," Andrew insisted, almost lifting her up off the chair. "Thanks so much for your time, sir, it's been…insightful, to say the least."

He dropped a twenty near his crystal ball and whisked Emily out the door. By the time they reached the end of the alley, he had been holding his breath so long that he should have been rightfully dead. He could barely grasp how a stoner witch could summarize the driving force of his life within moments of looking at each of their hands.

They walked, Andrew not sure where they were going, his mind rushing to put the words together. How could he even begin to explain this to her?

Emily, this is it. My whole life. It starts with a boy. And a girl. Right? That much is easy. But what to say next? How to make her understand?

How at eight years old, the boy sat in his bed one night, fingers playing an imaginary keyboard on the fringes of his bedspread, when his mind began to race with the wild blur of her, this girl, like an unloosed spirit, as the music wove new and thrilling patterns before his eyes. And she was there, always, from that day on. This girl, this same girl with the reddish hair, speaking to him, running joyously through his mind. How at fourteen, the pulse of his music had changed, with furor and rebellion. How he didn't understand it, and he could only feel and ache and need. And then there was sex. And suddenly everything was sex, and she was sex, and she was his. Especially at night, in the quiet stillness. How at eighteen, words of black wit and a newly tried-on sophistication invaded his manners, his lyrics, his being—and fit like a coat that was too large though perfectly comfortable. It became the armor he wore to this day to battle everything, except her.

How could he confess that friends, family, and even sanity could slip away, but she was always there. For him. She would take one look at him and run screaming. Any sane person would.

Right now he had to focus on a way to tamp down these emotions, the ones that were demanding that he confess, *Yes, damn it, it's true. All of it. Always you. Never another. There couldn't be, there could never be—only you. In my very blood. That man is right. He is absofuckinglutely right! Don't you feel it?*

They walked in silence to the bistro, their shoulders inches from each other's. Their reflection in a storefront window caught his eye. Although she was tall, Emily fit perfectly against his side, and he imagined how her body would feel against his, how his arms would hold her. The cool breeze blew back her hair, and she wrapped her arms across her old-fashioned sweater to keep warm. He considered surrendering his leather jacket but hovered his hand near the small of her back instead as they crossed the street, not trusting himself to do more.

The bistro proved to be like the countless others Andrew had hidden out in throughout his life. There were the familiar old art deco tiled floors, brick walls, a smattering of art and movie posters, and a lone little spiral staircase that led to nowhere. The air smelled of coffee and sugar and fresh cut flowers.

An effervescent young woman escorted them to a small table where they slipped behind their menus. Ella Fitzgerald sang out to them from somewhere.

Soon the restaurant filled up around them — students and professors by the looks of them, either intent on their companions or their laptops, a few tourists, and one couple that lay entwined on a sofa, kissing underneath a movie poster of *The Maltese Falcon*.

"I'm sorry about what happened back there, to mortify you like that. I wouldn't have brought you in the store if I'd had any idea how crazy he was."

"Mortified? No. It — I wasn't mortified, though it isn't something you hear every day, when you think of it — tied to someone through all eternity? Quite a commitment…" Andrew's voice trailed off as he struggled to find something else to say in response to the look of earnestness on Emily's face.

"At least apologize to your girlfriend for me, please. I don't think she'd appreciate all that talk of concubines, but I guess that's better than being your slave." She cringed at her words and bit her lip as though trying to stem the possibility of anything more escaping.

Luckily, an old shuffling waiter took that moment to interrupt and take their order.

"I'll have a pot of Earl Grey, please."

"Make that two," Andrew added, then dropped his voice to a more conspiratorial tone. "By the way, what is the exact definition of concubine? I forget. It's Chinese, right?"

"It's from the Latin," the waiter replied in a stage whisper, causing both of them to turn their heads. "Would you like anything to eat with your tea?"

"Scones with lemon curd, please."

"Thank you, miss. You see, the word is found in Old French and Middle English too, with Chinese and Muslim variants. It's a splendid word, isn't it? Concubine. Always reminds me of hookah pipes and intrigue. And you, sir?"

Andrew's eyebrows rose. "I'll have the same. Thank you."

They watched him trundle off, waiting until he was out of sight before they started laughing.

"Well that explains it," Andrew said. "I was rubbish at Latin, rubbish at most things, I'm afraid. No patience for it. It killed the philosophy major."

"You were a philosophy major?"

"Philosophy, poetry, music, then —"

"How many degrees did you get?"

"None."

"None?"

"I tend not to finish things. Except for pints and packs of cigarettes, but I've given them up — mostly — the cigarettes, that is."

She tilted her head. "You finish songs."

The look of sincerity on her face unnerved him. "It's the only thing I can finish these days…But you never answered my question. What is the definition of a concubine?"

"You seriously don't know?" She leaned forward and dropped her voice, deepening their conspiratorial nature. "Well, it comes from the Latin verb *concumbere*, as in, 'to lie together.'"

Andrew devoutly wished for that cigarette. "I take it you're an English major," he said carefully.

She nodded. "And psychology."

"Which is worse?"

"Psychology. Without a doubt."

"No, which variant is worse."

"Oh. The Muslim. Definitely the Muslim."

"Which is?"

She hesitated. "A woman residing in a harem and kept, as by a sultan, for sexual purposes."

His heart skittered like a rock down a cliff. The waiter appeared with their teapot. Andrew drummed his fingers, waiting for the old man to depart. At last, this was his chance. He finally had her alone.

"As for my girlfriend," he said with a deep breath, placing the pot down after pouring each of them a cup, "I believe she would not care as I do not have one."

"What?" Her eyes found his and blinked several times. Confusion and puzzlement passed through their gry depths until they settled on realization. "I'm so sorry. It must have been awful."

"Excuse me?"

"The break up must have been hard."

No, she couldn't. No. Oh, bloody hell. This was turning into some drawing room farce. Emily thought he had endured some horrible break up with his muse, this suddenly very existent nonexistent woman, for which he was going to punch the piss out of Simon and Christian for bringing her up in the first place. And now Margot's story would only corroborate the existence of a nonexistent break up.

The heat of guilt swathed across his face. The more he struggled to come up with something witty, or at least truthful, the more he flailed and the more tortured he knew he looked. Emily seemed to be suffering along as well. Clearly, she didn't know how to deal with him. Clearly, he didn't know how to deal with himself.

"It was nothing," he ended up saying. "Truthfully, it was nothing."

"Do you want to talk about it?"

"No," he said bluntly, his head reeling.

"So…um, you're a musician? That's wonderful."

He nodded in relief. His fingers found the pair of little silver tongs and he began shoveling cubes into his cup until he glanced up at her. "Sugar?"

"Just cream. But thank you."

He glimpsed about the restaurant. "It's a rather interesting place."

"I like it. It refuses to change."

He placed the tongs down and sat back, trying to control his nerves. Why was this so difficult? He'd waited forever for her, and now he could find nothing to say. Maybe he'd answer the questions all women asked him after they played the "you're a musician" card; it was always the same. What made you want to become one? Don't you find life hard on the road? What's your inspiration? What he was not prepared for was her response.

"Andrew, do you really believe in ghosts?"

"Pardon?"

"You promise you won't think I'm crazy?"

Oh, girl. I've built my life around the fantasy of you and am battling every nerve ending in my body not to lunge across the table and kiss you right now, so who's crazy here? "I promise."

"It's just that this morning, right before I left for class, I swore I saw something, heard something in my closet."

She had gone so pale at this that he leaned closer to her. "Were you hurt?"

"No, that's just it. There wasn't anyone there. Just a voice and—oh forget it, this all sounds ridiculous. You must think I'm an idiot."

"Was it a woman? I mean, was it a woman's voice you heard?"

"Yes, how did you know?"

"Nora." It was Nora; Nora had been there. Andrew hadn't realized he'd said the name out loud. "No, Nora comes with your part of the house," he added quickly, hoping to dispel Emily's increasing concern. "Our flat has cursed lovers, apparently. They can't haunt the same spaces for whatever reason. At least that's what Neil told us."

"But you've never seen either of them, you said?"

"No." What was he going to say? *I haven't seen the dead man but he loves this woman Nora so badly I can feel it. Like it's seeping into my very bones.* "You asked me about being a musician. Any more questions regarding that?"

She grasped her teacup, aware that she'd been warded off this line of questioning. "Are you—are you going to be staying in San Francisco long?"

"I would like to, but it depends. You see, we've decided we needed some time off from the road. So much has happened in the past year, we've become so popular so fast, that when Neil offered us the chance to stay here we couldn't say no." He went on to tell her of what had occurred in London. "We just wanted to decompress or detox or whatever the hell Christian calls it. Plus, I've always wanted to write here—can't tell you why." *Because it's a lie, you idiot.*

"Again, I'm so sorry for disrupting your show. I knew I was going to be sick and I had to get out of there. But I enjoyed it, really, I did. You were incredible."

"That's kind of you. So you're telling me I shouldn't quit my day job?"

"No! Unless you want to disappoint half the female population of San Francisco. Not to mention the table of girls over there. I think they've caught on to who you are."

"Marvelous…So, Christian mentioned something about a dinner?"

"Oh Lord." Emily laughed, her face a blur of happiness. "Please cook. Promise me you'll cook. Please. Or we'll all end up dead."

Contentment stole over him. Her hair caught on her sweater buttons again, and he uncurled it, holding the strand between his fingers.

"Stupid buttons, I'm going to chop all this hair off someday."

"No!"

Emily looked at him in surprise and blushed, pink warming her face.

"It's lovely," he stammered.

"Really? The curls are hopeless, and it's too short to let down a tower, you know."

For a heartbeat he did nothing but stare at her. "If you were in a tower, I wouldn't need this to reach you." He didn't know what made him say it. It was juvenile and awful and cringe-inducingly awkward—yet absolutely true. And now it was just out there, hanging tremulously like that strand of Emily's hair between his fingers.

"Your check. No rush," the waiter announced.

Christ! He closed his eyes and silently cursed a blue streak, causing Emily to recoil from him as though she had been burned by a stove.

Andrew knew he had scared her. She almost appeared panicked. He grasped for something to say but could come up with nothing.

"Andrew?"

He was wired so tight he cried, "Yes!"

"What—what made you go into music?"

His mind stuttered in a million directions. What could he say? *You?*

"Trying to avoid a beating." That seemed to take her by surprise, and he fumbled to recollect the essentials. "I was four or five years old, I think. My parents took me to a symphony. I was a royal bother according to mum. *Dolor de cabeza*, she used to say. She's Spanish, and met my father when she was at university. Now, my father would have called me a royal shite, more likely. He is—was—from Oxford. He was ready to sell me at that point, so I decided to pay attention."

She smiled; it was all he needed.

"They played *Fanfare for the Common Man*." His hands inadvertently played the table as he spoke, and he hummed the beginning bars. "There are sounds that have such a transcendent effect when you first hear them that they're near alive. No, they are alive. Hell, I know that sounds so pretentious, but giving up that control or being controlled by something with that much power—and to know that I could create that music, that I could spend my life losing myself in it—well…there was no going back. Even that young

I knew that everything in the world wasn't right, but I had an idea of what I was capable of after that. It changed me forever. It changed everything."

She stared at him. The whirl and hum of the restaurant became distant around them, her face remaining perfectly still. He knew her cheek would fit perfectly in the cup of his hand.

"Oh Christ, sorry, I've been rambling. I tend to do that. Feel free to smack me or do something equally violent next time. Now what about you? Seems you fancy poetry and tolerate psychology."

"And if I don't pass Vandin's class, I'll shoot myself."

"Why?"

"There's a writing conference at Squaw Valley this summer, a special one, and very few writers were invited. There's this manuscript I've been working on, and I'll have the opportunity to work on it with an agent. I've published articles and short stories before, but never anything this major. If I don't pass, I can't graduate. I'll need to retake the class in the summer and that means no conference. So yeah, it's hemlock for me if that happens."

"Why can't you take the course in the fall? Just postpone it?"

"I need to start working full-time by then. Scholarships only go so far, you know. I haven't got much money."

He could tell by the look on her face that she knew he did. *Another demerit, Hayes,* he thought. Do not pass go, do not get the girl.

"And your professor doesn't seem like a reasonable sort of chap, right?"

"Yeah, and if I don't get 'my head in the game' as he says, I'm toast. But if I can find a subject for this last research paper that he doesn't shoot down, I'll be golden, I think."

He didn't know whether she was trying to convince him or herself with that last comment. Either way, he didn't want that man within ten feet of Emily. What kind of prick got off demeaning a woman like that? And what the hell was this about her having to get his approval…

It was then that he had an idea.

"The bloke fancies ghosts, so why don't you research ours? Prove they exist?"

"Dr. Vandin? He's spent years trying to debunk the idea of ghost hunters, thinks it's crackpot science — 'bullshit' was the precise term he used during one lecture. He'd have me committed, or with my luck, the ghosts would decide to haunt another house the moment Pavel stepped over the threshold."

"Pavel?"

"Vandin, I mean."

Why would she use his first name? She couldn't be—no, that was ludicrous. But then, he didn't know Emily's history. In truth, he knew precious little about her. Emily Thomas was a complete unknown to him. Maybe she already had a boyfriend? Maybe they would have animalistic sex every night in that house for him to hear? Maybe he was just too bloody late?

"The ghosts," he said, startled by the passion in his voice. "They're searching for each other. That's why they moan—they can't find the other, no matter how hard they try. Someone needs to discover why. Uncover their mystery, help them become reunited. Don't you think it's worth a shot?"

"But—"

"Souls like that deserve to be together. Imagine loving someone so violently, so passionately, and not being able to touch them, to be with them, to hold them. And wanting that so fiercely."

His hand clenched his cup, adrenaline he couldn't control coursing in his veins. "Emily, what's worse than unrequited love?"

She did not respond.

"What's more wretched, more horrible than that?"

Her eyes lowered to her teacup; she studied its contents and gave a choked laugh. "Nothing."

She took a sip and said no more.

Thoughts of Emily tortured Andrew the entire week long. Somehow, some way, he needed to make it up to her and recover from their disastrous lunch. But he had no clue where to begin. She must have thought he was mad, acting the way he did. The poor girl had said nothing the whole drive home. They parted ways in the lobby with stiff nods.

Once he stepped through his front door, he steeled himself for the expected grilling from Simon and Christian. Running out of the house to chase after a girl you just met should elicit some form of rebuke. But nothing came. Perhaps they could sense his foul mood. Although when he told Simon he had run into Emily on campus, Simon couldn't help asking if it was with the truck. Christian, as Andrew had expected, was a lost cause, his renewed friendship with Zoey making him ungodly cheerful. As a result, they were subjected to endless tracks from Little Feat under the reasoning that it was their favorite group growing up. There was only so much fucking *Dixie Chicken* a man could take.

By the time Friday rolled around, Andrew was not only heartbroken but "Feated" out as well. Or as Simon said one night in the kitchen while banging his head against the refrigerator, "I bloody surrender. I am fucking de-*feated!*"

Emily had proved as invisible as the ghosts. He wasn't sure if she would ever speak with him again, sure she was living under the impression that he harbored some great unrequited love. Occasionally they would see each other coming or going. She would nod shyly but nothing more. Miserably wretched, he busied himself in trying to make some semblance of order in their flat, which proved challenging as they were living in a bleeding blueprint of a house.

Friday afternoon found Andrew working in the dining room on his laptop, sheet music splayed out across the table, his ratty old Cambridge T-shirt still sticking to his back from a pickup basketball game he had enjoyed earlier with Simon and Andrew at the school playground down the street. His sweaty hair was almost sticking up on its own due to the countless times he'd dragged his fingers through it.

Simon was not in any better shape and sat across from him idly drumming on an empty plaster bucket while staring in turn at an abandoned copy of *Genius: The Life and Science of Richard Feynman* and a *Playboy* that lay discarded nearby. A lit cigarette burned in an ashtray at his feet.

Christian was lost in the kitchen, preparing for what he kept referring to as *The Dinner*, pausing only to chastise Simon to smoke outside and question why he couldn't get his porn off the Internet like any decent perv.

Andrew was doing his best to ignore this, focusing instead on the growing ash on the end of Simon's cigarette.

While balancing on a ladder and yanking out some old knob and tube wiring, Sid took the opportunity to announce, "Those ladies upstairs. What do you think my chances would be if I asked one of them out?"

"Bad idea," Simon replied.

"Hey, I didn't even tell you which one."

"Doesn't matter. Although good luck with that Margot, my friend. Fiend of a woman if I ever saw one."

"I didn't think you remembered her name?" Andrew faced Simon. The ash fell off the end of his cigarette as Simon glowered in his direction.

"Well the big one, she's kind of cute. A whole lotta woman there."

An aproned Christian entered the dining room holding a large piece of cutlery. "Excuse me, man?"

"How are the short ribs coming there?" Andrew asked, smacking his hands down on the table certain that the last thing this place needed was a murder and yet another ghost.

"They're fine. And her name is Zoey, by the way. Cut out that 'big' shit, okay?"

"Yeah, or she'll knock you on your ass," Simon said. Little Feat blared from the kitchen.

"So what, that leaves the booky one," Sid pondered aloud, screwdriver in hand. "She seemed awful nice when I was up there last. A little hard to read, though."

"Yes, that would be Emily." Andrew sighed.

"So, you don't mind if I..." He jabbed his screwdriver in and out of a hole in the wall.

Andrew tilted back his chair. "Do you wish to die young?" he uttered in a barely controlled voice.

His declaration caught Simon's attention. "What? Has love come to Andy Hardy at last? When did this happen?"

"Nothing has happened. I told you, I ran into her on campus when I was trying to find us some rehearsal space, remember? And I don't think she'd care to be screwed, so to speak."

Christian and Simon exchanged looks.

"Don't you think your muse will mind?" inquired Christian.

"About that. Excuse me, Sid, would you mind giving us some privacy, please?"

Sid's stocky little legs lumbered down the ladder. "Gotta fix the john, anyways." He trotted off down the hall.

"You know the other day in the attic when you gentlemen decided to humiliate me with your gushing description of my muse? Thanks a ton for that, by the way. Margot asked me about it, actually she cornered me, but that goes without saying. Anyway, she asked me if I was dating her—this muse. I couldn't stand there and explain. It would have made me look like a—"

"A psycho?"

"Thanks, Simon."

"A wanker?"

"Shut up, Simon."

"A psychotic wanker?"

Andrew lunged across the table at him. Sheet music went flying.

Christian pulled him back. "Yeah, we know. Zoey told me all about it. You actually told Margot that you were dating her?"

"We broke up."

"This imaginary girl and you," Christian clarified.

"Yes, I just thought it would be easier that way."

"Oh yes, tons." Simon guffawed.

"So what do you want us to do?"

"In a word? Lie."

"Wouldn't it be easier if you just came clean?"

"Are you mad?" cried Simon. "Can you hear him trying to rationalize that one? 'Oh, pardon and all, but I may have communicated that the woman I said I was screwing I am no longer screwing, due to the fact that she was a figment of my imagination. But she has inspired all my music—and I would be lost without her—so no need to apply, no woman could compare.'"

Andrew held up the middle fingers of both his hands.

"What a tangled web, Paulie," tsk-tsked Simon. "So the party line is you dated this muse but she's history, so now you can put forth the moves on this Emily?"

Andrew slowly lowered his hands and spanned his fingers over the sheet music.

"Not to worry. Whatever you want. I'm only informing you, if you haven't realized it up to this point in your illustrious career of fucking, that little girls don't like it when you lie. Especially about other little girls. Especially about imaginary little girls."

"Listen, Andrew," Christian intervened, "I don't agree with you, but I get it. Now, can you two stop goofing off for a second and come in here and help with the food? The dinner, remember the dinner? We're hosting tomorrow night, right? So far we have no food, no alcohol, no decorations, nothing."

"Decorations? What is this, a wedding?" Simon said. "We just met these women."

Christian clenched the butcher knife tighter. "It's potluck."

"Fine. I'll supply the alcohol and the cigarettes."

"Zoey told me this morning she wanted everyone to bring a dish from where they were raised. Thought it might help us all get acquainted. I figured we could eat in the attic or on the roof if it's warm enough. But short of some sawhorses covered in dry wall, we've got squato. Some fine romantic dinner this is going to be. I'm about to march up there and take Zoey out and let you guys hang yourselves."

"Romantic dinner?" said Simon. "Do my ears deceive me? What is it with this place? I refuse to drink the water anymore. Speaking of which, does anyone fancy a pint? It's five o'clock somewhere, right?"

Suddenly, words reverberated inside Andrew's head. *Romantic dinner. Not just any dinner, Andrew, a romantic dinner.*

Yes. Yes, that's what he could do. He could start over, use the opportunity to redeem himself. He'd remain calm this time, be a gentleman, and not frighten Emily to death. Make it a night to remember—a night she'd never forget. *Yes.*

"Okay, here's what we're going to do." With a new-found surge of confidence, Andrew started firing his ideas at Christian and Simon. Christian joined in, whether caught up in Andrew's enthusiasm or in an attempt to get him to calm down, he truly didn't care. Evidently they were so loud that a few minutes later they heard stomping on the ceiling. At least Andrew thought it was the ceiling. Then the moaning started, and a second later a wail came from the direction of the bathroom.

A second later, Sid flew down the hallway, a white-faced crew-cut of a blur, shrieking at the top of his lungs as he barreled out the front door.

The three men momentarily stared at each other and then tore ass toward the bathroom. Christian was the first to reach it, and he stopped short. Simon and Andrew nearly toppled over him. Frantically they stuck their heads around the doorway, one on top of the other, and into the room.

"Holy shit!" Christian cried to Andrew who could only say, "It's true, man, it's really true."

Finally Simon, as though he'd been waiting all his life to say it, channeled a week's worth of Little Feat torture into one breath, and grinning ear to ear, threw back his head and wailed, "There's a dead man. In the bathtub. With a martini!"

Sure enough, a handsome apparition clad in a double-breasted suit with a boutonniere sat with his legs crossed, relaxing in their claw foot tub. His ghostly arms rested on the sides. His opalescent fingers clasped a martini glass.

In elegant silence he toasted them, then winked and raised his spectral glass toward the mirror over the vanity on the opposite side of the room. There, in a flowing script, were the words:

The cabinet under the stairs

"Doesn't he mean cupboard?" asked Andrew.

"How the hell do I know?" Christian retorted. "But what stairs? Which cupboard?"

They looked back to the tub. It was empty. He had vanished.

Like a shot, the three of them ran out to the lobby, pushing each other aside like children, eager to be the first there. Sure enough, under the long table that held their mail was a small door.

"After you, Simon," Andrew said, his heart pounding in excitement as the three crouched down to open it. What would they find: a treasure map, money — a body?

"No, after you, Paulie boy."

Andrew looked back and forth between his friends. Surely they weren't scared. He motioned to Christian, but he held up his hands in refusal. *Tosser.* He took a deep breath and grabbed the small hook in the door and pulled. The door creaked open stiffly from years of disuse.

They peered into the darkness.

"We love you, man." Christian smiled ear-to-ear.

"Holy hell!" cried Simon.

Which left Andrew nothing to say but, "Thanks, Nick."

If history books recorded such things, they would note that the Lost Boys' assault on their neighbors' hearts began on that Friday, at around six p.m.

An invitation addressed in a calligraphed hand arrived for Ms. Margot Larson, Ms. Zoey Cohen, and Ms. Emily Thomas that evening, slipped discreetly under their door.

Mssrs. Simon Godden, Christian Wood, and Andrew Hayes
request the honor of your presence
in the Conservatory at 8 p.m. tomorrow evening.
Formal dress is requested, but you may dress as you desire.

"My God, someone wrote this by hand. No one does this anymore. Do you see the way the ink ebbs and flows through the script? It's been written with a nib pen dipped in India ink. It looks like something from…" gushed Zoey.

"From Captain Wentworth," Emily whispered, foregoing the thought of Darcy, who probably wrote more neatly but never captured the exquisite anguish of his situation.

This beginning foray, while impressive in its own right, was followed by a stunning display of romantic maneuvering. A massive bouquet of wildflowers from the backyard was delivered at eight that evening—left in a martini shaker, no less. This romantic storming of the Bastille left the women with nothing to do but to circle the wagons. They spent the rest of the night determining what armor they needed to wear into battle. Zoey was enthusiastic, having evidently forgiven Andrew for his former transgressions; Margot was uninterested, having not forgiven Simon for any of his. Emily was simply panicked.

Later that night she lay in bed, unable to sleep. For the previous week she had avoided Andrew at all costs, and in less than twenty-four hours she would have to face him. They would stand awkwardly in that attic, all forced conversation until polite manners would dictate they could leave. How had Christian pressured him into this? Formal attire? Dancing? Part of her wished he had orchestrated this for her, but that would be absurd. He was blatantly in love with someone else; she had rarely seen a man that affected, and her irritation was only surpassed by her jealousy. For no matter how casual he appeared to be about his ex-girlfriend, this muse of his, his words spoke otherwise. She remembered their conversation at the café, the vehemence in his voice and his barely controlled emotions, and she found it ironic that never before had unrequited love become so popular.

She wouldn't go tomorrow night. There was no other choice. She glanced at the clock; it was nearly midnight. She had gone to bed in only a white nightshirt that Zoey had loaned her because her room had been broiling, no doubt thanks to Sid's crew disappearing before fixing the pipes. Unwilling to stay in the house past dark, they flocked out the doors at five each night no matter what state the house was in, leaving the inhabitants to the vagaries of ancient radiators. Chilly now, she rolled over on her side and pulled her blanket up around her shoulders, convincing herself it was the right choice. The room seemed to grow colder. Familiarly colder.

"Nora?" she breathed into the darkness. Her closet creaked open. A sharp gasp iced her throat. "Nora, I know you're there."

Silence.

"And I'd like to say—I'd like to take this opportunity to introduce myself. I'm Emily Thomas. If you want to borrow the coat, feel free. Just don't murder me in my sleep, please."

A ghostly feminine chuckle came from the closet. The door blew open a crack, and a slit of light was visible from the back wall.

"Nora?"

The chuckle continued, and the door whispered opened a fraction more. Andrew's music seemed to be coming from the back of her closet. How was that possible?

Emily slid out of the covers; her toes curled on the cold wood floor as she crept over to the closet. The knob froze her fingers just as before. And just as before, she was terrified. "Please let it not be some specter like at the end of *Raiders of the Lost Ark* that spirals around my head before it eats me."

"That, my dear, would be gauche."

Emily stopped dead. She was about to rush back into her bed when a melody, so lovely and plaintive, captured her. As if drawn by an unseen hand, she crept forward and into the closet toward the sliver of light. She brushed her coat aside, and seeing a door knob that protruded from the back wall, twisted it. With a creak the door opened, and she stepped into a narrow, dimly illuminated hallway. A secret passageway.

The only thing she could decipher was that it must have served as a back stairway, a butler's stairs, when the house was built. One old, ornate sconce covered in cobwebs lit the dusty hallway. The passageway went in both directions. Instinctively she turned left, the music becoming more distinct as she silently took step after step.

She ghosted along until she reached a dead end. A small section of wood flooring had been removed, and the opening shimmered with a dim glow. Bolts circled the cut-away; perhaps someone had butchered the floor to anchor a light fixture long ago. She peeked down through the opening.

She could see into the room beneath her through the filigreed canopy of a wrought iron chandelier that bathed the room below in near candlelight. Sheet music lay on the floor like drifts of snow and shadows of bookcases lined the walls. On the floor, a tea cup sat abandoned.

And there was a man. A man in flannel pajama bottoms and no shirt. The sight of him staggered her.

Alone, Andrew sat on a bed with his eyes closed; she could tell that in the dim light, at least. He was strumming a guitar. A more heartbreaking sound than she had ever remembered hearing filled the shadows around him.

He kept repeating the one refrain over and over, speaking softly to himself, and then starting again. His fingers moved over the frets — nimble, long, intelligent, seductive. He began to hum, a quiet desperation in his voice as though he had traveled all night and could spot the lights of home.

The words of Browning she knew by heart.

The gray sea and the long black land;
And the yellow half-moon large and low;
And the startled waves that leap
In fiery ringlets from their sleep,
As I gain the cove with pushing prow,
And quench its speed i' the slushy sand.
Then a mile of warm sea-scented beach;
Three fields to cross till a farm appears;
A tap at the pane, the quick sharp scratch
And blue spurt of a lighted match,
And a voice less loud, through its joys and fears,
Than the two hearts beating each to each.

Tears burned in her eyes and muddled the vision of him: his eyes closed, his head bowed as he finished, as though he had indeed stepped through that door and was lost to that woman. He stopped and put his hand over the strings to silence them and laid his head back with a sigh. The guitar pressed against his naked skin, his arms folded around it as if it were a lover.

Emily had never seen anything so erotic, so sensual. She couldn't stay. She had to leave. Silently as the grave, she stole back down the passageway, back to her room, back to the security of her bed. She desperately needed time to think.

It was when she neared the sconce that she saw it. An old-fashioned steamer trunk. It sat in the shadows at the end of the hall in the direction she hadn't taken. A wave of apprehension rose within her at the sight. What was it doing here? And what, more importantly, was inside it? Part of her was afraid to know, wanting to escape to her room and bury herself under the covers with her memories of Andrew, but curiosity kept her locked in place.

Upon closer inspection she could see that the steamer trunk was old, covered with dust and travel stickers from faraway lands and exotic places. Whose was it? Was it Neil's? Maybe, but it was so long forgotten…Could it have been left here by a previous owner? And how was she even going to open it — she hadn't a key.

Then she noticed: it wasn't locked.

Hesitantly, she ran her hand over the worn leather and brass buttons that decorated the exterior. Her finger brushed over an aged, peeling sticker that read, *Le Grand Hotel, Monte Carlo*, then another that read, *Cunard, White Star to Europe*, and one that looked very worn, as though it was the first one ever placed on the trunk: *The Mendocino Hotel.* Her finger stopped when it reached that one. She swore she felt someone sighing behind her.

She gripped the latch and flipped it up. The trunk exhaled, as though it had taken its first breath in years. With a trembling hand, she slowly opened the lid.

She saw the shimmer first, and then she saw the color. Her heart leaped into her throat. A concoction of the most stunning workmanship lay within. It was a blue sapphire dress, 1930s classic couture, tea length and perfectly exquisite. Her fingers reached out to touch it. The satin felt alive. A pair of matching shoes was nestled next to the dress, and beside them sat a velvet box wrapped with a bow.

She suddenly understood what armor she would wear tomorrow night, how she would survive the battle. How she could face Andrew Hayes.

"Oh, Nora," she whispered, her breath whispering before her in white puffs. "Thank you."

"Take no prisoners, darling," a ghostly voice replied. "Remember. Take no prisoners."

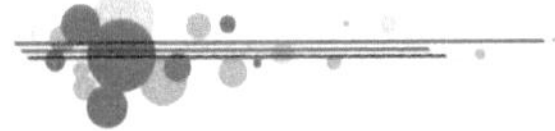

Glenn Miller warbled from the gilded lily gramophone horn that the men had hauled up from the cupboard under the stairs. Simon, Christian, and Andrew sat in the roof garden after a hectic day of lugging and hammering; they were enjoying a rare moment of peace as they watched the sun leave its last glow in the sky, the day slipping on its dinner jacket of dusk.

Andrew surveyed their handiwork from under the paper lanterns and tiny white lights they'd strung around the room and exhaled in satisfaction at a job well done. They had found these as well as other oddities, from bolts of gossamer material to a king's ransom of silverware, in the cache under the stairs. Christian's dance floor looked nearly professional, and the table was set to the hilt. The bar in the conservatory resembled something Bogart and Bacall could call home, and Christian had even carried up a keyboard in case he got in the mood to play. The sight, however, struck Andrew with an aching sense of déjà vu; this was not the first time this place shimmered as it did now. Nick had shaken martinis here; he knew it in his bones.

"It's a bit like throwing the baby out with the cart, don't you think?" Simon asked.

"The place was a dump," Christian argued. "Where were we going to have them sit? On bags of cement? Toolboxes? And those planters? The crew's been using them for fucking port-o-potties, man."

"It's putting the cart before the horse, and throwing the baby out with the bathwater," Andrew stated.

"Babies, horses — it's overkill, I'm telling you. Less is more."

Was it overkill? Yes. Andrew accepted the fact that he had a difficult time doing anything halfway. He wanted to ensure a friendship, not overwhelm her, but between this and their invitation he was definitely verging on overwhelming. Still, old things charmed Emily. Old things and poetry, like her Browning. And if worst came to worst, he could blame the whole thing on Christian.

"I can't believe you're wearing that army jacket," Christian scolded Simon as he dragged a silver ice chest full of champagne to the bar. "Do you own any other clothes?"

"No."

"What color was it originally, do you remember?" Christian shot a withering look over his shoulder to Andrew, whose arms were loaded down with the food Zoey had dropped off earlier.

"Who knows? He's wearing a shirt. Be thankful," Andrew replied.

For their part, Christian and Andrew had opted for a pair of old tuxes from university that had somehow survived the long trip, although Andrew had lost his bowtie at some sort of drunken debacle years ago where he had barely escaped with his guitar.

A little while later, after Andrew had finished lighting the two monstrosities of candelabras on the bar that Christian insisted they put there, Andrew heard him yell from the roof. "Hey! You figured out what that white fabric was for! Awesome."

"I didn't touch this," Andrew said flatly, staring at the fabric draped romantically in a canopy over the table.

"Simon!" Christian yelled.

Simon stepped out the door, and the look of surprise on his face told them he had nothing to do with it either. Although surveying the decorations, he shook his head. "Man, they're going to swear we're fucking poofs."

"Okay," Christian said with a forced lightness. "I'm going to make believe no one did this. Dead or otherwise. Want a drink?"

This was not the first time things had mysteriously arranged themselves on the roof since they'd finished work. Silverware moved about in different order around the place settings, extra wine glasses appeared out of nowhere, flowers that no one remembered picking materialized from the back garden in various vases about the room. So many flowers, in fact, that the closed space of the conservatory felt heady. All this while the scratchy records played, coaxing awake the stars that glimmered through the glass roof.

"They should be here by now," Christian said, knocking back another martini with the others at the bar. "What do you suppose they're doing?"

"Sharpening their claws," Simon replied.

Despite Simon's sentiments, three sets of eyes remained fixed on the door. A soft knock was followed by Zoey's electric smile. She looked startling, like a voluptuous version of Audrey Hepburn in *Breakfast at Tiffany's*, her long black dress and her long white gloves encasing tight mounds of exuberant flesh, untold amounts of rhinestone clips holding her wildly streaked hair hostage. Christian trotted over to meet her, and after giving her a smack on the cheek, took a large dish from her hands. Her eyes widened in shock at the room, her mouth hanging open as she began to gush uncontrollably.

"Oh, goddamn, Christian, it's…it's gorgeous. You did all this? I can't fucking believe it. Where the hell did you find all this shit?"

"She kisses him with that mouth." Simon sniggered in Andrew's ear as Christian's face beamed with pride.

"It was nothin', chere. Nothin' at all."

"He is so whipped."

Andrew elbowed Simon in the ribs.

But Simon had paused. Andrew turned his head to follow Simon's stare.

Margot entered the room with her customary mathematical precision. She wore a dress; Andrew guessed one might call it that, navy, skin tight, short, and angled. She surveyed the room passively as though she were entering a lecture hall, yet seeing the uncustomary flash in her eyes as she tossed her black hair, it was difficult to remember this woman ever taught anything legal. Then a voice spoke from behind her.

"Hello."

A vision from Andrew's memory stood framed by the doorway. A strapless blue gown graced her body, the creamy satin cinched around her waist held by a diamond clip. His eyes rose to her face. Her throat was bare except for a delicate necklace of sapphires, and the lights shimmered in the diamond and sapphire comb that swept up her hair in twist. A few loose tendrils curled about her face, her eyes darkened by shadow.

Nora.

Something inside of him reached out to her. *No*, Andrew said to himself. *No.* Emily, he was gazing at *Emily.*

At that precise moment her gaze fell to the floor as though she had heard him. She backed up, clearly embarrassed, and muttered something to herself, shaking her head in protest. A second later, she stumbled forward through the doorway as though shoved and straight into his arms.

"You look beautiful," they both said at the same time, looking everywhere except where they wanted.

He took her arm with a chuckle and led her toward the bar to join the others. "To warn you, the dinner menu's a tad bit interesting," he said, running his free hand through his slicked-back hair. "Turns out an international smorgasbord is fairly odd looking. Best to see what we're dealing with here."

They wandered over to where the platters sat on the candlelit table on the side of the room. Each dish was dotted with name cards. Andrew couldn't remember them being there before.

"I brought pizza from New York City," Emily said with her head held high.

"And good thing, that, we'll have something to eat amidst all of this," he told her, gaining her grateful smile. "Christian brought jambalaya and étouffé all the way from New Orleans."

"Zoey prepared her famous New Jersey…I'm not even sure how you pronounce it, actually, but go easy on that, okay? Wait, what is that?" She pointed to an odd loaf of what looked like Irish soda bread.

"It's Spotted Dick," Simon shouted proudly as he made his way from the bar. Margot choked on her drink. "You can call it Spotted Dog, but why bother?"

This was more than enough to grab the room's attention, and soon they were all standing before the table.

"Well, at least it doesn't look like an actual dick, but this…" Simon gestured down to what resembled a flaming red hot bratwurst. "Who pray tell brought 'Red Snappers'?"

"That would be me," said Margot with a black-widow smile. "Maine's finest. You should try them." With that, she speared one on a toothpick and shoved it right into Simon's mouth. To his credit, he chewed thoughtfully, swallowed hard, and after his tongue was done floating over his teeth said, "Yeah, just as I guessed. Tastes like a fucking hot dog."

Margot actually smirked at that and popped one in her mouth with a flourish.

"Would you care to see the roof?" Andrew asked.

"There's more?"

Before Emily knew it, he had led her to the dance floor. An old record wobbled on the gramophone, Billie Holiday lamenting lost love. Without thinking, he took her hand and twirled her around.

"Where did you learn to dance?" she asked his shoes, her lashes brushing her cheeks. He tilted up her chin with his finger. Her eyes met his.

"That's better. Don't pay attention to my feet. Pay attention to me."

She laughed.

"So, where did I learn to dance? Hmmm. I suppose from my Uncle Daniel. He lived in New York City, and I used to spend most of my summers with him when we weren't in Barcelona. He thought all education could be boiled down to knowing how to hold your fork, how to play the horses, and how to f…"

"Yes?" Emily persisted. "Knowing how to…?"

He smiled and dipped her. She whooped a bit, startled when he raised her back into his arms. "Dance," he lied.

They twisted, still in each other's arms, to peer at the other side of the garden. Christian was holding up some serving piece to Zoey, explaining the minting process by the sounds of it. Simon and Margot were back in the conservatory, both sipping champagne while continuing to eye the assortment of food lining the table.

"I bet he's wondering if she poisoned anything," Andrew said.

"No. She's dressed for hand-to-hand combat."

"This should be fabulous, then."

While the group gathered to sit down for dinner, music blared loudly in the background, as though someone had suddenly jacked up the volume of the gramophone. A familiar sound like a keyboard accompanied it, and a warbling voice sang out about needing someone to carry him home and bury his body in San Francisco.

Conversation stopped dead. Dead, in Andrew's opinion, being the operative word. He cleared his throat. "Hoagy Carmichael," he offered brightly. Then he glared behind him into the darkness. "Nick," he hissed under his breath, "cut it out."

The music softened.

"We found the gramophone in the house," explained Christian. "In a closet under the stairs."

"You mean a cupboard under the stairs," corrected Margot, passing the bread basket to Simon. "Isn't *Harry Potter* required reading where you people come from?"

Simon's fork hit his plate.

"So, are you all at university like Emily?" Andrew asked, trying not to laugh.

"I graduated a few years ago from art school," Zoey explained. "So to keep my art alive, I tile people's bathrooms."

"Bathrooms?" said Emily. "She's done kitchens in Pacific Heights, patios in Marin, and the lobby of a law firm down in South of Market."

"It's a lot more glamorous than it sounds," Zoey was quick to point out. She launched into a hilarious rant about the eccentricities of several of her wealthier clients and spent the remainder of the meal regaling them with tales of one, in particular, who wanted the master bath of her house re-designed specifically for her sixteen ancient, evil, asthmatic cats.

"I'd love to see that house," said Christian, wiping the tears from his eyes. "Never been to San Francisco before this."

"What? Never? Have any of you?"

The men shook their heads. Zoey gasped in mock horror and immediately decided that the three women would give them a tour of the city, if not the following day, then soon. Christian looked thrilled at the announcement, Emily surprised, Simon bored, and Margot annoyed.

Trying to lift Margot's mood, Andrew remembered his manners and asked her what she did for a living.

"Margot is our resident rocket scientist," Emily announced, having cleared most of the plates and returned with dessert. "She studies space dust."

"Thank you. You didn't have to do that," Andrew murmured to her under his breath with a nod to the table.

Margot took a long sip of her champagne. "Rocket scientist, no. I teach vacuous headed freshman elementary physics. My research is in primitive meteorites like Emily says."

"Like chunks of old stars?" asked Christian.

Margot placed down her champagne and smiled. An eager student in her midst. "Presolar stardust to be more specific, and yes, bits of stars that we analyze in the lab, but not exactly in the way you're thinking. It comes from the debris of red giants and supernova explosions and —"

Simon coughed so hard that Zoey was forced to pound him on the back.

"You're not the same M. M. Larson who co-authored that report in *Universe* two months ago, are you?"

"Yes," Margot answered in a voice Andrew doubted many had ever heard her use. It preened. "I was quite proud of that."

"Well, love, I hate to tell you, but I think you got it all wrong."

Oh bloody hell, Andrew thought.

"Really."

"How about them Giants?" cried Christian, equally troubled by the look on Margot's face.

"And what in your rock star, ass waving, lip pouting C.V. qualifies you to say so?"

"Well, you know that Randall tried to defend that same stand in last year's edition of *Cosmos* only to have to retract it because the work Plisko had done in Russia wasn't available at the time, since it was still undisclosed due to the some military security restrictions. Tell me you knew about Plisko? Everyone knows about Plisko, come on."

Margot seemed to be percolating in anger. "Plisko is irrelevant —"

"Dick, anyone?" Zoey chirped. "I mean Spotted Dog."

"Andrew, you throw such interesting parties," Emily whispered near his ear. "I take it Simon majored in physics?"

"Can I top off anyone's drinks?" Christian asked on his way to the bar. Five hands shot up into the air.

"So Andrew," asked Margot in a tone that told him she was done with Simon, but not yet done drawing blood, "you're from London, then. I didn't see anything from your home on the table."

"I brought the paella by way of Barcelona, but Chelsea is home, yes."

"And your parents, what do they do?"

"My father was a barrister, he's deceased. My mum is a barrister as well, though she no longer practices. She tends to nurture hopeless causes now, mainly charities and schools."

"And us, of course," Simon added.

"So, no musical talent. I find that odd — usually there's some genetic influence in there somewhere."

"Oh, my father was classically trained. As am I."

"Really? What instrument?"

Andrew felt the rigors of cross examination but retained his smile and brevity. He did not enjoy speaking of his family. He had not dealt well with his father's death; he had been touring when it happened, and the finality of it hit him harder than he was willing to realize. But the grief he knew he should feel never came. Only the sense of being cheated remained and guilt for all the things left unsaid. "Violin," he answered.

"Good golly, Miss Molly," Christian hooted from behind the bar. He hefted up a case up from below. "Lookie here kiddies, lookie what I found!"

"I shudder to guess," Andrew muttered, though thankful for the interruption.

Christian pulled a large green bottle from the case. "Absinthe. Can you believe it? Wait, this shit's from Paris. Oh sweet Lord, look what's in the bottom."

Curiosity piqued, the group drifted to his side as he took out a wide assortment of absinthe glasses and spoons. Andrew had seen it in action at his Uncle Daniel's. Not a pretty sight.

Christian metered out the spirit into six glasses and went to pass them out.

"Wait. We need some sugar cubes," Andrew said evenly, not sure he wanted this bunch partaking in this particular brew. "And water."

Zoey returned from the table with a few cubes clasped in her hands as well as a carafe.

"I learned to do this on the Food Network." She smiled up at him as she placed the silver slatted spoons over the glasses and topped each one with a cube of sugar. "Okay, pour, right?" she asked. Andrew nodded.

As Zoey drizzled the water over the cubes, the green liquid transformed into a ghostly white.

"Isn't this supposed to induce psychotic delusions?" asked Margot with a not-so-mild hint of apprehension in her voice.

"Myth," Emily said in quiet fascination. "Learned it junior year. The most commonly reported experience is a 'clear-headed' feeling of inebriation—a form of 'lucid drunkenness.' Although, Oscar Wilde said something like he felt as if he had tulips growing on his legs."

"Wicked," said Christian.

Andrew cocked an eyebrow at Emily, and she nodded. He smiled and took her hand. "To the Green Fairy," he whispered close to her ear, causing her to shudder and squeeze his hand back in excitement.

"To The Lost Boys for finding all these wonders," toasted Zoey.

They raised their glasses and tentatively drank as one. The anise burned Andrew's throat like licorice fire; he tried not to cough. The girls had equal responses, from fanning their mouths to hisses. But he knew from experience that the more they sipped, the smoother the absinthe would go down.

They sipped, and sure enough the absinthe flowed, and the Green Fairy led them over to the wicker sofas and curled up beside them. There they laughed and talked for hours about where they grew up, their parents, their families. Andrew learned that Emily's mother and father were both doctors—one of mathematics, the other of psychology—both retired and both adamant that Emily teach. They did not support her writing, viewing it as frivolous, something to pursue in her spare time once she found real work. Their financial support seemed as tenuous as the emotional, something Andrew both could and could not relate to. He took another slug of absinthe. And another. He laced his hand within Emily's, and soon everything became warm and lost in candlelight.

Sometime later Christian disappeared, and "In the Mood" blared from the roof. They all strolled out to the dance floor, pleasantly buzzed. A second bottle of absinthe had mysteriously appeared and swung from Zoey's hand. Andrew felt pretty sure Tommy Dorsey would roll over in his big band-loving grave if he saw Zoey and Christian's interpretation of swing. Simon held on to his drink at the edge of the dance floor, but Margot had retreated and sat on the edge of a planter watching, her foot twisting almost imperceptibly to the music.

"Can Simon dance?" Emily asked with a little hiccup, her shoulder brushing Andrew's.

"Like nobody alive."

"Then why isn't he?"

"Fear of failure."

Finally Christian, gasping for air, announced, "Enough!" and trotted over to the gramophone, pulled out an album, and smiled. He gently placed down the needle. The haunting swells of violins misted through the air. Eyes burning, he found Zoey. "Come here," he whispered, and rather than wait, walked toward her, enclosing her in his arms. They rocked in the blissful contentment of two stowaways.

"Dance with me," Emily commanded Andrew. She swayed slightly, the air heady about them. Her eyes reflected the stars, each and every one. He reached out his hand.

"Are you ready?" he whispered. She nodded.

He took Emily Thomas in his arms. Truly took her in his arms. He was holding the woman of his heart against his own, in a room furnished by a dead man, while a table of Spotted Dick, jambalaya, and red hot dogs lay half-eaten nearby. It was bloody perfect.

"Stardust" continued with its music of years gone by. Her nose, straight and small, twitched against a fluttering of curls. He could not look away from a face this beautiful — the force was too strong. She must have felt it too, and her body nestled closer.

Closing his eyes, he sang to her. This old song, these old words, as if he had sung them to her before, as if he had held her gorgeous and radiant, their bodies moving in a tempo lovers had known for all eternity. The haunting melody echoed along the garden wall, and he was with her "once again."

"Andrew," she breathed into his neck as though she were unsure. His hand found her face and lifted it. His breath caught as he saw tears glisten in her eyes, reflecting the candlelight. There was an invitation in her gaze; he knew it.

Was this the right thing? Was it too fast? Could he stop once he started? He had never doubted his control so much. His gaze, taking the place of his lips, moved from her face to her neck, to her shoulders. Something wicked and untamed rose up in him. The smell of the night air perfumed her skin, and her eyes flashed with a longing so familiar his step faltered for a moment.

There were other people here. His mind was telling him this. You cannot ravage this girl. You cannot peel her dress off as slowly and wantonly as you desire. You cannot lay her down and cup her head against your shoulder and whisper what you'll do to her, what you'll make her feel, what you'll make her cry out. You cannot. But bloody hell, you want to.

"Andrew, I need to tell you something. In the park, I…I did see you play. Once. I wanted to tell you, but I thought you'd think I was some crazed fan. I know how I'd feel if someone stalked me — I'd be terrified. And I know you must get that all the time. Not that I stalked you…" She seemed conflicted now, as if she had backed herself into a corner. What she saw in his face must have given her courage to go on. "I know how you crave your privacy. I thought you'd think less of me, somehow, that it was better if—"

"If what?"

"If you didn't know what I felt."

"And what do you feel?"

She said nothing; they had ceased dancing. The air in the room had gone entirely still as they stared at each other. Her eyes were so light, they were almost silver. Then without warning, her hands found his jacket and her lips found his. The taste of music, of light, coursed through him. It sang like a spirit, loose and wild. Then his body stiffened in realization. The truth of what was happening slammed into him. Emily Thomas was kissing him, and he was blown away like Margot's stardust. He kissed her back like a madman. He had no choice. She melted in his arms, giving herself away. With all his strength, he tried to make the kiss gentle, lingering, not filled with the force that fuses metals and explodes stars. He failed miserably.

He reluctantly pulled away, the taste of licorice and Emily still ripe on his tongue. Taking a ragged breath, he kissed her forehead first, then her eyes, then her lips. He rested his forehead against hers, and they rocked back and forth, cocooned in each other's arms.

"Andrew," she whispered, her lips pressed to his ear, her fingers gently laced through his hair. "I need to tell you something else."

"Hmmm…" he nuzzled into her cheek, euphoric, in space. *Tell me anything. Tell me you love me. Tell me you want me.*

"I take no prisoners."

He chuckled and kissed her again.

"Oh, and Andrew?"

"Yes, Emily?" he responded dreamily.

"Margot and Simon just set fire to the canopy."

Why wouldn't it stop? Please make it stop. Someone, anyone. Make the sunlight stop.

Emily peered from under her ice pack and moaned at the flash of brightness. "What time is it?"

"No effin' clue. I think it's a.m., though," Zoey mumbled. She was stretched out on the living room sofa like the spoils of war. Her multi-colored hair medusaed around the collar of her pajama clad body, and the back of her hand tumbled over her eyes like she should be tied to some railroad track. Margot was hunched over in the nearby club chair and curled up in a ball, looking like black-haired death.

Emily had chosen to lie on the floor, as it was the only surface that wasn't moving, although the ceiling rippled every now and then. Oscar Wilde was right about absinthe—tulips could be growing from her legs, or maybe they had replaced her legs, since she actually had to drag herself from her bedroom a few minutes ago, roused by the wounded animal sounds of her friends.

In their war with The Lost Boys, they had lost the latest battle brilliantly and went down in a blaze of glory. Now where was the ravaging and pillaging? Or had they slept through that too? God, she hoped not. How much more mortification could she have endured in one night? She moaned at what must be going through Andrew Hayes' mind this morning.

"That bad?" asked Zoey.

"Worse," Emily muttered back and placed the icepack over her face as the room began to reel again. Her hand pressed down on the cool hardwood floor to steady herself. He was there beneath her, just a few beams and joists away.

Though perhaps he was still asleep, a casualty of war himself, nursing his own wounds and lying there on the floor with his wild hair, his sweat pant clad legs falling lazily apart, a hand tossed over his eyes. Or maybe the party was just business as usual for him given his lifestyle, and he had already finished running five miles after shot-gunning his third Red Bull. Or maybe he was hiding from the bat-shit crazed she-devils he'd experienced last night, and music would be blaring through the floorboards any moment in retribution. Oh, please God, not that. The inside of her skull would shatter out her eyes.

"Just so I understand," Emily said, titling her face to the side to get a good look at Margot from underneath her ice pack. "You were explaining a comet's trajectory to Simon using a candelabra and a flaming piece of red hot dog?"

Margot pawed her question away like a bear coming out of hibernation, as if the thought was apparently too gruesome to discuss. Then one of her eyes peeled opened. "Did you really have to heave the ice chest over the both of us? Was that necessary?"

Actually, it was Andrew's quick thinking that had saved the day. Emily tried to help, but he hauled her to his side as he muttered something about ruining her beautiful dress.

Margot had stood there dripping wet, hair plastered over her eyes, nipples erect, and her black thong clearly outlined when she commenced wailing the litany of the saints. Simon stared at her as if she were the second coming of Christ, although Emily was pretty sure Jesus never used verbs like that, nor in that particular order, or for that matter even owned a push up bra. Christian and Zoey, who were still dancing while Rome burned around them, narrowly avoided the ice that scuttled around their feet.

Once satisfied the fire was completely out, Andrew stepped back and with a curse chucked the empty chest aside where it clattered loudly on the tiles. His eyes met Emily's. "I should have let them burn."

The anger in his tone, the ache in it, was the sexiest sound she had ever heard, and she shuddered in response. Mistaking her trembling for a chill, he immediately took off his jacket and draped it over her shoulders and ran his hands roughly up and down her arms. She nestled closer in response and felt the heat of his lips on her forehead.

"Oh, Emily…sweet girl."

Her body caught at his words, remembering their frantic embrace from moments before. But it wasn't only that kiss that ignited her memories; it was the kisses before that, and before that still. It was the kisses from another lifetime that reverberated through her, and laughter and music, brassy and loud. The crush of bodies surrounding her on a dance floor, swinging and twisting as a pompadoured man crooned at an old standing microphone in front of a row of trombones and big band music stands. And she felt the ferociousness of a man's arms surrounding her, grabbing her, spinning her, kissing her wildly and without restraint. *Sweet girl. Sweet girl.*

Suddenly from across the room they heard a scream. Their embrace shattered, and they whipped about to see what had happened. Simon lay on the floor, dazed, his lip bleeding. Margot towered over him, her stiletto bearing down on his chest, her fist raised, raring to punch him in the jaw—again. Andrew swore under his breath and launched himself across the dance floor.

Five expletive-filled, snarling, punch-blocked minutes later, the fires were finally put out and the boxers had retreated to their respective corners. Beyond mortified, Emily gathered up her two inebriated friends and promptly escorted them out the door before anyone could wreak more havoc. Her last image of Andrew was that of his tall, tightly wound body, sleeves rolled up over his forearms as he studied the canopy in disgust, his eyes opaque in the smoldering remains. It left her with an inexplicable feeling of sadness.

Zoey's cell phone rang on the end table, blaring a syrupy version of "Wouldn't It Be Nice?" into Margot's ear. In stake-through-the-heart fashion, she smashed it with her hand and nearly threw it against the wall, only deciding on Zoey as a target at the last moment before she returned to her fetal position.

Once Zoey had slinked off to her bedroom with her phone, Emily propped herself on her elbow and looked at Margot. What had passed between her and Simon last night before they committed arson had clearly unnerved her. She appeared pale and severe in the morning light, the remains of her mascara giving her a prizefighter's aura. "What's wrong?"

"I thought that was obvious. I don't like being made a fool of."

"He didn't make a fool of you."

"No, I was entirely capable of doing that myself."

"Margot."

"I don't want this, any of this, understand? Just because you two have decided to play house doesn't mean I have to make it a threesome."

Emily felt stung. "What are you afraid of, getting hurt?"

"Please, I'm nearly thirty. I'm too old for that dreck. And he's what, twenty-three, twenty-four maybe, and that's chronologically—let's not even try to determine where he falls emotionally. Every time I'm near that man, he's either snide or openly hostile. I have to deal with a thinly veiled version of that with the good ol' boys on the faculty every day, so I have no desire to allow some faux-intellectual rocker to do the same."

"If you gave him a chance—"

"He doesn't want a chance. He wants a fuck. Which would be all fine and good if I wasn't sharing a roof with him. No, I take that back. It would never be fine and good, because what he really wants is a conquest."

"Isn't that all you've ever wanted?"

She didn't answer right away. Emily could imagine her rubbing her long fingers together, the way she did whenever her words hadn't matched her thoughts.

"I like order, Emily. I like the scientific process, the ability to predict an outcome. I'm not some romantic-comedy girl who meets a boy she hates and once they're thrown together enough they fall madly in love. That's too much risk—it's chaos, actually. It's not a state I wish to enter."

"But you believe in love, right?" Emily pressed in a voice that made her question whom she was asking.

"I believe that last night was a result of absinthe goggles. That whatever transpired between all parties, good, bad, or indifferent, was a direct result of psychotropic alcohol. We were drunk and high. If you want to call that love, then by all means, be my guest."

Emily's stomach churned with the insecurity that lives in every woman, no matter how accomplished or beautiful. It was the drop down a missing step, the wobble and the recovery, made with a laugh and a tight swallow. Margot was right; everything to do with Andrew was chaos. A constant falling.

At that moment, Zoey returned from her call with a huge smile and the announcement, "Simon made us all breakfast. In apology. He wants to know how we like our eggs and take our coffee."

Both women turned to her in alarm. "What?"

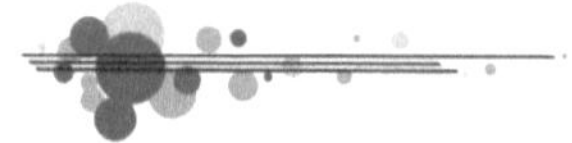

The front door shut behind Emily, and before she knew it, she was running. Having secretly slipped out of her apartment clad in a hastily assembled outfit of jogging shorts, t-shirt, and a jacket, she had left behind her roommates while they dressed for a breakfast she had no intention of attending.

Sweat soon covered her face and neck, and before long her muscles burned, the hangover dissipating in the exercise. She reached Golden Gate Park, the surrounding greenness drenching her senses, the air salty and foggy at this early hour. The coolness felt sharp against her hot face, a stark relief. The Conservatory of Flowers passed in a blur. She ran, not even stopping to enjoy the quiet emptiness of the rose garden.

You're a coward, Emily Thomas, a coward, the fog seemed to whisper to her, but she ignored it, willing her body to run faster; the macadam whizzed by like a black wheel under her feet. Nearing the ocean, she yanked her jacket around her as the fog became denser, and soon she could barely see three feet in front of her. She was forced to stop and slam her hands down on her knees, panting madly.

"Well, what am I supposed to do?" she cried, dragging in a gasp of air. "What the hell am I supposed to do? I can't face him. The first thing out of his mouth is going to be 'about last night, Emily…'"

The gray shroud remained silent, a distant fog horn sounding mournful and lost. She felt the need to cry with it, so lost in her emotions. She backhanded away a tear. "Oh, damn it to hell."

The wind blew coldly in reply, and she shuddered. She took a few steps forward, trying to find a place to collapse, when she realized she was standing on the edge of a small lake and there ahead of her loomed a series of tall, stately columns.

The Portals of the Past crept out of the mist. A grand and ghostly structure, a portico without a house, it was a survivor of the great earthquake and fire. Now surrounded in cattails and tall grass, it had been moved to the park for remembrance. She stared at it, swept up in its mystery—a symbol of perseverance, regardless of tragedy. The wind blew bitterly, and she wrapped her arms around herself.

"So beautiful," she said. "So lonely."

At her words, her skin tingled like ice. The spirits of long ago that haunted this grove seemed to whisper into the gray air. *All you have is now. Now. And then soon, no more.*

She swallowed down a nameless ache in her throat. "But I'm afraid."

Of what.

"Of pain, of rejection, of losing him."

Never.

The word hissed through the rushes of the lake. *Never.*

"Then what should I do?"

In answer, the skin on her arms broke out in goose bumps and a shiver ran down her spine. Standing amidst the columns was a frighteningly beautiful woman, a striking woman. Her short red hair curled about her porcelain face. Her dark eyebrows arched in question. She was clothed in a stylish gray suit and pumps, and she glimmered as she walked. Yet she wore the shadows of death in the hollows of her cheekbones and the cautiousness of her eyes.

"Nora?" Emily whispered.

"That would be Noreen, my dear. But Nora will do."

Shaking from head to toe, she ventured, "Thank…thank you for the dress, it was yours, wasn't it?"

The ghost nodded and smiled, though her image rippled a bit when she did so. "Was it a success?"

"Well, not exactly. I mean, didn't you see?"

"I can't go up there." Her sultry voice shook a bit, but she raised her chin and persevered. "It's all part of the rules, you see. Dreadful business. Nicholas has his rooms, I have mine. And never the twain shall meet. Makes for awful dinner parties. I had to entertain Dashiell and Lillian all by myself last month."

Emily collapsed onto a stone stoop, her knees weak. "You, ah, there are others of you?"

"Of course! It's San Francisco after all. People are simply dying to come here. Sorry, not the most tasteful of puns." She smiled for the first time.

Emily's mind exploded with questions. She grabbed at the first one. "How can you be here? I thought you'd be stuck in the house? Isn't that what happens with, I mean…beings such as yourself?"

"Ghosts, Emily, always use the proper word, no matter how uncomfortable. You're a writer for goodness sakes. I can be here because I was here in the past. Nicholas and I often came to this spot to picnic. Thank goodness this city is littered with historical remnants. It'd severely cramp my social season otherwise."

"Wait, you, did you say Nicholas?" No it couldn't be. "My God, you're, you're really real? I thought they were just characters in a book."

"That's what Dashiell would like you to think. He tended to base his characters on his friends, including us, as if that would fool anyone who knew anything. I was always a bit insulted, though. Nicholas worked for his money, and I rarely, if ever, drank, but after that book was published everyone thought we lived with martini glasses plastered to our hands. And don't even get me started about dogs. People never called us Nick and Nora until after that dreadful book, not to mention the movie. Nicholas just laughed the whole thing off. He adored calling me Nora just to get a rise out of me."

"But why can't—why aren't you two together?"

"That, my dear, is the million dollar question. One we almost found the answer to, but unfortunately Nicholas decided to drive that car of his too fast and here we are."

"I'm so sorry, it must be awful. Being separated, I mean." Emily wasn't sure how the whole being dead thing fared, but she felt it best not to delve into it at present.

"Awful? Well, I wouldn't be that melodramatic, but yes, I miss the man terribly. I became quite fond of him, you know. No one can foxtrot like Mr. Chamberlain."

"Chamberlain? Nicholas and Noreen Chamberlain?"

"Much better than Charles."

"When did you, um, die?"

"July 1st, 1935. Our Death Day. This year I suppose I'll have my party at the Columbarium where my ashes are housed. It's easier for the older guests, and there's plenty of room for dancing. Of course, Nicholas will have to have his at the Flood Mansion, as always." She sighed; a part of her seemed to disappear with it.

"Do you know why you can't be together?"

"We have no clue where his body is. That seems to be part of the problem. I think we need to be laid to rest together. Once we're laid in the earth, well, then I'm hoping—" She broke off and tried not to look at Emily.

Suddenly Emily was struck with an idea. "I—I could help—look through some records, there's the Internet now, you can find just about anything on it…A body might be a slight problem—but I could try. If nothing else, I need to repay you for the loan of the dress."

Nora paused and stared at Emily, her eyes narrowed, silver in the fog. She took a step toward her and then paused. "I believe you need to help yourself before you can help me."

"I don't understand."

She hesitated again, as though she were being kept from saying any more. "We'll talk again soon. Now go home. It's where you belong."

"But Nora, I can't—I just can't…"

"Did you take no prisoners like I told you to?"

"Yes, but—"

"Did he kiss you?"

"Well yes, but—"

"*Yesbuts* live in the woods, Emily. And you live in a house, not the woods, and so does that brilliant young man. Life is to be lived, not to be avoided." Her tone altered, it became more urgent, troubled even; her gaze traveled out across the lake, her eyes darkening in concern. She spoke quickly now, her attention focused on some unseen threat. "Live, Emily, live while you can. I have to go. Time is running out. If you can help me, you need to find him. Quickly. Time…is…running…out."

Like her words, she dissolved into the fog. Nothing but the silent columns remained.

A black tremor swept through Emily at the warning. She had just spoken with the ghost of Nora Chamberlain, the real-life woman, not some imaginary character from a book, and she seemed in trouble, some untold trouble. No, no, it couldn't be. She must have been hallucinating. Lord, how long did the effects of absinthe last? Yet Nora's ominous words echoed in the stillness of the lake. *Time is running out. Find him.*

Without another breath, she jumped to her feet. *Find him, find him, find him* echoed with each footfall as she began to run. Find Andrew. She had to find Andrew. By the time she reached the end of her street, her lungs burned in her chest from the force with which she had pushed her body. She was drenched in sweat, her hair wild. She took two more strides to reach the chain link gate near the playground, and she hung onto that for dear life.

Gulping in mouthfuls of air, she stared at the sidewalk. What would she do or say to him when she walked through the front door? How would she even start? Eventually, her breathing returned to normal, and she knew she couldn't postpone the inevitable anymore. Better now than never. They'd think she was a lunatic soon enough. That's when she noticed the figure on the swings.

He rocked back and forth with his head bowed low while his sneakers scuffed the sand beneath him like a little boy, or as if he was in deep thought. He wore running shorts and a thick zippered jacket, dark-brown hair windblown from what looked like a long run in the foggy morning air. His hands twisted the chains of the swing this way and that, clinking echoes through the empty playground.

Andrew.

Emily's heart lodged in her throat. What should she do? *Find him. Find him.* Yet she caught herself. Which him? Nick or Andrew?

With a deep breath, she made a decision and swung open the gate. Hearing the scrape of metal, his head rose and Emily halted. She could see the pulse in his neck—he had been running as well. He watched her approach. She took a few more steps and stopped, unable to go on. Then silently, without taking his eyes from hers, he held out his hand, fingers splayed open. She stared at it—his lovely long fingers—a musician's hand. The meaning was clear: *come to me.*

She stretched open her palm and met him, pressing her hand to his. He closed his eyes. The lines of their palms, so much the same, joined together. He kept his fingers open, though, his hand shaking slightly, from his run, no doubt. His eyes finally lifted. She took the swing next to him, never once removing her hand.

"How many fingers?" he asked, their hands still pressed together. The odd question made her take notice.

"Ten," she said.

"Funny, I only see five." He curled his slender fingers between hers. His hand was cool, inviting. "Ah, now there are ten. How's your head?"

She grimaced slightly and pulled her jacket around her with her free hand.

"About last night," he began. "I did something and…you need to tell me…I'm asking you…shall I stop?"

His words rambled through her mind before they slowly dawned on her. She nodded, pressing her lips together, not breathing. "That depends."

"On?"

"On you."

"I would like very much not to stop."

He pulled her swing closer. His breath warmed her face, and his lips brushed over hers, tentatively, but with a sureness that made her head spin.

"Emily."

She felt him seize her, hoisting her up into his lap and enclosing her shoulders in his arms. She shivered in response, and he opened his jacket wider, letting her slip in and drop her head onto his shoulder.

"Shall I stop?" He began to swing. His hands held her close as if she would fly away. She could feel his sweaty skin under her — feel his fingers firm against the naked skin of her shoulder blades. "Shall I stop?"

They were pitching so high now, the swing unable to go any higher. His lips pressed deeper into her skin. "Shall I stop?" he whispered.

She couldn't tell him no.

It was only when they heard the patter of small feet and the laughter of toddlers that they pulled apart.

Andrew swept Emily off the swing and carried her in his arms to the top of the slide where he pulled her into a plastic tree house. She was laughing so hard as he tried to squeeze his lanky body into a space meant for people half his height.

"Come here," he smiled mischievously. She scuttled over but bashed her head. "Ow." She fell forward and landed on him, her legs straddling his lap.

"That's better," he whispered, and his mouth found hers. He kissed her, and she tried to pull away to gasp a breath.

"No," he commanded, his lips trailing down her neck to her shoulder. "You're salty," he whispered against her collarbone.

"I'm sorry, I was running."

"No, I enjoy it. I haven't eaten breakfast. My date, you see, didn't show up."

She tried to respond, but his hands were slipping their way up the bare skin of her sides. She fell into him madly without knowing what she was doing, and when she threw her head back it smashed against the plastic walls.

"Owwww!" His hand was immediately there, and she felt his chest vibrate with laughter.

"Serves you right. I even made you a pot of tea. My sole contribution, but it took me all morning to boil the water."

"With sugar and cream?"

He nodded. "Seriously, where were you?"

"I went for a run. I thought that maybe you might have had too much absinthe last night, and I, well, I didn't know how you felt about things…"

"Sweet girl." His lips brushed hers. "Don't."

"Why were you here?" she asked as he began to nibble on her earlobe, causing her to sigh softly.

"I went to pursue you."

Her senses were on fire with the scent of him in this tiny space, sweaty, musky, all sunlight in the woods. He snaked his arms around her neck and kissed her. She tasted him, wanting him to be real. Here, alive, and now—just as Nora had said.

"Andrew," she managed to say, the thought of Nora grounding her back in reality and making her aware that if she didn't do something soon, a second later they would most assuredly be naked and making wild love in a five-by-five yellow plastic house. "If I tell you something, will you promise not to bundle me off to some mental hospital?"

"They're nasty places—" his lips drifted to her temple "—and the food is for shit."

She laughed in his arms and forced herself to concentrate, not be swept away. "I saw Nora." His lips didn't stop. She went on. "The ghost that lives in our house." She could feel him smile at the word "our."

"Yes?"

Leaving out the details of the hidden passageway and her midnight voyeurism, she told him about her recent experiences with Nora.

Andrew paused his kissing. He drew back, his face surreal in this small space, unshaven as it was, with eyes that glimmered as his sharp intelligence crept back into them. "What do you suppose it means?"

"I don't know, but I feel beholden in a weird way, like I'm supposed to help her. Like I was meant to help her—help them. I just can't sit by and watch them pine away like that. I know it sounds ridiculous. A few weeks ago I wouldn't have believed it, but I believe it now, don't you?"

Andrew studied her for a long while. "Perhaps we should scour the house a bit more. There may be something of them left behind. I suppose I should ask Nick about it, as well."

"You…you saw Nick? When?"

"Who do you think supplied the party favors—and the music for that matter?"

She stared at him in shocked disbelief. "So what does this make us then? The next Nick and Nora, off together to solve the mystery? All we need is a wire-haired terrier and we're set, although I think it was a schnauzer in the book, right? But I forgot, she really doesn't care for dogs." She laughed, only to notice that he hadn't. Oh Lord, she thought, nothing like plowing into commitment before they even had their first date. She felt herself turn crimson and wanted to melt through the plastic floor.

"Look at me, Emily." She refused, swallowing down the knot in her throat. "Emily." Andrew raised her face to his. "I'm not playing here, just so you know. Rather fond of you, if you haven't noticed."

Still avoiding his gaze, she quipped, "Here I thought you were showing appreciation to your fans."

Andrew's fingers brushed back the hair that had fallen in her face. "Evidently you weren't listening. You heard what that man told us: you're my slave, my concubine…my lover." He drew out each word seductively as his finger brushed along her bottom lip. "My lover. My lover. My—" His last words were smothered by her lips.

"Your muse," she sighed, her mouth on his neck, her teeth grazing the corded muscles there. Andrew groaned and clutched her hair in his hand when suddenly he stilled, as if her words had finally registered in his mind.

His muse. All her hopes and fears were exposed in that one sentence, bounding around those little plastic walls. Her stomach clenched. Logically she knew there was no room in a love affair for three people, and if Andrew still longed for his old girlfriend, she needed to know where she stood before she went on. But emotionally she had laid all her chips on the table and was scared to death.

"Sorry. Didn't want to bring up the past," she blurted out, trying to keep her voice as business-like as possible. "It's just that, you see, I'm sort of fond of you myself, and I don't share very well." Nora's words resounded in her head. *Take no prisoners.*

"Look, I understand you're only here for a while. You're a musician after all, you live on the road, right? But I don't want to be a fling, I don't fling very well, either. I don't have flingy parts. All I'm asking for is honesty. It's kind of mandatory for me. So if you're still in love with someone, that's okay, I don't want to take away your memories. But I won't be a consolation prize. I need to matter. I need us to matter."

Andrew didn't say anything. He just stared at her. He came closer, the energy pouring off of him, burning the air around them like the moment on the stage when he had shouted after her. She felt the danger in him and it thrilled her—as she was sure it thrilled all the women who heard him play, as she was sure it had thrilled his muse. But she needed to know, she needed to hear him say it.

He cupped her face in his hands. "You matter, Emily, more than you could possibly comprehend. I'm here, I'm not going anywhere. I want to be here. I've wanted to be here for a long time. A bloody long, long time." He kissed her, a kiss a soul could drown in, and rested his forehead on hers. She could feel his heart beat against her chest.

"Me too," she whispered back.

It wasn't the answer she wanted, but it was the answer she needed. She might not be this muse of Andrew's, even if the palm reader had told her so, but he did care—she knew that, she could feel that. She had asked Andrew for honesty, which he had given. What more could she expect? They had only just met, and somehow she knew that muse was a once in a lifetime title; perhaps it had just skipped this particular lifetime.

"Hey, mister," a tiny voice barked from below. "You gonna be in there all day?"

Andrew smiled. She dropped her head and laughed softly against his chest. Her emotions were still so raw she didn't know what to say. Her stomach, however, decided it for her and growled loudly. He chuckled at the sound, his lips pressed in her hair.

"So, where can a girl get some breakfast around here?" she asked. "I'm starving."

"Funny you should mention that. I know this great place, a little rustic, but the music is really first class." He hugged her to him, brushing his fingers against her cheek one last time.

No one seemed to notice Andrew and Emily's entrance into the kitchen with the exception of Zoey, who looked up at them from the table with a shrewd smile.

As Andrew slinked to the sink for a glass of water, he passed Simon silently lording over the stove. The letters on his fingers stood out as he clenched the spatula. He had added a fishing hat to his earlier wardrobe of a faded *Che Guevara for Pope* T-shirt and camouflage jeans.

"You're looking mighty keen, Paulie. Have a nice run, did you now? We were going to send a search party for the both of you."

"Bugger off."

Margot stood by the stove next to Simon, her arms folded over her starched white shirt as she inspected his progress.

"It's all in the wrists," Simon told her nonchalantly as he flipped a crepe high into the air. "You should really cook them on the bottom of the pan, but it's quicker this way. Care to have a go?"

"I don't cook."

Simon ignored her and covered her hand with his, catching a crepe as it flashed in the air before them. She yelped in surprise.

Simon steadied her. "Nothing to get nervous about. If you drop it, I'll make more."

Her pale lips disappeared as she concentrated on flipping the crepe onto a plate on her own. "So, you really think Plisko has a leg to stand on?"

"Yes."

"Why?"

"You're a smart girl, you know why. But as my aunt used to say, 'you need to build a bridge and get over it, love.' No one's ever one hundred percent spot-on about anything, or anyone for that matter. That's the nature of experimentation. You try and you fail, and you try again. It's definitely the nature of cooking…you'll want to save that one before it burns."

She rescued the crepe, removing it from the pan with a good deal of determination. Simon nodded at her and began to crack eggs. "So. What are you up to this week?"

"I…I have a papers that need grading, and I'm going out to Berkeley to do some research on the ATA."

"The Allen Telescope Array?" Simon asked, whisking the eggs in a bowl and handing it to her.

"Yes," she answered after a moment's hesitation.

"The one where they're partnering with SETI?"

"How did you…how do you…Well, yes. I'm going to be using the telescopes on campus, but I got lucky and pulled the graveyard shift, three a.m. It's when we'll have a stellar view of Jupiter. Would you like to see it?" Margot ventured. "I can bring guests."

"I don't know. If we're going at three a.m., I'd think you might be trying to get flirty with me."

"No, that's not what I meant. Strictly professional."

"Then what's the point?"

Margot peered toward the stove with the hint of a smile. "Your eggs are burning."

The rest of breakfast passed in a limbo of silence. In the shifting sands of relationships, there was no traction to begin any conversation. Salt and pepper were passed, the butter dish made the rounds, and coffee was poured before Zoey asked, "So Emily, how about you? What will you be doing this week?"

"I'm ghost hunting," she answered without hesitation.

The entire table went silent.

"What Emily is trying to say is that she is researching the history of the previous tenants of this house to discover how it may be relevant to the occurrences of disruption over the recent past, and she's going to publish the results as the final paper in her psychology class," Andrew explained, trying to gloss over the essentials lest they think both of them were lunatics.

"Ghost hunting? Does finding Nick in the bathtub count?" Christian asked.

"There was a ghost taking a bath in your flat?" Zoey's mouth didn't shut, but stayed in a shocked "O."

"Nah, he was dressed in this kick-ass suit and sipping a martini."

Andrew dropped his head into his hands. So much for subtlety.

"But I thought, I thought you were just making it all up about this Nora person?"

"She is a ghost. Was a person. I think she's sensitive to such things," Emily corrected her. She proceeded to describe to an astounded crowd her experience with Nora in the park.

"This is so cosmically relevant. Can you imagine, torn from being with the one you love? How do I help? Where do I sign up? Christian, you have to get involved in this with your aunt's voodoo shop and all, baby," Zoey said and clutched his hand in hers.

"Her place basically sold antiques, chere. Silver, jewelry—"

"Shrunken heads," Simon commented with a raised eyebrow.

"Well, I could probably use the extra manpower. We'll need to search the house for what might have belonged to them, anything that may have been left behind—diaries, letters, newspaper articles, anything that might help us in understanding their history. I'll see what I can find online too, and I suppose if all else fails, we search the city."

"So let me get this straight," asked Margot, clearly not convinced yet. "You're going to tell your professor, who happens to specialize in debunking anything related to the supernatural, that you're writing about reuniting the ghosts of lost lovers by finding a dead body and solving the mystery of their separation?"

"Yes."

"Are you out of your mind? He's going to fail you."

"But just think what he'd do if I could actually get some real data for once."

"It'll be the first time grave robbing is part of field study," Simon pointed out.

"What?" Emily turned to the solemn faced drummer.

"No, he's right," said Margot. "According to your friendly ghost friend, you'll have to first steal her ashes from the Columbarium, a huge basilica loaded with thousands of crypts, which is ludicrous in and of itself. And don't forget that the other remains could be who the hell knows where. Either way, you'll be plundering one grave at the least, which is, if I'm not mistaken, a criminal offense. And are you even sure this'll work? Jesus, I can't believe I'm actually having this conversation. Ghosts. This makes no sense whatsoever. And what about Vandin?" Margot pressed.

"I'm not sure how I'm going to present it yet, but I have a meeting scheduled with him."

"When?" Andrew asked.

"Next week. I can't remember, exactly."

Andrew could tell she was lying. Had she even made an appointment yet? Despite her evident independence, this was one thing he wasn't thrilled about her doing on her own, and he made a promise to himself that he would be conveniently sitting outside Vandin's open office door during that meeting. There was no way he was going to allow her to be alone with him, not after what he had witnessed in his classroom.

"So when do we start?" Zoey asked.

"Finish your brunch first," Margot told her with a disgusted shake of her head and flipped a crepe onto her plate.

"Not bad," Simon murmured.

The next week was spent in research during which Emily and Andrew were rarely apart. The days passed, and they found themselves lost in each other. They talked about everything and anything, until they found they could not stop, until they were hoarse, even though their minds still swirled with the need to hear the other's voice. They laughed, listened, and carried on like lost mates reunited after a lifetime. She didn't pander to him, something that surprised as much as pleased him. She confidently parried his intelligence and wit, and in turn, he didn't let her retreat without a fight, didn't accept anything less than all of her. When night came, he didn't want to leave her side.

He didn't see the growing concern of his band mates, in particular, Simon's critical stares at his "infatuation." It was all too easy, he thought to himself. It was the thrill of falling without the crash. But he didn't care. He was far too lost.

Early one morning, Andrew and Emily set off to City Hall to unearth any records they could find regarding the ownership of the house. They eagerly walked hand-in-hand up the stairs and into the great basilica. Emily laughed as she had to pull Andrew by the hand, his head lost to the towering stone and light.

"Come on, you. You're acting like a tourist."

"Bloody gorgeous."

"I know, the renovation is spectacular."

"I didn't mean the building."

She blushed and swung his hand. They spent the following hours trying to find the proper office to obtain the tax roll to determine when or if a Nick or Nora Chamberlain owned the house they were now living in. Andrew marveled at her tenacity, and she told him she marveled at his patience. After an hour of searching, they were about to give up hope when Emily pulled hard on his sleeve. "Look." She pointed to a listing on the tax record that read, *The Chamberlain Detective Agency*.

"Do you think?" Her eyes found Andrew's. "Do you think that he may have been a real detective after all? Nora said they were the inspiration for the Charleses."

"I always thought Dashiell Hammett and Lillian Hellman were the basis for Nick and Nora."

"No, but Nora told me she parties with them."

"Emily, really."

"Let's see if we can find anything else." She smiled at him, gave him a fast kiss, and pushed her curls behind her ears, thrilled to continue.

An hour later they had, unfortunately, come up with no information. There were no more records involving The Chamberlain Detective Agency, no liens, no tax bills, nothing. Around lunchtime they threw in the towel, thanked the weary clerk who had helped them, and headed down the sweeping steps to the floor of the rotunda.

"The acoustics in here must be amazing." Andrew hummed under his breath, lost in his thoughts, his hand twitching at his side.

"You never stop thinking about it, do you?"

There was no need to ask her to qualify what she meant — he knew. His music. The Lost Boys. "No, I can't. Sorry."

A small wedding party gathered on the mezzanine above them, and they heard a violinist and cellist begin to play. The strains of music flowed out to meet the sunlight.

"Wait, stop. Let's listen." He took her hand in his and led her to a nearby bench. They sat down; he wrapped his arm around her.

"That's Beethoven, a duo for violin and cello. If you listen very carefully, you can hear how the violin and the cello trade the tune back and forth, give and take, and then support the other when one has the melody line. See, right there? It's like a conversation between the two instruments — it's balanced — no one voice stands out above the other. Stunning."

She looked up at him, his eyes slightly closed, a smile making its way across his lips.

"Would you play the violin for me sometime? I need the encouragement. I thought we'd find more here, and there was nothing online, either. We're never going to find him. Even his own wife doesn't know where he's buried."

He kissed the back of her hand. "We've got time."

"No we don't," she answered with a frown. "We don't. She said so." She dropped his hand and stared at the wedding party before walking to the door.

"Hey, slow down," he shouted after her. "What's the rush? Why are you so upset?"

"It's nothing. I'm sorry."

"No, it's not nothing. Talk to me."

"It's just that I've never — I've never been with someone that — I'm not good with long distance relationships."

"I don't understand."

"Your music is your life — it's what you do."

"Yes, but it doesn't matter."

A field trip of small children marched by wearing matching bright green T-shirts, parents shepherding them along. Would she ever want that kind of life; would he? Her eyes followed them as well.

"Buy me lunch. I'm hungry," she told him and laced her fingers in his. "And I'll stop acting like an idiot."

"We have time, Emily." But as he said the words he knew she did not believe them.

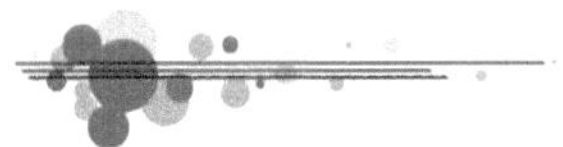

Their next stop was the main branch of the San Francisco Public Library. As they entered the building, Emily's bad humor from before seemed to evaporate. The hushed whispers and musty smell of old pages filled even the modern lobby. He could see her eyes sweep from floor to floor, entranced no doubt with the desire to disappear into the stacks and be heard from no more.

"This way, please." A smartly dressed woman smiled up at them from behind the help desk and led them to a microfiche room.

She spoke quietly so as not to disturb the other visitors and directed them on how to retrieve the files surrounding July 1st, 1935, the date of Nick and Nora's death. The room hummed in the suffused light of the machines, the swish and whir of images passing through the screens. They were about to divide the film and sit at separate cubicles when Emily placed her hand on his arm.

"Stay with me."

He pulled up a chair next to hers and draped his arm around her back as she readied the machine. Soon pages of the newspaper drifted by—old advertisements, black-and-white photos, and banner headlines, as though they should have their own soundtrack from a scratchy and muted record. Emily's face glowed blue-gray in the reflection, her eyes wide and almost silver. July first, July second, July third…Emily moved the slides faster as if knowing what to look for. Andrew blinked, the light beginning to hurt his eyes. The date scrawled along the top of the screen, and he blinked again, the pain becoming sharper. Faster and faster the pages flew, a blur of text and photos and advertisements. Soon the pain became an ice pick behind his eyes. His hand rose to his temple, and he felt nausea rise in his stomach. Faster and faster still, Emily's eyes scanning every detail somehow, until the images slammed to a halt. The word *Obituaries*, in a somber font, hung across the top of screen.

NICK CHAMBERLAIN MEMORIAL RITES HELD FRIDAY

A memorial service was held for Mr. Nick Chamberlain at 9 o'clock at the Flood Mansion on Friday evening. Mr. Chamberlain was killed in an automotive accident on July first near Mendocino when his car lost control and plummeted off the roadway. Mr. Chamberlain was famous for his high-profile work as a private detective, as well as being instrumental in working with law enforcement to solve certain notorious crimes, especially the Walter's Heist and the murder of famed film producer, Emile Latournow.

Andrew couldn't read any more, the pain too much to take, and he staggered out of the room. Emily looked up from the machine as he turned the corner, and the color stripped from her face as she saw his hand clench the doorjamb. Pale and shaking, he slammed open the door of the men's room and vomited in the closest stall. His head exploded. The sound of the sea and squealing tires roared in his ears. The sweaty feel of a steering wheel burned under his hands as he curled his fingers on the cold antiseptic tiles.

"Andrew! Andrew!" He could hear Emily calling from the hallway, but he didn't move. He couldn't face her. He was losing his mind, he knew he was. He had believed that once he found her this would stop, but the truth was, it was only getting worse. He was trading in one form of madness for another.

Andrew remembered the blunt voice of the doctor from long ago as he explained his diagnosis to his mum, and the scratch of his pen as he made notes on his chart.

"He's quite advanced for his age. Startling, really. We often see spells brought on by this level of precociousness."

The room was cold. His mother clenched his arm, and he could feel her love and worry evident in the press of her fingers, as though she could bring her young son back from his depression by the sheer force of her will.

"I see this form of neurosis often with child prodigies—it's the dark side of their enormous talent, in a way. Andrew seems fixated with a figure he links to his music. This obsession, while common, can prove unhealthy if it is not absorbed into the active, creative mind. I believe that in pushing it away, he is taking the first step toward independence."

"What can I do? What can I do to help?"

Andrew could not look at her. Her voice was so sad, and he knew he was responsible for making it so. He kept his eyes shut, feeling he had hurt her too badly to ever achieve forgiveness.

"He needs rest, and I strongly suggest you begin counseling to allow him to remove this unhealthy fixation from his mind."

"No!"

Claudia's hand tightened. It was the first sound her ten-year-old had made in several days.

"No! I don't want her to go away."

Claudia looked at him, not with fear or scorn, but with her patient compassion. *She doesn't have to*, her eyes told him.

So Andrew agreed to all the tests and the talks to pacify the doctors and all involved. He was bright enough to know what to say and do so they would think he was fine. Cured, as they would later exclaim.

Then years and years later…the 215th straight day of touring. They took their last encore and departed the stage. The recent loss of his father had compelled him to perform, plan, and write, to drive himself faster than his grief. He needed his muse more at that moment than ever before, and he hated that he was so weak as to want a fantasy. Paper-thin exhausted, all he wanted to do was to collapse.

"Fuck you," he remembered screaming at her in his mind. "Just fucking leave me alone." He flung his guitar to the ground and stalked off to the dressing rooms. Sitting before the mirror, he could hear her pleading with him, begging him to stay. "Bloody go to hell."

The next night, in the middle of the set, he reached out to her as he always did with that particular song. She was gone. He couldn't remember her, not a detail, not a whisper. Suddenly a vision came into his mind, a car careening against a guard rail, a woman's screams, her screams, his muse's scream. His hands couldn't move; he stopped dead in the midst of the refrain. His skin felt freezing and clammy, his hands trembled, and his heart was pounding so erratically he swore he was dying from a heart attack. Christian and Simon covered as best they could, long enough for him to stumble backstage.

"A breakdown," the shrink later informed Simon and Christian, both ashen-faced and silent. "He can't keep on like this. It's insane. He'll drive himself into an early grave."

So they forced him to stop, to take a breather, because he couldn't do anything else. And now, now he was spiraling out of control again. Except the vision was clearer now — a living nightmare.

They said little on the ride home. Andrew had claimed lunch had waylaid him and sat next to her on the MUNI shivering, his arms wrapped around his waist, causing her to worry even more. By the time they reached the foyer of their house, she walked him into his flat and waited until he was in bed before she left. It wasn't until later that night, when the house sighed and settled around him, that he heard a soft knock on his bedroom door.

Emily entered with a smile and a tray of broth and tea. Andrew realized it was the first time she had entered his room, and he smiled back up at her, uncharacteristically self-conscious. After placing the tray on his bed, she walked to his window and ran her fingers along the ledge. She turned and surveyed the walls, the wrought iron chandelier. An empty wine glass sat on his nightstand, sheet music lay strewn across the bed, and a pile of dirty clothes was heaped in the corner. She stared at the floor before looking into his eyes.

"You feel better?"

"Yes, better. I never had the chance to ask you, but what did the rest of the obituary say?"

"Well, it's strange. There was no listing of next of kin, nothing, and no mention of Nora of all. How could that be? She was his wife, yet it's like she didn't even exist. The only thing I know is that Nora's ashes are somewhere in the Columbarium."

"You still plan on nicking them?"

She shuddered slightly. "Would you go with me? I've never been there, but from what I know, I don't…I don't much care for closed up spaces. I'm a bit claustrophobic." She glanced up at him, embarrassed.

"Of course I'll go with you."

She blew a piece of hair out of her eyes in relief and glanced across the room, strangely nervous. "Is that yours?" She nodded toward an old violin case propped up in the corner.

Andrew had unearthed it from under his bed after he had returned, driven by the nostalgia awoken in him after hearing the classical instruments.

"No. It's my father's, actually. He gave it to me." He went to the case and opened it. The musty scent brought up a wave of melancholy. He felt Emily stand next to him, and he took a breath before he continued.

"John Hayes only believed in classical music. To him, only the masters mattered. He played them constantly. 'Technique,' he used to say to me, 'it's all in the technique, son.' Somehow phrasing and feeling didn't count as much. Well, until I showed him otherwise." He took out the bow.

"Did he like your music? He must have been proud."

Andrew tensed. His relationship with his father — how could he make her understand? How his father had the desire but not the ability, and when he discovered he had a son with the ability but not the desire, it had devastated him. "My father's dream was for me to become a classical pianist or violinist. I was equally skilled in both, you see. He didn't approve of my ultimate choice of professions. We weren't on speaking terms at the time — when he died."

"Oh, Andrew, I'm sorry."

"It's strange, you know. Now that we're having some success, I feel like I need to prove to him that it's justified — that there's honor among thieves, that we're just not some loud, ridiculously-dressed burden on society."

"Is that what he used to call you?"

"Pretty much…It's hard when you love someone, love someone like I loved him — he was the world to me. Him and Mum. And he was so much larger than life that I just believed everything he said was gospel. How could I fancy myself a rocker? It was absurd. But that's how my music came to me. Here."

He led her to sit on the bed and took some time tuning the violin. She eyed him in surprise as if he had begun speaking a different language. He studied the strings for a moment and rested his hand on them. "My father loved this."

He began to play, reliving the sorrow hidden in the music. When he finished, he closed his eyes and took a labored breath. The last time he had played Bach's *Chaconne* had been for his father when he was still alive, when he was still proud. He placed down his bow and looked to Emily. A silent tear fell along her cheek.

"I could never let that leave my music, Emily. But I need to…I need to scream too, to get it out of me. That's why I play the music I do, why I'm not in some philharmonic somewhere. I just wanted to scream loud enough and long enough so someone would listen, someone would understand, that somehow I could finally find a way to reach…" He faltered.

"To reach what?"

The only sound in the room was the light rain that had begun to splatter on the windows.

What could he say to her? How could he explain to her that she had possessed him since he was a child, that he had been institutionalized, had a break down not once but twice, all because of her? No, she would run, leave him. And now these horrid visions had made him doubt his own sanity again.

"So tomorrow, it's a school day, yes?" he went on matter-of-factly. "What then? Going to the water department, the historical society? By the way, I never asked you, has that shite approved your paper yet?"

"No, but I'm sure he will—he said that any topic covered this semester was fair game. Hauntings were covered, end of story. Andrew, are you all right?"

"So, when are you going to see him?"

She seemed startled by his tone and cleared her voice. "Soon."

"I want you to promise me something. Would you do that for me? Would you promise me that you'll let me come with you?"

"You don't have to worry. I'm a big girl—he's nothing I can't handle."

"Some battles shouldn't be fought single-handedly."

A strained silence hung between them. Moments passed without either saying a word.

"I've put in a call to the secretary at the Columbarium to see if Nora's ashes are there."

"Remember, I'm going with you there, as well," he told her.

"If I haven't mentioned it, I love it when you're like this—it keeps that Byronic hero image alive."

He grimaced at her and chuckled bitterly. "Let me guess, Simon told you about the article. 'Mad, bad, and dangerous to know.' Is that how you see me?"

"You're too handsome and too tall to be Mr. Rochester, but you're dark like him, all that Spanish swarthiness of yours," she said wryly in an attempt to humor him, but his face remained fixed. His walls were flying up around him faster than she could ever hope to block.

"Is that how you see me?" he repeated.

His reticence must have intimidated her, and she pushed back. "I know for a fact you don't have a dead wife hidden in the attic. And I'm sure you would have told me if insanity runs in the family, or you have some deep dark secret that would cause me to run away and nearly starve to death on the moors."

Even in the darkness he could see her forced smile.

"Andrew, I'm only joking. It doesn't matter. I'm more like Jane Eyre than you're like Mr. Rochester. Although I don't think I'd do well with strange people stalking me." She caught herself. "I mean ripping apart my clothes and all. No one wants to be stalked. You of all people must know that."

She looked miserable staring at him now, her hands plaited in her lap.

Before she could open her mouth to say anything else, he looked her straight in the eye. "No. Stalking someone, tracking them like that? It would be disgusting."

It was the voice of a man he hardly recognized. In that instant, he wondered if Emily calling him a "tortured Byronic hero" hadn't been far from the mark. Years of studying literature had made identifying the hallmarks easy — he could almost recite them: intelligent, mysterious, and charismatic; socially and sexually dominant; brooding; a troubled past; and…riddled with self-destructive secrets. All these secrets, secrets he had not yet told her, may never tell her. There was a Bertha Mason alive in an attic of his own making.

Love was anarchy, chaos.

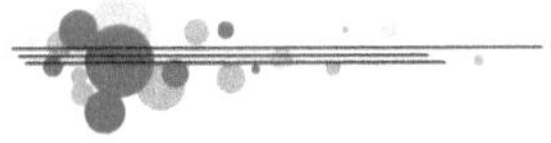

That night he lay in bed, his violin cast aside, Emily long gone. The radiator, unable to be turned off, was pumping torrents of heat into his room. The ghastly temperature had forced him out of all of his clothes; he was covered only in a loose pair of cotton running shorts and a thin layer of perspiration.

He glared at the clock. One a.m. He closed his eyes and imagined what she might be doing right now. Was her mind as wracked as his? She had left bothered and with few words. But what of her body? The bond between them that the bloody fortune-teller saw told of concubines and mistresses and slaves. Now, here at night, his want and need for her came together into something so primal that if he ever gave in to it, he feared for her safety.

He shoved off the shorts till he lay completely naked on the bare sheet and grasped a hold of himself hard, the dim light of the moon washing him in silver. He had never wanted anything like he wanted this woman. His body ached to the point of agony, and it felt like raw anger in his fist. He needed release—he had to have it.

He closed his eyes and imagined her glorious body lying underneath him, spreading her legs, tasting every inch of her, making her scream his name over and over as he licked a line along her hips, the arch of her ribs, the warm curves of her breasts. Gazing down into her gray eyes he would take her, feeling her clench tight and wet around him, both of them covered in sweat and joy.

He tightened his grip, raging in desperation. He groaned; in his mind he lost himself in the cascade of her hair and gouged his fingers into the hot skin of her bare back and made her his. Over and over until there was no end and no beginning, till there were only lovers. Till he was pounding so brutally into her she could only arch her back and submit.

"Fuck, I love you."

His head twisted to the side to muffle the cry as he came, hot and wet through his fingers. His body battled like a strangled thing. In his longing he swore he heard her gasp his name and could feel her near, the palpable presence of love.

"Stay!" he gasped into the darkness, his body still tense from the force of release. "Stay."

He slammed his arm over his eyes in bitter agony and exhaustion. "Stay…just…please. I love you."

Eventually too tired to fight any longer, sleep pulled him into its darkness. But as he closed his eyes the last time, he swore he heard the sound of ghosts passing in the night.

Emily rested her forehead against the driver's side window of her car the next morning, letting her breath fog the glass. The sun cast its rays across their street.

I love you.

She had heard him utter those words, all those words, every one of those fiercely tender, evocative words. Words she wished she could gather up in her hands at this moment and hold to her cheek to feel their warmth; her car was so cold. Had Andrew known how she had captured those words and others even more elusive, he would be livid. She had stood in the darkness of the passageway gazing at him in secret, watching his exquisite naked body twist and writhe as he raged against himself, all sinews and sweat, and the words he had cried made her need him with a hunger that made her feel inhuman.

"I love you." She whispered the words out loud, setting them free.

He had told the night only; she knew that, but she was part of the night, part of the shadows. And she knew that some would think she shouldn't have been there. Privacy was already in short supply in a crowded house with snooping ghosts. But when she saw him strip, she couldn't look away.

She wanted to believe that he had said those words to her, but she couldn't banish the image from her mind; it would not leave. His revulsion at being stalked. Had his muse stalked him and was he in love with her still? Or worse yet, had he stalked her, and was Emily someone he was using to take her place? Either way, it proved disastrous. And she, herself, how could she explain to him that she had watched him from a park bench, only to be near him, to see him the only way she knew how?

"I love you," she whispered again. For she couldn't deny it any longer. She loved him with all the mess and heartache and euphoria she'd spent a lifetime hiding from. It was as if her bones and blood were owned by him. "I love you." Her words were alive in the world now, a world that had changed as if someone had let loose the color of bliss.

It took Emily no time at all to reach Dr. Vandin's office. There were few cars on the street at that early hour, and fewer still in the college parking lot. She trudged down into the bowels of Payne Hall. Vandin's office sat at the farthest end of nowhere, a lone door illuminated by fizzing fluorescent lights, long glass coffins to a handful of dead flies.

Sitting outside on a metal chair, she tapped her foot nervously, the sound echoing through the empty hallway. Discarded flyers had fallen like leaves from the sterile bulletin boards that lined the labyrinths of cement walls and constituted the only other thing present, except for the stale antiseptic smell of the linoleum. She wondered how Vandin had come to be relegated to the basement. He probably once had a wood-paneled office with a view of some sun-spangled quad. But she knew from rumors that his star had fallen, the drinking, the undergraduates, the excesses of living too hard.

Andrew would be furious he if knew she had come without him, but she knew it was best not to make a scene. She had seen his temper. Still, the thought of what she was about to do made her pull her Chanel jacket around her shoulders and curse herself for the hundredth time that morning. She smoothed down the black crepe skirt that draped her stocking-covered legs. If she was going to go through with this insane mission, she intended to look the part: an intelligent, soon to be *summa cum laude*, well-coiffed, well-heeled graduate. Not some romantic believer in destiny and soul mates.

The door to Dr. Vandin's office swung open. The strains of jazz preceded a much disheveled and very wide-eyed student. She cast Emily a haunted look as her hands swept about her trying to repair the irreparable. She toddled down the hall, one loose shoe wobbling like a beat up toy train.

Emily muttered under her breath. The saxophone finished wailing just as the metal exit door slammed shut behind her.

"Ms. Thomas?" his voice barked from the office.

She closed her eyes and said a silent prayer to the patron saint of insanity, St. Dympha. Margot had informed her of this when she told her she was coming here this morning.

"I don't have all day. Are you going to sit out there and make me shout, or are you going to come in and grace me with your presence?"

She had been alone with him only once before in his lab. He had been different then, attentive, professorial, interesting, and interested. She, however, had not. As she passed through the door, she promised herself that it would stay open at all costs.

The office reflected the man. Bookcases were stacked with gilt-edged references and his bestsellers. Burgundy walls were decorated with diplomas and pictures of him from all over the globe, and a world map was impaled by a swath of red pins. She glanced to the far wall; a flurry of Thai pillows and a woolen throw lay wantonly on a leather couch as though he had spent the night. An empty bottle and two glasses sat nearby. No, he had definitely spent the night, and apparently not alone. Two suitcases stood near the door.

Dr. Vandin sat behind a massive mahogany desk where God knows what had taken place during his tenure. He paused only to glance up from his papers before he returned to his work. "So, I take it this isn't a social call."

"No."

"By the looks of it, you should be litigating a case, but you don't care for the law, do you? All poetry, if I remember. Verbose dead men and unproductive live ones. What a calling, Ms. Thomas. Love is a familiar. Love is a devil, blah, blah, blah."

"There is no evil angel but love. *Love's Labour's Lost*, Act One, Scene Two," she answered simply.

His eyes shot up at her. "Yes…well, sit down, don't stand there. It is annoying to watch you fidget."

"I'm here to go over my final paper." She handed him her binder.

"Oh yes, that. Mind if I smoke? I think it will be necessary." He lit a cigarette, not waiting for a response.

"It's a non-smoking building."

"Yes, I have never seen it smoke, myself," he returned in a practiced line.

"There's an outline in the beginning as you requested, and you'll see I've already started on the research."

He took long drags on the cigarette and blew the smoke up toward the ceiling where it spiraled like a serpent. He read slowly, turning back and forth, apparently in an effort to check and recheck information. He wore a button-down blue shirt with faded jeans, more yuppie than usual, and she noticed a wrinkled tie slung over the back of his chair as though it had been previously been used for other purposes. Her stomach turned at the thought. She coughed into her shoulder as the smoke built up in the confines of the room.

Finally, he lifted his head and looked at her with a combination of disgust and fascination.

"Ghosts? Truly, Ms. Thomas. You are special, are you not? The laws of science do not apply in your case." He nodded his head toward the wall behind him and took a deep puff from his cigarette before making a show of snuffing it dead in his ashtray. "Do you know what that map represents? Do you know what those red pins denote? They all constitute places that have been purported to be haunted. All that bullshit, all across the world — and I've disproved each and every one. Frauds, hoaxes, shams — set up to gain notoriety, increase tourism, and line the pockets of the charlatans that shovel that manure from one haunted inn to the next haunted castle. Don't tell me. Is your landlord holding ghost tours in the evening? Are there visitations? Does that boyfriend of yours play his guitar in the background to set the mood?"

Their eyes fixed together like the edges of knives. Then Emily halted. How did he know that Andrew played the guitar? He could have heard about the band from the students in the class; there were faces in the lecture hall that day that she remembered seeing at the shows. But to be that interested?

She took a steadying breath to calm herself. Maybe she was being paranoid. All she wanted was to get in and out of there with the least possible confrontation. Let her exit this horrid room with his grudging approval and she could write her paper, graduate, and get to her writer's conference. That's all she wanted from him.

"If you'll read farther down, you'll see that my thesis deals with the existence of residual energy based upon an emotional event or trauma. I never mentioned ghosts."

"Energy, ghosts, Akashic records, spirits — it is all the same. And what is this emotional event, exactly?"

She swallowed hard. "Love."

His mouth twitched into a smirk, and he rocked back on his chair before bursting into laughter. "Oh, spare me. Let me understand fully — soul mates, yes? They were parted in life and now search for each other in the afterlife, only to find peace once they've been reunited. Do you know how many times that tripe is passed off as science? Come now, Ms. Thomas, even you are smarter than this.

"You wish to write a paper? Write one about the active mind creating a fantasy that supplants reality. That the collected neuroses of fixating on one ideal takes over your life and you believe the lie, that fantasy is the only truth. Now *that* is the most dangerous and deadly deception of all. Whole industries are based on that disease. Novels, movies, television. You wish to believe in these ghosts because you believe they are lovers unable to rest in peace until they find each other? Just like you might believe there is one person out there in the world for you."

"And you don't?"

He hesitated. "No. No, I don't. There is only wanting and taking. Anyone that is saying anything else is selling you something. People love you or say they love you to get something they want from you. They can couch it in any euphemism they think fit—but in the end, they are all trying to use you."

The passion in his voice stunned her.

"And you sit there looking at me in disgust because I am honest about this. I see in you a brilliant, beautiful woman who for some extraordinary reason did not say yes to me. But I am your professor, aren't I? And there are rules. But I would bend them for you, break them if you'd like. But you're in love with him, aren't you?" His voice was low, an accusation more than a question. He rose from behind his desk and walked to the bookcase by the door.

"I could tell by the way that you looked at him, all knight in shining armor, wasn't he? So poetic. But Emily, do you not see that he wants what I want, what every man wants? It's merely that he is lying. He will tell you all the sweet things you want to hear, all that rubbish about love, but it's not you he is in love with. It's an ideal he has in his mind, you know that. The more artistic, the worse they become. He will call you his muse and write all the music in the world to you. But it is not you. And in a little while, after he's done fucking you, he will see your faults, see you for what you really are, and look for that muse of his somewhere else."

He took two steps from where he stood, turned, and shut the door. His back remained to her.

"Dr. Vandin, open the door."

"Funny that a musician would want someone like you. He must have deluded himself a great deal. Don't they usually strive for the blondes with large…vocabularies? Look in the mirror, Emily. You know what you'll see in the reflection: a driven woman that knows what she wants and will not let anything stand in her way. That is who you are. That is who I saw that the first time I laid eyes on you. You and I are a very much alike. There is fantasy out there, and there's reality in here."

"Open the door."

"You're not listening to me. You, an obscure little college student. A nearly famous rock star is really going to drop everything and remain here for you? Use your mind, Emily. He is using you, and you're in too deep to see. It is the same way people perceive ghosts. They want to believe because it is so romantic and mysterious, so out of their hands. But nothing is out of our hands. We're scientists. I only believe in things I can see and touch."

His shoulders shifted under the pressed lines of his shirt as he breathed. "I know you feel the same. I could see it in your eyes from the start."

"Open the door."

He walked slowly back to his chair. "You let me kiss you once." He took the tie off the back of his chair and held it in his hands. The silk slipped through his fingers like a rope. "Why was that?"

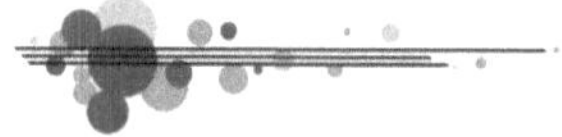

It was Monday evening, and Simon, Christian, and Andrew had just returned from a game of basketball. Their shoulders and legs burned from the grueling workout. Simon proceeded to shower while Andrew and Christian sat on the dusty tile floor of the bathroom and chatted about their day. Simon and Christian had gone down to Santa Cruz earlier to look at mandolins, Christian's latest obsession. When they returned, Andrew had begged them to shoot a few hoops. All day he had been riddled with an anxiety that he could not shake.

His only break had come in an unexpected visit from Neil, who had appeared when Andrew was about to go mad trying to salvage a song's lyrics from not sounding for shit. Neil had appeared just as bothered as Andrew, although about what, he wouldn't say. Yet he had given him excellent advice and they had spent a productive hour lost in the effort.

Simon stepped out of the shower and yanked off a towel from a rod which crumbled from the wall. "Fucking Sid. When is he ever going to finish anything in this house?"

"Nick scared him off," Andrew replied.

"What, he's only working upstairs now? Where's Emily? I thought you two were inseparable."

"I don't know."

"What do you mean, 'I don't know'? How'd you manage that? Did you tell her 'bout your imaginary friend? Ah, sweet Jesus, don't tell me you ran your mouth. Aw hell, look at your face. You did, didn't you? What's your fucking problem? You finally got a molly that's live and breathing and you go and cock it up. So what'd you do now?"

"I'm the quintessential Byronic hero, apparently," Andrew muttered bitterly.

"He does brood better than anyone I know," Christian concurred.

"Well, you're better off, if you ask me. It was getting too serious — you were losing your focus."

"I didn't ask you and my focus is fine. By the way, I finished the lyrics on 'Under Red Tables.' Actually, Neil finished the lyrics."

"Neil?"

Andrew had just finished explaining the visit when a knock came from the front door. Simon tightened the towel around his waist before he strode off to answer it.

"Welcome, welcome, welcome all," Simon bellowed, arm outstretched like some sarcastic game show host before stopping short. Zoey and Margot stood on the other side, their faces riddled with concern. Margot clutched a cell phone in her hand.

"Can we come in?"

Simon swung the door open, and they marched in and stood by the fireplace. Margot looked directly at Andrew. "Has Emily called? Have you seen her tonight?"

"No," Andrew said, then taking in the severity of Margot's expression, pressed, "What happened?"

"She made me promise. That's all I'm saying — she made me promise, and like an idiot I agreed."

"Where is she?" Andrew asked, his voice flat.

"We don't know."

"What do you mean, you don't know?"

"She had a meeting with him early this morning, and we were supposed to meet for lunch afterward, but she didn't show up. She should have been home hours ago. I called her cell phone but she didn't answer. I found it in her room — she forgot to take it with her."

"Who's him?" Simon asked.

"No, she couldn't, she promised me she wouldn't," Andrew said, frowning at Margot.

"Who's him?" Simon repeated.

"That shite," Andrew shot back, unable to understand how she had done such a stupid thing.

"Well that clarifies things."

"Vandin, the professor who tried to —"

"Tried to what?" Simon pushed.

"To fuck her, Simon," Margot said bitterly. "Please. I want to go to the college and find her. We can take my car — we can all fit in it," she added quickly.

"Wait," Christian interjected. "She's probably doing research and stayed late at the library or something. It's not like —"

"No. It's exactly 'like,'" Andrew muttered. "You've never seen him in action."

Andrew sat in the front of Margot's car, with Simon and Christian crammed into the backseat around Zoey. The sun was setting red on the horizon as they ran the second light in a row. The street tunneled before them; people out on the warm night jumped into it, jaywalked, darted around street corners. He wanted to lean out the window and scream at them to move.

Next to him, Margot clenched the steering wheel. "It's been hours. She's never like this. She's reliable, dependable…"

"Yes," he said. "Yes. She's fine. Nothing happened to her. She's fine. Stop."

Christian pocketed his phone. "No one's answering at the department—it's an after-hours message. Will anyone be there at the building to ask?"

"It's a college," Margot replied curtly. "There's always a body somewhere."

"Fine choice of words," Simon murmured.

"Watch out!" Andrew yelled. Margot swerved, nearly hitting a bicyclist.

"So this professor…" Christian began. "Why the hell didn't she report him? I mean, that shit's not right. There are rules."

Margot gunned the engine down a mercifully empty patch of street. "I don't know, but she wouldn't. And Emily wasn't the first, apparently. She should have put his ass in a sling a long time ago, but it would have been her word against his. She needed this final credit, and in the end I suppose she decided it was easier to just tough it out. And to think, I actually teased her about him." She yanked the wheel hard to the left. "It was her last class. All she wanted was to get to that conference this summer. It's all she ever talked about. Well, all she used to talk about…" She shot her eyes to Andrew and back to the road again.

"I really think we're seriously overreacting here," Christian said. "Let's get to this jerk's office first, and we'll go from there, okay? He's a professor, and we're all jumping to some pretty harsh conclusions. He isn't going to jeopardize his job, he's not crazy. She's probably holed up somewhere studying, or she found some information about Nick and Nora and lost track of the time."

"He doesn't care about his fucking job. He's a visiting professor," Margot said. "He's leaving at the end of the semester, probably to go off and find better hunting grounds before the administration catches up with him. A man like that never lasts long at any school, even ones that'll look the other way just to have bragging rights to a such a famous professor on their faculty. And trust me, I've seen enough of what gets 'looked over' in my department."

Andrew stared out the side window, prey to his mounting unease. He blamed himself for this. If he hadn't closed up on Emily last night, maybe she would have told him. He had scared her away again, and off she went to do this alone.

If she was safe—which he knew she would be, of course she would be—he promised himself he would tell her everything, he would come clean; the lies, the evasions, everything would go. He didn't want to think of her face as he had seen it in that lecture hall. He didn't want to think of her being humiliated, bullied.

The car slammed to a stop. Andrew jumped out before the engine died, with Simon and Christian following. They stared up at Payne Hall, silhouetted in black against the scarlet of the evening sky. Lights glowed in the windows like unblinking eyes.

"His office is in the basement, I think," said Margot. "We can take the stairs."

A handful of students hung about in the lobby, tired and weary-eyed. Andrew zeroed in on the directory. *T—U—V…* There it was: *Vandin, Room 61.*

His feet pounded along the peeled linoleum floor; his hands shoved open the metal stairway door. Andrew could feel Simon next to him as they stomped down into the bowels of the building. Whatever his opinion on all of this, he had not said a word, though Andrew was in no mood to hear it. Zoey and Margot's footfalls echoed behind them.

The doors crashed open as they reached the bottom floor; they stood together for a second to get their bearings. The hallway was dim, with weak fluorescent lighting, like a hospital ward. Andrew's skin prickled; it even smelled the same.

He could picture Emily here. Alone, waiting. What the hell had she been thinking? Why didn't she turn around? It was a naïve stunt to pull; she knew what Vandin was and how he felt about her. For the first time he felt angry, infuriated at her willful stupidity.

They rushed down to the end of the hall and reached a door. The placard read: *Dr. Pavel T. Vandin, Professor.*

The door was locked. Andrew pounded against it. No answer. He shouted Emily's name. No answer. He slammed it with his open hand.

"She's not here, Andrew. It's been too long," Zoey told him.

"He's just left for the day, that's all. We'll look for her somewhere else. It's after hours, no one is here," Christian placed his arm around Zoey, hoping to calm the anxiety in her voice.

"I want to be sure," said Margot and ran over to a janitor who was pushing a mop down at the far end of the hall. Seconds later she returned with him in tow; he was holding out his keys, his eyes beaming, eager to help.

"What did you say to him?" Simon whispered to her.

"You don't want to know."

He unlocked the door and pushed it open. In the darkness, they could only tell the room reeked of cigarette smoke and emptiness. A moment later, the overhead light flickered on.

"Holy shit!" the janitor cried at the sight before them.

A small reading lamp had crashed onto the carpet, its shade broken. Papers lay strewn across the desk but even more were heaped violently on the floor. Books toppled over each other in the bookcase, and pictures framed in broken glass lay scattered on the floor as if something or someone had been hurled against the wall.

Andrew griped the doorjamb as the room spun in and out of focus.

"We have to call the police," Zoey said numbly.

"Oh Jesus," Margot gasped, her face ashen. She stood in front of a wall-sized map that hung behind the desk and stared at her feet in revulsion. She knelt down and turned her face away like she was going to be sick. When she got to her feet, she was grasping something in her hand. An ashtray. A heavy glass ashtray. But something was wrong.

"There's blood on it." It slipped through her hands and crashed to the floor, a wet trail of crimson left on her fingers. "There's blood…all over the floor." She wobbled like she might faint and grabbed the side of the desk for support.

"Are you sure?" Andrew looked back to Margot.

"It's sticky. It's still sticky." Her fingers rubbed together, and she bit her lips and swallowed down whatever words or bile would come next.

"Listen," Andrew said. They turned to face him in a haze. "Christian, go with the janitor gent and get campus security, they'll know what to do. Margot, you need to focus on where else would she go. Does she study anywhere? Could she have driven…?"

"Wait. You said she drove here, right? Is her car still in the lot?" Simon demanded.

Once back in the parking lot, Andrew yelled out to the others. "What does she drive?"

"It's an old, green Citroën. You can't miss it," Margot answered, her eyes scanning the dim lot.

There must have been an evening class, because the lot was still full this time of night making their search difficult. After several minutes, they heard Christian shouting. "It isn't here. It isn't here. Well, maybe that's a good thing, maybe—"

"What? Maybe she got away? Or maybe he got rid of her car? Maybe he drove her somewhere so he could—" Simon's steady hand gripped Margot's shoulder.

Andrew stared at everyone, Simon and Christian, especially. With a labored breath, he spoke clearly and with little emotion. "We need to talk with security first. Margot, find Vandin's address in case they can't help. Zoey, ring whoever's the secretary of the department and get Vandin's schedule for the day, did he check in with anyone, anything like that." He told each of them to focus. They all knew what they had to do; they all were to reconnect every ten minutes via cell phone.

Simon looked at Andrew. "I think we need to phone the hospitals, just in case."

Margot's eyes widened, and she nodded her head; her fingers shook as she began searching for the numbers.

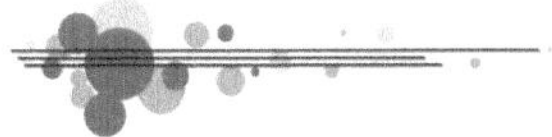

Hospitals move at a snail's pace. Unless you're gushing blood or have lost a limb, you wait. Broken spirits, Emily was to learn, count for much less.

Emily sat on a gurney, her hands like ice as she stared down at the borrowed cell phone, ready to call Margot, but she didn't know how to find the words. Shock had taken her. Gored her. She closed her eyes and relived the memory…

"Open the damn door." She was there in the office, trapped in quicksand, unable to move from the chair.

"There doesn't have to be strings attached. Like I told you before, we are two discreet, consenting adults…"

"I can sue you. For sexual harassment."

"I know, but you haven't. Why is that? Because you know how very difficult it is to prove. And I could just as easily argue it was you who instigated the liaison. You did, didn't you? Little Miss Thomas, infatuated by a father figure. An Electra complex. A classic evolutionary path: the younger woman drawn to an older man because she perceives he has the authority, the status, and the wealth to take care of her. Society has changed very little, Emily." The tie remained taut in his hands.

"Put that down and open the door, now."

"Or what? You'll scream? You didn't think she protested a bit, my previous appointment?" He studied the tie as he said this, as if testing to see how strong it really was. "You know another thing that's hard to prove?"

Sheer black fear swept through her knowing exactly what he would say. He took a step closer and smiled. "Especially since we have shared such a close relationship. Working together, you trying so diligently to get the job in the first place. The way I tease you in class, and the way you never complain. People might already think something is going on between us. No, I could merely say you preferred it rough, that you like to be bruised. Is that how he gives it to you? Does he like it hard and rough?"

His hands twisted the tie completely around each fist till there was nothing but a cord in his hands. Her lips bit back the tears that stung her eyes. Her mind clamped down on a singular thought: escape. The door, she had to get to the door.

He lifted the tie and held it aloft, arching his back. With a dark chuckle he lowered it, placed it under his collar, and yanked hard on the ends as he drew one through the other, making a perfect knot. Like he was leaving for work. Like he hadn't mentally tortured her. Like this was the way he was. A sadistic psychopath.

"I'm traveling to London for a seminar next week, and my flight leaves soon — I don't wish to be late. And to prove to you that I have a heart, you go ahead and write that paper of yours. It's an interesting story, and if nothing else, it'll give me something to look forward to when I return," he said with cool aloofness.

An ice-cold pulse thundered in her veins. White blotches tore at her vision. The room was freezing. Shock. She was going into shock. *Don't faint, don't faint, please don't faint. He'll hurt you. He will. He's taunting you now like you're his play-toy.*

"Though remember when you write this *piece de resistance*," she heard him say through the miasma, "ghosts are not based in reality, neither is love. They are both figments of the imagination to keep us from the void, from madness. And Ms. Thomas — " he nodded to the door " — don't look so upset. The door was merely closed. You were the one who believed it was locked. You could have left at any time. You were the one who chose to stay." With a nod, a blackish-gray lock from his slicked back hair fell on his forehead as he reached for his luggage. "Oh, and turn off the lights when you leave."

He turned to go.

As if his words were law, the lights suddenly went out and the room plunged into darkness. The temperature seemed to drop ten degrees, and Emily's skin froze as she clenched the armrest. He was playing with her after all; he had no intention of leaving.

A woman's voice whispered, "Riiing…arooound…the…rosssey…"

She could hear Vandin start abruptly near her. She recoiled blindly.

The icy voice warbled on. "Pockets…fuuuuulll…"

The door creaked open on a breath, then slammed shut on its own. The small light on his desk fizzled to life. Vandin's labored breaths came in short white puffs through his nose like a dragon.

"…of poooossseys…"

Fright as she was meant to feel, fright that made her hardwired to being alive, filled Emily. But a small part of her brain, the part that was still functioning, knew. She could feel her; she knew this familiar fear. She was never so glad to be terrified in her life. She knew that eerie, sultry voice.

Vandin wheeled around, his eyes like slits, trying to get a bearing on where the ghostly voice was coming from.

"Asshhhhes!" A laugh erupted from nowhere, a sound to freeze the blood in your veins.

All at once, a framed picture flew from the bookcase. The voice rose in anger. "Ashhhessss…"

Then another frame shot out, crashing to the floor. And another. A barrage of books followed, forcing Emily to cringe into the chair to avoid being hit. From behind, the desk pins ejected out of the map like machine gun fire, flying across the room. They impaled Vandin's arm. He howled, cursing in pain.

"All faaaalll…"

The small lamp toppled over, the shade demolished. Dr. Vandin's back was to Emily as he twisted around wildly, frantic to find the source of the destruction. Suddenly his body staggered backward as though he had been punched in the face. He fell to the floor; a heavy glass ashtray lay at his side. He turned. His nose spewed blood, his shirt and tie were smeared with it, and ash covered his face. He looked like a ghoul.

The voice sang out loudly. "Down!"

"Nora!" Emily yelled out loud. "Noreen!"

Vandin glared at her, holding his nose like a stuck pig. "What are you doing? How are you doing this? *How are you doing this?*"

"She isn't!" Nora wailed, and with a bone chilling cry, the door flew open. "But I am, you pig! Boo!"

He scuttled backward like a crab. One hand tried to stem the tide of the blood that left a trail behind him, the other grappled for his luggage. He threw himself out the door. The sound of his terrified footsteps thundered down the hall.

Emily sat there, unable to move, unable to breathe. Adrenaline raced through her body; she tried to speak, but she couldn't open her mouth.

"Emily," Nora whispered, her voice weaker, farther away. "I can't stay. I've only been here once, the bonds aren't strong. Never much of a poltergeist, I'm afraid. At sunset, tonight, the Columbarium. Please, Emily, we don't have much time. At sunset, the Columbarium. You need to understand. But first, Emily—you have to find her."

"Wait," Emily shouted. "What? Who do I have find?"

"That girl, the girl from before, find her. And Emily…" Her voice was nothing but a wisp now. "Be strong." Then there was silence broken only by a soft exhalation, and Emily swore she whispered, "Love the jacket… my favorite."

The full force of what had just happened to her hadn't yet hit; she didn't know what would happen when it did. Despite everything, she was gripped with the overwhelming desire to drop to her knees; she was so thankful, so god-awful thankful.

All at once the ghost's words reverberated through her mind: *the girl from before, find her. Be strong.* And she understood. Emily ripped through the papers on Vandin's desk, her hands still shaking but her mind laser sharp in its purpose. She found what she wanted. The girl's name was written on his calendar blotter next to hers, with three stars beside it. Her stomach roiled in disgust.

Nora was right. She was always right.

"You're dead," Emily muttered. She tore out the page and shoved it in her pocket. Then in a fit of uncontrolled rage, she swept everything off his desk onto the floor with a loud crash.

Emily found her. Her name was Laura Schandler. She was a freshman, from Wichita, Kansas. Her father was a pastor; her mother taught Sunday school. Through the crack in the door, Emily could see her eyes were red and swollen and afraid.

"But he said I was special," said her little girl voice. She still wore the same clothes. She said her parents would be furious. They had homeschooled her, raised her to be a good girl. "I didn't want him to do that, but everything happened so fast."

Be strong.

"You need to go to the Administration Office. It's the only way."

"But I can't, my parents…"

"No, it's all right. Shhhh. It's all right. I'll stay with you. Your parents love you. They want you safe. If you don't report this, he'll keep doing it to other girls. I'll stay with you, I promise."

And Emily did. She sat next to her at the counselors, who immediately called the police upon learning that Laura was only seventeen. She held her freezing cold hand when Laura began to panic and did not let go on the ride to the hospital, or in the examination room.

It was very late by the time they finished, after their last statements were taken by the police who promised to remain in touch. Emily dug in her purse to find her cell phone, but it was nowhere to be found. She asked Laura if she had one she could possibly borrow. Laura handed it to her with trembling hands.

Emily stared at the phone. She opened her mouth to ask Laura how to dial, as it was so unlike her own, only to look up and realize that Laura's face was colorless. How could she explain to Margot what had happened while she sat next to this scarred girl? She opted to text, hoping she was doing it correctly.

I'm fine. Will be late. Don't worry. E.

She prayed it was good enough for Margot.

"Thank you — for taking care of me," Laura whispered.

"No need to thank me. Remember, you're not alone. You're going to need to be strong, though."

"You too."

"Yes."

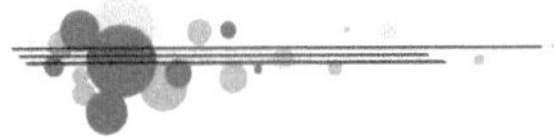

The phone booth on Stanyan reeked of urine. She held her breath and called home. The line rang and rang and rang. The answering machine wouldn't pick up. Hell. Where was everyone? She struggled not to hit something, feeling more and more alone.

Her heart beat harder with the thought of calling Andrew. But how? Madly in love with the man and she didn't even know his phone number. How could that even be? Maybe it was a good thing; she could only imagine his reaction to all this.

Promise me that you'll let me come with you? I've seen how he treats you. I don't want you near him alone.

She'd deal with the fallout later. Right now the sun was setting; she was running out of time. She swore as she rummaged in her pockets for change. Across the street a bunch of crack heads were starting to pee on her car. Hell! Wasn't the phone booth good enough? Slamming the phone down in disgust, she raced back across the street. She'd try again, after… after whatever Nora wanted had happened.

The sun left a red slash in the sky as it dipped below the horizon; the trees stood like black sentinels against it. Just beyond, the basilica came into view. The Columbarium. She had never stepped a foot inside. She was too daunted, for one simple reason: the place teemed with the dead. She could feel them the few times she had driven past, and hated the thought of being confined so close to them.

Her roommates had dismissed her fears as crazy, but it was one of the reasons she enrolled in Vandin's class — to banish her belief in ghosts — long before they had intruded on her life. As a teenager she had lost herself in Poe and Lovecraft. The lurid fascination with the macabre had never left her, but it didn't make it any easier to enter the place.

When she reached the door, her heart sped up. The sign read: *Visiting hours 8:30 a.m. to 5 p.m. Silence requested.* She checked her watch. It was almost five; she'd made it just under the wire. The heavy bronze doors opened like those of a cathedral, and immediately the scents of incense and age assaulted her senses. As she entered, her heels clipped on the marble floor. She looked up and stopped short in wonder.

A beautiful rotunda towered above her head, and stained-glass windows ringed the upper dome. The entire interior was made up of level after level of open galleries with corridors leading off of them, much like the spokes radiating out from the center of a very expensive wheel. Ornate wrought-iron railings circled every tier, and she guessed each corridor would house the vaults that held the cremated remains.

Her attention was drawn ahead to the floor of the rotunda where a finely appointed table stood, topped by an ornate urn. Rows of chairs were lined up in front of it. A small gathering of mourners sat there, heads bowed. A sign read:

Lipswitch Internment

Reception to follow

A pianist and harpist played off to the side. A haunting melody floated from their instruments and enveloped the room. Emily could feel the weight of the day settle heavily upon her, the poignant sound making her heart draw tight. She drew back into the shadows as a man in a uniform spotted her and immediately trotted over.

Emily gaped at him in surprise as he smiled back in the same witchy-stoner way he had at his shop. She'd never mistake all those tattoos. Evidently he had no problem recognizing her, either.

"Yo. If it ain't the Muse-lady! Dinesh said you'd come here, I just didn't believe him." He smiled broadly and motioned to the man behind the piano.

A long-haired Indian stoner, whom she could only assume to be Dinesh, nodded at her in response like Lurch from *The Addams Family*. He kicked the emaciated bald guy bent at the harp, who looked over his shoulder at Emily. She heard him utter, "Holy shit," over a woeful chord. A few of the mourners' heads popped up in alarm.

"What are you doing here?" Emily asked in disbelief.

"Shop's closed on Mondays. Just working here to earn a little extra scratch. That's Buck next to Dinesh—they're aiding the dearly beloved with the passing of their dearly departed, yada, yada, yada. Little do they know, Mr. Lipswitch's hanging out on the third floor balcony with his wife. She's bitching about all the people who didn't show up. Can't you see him, the fat dude with the mustache?"

Emily peered up into the dim gallery. "Um, no. I don't think so. But I think I'm a one-woman ghost watcher, though. You can see them all? Every one?"

"Yeah. It's a bummer, though. Seems like they've all got something that's harshing their mellow. One ghost can't stand to be near his ex-wife's ashes 'cause it's eating away at what's left of him. Another one is rotting from all the shit she dumped on everybody in her life. Issues, issues, issues. A nasty bunch here, if I do say so myself."

Emily wanted to hug him at that moment; he was the first smiling face she had seen all day. The realization made all the strength she had girded herself with to survive the past few hours nearly crumble away.

"Dwayne, your name's Dwayne, right?" she asked, fighting to keep her voice even.

He gave her the thumbs up and showed off his rather fancy nametag. "Dwayne Cobshib."

"Pleased to meet you again, Dwayne Cobshib. I'm Emily, Emily Thomas." She shook his hand with a brisk, business-like nature which confused him a bit. "I need your help. I need to find someone, well, the remains of someone who I think is here. Is there a directory or book or anything I could check?"

He looked uncomfortable. "Uh, actually, I'm pretty new here."

"How new?"

"My first week. Dinesh got me the job."

Emily groaned.

"Yo, yo, Muse-lady, don't start freaking. I don't think there's anything like that, anyway. You know, privacy and all. Some really famous people are boxed up here."

"You don't suppose you could ask, um…" Emily glanced up at the gallery where she thought Mr. Lipswitch might be standing.

"Whoa. No way. It's a member's only club, and they're tighter than a nun's budget with that shit. They take those secrets to the grave."

"Well, what am I supposed to do? She told me to be here at dusk, and I came without even knowing why. Do you know what I've been through today? Do you have any idea? Now I'm standing here in some God-forsaken crypt, the reason for which I have no idea, my friends are probably apoplectic wondering where the hell I am, and all I want to do is go home and forget this whole day ever happened. Do you understand? Do you?!"

It was the moment she knew was coming, she just didn't picture it happening in front of a security guard/palm reader, the entire grieving Lipswitch family, two stoner musicians, and countless disembodied dead people. Grabbing him, her face inches from his, she began to shake the shoulders of a tattooed man who weeks ago had told her she'd spent lifetimes loving the man who was probably going to kill her the minute she walked in the door tonight. "Do you understand?"

Dwayne looked petrified, like someone had just handed him a ticking time bomb, which wasn't far from the truth. He awkwardly put his arms around her, guiding her off and up the stairs with Emily resisting all the way until they reached the top. A couch was tucked in the corner, the back covered in an abundance of velvet pillows.

Emily finally gave in to his efforts and felt a stray tear steal down her face as she turned her head into the pot-reeking softness of his shoulder. He sat there as she unloaded her whole day, her whole week, her whole month into his tattooed arms.

Finally, after what felt like an eternity, her voice raw from the telling and a few more of her tears shouldered away, the equally wary faces of Dinesh and Buck poked around the corner. Dinesh ventured closer and offered her a large glass of wine that she took with shaking hands.

"Drink up, sister. You look like the dead."

She snorted and gulped the wine down in one swallow. It hit her stomach like a fist. Dinesh glanced at Buck who begrudgingly handed his glass over. "But it's good vino, man. Those Lipshit people are loaded."

"Lipswitch," mumbled Dinesh.

The second glass disappeared without a hitch. Warm tendrils of alcohol spiraled down to Emily's feet.

"Look, we'd really like to help," said Dwayne, "but we got another gig across town. There's a Wiccan spiral dance over on Valencia. We promised Dinesh's girlfriend, Lucretia, we'd be there like a half hour ago. She's gonna turn me into a newt or some other shit if I don't get going. Man, witches…"

Buck didn't utter a word, just looked apologetic and shrugged his shoulders as if to agree with the vagaries of the supernatural.

"Meet you in the van, dude," said Dinesh as Buck followed silently, and with a wave goodbye, their footsteps clodded away leaving Dwayne staring down at her.

"Look, it'll probably get me fired, but why don't you stick around and look for those cre-mains? Just flick the lock on the door when you leave. It ain't like you'll be getting any visitors this late at night. I'm just gonna close up the office downstairs. Can you believe them giving me an office? Righteous.

"Oh, yeah, here, if you have any problems." He patted his jacket and withdrew a card.

Emily held it up in the dim light:

Dwayne Cobshib

Palmist, Tarot Card Reader, Spiritualist, and Security Guard,
The Columbarium

His phone number was listed, followed by the e-mail address of *ghotz-seer@dead4u.com*. She managed a smile.

"A séance might be just what you need," Dwayne informed her. "They really like to dish the dirt on each other. The secret is to find the right spirit guide to allow the positive energy to flow."

Emily nodded weakly and wondered how she had gotten to this point, sitting in a crypt after hours, chatting about communicating with the Great Beyond after barely escaping the clutches of a very live man with the help of a very dead woman. She hung her head and chuckled miserably.

"Thank you, Dwayne. I suppose I'll just start looking around. Guess here's as good a place as any. You wouldn't happen to know how many um, uh, remains are here?"

"Ehhhh, about seven thousand."

Her heart fell to her lap. Seven thousand! How the hell was she going to find Nora amidst seven thousand vaults?

"Although there's a bunch that are gonna be moved to other locations tomorrow, so it'll lower the number by a few."

"Moved to other locations? Which ones?"

"They're marked with a red tag. Something about money running out from the estates or something. Bummer, though. It's going to make for a ton of even more pissed off spirits."

Hope rose up in her. Time was running out. Is that what Nora meant? Time was running out before her ashes would be sent to God knows where? And if they were lost, there would be no way to reunite them with her husband.

"Oh, one more thing." Dwayne handed her his flashlight. "You're going to need this. The lights are on a timer. They'll be going off in a few hours."

Great. She was going to be left in the spookiest place in San Francisco, victim to a thousand ghosts, with only a flashlight to protect her.

"Who you looking for, by the way?"

She told him, and he shrugged his shoulders. "Look, gotta run. Dinesh hates to wait. Good luck there, Muse-lady."

Even with the lights on, the lower floor, with its heavy, breathing silence, preyed on her nerves. Every corridor was lined with countless vaults up and down their high walls, making her search seem doomed. With each step, she could hear the unmistakable fall of footsteps behind her. They ceased when she paused. The chill of the air brushed against her hair as though someone—or something—had breathed against her ear. Looking over her shoulder, her heart plummeted into the pit of her stomach when she saw the emaciated shape of an eyeless face slither into the shadows.

Swallowing down a mouthful of fear, she began searching for the vaults with red tags tied to their locks. Most were little niches with glass fronts, and they usually held an urn or some other receptacle for the ashes and other memorabilia from the departed. Some even smoothed her jarred nerves: a teapot, a piggy bank, a cocktail shaker that she double checked, sure it had to be Nora's, but it wasn't. Pictures of family were on display inside too, as well as decorated boxes and letters. Her hand dusted along as if greeting these people by name, seeing their lives defined by such heartfelt things. Other vaults brought back her trepidation. They were old, forbidding metal drawers, ornate gilded fronts with no visibility to the secrets within. As she crept about, her belief solidified that Nora's warning must have meant that her ashes were in jeopardy of being lost. Time passed, and with each weary footstep, the gravity and weight of the day began to sink in.

There were no such things as ghosts, Vandin had said, mocking her. But she knew there were, and now she could feel them creeping out of the shadows to stalk her progress. No longer did they seem the dismissive lot that Dwayne had spoken of. Some felt lifeless in their stillness, some lurking, some waiting and watching. The hair on her arms stood up, her body keenly aware of their presence. Vandin's voice whispered among them: *Ghosts are not reality, neither is love. They're both figments of the imagination to keep us from the void, from madness.*

That's when the lights went out.

Suddenly the air whispered with a thousand voices, hushing and hissing; the darkness about her was heavy with their swirling shapes. She flicked on the flashlight but it shook in her hand as the bulb began to wane. She jostled it a little more, but only an anemic sliver of light shone in the night. Faceless beings began to sweep around her, white, living cobwebs, moist and freezing as they passed. A palpable resentment filled them as though she had invaded their sanctum, stayed too long in a place she did not belong.

Their growing crush made her clutch at the wrought iron railing, compelling her to take one step at a time as she fought against the force that sought to drain her, to drag her down. She closed her eyes in an attempt to banish them, but she felt their souls lash at her skin, equally enraged and fascinated by her humanity. Vandin's words reverberated again in her mind: *To keep us from the void, madness.*

No. She was in control, she insisted to herself, not the fear around her. Looking up she saw the top of the basilica — the last place she needed to search. Struggling to navigate the remaining flight of steps, she could feel the ghosts' increasing hostility at her trespassing, their curiosity turning heated. All the air seemed driven from her lungs, and the walls of crypts threatened to suffocate her. Intense claustrophobia seized her. She remembered the awful childhood memory of being locked in a hallway closet. A wild mouse was trapped along with her. It scratched madly in the corner, its red eyes flashing in the thin line of light under the frame. Only a few seconds till she passed out. She thought of the cool night and the sweetness of the air, but she couldn't move.

"Nora!" she shouted into the blackness.

"Norrrraaaa!" returned to her unanswered. She had to get to out to open space. She couldn't breathe. Unseen hands shoved her closer to the edge of the basilica's railing, the marble floor barely visible from on high, its tiles pulling her to them like lead weights.

"Join us," she could hear the voices whisper. "One more step, Emily." Her hands clenched the metal handrail, her palms slicked with cold sweat. Long-dead fingers speared her shoulders and combed through her hair, leaving a chilled touch in their wake.

"No, let her be," another voice muttered. "She doesn't belong here. Make her go away," a child cried. A thin, dry voice spat, "She'd be better off dead." Paralyzed, she felt arms heave her up the railing.

"No!" she screamed into the night. "No!" She wrenched away from the death grip and threw herself toward the stairs. A hand reached out and grabbed hers, but she slammed her body hard against it.

"Emily," she heard a woman shout.

Emily twisted about, hearing Nora's voice. The emptiness and desolation of this place took root in her. "Nora!" Emily cried out in return.

Then silence. A horrible, chilling silence swelled up in the darkness. And a rattle, a wheezing death rattle sounded from down far below on the marble floor. The lurid sound of a dead limb being dragged across the tiles. Terrified, Emily froze on the landing. Fear paralyzed her. Step by step, the thing lumbered up the rings of the basilica until something rose out of the pitch black. Rags covered milky eyes. Dead black nails covered gray veined fingers.

"It's only a dream, it's only a dream," Emily prayed. She stepped back, and her foot caught on edge of the railing. She stumbled, vainly grappling for a hold. "She's meant to be a ghost," a dry voice hissed as Emily's head crashed hard against the stone landing, and she heard no more.

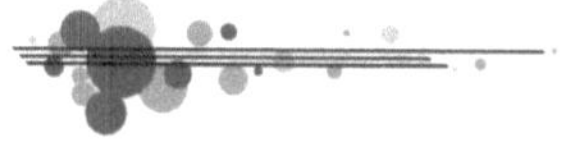

Somewhere around midnight Andrew hit the wall. Margot and Zoey were no better, having turned themselves inside out with worry. They had not found Emily. They had not found Vandin. They had found nothing.

Andrew had torn through every building on campus where she might be. Every stack, every cubicle, every corner, every shadow. Vandin's house was sealed up like a crypt, according to Christian. There was no car in the garage. Simon had gone down to Haight Street, to every bar and café, and Zoey had tried to call any students that might have him as their professor;

no one knew a thing. Campus security had sealed off Vandin's office and promised to contact them in the morning.

The five of them sat around the girls' kitchen in the dark. Candles glowed about them, throwing their shadows on the walls. The power had been on and off all day; a note from Sid was taped on the refrigerator, apologizing for the inconvenience and promising it would be better first thing in the morning.

The clock ticked in the kitchen wall. Tick. Tick. Tick. *She's hurt.* Tick. Tick. Tick. *She's afraid.* Tick. Tick. Tick. *She's bleeding…*

Andrew's cell phone rang. For a split second he hesitated to answer, and then his hand flashed to it. "Emily!" he yelled.

Silence on the other end. Moments later a soft voice replied, "Andrew? Andrew is everything all right? I had the worst dream, I—"

"Mum?"

"You're not hurt, are you? It was so horrible."

"Mum, I'm fine," he lied. "Where are you?"

"I'm in New York. I came over to visit some friends, and I was planning on surprising you. But the dream—it was rather terrible—and you know how I am." He could hear her drumming fingers on the other end of the phone that matched his own. "I was worried. I hadn't heard from you since you flew out there. It's so unlike you."

"I've been busy, I am sorry. Listen Mum, I love you, but I'm waiting for a call, it's rather important, do you mind?"

"Not at all. I'll ring you later in the week. You promise me you're all right though?"

"Yes," he lied again.

Five pairs of tired and anxious eyes stared back at him as he put down the phone.

"Claudia, my mum."

Scrubbing his face with his hands, he let out a howl and slammed back on the stool. "That's it. I can't sit here anymore. I've got to do something. Where are the car keys?"

"You're too knackered to drive by yourself. I'm coming," said Simon.

Margot glanced at him. He had shown his true colors tonight, and it wasn't lost on her. Her eyes followed him as he went to get his jacket, and they did not look away as he slipped it on one arm at a time.

"If you hear anything," Andrew said to everyone on the way out, "if she calls. If anyone calls…"

"You'll be the first to know, Andrew," Christian finished.

The night was still warm, almost humid. He left his jacket behind—his button-down shirt and jeans were enough—and he shoved his cell phone in his pocket. A thin layer of fog blanketed the streets.

"I'll drive," said Simon, and Andrew didn't argue. He got into the passenger side of the truck and shuddered from a chill he could recognize as exhaustion.

The engine turned over, and they pulled away, the tires kicking up gravel. Desperate for distraction, Andrew flipped on the radio. An oldies station played. It was Billie Holiday singing of body and soul.

"What station is this? You had me convinced the truck only got classic rock and public radio," said Simon, his voice stretched in feigned lightness. "Where do you want to head?"

"Just drive. Anywhere. Everywhere. Places she might be. The whole bloody city if we have to…"

The city passed by in a neon blur. Andrew stared unseeing at everything, hoping against hope to see her car. But all he could see was the hell that was Vandin's office. The destruction. The ashtray. The blood. He laid his head against the windshield and moaned.

"Are you gonna lose it? Do you want me to pull over?"

"No!" He sat back up and folded his arms across his chest. "Or do you mean am I going to lose it, like go mad again?" he said bitterly.

"Well, yeah, there's always that possibility, but I didn't want to sound like a shit."

Andrew ignored him.

Simon changed stations, hoping to banish Billie's misery. The blaring strains of Warren Zevon filled the cab as he wailed his ragtime obscenities of raping and killing and burying little Susie's bones.

"Enough of that shit," Simon muttered, and he bashed the station back to the oldies.

They rode on listening to Lady Day, but Andrew could only hear "Excitable Boy." Simon lit a cigarette; the tip burned in the darkness.

"I love her." Andrew's face was pressed to the passenger side window. His breath etched the glass.

"I know. Didn't take much to see. Though I don't quite understand it, and I still think it's a disaster in the making, but I'd rather you fixated yourself on someone breathing. Just don't get too serious, you barely know the girl. You're gonna get fucked up all ways to crazy when she breaks your heart. 'Cause you know she's going to. We'll be on the road and she'll be here. She doesn't seem like the kind of woman who wants to ride in the back of a truck. A bit too posh for sharing hotel rooms and mini-soaps."

"So you don't think this is crazy?"

Simon glanced at him sideways and chuckled darkly. "Crazy? Absolutely. But I've seen a ghost, I've set fire to me own home, and I haven't had sex for almost six months. Who's crazy here? Bizarre in a way, though, like all that soul mate crap is true. Maybe you two will end up being buried together — a long time from now, though. I'm not nearly rich enough yet. You want a smoke?"

Andrew eyed the offered cigarette but shook his head and returned to stare out the window. "Do you think anything's happened to her?"

Simon hesitated. "People do some sick things in this world. When I was kid, people went missing, all the time, every week. Sometimes they were found, sometimes they weren't. It's a fucking twisted world. But I still say she's probably reading in some shop somewhere, researching your ghosts."

The cab had become cold. Billie finished, surrendering herself in body and soul. The announcer came on, and Andrew forced his mind to concentrate on Simon's words to keep from despairing: *Researching ghosts. Maybe you two will end up being buried together…buried together.*

"Wait," Andrew cried. He grabbed his cell phone. A few seconds later he had found the map. "Turn left," he ordered. Blocks flew by. Houses, shops, buildings all washed away into the night. "Then at Anza, right here!"

Finally, the immense copper-domed basilica of the Columbarium loomed before them. The adjacent parking lot was completely dark except for the one street light that cast its illumination on a single car. A green Citroën.

"Emily!"

The tires squealed as Simon slammed on the brakes. Andrew threw open the door while the car was coasting to a stop and almost fell to the pavement. He was running. He was running and choking.

The Columbarium's door loomed before Andrew. He lunged for the large metal handles and pulled violently, expecting them to be locked. But they parted. He threw himself into the darkness.

His eyes fought to adjust to the black fog around him. He swore he heard whispers above and wrenched his head to look. "Emily!" he screamed. His terror echoed back to him. "MILEE, MILL-eee…"

He ran toward the outline of a table a few yards away and knocked into a chair. It crashed over and clattered loudly in the silence. He screamed again. A shape listed on the other side of the room. "Emily!"

"Shit, Andrew. It's me," hissed Simon. "I can't see a damn thing."

Andrew squinted, forcing his eyes to adjust to the dark; they narrowed in on the steps and the galleries above.

"You go down. I'll go up. If you find him, he's mine."

Tearing up the stairs by threes, he raced around each floor yelling her name. Peering down each corridor, he saw nothing except the passing of his shadow. He could hear Simon shouting from below.

He reached the top tier and stopped short. He staggered backward. Emily was lying on the floor. Her hair was splayed out around her, a thin trail of blood near her head. It glowed purple in moonlight.

"Oh God, no. No. No."

He dropped to his knees beside her and took her in his arms. "Emily, Emily, sweet girl, wake up. Please, oh Christ, please. Don't, don't. *Don't.*"

He felt her move, and his heart exploded as he sought out her face. "Are you hurt?"

"Andrew? Is that you?" She shook like a storm, and he held her, rocking back and forth.

"Where is he? Did he hurt you? Where is he?"

"I'm all right. I'm all right now." Her fingers reached toward her head. "Ouch."

Andrew saw a thin gouge near her scalp, a tiny line of blood had dried down her cheekbone. "Did he do this?"

"No. I'm not hurt. I must have hit my head. There were…I thought I heard voices. And then…Oh hell, I can't remember." She stopped, looking around as though searching for something she had lost, before she returned her pained gaze to Andrew. "Didn't Margot tell you? Didn't you get my message? What time is it? How long have I been here?"

"No. We didn't hear anything. I've been insane with worry. Jesus Christ, Emily. We saw the office. What happened? We thought, I thought, oh fucking hell, how could you do that?" His voice broke, and he looked away.

Simon's steps came up the stairs. "Mother of God, are you okay? That's a right good bleeder."

"I'm fine."

"Anyone else here we should know about?"

"Not here," she said weakly and struggled to sit up.

Andrew backed away slightly and Emily looked at him; a trail of tears had dried on her face. Her hand pressed to the cut on her forehead. "I must have hit the railing. Andrew, I'm sorry you were worried. But everything happened so fast."

"What happened?"

"I went to his office." She told them about Vandin, what he had done. Then she spoke of Nora and the destruction, and Andrew didn't even care if Emily had done it all herself. He wanted to punch the teeth out of the man's face. Her voice quieted when she got to the part about the girl and the hospital. Finally, when she was done, she stood. Rays of moonlight filtered in from the small, stained glass windows around them. She looked like a ghost, Andrew thought, with the trail of dried tears and blood on her face.

Simon cleared his throat. "I've got some important phone calls to make…meet you outside. Um, take your time."

They waited until they heard the door thud shut down below; then Andrew stood as well and took her hands in his hands. "You're safe now. You're safe with me. Do you understand?" She nodded. "But why did you go there alone? Why didn't you let me come with you? Emily, what were you thinking? Do you know how worried, how insane we all were? He could have—bloody hell, Emily!"

Her brow creased. He took hold of her by the shoulders. "You can't… nothing can happen to you, do you understand!"

"But I thought, I just thought that—"

"No! You didn't think. If you had thought, you would have never put yourself in that position, taken that kind of risk."

"So this is all my fault? I had no idea he would—he would do what he did. Do you think I would have gone there if I did? If I knew?" Her breath came out in ragged bursts, and she shook off his grip.

"Do you know what the worst was? It wasn't how he mocked me, how he demeaned me, how he held that god-awful tie like he wanted to choke me. It wasn't sitting in that hospital room watching that girl's face cringe as they scraped her body, knowing that it could have been me there…It was what he said, what he said about you. How I was something you'd throw away when you got tired of me. How he said you'd call me your muse and when you were done fucking me, you'd leave. And you know why that hurt? Because it's true! I know it's true. You love someone else, you always will. You can't love me, not the same way. And it's killing me, you know why? Because I love you, God help me I do, more than anyone. Ever. And I wish I didn't. I wish I could stop."

Her words crashed off the walls of crypts. Exhausted and vulnerable and exposed, she was the most moving thing he had ever seen.

"You love me?" he repeated the words in disbelief.

"Yes." She wiped her running nose with the back of her wrist. "I do."

Too shocked to do anything more, he stood directly in front of her and tried to make her understand. "Emily, there is no woman out there. Only here. Only you. Only ever you. You are my muse. I searched my whole life for you, traveled across half the world to find you. You! Your eyes, your lips, your face. I love you. I've always loved you, only you, and that is the only truth. I love you. I was afraid you wouldn't understand, that you'd think I was mad." He reached out and took her hand again, squeezing it, willing the words into her flesh. "I love you, Emily. Only you."

Her hands rose to his chest, to edge him away or toward her, he could not tell.

"You're shaking," he said.

Tentatively, he took her face in his hands. Moonlight bathed the bare skin of her pale neck, making her look opalescent. He wanted to feel her, he wanted to taste her, he wanted her, all at once. Yet he didn't move. "Do you understand?" he demanded, desperate to know that she did, that she didn't fear him, or think him mad. That she wasn't going to run away.

"Do you?" His fingers sought her shoulders and shook her, so that her back was now pressed against the vaults.

"I love you," she told him, not taking her eyes from his.

"Do you understand?"

"I love you," she repeated adamantly.

"Emily, answer me."

Her cold fingers rose to cover his hands, and she tilted her head until the moonlight swept over her face, illuminating the answer there. She kissed him, still shaking, her breathing amplified in the silence.

"No," he cursed himself, he needed her to understand. He needed to know she would not leave. "Emily."

But she remained silent. She lowered her hand between their bodies again, her fingernails gouging his chest. His back arched in fierce arousal from the twin sensations of cold and desire.

"Wait." His voice was hoarse with want. "I need you too, but I don't want you to regret—"

His words didn't matter. Was she in shock? Perhaps. But whatever it was, Emily was as he had never seen her before. She struggled to free herself from her jacket, twisting her shoulders until it fell discarded on the floor, the buttons tinning against the tiles.

Somewhere he knew someone was waiting for them, that they were standing amidst tombs of ghosts, that this woman had almost been attacked, but none of it mattered. He kissed her for what felt like a lifetime and yet only a breath. His lips trembled on hers as his hands slowly swept away her blouse, the straps of her bra, and he heard her groan as he brushed his hands across her breasts, and that sound, that lone sound, ignited something long dormant inside him.

Both of them driven by madness, their hands were frantic to reach his shirt. She tore the fabric downward, buttons cascading on the tiles like rain. Soon flesh met flesh, and memories scored his mind. Her breath hot against his ear, she whispered words that he knew, words she had screamed, whispered, teased him with for ages. Were they from his memory when he longed for her, or from the edges of somewhere, the cusp of a dream? He scoured his mind as his hands explored her body, her breasts, her thighs, the thin bones of her hips. The presence of something out of reach taunted him, angered him, thrilled him and drew him closer. He wanted to scream her name, but he could not find the words.

His tongue tasted the wine on her lips, and he heard her say, "I love you," like a confession. "I love you, I love you, Andrew, I love—"

Suddenly her body tensed as though someone were standing directly behind them. He lifted his head from the heat of their entangled bodies to gaze at her face. Her eyes were wide, her mouth agape. He turned, still clutching her to him. Her breath buffeted against his bare chest.

There, on the opposite wall, rays of moonlight illuminated a solitary niche. A red tag hung by the glass window.

A name was engraved on a brass plate centered below the ornate frame. He frowned, unable to understand. He could hear Emily inhale. His hands tightened around her.

APRIL 18, 1906–JULY 1, 1935
MISS NOREEN THOMAS
BELOVED OF NICHOLAS CHAMBERLAIN

ndrew's arms held her, and the warmth of his breath encircled her neck, but even with those tethers Emily had departed her body; she had floated to the apex of the basilica and was staring down at the vault.

Noreen *Thomas*. No. No, it couldn't be. *Noreen Thomas*. Every nerve in her was riveted on the brass plate. There had to be some mistake. Nick and Nora were married, were transformed and idealized by Dashiell Hammett into the dashing, debonair couple that swilled martinis and bantered and were dragged across town by their dog, Asta. It should say Noreen Chamberlain. Not Noreen Thomas. Nora Chamberlain.

Miss Noreen Thomas

Beloved of Nicholas Chamberlain

Yet as she gazed at the lettering, she felt the chill as if viewing her own gravestone. Numbly, she stepped from their embrace. "Her name. She has my name."

"Thomas is a fairly common name, Emily."

"No." The pull of the niche and what lay inside was becoming stronger by the second, and nothing that Andrew could say would change that. "What if I'm related to her? And that's the reason why she haunts me, why she's only spoken to me?"

"You're forgetting something. It says *Miss Noreen Thomas*. They might never have married—they might never have had children."

"Of course they were married, everyone knows they were married. They were in love."

"Noreen Thomas," Andrew said, reading the words engraved there.

"Yes, don't you see?" She looked at him imploringly as his eyes narrowed on the niche. "There is a reason why she sought me out. I'm her family, the only one who can help her. That has to be the explanation to all this."

He didn't respond to her, and she thought it was because of his fascination with the niche, the way his gaze didn't break from studying it, but then she realized where they were standing and what had just occurred between them. The full weight of the last several minutes crashed into her. His stiff posture, his indifference—he was regretting what he had done, and he couldn't bring himself to look at her. She suddenly felt even more naked than ever, and she turned her face away, beset with the burden of how to act, how to react.

"Look at me."

Andrew brushed the damp hair from her face, but she wouldn't face him.

"First thing…I love you."

He brushed away another lock and frowned at her, unsatisfied.

"Second thing. I love you."

He kissed her, gently this time, and when he gradually drew away, his lips still touched hers. "Third thing. I love you. You need to know that. Emily, look at me," he said in exasperation and raised her chin with his finger. "This is not where I envisioned us being together. Not where I wanted to tell you that I love you…I had dreams, fantasies…truly…of somewhere romantic and…preferably with fewer dead people."

She tried not to smile.

"Emily, all that I said, all that I told you, everything is true. And it will still be true when the sun comes up in a few hours, and when the sun goes down tonight. Always. Nod your head if you understand."

She nodded her head.

"Now, nod your head if you have any idea how much I love you."

She nodded again.

"Good. Now nod your head if you have any clue where my bloody shirt is."

She laughed in earnest now, and he chuckled himself. There was still so much to say, but now was not the time. Yet as Andrew, all shirtless and tousled, found her jacket and bra and handed them to her, the sound of Simon's footsteps came clipping up the stairs. Before either of them could react, he whipped around the corner. At the sight of Emily clutching her crumpled jacket to her chest and Andrew sweeping his fallen shirt from the floor, he let loose with a string of Gaelic curses so loud he nearly shocked them out of their wits. With an immediate turn of his heel, he spun around and placed his hands to his hips before he addressed the top of the basilica.

"I never pegged you two for 'doing the deed with the dead.'" He wickedly enunciated each *D*, clearly relishing the fact that he had caught them red-handed.

"Simon," Andrew warned. He started to button his shirt only to realize there were no buttons.

Simon then turned to Emily, a self-satisfied smirk tilting his long, skinny face. He peered at her over the edge of the opaque circles of his glasses. "I believe it's safe to say that everyone in here believes in the second comin' now."

"Simon."

"I bet you sat in the truck and worked out each one of those, didn't you," Emily announced primly, finishing dressing. "It doesn't matter. I found it."

"Did you now? I'd thought you'd lost it."

Andrew lunged, and she grabbed a hold of his shoulders seconds before Simon stepped out of reach and snickered devilishly.

"No, Nora's vault." She cleared her throat, gradually letting go of a disgruntled Andrew as she motioned with her head to the small vault across from them. "Only she's…"

Simon squinted into the dark. She watched the reaction on his face pass from incomprehension, to bewilderment, to flat out astonishment. "Well, look at that. Is she like your granny or something?"

"Not my grandmother—her name was Loraine—and I know she was a Mrs. Thomas."

Simon stared down the stairs into the silent darkness, not paying her much heed. "I'm thrilled you found the old lady and all, but would you mind if we bolt soon? This place is giving me the willies, and that's just from smoking in the car park. Also, I hate to be the bearer of bad tidings, but one of San Francisco's finest cruisers keeps circling the block. I reckon they suspect someone's casing the joint, and I have no desire to become acquainted with law enforcement again if I can possibly avoid it."

"But we can't leave. They're taking away Nora's ashes tomorrow."

"My regrets," replied Simon; he glanced back down the stairs, undoubtedly sure the police were going to storm the doors at any second. "But don't they leave forwarding addresses? You can go visit her there."

"No! You don't understand, we can't leave her here. We have to take her with us."

Both Andrew and Simon looked at Emily like she was speaking in tongues.

"We, white man?" asked Simon incredulously.

"Emily, luv," said Andrew more softly, but with the same underlying level of skepticism. "You can't…I mean what you're proposing, I believe, is considered theft."

"How would anyone know?" She threw the question back at both of them. Clearly they didn't understand the importance of saving these ashes. "We can just replace them with dirt or rocks, no one will know the difference. The lock, though," she began to murmur to herself. "That's going to be tricky. I wonder if the keys are in the office?"

"I don't think the lock's going be your problem," said Simon, his voice a little off. "The lock — it's open."

All three turned their heads. The lock that had been fastened shut just a moment before now dangled open.

As Emily stepped toward the vault she could feel both Andrew's and Simon's hands reach out to restrain her, but it was as if the crypt were calling to her like Pandora's box.

The lock felt cool in her fingers and slipped off easily. She slowly turned the knob and pulled. The vault sighed, letting loose a long held exhalation; the gust of air was like a thousand whispers, and they blew across her face smelling of smoke, lavender, and death. Gulping down her fear that Nora's frigid dead hand would latch hold of hers, she reached further inside, and her fingers tightened around something cool and metal. She pulled it to her.

In the moonlight she could make out that the urn was clearly expensive, solid silver by the look and feel of it, and ringed in an elegant design of simple vines.

"It's beautiful," she whispered.

"It is." Andrew took the urn from her hands and holding it up, gazed at the flowing pattern and the gleaming silver.

She had seen this design before, but she couldn't place it. However, she had no time to ponder it now and reached back inside the vault to feel if anything else was left inside. Her fingers brushed up against the sharp edge of something hard, and as she strained to retrieve it, the thrill of the mystery bubbled up excitedly within her.

It was an old-fashioned keepsake box of a strange construction, also engraved in the same pattern, but with a built-in combination lock several numbers in length. She shook it, and something rattled inside. Andrew's eyes widened in fascination. "We're taking this," she said.

"Ra-ther," Andrew answered, grinning like a cat.

"Theft? Does anyone recall the word theft? Three to five and out in two for good behavior?" Simon said, trying to get their attention.

"Now all we have to do is get something to transfer her ashes into and something to replace the ashes in her urn," Emily said, overcome with the spirit of the adventure. "Simon, you run down to the office. There's got to be a box or container down there. Andrew, I think I saw a potted plant near the piano…can you go grab it?"

Somehow her enthusiasm must have finally rubbed off on the belea-guered drummer, or he had just given up the fight, for he threw up his hands and headed back down the stairs. Andrew gave her a kiss and a roguish smile before taking off after him.

Minutes later he returned. In his hands he held a sad looking potted plant. She glanced down at it with a grin and proceeded to disembowel it, leaving a pot full of dirt and gravel behind.

Simon's footsteps raced up the stairs and then halted as if he were catching his breath, or biding his time. "How's this? I found it in a locker in the office," he announced as he stepped into the moonlight and presented it to Emily with a deadpan expression on his face.

"You have got to be kidding me? No! No, no, no, no!" Dumbfounded, she stared at him and shook her head vehemently, appalled beyond words. "You are not, I repeat not, going to put Nora's ashes inside—a *bong!*"

The glass monstrosity gleamed in the moonlight.

Simon scrutinized what had to have been Dwayne's bong. "Hey, it's the only thing down there. Listen, those fine officers just got out of their car, so if you want to get arrested for breaking and entering we can stand around here and chat. Otherwise, dish 'em out darlin'. At least the thing is dry."

Andrew bit his lip to keep himself from laughing, but she could see a small muscle spasm at the corner of his mouth. This had undoubtedly pushed him over the edge. He looked exhausted and weary and gleeful all at once.

"Oh, Nora, I'm so, so sorry. Please forgive me." Her eyes rose to heaven. Simon guffawed. "Yeah, laugh it up, big guy, you don't have to live with her. She's going to be incensed."

"Better than being *incense*," snorted Simon.

"More like she's going to be plagued with an eternal case of the munchies." Andrew fell over into a fit. Simon joined in.

"Men…" Emily muttered and opened the urn, praying she didn't drop a speck.

After she finished transferring Nora to her new, Maui-wowie home, the downstairs door creaked open. The three of them froze, eyes wide like saucers. Simon grabbed the bong and hid it in his jacket, Andrew grabbed Emily's hand, and they all flattened their backs against the farthest wall.

Agonizing minutes passed while what sounded like two determined police officers prowled around downstairs. Emily stood cramped and frozen between Andrew and Simon, her mouth dry. Suddenly, the rays of a flashlight doused the air around them. They plastered themselves further against the crypts, so hard in fact that the locks stabbed into their backs. Emily's heart was beating so rapidly she swore her blouse fluttered up and down.

Just then, steps, deliberate and heavy, echoed from the bottom of the staircase. She looked to Andrew in panic. Cool as ice, he merely shook his head and crouched down. His long fingers swept up something from the floor. Like a cat, he crept soundlessly to the edge of the gallery and tossed whatever it was to the floor below.

It rattled along the marble, causing the footsteps to seize and change direction. After several pulse-hammering minutes, two voices muttered in turn, "Fucking rats…Yeah, hate those things."

Her mouth hung open. "Rats?" she mouthed wordlessly to Andrew.

He nodded. "Near the piano."

"What?"

He swiftly placed his hand over her mouth.

It seemed like an eternity, but eventually the door shut below, the police evidently satisfied no one had broken in. The sound of their squad car disappeared into the night. Without a second to lose, they quickly replaced Nora's urn and locked the vault before racing down the staircase.

She took a moment to glance back up to the basilica. Andrew's eyes followed her gaze; his hand covered hers.

"We'll always have the Columbarium," he whispered in her ear, leaving a kiss on her temple, and then yanked her swiftly toward the door.

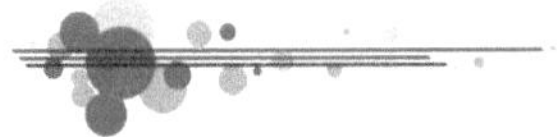

When the next morning came, it was overcast. At least Emily thought it was overcast, but when she dragged herself out of bed and squinted through the curtains, she realized the morning was night. She had slept through an entire day.

She found Zoey in the dining room wearing a macraméd poncho and leggings, samples of tiles and grout boards scattered over a table cobbled together from a sheet of gypsum board and stacks of magazines.

"She's awake," she exclaimed and raced over to give her a hug. Not letting go, Zoey walked with her into the kitchen where Margot, still in her slacks and blouse from work, sat in front of her laptop, sipping what looked like scotch.

She made a few more strikes to the keyboard before eyeing Emily flatly. "I'm glad you're alive, but you have got to be kidding me." She nodded toward the fireplace where Nora sat on the mantle. Emily grimaced and sat down, but not before Zoey began to dish her out some dinner from pots still warm on the stove.

"Now, just to clarify. Last night you stole the ashes of the ghost who saved you from that disgusting pig of a professor, and now she's living in a water bong on our dining room mantle."

"That's about it."

Margot tilted back on her chair and leveled Emily with a withering stare.

"Aren't you leaving out one itsy bitsy detail? I'm assuming due to the fact that you were pawed over, and he didn't have any buttons left on his shirt that when he carried you half asleep in the door last night —"

"I love him and he loves me."

Margot's chair hit the floor.

"I know it sounds crazy. I know we've only known each other a short period of time. I know he's a musician that lives on the road. I know, I know, I know! But I've loved him since I saw him in the park."

"Park? What park?"

"I went to watch him play his guitar. Every day. He used to play at the end of Haight Street, by Kezar, every day for hours, and I just sat there and watched him. Yes, I stalked the man, good, feminist, intelligent woman that I am. But after the first time I saw him perform, it was just, I can't explain it. I know it makes no sense."

"No, it doesn't."

"It's even worse than that. Remember that witch shop? I took him there. This stoner pulled us into a corner and read my palm. He says I'm Andrew's soul mate."

"Margot," Zoey uttered. "Did you hear that? They're soul mates. It's destiny. Fate."

"Whatever it is, are you sure?" Margot questioned. "It's awfully fast."

Emily ran her nail along the edge of the soapstone island. "Sometimes I wish it were faster. All I know is that I want to be with him. I want to hear him speak and watch him play. I want to kiss him and laugh with him and listen to him sing and see the world by his side, but at the same time, I could just watch him, that'd be enough."

"But what about him? What about this other girlfriend of his—the one he broke up with?"

What about Andrew? Emily had had so little time to consider his words. He had called her his muse, told her there was no one else, and that there never had been. Only her. *That is the only truth.* But what did that mean?

"God, you've got it bad, don't you." Margot whistled, scrutinizing her roommate's face and slowly shutting her laptop. "Promise me one thing."

"What?"

"These guys…this situation is highly abnormal. They won't stay here for long, and it's not just a question of them having to go out on tour. They've chosen that lifestyle. It's addicting, that adulation, that attention. And all those women? Life in any one place is going to become boring pretty fast after what they've seen. I know he's attractive…but what attracts you is the same thing that attracts every woman he meets. He's charming because it's helped him succeed. Darwin would have loved him—he adapts to suit his needs incredibly well. You think you know him, you may even think you're in love with him, but there's been no time to really get to know him, to know how he will react to fame and pressure. And there won't be. I don't want you to get hurt."

"I don't want you to get hurt, either."

Margot didn't respond. Whatever her relationship was with Simon, she was holding her cards close to her chest. Instead, she returned her attention to her laptop, but not before Emily saw a flicker of vulnerability pass through her eyes.

"So what's up with that box?" Margot waved her hand to the counter where the locked metal tin they had withdrawn from the vault sat. "The guys tried all ways to Sunday to open it today. No luck."

"They were here? Andrew, Andrew was here?"

"You were out for a long time. He sat on the floor up against your bedroom wall and watched you sleep. Played his guitar. Christian finally got him to sit here and eat dinner — they just left. Oh, and Simon rearranged Margot's holy card collection. He put Teresa of Avila front and center. He said you'd understand."

"Oh God," Emily moaned, envisioning Margot's miniature reproduction of the saint writhing in all her mystical orgasmic ecstasy.

"I know," answered Zoey. "I can't believe she would let him touch her holy cards."

"So this ghost of ours," Margot said tersely. "She has your last name."

"Or I have hers."

"A relative?"

"Maybe a coincidence." Emily remembered Andrew's words, but she still didn't believe them.

"There are no coincidences and there are no accidents. Nothing happens unless someone wills it to happen," Zoey said knowingly.

"Your swami?" asked Margot.

"Not unless he's William S. Burroughs," said Emily with a smile, remembering the quote. "But he's dead."

"Does that really matter anymore?" said Margot as she marched off to bed. "Oh, I almost forgot, he left this for you." She retrieved a small envelope from the mantle and handed it to Emily.

To Emily Thomas, resident Sleeping Beauty

Margot rolled her eyes and continued down the hall, but Zoey remained, forcing Emily to keep twisting this way and that to stop her from peering over her shoulder.

Emily,

By the time you read this, you obviously will have awoken. Believe me, the temptation was great to storm your flat and kiss you awake myself, keeping the fairy tale tradition alive in this place.

I hope you're feeling better, and if so, or perhaps if not, I'd like to take you to dinner Friday night. Seven p.m. Please wear one of your old, odd, and breathtaking dresses. Escaping should not pose a problem, as I believe Christian will be extending his own invitation for the evening, the cheeky bastard. This, however, should not be construed by anyone as a double date (Zoey, that means you, if you are reading on). Single, as in Emily and me. You and I, Emily. Full stop.

One more thing, I hope you realize how terribly dull this house is when you are asleep. The only excitement we had was trying to keep the painters from smoking Nora. Hence, she is with you.

Unfortunately, we have to leave for L.A. in the morning. But we'll be home soon.

I miss you, Emily. I need to speak with you. And touch you.

Till then.
Yours,

A.

Emily read it two more times. By the time she had it memorized a sense of euphoria filled her. The world had become filled with promise. She could finish school, be with Andrew, find Nick's ashes, reunite lost lovers, go to her seminar, publish her book, afford rent…do everything and anything.

"By the way," Zoey said, gathering up her tiles for the night, "a detective called while you were asleep. An Anthony Obester. He's assigned to that girl's case. He left a number where you should call him tomorrow. Sounded pretty concerned."

Hell. Emily had almost forgotten. She wasn't free and clear. It was just the calm before the storm. Dr. Vandin was still out there. Somewhere in London. Free.

"I'm proud of what you did, how you helped that girl," said Zoey on their way to bed. "Very proud."

Emily folded up Andrew's note and placed it in her pajama top pocket, close to her heart, where she needed it most.

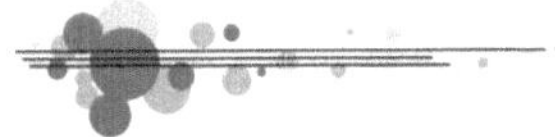

The days seemed to drag while the boys were away, but Friday night finally approached. Andrew's note lay on her nightstand; Emily took it in her hands and gazed at it for the hundredth time.

"I miss you," she said to the shadows.

She threw off the covers, sweating and restless. The radiator knocked, pumping heat into the room, some passive-aggressive gesture by Sid, no doubt. Over the last few days he had seemed intent on rendering the house inhabitable, thereby either freeing him of the burden of the remodel or forcing the girls into the least amount of clothing possible.

The specter of Vandin should have cast the house in its own icy pall. And images of the Columbarium clawed at the edges of her mind, but the harder she tried, the less she could remember from that night once the lights had gone out. Although her roommates had done their best to keep her busy and draw her into the relief of routine, it didn't stop her from jumping at the odd sound or catching her breath when a worker turned a corner too quickly. All of this made her miss Andrew even more. He had spoken with her each day to make sure she was all right and kissed her tenderly before he had left. But she missed him the moment the door closed. Everything felt flat and lifeless in his absence.

When not moping about accordingly, she'd spent the time knee deep in research or juggling the demands of her remaining school work. There was little new information she had uncovered about the Chamberlain Detective Agency. It had operated out of the house, but its clientele had been secretive; the majority of the cases it handled were evidently not the stuff that was recorded in newspapers. Noreen Thomas had been listed in a few society affairs, and Nicholas Chamberlain was mentioned sporadically in regard to various crime stories, but she could obtain nothing more about them. Except for the odd circumstance that Noreen Thomas's obituary was not recorded in any major San Francisco newspaper, or at least not one that Emily could find. Her eyes were sore from the endless rolls of microfiche she had scoured through in the last few days.

Her frustration was fueled by that fact that the box they had recovered from Nora's vault still remained locked tight. Emily had turned the numbers to correspond with their birthdays as well as the day of their deaths, but nothing worked. She thought of prying it open, but worried she might damage whatever lay inside. What she needed was more information, anything that would cast more light on their mysterious lives. She had reread *The Thin Man*, hoping to glean some secret, but the characters Hammett wrote of were now mere echoes of the ghosts she was learning about. She searched the house again from stem to stern, and had done everything but slash the lining of Nora's trunk to see if anything was hidden inside.

That thought stuck in her head as she looked to her alarm clock, which read one a.m. Since she couldn't sleep, she would investigate the trunk again, comb it completely, and then search for anything else hidden in the shadowy passageway.

The chill that normally permeated the roughhewn walls and exposed joists was replaced by Amazonian heat. She cursed Sid yet again and crept along to where she had last left Nora's trunk, but a rectangular patch of undusted ground was all that remained in the spot. Emily shook her head. No, she distinctly remembered it there. She couldn't have been mistaken — this is where she had knelt down — those were her footprints. Disturbed, she turned and headed back in the opposite direction in search of it.

The heat was nearly stifling now, and a thin layer of sweat soon covered her, making her nightshirt stick to her body. She stopped herself and leaned against the wall, feeling faint.

A familiar ache held her in place. There at the end of the passageway was the space above Andrew's room. The image of him lying there in the moonlight flooded her senses. Why couldn't she think of him and maintain her hold on reality? It was as if a thousand women filled her mind and were calling out to her. She fell back against the beams and gazed down at the lines in her hand. Were they? Were they the lifetimes of concubines and lovers and mistresses? That's what Dwayne had said. Were they all teeming within her, craving what they couldn't have? Did their desires intensify with each passing generation, leaving her to shoulder the weight?

Yet there were no wives and mothers in those lines, she could feel that. It was as if all the women that might have shared her past were created for one reason and one reason alone: to tempt, to seduce, to ensnare. But not to stay.

Unable to dwell on it any longer, she managed a little farther in the heat, careful not to make a sound as she approached the faint light that was coming from the slits in the floor. He was home! When had he returned? She took one more step, then another, her body drawn to his. She went to kneel down when she heard a sound behind her. She tensed and spun around, her hair whipping about her shoulders.

"So this is where you are," Andrew said. He did not greet her, nor ask how she was feeling, not even after days apart. He merely stood stock still a few feet away, a wall sconce shedding light on his body. He wore a pair of pajama bottoms and nothing else. They hung low on the smooth, angled bones of his hips.

"How many times, Emily?" He glanced to the source of light shining from the floor. He took another step forward, his bare feet silent in his stalking. "Did you like what you saw?" His eyes were violet in the light, volcanic, not a glimpse of their pure blue remaining. He was on the hunt, every muscle of his arms and chest poised to spring. "You watched me, didn't you?" He smirked but didn't let her respond.

"Secret passageways always have an entrance and an exit, everyone knows that. Such a fairy tale place, this house. Which fairy tale is left?" He bit his bottom lip as he said this, and a lock of hair tumbled to his forehead. His eyes fell to her body, watching the lines of sweat trickle down her neck.

The sane part of her knew there were questions she needed to ask him, and she could tell from his eyes that he wanted to answer them, that he wanted them to be quiet and close and calm, but somehow the thought of being denied each other demolished everything else.

Ever since that night at the Columbarium, something primitive and raw had passed between them, something long held captive and straining to be let loose. That's what it felt like. Like she was possessed. Whenever she was in the dark and alone with this man, she ceased to be simply Emily Thomas, and he ceased to be simply Andrew Hayes. What were they then? Her mind burned with memories of lovers she could feel but not see. Was that who they were?

"La Bella y la Bestia," he whispered, the first time she heard him speak Spanish. "That's the only fairy tale that's left." He moved toward her soundlessly. "You know what I always found fascinating about that story?"

She shook her head, her fingers reaching behind her to find the dead end of the wall.

"That last moment, when the beast is transformed. The look in her eyes when she sees the prince. There's that second of hesitation when she longs for the beast. She wants the animal."

"I know."

He was close now. Too close.

"Did you get my invitation?"

"Yes…thank you."

"Tomorrow I will be the prince, I swear. But tonight, I can't…please don't make me. All I need is to taste you. Your mouth, your body…please." He loomed over her, his face inches from hers. His teeth found her neck; his hands took her body.

"Emily," he gasped. "Emily, please…"

"No," she said, and without hesitation or conscious thought she reached out and took hold of his shoulders and pressed his back flat against the wall. The ghosts of all the women within her smiled seductively as she knelt down before him. "It's my turn."

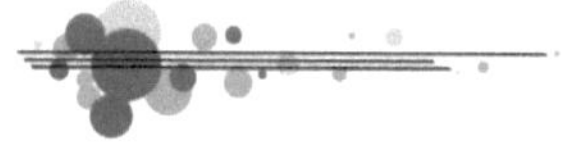

They had collapsed into each other's arms immediately afterward, kissing and groping, sweaty and sliding. What a tangled, sodden mess they were. Delicious and disheveled, he wanted nothing more than to have her, he truly did, with her hair so wild and her face so flush, there on the splintered and dusty floor. But this was Emily; he had to get that fact into his head. This was Emily, but what she had done to him, what her tiny hands and supple mouth had ignited in him made him wonder if what the mad fortuneteller had said was true. And it was beyond glorious. Her mouth on him had fueled all his pent up desire, and with it a fuse was lit. It was an explosion without sound, only force and light. And all at once the dreams he had dreamed before seemed small, and all the wants he had wanted were gone. Yet here in the dark, he wanted nothing but to turn her inside out with lust.

He had to chastise himself: *remember, this is Emily, your muse. Emily.* But in the darkness, in this beastly heat, she was a secret to him.

Doubting how long he could trust himself, he cradled her in his arms, and in one fluid motion swept her up against him. Her eyes widened as he stood and began to navigate the hallway, heading back to her bed. She made no sound when he stepped through the door to her closet, no sound when he placed her on her bed, but only watched him with those cool gray eyes, daring him to walk away.

He lowered himself down until the lengths of their bodies were one. He propped himself up on his forearms to gaze down on her.

"How did you find me?" Emily asked.

"In the passageway or before?"

She tilted her head, as if not understanding for a moment, and smiled again, brushing the back of her hand against his face. "You'll need to shave for Friday."

"You don't care for it?"

"You look like Simon."

"If you tell me you harbor a secret love for my drummer, I'll just kill myself now."

"I like you smooth."

"There are places on your body that may object to that."

He could feel her twist below him, and he groaned softly and began a story. He had to. It was the only thing keeping him from attacking her.

She stilled as he told her how he had seen her in the Skellar. That first night. How everything had changed, or begun, in that one moment.

"As far as finding you, I didn't have much to go on, just the belief that I would find you some day. Something I've always known, though, my entire life."

She studied him. He was sure she didn't understand, couldn't grasp it. He was having a hard time understanding it too. But it didn't seem to matter.

"Your whole life?"

"The promise of you, yes. I can't explain it. I've felt you, envisioned you in my mind, since I could remember. When I actually saw you that night, well, don't you recall how I went barmy on the stage? It's quite disconcerting when fate decides to manifest, well…your fate right in front of you. If only I had seen you sooner, spoken with you—"

"I wouldn't change anything. No, you are here, now. For as long as you can be. That's all that matters."

Her voice was meant to be strong, but there was a cheerlessness to it he didn't like because he knew it was the truth. They would eventually have to leave this place. To go on. Return to the road. And very soon. But at this moment, in this moonlit room, breathing the same air, he could not think of parting from her.

"When did you come home, by the way? Why didn't you wake me?"

"It was so late."

"Now you're going to tell me how you found me tonight."

"And divulge my deepest, darkest secrets? Never."

"Where's the other entrance?"

"Do you know our pantry holds a ransom of Cheez-Its, spray cheese, Cheetos, boxes of Easy Mac—a case of them, by the way—because one can never have enough unnatural cheese—beef jerky, pig rinds, Ramen noodles, corn nuts, Nestlé Quick, Captain Crunch, Cocoa Puffs, Pop-Tarts, SpaghettiOs, and syrup."

"You have an incredible mind for detail. You should write."

"I'm bollocks at anything that doesn't rhyme. Now no editorializing—this is my story."

She laughed again, and he kissed the side of her mouth. His lips hovered there as her smile widened.

"It doesn't contain tea or booze, that's the vital fact. So…in a fit of frustration that my pantry could help us survive a nuclear holocaust but didn't contain a drop of alcohol, I slammed my back against the pantry wall only to find the wall did move. As in shift. As in creaked backward."

"Oh my."

He trailed his lips along her jaw. She giggled in pleasure.

"Now, when fate presents you a hidden door, you open it. When fate hands you a hidden stairway, you climb it, rather excitedly, even if it is littered with cobwebs and spiders and you are half convinced the bloody planks below your feet might splinter into dust and plunge you to your death. Even when you stub your toes on some old trunk, you just keep going."

Emily had stilled beneath him.

"Wait. Did you say trunk? As in an old steamer trunk?"

He eyed her questioningly. "Yes. It was right near the top of the staircase."

"It was moved. The trunk, it wasn't where I left it. Someone must have moved it."

"You've seen this trunk before?"

She blinked at him and exhaled slowly, summoning up the courage to tell him how she had first found the trunk. He had buried his face in the pillow and was laughing by the time she finished her tale.

"But the trunk," she cried, smacking him on the shoulder. "If you didn't move it, who did?"

He shrugged.

"You don't suppose?"

"What? That Nick lugged the thing himself? Or Nora? No, I am done supposing with this house. It could have been Sid, for all we know."

Emily made a face. But the wheels were turning in her head. "Go on with your story. I want to hear the ending," she said distractedly.

"I found you. You know the rest of the story. And now I'm here."

"And now you're here," she answered.

Suddenly the air felt different in the room. He became aware of their naked skin touching, of the rise and fall of their chests. He knew what would happen next. But it couldn't. Not yet.

"Emily, I need you to understand something."

Their noses were almost touching, her breath mingled with his, their lips so, so close.

"When I make love to you…when we make love…it needs to be somewhere we can be completely alone. Where no one can interrupt. Where we can stay in bed all day and all night. Where what I will make you feel…what I will make you whisper and cry out…can only be heard by me."

In the moonlight, her skin glowed pearlescent like the inside of a shell, her eyes wide.

"I have to leave you before I break all the promises I've made to myself."

"Please. Don't go yet."

He hesitated. He shut his eyes, hoping that if he could not see her, he would be able to walk away. He knew she was asking him to stay in ways he couldn't. Stay in this bed. Stay in San Francisco. Stay.

Things had to be different with Emily. They had to be. As much as he craved her to the point of madness, as much as he was at war with himself not to take her right now—to take all of her, over and over again—he needed this moment to be different. They needed to be different.

"Sing to me."

The simple request made a rush of relief break from his lips. Yes, that he could give her tonight. Every night, if she asked. He sang until her breath passed into sleep.

When at last he took himself away from her, his mind was a whirl of every emotion; he badly needed air. He slipped back into the hallway and shut the door to her wardrobe, exhaling heavily against it. Eager to put a safe distance between them, he retraced his steps to the stairway. Andrew had almost reached it when he spotted the trunk. Nora's trunk.

Something about it, something he couldn't quite place, held his attention as he approached it. With a growing interest, his hands ran over the leather straps, the hammered studs, the faded travel labels. It was old, no doubt, and well-traveled based on its wear and the preponderance of stickers. He smiled and knelt down before it, oblivious to all around him.

Filled with the same fascination that coursed through him as he stood before Nora's niche at the Columbarium, he hastily flipped open the clasps, but with an ease that felt like he'd done it countless times before. As the lid rose a familiar odor assaulted his psyche. He teetered on his knees in shock. Without warning, memories like an old movie, cut up and out of focus, lashed across his eyes.

A seaside. Cliffs. An old hotel.

He blinked, trying hard to capture at least one of the images. Then from the depths of some long hidden place, a woman's scream pierced the night, wailing and horrible. "Nooooo!"

He fell back onto his hands. They skinned on the splintered floor; his heart blazed in cold and painful beats. He could barely breathe.

"Nooooo!"

The pain was excruciating; blazing hot needles plunged in his eyes. He threw his hands to his temples and nearly screamed. The shrieking wouldn't stop. They lurched like twisted, screeching metal, an endless cry of anguish.

"No," he screamed back. "Stop!"

When he thought he could take no more, that the pain would tear him apart, it ceased. Then blackness, nothing. Silence. Just a trunk in the dark hallway.

"Christ," he muttered and scrubbed his face with his trembling hands. "Christ." It was the same awful screaming that had assaulted him at the library. The same voices, the same tortured helplessness.

Tentatively, as though he were approaching a wild animal in a cage, he went back to the trunk. He reached out like it was a hot stove, daring to touch it again.

Nothing.

He threw his hands against the sides, taunting it, striking it for the pain it had inflicted. Still nothing. In a burst of fierceness, he threw open the top. It was empty. His hands reached down and knocked hard against the base of it, and a dull echo sounded. It was a false bottom. He wrestled with the panel, gouging his fingers into the small space lining the edges, prying hard until it gave way, breaking free into his hands. He tossed it away where it rattled to a stop on the splintered floor.

Not knowing what he would find, he peered down into the trunk, torn between dread and expectation.

"Well, bloody hell," he muttered and rocked back on his legs, shaking his head in disbelief as he reached down and pulled out a stack of letters. They were bundled in a red ribbon — that was all. No bones, no blood. Only letters.

They were addressed in a florid script that was difficult to decipher in the dim light. His heart sped up as the name came into focus:

Mr. Nicholas Chamberlain
of the Chamberlain Detective Agency.

The return address: *Miss Noreen Thomas.*

Nora. In a rush of excitement he left the trunk behind, and with an armful of letters he rushed down into the pantry. After he shut the door behind him with a definitive click, he turned on the light, grabbed a bottle of water from a nearby shelf, and sat down on the pantry floor. Too keyed up to possibly contemplate sleep, he took a long drink and hungrily eyed the envelopes that lay in his lap.

They were pricey by the looks of them, made of fine cardstock and of an elegant design, and they still held of a hint of lavender. He quickly opened the first on the stack:

April 13, 1933

Dear Mr. Chamberlain,

I enjoyed meeting with you last Tuesday in regard to my strange, and I'm sure, rather unorthodox case. I do understand that supernatural matters are something with which your firm does not normally become involved. I, too, would much rather not be involved, but the fact remains, I have a house and a ghost, and I only wish to have the former.

I will be hosting a birthday party for my dear friend, Lillian Hellman, this Saturday evening at eight o'clock at the Sir Francis Drake. You may consider it forward of me, but it would be a fine thing if you could attend. There will be copious amounts of martinis and stimulating conversation. You may wish to partake of both, or the former only.

Sincerely,

Noreen Thomas

He hurriedly read the next.

May 1, 1933

Dear Mr. Chamberlain,

Thank you for your recommendation of the spiritualist and medium, Mr. Kowacz. While his turban and accent were quite impressive, his results were not. He informed me I have not one, but two ghosts now. Either he is a magician capable of pulling them out of said turban, or he intends to grease his way into my heart—or so was the sentiment expressed by him—although with the Hungarian accent, who is to know?

*I also wish to thank you for the bouquet of
calla lilies. They were delivered earlier this week,
black bows and all. While I realize the humor
behind them, you should know I adore them.
They remind me of your scrawny neck.*

I remain, your annoying client,

Miss Noreen Thomas

He placed the letter aside as his eyes raced to the following.

June 26, 1933

Dear Mr. Chamberlain,

*No. I will not go out with you to hear Mr.
Armstrong play. No. I will not accompany you to
the races, and no, I will not fly off with you to
Mendocino.*

*Please leave me alone. One more word of advice:
I am available next Saturday night for
cocktails. And only if you say please and arrive
on time.*

Noreen Thomas

He read more, an observer to a charming, sophisticated, and witty
war of words. At long last he laid his head back against a sack of rice and
closed his eyes, the letters still in his hands, a smile on his lips. He imagined
all the hoops Nora had made Nick jump through. How he had probably
never met a woman like her in his life. How maddeningly in love he must
have been. He yawned and felt, not for the first time, an extraordinary
kinship with a ghost.

"Neil called," Christian yelled out to Andrew as he came through the front door from his morning run. "He told Simon he wants to meet us for lunch today if we can make it—with an associate friend of his. Isn't that awesome?"

"Tremendous," Andrew said, assuming it would be yet another promoter or some club owner. He found Christian in the kitchen eating cold pizza out of a box. He angled around him to reach the sink and grab a glass of water, and Christian eyed him suspiciously while he drank.

"You seem rather preoccupied."

"No. Just buzzed. It was a good run. Brilliant about Neil, though."

"Since when do you think anything about Neil is brilliant?"

Andrew shrugged and backed up to make way for two workmen who were carrying a ladder. They looked this way and that as if expecting the Grim Reaper to descend at any second.

"First day?" Andrew asked them, to which they nodded grimly and scurried through the kitchen and out the back door.

"You realize you scared the living bejesus out of me last night," Christian said, taking a seat at the counter. Andrew continued to sip his water, careful to study the calendar taped onto the refrigerator. "I mean, it's one thing to whip open the pantry door in the middle of the night hoping to find a box of Oreos, but it's a whole other deal to trip over a half-naked guy dead asleep on the floor covered in scratch marks and letters. I swear to God Almighty, between these ghosts, ashes in bongs, and things going bump in the night, I might as well move back into the basement of my *tante's* shop."

"Zoey wouldn't allow it," Andrew said, the glass still at his lips.

"Probably."

"Funny thing, though," Andrew pondered aloud, "but did I or did I not notice two glasses of milk and some Oreos near the ice box last night? And if I recall, you don't fancy them. More of a Famous Amos man."

"Fig Newtons, actually."

"Case closed."

"You will explain all of this when I get you drunk someday," Christian added.

"You are going to have to get me royally pissed to even have a prayer of getting any information. And then I will be forced to kill you. So what time and where is lunch?"

"Huh?"

"Lunch. I trust Simon got the details this time — remember when he said he'd meet us by the taxi stand in Manhattan?"

"Yeah, the one on the corner." Christian shook his head and laughed. "It's at two. Why don't we all go together — or are you going to be lurking in the foyer for Emily till then?"

Andrew refilled his glass. "No, I believe Emily can take care of herself… frighteningly well, in fact." He took a long swig to hide his smile. "Actually, I'd love to do some writing, and I need to run some errands, so text me the address and I'll meet you over there, okay? Where are you taking Zoey tonight, by the way?"

"Hell if I know. That girl's got high expectations."

Andrew toasted him. "Here's to high expectations, then."

"Is there something about that pantry that I should know?" Christian pressed, clearly too intrigued to leave it alone.

"Trust me. It doesn't contain Fig Newtons."

Andrew placed his glass down and headed off to his room to grab the stack of letters, then shot upstairs to the conservatory. He was impatient to finish reading them and wanted the privacy. It was still far too early for Emily to be awake, and although he was looking forward to presenting them to her later, a piece of him wanted to read them on his own first.

Bright light greeted him when he opened the conservatory door; it streamed in through the glass ceiling and washed the room in blue. The worn wicker furniture and orchids were back in place after the party, and he noticed the keyboard still sat near the door to the roof. Good, he thought as he made his way to a couch, maybe when he was done he could get some writing finished as well. But no sooner had he taken another step than his head snapped back in the direction of the keyboard. Surprisingly, the bench before it was occupied.

There sat a dapper, mustached, and vaporous man who crooned a heart-felt rendition of "Hong Kong Blues."

Fear was Andrew's first reaction. His heart skipped a few beats as though he had been splashed with ice water. He had seen Nick before, but that was only for a split second before he disappeared from the bathtub. Now the ghost seemed in no mood to vanish any time soon.

"Funny, I've heard that somewhere before." Andrew steeled himself and approached the suave apparition who had closed his eyes while he tinkled the ivories, shimmering away. Overcoming his fear, he gestured toward the bench. "Mind if I take a seat?"

Nick shook his head and continued to play. With a bit of trepidation, Andrew sat down next to him. He didn't know what to expect sharing a piano bench with a dead man. He expected it to be cold, which it was, disconcerting, which it definitely was, but not oddly familiar, which it was as well, beyond a doubt. Maybe it was because, even as a ghost, Nick could still play a mean accompaniment.

Andrew took the counterpoint, and a small smile broke at the side of Nick's mouth — or vapory what-have-you.

"That's part of the plan, yes? We need to find you?"

Nick didn't respond.

"You don't happen to hang out on Haight Street at night, by the way? Very different wardrobe, though." The chill Andrew felt made him recall the shopping cart man he had run into after he had stormed out of the club in his frantic search for Emily, but by the looks of things, Nick didn't do homeless.

"So, how'd you like Grant's tomb?" Nick asked, changing the key and the subject.

"What? Grant's — oh, you mean the Columbarium?"

"Right in one."

"Well…it definitely had its moments."

"So I've heard."

Andrew glanced over at him and back again feeling slightly unnerved. "A bit of clarification here. You, you…spirits converse with each other?"

"We may."

"But you can't speak to Nora because…"

"People have their theories."

"Which are?"

"You'll have to ask them."

"Which them? Who do we need to ask?"

"You're a smart kid, figure it out."

Andrew huffed in frustration, tired of getting the spectral run around.

"You know that Nora's downstairs now. We, well we—"

"Moved her to her summer home? She must be thrilled."

"It doesn't bother you? Her being here, so close?"

"Those ashes you brought into this place, that's not the woman I love. Gravel's not my type, I'm afraid."

"Really?" Andrew's tone was unconvinced. "What's your type then?"

"Redheads with wicked jaws."

Instantly, the image of Emily and her beautiful lips, kneeling in front of him, assaulted his memory. He nearly fell off the bench.

"You know, Andy my boy, in my day that kind of behavior either warranted a twenty on the nightstand or a diamond bracelet around the wrist."

"How, how the hell did you—"

"You're a spirit yourself, kid, in there somewhere. And I hate to tell you, but your aura is showing."

Andrew glanced down at his body then back at Nick, fighting to keep his mind away from the memory of Emily's nails as they dragged down his chest and how her tongue and the heat of her mouth felt…

"Please, this is my house, you know. You're offending my girlish sensibilities, not to mention the young lady's."

"What do you mean?"

Nick stopped playing. He became very still and stared down at the keys through the mist of his hands.

"I mean, what are your intentions? Emily is very important—she's an extremely special young woman."

"I know that."

"Do you?" There was a lethal calmness in his tone.

"I…I think I know that better than anyone. And as far as my intentions, well they are, I mean I plan, I've been trying to keep—"

"What?" Nick snapped. "You're going to string her along until you rush back to the roar of the greasepaint and the smell of the crowd? Seems pretty cheap, and I never pictured you as a cheap anything. Thought you came from better stock than that."

"Listen, I don't see how you can sit, um…hover there and lecture me about intentions. I love that woman. Got it? And whatever happens between us, well, it's bloody well between us and no one else. And one more thing, I failed to see your last name next to Nora's on that plaque. You were off living in sin, or whatever you called it back then, long before Emily and I were even born. That must have caused quite a scandal. I can't imagine your family must have been too proud."

Nick darkened; the room chilled. Andrew had hit a nerve, and a very sore nerve from the feel of it. "Family doesn't always make things easier, do they? It's best not to speak ill of dead ancestors, though. Much better to save that for the living, right?"

"I don't think so—I'm quite fond of my family," Andrew responded.

"So you say."

"Were you always this much of a delight in real life? It's amazing Nora gave you the time of day. Ah, but she hired you for a job, didn't she? I found the letters, by the way. She was haunted by ghosts too. Interesting coincidence. Were they as much of a pain in the ass as you are?"

"You'll go straight to hell, reading other people's mail. That's what the old mater used to tell me."

"Sounds like a peach."

"No, not a peach. More like a vicious-tongued, superstitious old nut. Holed up in that boarding house on the coast with her Ouija boards and crystal balls."

"She was a medium? Your mother was a medium?"

"No, she was a nut, plain and simple. Crackers, pure crackers. But I thought Nora was the same when I met her too. Believing in ghosts and all that. What my mother believed, though, that was ludicrous, preposterous."

"What did she believe?"

Nick started to play again and did not answer.

"What? What did she believe? Damn it, why can't you ghosts ever answer a direct question?"

"There are rules. Forces. Things we can't interfere with. Destiny."

"You didn't marry Nora."

"Oh, I'd planned to, even had the rings. I had everything I'd ever wanted in that car when we drove off to elope. But, well, you know what happened."

Andrew recalled what Emily had told him. About Nick's propensity to drive fast. Then it hit him like a cold hand clamped over his mouth. The flashbacks at the trunk: the hotel, the cliffs, the screaming. "You…you were on your way there when you died? Christ, I'm sorry."

"Well, I do believe the little man cares."

"No, seriously."

"Put quite a damper on the honeymoon, trust me."

"Nick, listen. I know this doesn't make any sense, but I feel responsible. I…I would like—no, I want to help you. We all do. But we can't do it alone. You have to help us. I know you say you can't give us answers, but is there anyone, anyone we could…contact, someone who you were close to?"

Nick shrugged and began playing again, his eyes focused on something far away.

"You know what to do, you've always known. But remember, just because you know what to do doesn't mean you know everything. People, people you think you will understand, they may turn out to have secrets you never could fathom. Secrets that could hurt you. Your only hope is to trust your instincts. Seize life with your hands, live it. But don't do it faintheartedly. It needs to be all or nothing. That's the only thing that will save you in the end."

"Save me?" Andrew didn't like the sound of that at all.

Nick started to wisp away. He played the last strains of the song. "Make sure you show her a great time tonight, kid. At least get something new to wear. She likes the old stuff."

"Nick? Nick, damn it, come back. Nick!"

Andrew slammed the piano keys. Nick was gone. But his warning echoed in Andrew's mind.

Seize life with your hands…secrets you could never fathom…the only thing to save you.

Why did he need to be saved? From what? From whom?

He left the bench and wrapped his arms across his chest, staring out of the glass panes to the far off hills. A bank of fog had gathered on the horizon, waiting to blanket the city. The sun had only a few hours left.

What did it all mean? Who were they supposed to contact? And how was he involved in any of this? He understood Emily's need to reunite the lost lovers and wanted to support her, help her in her pursuit, but why did he feel he was now being pulled into something personal, something he was responsible for but over which he had no control?

Filled with anxiety and having no desire to remain in that room a moment longer, he abandoned the letters, telling himself he would show them to Emily after they returned from their date. He stormed down the stairs.

Seize life. Live life. That's what Nick had said, and that's what he would do. He could govern very little of his life, being torn in so many different directions, but what he could control was his time with Emily. And whatever time they had would be brilliant.

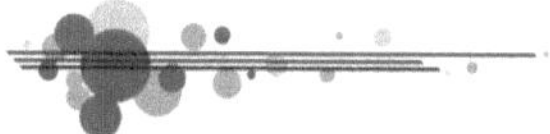

Needing to escape, Andrew headed down to Haight Street. It was still before noon when he arrived, and the street was practically vacant; apparently, most of its denizens had yet to awaken.

Tie-died window displays and Grateful Dead memorabilia mixed with cafés and head shops. The scent of cigarettes and urine and spilled coffee wafted up from the sidewalk under his feet. He walked for a while, stopping in a record store here and a bookstore there, places where he had placed flyers a few weeks before, trying to kill the few hours before his meeting with Neil.

At one corner a familiar shop caught his eye. A cluster of headless mannequins stood in the window, clothed in everything from Victorian top hats to 1970s beaded dresses. A black frockcoat stood out from the rest, draped on the shoulders of a striped dressmaker's dummy. It was Emily's shop.

A bell sounded as he entered, and an old woman shouted out from the back of the shop, "Be with you in a minute."

The scratchy, muted horns of Tommy Dorsey's "Smoke Gets in Your Eyes" danced their way about the shop. By the time he navigated the circuitous path around the knickknack laden tables and overstuffed clothes racks, the boxes of musty books and record albums, and on to the counter, he was humming the tune.

The little white-haired woman he remembered from before came scampering toward him, her hands held up, her eyes bright as though Andrew was the first customer of the day. "Excuse the mess, I'm doing some spring cleaning and everything is all over the place. Oh—oh I remember you! The handsome borscht fellow!"

"Pardon?"

"You're Emily's friend, the homeless musician. So nice to meet you. My name is Myra, Myra Freidlander. We've never been formally introduced, but I've heard all about you. You're Andrew Hayes." She shook his hand daintily, a smile illuminating her inquisitive face.

"Pleased to meet you as well, and yes, I'm Andrew Hayes. But I'm not homeless."

"I know, she told me."

"Really? What else did she tell you?"

"You know how Emily is. I just have to infer the good bits myself, but I'm usually not far off. So, Mr. Andrew 'I'm no longer homeless' Hayes, with the caramel skin and the ought to be illegal blue eyes, what brings you to my store?"

Andrew felt himself blush, the way he did on stage whenever anyone called out something the least bit provocative. "There's a coat in the front window. The black one. I was wondering if I may—"

"That would look breathtaking on you. Let me get it."

Myra rushed off. Andrew was amused, watching her tiny body wind between the plastic mannequins on display in the front window. Myra, however, proved more nimble than Andrew would have ever expected, and with a cry she emerged through the bodies triumphant, the black frock coat held high.

"Here you go—can't wait to see what it looks like on those amazing shoulders of yours."

Disarmed, he took it from her and offered her a hand down from the window along with a heartfelt smile. In return, she blushed a shocking shade of red and batted her eyelashes.

A three-way mirror sat in the back of the shop. He slid on the coat and checked his reflection, shoving his hands in his pockets as he was wont to do. It fit like a glove and looked surprisingly decent, especially for being so old.

"You need a coat like this. The weather's been awful, and Emily would love it."

"I'll take it, then."

Myra rang him up at the counter, Tommy Dorsey's horns having given way to Benny Goodman's clarinet. "I like your choice of music," Andrew offered.

"Of course you do, who wouldn't? That was when they knew how to play. You could understand every word they sang."

He smiled and wondered what Myra would make of The Lost Boys. Probably the same thing his father had. He could only imagine what that proper man would think of his life now. Piano playing ghosts in the attic issuing warnings. Fame around the corner. A woman who made everything else pale in comparison.

The emptiness of missing the man he had never said goodbye to sat in his heart like a weight. Despite their estrangement, could he only look back to appreciate their good times together and forget everything else? Was nostalgia that strong?

He drummed his fingers on the counter and glanced down at the vast selection of jewelry on display. Old vintage brooches, bracelets, and necklaces lay on trays of velvet. His eyes inventoried the collection while he waited.

"Is Emily partial to anything here?"

Myra's eyes met his, and they sparkled in a kind of elfish delight. "Oh, she loves them all."

The earrings in the front appeared to be the clip-on kind, decorated with glaring chunks of costume glass which seemed more appropriate for someone's grandmother. Next to them were hefty looking cameos of Greek goddesses in profile, and to the right of those were strings of odd-shaped pearls with rhinestone clasps. He seriously doubted Emily would care for any of these pieces, and if she did, their very weight would surely topple her to the ground. Almost giving up, his eyes strayed to the back corner of the case and he stopped dead. There, set aside in its own velvet box, was a ring: platinum, inlaid with diamonds, and encircled with a vine pattern. He knew that design. They were the exact same vines that decorated Nora's urn. And the exact same pattern that decorated the keepsake box.

Finding his voice, he calmly asked the woman, "That…that ring. Where…where did you get it?"

"This one?" Myra laughed to herself as her fingers flitted in anticipation, and she retrieved the box and brought it up to the counter like she was displaying her first born.

"It's lovely, isn't it? Pure platinum, and the color and clarity of those diamonds laced in there are almost overkill, if you ask me. The workmanship alone—"

"How much?"

"Oh, I'm sorry, this is reserved for a friend. I couldn't possibly—"

"I'll give you twice the asking price."

"If I'm not being too bold here, what do you intend to do with it?"

"Emily. Emily would love this ring." He didn't know if Emily had shared the details of their recent finds with Myra, and he had no intention of doing so now. But he had to have this ring. He had to have it for Emily.

"Well, you know, times being what they are, I suppose I could—"

"Three times."

Her jaw snapped shut. "Would you like me to gift wrap it for you?"

"No need. I'll take it with me," he insisted.

When she was done ringing him up, he slipped on the coat and placed the small velvet box in the pocket. His fingers remained there as he exited the shop, brushing Emily's ring like it was a talisman.

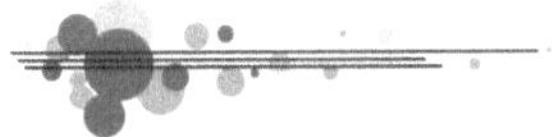

The restaurant Neil had chosen for their meeting was located on Valencia Street, a bit hipper but no less edgier a neighborhood than the Haight and lined with the urban staples of unpronounceable restaurants and avant-garde art galleries. Their restaurant appeared to be an amalgamation of both.

"Where were you?" Simon yelled as Andrew rushed out of a taxi. Dressed for once in a button-down and jeans, his army jacket nowhere to be found, he was pacing outside the restaurant door. He had combed his hair and his glasses were pushed firmly up the bridge of his nose, casting him more in the light of a Stanford MBA than that of a drummer in a rock band on the verge of greatness. Christian, a picture of relaxation in a leather jacket and cords, was leaning against the faux brick façade, texting. He raised a hand in greeting but didn't look up from his phone.

"I got waylaid. Not to worry, we're on time."

"Barely." Simon shoved open the stained glass doors. "After you, Paulie," he said grandly but not without an undertone of reproach.

The host led them to a large table near the window; the sun reflected off the severe place settings and starched white tablecloth. A painting reminiscent of Chagall hung directly above and featured a woman whipping a herd of cows.

"Andrew." Neil stood and held out his hand in greeting, a rare smile on his face as they approached the table. "How's the house? How's the writing?" he asked as he shook Simon's and Christian's hands in turn. "You received some excellent write-ups from your shows in L.A. Did you happen to catch them?"

Andrew waited for his standard dislike for the retired manager to rear its ugly head, but it didn't. It was good to talk to him, to hear the businesslike clip of his voice and feel the contained excitement that seemed to always be brewing under his surface. By the time he sat down, he felt relaxed in spite of himself.

"Yeah, we did, thanks. The house is a nightmare, nothing new there. But we managed to nail down some rehearsal space at the university, and I'm writing—on and off." He wondered what the hell Neil would think if he knew what had transpired in his life during the last week.

"What? Your neighbors don't approve of your playing?"

"Define playing," quipped Simon under his breath with a raised eyebrow in Christian and Andrew's direction.

"Well, thank you for coming today on such short notice. This all came about rather quickly. Evidently one of her people saw you in L.A. and things really started moving," said Neil, taking his seat. "It's a wait-then-hurry up world sometimes, isn't it? I want you to know before we begin that you are under no obligation—" He opened his mouth as though he wanted to say more, but his eyes locked on a figure who was making her way to table. "Ah, there she is. Gentlemen, may I introduce you to a colleague of mine, S.J. Gordian of Voodoo Pink Records. She's represents—"

"The Stands, Violet Afternoon, and the Havershams," Andrew said, amazed. "Three of my favorite bands."

"Very good. And here I thought you were just the tortured artist type from all the buzz I've heard about you. You must be Andrew Hayes."

A willowy blonde wearing a stylish suit of light green and needle-sharp black pumps, her hair constrained in a tight chignon, held out her hand.

Andrew shook it, and her full lips creased into a smile, her lipstick the palest of pinks. She was of an indeterminate age, both nature and success evidently playing in her favor. Like most agents, she was anchored between the wildness of twenty and the gamesmanship of forty.

"Pleased to meet you," he replied briskly.

She shook the hands of Simon and Christian, causing them to stammer their greetings before they all took their seats. She perched on the edge of her chair and loosened her gossamer scarf, the color of a crisp dollar bill, as she ordered a drink from the waiter.

"So, Andrew, how long do you intend to hide away here in San Francisco?"

The remark caught him off guard. Emily had asked him almost the same thing, but where hers was full of hope, S.J.'s question was a challenge.

Why are you wasting your time here? Where is your drive? Your ambition? Don't you want to amount to anything?

He was about to respond when Neil cut him off, his voice a little more forceful than Andrew ever remembered. "These gentlemen have been touring nonstop for quite a long period. Nonstop — you remember what that's like, don't you, S.J.? I believe they need some time to recharge, to recall why they do what they do. It keeps them sane. Don't you agree?"

S.J. cast him a sideways glance. "Not all of us can afford to sit back and enjoy the fruits of our labors, Neil. And all play and no work makes for a very unmarketable Lost Boy."

Andrew sat back, interested to watch these two powerhouses duke it out. But the conversation from that point on remained coolly cordial, with Neil dominating most of it, so much so that Andrew soon became aggravated. After all, she wasn't here to be lectured to as Neil had the annoying habit of doing. In fact, it wasn't until the salad, when Neil was asking her about signing an obscure new group from the slums of Dubai, that she had her first opportunity to speak. She praised their talent, their ability to succeed in the face of certain failure.

"Oh, but I forgot, they would interest you, wouldn't they? You've always been my inspiration, Neil." She raised her glass and toasted him. "Gentleman, your landlord is a legend in the business — quite a story."

Neil leveled her with a look that prompted Andrew to ask, "What story?" But Neil was not forthcoming with any details, which only intrigued Andrew more. "Seriously, I'd like to hear it."

Neil averted his eyes as if to say, *do what you want*. The tension between him and S.J. was quickly becoming palpable.

"They covered Neil in this incredible documentary, if I remember correctly." She leaned over to Neil, placed her hand on his, and murmured, "Please correct me if I get any of this wrong. I don't want to exaggerate any of the details," before she turned her attention to Simon, Christian, and Andrew with a conspiratorial smile and a wink.

"It was incredibly well done, almost Dickensian. I remember how the announcer went on and on. Bought up an orphan in London, lived on the streets, forced from foster home to foster home. Finally taken in by the St. Johns, a poor but good-hearted family in Oxford. God, you really should have had your own theme music. Isn't that right, Neil?" She smiled serenely at him in the torturing style of an old acquaintance before she leaned over and whispered. "You see, gentlemen, the St. Johns never realized what a genius they had on their hands until young Neil went off to school. Brilliant, sucked it all up. He managed to get full scholarships through university. Then he shocked his family and decided he wanted to go into the music business, quite an unorthodox choice when he could have been a doctor or a lawyer, or even the Prime Minister if he'd wanted. Didn't even finish school, left England in a flare of a rebellion. Left his family, left everyone. He never returned until years and years later."

Neil had remained quiet at the growing grandiosity of S.J.'s story, but the laugh lines near his eyes had deepened, and for the first time Andrew could see his urbane façade slip. The street punk, all brains and stratagems, working the world to survive, had wormed its way to the surface.

"Well, the rest is history," said S.J. airily. "Went on to show everyone, prove he could do it on his own terms. Hurray for you, Neil." She raised her glass and they all toasted. "Although, I am sad about Faith. She was lovely, just lovely. Life is horrid that way." She patted Neil's hand again.

The waiter appeared with their entrees. S.J. chewed slowly. Neil hardly touched his food and ordered another drink.

"I think that's commendable," said Andrew, eventually breaking the silence. "Doing what you want in spite of what your family thinks. It takes guts."

Neil looked at him as though he hadn't heard him properly and blinked several times.

"I did the same thing. It's not easy."

"No, no it isn't," Neil replied quietly.

"I must say," said S.J, slicing off the wing of her chicken, "I got a cut of your latest album. It's remarkable, like nothing I've heard in a long time."

Andrew didn't want to look away from Neil. His face held something he had never seen before, but S.J. caught him off guard. "Though everyone knows there's no money in recordings. They exist solely to promote you."

Here she pointed to Andrew alone. "The question you need to ask yourself is how big do you want to get? If you want to remain breaking your backs, then keep playing those small venues. I'll admit, you could possibly eke out a decent living, a good day job. But your talents are going to be wasted. The large arenas, the merchandising off of that, there's where the money is."

"We've never been focused on the money," Andrew said dryly.

"I wouldn't go that far," said Simon, who seemed engrossed with S.J.'s speech. "Money's not the root of *all* evil."

"No, it isn't. What I meant to say is that I care about our sound, our music. I'm not going to—"

"Sell out?" S.J. finished his sentence for him. "Do you know how many people end up in the dust bin and on vh1's *Where Are They Now?* with that kind of attitude? Don't be so naïve. You have talent, and a lot of it. You think anyone of any repute in this business wants to give it away for free? If you want your sound to be known, you have to get it to the most people possible. That's where I can help you."

Andrew could tell by the looks on Simon's and Christian's faces that her blunt approach had hooked them. Although Andrew was shrewd enough to know what she was saying was true, he just didn't trust her. But he didn't trust Neil, either.

Neil cleared his throat as though he wanted the conversation to wrap up. "Aren't we here to talk about the photo shoot?"

S.J. placed her napkin on the table, meeting his frosty glance straight on. "A friend of mine works at *Rolling Stone*—you may have heard of him—Glenn Sommers. He also happens to adore your music. He's—actually the magazine is—interested in doing a cover on The Lost Boys."

All the motion at the table ceased. A cover on *Rolling Stone*. Bloody hell. For a second Andrew let the almost-famous moment wash over him.

"With my representation, he could arrange for this to happen. Immediately, if not sooner."

"The photo shoot, though, there wouldn't be any obligation," said Neil, an edge to his voice. "I was under the assumption that *Rolling Stone* wanted to do the cover, regardless. Right, S.J.? The Lost Boys could do the shoot and still have time to consider your offer before entering into a relationship, am I correct?"

"Yes, of course, but we'll deal with the minutiae later. The most important thing to concentrate on now is the next steps. To start, I'll get in touch with you about the dates and arrange a meeting with Glenn. We should probably do that at my San Francisco office. It's smaller, of course, but it'd be easier than L.A. Until then, please think over what we've talked about. Not to brag, but I am in demand, and I don't play with boys I don't like. Either way, you gentlemen can't hang out here forever. This isn't the Summer of Love—you need to be out there in front of your fans on a national tour. A real tour. *Rolling Stone* is just the beginning." Her eyes fell to Simon. "There will be the financial implications of how to properly invest your increased cash flow, and I can hook you up with some brilliant financial advisers who work miracles. Of course, you'll need to allocate some to your increased security detail in order to keep those fans of yours from tearing your shirts off, but that's only to be expected." She smiled, and the sunlight glimmered off her straight, too white teeth. There was a slight space between the front two that Andrew hadn't noticed before. Her lips covered them when she saw his eyes lower to it, as though she had long practiced keeping the imperfection hidden. She kept speaking, her gaze shifting nearly imperceptibly to Christian. "But seriously, the countless fans you've never reached before will be amazed by your talent. I can't explain the feeling. I've seen it so many times with my clients, of how proud the people you love will feel to see you up there and know that you've realized your dream."

She began to tie the scarf around her neck as she set her sights on Andrew. "But at the end of the day, there is nothing like success to really prove you're worth it. That despite whatever anyone else says, your music is good. There won't be a person out there who won't know the beauty of it, or know who you wrote it for."

With that, she stood and released them from her spell. They fell back to their chairs. "Thank you, gentlemen, it's been a true pleasure. But I apologize, I must be off, I've got a four-thirty in Atherton. Neil. Andrew.

Gentlemen, I'll be in touch." Her hand brushed Andrew's shoulder, and she left them with a smile.

The whole table seemed to reach for their drinks at once. Neil looked troubled, while Simon and Christian looked like a bomb had dropped on them. And Andrew realized that this S.J. Gordian, whoever she was, spoke the truth. She could change their lives forever. And she wanted to. Taking a deep, unsteady breath, his fingers reached back to the outer pocket of his coat to touch Emily's ring.

It was almost ten in the morning when Emily awoke from a dream, her body twisted in the sheets, her skin sweating. Her vision contained no sunlit rooms, however, no gramophones warbling, no breeze from open windows rustling the curtains as she had experienced before. No, this dream was dark, more sinister. Andrew in a long, black coat, his figure stalking closer and closer to a woman she couldn't see. She watched as his hands grabbed hold of the unknown woman's and held them against a brick wall, his eyes liquid in the light of a streetlamp, his fingertips blazing up the bare skin of her thigh. "Be still," he hissed, his mouth a flame's breath away from the woman's. "Don't move, understand?" His hands snared her wrists. He shoved her hard against the bricks, burning into her, and kissed her fiercely.

Emily struggled to reach him, but when she did he recoiled from the sight of her as if she were poisonous. Then before her eyes, the corporeal nature of his body began to dissipate. She cried for him to stay, but he staggered backward, clutching the dream woman to himself until only mist remained.

"No!" She sat straight up. The chipped and peeling paint on her bedroom walls had replaced the brick wall from her dream. The muted sounds of morning came from outside her window, the piercing song of birds and the faraway rush of cars, instead of the silence of the night.

In a savage mood, she threw herself from the bed and caught sight of her reflection. There, in her floor length mirror, a creature stared back at her. It was full of wild, unkempt curls, a face overtaken by luminous eyes ringed in thick black lashes and the thin arch of brows. Her fingers reached to touch the flush of the woman's cheeks, the terror of her hair.

"Dreams are a manifestation of the fears and wants of our subconscious," she whispered to herself, remembering what Vandin had once said. "Nothing more."

Wanting was not new to Emily, but this kind of nameless longing was. It gnawed away at her like a hunger. She hated the hold Andrew was fast having over her, she hated the idea that his life meant him spending stretches of time away from her, and she hated the fact that this didn't bother him, that he could easily live a life free to enjoy all his desires. Usually calm and levelheaded, she was fast becoming greedy and petulant. She didn't like being in second place.

Hoping to alleviate the tension twisting within her, she headed for the shower and let the hot water pour over her neck and shoulders. She concentrated on the pressure of the stream, focusing on everything that had happened to her in such a short period of time, as if she were scripting her own Gothic novel. The man of her heart had found her and taken her soul in the process. Meanwhile, her psychotic professor was out there somewhere, and God only knew what would happen when he returned. Add to that her personal quest to unite dead lovers who were half in this world, half out, and who also happened to be haunting her home, and she raised her head, closed her eyes, and let the white-hot water pound her face, hoping she might drown.

From somewhere in the house the phone rang. Once the answering machine refused to pick up the call she shouted out to her roommates, but it continued to ring off the hook. Wrapped in her robe, she trudged down the hall to the kitchen dripping wet and grumbling curses, her toes curling on the cold floor as she snatched the phone.

"Yes!"

"Hello, may I please speak to a Miss Thomas?"

"Speaking."

"Emily?"

Part of her froze — for a split second she was convinced it was Vandin's voice; it had the same halting nature, the same cadence. But this voice was lighter, calmer, and almost familiar, with the hint of a Brooklyn accent.

She chastised herself for her nerves, and wondered if she would ever stop jumping at ghosts that weren't there.

"Yes, this is Emily. Who am I speaking with?"

"I'm sorry. It's Detective Obester, Anthony Obester. I've been assigned to Laura Schandler's case. You probably don't remember me, but your father knew mine really well. They taught together at NYU. We lived in the brownstone across from you in the West Village."

The name rattled around her brain until a memory of her old street came to life. "The big kid with the curly hair and the braces?"

"Guilty as charged."

"Ah, I remember you. You used to walk me down the block to get ice cream." She let loose a huge sigh and smiled. "So, Anthony Obester, what brings you all the way to San Francisco?"

"Fell in love with a girl out here and never left. Two kids and two mutts later I'm still in the department, haven't managed to wrangle myself out of here yet. Listen, I wish this were a social call, but like I said, I've been assigned to that case and I have some questions I need to ask you. Do you have a few minutes?"

"Of course."

"I don't know if you're aware, but Dr. Vandin is still out of the country."

"Yes...London, I think, on business. He said it was a conference."

They spent the next few minutes reviewing the details of the case. The detective verified Emily's position as his assistant.

"There's nothing much we can do until he returns, but we've also made a few inquiries around campus. It seems the man's a player, cycles through students on a pretty regular basis. Do you know of anyone else we might be able to question?"

"No, no I don't...I didn't realize. I didn't think he ever acted on anything, truthfully. When I first met him, I thought it was all bravado, part of his image. He can come across as very charming, larger than life, and I can see how women are drawn to that."

"Did you two ever have a relationship?"

"No, of course not, no! He kissed me — once — when I first started to work for him. I was surprised. He caught me off guard."

"Did you say anything to him afterward? Was he under the assumption that you wanted to pursue a relationship?"

"I made it very clear I didn't. And I don't see how this matters at all in this case. He shouldn't have done what he did to me or to Laura."

"I don't mean to upset you, Emily, but you need to understand that his lawyers will use every trick in the book to make you out to be a liar. They'll try to make it look like you have an axe to grind and you're getting revenge by colluding with this girl to invent a story. Just wanted to let you know that being a witness is going to be a difficult experience for you."

"I know, but I couldn't sit back and do nothing."

"No, you did the right thing. But if he contacts you in any way, let me know immediately. From what we've dug up, the man's got a temper, so be careful, be aware. There were some rumblings from the last post he held that weren't too nice. Don't go anywhere alone if you can help it. Got it?"

"Yes."

"And one more thing. If you leave the city, let us know where you're going before you leave, just until we can locate Vandin. Plus, it'll keep your dad from killing me if he thought I wasn't looking after his kid. Look, you can always call the department, but I'll give you my personal cell too. Best to use that one—you can reach me there day or night." She scribbled the number down on a nearby notepad. "I'll be in touch. Sorry it had to be under these circumstances, but it's great hearing a voice from back home. Take care of yourself."

He hung up, leaving her to stare at the phone, a knot tightening in the pit of her stomach. Vandin was out there, somewhere. The call had only solidified the feeling that she would never be free of him, that he would never leave her alone. The house seemed hollow and cold, and she glanced up at the ceiling devoutly wishing she was in Andrew's bedroom, under his warm covers, nestled into his side, and his lips on hers telling her everything was going to be all right.

"No," she said to herself, putting an end to her self-pity. "Take care of yourself."

She closed her eyes and went over the call again in her mind, detail by detail. She thought of her parents. *Take care of yourself*—it was her mother's mantra. They were the words of a woman who did not believe in warm covers or nestling, whose relationships were known only for their long years of silence interrupted by acute periods of politeness.

The reality of her mother's inner life was not lost on Emily, who noticed everything. The novels left on her mother's nightstand whispered of desires and passion far more chaotic than she would ever allow in her own home.

Whether she was telling Emily *take care of yourself and love will follow*, or *take care of yourself so love won't*, Emily could not decide. But either way the message was clear. After all, when Andrew went back on the road, she wouldn't have him to rely on. Why was she even thinking like this? Austen was right: women's minds jumped from admiration to love and from love to matrimony in a moment. Andrew and she had just met, and here she was wondering what they would be like when he returned to the life he had been happily living long before there ever was a *they*.

Take care of yourself.

Yet how could she think of being without him? They would have to make it work — it was their only choice — but she knew long distance relationships rarely worked for long; she had told him as much. It was an artificial life, one of trying to fit weeks into days and days into hours until the goodbyes were wished for, if only to speed along the pain of separation. But the life he had on the road involved throngs of adoring, screaming women, all night, every night. She had seen him perform and witnessed it. How could she even hope to compete with that at her writer's seminar, typing away on her laptop? What kind of connection could that possibly provide?

Before she knew what she was doing, she had dialed her parents' phone number. She hadn't spoken to them in weeks and readied her mental checklist that she used for every conversation: grades, graduate school, the weather, and an occasional attempt at tenderness. The phone was answered on the fourth ring.

"Mom?"

In the background she heard the drone of female voices, a sharp laugh, the clink of glasses. "Emily? What a surprise — your father and I had you down for dead."

"Sorry to disappoint."

"Stop being facetious, dear. Now isn't a good time, my book club is wrapping up. Can you call back tomorrow? No wait, that won't work, I have my seminar. This is all very annoying. I don't have my planner handy."

"No, no, Mom, is Dad there? I need to talk to Dad."

"He's gone to Vermont with his colleagues, won't be back until Sunday night. You must remember, it's their annual male bonding pilgrimage, off to re-connect with their cave dweller in a sweat lodge somewhere or some such nonsense. God knows what they really do up there."

"Crap, I really wanted to talk to him."

"Language, Emily."

Emily wondered how her mother could imply her father was off buggering his work buddies and she couldn't even swear.

"Listen, sweetie, I have to go, they're waiting for me."

"Hold on, Mom! I need you to ask Dad…No wait, write this down, please."

"Emily, this is a tremendous imposition."

"Please."

"Fine, what is it?"

She hadn't thought through how to phrase it without arousing her parents' suspicions. And she was out of practice on how to properly lie to them.

"Ask Dad if he had any relatives, it'd be a great- or great-great-aunt, maybe, that was named Noreen Thomas."

"Is that it?"

"Yes. And tell him I ran into Anthony Obester at the grocery store the other day. He's a son of a friend of Dad's from NYU. He works out here now." There, that might cover her if word ever got back to her father.

"Is that it?"

"Yes. And Mom, I love you."

Emily's voice broke a little when she said it. She missed her mother, and she wished she could explain everything and have her rationalize away her fears like she always did, but she didn't want her to worry.

"Emily, is everything fine? Are you in trouble?"

"No, Mom, everything is great. I bet the forsythia is blooming in the front yard, right? Or did Dad manage to cut it down?"

"No. I will never let him touch the hedge clippers again without my direct supervision. Emily, really, I have to get going. We can chat later."

"Yeah, I've got to run myself, I've got a date—"

"With a man?" Long pause. "Just two questions: are you graduating on time and does he have a job?"

"Thanks for putting it in that order. And the answer is yes. To both."

"Good. Because I'm too young to be a grandmother."

With an aggravated sigh Emily ended the call and set herself to conquer the last stack of school papers, thinking that once she finished them she could concentrate on Nora, devote all her attention to finding Nick's remains, and hope that she could create one happy ending in this world.

Somewhere around two, Margot and Zoey tumbled in the door laughing, and the sound was heaven to Emily's ears. They found her drowning under the weight of notebooks, her laptop, and reams of paper sprawled out around her on the dining room table, not to mention her own growing glumness.

Margot wore a rare smile on her face. "I'm done with my hopeless students. Finals. What a lovely word. Say it with me, Emily. Finals."

Emily glared at her. Zoey rubbed her shoulders, and her head slowly hit the table. "Why is she smiling?" Emily muttered out of the side of her mouth while Zoey's hands continued to knead her tight muscles, causing her to puddle underneath her fingertips.

"Simon is taking her to a baseball game," Zoey teased.

"You're kidding?"

"No, he's taking her to a baseball game on their first date. Can you believe it? A baseball game!"

"What I want to know is where in the *How to Get a Girl to Fuck You* manual are athletic events listed?" Margot muttered.

"Right next to hunting and bowling." Zoey laughed.

"And it's not a date. I want to go on record about that. It's two adults paying their own way to sit in a freezing cold stadium and watch grown men stand around on the grass and scratch themselves."

"So what are you wearing to 'watch grown men stand around on the grass'?" Emily asked.

"Clothes that absorb beer and spit," Zoey suggested. "I can't believe you're really going on a date with him."

"I repeat, it's not a date."

"Why don't you wear a Giants T-shirt and jeans?"

Margot frowned at Emily. "What? And look like I'm selling churros? No way in hell. Speaking of which, tonight is your first official date with Prince Charming, isn't it, as I'm sure the dinner on the roof and the crypt didn't count."

"No, they don't. Not even the crypt."

"Where is he taking you?"

"I have no idea."

"I love that restaurant. I've been there a thousand times, very French, very romantic. Where are you going after dinner?"

"The same place. All I know is he wants me to wear something old."

"Wear that pale pink dress, the sleeveless one with the beads, the one that makes you look like a flapper. Virginal, yet adequate access to the neck and breasts," Zoey told her. "Practical and efficient."

"And what about your date with Christian?"

"He won't care. I'll be out of whatever I wear quick enough."

At precisely seven p.m., a knock came from the door.

"Good evening." Andrew stood there wearing a pair of tailored navy pants and a starched white dress shirt; his coat was draped over one arm while the other was held behind his back. A boyish smirk played across his features as he looked into her eyes, and then his gaze halted as though he had caught himself, as though he was seeing her for the first time. "Christ, you are beautiful, aren't you?"

She wanted to look away but she couldn't. He hadn't bothered to shave after all; the roughness of his jaw stood out in stark contrast to the smooth, naked skin visible from his open collar. His hair was slicked back, but, as always, only barely contained.

"Here." Andrew handed her a simple bouquet of wildflowers. "It comes from my private stock."

Her heart melted. She took the bouquet from him and raised it to her face. "The back garden?"

"I would have emptied every florist in town, if I had my way."

"No. They're perfect. Thank you for the restraint."

He smiled and reached out for her hand, kissing her knuckles fervently. "Finally. Jesus, Emily, I've been waiting all day. It's been killing me. I've got so much to tell you."

Downstairs a taxi was waiting. The evening was cool and foggy. The street lamps cast oval puddles of light along the sidewalks. People hurried along, zipping their coats and shoving their hands deep into their pockets, their faces hunkering down against the wind.

As they drove, she tried to nestle closer to him as best she could, reveling in the warmth of him. His body felt excited, like a spring next to hers; his left hand was drumming a chord on his knee while his eyes darted about taking in the scenes of the night.

"Where are we going?" she asked, unable to stop herself from placing her fingers over his.

He gave her a conspiratorial wink. "'Tis a secret."

"Your accent gets broader when you're excited, you know that?"

"Then it's a miracle you can even understand me tonight," he murmured.

She blushed and laughed. "What's going on? You look like you're about to explode. When are you going to tell me what happened today?"

He didn't answer her. Instead, he pulled her to him and kissed her. His fingers ran through her hair and lingered on her neck. With a deep sigh, he drew away and kissed the tip of her nose before he sat back, satisfied.

"You don't play fair," she managed to say.

"I wasn't playing."

They drove a little farther, and Emily knew whatever trepidations she had about this man and about their future crumbled in his presence. He was too full of life, too charismatic, and his high spirits rendered him unspeakably sexy. She felt what all his fans must feel being near him — the need for more.

"Here's fine," Andrew told the taxi driver, who pulled the car over at the end of a dark alley. Emily looked around. It was eerily lit by only a single gas-lamp style street light, but before she could register where they were, he was at her side, his arm around her waist.

"Where are we going?" she asked as they walked onto the avenue. He didn't say a word; his arm merely pulled her closer to warm her from the chill.

They stopped a block farther up, near a row of darkened doors. A sign hung above:

ANTI-SALOON LEAGUE, SAN FRANCISCO BRANCH, EST. 1920

Andrew rang what appeared to be a buzzer. She frowned at him, but he merely cocked an eyebrow and smiled, only adding to the mystery.

A long rectangular slit in one of the doors opened, revealing a pair of eyes.

"Password?" a gravelly voice requested.

"Books," replied Andrew.

Several locks unfastened with a series of clicks on the other side. Andrew cast her a conspiratorial glance and squeezed her hand.

The large door creaked open, inviting them into a foyer. The walls were lined with a lush maroon, brocade wallpaper, and candlelit sconces reflected across the dark wooden floors and the pressed-tin ceiling. Her eyes widened in disbelief. They had stepped back in time to the 1920s.

A man in a bowtie and suspenders met them. Andrew whispered something to him to which he replied with a discreet nod before escorting them down a long hallway. The smell of cigars and leather bound books hung rich in the air. At any moment she expected to see Al Capone or John Dillinger pass by with a dew-eyed starlet on their arm.

"Right this way."

They entered a grand room buzzing with subdued conversation, not a vacant seat to be had. A beautiful mahogany bar dominated the room. High-backed booths filled the remainder, all occupied with high-toned people intent on inhabiting their own worlds. Above their heads a tremendous chandelier warmed the room in amber. Somewhere nearby a piano swooned jazz.

A maître d' materialized out of nowhere, nodded to the tuxedoed man in somber thanks, and escorted them to a booth in the corner.

"Would you like me to take your coat, Miss?" he asked.

Before she knew it, Andrew's hands grasped her shoulders instead. The coat slipped off the beads of the dress like water. She heard him catch his breath. He deposited her coat in the outstretched hand of the maître d'. "Here is the libations list, Mr. Hayes," he said, and glancing at Emily's newly exposed arms a trifle longer than necessary, he added, "Enjoy." Then he returned toward the door.

Her eyes drank in the Prohibition splendor of the place. She felt like someone who had stepped out of time in her flapper dress, its pink beads draping her body like countless strings of pearls. Smiling madly, she turned to face Andrew, her long earrings brushing against her bare collarbone, a spot on which Andrew's eyes were now fixed.

"You need to speak easy to me now," Emily said.

His eyes flashed back up to her face. A most dangerous look darkened his features, yet he said nothing.

Discomfited by his continued muteness, she bristled and said, "I had to wear the dress. I'm a girl, you know."

Andrew reached across the table and draped his warm hand over hers. "That is a fact every man in this establishment is now painfully aware of."

"Well then, I should warn you that I'm wearing a garter belt. I'm not exactly sure I have it on right, so if I start fidgeting, I have an excuse."

A flame of something wicked passed through his hooded eyes. "I'd be happy to lend a hand in that department."

"With the garter or the fidgeting?"

"Tell me about your day, or we're never going to get past the first drink."

She told him of the basic details, school work, and the phone call with her mother. She sighed as the warmth of close-gathered bodies and the rich commotion of conversation hummed about them. Candles glowed on each table, reflecting the patrons' eyes and casting their silhouettes against the brick walls. He gazed at her as she leaned back into the corner of the booth, both of them suffused in the deep contentment that permeates two people aware of themselves and no one else.

Then she told of him of her conversation with Anthony Obester.

"He gave you his personal cell phone? Is that normal procedure?"

"He thought it would be best, and I think it's a bit overprotective, but he is a friend of the family."

"You know him?"

She watched his eyes narrow, his lips purse just a tad. Tickled by his jealousy, she could not pass up the opportunity to tease him.

"Your drink selections?"

Andrew's eyes didn't release hers as he addressed the waiter. "The Pol Roger Brut, thank you."

"About this detective…"

"Anthony and I were very close. We spent a lot of time together."

His lips pursed harder. "Really."

"He took me out on a lot of dates. I may have broken his heart."

"Poor him."

"But it's hard to remember. I was four, I think."

A smile slowly creased the side of his mouth. "Detective Obester had excellent taste, even then. I won't have to kill him now. Though, seriously, what he said makes sense. Vandin is unstable — you shouldn't be near him."

"So noted. I'll be careful."

Moments passed. Andrew had begun to run his fingers around her wrist, studying the small bones in careful attention.

"Tell me about what happened today now, please."

Blinking at her as though he was unaware exactly what she had asked him, he smiled and laughed as if remembering a joke. "Christ, where to start?"

"Why not start after you snuck out of my bedroom."

"I found your trunk, by the way," he told her and released her wrist, his tone oddly contained, but he went on to tell her about the letters. She sat transfixed as he related the nature of the correspondence. "And I had a run in with Nick."

"Seriously? He actually spoke to you? What did he say?"

He found her eyes and told her.

"Died on their way to get married? God, that's horrible. But what was that about 'saving you'? Why do you need to be saved?"

"I wish I knew. He's not the world's most straightforward kind of a ghost, I'm afraid. He seems to think I know what to do, whom to contact to help us, and whom to trust, even. Plus, did I forget to mention, he had one mother of a mother. Evidently, she was big into spiritualism, and whatever she believed, he disliked her intensely for it. Maybe she tried to drive a wedge between Nora and him, who knows? But the more I think about it, the more I think she's definitely involved in this somehow. I hate to add one more thing to the search, but I think we might need to find out whatever happened to Mother Chamberlain. Have you had any luck with opening the box?"

Emily shook her head. "I'm about ready to pry the thing open with my bare hands, but I'm just afraid it might destroy something inside. You know, I think we should have that séance Dwayne suggested, whether we want to or not."

Andrew laughed. Perhaps he was envisioning Simon communicating with the great beyond, or Margot, for that matter. The champagne arrived too elegant to swallow.

"So Simon wore a tuxedo to a baseball game?" Emily asked. The Irishman had shown up for his date with Margot wearing a full-fledged, cuff-linked, sharp pressed, bow-tied tuxedo that left her roommate speechless. *Home run, Simon*, Emily had thought. The drummer had knocked the ball out of the park before he'd even left the house.

"I couldn't restrain him. He felt the need to celebrate."

"Okay. What's up with you guys—what aren't you telling me?"

"Wait, don't drink yet, I want to propose a toast." He lifted his glass, eyes sparkling. "Here's to the next band, the brilliant, most bloody talented band, I might add, to be featured on the cover of *Rolling Stone*. The Lost Boys."

Emily's jaw dropped; she blinked repeatedly in utter amazement. Andrew's smile beamed, lighting up their dark corner like fireworks, and without a thought she launched out of her seat and threw her arms around him, nearly crashing over their champagne.

"It's a photo shoot too." His smile, if possible, became even more magnificent as he took a sip of his drink and grinned cockily. "Cover of *Rolling Stone*, hell, it sounds like the bloody Dr. Hook song. You know that went to number six on the U.S. charts in nineteen seventy-three? Boggles the mind."

"Andrew. Why didn't you say something sooner? Andrew! Really? When are they going to do the article?"

He went on to explain their meeting with Neil. Emily had to continually goad him into telling all the details; he was barely able to control his excitement.

"It's great that this S.J. person wants to help you."

"She wants to do more than that—she wants to sign us, take us on as clients."

"And that's a good thing, right?"

"I honestly don't know. She represents some incredible groups, but there's something that doesn't sit right, especially between her and Neil. There's a tension there you can cut with a knife. But you never know with Neil. My guess is that they're old lovers. He seems rather bitter, and she was goading him on something fierce. I've never seen Neil put in his place like that. You should have seen her. It was refreshing, to say the least."

Emily blinked twice at his choice of adjective. "Well…then do the photo shoot and don't use her, trust your gut."

"Funny, that's what Nick said to do."

"Then here's to Nick." They clinked glasses. He kissed her, only breaking off when they heard the discreet cough of the waiter.

"Would you please follow me to dinner."

Andrew grabbed her hand. As they walked, her dress whispered as the beads clicked together. His fingers moved to smooth her back in a drumming a pattern, as though intrigued with the sensation. She glanced at him in question.

"I'm composing." His lips were near her neck, making the bare flesh on her arms tingle.

They entered another room, an old private library from the looks of it, displaying brick walls filled with shelves of books. Over dim candlelight, they enjoyed what turned out to be an exquisite meal with wine that tasted like honey, although she noticed Andrew barely touched his entrée. And his hand was never still, like it had a life unto itself. All of this didn't bode well for Emily. She could see the signs; he was distracted, his mind already a million miles from here and back with *Rolling Stone*, back out on the road. Finally, at the end of dinner, he caught her staring.

"Still composing?"

"Yes." His fingers reached out to brush lightly along the curve of her shoulder, his eyes narrowing. "I want to play you."

She gulped down a mouthful of wine. "Play away," she said, feeling her face blaze.

"But first, I need to talk to you."

She took another sip. She braced herself for his words. He could only be lost in such deep concentration over one thing. Here it goes. *It's all been grand, but…*Stupid, stupid, love struck girl, she chided herself. You walked into this with both eyes open; you only have yourself to blame. It seemed horribly ironic that Vandin's words would reverberate in her mind. *You, an obscure little college student. An almost-famous rock star is really going to drop everything and remain here for you?*

"When we were talking with S.J. today—"

"Is she pretty?"

"Pardon?"

"This S.J., is she pretty?"

"Well, she—"

"That pretty, huh."

"For a blonde, yes."

"Ah, a blonde."

"I prefer auburn-haired women with wicked jaws, myself."

She grumbled and looked down. She didn't want to be handled or placated; she wanted the truth. Just get it done with.

"Are you going to let me talk or are you going to have her in the sack with me before we order dessert?"

"I'm not hungry."

"You'll want dessert. It's a homemade cherry tart."

He took her fingers in his and raised her chin with their joined hands. It was apparent that whatever he was going to say was difficult for him at least; he seemed to struggle to find the words.

"We're going to have to start touring again. As much as I never want to leave this city, I have to. Goes with who I am, I'm afraid."

Her heart fell to the pit of her stomach. The last few weeks began to flash before her eyes; everything seemed large, loud, and out of focus. He was saying goodbye.

"No!" The forcefulness of her voice caught the attention of some other patrons. He tightened his grip. He must have known how she would react, and he was trying to soften the blow. He seemed embarrassed, tongue-tied, and a sense of humiliation filled her. She swore to herself she would not make a scene. Her eyes flew to the nearest exit sign. She had to get out of there. Instead, he took a deep breath, and when he spoke again, the lines of concentration deepened around his eyes.

"I found something today. I believe it belongs to you."

He reached back into his coat pocket and took out a small velvet box, and placed it on the table.

Emily sat unmoving. Her hands had gone quite cold.

"It's better if you open it," he added quietly as she sat there staring at it.

Louis Armstrong crooned from far away, and she could hear someone breathing more heavily. She raised the lid slowly. Nestled within the box lay the ring she had adored, the ring from her shop, its platinum and diamonds reflected the candlelight. "My ring, how did you know?" she mumbled incoherently, the lump in her throat making speech difficult. "And the pattern, the pattern, my God, I never noticed, it's the same. The same as the urn. And the box."

"Yes, it is. It's fate."

Andrew took the ring from her and gently put it on her left ring finger. He then clasped her hands to his, raising them to his lips. He was shaking. Holding himself steady, he let out a long breath.

"Emily," he went on, his voice seemed to have dropped an octave. "I have something to ask you. I know I've only been with you for a heartbeat of time. But you've always been with me…I'm asking you…what I want to say…what I mean…I would very much like for you to wear this. Always. I don't have much to offer right now, not living the ideal kind of life for us, I'm afraid, but I will someday, I promise you. And if you'll wait, if you want to wait, I never want to lose you…"

She was already in his arms before he could finish; she grabbed him around the neck and hugged him within an inch of his life, and they laughed so hard they nearly fell out of the chair. Andrew took her hand and kissed it again.

"I'll take that as a yes. I'm total rubbish at these things, I'm sorry."

She was crying now in earnest. Andrew was chuckling, alternately kissing away her tears and pulling back to look at her in complete adoration. They were lost in time, kissing, laughing. Happiness as she had never before felt swelled inside her. Andrew looked how she felt, coupled with perhaps a huge wave of relief. She had never seen him smile like this; he looked on top of the world, like he could scream and shout. Like he did on stage.

"We need to celebrate properly."

"How?"

"A holiday."

"A what?"

"God, you Americans. A holiday. A weekend away. As in this weekend when, for once, we don't have any gigs. As in I can't wait a second longer to finally roger you senseless in a bed."

The waiter placed down the cherry tart at that exact moment, his eyebrows raised into his hairline. He gave a short cough signaling his discretion and disappeared.

"How did you know?" she finally managed to ask. "I mean about the ring. You know I had it on reserve. I must really rate with Myra. She sold it to the first pretty face that walked in the door."

Andrew smiled wickedly. "She didn't. It was a fierce negotiation. And she had already seen my pretty face once."

His eyes darted briefly to the tart.

"You haven't eaten all day, have you?"

He shook his head, grinning madly as he cut off a massive piece. "Bloody nerves."

A quiet descended over them. Over Andrew's mandatory tea, Louis Armstrong sang on about kisses and dreams, and she was sure his fingers played the melody on the side of his cup. As the song ended, his eyes narrowed, his gaze trailing across her body almost possessively.

"Let's get out of here. Now."

She nodded.

The bill and her coat arrived. Andrew rose and helped her with her coat, drawing his touch across the nape of her neck as his long fingers drummed seductively on her shoulders.

"Composing?" she asked hoarsely.

"Always…Ready?" he whispered, brushing his lips against her neck and sending a cascade of chills down her spine. The maître d' escorted them from the room. "There are five secret exit tunnels from our establishment," he explained. "The one specifically designated as a Ladies' Exit is the most obscure. These other tunnels allowed for a quick underground getaway all the way up to Geary Street, further up at Jones Street, and two exit to O'Farrell Street. But the Ladies' Exit grants safe passage all the way to Leavenworth Street, a full block away. Would you like to use it?"

She nodded to the maître d' and hazarded a glance back. Andrew slipped on his coat. She halted, unable to move another step. It was the same coat, the same coat as from her dream this morning. She grasped onto a nearby doorframe for support as the wave of memories crashed into her. Andrew glanced at her, and she swallowed, sure her face betrayed her thoughts.

A partially open bookcase led down into a bricked tunnel. The maître d' gestured ahead. "Continue on this way, you'll find an exit at the other end. A most pleasant evening to you both."

In silence they walked, hands laced tightly, hearing only the sound of their footsteps and the roughness of Andrew's breath. Emily fought the urge to look at him, torn between the need to touch him, to feel his skin underneath her cold fingers, and the need to explain what she had dreamed, not just today but ever since she had moved into the house. Every second she wanted him to stop, to turn to her, but he continued on.

He halted as they reached the door at the end of the passage. Her heart sped up in her chest. Here is where he had kissed the other woman in her dream, taken her savagely against these brick walls. The realization made her begin to shake. His hand grasped the doorknob, and he shut his eyes. His jaw tightened as he wrenched the door open.

As promised, the tunnel led them close to the alley where they had been dropped off by the taxi. They neared the darkened end, and Andrew reached out to hail a cab. *No.* This was not how it was supposed to be. Unable to control herself any longer, she clenched her fingers about his other hand and pulled him toward the alley.

Once they were lost to the darkness, she dropped her forehead to his shoulder. "Andrew, please. I've been here before. We've been here before."

His touch was hesitant at first, tracing the curve of her cheek. Her heart pounded near her throat as his fingertips brushed across her lips and slid down to rest on the nape of her neck.

"I know."

"How do you know?" she whispered, her hands clasping the edges of his coat. "Andrew, my dreams, it's not déjà vu, they're too real. Like right here, right now, I know what will happen. Please tell me you don't. Please tell me you haven't been dreaming."

"I can't." He looked anguished; whatever he had seen he was not about to share it with her.

The beads of her dress rustled in the wind passing through the vacant alley. "Andrew, talk to me. I'm losing my mind. What have you dreamt? What have you seen? Please tell me."

"They're simply dreams. That's all." He wrapped her in his arms and kissed her, pressing his chin forcibly against her cheek afterward. "That's all."

"Then is this a dream?" Her voice challenged him. With unexpected daring, she took his hand and skimmed his fingers along her stockings, closing her eyes in desire as she dragged his hand to the bare flesh above her garter. "Feel me. Feel what you do to me."

"Emily," he hissed, his lips lost in her hair.

His fingers hesitated, his breath stormy and torn. She ran her lips along his neck and kissed him passionately. He muttered a curse, and she could feel his body clench. His hand twitched against her, his fingers and thoughts betraying him. *Yes, come to me, you're mine now, not hers, I won't let you escape.*

"Be still," Andrew whispered, his mouth on hers. "Don't move, understand?" She could feel the war rage on in him. Suddenly, his hands held her wrists to her sides and he shoved her against the side of a nearby car, burning into her.

"I love you. Fucking hell, you know I do. I always will. But if I took you now, it would be like an animal. Do you understand?"

Their foreheads pressed together, his hands hauled her onto the hood of the car, her dress thrashing against it like rain, and he roughly hitched her leg over his hip. She could hear the metal creaking below her as he kissed her hard, his mouth slowly lowering to claim her neck. His breath panted along her throat, his hands caressing her shoulders. With a growl, he shoved her dress aside. His teeth raked across her collarbone to her breasts, making her throw back her head in rapture, her hair wild shadows in the night air. He kissed her again, not wanting to be parted from her mouth.

With every touch he told her what he would do to her, in obscene detail, his words mixing with grunted curses that made her nails claw for a hold on the metal grille.

They moved as though possessed. Somewhere a saxophone was wailing; a siren blared. She curled into him, gasping his name and obscenities to the night air, and the words swirled around them like untamed phantoms. He was feral and merciless. She fisted his hair in her hands, the stubble of his clenched jaw burning her neck.

Soon she trembled helplessly, so close to the edge she could only whimper. Her hips had begun to buck hard against him, matching his fierce rhythm. She held her breath as she arched her back, trying desperately to hang on. His fingers plunged inside of her body, and she exploded, waves of ecstasy pulsing through her as she slammed her drenched body against his, her legs stiff, every muscle taut and screaming. Wave after wave after wave. His mouth wet and unrelenting on hers, his fingers demanding she come again and again.

Inhuman, divine, all love, everything.

Shattering, she screamed out, falling…falling. Her body would have collapsed onto the cold metal of the hood, but a pair of strong arms caught hold of her. For countless precious, perilous minutes he held her roughly to him, cocooning them together. Panting, desperate to hold on to each other, they felt the earth whip by underneath their feet.

"I'm sorry," he kept whispering into her neck, his voice nearly breaking, his forehead drenched in sweat. "I'm sorry. I know you wanted it, but I couldn't take you here, not here, not here."

"No," she kept repeating back to him, still shaking. "No. God, that was—I love you, love you. No."

Their strangled voices echoed in the stillness, leaving ghostly halos of breath about them.

"God, I love you," he said, rocking her back and forth in his arms. "I love you so."

She raised her eyes to the night sky and breathed in a huge lungful of cool air, letting the fog envelop her, damp and soothing on her feverish skin. The street lamp bathed the air in gold. For the first time she noticed the street sign on the alley.

Dashiell Hammett Street, it read.

When they were able to move, they gradually, reluctantly, fumbled their clothes back into place. Andrew kissed her, a slow drugging kiss, not stopping until their bodies and hearts were quiet, calm. One.

"I love you," she told him, unwilling to let him go.

"Oh, sweet girl, you have no idea—"

Without warning, a voice came from behind them. It cursed loudly.

Immediately, Andrew tensed. His eyes found hers—*don't move*, they warned.

A figure stepped into the end of the alley. Emily's heart pounded in fear, and feeling it, Andrew turned, blocking her from view and holding her against the car. She dared a peek over his shoulder and saw four bodies in the shadows. They were outnumbered.

One stepped out into the light. Emily stiffened into Andrew's shoulder.

"Bloody hell, do you two ever do it anywhere normal?"

Simon stepped into the lamplight that bathed the entrance to the alley. His bowtie hung undone around his neck, his tuxedo flapped open in the breeze, and his arms stretched out in the same mocking disbelief that matched his words.

"Crypts, alleys? What do you suppose is next? Crawlspaces? For God's sake, get a bloody room, why don't you."

With a stifled string of curses, Andrew relaxed his stance, though his arms still held Emily against the car. Her head dropped onto the heated muscles between his shoulder blades, and she could feel his heartbeat pound out the same jagged rhythm as hers.

Andrew turned, and completely ignoring Simon, he gently raised his hands, cupped them about Emily's shoulders and looked her full in the face, his eyes brimming with concern. Caressing the side of her cheek with one hand, he straightened her coat with the other. "Ignore him," he whispered.

"But—" She could feel the embarrassment blaze upon her cheeks and didn't know where to look. How much had they heard; how much had they seen?

"But nothing. He's probably just jealous." He smiled, and she couldn't help but smirk a little in response, especially when he gave her a clandestine wink. "Crawlspaces?" Her smirk widened, and he drew her into hug. "You're mine, girl, all mine. Nothing else matters. Understood?"

She nodded and laughed into his chest, lost in the folds of his coat. "Good. Now take my hand. Brilliant. Deep breath. Ready?" With that they turned around and exited the dark alley to face the crowd and the music.

Zoey was apparent first. She had her hands shoved deep into the pockets of her purple faux-fur coat, and her face appeared awestruck as she rocked from foot to foot on the sidewalk. Next to her, Christian was staring at his own feet, his dreads swinging as he fought back a round of sniggering. Simon had lit up a cigarette while waiting for someone to say a word, but Margot, in her Giants T-shirt and leather jacket, swiped the cigarette from his hands took a deep puff and blew it off to the side.

"And what brings you to this neighborhood, exactly?" asked Andrew tersely.

"Well," ventured Simon, "we heard the screaming from around the corner and we—"

"Idiot!" Margot reprimanded him. "What this moron meant to say is that he and his friend dragged us over miles and miles of crumbling sidewalks to interrupt your romantic dinner thanks to *someone* turning off their phone. All this to go to this supposed jazz club, since they found out a Mr. Memphis or someone is playing there tonight. I'd like to add that neither of them is wearing goddamn three inch heels." She pointed to her black boots with a scowl and threw the cigarette into the gutter.

"Memphis?" Andrew said. "Memphis is playing? Where?"

"Over on Columbus," answered Simon, his grin widening at the effusion in Andrew's voice.

Before she knew what was happening, Emily was being hauled down the street; she cast a frantic, fleeting look back at Margot and Zoey who looked equally shocked, tripping and tumbling as their dates dragged them down the avenue like just another one of their equipment cases. The moment they started to protest in earnest, a red awning bearing some illegible name came into view and they were whisked inside.

Once stationary, euphoria and vulnerability battled for equal footing inside Emily. She wanted nothing more than to be alone with Andrew, and even the press of his lips to her temple as they passed through a set of thick velvet drapes to the club beyond did little to shake off her ever growing feeling of helplessness.

The room was dusky, as if the smoke that had once permeated every square inch had never truly blown away, and it was packed with people crowded around café tables, their faces illuminated by a collection of mismatched votive candles crammed into shot glasses. The only other light was provided by a nicotine-stained crystal chandelier.

She watched as the men shelled out a king's ransom to a host, who led them to two tables pushed together in front of the small stage where a drum set and two guitars sat idle.

"Excellent," said Andrew. "They must be between sets."

In desperate need of a moment, Emily excused herself and headed for the restrooms, her roommates, unfortunately though not unexpectedly, in tow. Sensing her mood, they did not cross-examine her too harshly, and she made it a point to keep her ring out of sight, not wanting to explain the significance of it right now. They would have too many questions she couldn't answer.

But unable to keep from venturing into that forbidden territory for long, Margot cleared her throat after having finished reapplying her lipstick to her satisfaction. "Back there in the alley, that's quite unlike you. Highly unlike you."

"Maybe," Emily answered quietly.

"You're being careful, right?"

"It wasn't exactly like that."

"So you're saying that screaming was because he was…because you were…sweet Jesus…But all joking aside, you should be careful regardless, they're heading out soon. You know that, don't you?"

Zoey's smile vanished. "When did you hear that?"

"When do you think? While standing in line for garlic fries and a beer. Things are heating up for them, with *Rolling Stone* and all. Simon thought they'd be back on the road in a few weeks, if not sooner."

"Weeks." Zoey repeated the word, watching as the water washed down the drain.

"Weeks," Emily repeated. She knew Andrew had to go on tour soon, he had said as much at dinner, but hearing "soon" quantified was another matter entirely. She twisted the ring on her hand, now hidden deep in the pocket of her coat. She realized that her fear of losing him for good had been replaced with the truth she couldn't avoid, the truth she kept coming back to again and again: how would she fit in with his life as a musician when they were always separated by time and distance? She had been in a few relationships before, but nothing like this. Nothing could compare. Yet for all they had in their favor, they had so many things going against them. They knew so little of each other. How were they supposed to build a lifetime together when they were destined to spend it apart?

Yet as she made her way back to the table, she promised herself she wouldn't dwell on the unknowns right now; tonight was a night to celebrate. They were together, and he had traveled halfway around the world to find her, a world he was about to take by storm.

Her determination, however, made the color bright on her cheeks, which Andrew mistook for embarrassment. His eyebrows rose in question as he stood and pulled out the chair next to him, taking her coat from her shoulders. With one arm draped around her, he pulled her close to his side, his fingers lingering on the beads of her dress.

"You're blushing."

"I did not break under interrogation, you'll be happy to know," she murmured back to him.

"Then they don't know how to interrogate you properly."

He leaned forward menacingly, and she drew away from his clutches in feigned alarm. But a moment later, his eyes darted toward the door to see Neil St. John entering the club. On instinct Emily raised her hand, causing everyone else at the table to look in the direction in which she was waving. Neil nodded in response, although a bit bluntly, even given his normally aloof demeanor. It was then that Emily noticed the woman by his side.

It was as if *Vogue* and *The Wall Street Journal* had mated and out of their pages had sprung this creature. That was the only explanation Emily could think of as she stared at her. She dressed as though she were French, in a burgundy trench coat and matching open-laced heels, and seemed able to accessorize to the smallest detail, down to tying the perfect knot and choosing stunning yet understated jewelry. Emily felt sure that she would even smell expensive. The woman's hair was the only thing that appeared ruffled, falling loose around her face in long, creamy curls. Creamy, blond curls.

*Ahhh…*Emily finally understood Andrew's earlier reluctance at dinner while describing the agent, whom she automatically assumed had to be this woman. Why did men have the uncanny knack to forget essentials when it came to other women?

To her left stood a handsome man with thick black hair, his glasses and leather jacket also black and stylish. He seemed bored with the surroundings and attentive only to her. They were escorted to a table on the opposite side of the room, the last empty one in the house.

Emily was about to ask Andrew about the woman when she realized she had lost his attention entirely. An elderly black man had shuffled up onto the stage, the room quieting down in respect as he did so. The man's gnarled hands tuned the guitar he took off the stand. Age spots and dark moles spread out across his cheeks so that his leathery skin appeared mottled; his ears and nose had grown large with time, filled with an outcropping of gray hairs. His teeth, what were left of them, held his smile. Despite the ravages of time, his face looked beautiful to her; it was so very alive.

Andrew sat enthralled by the sight of him, his mind miles away, and Christian and Simon seemed just as smitten. After the old man finished up his first number to warm applause, he cleared the gravel from his throat as if getting ready to tell a story. The microphone squawked a bit when he adjusted it, making him cringe in surprise before he settled back on his stool with a smile.

"Now don't you think I don't see you out there in the shadows, boy, 'cause I do. These eyes may be gettin' on, but the mind's just as sharp. You hop on up here if you know what's good for you, 'cause I ain't getting no younger. Yeah, you boy, get your boney English ass on up here rhat now."

Andrew obeyed without question, and ducking his head with reserve, he walked to the stage. A murmur passed through the crowd, and Emily swore she could hear Andrew's name being repeated on many lips, along with the familiar sound of a bevy of women's sighs, of course. Andrew held his hand out in greeting, but the old man looked at him with a kind of "pshsaw" gesture and grabbed Andrew into a massive bear hug before slapping him on the back.

Emily leaned back in her chair, dumbfounded. In response, Christian slid his chair next to her and smiled. "His name is Clarence Memphis Green. He is one of best, if not the greatest, bluesmen alive. Extremely underrated, though. He also adores Andrew."

Her eyebrows rose as she met Christian's serene face. Christian was a musician, and like all musicians belonged to a club that folk like Emily could only admire from afar. "Andrew rode on a freight car with Memphis for weeks. Nothing but his guitar and the clothes on his back. Wrote some of the most incredible music afterward."

"But I thought you were touring all the time. When did he do that?"

Christian's face stilled, and his eyes flickered at her and then to Andrew. "A while back. We were down South, near my home. Andrew had—well, he was really burned out, that's all—we call it his Jack Kerouac phase. He just rode the rails and slept on hay and learned from the master. He said Memphis didn't know what to make of him in the beginning, swore he was Mexican, but couldn't understand what a skinny Mexican kid was doing with an English accent. But you know Andrew, he could sell coal to the devil, and it didn't take long before Memphis took him under his wing. He's like a son to him, I guess. Being a bluesman, you're never in one place long enough to have one of your own."

Christian's words stayed between them. *You're never in one place long enough.* She ignored them and instead asked him pointedly, "Why would he go off all alone?" But at that moment Memphis had started to hum.

He had handed Andrew an old guitar, which Andrew took reverently before he sat down on a nearby wooden stool and began to play. Soon the humming joined the moving chords, and Andrew closed his eyes.

The regular din of conversation had ebbed away; the audience had become transfixed by the sound of wood and strings. Emily watched the crowd take Andrew in, and from across the room she saw Neil stare at him as well, with what could only be described as pride. The sight made her throat unexpectedly tight. She had heard enough about Neil's history to learn that while he had always appeared cordial to her, he was not a happy man, and definitely not a satisfied one. Now, it looked as if he had found a missing piece.

Memphis began to sing, pulling her attention back to the stage. With subdued respect, Andrew accompanied the bluesman. The song twanged sadly and ended with an old spiritual refrain, one everyone knew and could sing, and a few did so.

After the applause, Memphis took the microphone. "Well now, that ain't too bad, don't y'all think? Why don't you do something? Some of what I learned you." Hoots of agreement came from all around, making the old man smile and shake his head.

Andrew raised his eyebrows in surprise. He must have known the old man wouldn't take no for an answer, and the continued shouts from the crowd only added to the inducement. With that, Memphis positioned the microphone in front of Andrew's seat. The bright light focused on the stage made Andrew squint out into the audience.

"Thank you, sir," he said with deep affection. "What should I play?" He strummed while he addressed the old man, as he did whenever he held a guitar, playing, always playing.

"Do that little one she liked so much. The one you used to do for her when your heart was all busted up, when she went away."

Andrew's strumming caught; he was studying the strings now, something she had never seen him do. He appeared to be stalling for time while his fingers began to plink away at the notes, and he tried to find his bearings. When at last he raised his eyes, they were a sea of blue glass. He spoke quietly into the microphone. "This is for her. For my muse. Because I found her, and because she said yes."

The song was simple, more poem than anything else, and his voice was rife with heartbreak. Emily could hear Zoey sniffle next to her, and Christian chuckled softly and pulled her closer in response. Simon said nothing to Margot, though he had not moved his hand from where it lay next to hers on the table.

Andrew's strumming grew stronger and fiercer. Feelings overflowed in her. Jealously. Anger. Confusion. Love.

What did the old man mean "when she went away?" When his muse went away? But she was his muse. She remembered Andrew's words, that the thought of her had been with him his whole life. But she had always believed him to mean something romantic, not painful, not controlling. Not real.

Finally, the music quieted to only the vibrations of the strings and the whisper of his voice. When he finished, Andrew placed his hands on the strings and closed his eyes as he did whenever he played anything close to his heart. The applause was shattering. Memphis sat back as if to say "look at your bad self," and gave him one last smack on the back before Andrew politely waved to the crowd and hustled his way back to the table.

Once there, he took a long drink of water and sat back in his chair, clearly self-conscious. Memphis began another song as Andrew glanced at Emily, his glass still at his lips.

"That was—"

"For you," he said quietly, and swallowed a huge gulp.

"You traveled with him, in a train?" cried Zoey in disbelief; evidently Christian had told her the story as well.

"With chickens."

"No. You're shitting me."

"Right hand to God." Andrew waved the waitress down for another drink. "I get wicked thirsty when I sing, sorry." He glanced to Emily before returning his attention to Zoey. "Yes, I spent some time with him, and it was amazing. Ah, Neil's still here." Then he looked past them and waved his hand in an effort to change the conversation.

"Andrew," Emily asked. "About what Memphis said?"

"Andrew, your fans cometh," Margot said, her voice less than gracious. She gestured to the blonde who had gotten out of her seat and was slinking toward them.

"Fan doesn't seem to suit her job description," Emily muttered.

"No it doesn't, but they're coming over now, and I'd hate to have to snog you senseless on this table to prove a point. Be nice."

"Andrew, gentlemen, what a pleasure," S.J. said, her voice dark like smoked glass. She glanced between Margot and Zoey before her gaze settled on Emily. "This is my colleague, Robert Bolen. He'll be working with Glenn Sommers, the writer from *Rolling Stone* I mentioned over lunch today. Fancy running into you tonight. I didn't realize you guys hung with itinerant bluesmen."

Emily dug her nails into Andrew's knee. "Ow. Um—yes. S.J., permit me to introduce Ms. Zoey Cohen, Dr. Margot Larson, and Ms. Emily Thomas. Ladies, this is S.J. Gordian."

S.J. nodded in greeting to each of them before stopping at Emily. "What an interesting name. Emily Thomas—it's rather old fashioned."

"And yours too. Rather mythological."

Neil appeared at that moment, saving Emily from ruining Andrew's career.

"How is everyone doing this evening? Mr. Green is amazing, isn't he? And you, Andrew, you were—"

"Phenomenal." S.J. zeroed in her attention on Andrew, ignoring the rest.

"If anyone is phenomenal, it's Memphis," Andrew replied, blushing as he finished off the last of his drink.

"There's a distinct difference between hearing music on a track and hearing it live, from the lips, as it were. Don't you think, Neil? How long have you known about this man, really? Were you holding out on me?"

"Of course I was," Neil said with more than a hint of condescension. "It's what keeps me awake at nights. How to make your life even more difficult, S.J."

Robert snapped a few shots as if this was his only form of discourse.

"It seems Mr. Green has a question for you," S.J. whispered to Andrew.

He excused himself, leaving an awkward silence in his wake, but he soon returned, and his face was alight with enthusiasm. "He wants us to play."

"You're shitting me," Christian muttered. "Really?"

"Our choice."

"Hell," was all Simon could utter.

"So what's it going to be? Nothing sedate. Boy band rubbish, mate?" Andrew asked Simon and neatly ducked a blow.

"Boy band what?" S.J. asked.

"You know," said Christian, barely able to talk through his laughter. "It's Simon's deepest darkest secret. He wants to be every twelve-year-old girl's fantasy. Two guys wailing into one microphone with the big bad drummer in the middle, pounding away."

"Then by all means," said S.J. enthusiastically.

With evil smiles all around, the three men jumped up onto the stage. Memphis took the microphone.

"Looks like we got ourselves an extra treat this evening. I've heard these boys play, so y'all might want to hold onto your woman or man or whatever you got next to you, but that's just 'cause I'll be playing along." He chortled and moved his chair to the side, taking out a harmonica and beaming from ear to ear.

Simon took his place behind the drums, sizing them up, and Christian draped the bass over his shoulder and strummed a bit, getting comfortable, while Andrew took hold of the guitar he had been playing.

"Oh dear God," muttered Zoey at the sight of all three of them up there.

Christian was right. There was something about two men at one microphone and one behind a set of drums that could make even a twenty-something group of women with ample education fall to pieces. Andrew started counting off, and then his hand struck his guitar. Zoey started screaming as the beginning chords exploded. Christian's face plastered against Andrew's as their lips blazoned the lyrics into the microphone. Simon pounded the drums with wanton frustration of a song about sex, about wanting it and not having it, then having it but not getting enough of it. It was a wonder they remained standing.

Christian, usually sedate on bass, had his face contorted into some gorgeous pseudo-coital expression that was riveting. And Andrew, oh Andrew, he was just too elated, too on fire to do anything but smile and cock his head like a teenage boy, then fall back, purse his lips, and tear into a wild, inhuman riff. By the time they hit the bridge with the requisite "oooos" wailed in tandem and their sweaty cheeks pressed together, the crowd was on its feet.

Possessed by the sound, people began to dance, rocking, pounding their feet. Those who weren't dancing stood on chairs to get a better look at the stage as Simon smashed away on the drums and Andrew improvised, his fingers on fire.

Out of nowhere, Neil took Emily's hand and pulled her out of her seat. He swung her into the horde and began to dance, and they laughed so hard they almost fell down. It was a side of him she had never seen. A wave of elation crashed over everyone, and they were singing and dancing; the old were young again, and the young were unleashed. The photographer was firing pictures off so fast he seemed like a strobe light with legs. And S.J. was mesmerized.

Neil spotted her too, and made a sound in the back of his throat as he spun Emily around hard.

"Neil," she shouted over the din. "What's wrong?"

She could only hear bits and pieces of what he was saying; the riot around them was too loud. "She promised the photo shoot, that's it. That's the only reason—she would have never—And now she wants to sign them. They need someone else. She'll only—never mind. Forget it."

Determined to keep him talking and knowing from the look on his face that she probably would not get any more information about S.J. from him, she plumbed her mind for anything they might have in common. "I've been doing some research about your house for a paper of mine for school. I was wondering if you knew anything about the previous owners. Or any history of the house."

"I bought the place about ten years ago in an estate auction," he yelled to her over the commotion. "I never met the owner." They danced a bit more before he lowered his lips to her ear. "My wife was getting her treatment at UC, the location was convenient, and she adored it." She had to strain to hear him now and stood on her tiptoes. "She didn't want to die in a hospital. We had hospice until the end."

She looked up to him. "I'm so sorry."

Before she could ask another question, The Lost Boys finished with one last scream. The crowd went wild, stomping and clapping and demanding more, but Andrew shook his head and held his hand out. "Thank you, good evening," he managed to shout through the racket. "'Twas a pleasure." Christian and Simon smiled and waved, and with that they trotted off the stage.

Neil looked on as Andrew took Emily in his arms and swirled her around, laughing as he kissed her. He was riding the high of performing, buzzing with infectious energy. People had started to swamp them, asking for their autographs. The guys signed a few bar napkins graciously; Simon grinned as two girls giggled like crazy and snapped his picture on their phone. Across the room, S.J. began to make her way toward them.

"Let's all get out of here," Andrew announced to their table.

"Excellent idea!" Without hesitating, Emily grabbed his hand and all of them, Neil included, headed for the door.

They dashed into two taxis, yelling back and forth on where to go next, and decided on a nearby club in an attempt to burn off their newfound energy. Once there, Neil opted out of dancing, and with a rare smile at Emily claimed the best partner was taken and excused himself to make a few calls at the bar.

"We won't be long," she promised him and felt a twinge watching him stand alone.

After slamming down endless shots, the guys hauled the girls off to the dance floor and into a throng of gyrating, feverish bodies, the music blaring in their ears. Emily couldn't make out Christian or Zoey in the flashes of light that pierced the blackness as the beat pounded up through the floor. Simon was visible, along with what remained of his tuxedo. He shook a pack of cigarettes in Margot's direction and cocked his head toward the exit.

"No! I want to dance," she said in a challenge. He threw the pack over his shoulder and swung her madly into the crowd. Emily could almost hear her laughter over the blare.

That left Andrew. Smiling like Satan himself, he circled her slowly and then placed one hand on her hip and one on the side of her face. He seductively drew her to him, leaving nothing but his lust between them. His lips trailed along her cheekbone.

"You were made perfectly to be loved—and surely I have loved you, in the idea of you, my whole life long."

He spoke the words of Browning as though he had written them. His arms wound around her waist, and he kissed her with abandon, then pressed against her, melting into the music. Her mind raced with unanswered questions, but she could only throw her head back as his mouth devoured her neck, her eyes falling shut.

The music and the tequila ignited stars of arousal behind her lids, a maddening, dizzying hunger rampant again between them. He could feel her surrender, and he forced himself hard against her, the song getting louder and raunchier by the second. He gazed down at her, his hands tight on her hips.

"How? How can I want you like this? I was raised better than this, you must know. With manners and etiquette. So proper, so poised at all times. If you cut me, I swear it'll run blue. My father's people were all the epitome of English culture, Emily. My mum, Christ, she'd die a thousand deaths if she knew what I'm thinking of doing to you right now. There's sanity in this head, I swear.

"I wasn't raised to want to keep you tied up in a bed. I wasn't raised to want to keep you as my slave, my whore." His mouth was hot against her skin as he gasped the words, making her moan. "I adore you beyond reckoning, but one look from those exquisite eyes and I'm no longer sane. And it terrifies me as much as I crave it. Crave you. Because the longer I'm with you, the longer I touch this skin and kiss this mouth, the more I can't control it, and it kills me and…I love it."

His mouth collided with hers. She kissed him back, channeling all the passion and fears she possessed, letting him know she felt the same torture, the same inexplicable longing, and she feared drowning in it too but was unwilling to do anything to stop it.

We are lost. So gloriously lost.

Later, after the men had mercifully burned off some of their energy and the women had begged for a reprieve, they ended up at a neighborhood favorite, Mad Dog in the Fog, an English pub not far from their home. There they offered the type of Guinness Simon demanded, the darts Christian was dying for, and the booths where Emily could put her aching feet up while keeping Andrew at arm's length. The women were exhausted, but by the looks of things, the men had just started the evening. Neil had not yet bid them goodnight but sat tending his drink, watching them all.

Somewhere after the second round, the bartender announced that it was trivia night. The somewhat blitzed bunch looked to Andrew, and he waved his Guinness in the air as if to say *bring it on*.

The topic was 1960s music. Periodically, the bartender would shout out some question to which the three of them would fire back a response. It quickly became embarrassing; death glares came their way from both a group of tourists and a rather drunk Irish soccer team. During an intense moment of Christian and Simon arguing over whether it was the heroin or the alcohol that killed Janis Joplin, Neil leveled Andrew with a cool stare. "If S.J. wanted you before, she's going to really want you now, you know that. That little performance back there clinched the deal."

Emily couldn't tell if Neil had spoken in jest. Andrew merely sipped his Guinness and shrugged his shoulders. "Doesn't matter. We're doing the photo shoot, period."

"What?" said Simon, breaking off from his argument in mid-sentence.

"I don't trust her."

"But what happens if I do?"

"The woman's a shark."

"And your point is? What better kind of person to have rep us? We don't have to love her — we just need her to do her job."

"Can't we have both?"

"Yeah, and I'm going to grow a third tit. 'Tisn't possible, Paulie."

Neil put down his drink. "I wouldn't say that." The three men stared at him. "There are a lot of talented people out there, seasoned people, people who know the ropes, who would be lucky to take you gentlemen on. I know quite a few."

Andrew shot Simon a long look, a look that had *I told you he wouldn't take us on* written all over it. "So you changed your mind about managers, Simon? Since your previous plans seem to have fallen flat?"

"No, I'm being realistic. Isn't that the word you're always using? So the way I see it, one in the hand, as they say. We can't wait around forever. This woman is at the top of her game, right? She's also fronting some serious talent, so why not let her work her magic for us? Andrew, shit, we can't go back out there and have you do it all by yourself again. We're in this to make it, and I don't want to make it without you, but I don't want to wake up one day and be some gray-haired old geezer telling my kids about how I played backup for some other band. Some band they idolize. Fuck, the only thing more pathetic than old rocker has-beens is old rocker wannabes. This is our time, man. What are you afraid of?"

No one said a word. Andrew silently stared up at the bar.

"You three are the best I have seen in a long, long time," Neil said levelly, breaking the tension. "Plus, you're intelligent and grounded. You're willing to work hard, and you're loyal to each other. Simon is right. Your time to step up is now."

"Neil…" Andrew began.

"Let me finish. You need to think about this, talk about it amongst yourselves. It's a huge step, an important and hopefully life-long relationship, not something you can decide over a few beers. S.J. is very successful — that is true — there's no denying that. But there are other things to consider."

"You don't want us to sign with her, do you? Why?" Andrew asked.

"My feelings about S.J. should not factor into your decision."

"Like hell they don't. What gives?"

Neil looked uncomfortable; he took a swig of his drink before he spoke. Emily had never heard Neil speak so candidly. This whole evening was full of surprises. "S.J. is famous for her mergers and acquisitions, insofar that she signs the talent then vivisects the band. Her *modus operandi* is to front the group, then go in for the kill and launch solo careers. I've seen her do it with her last several bands. It's a pattern."

"So you don't trust her?" Christian leaned forward on the table.

"I don't trust anyone in this business. Let's just say I don't care for her technique. I could be wrong in this case, but I never am."

"Never?" Andrew asked, clearly intrigued by the content and tone of what Neil had just said.

"Only once." Neil stared back at Andrew, his eyes a million miles away and yet totally focused on the young man that sat before him. "About a woman, actually, a very beautiful woman, but I get maudlin when I drink, so there."

His eyes flashed to Emily, who knew he was thinking about his wife, and something inside of her wanted to reach out and take his hand.

"What I want to say to you gentlemen is that most of all, you need to do what feels right. Trust me, I know. This business has been in my blood since I heard my first live band. When I hear you play, I remember what I felt like back in London in the basement of that club, when I was younger than you are now. I'd forgotten that. You really don't understand how great you are. It would be an honor for anyone to represent you. Just give yourselves a little more time before you make any commitments. You need to know who to trust."

The band looked thoughtful and sat back in their chairs; the air around them seemed electric, alive with beginnings and fraught with peril.

"Whatever we do, we do it together, understood?" Andrew said. They all nodded. Without another word, the three of them held up their glasses and smashed them together.

"Okay, enough of this," Christian cried. "Now let's celebrate—Jesus, we're going to be on the cover of *Rolling Stone* for fuck's sake!"

"Waiter!" cried Andrew, laughing. "Another round!"

They all cheered and raised their glasses. "To The Lost Boys!"

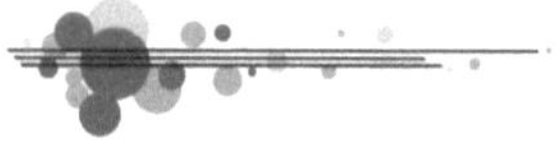

By the time they staggered up their street, they were all pleasantly buzzed and singing at the top of their lungs. A few neighbors' lights went on, and several dogs started to howl.

Christian howled in return. His arm hung over Zoey's shoulder. She had a long-stemmed rose in her teeth, one of their winnings from the trivia contest.

Simon and Margot orbited each other. Simon eyed her over his glasses, shepherding her to stay on the sidewalk and not stray into the hedges and bushes that lined the road. Behind them, Neil held a bottle of wine, and although equally tipsy, he was definitely the adult supervision of the group. In the back of the pack, Andrew would stop Emily every few feet to kiss her and break into either laughter or song, using a Guinness bottle as a microphone.

They passed a tree, and before she could stop him, Andrew swung himself up into the branches.

"Andrew!" she hissed. "Get down! You'll break your neck!"

"'T'ain't my neck you should be worried about, darlin'."

"Your hands then!"

"'T'ain't me hands neither."

"Why are you speakin' Irish?"

"I was going for Scottish. Bugger."

"Get out of that tree this instant, we're losing them!" She pointed to the wayward party wobbling on ahead.

"Only if you promise me sometin'."

"Anything, but please get out of the tree."

A second later he began to climb dangerously higher and higher into the branches. Without warning, he sailed down the trunk with a whoop. She screamed.

His hand caught hold of a limb, and his face slung down inches from hers. She screamed again. "My ears, woman. Please. Now listen, I shall only get out of this shrub—"

"It's a tree."

"Whatever. I shall only get out of this tree-shrub if you promise me something. Else I'll sit in here like I'm in bloody Greenpeace."

"You're insane, you know that? Yes, anything, what?"

"Marry me."

Her heart skipped a beat, and she stared at his sloppy smile and tried not to laugh. "Didn't we just—anyway, you cannot propose to me hanging from a tree."

"Then I shall get down on one knee. See. There. Emily Thomas, would you do me the honor—aaaaahhh!"

In a flailing rush of leaves and flying arms, he fell off the branch and crashed into a bush below. White flowers exploded everywhere. She launched over to his prone body and tried to pull him out, but before she could find him in the darkened mass of greenery, two arms shot out and grabbed hold of her.

He rolled her out of the bush, over and over onto a lawn. Once she had caught her breath and stopped laughing, he stared down at her, and when he spoke, his voice was strangely hoarse and surprisingly sober. So sober, in fact, she wondered how drunk he really was.

"I love you, Emily." His breath was uneven and tasted of barley, and his eyes glowed like the stars in the sky above him. "Marry me. Now, not later."

She blinked back at him in shock. He probably wouldn't remember a word of this tomorrow morning, she knew that, and for some inexplicable reason it made her want to cry. Swallowing down her hurt, she shimmied out from underneath him. Too overcome to say another word, she stumbled to her feet and, after a second, latched onto his hand and yanked as hard as she could. He staggered upright, crashing into her, his arms flailing around her waist.

"Easy there, cowboy. Let's get you home."

He began to sing as they hobbled along, and she blew the hair out of her eyes. Her mind raced in circles, wondering if his drunken proposal was how he truly felt, if those words were locked in his heart and he couldn't find the courage to voice them earlier. And were they the words she truly wanted to hear but was too afraid to ask?

She hazarded another question, knowing that if he was indeed drunk, she wasn't playing fair. "Andrew, why did you go on that train with Memphis?"

He glanced at her from the corner of his eyes and grinned. "I liked the chickens."

"What the fuck?" Simon cried ahead of them.

A dilapidated Volkswagen minibus sat parked on the street in front of their house; its windows were fogged over and the sides dented. The bumper was held in place by a slew of stickers that read: *My other car is a broom, Every day's a holiday when you're pagan!* and *Get a taste of religion. Lick a witch.*

Andrew and Christian started inventing their own sayings, causing the next-door neighbor's dog to yowl, finally settling on *Something Wiccan this way comes.*

"That's cleber," Emily told them, beginning to feel the result of the countless drinks she'd ingested tonight, but still wanting an answer to her question.

"Berry, berry cleber. That's why you love me," Andrew replied.

"Berry, berry much."

"Andrew," Emily ventured, finding courage from God knows where, knowing she might never have another chance. "About what you said back there on the lawn, a little clarification would be nice—"

"Huh?" said Andrew, staring at their house. Candlelight was shining from the lower bay window. All at once, Emily got a sinking feeling in her spinning head that had nothing to do with alcohol.

The five of them tumbled up the stairs, and after much fumbling, Neil finally took hold of the keys and opened the door. He handed them back to Andrew who, with a growing sense of sobriety, quickly unlocked his front door and swung it open.

It was dark and difficult to see at first. The air was heavy with pot, but candles lit the room well enough to make out a series of shapes. Emily frantically pushed Zoey aside and approached a large table draped in a dark velvet cloth and covered with lighted tapers, chairs surrounding it. Three were occupied.

"Dwayne?" she stuttered, immediately recognizing the tattooed palm reader-security guard. "What are you doing here? Oh God." She spun about, panicked. "Where's Nora? Tell me you didn't smoke Nora."

Dwayne looked to either side, where Dinesh from the Columbarium and a man she didn't recognize sat, and began to open his mouth. Suddenly, a beautiful woman stepped out from the shadows.

"Andrew," she cried in greeting, arms outstretched.

"Mum?" Andrew stammered in disbelief.

"Mum?" Emily gasped. "Oh hell." She tried to straighten her clothes and hair.

"C.C.?" Neil whispered. A look of amazement blanketed his face.

At the sound of his voice, Andrew's mother stopped dead in her tracks. "Lainey."

"C.C.?" Andrew did a double take between his mother and Neil.

"Lainey…" she said tentatively.

"Righteous!" Dwayne cried.

"What the hell are you people doing in my living room?" demanded Simon.

Thank God someone had a knack for the essentials.

"Yo, Muse-lady, you live here too?" Dwayne crowed, stepping away from the candlelit table to greet Emily.

The rest of the crowd remained silent. The previous rapid fire greetings had rendered everyone slack jawed and speechless. Emily was most concerned about Andrew, not sure what he would say or how he would act given his current state of drunkenness, but the steady stare he leveled at his mother told her he might be far more sober than she suspected.

"Righteous seeing you again!" Dwayne beamed. "Imagine me standing in your living room when only a few days ago you were running up and down my al-ter-na-tive working establishment." His mangy mop of hair bounced like a bobble-headed dashboard dog while he turned about, taking in the demolished state of the walls and ceiling before swinging his hazy focus back to her. "You're looking better than the last time I saw you, I've got to say—had me kind of concerned there…still a little gnarly with the sticks in the hair and all, but who am I to judge, right?"

Her hands flew to her head, feeling the undeniable presence of twigs and blades of grass. Oh God, what must she look like?

"Hey, you ever find those ashes you were looking for?"

Nora! She had totally forgotten about Nora. The living room reeked with the smell of pot, and she panicked with the thought that her ashes might be burning, but then she remembered: Nora was safe on their fireplace mantle upstairs. A lungful of trapped air escaped her, and she stuttered a few unintelligible words, grappling with what she could possibly say to him.

Well, yes, Dwayne, I did in fact find Nora's ashes, thank you very much. And I smuggled them out in the business end of your bong—hope you don't mind.

From the foggy grin on his face though, Emily was fairly certain Dwayne didn't miss his bong, as he was busy putting out a recently sparked doobie in his Starbucks cup. But what in the world was he doing in the middle of Andrew's living room surrounded by his fellow baked comrades in the midst of what looked frighteningly like a séance? It was either that or the most bizarre Goth poker game ever.

"Emily…it's Emily, right?" Dwayne asked her on the Q.T. with a whisper in her ear. "Which one of these amigos is named Andrew? Please tell me it ain't John Lennon over there." He gestured toward Simon, who had already lit up a cigarette. "Or is it the guy that came in with you to the shop? Now that would be totally awesome. The uptight English dude with the matching palm who owns, like…your soul? No offense, I'm talking, like, metaphysically."

"Andrew?"

"Righteous." Dwayne waved at Andrew in recognition, then looked back to her with a faraway glaze in his eyes. "Man, that's one lucky bastard. I wish I had a woman who was put on this earth to be like my number one love slave. Imagine lifetimes of that shit. Yo, it must be like a supernova when you get it on. How do you stand it? Hard wired to want nothing but to sa-tis-fy…Listen, if you ever get tired of him, change your mind or anything, wanna branch out…"

Andrew stepped forward and clamped his hand on Dwayne's shoulder. "Not in this…or any other lifetime."

Dwayne stumbled back a step or two as Andrew's tall, black-coated figure loomed over him. "Nice to see you again, man," Dwayne replied, his soul patch and mustache quivering a bit in apology. "Sorry to be crashing your pad and everything, but dude, you gotta put us out of our misery. Dinesh and I haven't been able to sleep, like for seventy-two straight hours. Seems there's a friend of one of your friends here that's dying—well, he would die if he could—sucks to be him, I guess." He snorted at his own joke.

"Dwayne." The third man of their trio, the one Emily didn't recognize, chided him. His long black hair shook, and his multiple facial piercings clacked together like beaded curtains.

"Egan here's right," said Dinesh, the musician Emily remembered from the Columbarium. The black-haired man nodded in acknowledgment and shook the sleeves of his flowing purple caftan that was embossed with gold stars. "Don't dis the sprits, man. Karma is a bitch. You'll come back as a 'possum or some other shit."

"Sorry, it's just that this spirit is righteously empowered and needs to talk. Gave us directions to your domicile and everything. We were camping out here most of the night and saw C.C. here, I mean Claudia, sorry Mom-lady. Well, we saw her dropped off in a cab, and since your door was already open—"

"What do you mean our door was open?" Andrew turned to his mother. "C.C.?" His sharply-arched voice rose along with his eyebrows.

Tall and handsome like a Goya painting brought to life, Andrew's mother was still standing motionless across the room. Her eyes reflected the candlelight as they flashed away from Neil. Sky blue and surrounded by the same black lashes as her son's, they blinked wide and questioning. The soft, light-brown planes of her face, again so much like Andrew's, were framed instead by thick, black waves that had fallen loose from a wide braid at her neck, which her fingers fussed with distractedly.

"Yes?"

"The door, Mum?"

"Andrew, the outside door was unlocked when I arrived—and your door was wide open. I thought you were home, especially after Mr. Cobshib explained his situation." She took a step closer to him and lowered her voice, a voice that bore a faint trace of a Spanish accent and the lilt of an English one. "Dear, you know how I am with anything to do with the supernatural. And after my dream and then our phone conversation when you sounded so terribly upset, I cut my visit short in New York and rushed out here. He claimed to know you, so I let him in. He, um, looks like the type of person you might know in your profession. A roadie? Is that what you call them?"

Emily could hear Simon chuckle next to her.

"Christ, Mum."

"Language, Andrew."

He scrubbed his hand across the back of his neck and made halting introductions. The guys evidently knew Andrew's mother well and hugged her warmly, maybe a bit too warmly due to their gargantuan intake of alcohol. She didn't seem to mind and responded with smiles and ruffles of their hair. Emily was devoutly thankful that Margot and Zoey, given their own inebriated state, merely nodded to her politely. All she needed was for Zoey to launch into a play by play of what had transpired earlier on the hood of the car…

Finally, Andrew came to Emily.

"Emily, may I introduce you to my mother, Claudia Hayes. Mum, this is my—"

It seemed that Andrew was having difficulty in finding his words. "I found her, Mum," he said softly. "May I introduce Miss Emily Thomas. My muse."

Did Emily imagine it, or did Claudia's eyes widen in alarm at the sight of her? And did Simon actually swear? "Andrew," she uttered his name in stunned disbelief.

"It's a pleasure to meet you, Mrs. Hayes." Emily went to shake her hand, but Claudia recoiled. Emily looked to Andrew, whose shoulders had tensed, his lips pressed tight.

"Why do you look so surprised? I told you I was going to find her, and I did."

"Andrew—this is—I just can't—this is…"

Claudia's voice trailed off, but she continued to stare. Emily had no idea why Claudia looked at her in such a way; she actually appeared distraught. Had something died in her hair? Did she have love bites all over her neck? She glanced sideways at Andrew, but his sight never wavered from his mother.

"Oh, Andrew—"

Something passed between them, and his chin rose in defiance. He was as hurt and angry as Emily had ever seen him. His voice was strangely tight as he stepped to the side and made the last introduction. "Neil," he said, though he did not look at him, "this is my mother, Claudia Hayes. Claudia, Neil St. John. I believe you two may have met?"

Met. The word hung ominously over their heads. Claudia looked like she had seen a ghost. Neither of them said a word, and neither of them moved an inch, only adding to the already stifling soap opera vibe in the room. There was nothing quite like meeting your lover's mother, Emily thought, while his mother's former lover was standing right behind you. They had to have been lovers; no one would look at another person like that unless they shared a past.

Neil reached out and took Claudia's hand. He tried to touch her casually, with a fluid gesture, in an attempt to mask the pure ache in his face and lessen the determined lines near his eyes where the muscles were so tight they lashed the skin across his cheekbones to the edge of his temples.

"I hate to break up the love fest here, fellow travelers," the caftan-wearing stoner priest named Egan announced, "but we cannot leave until we have a circle."

"A what?" Simon demanded.

"An open circle, to let the spirit world communicate with us," explained Dwayne. "Egan here is the best. He usually does closed circles, but he's doing me a favor to help me get some sleep. Slumming, like."

"It's two-thirty in the morning! Can't he do his fucking slumming somewhere else? Um, sorry, Mrs. Hayes."

"What? Oh, that's fine, Simon," Claudia murmured.

"You mean we're going to have a séance? A real live séance?" Zoey asked, wobbling tipsily on her chair.

"We don't call them séances anymore," Egan corrected her. "Please, everyone take a seat. The spirits are restless and may not linger long."

"We can only hope," Andrew muttered and raked his hand through his hair.

"Can't we at least have a cup of coffee before we communicate with the great beyond?" Margot begged through a hiccup, her boots clutched in her hands.

"Caffeine impedes the connection to the spirit world."

"Oh, puh-lease. Caffeine is the only damn thing that's going to keep me connected to this fucking world. Um, sorry there, Mrs. Hayes."

Claudia laughed softly and blew the hair from her eyes. Emily heard Neil's quick inhalation of breath from behind her.

"An underpinning of non-belief is going to hamper the flow of energy. I detect a strong level of animosity from the ebony-haired one here."

"Oh no," Emily mumbled under her breath. Andrew's eyes flashed to hers conspiratorially.

"You have a problem with Dr. Larson, mate?" Simon asked, the tattoos on his fingers visible on his fist.

Egan stuttered at the barely contained ire simmering before him. "None that I will speak of anymore."

Andrew rubbed his hand along the back of his neck again, clearly exasperated with the whole situation. "Well, good. Now give me one bloody good reason why I shouldn't be falling into bed right now."

Dwayne stood. "Noreen Thomas needs your help, dude!"

"What?"

"This Noreen Thomas, Nora, you call her, her vibrations are off the map, and she's in such a highly agitated state that she can't make contact, so a fellow spirit has stepped forward. Luckily, Egan here is adhering to a pretty strict drug regimen to keep his mind limber enough to absorb all this energy. I can't do it quite as well. Anyway, this spirit, the one who won't let me sleep, says he has some info—highly vital info in regards to Emily Thomas."

Everyone turned to gape at her.

"I'm Emily, Emily Thomas," she mumbled rather thinly.

"Dwayne," murmured Egan, "you said she was pretty, not beautiful. I had no idea. And this is the woman with the palm? The eternal concubine?" His eyebrow studs waggled lasciviously.

Claudia's breath caught. Emily cringed. Love slave, concubine, what a wonderful first impression she must be making…

Andrew clasped Emily's hand more tightly in his, sending death glares at Egan. He lowered his face to hers. "Emily, luv, would you like to do this? Would this help? If you don't want to we can send them packing. I'd be more than happy to oblige in that regard."

She nodded her head firmly. But at the same time, an unexplainable sense of unease began to well up in her, and his eyes darkened as though he was feeling it too. He opened his mouth to speak when Egan cried, "Excellent," and settled down in a chair, his robe puffing up around him, with his hands held out beckoning for all to join.

Andrew drew Emily closer to him, tilting his head to her ear. "Emily, what's wrong?"

She shook her head.

"Tell me."

"Nothing." She fought to hold her voice steady. Goose bumps had broken out up and down her arms, and her teeth had almost begun to rattle. The exhaustion, the excitement, and the alcohol must have frayed her nerves to make her this irrationally afraid.

Clearly unhappy, he drew out a chair for her, and across the table, at the exact same moment, Neil drew out a chair for Claudia. Each man observed the other from across the candle flames. Emily took hold of Andrew's hand and dragged him down into his seat.

"Thank you for not pulling your gun," she whispered. He didn't answer. His eyes were riveted upon the sight of Neil and Claudia's intertwined fingers.

Egan announced that they should close their eyes and bow their heads as if in prayer. The room fell quiet as a tomb. Minutes passed. Andrew's pulse beat steady in Emily's hand, his grip never lessening.

"What should we do next?" Zoey's voice was an insistent whisper. "Aren't we supposed to say something? I'm pretty sure we're supposed to say something."

"Shhhhhhh!" Egan hissed.

"Sorry, dude," Christian apologized, a thinly veiled look of remorse on his face. "But it might inspire confidence if you did say something."

Egan scowled at him and then gave a scathing look at Dwayne, who shrugged miserably. A few moments later, Egan began to make an "Ohm" sound, his piercings rattling. The temperature of the room dropped precipitously, causing Emily, already very familiar with the sensation, to shudder. Andrew laced his fingers protectively through hers, knowing what was to come.

"Love is the vibration of communication in the spirit world. Its presence enables transference to take place. Let us feel the love here between us, about us, above us, below us. From the pinnacle of our scalps unto the finality of our toes."

Zoey's knee banged the bottom of the table, and a rash of giggles choked in her throat. Oh good God. What was she up to now?

With a loud smack, Egan slammed a book onto the table, startling the living daylights out of everyone. Emily peeked through one eye and with a gasp saw it was *The Thin Man*.

"The circle is a safe place, the circle is an open place, the circle is one. We call upon the spirit of Dashol — Dashnel — Dashing — "

"Dashiell!" Emily hissed. Andrew squeezed her hand.

"What the lady said. Dashiell Hammett. You have something to tell us, something that this Nora Jones — "

"Thomas!" Emily seethed, making Christian rock with barely suppressed laughter.

"Something that Nora Thomas wants to impart." Dwayne took over. "Yo, spirit dude, writer of books about weight loss, help us in this hour."

Zoey toppled over in a spasm of laughter.

"What? That's the title," Dwayne reasoned aloud. "*The Thin Man.*"

Zoey used the momentary diversion to stretch out her leg, causing Christian to clench his eyes shut and mutter in prayer. Oh God, she wasn't doing what Emily thought she was doing. Not here. Not now.

"Mr. Hammond, sir," Dwayne continued, "Mr. Hammond, you seem like a talented dude. A writer and maker of organs."

With that, Andrew began to laugh, and Emily couldn't stop herself either. The tension of the last few minutes seemed to evaporate as Andrew squeezed Emily's hand even tighter, raising it to his lips to kiss. *God, I love you*, he mouthed silently, using the back of her hand to wipe away his tears. *You know the weirdest people.*

Dwayne coughed discreetly and resumed. "Mr. Hammond, join us in this circle and say what you need to say. And let me get some friggin' sleep, if it ain't too much to ask."

Christian went to open his mouth, sure to launch into some off color comment about organs, when a voice poured from his lips that made the hair on the back of Emily's neck stand on end.

"I'll be right with you, but at the moment I'm enjoying this sweetheart's most talented toes."

Zoey shrieked, and her foot presumably flew from Christian's crotch as they heard it hit the floor.

"Hell. It's been a long time, sister. Hate to offend, but Lillian was never into such feats."

Zoey's face paled as she stared at the hard-boiled voice coming from Christian's mouth. The room fell deathly still.

"Nice digs, this place. Always liked this house. Nick and I got drunk in that attic too many times to remember and played that gramophone of his till all hours. If people only knew how much I lifted off that man. They don't make 'em like that anymore. Not like Mr. Nicholas Chamberlain, that's for sure."

Not one soul bothered to shut their eyes anymore; they were all staring in horror at Christian, who was no longer Christian. Zoey appeared the most on edge, having just given a foot job to a dead man.

Neil sat up straight, his fingers clenched around the hand of an increasingly stricken Claudia.

"A heartbreak what happened with him and Nora, though. Now that was some dame. You could learn a thing or two from her, sweetie." Zoey recoiled in her chair and crossed her legs. "Nick didn't stand a chance, no man did around Nora. They were one of a kind, those two. Damn shame though, first the cliffs and then not being able to be together, even in fucking death. Uh, sorry there, Mrs. Hayes."

Claudia squeaked in fright.

"Now, which one of you fillies is Emily? Nora said she looked like a bookish version of Gene Tierney with good teeth, so that would be…" Christian scanned the circle, his expression sharp and shrewd, and his eyes glowed white in the darkness. They stopped dead, fixated on their target. "That would be you."

Emily was so scared she couldn't breathe, but she couldn't look away either. Andrew grasped her hand more fiercely.

"Hell. It's true, isn't it? She told me, and I wouldn't believe it. It's happening all over again. Damn," the spirit muttered.

"What's—what's happening again?" Andrew demanded. The spirit said nothing.

"He can't tell us, Andrew. There are rules, right? Nora told me about the rules."

"As smart as you are stunning, Miss Thomas."

"Is Nora all right? Is she in trouble? What does she need to tell us?"

"I can't say much, but I can give you the goods on who will. She's got it all in spades—all the information you'll need. But I've got to warn you, if you find her you're in for a world full of hurt."

"Why?"

"'Cause she wants you dead, sugar."

Andrew launched up from the table. Emily tried to seize hold of him, but he pushed her away.

"What the hell is going on?" he demanded through fixed teeth. "Christian, cut this shit out."

"It's not Christian you're talking to, lover boy. What's the matter? You want me to move locations?"

With that, Zoey seized and Christian's eyes flashed open. "Jesus, I feel sick," he groaned, blinking in confusion.

"There, you happy now?"

Andrew spun to face Zoey. She was speaking in the same exact voice that had come from Christian. He sat down in shock. "How? How are you doing this?"

"I hate to tell you, but all that medium bullshit is true. There's something about a drug-induced consciousness that allows us to break through. We can fry the less malleable mind."

"But you're not speaking through one of them, you're speaking through her."

"Yeah, I am. The medium's the conduit, but I can choose another body once I'm through. Hey, blackie. God, you're a looker." Christian and Simon stared in perverse fascination at the sight of Zoey hitting on Margot.

"Why not show up as a ghost?"

"We're limited to whom we can speak to in that form. Once we got a body, we're golden, as long as you don't die on us."

"Why?"

"It's near impossible to escape a suicide, and if we do survive, what's left is pretty gruesome. So, you want to sit here and talk about rotting ghosts, pal? Or you want to save your woman?"

Andrew nodded.

"I've only got limited time, so I'll cut to the chase. Nora is out of her mind, and she can't tell me why, but I've got my suspicions. If it's anything like last time, it can't be good. She wants you to find this Lady in Red, that's what people call her. The Lady in Red. Nora says you'll understand if you follow the message in the ring. The Lady in Red knows where Nick's ashes lie—and she knows all about the curse."

Suddenly Zoey convulsed. Christian launched to his feet and grabbed hold of her as she lurched back in her chair. Her eyes flew open, and she gasped; then just as quickly they rolled back into her head. "Shit, shouldn't have said that. Information overload. You need to act now. Follow the clues, that's the best you can do. If I tell you any more, I could hurt this girl. But listen, Emily, you are in some seriously bad danger."

"Why?"

"The ring. Use it. Nora's engagement ring. Your lover's gift to you, use it to solve what you haven't been able to." Again Zoey contorted. "The connection's ending. I've told you too much. I won't be able to pass through again."

"What danger? What danger am I in? Tell me!"

"Emily, don't fail. You can't fail!"

"Why? What will happen? Please!"

Zoey thrashed as though she was being beaten in the gut. Her hands flew to her hair, her face twisted in pain. Christian began yelling but not loud enough to block out the last two words that fell from her bloodless lips.

"You'll die."

With that, Zoey lashed backward like a contorted ragdoll, then fell forward, her multi-colored hair tumbling over her face. Egan cried out and collapsed onto the table as Andrew looked at Emily in horror.

The circle had ended. Dwayne grabbed another joint.

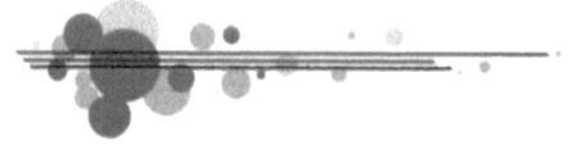

They were all alive. That's the best that could be said, Emily thought ruefully.

Huddled in the girls' kitchen, some were smoking while others were drinking. With the notable exception of Andrew, Claudia, and Neil.

Neil had departed immediately after the circle, pale and somber; he didn't even bid them good night. Lord only knew what he was thinking. Maybe they would all receive an eviction notice the next day.

The stoners, on the other hand, were heading out to party, totally jazzed that they had connected with the "next plane of consciousness." Before they left, they made Emily promise to use their services for any further spirit communications, and even tried to offer her a joint in thanks. Andrew had slammed the door shut in their faces.

After a wordless but forceful hug, he promised to join her as soon as he could and went off to get his mother situated for the night. Emily shuddered to imagine what that conversation would entail.

"If you ask me, it's all bloody bullshit," said Simon, scrambling eggs. The coffee had finished its hissed percolation and warmed the air with its familiar aroma. "And what did that Egan bloke mean about 'the spirit delving in areas far outside his purview'? Or why the hell did Andrew introduce you as…oh never mind."

Christian had his arms around Zoey, who was wrapped up in a blanket. He hadn't left her side since she'd convulsed on the table. Luckily she was unharmed, only pale and shaking and prey to periodic fits of laughter.

Margot, meanwhile, was deep in thought as she started to pour the coffee. Emily would have sworn her PhD mind would have dismissed everything as mumbo jumbo, but that wasn't the case. "It's all physics," she mumbled to herself. "The greater the force the spirit exerts on this world, the greater the natural world forces its way back. Rules. To every action there is an equal and opposite reaction."

"Rules, really?" Simon chided her, holding the frying pan out ready to serve. The kitchen clock read four a.m. They all looked like death warmed over.

"I don't know what to believe, honestly. All I know is that whatever it was, it wasn't Christian or Zoey. And it frightened me. And I don't do frightened."

Simon cast her a smile. "Nothing's going to happen to you, blackie."

"I'm not worried about myself. I don't have a death sentence hanging over my head. And what was all that talk about a ring?"

With great reluctance, Emily slipped the ring off her finger, sure something must be inscribed inside. No one said a word about its significance, though she was sure that would come soon. Simon, however, seemed especially irritated by the sight of it.

"Nothing that I can see." She shook her head, feeling tired and hopeless. A sense of panic was bubbling up inside of her. A ghost had just warned her that if she didn't act, and soon, she would be dead. Dead. Suddenly things had taken a horrible turn that she never could have expected. She needed to find Andrew and talk to him. She kept looking toward the dining room hoping to see him enter, but there was nothing there save shadows.

"Can I take a look at the ring?" Christian asked.

Emily handed it to him, and the diamonds and platinum refracted rainbows into the night. It was hard to believe it was truly Nora's ring. Had she worn it in this house? Had she ever taken it off her finger? Emily's hand felt naked without it, and she had only worn it for a few hours.

Christian ran his pinkie around the inside and frowned. "Hmmm." He reluctantly returned it. "So you need to find this Lady in Red, who not only wants you dead, but knows where Nick's ashes are located?"

"And this ring is supposed to show you how to find her?" Simon interrupted. "And if not, somebody's going to pop a cap in your head? Bullshit, I'm telling you. Hocus-pocus bullshit. It's fucking ridiculous, all of it."

"But Simon, I was talking with his voice, and you heard Zoey," Christian argued. "I keep telling you, you can't dis the ghost world, man. It's powerful stuff."

Simon shoveled a forkful of eggs into his mouth. "Where's Andrew? The food is getting cold."

"I think he's still with Claudia," Christian replied discreetly.

"Jesus, that can't be good."

Christian smacked him on the arm and nodded toward Emily.

"Well, it doesn't help that she met her old boyfriend and her son's nearly-dead muse all in one night."

Christian smacked Simon even harder.

"Maybe I should just stay away until I can figure this all out," Emily mumbled into her coffee. "Maybe it would be safer that way."

"Andrew won't let you out of his sight now," muttered Simon.

"I'll admit it was awkward," Christian said. "Claudia couldn't keep her eyes off you, and Neil couldn't keep his eyes off her. There's a story there—you've got to be blind not to see it. Did you see the look on Andrew's face when they shook hands good night? I thought he was going to punch Neil."

"Wonder if our old boy Neil dipped his wick where he shouldn't have?" Simon cut in.

"You are a tactless idiot. You know that?" Margot told him.

"You ever taken a good look at the two of them? Andrew and Neil? They even speak the same way."

"Of course they do, they're British. They sound like you, only more intelligent."

Simon took a big bite of his toast and rolled his eyes. "Nowha I ment." He washed it down with a swig of coffee. "Hey, listening to Andrew is my job. I'm merely saying that there are some uncanny similarities between Paulie and Lainey there. Yeah, and what was all that with the Lainey stuff if there wasn't something wicked in the state of Denmark?"

"Maybe it was his nickname?" reasoned Margot. "Like people undoubtedly call you 'clueless moron.'"

"Ah, but you're taking me to see the stars tomorrow night, so I must rate, right?"

Margot didn't respond, but Emily noticed how her cheeks blushed slightly as she made a point to busy herself with cleaning up the kitchen.

The crowd eventually dispersed, and Zoey and Margot trudged off to bed, but not before they each gave Emily a heartfelt though exhausted hug. All the while, Andrew had never showed. Emily knew he was done in and probably wanted to visit with his mother in private, but that didn't lessen the aching loss she felt for him. The house seemed so still, so full of shadows. With his mother hating her and ghosts wanting her dead, she desperately needed some peace of mind.

It was five a.m., and she lay awake in bed, unable to sleep. The room was entirely dark except for the light of her laptop. She was trying to Google *The Lady in Red* but kept coming up with old songs. Was it a person she was supposed to find? A ghost? She had no idea. And time was running out.

She threw her head back on her pillow in wretched frustration. She needed Andrew. He would know what to do, where to start. But most of all she just needed him. She felt thin and drawn to the breaking point, and something inside of her told her he did too.

She hesitated before the closet door wondering if what she was about to do was right. As she crept into the back of the closet, she promised herself she wouldn't stay long, she would make sure he was sleeping and safe, and then she would return. Tomorrow they could figure out this mess. Tomorrow they would not leave each other's side.

By now the passageway was well known territory to her. She closed her eyes and tried to hold the memories of those walls at bay, still so strong and potent in her mind, memories of their bodies, hot and entwined, of his hands — his perfect hands — powerful and wanting.

With a deep breath, she persevered until she reached the telltale bolts in the floor. Light flickered up from the slats; voices hushed but adamant joined them. Her heart sped up as she approached and squatted down on the floor to peer through the opening into Andrew's bedroom.

"I know what I'm doing, Mum, I've always known."

Andrew was pacing across the room, and what had to be his mother's suitcase was open on the floor. She sat on the edge of his bed. They looked as though they had been talking for some time, as neither of them had changed out of their clothes.

"But Andrew, have you truly thought about this? It's all happened so quickly. You saw this girl in a club, and now? Do you know anything about her?"

"I know everything I need to know about Emily."

"But tonight—what that thing—what they said. Someone wants her dead, and when that man said she would die—"

"Do you honestly believe all that rubbish?"

Claudia didn't answer right away. "I think the question is whether or not you believe it."

Andrew's gait hitched. He scrubbed the back of his neck with his hand and looked to the ceiling. Emily drew back into the darkness. "Nothing is going to happen to Emily. I would kill anyone who tried."

"But, dear, really, listen to yourself. Always so dramatic, always ready to grab your sword and slay a dragon. Are you sure it's not the resemblance? The fact that she looks so much like her, is that it?"

"Mum, it is real. Emily is real. Why don't you believe me?"

"Oh, Andrew. I have supported you through everything. When the doctors said she was a figment of your imagination, I trusted you. I've never stopped supporting you. But for all the inspiration this muse has given you, she's traumatized you so. I love you, and I don't want to see you harmed again."

Andrew walked to the other side of the room and slid down against the wall, his hands folded in his sides. "I love you too. Trust me—that is all I ask."

"When you were a child, do you remember? When you were in the hospital? I wanted nothing more than for you to get well, and your father thought you would grow out of it, abandon this imaginary friend of yours. But I knew better. I understood. I knew there were things in this life that can't be explained away, things that transcend the here and now, things that can change your life." She paused and placed her hands on her knees. "But your obsession with her, it was so strong, so passionate, I have to admit it frightened me. The way you spoke of her like she was next to you, the notes you left in the margins of your compositions to her…Maybe I was a little bit jealous too." She tried to smile but her worry eroded the effort.

"Then things seemed to improve. You were thriving and happy, and so alive. I stopped fretting, I thought you had found a place for her, 'assimilated her into your psyche' as the doctors used to say." She glanced up at her son, her voice thick with emotion. "But after that last breakdown on stage…Simon and Christian were so worried. You just collapsed there. They thought you'd had a heart attack. And the doctors were adamant you needed help. They were convinced you would end up killing yourself, and yet you did nothing. *Nothing.* Simon told me all you would say over and over again was that you had lost her. That she had gone. Then you disappeared on that train. I was frantic, Andrew. You left without a word, and I didn't hear from you for weeks."

Emily's heart was hammering uncontrollably in her chest at the sight. She had no idea of the intensity of Andrew's feelings. His muse. A woman that lived in his mind, his heart; that's who she was. Not Emily. His muse had left him, and it had destroyed him. For the first time she saw the ferocity of that passion, and it was beyond terrifying. Anguished images began to build: a man obsessed, fixated, mad. No, she struggled to remind herself, this was Andrew, her Andrew. Her sweet, playful Andrew.

"I didn't know what to think," Claudia went on. "One night I found your journals, the ones you left at home after university. I'm ashamed to admit it, but I read them. I thought they would help me understand. I didn't realize how very real she was to you, and the way you described her in such detail…"

"You read them? All of them?"

"I was scared you'd become obsessed, Andrew. That this creature could control you so. And when I saw her tonight — the way she looked, the way she spoke — I didn't know what to do. Are you certain, truly certain you haven't transferred your fixation onto this poor girl? Taken all your hopes and dreams and convinced yourself that she is the one?"

"No."

"Have you ever thought of what this means to her? To Emily? What happens if she doesn't live up to your expectations? Do you really want to break her heart like that? When you realize that she is not her?"

The memory of Vandin's words cut into Emily. *He will tell you all the sweet things you want to hear, all that rubbish about love, but it's not you he is in love with. It's an ideal he has in his mind, you know that. The more artistic, the worse they become. He will call you his muse and write all the music in the world to you. But it is not you. And in a little while, after he's done fucking you, he will see your faults, see you for what you really are, and look for that muse of his somewhere else.*

"But she is!" Andrew cried. "Don't you understand? She is, I know it. In my soul and in my bones. I'm not delusional. I'm not obsessed. I was meant to find her, and I did. God, Mum, can't you understand what Emily means to me?"

"She doesn't have an issue with your past, with the depth of your devotion, or with the fact that you've been institutionalized and were placed on medication?"

Andrew wrapped his arms tighter around his legs and looked away.

"She doesn't know, does she? Oh, Andrew, if you can't trust her with that, then how can you even expect her to deal with all the problems you'll face together? Do you even know how she would react if you told her? What she would do?"

Andrew said nothing.

"Don't you see, darling, you only love what you *think* she is."

"No, I love her. Emily."

"But you love your music and performing as well. Can she live with that? What is she going to do when you're on the road? What kind of life is that for her? What are her dreams? Do you know? Would she sacrifice those to follow you from city to city?"

He hung his head.

"You were born to be a musician. It's who you are. You know that, and there is no stopping it. I'm not saying that this Emily isn't a lovely girl, but wouldn't it be best to take some time, step back from this situation and see it for what it really is, and not attach yourself at such a young age? Allow yourself the space and freedom to achieve what you want?"

Andrew raised his head, slowly, deliberately. He regarded his mother a long time, his eyes flat. When he finally spoke his voice was lethally calm. "Is that what happened with Neil?"

Claudia's stilled. "My relationship with Mr. St. John was a long time ago."

"So you did have a thing with him."

"It ended. I knew what he wanted, what his dreams were. We were very young, and I knew it could never work. I would have held him back."

Andrew slid up the wall. Tension crackled from him, making the room thick in accusation.

"Why would you have held him back? You were brilliant and beautiful. What could possibly be so wrong with you that he would leave you?"

A silence so profound, so immense, froze the room. Claudia sat lifeless, white as a ghost. Andrew now stood facing her like he was facing a firing squad.

"Don't lie to me, Mum. I read Father's letters. Yeah. Surprised? It would seem we've all been reading things we shouldn't."

Claudia seemed to be holding her breath. Waiting. Teetering.

"When I was clearing out papers over Christmas, I found a stack of love letters he had written to you. I didn't mean to read them, but I missed him. Never got a chance to say goodbye—I just wanted to see his handwriting, the scrawl of it. Smell the paper. I ran my fingers over it…"

Andrew paused and swallowed down the lump that lingered in his throat.

"There was a love letter he wrote to you about the first time he saw you. Do you remember? You had met at a lawn party of a mutual friend. He told you how beautiful you looked, how taken he was with you despite your surprise when you met him.

"He wrote of how you had run across the grass asking the host where St. John was, that you had heard he was at the party. And when the host introduced Father to you, your face dropped in a strange sense of desolation—that was the term he used. 'A strange sense of desolation.' He joked that 'though I might have been a John of sorts, I was certainly no saint. It was a miracle that you even gave me the time of day, considering my hound dog visage.'"

He laughed bitterly to himself, his face studying the floor.

"It was only tonight that I realized something. Watching Neil walk away from the house, I finally put the pieces together. You weren't disappointed in Father's face, you were disappointed because Father wasn't who you wanted. You wanted Neil St. John, but got John Hayes instead. He was the wrong John."

Claudia's face shattered.

"Did he know?"

Claudia said nothing, fighting to compose herself.

"Fuck, Mum. Did Father know about him? Answer me! Did Father know about Neil?"

"Yes. Yes! I was always honest with him. He didn't care. And Lainey, he went on to achieve everything he'd ever wanted. It was all for the best."

"How the hell can you sit there and make excuses for him? How could you sit there tonight and look at him like that? You never once, ever, looked at Father like that. Christ."

"Andrew, sweetheart, you don't understand—"

"Oh, I understand perfectly. I could do sums since I was three. My birthday, your anniversary. It wasn't rocket science. You never cared, so why should I? But it wasn't Father that did it, was it? After reading that letter I figured it was someone named St. John, but Neil? Neil fucking St. John? He knocked you up and then walked out. Abandoned you. Abandoned us. While he went off to achieve, you found some poor sod who adored you and you married him. You let that bastard off scot-free, and you faked it, faked it your whole life with the other poor bastard who loved you, worshiped you. Oh, I understand everything. Perfectly."

"It wasn't like that — you have to listen to me."

"No wonder father despised it when I started a band. No wonder he wouldn't talk to me anymore. What a bloody kick in the bollocks that must have been. His bastard son — just a chip off the old block."

"No! Your father adored you. He never —"

"Were you even sure it was Neil? Or did you just fuck around? Is that how you paid your way through university?"

"Andrew!"

"How bloody ironic. I couldn't possibly have turned out the way Father wanted. What must he have thought? The insane boy with his pathetic guitar. He was probably convinced I'd turn out just like Neil. Just one step up from street trash." Andrew took another step closer to his mother, his eyes full of contempt. "Is that what this is all about, then? Is this what you've really been trying to tell me all along? That I'll fuck up just like Neil did? That I'm just like him? That it isn't in my nature to stick around?

"So what should I do? Give it all up? Leave Emily while I can? Maybe I should before I can ruin her. Before I make a liar and a whore out of her, just like that bastard did to you. Well — at least I didn't fuck her. Does that make you happy?"

Claudia slapped him across the face. The sound was lurid. Andrew turned, frozen, his body ungodly still.

"I only wanted —" She whimpered and made a move to touch him.

He flinched back like she was poison. "Go to hell. I don't care what you wanted. It was a lie. Everything was a bloody lie. I'm a bloody lie. I'm fucking out of here!"

He stormed from the room, slamming the door shut behind him.

Emily stood there in shock, glued to the spot, her pulse exploding in her head. Before she knew what she was doing, she was racing like a demon down the passageway. She hurled herself through her apartment and tore open the front door. Grabbing hold of the banister, she stopped dead, panting.

At the foot of the stairs Andrew stood trembling, his eyes burning red with tears, his jacket clenched in his fist. Their gazes riveted together, and Emily felt a panic like she'd never felt well up in her throat. He knew she had seen him. He knew why she was standing there.

"Andrew," she whispered.

"No. Don't." He held out his hands, ordering her to stop, his voice cold-blooded.

In that awful moment she could see it all. The tortured brow, the fierce chin, the biting lines of his cheekbones. She could see his father. She could see Neil. And she could see the heartbreaking resignation, the same haunting desire to flee.

"Stay away from me, Emily, I'm no good," he commanded. "I'm—" His voice faltered, broken like his spirit. "I'm not right—I never have been—I've lied. We're…we'll never be…It's all…it's all bloody wrong!"

His face held more pain than she had ever seen. He didn't want her—he didn't want them. Even with the specter of death waiting, he didn't care. Even with all the proposals and the promises, he didn't care. He hated himself too much. He wanted to escape, to disappear. To be done.

Without a word, he crashed open the door and ran.

eil apparently did not expect Andrew that early the following morning, or maybe he did, but nevertheless he showed no surprise when Andrew appeared on his doorstep still dressed in the same clothes as the night before. Neil would have been an idiot not to have known why Andrew was there and why he was livid. Yet the older man's face bore no shock, no remorse, and upon seeing the younger man, he remained as businesslike as ever, mechanical in his motions, though dark circles ringed his eyes.

Andrew had never before stepped foot into Neil's home, a modern, monolithic structure on Broadway; he had never even received an invitation. Now he was being ushered into his office, one of the countless rooms off an austere foyer with sweeping walls of glass and blocks of leather furniture.

Crisply dressed in a pressed white oxford and trousers, Neil spoke of trivial things, waiting, biding his time, before offering Andrew a seat that he refused. Andrew wanted to hate him, so cool and collected, standing there in front of his platinum records and awards, he truly did, but he could not find it in himself; maybe that was a good thing, he thought. Maybe it proved something, although what, he didn't know.

And he would have left. But when Neil stepped around his desk and rested his hand on Andrew's shoulder and Neil's eyes searched his, filled with such compassion and understanding and — and Christ, with pride — Andrew hauled off and punched him as hard as he could. Hard, brutal, and wanting revenge. His fist made a sick sound when it connected with the side of Neil's mouth, sending his head snapping back. Andrew instantly readied himself for the blow he knew he would receive in return, the shouts and the curses.

Neil's fingers found the blood on his lips, and he stopped. "I'm sorry," was all he said. "I am so terribly sorry."

Andrew had rehearsed what he would say. He had thought about it every step of the way there, but now the words flew out in a rage. "You fucking left her. And now you came back, for what? To play daddy? Some midlife crisis after your wife died, and you supposed you wanted a family now, now that it was convenient? Showing up in London, it was a scam, wasn't it? Offering us the house and some work, it was all part of a game. You never wanted to help. You didn't care about the band, it was all about you. About what you bloody wanted — to keep us holed up, take us out and parade us around, to see how it felt having a son before you decided to commit."

"It wasn't like that. It isn't like that."

"Did you ever once tell the truth? Did you even believe we stood a chance?" Andrew held the back of his throbbing hand to his mouth and fought to keep his voice from breaking when Neil began to speak. "No, don't say a word. I don't want to hear your excuses. You left her because she was pregnant with me and that didn't fit into your grand plan. That's why you never went back to London. You didn't want to hazard the risk of running into your responsibilities. Well, fuck you. We didn't need you then, and we sure as hell don't need you now."

"Andrew, listen. I…I wanted to help."

"I swear, if you come near me or my mum again, I'll fucking kill you."

"Stop. Listen to me."

But Andrew was already through the door, a whirlwind of destruction intent on tearing everything down if necessary.

It was late morning when Emily finally awoke. In those first few blurry moments she had forgotten everything, and before losing the grasp of sleep, the soft comfort of pillows and blankets and oblivion, she was happy.

Then the pain came; it poured through her veins like a drug, making her want to be anyone but herself right now. She wanted to wake, wondering if Andrew meant what he said when he was drunk in the dark, not sober in the light.

There never should have been a séance, she thought bitterly. They should have stumbled home together, tripping over the threshold. They should have kissed long and sloppily in the foyer, and laughing, he should have led her by the hand to his bed, and finally, finally, they should have made crazed, unrelenting, fantastical love. They should be waking now, hands trailing, mouths parting, tongues tasting. She would have never left his bed. He would never have left her body. Like lovers.

Like lovers who didn't have ghosts ruling their lives, didn't have spirits that wanted them dead. Who didn't have tour dates and writing conferences and she-devil rapacious agents stalking them. Who didn't have lies between them. Who only had each other.

If she didn't think about these things, she could make them go away. It was a trick she had learned as a child. When misfortune would strike she would force it from her mind, throw the fortress walls up, slam her back to them, and carry on as though nothing had occurred. That wasn't a C-minus she received on a test; she had tons of friends despite sitting alone on the bus; her parents really loved each other. Her life was fine, and her heart was intact. It worked. Most of the time.

After her shower she attempted to eat lunch, but the food tasted like plastic. When she was done studying for finals, she buried herself in her search for The Lady in Red but found nothing. Upon cleaning the house for the second time, she broke down and called Detective Obester. He was suffering from a cold, and his voice sounded like how she felt, straining to remain positive. No news to report. Nothing. Hearing the despondency in her voice, he extended an invitation to a family barbeque. Forget her problems for a day, he said.

She ended the call with a shudder.

Rays of sun streamed in through her bedroom window; the glass was so old that it seemed to run between the mullions like rain. In truth, she felt steadier in the sun, more positive. Things weren't as bad as she thought when it was so bright and cheerful outside. Andrew was angry—he had a right to be after everything he had learned—but he hadn't meant to take it out on her, she reasoned. He hadn't meant what he said about them. He was distraught; he needed time, space, to get his head together. They were fine, really. He would come back in a few hours, and they would hug and cry and kiss and everything would be back to normal.

Yes. *Of course.*

She smiled confidently, having straightened herself out so. There was nothing wrong with them. Nothing wrong with him. Nothing.

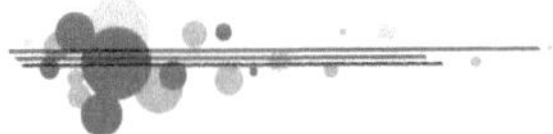

The blood tasted like metal in Andrew's mouth. He sucked one knuckle, the worst of the gashes, and his eyes squinted shut at the pain and the screeching morning sun overhead.

S.J. Gordian, the last person in the world he expected to see on this street, and at this hour of the morning, was uncoiling from a car parked directly across from Neil's front door. The sun blazed on the Jaguar's feline chassis. The sun blazed on her.

She regarded Andrew as though it was the most logical thing in the world that he should be standing there, with blood on his hands, unshaven and panting, at ten a.m. on a Friday morning.

"You know, I never gave you this." She reached into her elegant black bag and withdrew a business card, holding it tight between the tips of her fingers. She searched his shirt for a pocket, and when she found none, her eyes roamed lower.

Before Andrew could utter a word, her face was inches from his. He felt the claw of her nails, forceful and brazen as they slid into his trouser pocket. Like talons, they slowly scratched along his thigh as she released the card. Her sunglasses hid her eyes, but the smile on her lips told him they were laughing.

"You never know who to trust in this profession, do you?" She stepped an inch closer, not a sigh between them. Andrew didn't back down. Her breath held a mix of peppermint and coffee. "My home phone number is on the back. Why don't you stop by for drinks tonight? We can chat."

Her lips brushed his cheek, hot and moist with lipstick, and her nails dragged dangerously along the inside of his thigh. She waited. Slowly, she deliberately withdrew her hand, stepped back, and smiled.

Andrew knew there would be no need for explanations with her. She would open the door to her tasteful designer penthouse, knowing he had no place left to hide. With no thought of going back, and only twenty bucks in his jacket pocket, where else could he go?

They would have the required drink, and when they were done they would face each other. She would want him to undress her as she undressed him, without passion. Then she would turn, her nails gleaming in the candlelight, they would fuck.

He would shower and leave in the morning. No goodbyes. None required. There was no need.

"Andrew?"

Did she enjoy the look of self-loathing in his eyes?

"You really are amazing. Such talent, so gorgeous. We could do incredible things together, you and I. Think about it. I really do want to help you."

Her heels clipped up the steps, and her hand paused on Neil's door knowing he was still watching her. She looked over her shoulder, her blond curls victorious. "Ten o'clock, just drinks. Don't be late. We'll have fun."

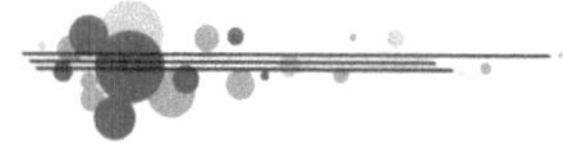

Sometime around six in the evening Emily heard a car pull into the driveway, and she was at the window before she even knew she was moving. The figure of Claudia, smaller than Emily remembered, was getting into a taxi, suitcase in hand.

Emily's nose stayed pressed to the pane, her breath fogging the glass, until the figures of Margot and Simon stole her attention. They walked tentatively toward Margot's car, each eyeing the other, about to depart for their sojourn to the observatory in Berkeley.

Restless, she retreated to the conservatory and sat curled up on a wicker chair tucked away in the corner. Outside the weather was getting worse; a relentless thin gray line had descended on the horizon: the harbinger of storms. She pulled her hooded sweatshirt around her and shivered uncontrollably, then began to pluck at a string on her torn jeans.

Footsteps echoed on the steps, and she bounded upright as Christian entered, Zoey at his side, her wide eyes soft and warm.

"Soot," Christian announced.

"Soot," Zoey repeated enthusiastically.

Emily frowned, unable to fathom what they were saying, and unconsciously rubbed her face, afraid that it might be dirty. Her fingers felt like ice cubes.

Christian held a candle in one hand. "May I borrow that ring of yours for a second? I'm not going to have it long, then you can have it right back," he said reassuringly. "I want to try something. I think there's an inscription on the inside, but I couldn't see it before. This might help."

Despite her misgivings and the foreboding she felt as she pulled it from her finger, her mind overruled her emotions, grateful to have something to concentrate on. He lit the candle and went to put the ring in the flame.

"No!" Emily cried out. "No, you can't!"

He held out a hand to calm her. "Soot. I'm trying to build up a layer of soot on the inside of the ring. I'm not going to hurt it, I promise."

She sat back, still uneasy, her brow creasing in alarm.

"I learned about this in a metallurgy lecture in college. It's really cool. I remembered about it last night, but I just found my notes a little while ago."

"I found your notes," said Zoey with a pleased smile. "His room is a sty. I can't believe you keep all that shit."

Christian shrugged. "I kept all your letters."

Zoey couldn't conceal her surprise. "All of them?" There was something small and endearing in her voice, and Emily thought she could hear Zoey's heartbeat in it.

"You see," Christian continued, "sometimes the markings in antique rings, especially older ones like this, are so faint or worn down by wear that you need to 'soot over' them to even see that they're there. Do you have any tape?" He looked to Emily, but she shook her head at him numbly.

"It's in our kitchen, hold on." Zoey ran off down the stairs, leaving the two of them alone.

"So Claudia went to stay at a bed and breakfast. Thought we needed our own bedrooms. Smart woman, that."

Emily merely nodded blankly.

"It's important not to heat the stones," Christian informed her as he swirled the ring around the flame, kindly ignoring what had to have been the distress on her face. Emily looked on in growing fascination as a layer of blackened ash began to build up inside the band.

When he seemed satisfied, he blew out the candle and held the ring carefully between his fingers, waiting for Zoey to return.

"Has…" Emily cleared her throat. "Has Andrew called you today? I…I haven't seen him."

"No. No, he hasn't."

"Oh."

Christian glanced at her, then back to the ring. "But his wallet and his phone are on the kitchen counter, so wherever he is, he won't be gone long, right?"

It wasn't the playful eyes or the continual smile that always struck Emily about Christian — it was his unyielding optimism. But it was an optimism she couldn't share at the moment.

"Wonder what went on, though. Man, it was one hell of a knock-down, drag-out fight. I heard the screaming and the door slamming at the end of it. He usually reserves that shit for Simon. I've never heard him like that with Claudia. He adores her, and God knows she loves him like crazy."

She swallowed at his choice of words and pulled at her jeans, praying that Zoey would return soon.

"But everything is all good — I mean between the two of you?"

"Yeah, absolutely. Sure."

Mercifully, the sound of Zoey's scampering saved Emily from lying further.

Christian took the dispenser from her. "Thanks, babe. Okay, now you take a piece of tape and place it over the soot." He pressed the tape gently but firmly onto the interior of the ring before carefully removing it. "Paper, I need paper." He shook one hand like a doctor in want of a scalpel.

A stack of pages lay scattered on a nearby table. Emily grabbed a handful, and then caught herself. It was sheet music, and Andrew's familiar script noted the margins. One of the pages swept from her hand down onto the ground, the word *Emily* inscribed at the top.

"He…here." She shoved the rest at Christian, unable to hold them. He took them, frowning in reaction to her ashen face.

"What do you do next?" Zoey asked, excited.

Christian returned his focus to the ring. "You place the tape directly onto the paper. The soot lifts the image of the marks like lifting a fingerprint. And there you go, a nice and easy-to-read copy."

Three faces peered at the bit of tape on the paper; three hearts beat in suspense. Zoey whooped in delight.

A string of numbers was revealed: 75510791.

"What do you suppose it means?"

"I have no idea," Emily whispered in fascination, feeling the first bit of hope that day. "But it's something."

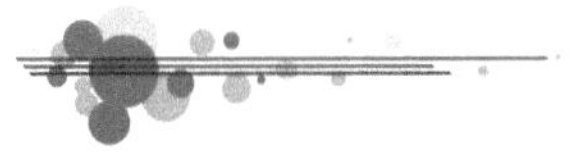

Word of advice, Andrew wearily noted to himself. *Don't ever attempt to bathe in a university building's lavatory. The sinks are useless, and the mirrors are for shit.* Not that he wanted to see his reflection.

"Christ," he muttered, standing there, teeth chattering as he wrestled off the tap. "What the fuck have I done?"

"Trashed everything you love, kid," the mirror mocked, like some smart-mouthed, enchanted looking glass from a fairy tale.

The soap tumbled from his hands; he would know that voice anywhere.

"And by the way, what kind of noble hero-on-a-quest shit are you playing at? 'Cause I ain't getting it."

"Nick!" Andrew whirled around. *Niiiick* echoed back off the tile walls. "Where are you?" *Yoooooouuuu.*

"So let me get this straight. You just flat out told her you didn't want her?"

Andrew couldn't see the ghost anywhere. "Yes," he shot back with venom, about to explain, his eyes still scouring the room for the apparition.

"Were you drunk?"

"No."

"High?"

"No!"

"Then kindly explain to me how a man who doesn't have a bottle in his hand or a broad in his bed can be so damn oblivious. That's your problem, kid. You cock off without thinking things through, without knowing all the facts."

"I know what I know."

"You don't know shit."

He stared at the mirror, hands quaking in anger and exhaustion. "Bugger off, Nick."

"You don't have time to screw up, kid. In fact, you don't have much time left at all."

"Stop it. I don't want any part of this ghost chasing anymore—I'm out. Find someone else. I'm not your man, and stay away from her as well. Go haunt some other goddamn place. She's suffered enough without death threats from dead people."

"Ever the hero," Andrew heard Nick snap at him as he stormed out the bathroom door.

Back in the hidden confines of the practice room, he huddled down next to the piano, his elbows on his knees and his head in his hands, with no desire to talk to anyone, human or otherwise. Bone chilled and shaking, he wrapped his busted up hand in a spit soaked towel left by some brass player, probably. Wincing in pain, he grimaced at the sight of his swollen fingers.

What the hell had happened to his quest? What kind of hero was he? Not the kind Emily deserved, that was certain. She deserved someone sane and stable, someone who wouldn't hurt her by the very act of existing. Someone safe. He looked at his palm, at those lines. Did Neil have the same ones? Was that what his future really held—that he'd only use women and not stay around to see it through?

Andrew's good hand groped above him like a drowning man reaching for a life preserver. He found the piano keys. Plink. Plink. Pllllllink.

With the determined growl, he hefted himself up onto the bench. Slowly one note came, then another, dredged up from all the anger that simmered within him. Music raged for hours in that solitary room. The intricate chords were an escape—they allowed him to forget. But how could he?

He had attacked his mother, cursed her for her regrets, called her a liar and a whore. Mum, a whore. And she had hit him. Which he deserved.

He had told Emily they were wrong, that he was wrong. Which he was.

He slammed the keys as the crescendo gathered force. Outside, the late evening fog had given way to blacker clouds, a dark reflection of his mood. He was poison to her, he knew that. Whatever twisted way their lives were joined only kept getting more violent, more unexplainable with each passing day. He would end it, cut it off so mercilessly and brutally she would hate him—with an act so heartless, so cruel, she would never look back and wonder. She would never, ever have regrets.

He felt S.J.'s business card cut into his leg, and he slammed the keys harder.

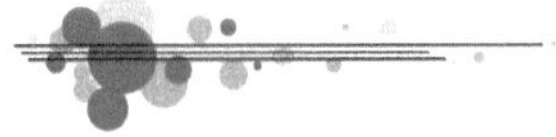

As the kitchen clock ticked on, Emily knew with certainty that Andrew wouldn't be coming home tonight. He had no wallet, no phone, and the weather was getting worse and worse. But where would he go? Images seeped into her mind: images of him sleeping frozen on the street, huddling cold and alone under an overpass; images of him sitting in a café with a girl offering him a warm place to stay for the night.

"Emily," Zoey said with a thinly masked attempt at levity as she finished washing the last of the dinner dishes. "Was it just your first fight, or should Christian be looking for a day job?"

Christian shot her a look, having poured himself another glass of wine.

"He only did what Vandin said he would do."

Zoey put down a plate and stared at her. "Emily?"

"I was the one who had believed in the fairy tale, who let myself think that I could be a part of Andrew's life, but I was wrong." She said more to herself than to anyone. She went on to relate the whole conversation she had overheard into their shocked faces. From Claudia's doubts, to Andrew's accusations, to Claudia's confessions, to Andrew's flight.

"And then…and then he stood there and said, 'Stay away from me, Emily, I'm not right—I never have been—I've lied. We're…all bloody wrong.' He really thinks he's no good. That he's just like Neil," she finished, wiping her nose with her sleeve, unaware she had been crying.

"But Neil is wonderful," Zoey argued. "He's cool and kind, and he really wants to help the band—you heard him. And he brought us muffins, remember? What kind of horrible man brings muffins?"

Christian quickly poured more wine.

"Maybe Neil didn't know?" Zoey looked into Emily's bleary red-eyed mess of a face with her brilliant eye-shining optimism. "Maybe Claudia never told him? You saw how he looked at her, in awe, almost. Maybe he's always loved her? Maybe she never told him she was pregnant and that's what she meant by not holding him back? So she wouldn't hurt him?"

"But she has! Don't you see? She's hurt him and herself and Andrew most of all. And now…Maybe it's better this way? Better to deal with it now, get it over with, than let it go on," she said bitterly. For she knew if she lost herself completely, unspeakable heartache was sure to follow. There would be no turning back from that pain. She would become one of those crazy women poets and perhaps put her head in the oven when he left again, which he would of course — it was in his nature to do so. She wasn't unrealistic; she knew falling in love with Andrew came with a price. Living in a fantasy world always did. "Andrew doesn't want…us."

"No, he didn't mean it, Emily," Christian said firmly, cutting her off. "He couldn't have meant it. He loves you, worships you. He always has; he always will. He probably hates himself pretty bad right now, and he has to be rocked to the core. Shit, I just hope he doesn't do something stupid."

"Like what?" She wiped at her tears with the heel of her palms, hiccupping down the rest of them.

The sky outside was dark and foreboding, a portent of storms. He leaned over and took a slug of his wine. "He wouldn't. Nah, he wouldn't," he said to the window.

But his face didn't look convinced.

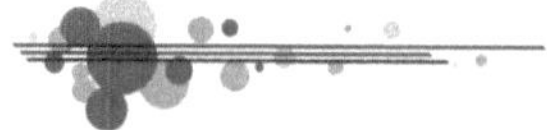

Beethoven had descended to Tchaikovsky and raged into Schoenberg. Andrew's fingers could no longer move. He desperately needed aspirin or alcohol.

He got both. Thank God for student unions. He looked at the clock on the checkout stand. Would he be too late?

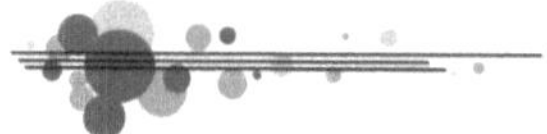

Zoey had her hand on Emily's back as they listened to the rain howling in sheets against her bedroom window. Christian had left them a while ago.

"I don't want to talk about it anymore," Emily said, slipping her shoulder away from Zoey's touch.

"When you were lost, he looked for you. He's lost now, don't you see? Everything that he's trusted has crumbled. I love you, but you two are so fucking stubborn I want to knock your little neurotic heads together sometimes. You're both wrapped up in your own fears, your own insecurities, your own worst case scenarios."

Emily blinked at her, shocked. "But he said —"

"I know what he said. But do you honestly believe he meant it? After everything you two have been through? Emily, he loves you. You love him. Christian was right. It isn't that hard. You can sit here and worry, or you can fight for him."

"But, Zoey, he's been hospitalized because of this idea of a muse. It's not some romantic notion to him. It's real. She's real. And he truly believes that I'm her."

"Would you leave him because of that? Because he's wrestled with that burden as best as he could? He is not a lunatic, Emily. Tortured, yes. Strong willed and driven, certainly. But at the same time he's incredibly passionate and brilliant. Think about it — he's had to find a way to live without you his whole life. You've only had to live without him for a day, and look at what state you're in."

"But what if he's deluding himself. What…what happens if I'm not really his muse after all? He'll leave. He's left already. Don't you see that?"

"But you're not his muse!"

Emily blinked. The rain rat-a-tat-tatted against the panes. *Rat-a-tat-tat. Rat-a-tat-tat.*

"You shouldn't be. You're so much better than her. Just drown the bitch."

Thunder rumbled. A beautiful sound.

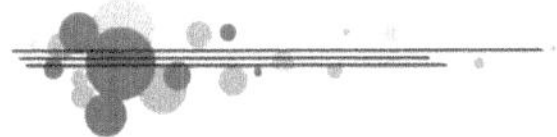

A gang of drunken frat boys spotted Andrew on his way out of the Student Union. They trailed him, laughing and cursing as he pressed on across the quad, his shoulders hunched against the pelting storm. This wouldn't end well, he knew it.

He should have run, but he'd be damned if a bunch of spoiled, rich prats were going to mess with him; he was in no bloody mood.

"Hey, you," one slurred, his words coming in fits and spurts in the driving rain. "I don't like your fucking face. You illegal? Go back to picking lettuce, chico."

Andrew buried his hands in his pockets; the rain, almost horizontal in its rage, sliced against his freezing body. He trudged on, leaving behind the sound of their boots squashing harshly in the thick mud. But the thundering storm had prevented him from hearing them near, and an alarm shot through him when he realized they were directly behind him.

"Listen here, faggot." Andrew felt a heavy paw of a hand grab his shoulder. "I said — I don't like your face."

He stopped dead. His jacket and trousers slapped to him like a drenched icy skin. He clenched his hands into fists as something inside of him snapped. The exhaustion, the anger, his own self-hatred. He wanted to fight. He wanted to hurt someone. Badly.

"Funny," Andrew seethed, "I don't like your fucking repulsive mug either."

The paw shoved him around and rose into the air, ready to come smashing down on his face. Andrew dodged to the right at the last minute, missing the blow by inches. The owner teetered around in surprise, but not before Andrew drove his fist against the side of his jaw. He hurled backward and fell into the slick, black mud.

Before Andrew knew it a massive form lurched at him from the darkness, and he wheeled to one side as his attacker went flying past him. The heat of the drunk's anger left a trail in the air as he fell face first next to his friend in the sodden grass.

Andrew bounced backward on his toes like a street fighter, egging them on. "That's the best you can do, you bloody pricks?"

With a drunken howl another hulk roared at him. Andrew hauled back and hurled his fist into the boy's stomach; he doubled back and fell, groaning. Grabbing his burning hand, Andrew bent over, holding it to his body, cursing and grimacing in the white hot pain.

Seeing him falter, a pair of beefy arms seized the advantage and grabbed Andrew from behind, wrenching his arms back. A flash of fear shot through him. Lightning bolts of searing fire tore up his hand. *Not my hands, fuck, not my hands.*

"Who you calling a prick, you faggot? You got a little gay boy voice, you fucking queer!"

The figure of a man lurched out of the dark rain, reeking of beer, and spat in Andrew's face. Andrew struggled against the clamped grip on his arms, but the iron hands wrenched him brutally back, exposing his chest like a punching bag.

The man leaned back and slammed his fist into Andrew's jaw; he felt the breath leave his lungs in a painful gasp. Another fist smashed into his gut. He doubled over, struggling to breathe.

Not my hands, please God, not my hands.

The headlights of an approaching car forced them to back off. With snide curses, they heaved Andrew onto the ground where he landed hard on the muddy grass. He plastered his hands into his body as he heard feet approach and the sound of boots seeping into the sodden ground.

Laughing, they ran, stumbling off into the night.

Groaning, Andrew lay writhing in a puddle of mud and grass. The freezing rain mixed with the heated trickle of blood from the gash along his eyebrow. The sound of gurgling seemed to be coming from his lips. He convulsed onto his side, holding his bruised gut, and coughed up what he prayed wasn't his teeth. Raw skinned and throbbing, he curled onto his side, fighting off the waves of pain.

"Fuck, I want to go home. Please, anyone, I just want to go home…"

Teeth chattering, he curled deeper into the ground, his cheek scraping against the cold, hard gravel. The taste of blood and stones stung his mouth.

What seemed like an eternity passed, filled only with darkness and bitter rain, the far off sounds of traffic, and the smell of the earth.

"Get up, Hayes!" A voice shouted in his head, stronger and more aware than he. "Get up, or you're going to damn well drown here, kid. Get on your feet!"

He felt himself dragged to his knees and struggled to stand. Nearly tripping, he blinked into the driving rain searching for the voice. Raising his face into the sky, blood and rain seeped down his throat. "I want to go home," he pleaded to the voice, or to God, or to whoever would listen. "Please, I just want to go home," he begged, his shoulders shaking.

Please.

Emily's voice whispered in the sheets of rain. *Home.* He stumbled, falling on one knee. A dagger of pain lanced up his leg. *Home.*

No, he couldn't. He wouldn't.

No.

It was wrong. He was wrong. Wrong. Wrong. Wrong.

His bruised and bleeding hand found S.J.'s card.

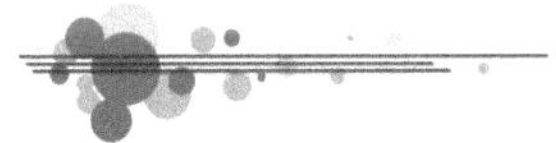

"You've been afraid ever since you met Andrew. And you've been running from him or shutting him out every chance you get. I don't know

what the answers are. But don't you want to find them together and not let someone else dictate them to you? Fuck nature. So maybe his father made some mistakes, and his mother too. But he's out there somewhere in the dark, in this torrential downpour, cold, alone, and heartbroken. Don't you think he needs a hell of a lot more nurture right now?"

"But he isn't coming home. Not tonight. He's running."

"No, you're the one running. Did you ever trust him, ever believe in him? Or were you in your own fantasy world? If you had trusted him, believed what he told you, you would have run after him the moment he turned and headed out that door. You would have grabbed hold of his shoulders and shook him until he faced you. That's what people who love each other do. Did you ever think that he never told you about his problems because he was afraid you would do precisely what you're doing right now — abandon him?

"It's late, Emily. Don't let him do something he'll regret. You're the only one who stands between him and something that will make him hate himself more than he already does. So what's it going to be?"

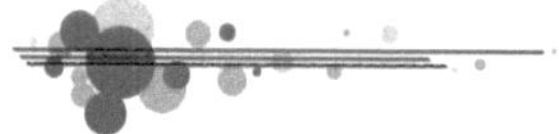

Trembling and stumbling like a wounded man, Andrew collapsed against the phone booth. His hair glued to his cheeks, he watched the rain trace bloody trails down the back of his hand as he fumbled the numbers. Finally, with chattering teeth, he crumbled against the metal ledge, the receiver in his hands. The entire world had gone silent except for the promise of the ringtone.

He thought the phone would ring many more times. That she would make him suffer before answering. She picked it up in one.

"Andrew?"

The phone hung trembling near his mouth. The card lay crushed under his heel.

"Where are you? Tell me and I'll be there," said Emily.

"No. I deserve the rain. I love you. Are you…are you all right?"

"Andrew, Andrew are you there? Andrew?"

"Home." It was all he said. It was everything.

"Yes, home."

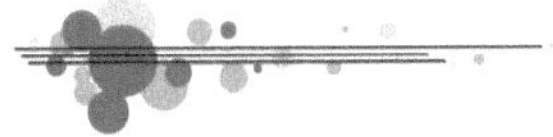

It was one a.m. Emily knew this because she sat staring at her watch, huddled in her robe on the stairway and waiting for him to return. When the sound of the cab finally came, her heart stopped. Up until that moment she didn't believe he would really come back to her. She bounded out the front door.

He stood there on the sidewalk, unmoving. She gasped at the sight of him. It was horribly real. Soaked, muddied, and stained with blood, his wet clothes were plastered to his bruised skin. His cheek was swollen as though pummeled, one eyebrow was split open, and he was drenched to the bone.

She flew from the steps and threw her arms around him, squeezing him as fiercely as she could, the rain soaking her robe. He cringed in pain, and she immediately pulled back, afraid she had hurt him. He was shaking, his teeth chattering.

"My God. You're hurt! You're freezing!" She rubbed his arms, trying to warm him.

"Yesss."

Lifting up his arm so she could slide under it, Emily bore his weight as best she could and hobbled him out of the storm and into the foyer. Despite his terrible condition he could still walk, but once in the house he wavered a little. She clasped her arms about him, his skin icy and trembling. Shivering herself, she closed her eyes for a heartbeat and tilted her head up into his soaked shirt, tightening her hold. With a cough, he bent his head and rested his mouth against the hollow of her throat, as if to find warmth; the stubble of his chin grazed her neck as her pulse hammered against his frozen lips. If she were not clenching him with both arms, she felt sure he would fall.

She tried to ask him what had happened, but he wouldn't respond. When he did speak, it was halting, a result of the intense cold he was suffering. "I am so sorry. So bloody sorry. I've treated you horribly. I don't know how to make it right. All I've ever wanted is you…not anything but…you."

His words cut off as though he wished to say more but had lost his way, his teeth still chattering. Without another word, she gathered him to her and led him up the stairs, afraid for a moment he might not be able to climb them. Once inside her apartment, she quickly found a blanket and wrapped it securely about his shoulders. She asked him if he wanted food, but he shook his head.

Fearful he might faint onto the floor, she led him to her bedroom. He hesitated before the door, his body seeming to quake from cold or nerves, she didn't know which. She gently opened it and took his hand, only letting go to turn on a small lamp on her bedside table. He remained leaning against the door as though he wasn't sure he would stay. She sat on the edge of the bed, heart hammering wildly, ready to grab him at any moment lest he slide down the wall. It was a long time till he spoke again, his voice bruised.

"I was terrified to tell you. To let you in, because I thought…you wouldn't stay. You'd never believe me…you'd be horrified."

He closed his eyes. She saw the cuts and contusions on his face and swallowed, wanting to tend to him but powerless to move, knowing from the tone of his voice he would push her away until he was done saying what he had to say.

"How could I explain to you that by some miracle, I found my muse — in that club, close enough to touch. And everything I dreamed about her was true. It was real, after I traveled halfway around the world to find her. I chased *her*, Emily — but I fell in love with *you*. You. No one else. I'm not mad, I'm not. Or maybe I am. I don't know anymore."

He stepped toward her, the blanket sliding to the floor, and leaning down, rested his forehead against hers. Her hands trailed up his arms and touched his face tenderly, brushing over the gashes and bruises; he closed his eyes, turning away not in pain but battling something, as though it took him lifetimes to utter these words. "Emily, I wanted to run. I've wanted to run away from everything, from my mum, Neil, from all the lies. Even from you. And from myself most of all.

"I've run from myself most of my life. But I couldn't this time. Because I can't leave you. I know I've lied to you. I know you're scared. You have every reason in the world not to trust me. But I love you. Strip everything away, and there is only that. That is who I am. God, I'm…I'm so cold."

She reached down, taking his freezing hands in hers. Searching for his eyes amidst the shadows of his face, she whispered, "Stay." She raised his fingers to her lips, speaking to him as softly as she could, "It'll be all right — we'll make it right."

He looked down at her, his eyes imploring. "Please. You need to understand. I want…forever."

"Yes."

"I want…never to be apart from you." His lips pressed against her forehead.

"Yes."

"I want…" His voice was so exposed, so full of yearning. She nodded, pushing back down her tears. They stood there for an inexorable moment, staring at each other, before Andrew whispered, "I want to love you."

He lowered his lips, and with a restrained breath, he brushed them against hers. Sighs of sighs of sighs passed between them.

He trailed his lips tenderly to her brow, her eyes, her cheeks. She could feel the trembling of his mouth as it ghosted against the curve of her jaw, his teeth grazing her skin as it came to rest against the hollow of her throat.

"Emily," he asked, his voice full of uncertainty. "Please…"

A wayward lock lay fallen upon the crease in his brow. Understanding, she raised her hand and brushed away the curl from his eyes. They narrowed slightly as she let her chin drop a fraction of an inch and raised it back. "Yes," she whispered one final time.

He slowly reached out with his hands and with stilted tenderness tried to undress her, but she stopped him.

"Your face, your eye? What happened to your hands? Oh, Andrew." She hesitated.

He shook his head. He let her kiss the cuts on his hand until he sighed. Still terribly worried about him, she took heart that at least his tremors had calmed down and his breathing had evened.

With a fumbling determination he tried to sweep away her robe, but she took his hands away and slid it from her shoulders. She wore nothing beneath.

"Home," he whispered, his voice as tentative and hopeful as the word. "My home," he went on, placing feathery kisses down one side of her neck.

She knew instantly what he was speaking of, what he needed above everything else in the world. She was the only thing he could ever hold onto. No world was safe, real or fantasy. Both were dangerous. But she would embrace his world of consuming love, curses, and ghosts, because he was in it. Overwhelmed with emotions, she could only reach out and pull him to her. All the fear and horror of the past days dissolved as they fell into each other.

"Home," she breathed back into the icy skin of his neck, tears finally falling from her eyes.

Andrew's breath caressed her shoulders as she undressed him; he cringed as she slid his shirt off his arms. It fell to the floor with the rest of his clothes, slick and cold. They embraced tenderly, his breath echoing her heartbeat until he gasped as skin met bare skin, warm skin to freezing.

"Andrew?"

She saw the savage bruises on his chest in the ghostly light. She recoiled at his injuries, her mouth open in alarm. His finger pressed her lips in silence, pushing her gently into the bed. With a sigh, he delicately trailed his finger down to trace the outline of her jaw. "I want to remember," he told her. "I want to remember this when I'm old. I want to remember what you looked like, how I had you, had you to myself in this bed, your eyes, your mouth. I don't want to let this go."

She raised her hand and touched the strong muscles of his neck, the icy skin of his chest, then over the cuts and scrapes, making tears rise in her throat. His heart pounded against her fingers as she searched his face, trying to make him understand how deeply she was his, how she could no longer exist without him, how they were inextricably tied to each other…how it seemed they had always been. The storm pelted against the windows, and she felt the power of Andrew's long sleek body naked against hers despite his injuries.

Nuzzled underneath his chin, she breathed him in, and reached up to kiss his face. In a tentative way she began to explore him, her fingers shaking as they felt his cheeks, his neck, and his shoulders. It terrified and thrilled her all at once to be this close to him. His breathing faltered as her teeth nipped his neck; she felt strangely powerful in that moment, as though she were healing him. Her hands massaged the firm muscles of his biceps, pressing him down into the softness of the blankets.

Rapturous, their bodies laced together. Twisting and turning in each other's arms, they would have cried in joy had they not been so consumed by the wonder of it all.

"I promise, I'll never…never leave you."

"I won't let you."

His head fell, and he laughed. He ceased to care that she was tiny or vulnerable; he consumed her, ravaged her with his lips, unable to deny himself. Grunting huskily, his long, muscled leg snaked around her, pressing his naked body into hers. Caught between the exquisite pleasure and pain it caused, he bit down hard on his lip. Emily drew away and forced down her desire, her body strung taut like a wire.

"We need to get you to a doctor."

"No. Come here," he demanded.

His arms twined about her, the wet curls of his hair brushing against her forehead. His touch flamed her in warmth, and blood coursed through her. His kiss, no less urgent now, brushed against her lips, parting them.

His hand explored the hollow of her neck and smoothed down her sides, his fingers caressing the line of her ribs as he pulled her to him. He lowered his mouth to taste her, his breath warm and fast as he took each nipple one by one into his mouth in hunger, twirling his tongue and grazing his teeth over her till, in exquisite agony, she arched her back again. He sucked deeply, making her nearly come from the raw need of his mouth. Then without warning, he softly bit down, his smile teasing her skin as she called out, aching in bliss.

Satisfied she would no longer protest, Andrew's hand slid its way down the damp skin of her back. He drew a breath and stared at her, his muscles strained and quaking. His eyes forbade her to look away. She dropped all pretense; all her walls tumbled down, and she lay there helpless, burning and sweaty against his thighs. His knees wrenched her open to him.

"Emily," he spoke through clenched teeth, clenched arms, and clenched body, pinning her to the bed, his weight trapping her. His hand claimed her lower back, and his cock pressed against the wet and aching want of her.

She nodded, transfixed.

Then with a violent growl he yanked her to him one last time, his eyes never leaving hers, hypnotizing her in their blue fire. Her body quaked as he took her, as though with that one thrust she would come undone, screaming. She twisted her head against the pillows as he held her captive beneath him. Andrew hissed, his lips near her ear, his breath warm and damp. "Always." His body drove each blessed word slowly and wickedly into her, owning her as no man had ever done. "You…are…mine…always."

Emily flailed underneath him, driven into the soft bed by his assault. Andrew moved in her like a man possessed by the very thing he wished to capture. It didn't matter that the fates were against him, denying him happiness—he had it now. It passed beyond that, as if years of withheld joy were being lavished upon him. He thrust within her, each time repeating the glorious, uncontrollable desire to laugh, to shout if he could. He would not leave her, he told her fiercely. He would not dare tear his body from hers. He was bound to her. He needed to make her understand what roared inside him—exhilarant, wild, and awed.

"Do you know?" his voice and his body demanded. "Have I shown you what you are to me?"

His lovemaking became more erratic, rough and untamed, yet still achingly tender. She was trembling so close to the edge that she could only whimper now and beg him with words so obscene it made him impale himself into her. She held her breath and arched her back, trying desperately to hang on as she cried out loudly, buckling beneath him. In that moment she felt the call of countless generations, lifetimes of souls from the past. They cried their own lovers' names, their rapture magnifying hers, having finally found what they had long lost, all gloriously, rapturously together. Each desperate and terrified of the loss to come.

Andrew dragged her ever more fiercely to him, his burning skin and the sharp stubble of his chin rasping against the flesh of her cheek. He buried his face into her neck and cried, coming hot and savagely inside her, his body contorting in exhaustion. In that last euphoric moment, he cried out one word, falling heavily onto her as though claiming her soul for his and his alone.

"Home."

In that first night.
She wraps the last blankets around
Your body,
Your hands reach
Her face,
Unable to, unable to breathe.
And she whispers sounds for you.
Sweet, sweet, sweet
sounds.
You surrender,
To her, her breath, to her,
To her last first night.
Night,
Andrew Hayes, 2009

Sometime in the night, Emily awoke. The rain still beat against the windows, their bodies burrowed beneath the covers making a refuge of their bed. Andrew's solid forearm lay curled across her breasts, his face nuzzled within the nape of her neck, his breath now warm and steady. Having felt her move, he tightened his hold. Not wanting this to be a dream, she slowly turned to face him in the silent ballet lovers do, scared he would disappear if she couldn't see him, and pressed in drowsy sleep the full length of her naked body to his. In the darkness, she drew her hands softly across the definition of his muscles, memorizing him. Then she remembered his injuries, the cuts on his face and the bruises on his ribs. She heard him inhale, his chest rising at her touch, and she stilled her hand, afraid she had hurt him. In turn, his hand reached out in the blackness, his fingers encircling her wrist.

"I'm still asleep," he murmured.

"If you won't go see a doctor, then you at least need to have a shower or a bath."

"Only if you join me."

"Are you ever going to tell me what happened to you? Or are you going to let me lie here and wonder if you took out your frustrations in a biker bar?"

Andrew groaned with that, and she knew whatever his story, it wouldn't be pretty, so she forced a lightness to her voice, hoping to cajole the truth out of him. "As long as you don't tell me you beat the shit out of Neil, I'll live."

He didn't respond.

She turned to face him. "Oh, Andrew."

"I believe that was what is referred to in the music business as a career limiting move."

Her hand stayed glued across her mouth as he described to her what had occurred at Neil's. He seemed miserable in the retelling, draping his arm over his eyes at the description of it all. In an attempt to turn a horrible situation less dour, she told him about his mother going to stay at a bed and breakfast and tried to convince him that it was a positive thing, that she wasn't leaving for good. Andrew was quiet for some time, and Emily let him be, knowing he had to work this out for himself; no one else could do it for him. The rest would right itself—it had to.

"I'm so sorry Andrew—I never should have eavesdropped on your conversation. I had no right to invade your privacy like that. It was a shitty thing to do."

"I love you," he replied before she could utter another word. "There is nothing to forgive. I should have told you myself."

He lay in silence for a little while longer. When he spoke at last, his face looked soft, like a young boy's in the faint light. "My father loved my mother. Worshipped her. He loved me. That is the truth. There is nothing in the world he wouldn't have done for her. And she cared for him through his illness. He was her friend; they were content—never argued, never raged, always the pinnacle of decorum and respect. But I knew she never loved him. There was no fire. Nothing of what exists between us." His eyes rose to hers, and the passion she saw there made her breath come up short.

He rolled onto his back and groaned, sore and aching, and scrubbed his face awake.

"You're hurt."

"Kiss me."

"But your hands, your face. You could have broken bones."

"I think I would know that by now. You have amazing healing powers, Emily. Please? The bed is warm. I am warm."

"We can do this the hard way or the easy way. Now let me see your hand."

He made a fist and extended his fingers, but he winced a bit when he did so.

"You know, if you don't do it yourself, Christian and Simon are going to haul you kicking and screaming into the emergency room. How are your ribs?"

"You tell me."

"Not a chance. Now talk," she ordered him. "Where were you yesterday and how did this happen?"

He flexed his hand again, testing his fingers, no doubt. "I didn't know what to do after I saw Neil. I ran into S.J., then I ended up on campus." He told her of how he licked his wounds in the practice room, how Nick had spoken to him. The fight on campus came as an afterthought.

Andrew watched Emily's face. Her chin rose and her body tensed. Legs still entwined, their toes barely touched.

"I'm so sorry they hurt you. I could kill them."

"I'll keep that in mind next time."

"And you saw…you saw Nick," she said, when she meant, *You saw her.*

"Yes."

"And later, when you were—hurt. Do you think that was his voice that was speaking to you?"

"I don't know."

The air in the room had cooled. She could tell he regretted mentioning S.J. His face had lost its ease, and his fingers had slowly begun to drum the sides of her thigh, piquing her concern. Yet after everything Andrew and she had gone through in the last twenty-four hours, she felt incredibly petty for reacting in such a way.

"Why do you suppose they keep talking about time running out? Nick has, and Nora too. Even at the séance, Dashiell said that everything is repeating itself. And a curse, he said The Lady in Red would understand the curse. It's got to be the curse that has kept them apart, right?"

"I refuse to believe in curses."

"Even if it involves me being killed?"

"Especially then."

And she could say no more, because he wouldn't let her; his lips ended all argument.

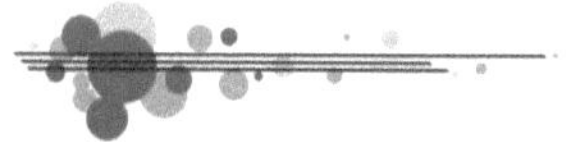

The door was open to the downstairs apartment, and Emily shouted a hello and promptly heard Zoey and Christian's welcome from back in the kitchen. Andrew had left her bed reluctantly a little while ago with a promise to meet her for breakfast there shortly.

They had outdone themselves. There were trays of muffins, sugar dusted scones, steaming platters of scrambled eggs and bacon, heaping bowls of strawberries, and one huge pot of coffee. Zoey had a mug filled and handed it to her with her trademark grin. Margot held up her own mug in greeting and sat clean and pressed at the edge of the table, intent on reading the morning paper. Andrew was nowhere to be found.

Christian was wrestling with the espresso machine, but having a rough go of it. He gave her a wonderfully woeful smile, then wiped his brow. "Please tell me he went to the hospital," she whispered to him as Zoey took over with the espresso duties.

"That hand is my livelihood, you better believe he's going there. He's getting dressed now, but I'm making the idiot walk home after they patch him up. What the hell was he thinking?"

"How much did you get?"

"Enough. Neil, of all people. I'd have let him hit me, instead. We're going to be thrown out on the fucking streets."

With glasses askance and hair sticking up in all directions, Simon shuffled into the kitchen wearing a decrepit bathrobe and humming, "Twinkle,

twinkle little star, how I wonder what you are. Up above the world so high, like—" He stopped short upon seeing the crowd gathered there. Margot studied him over the edge of her paper.

"What can I get you for breakfast?" Simon murmured as he took a seat by her elbow.

"I've already had mine, thank you." She quietly turned a page.

"So where's the prodigal son?" Simon asked flatly, scanning the kitchen. "Did he finally come home and make nice-nice?"

Christian choked on his coffee. Simon's confusion lasted for only a moment.

"Hope you weren't too rough on him. He's a pansy-assed boy. Did he insist on reading you poetry beforehand?"

Just then Andrew rounded the corner. He was dressed in an old flannel shirt and jeans, his unshaven face with its various cuts, scrapes, and bruises made him look thoroughly disreputable. He had even wrapped an Ace bandage around his hand.

Simon's face bloomed in shock at the sight of him. "Jesus Christ, Emily! What the bloody hell did you do to him?"

Andrew's eyes flashed at Simon. His eyebrow arched in unspoken threat.

"So, what the hell happened to you? Did you get attacked by a bunch of horny fangirls?"

"No."

"Fanboys?"

"Christ, Simon. No. And by the way, just for curiosity's sake, how does one study the stars during a thunderstorm?"

Simon swirled around his fork in the air and chewed. "It's not easy. So what did you guys do while we were gathering important scientific data?" he asked, glancing toward Margot while spearing another piece of cantaloupe.

"Andrew punched Neil in the face," Christian deadpanned.

"He what?"

"Is my personal life going to become common knowledge now? Because if so, I'll just call *Entertainment Weekly* after breakfast and save you all the trouble."

"So Neil really is—um—like your baby daddy? Oh blimey. And you really punched him?"

"Yes and yes. Enough said?"

"Mate, we've stayed in God knows how many shit-hole hotels and not once would you let us trash the premises. And now that we've actually got ourselves a house, you have to go and pistol-whip the landlord. You sure we're not going to come home and find our stuff turfed on the curb?"

Andrew rubbed the back of his neck and moaned at the ceiling.

"You can move in with us," said Zoey without hesitation, as if the thought of Christian playing his guitar on the street for spare change was too much to bear.

"I'm sorry," said Simon quietly to him. "I'm just having a laugh, you know that. That has to suck with your mum and everything."

"Yeah." He hesitated as though he wanted to say more, but clearly looked too uncomfortable to answer, so he turned to Christian instead. "What have you been up to?"

"I found a code in Emily's ring."

"What?"

Zoey immediately explained the details to them. The candle, the soot, the numbers.

"But we haven't found out what the numbers could mean," she concluded. "Emily's looked up everything we could think of, addresses, phone numbers, even longitude and latitude."

"How many numbers is it again?" asked Andrew. His expression had stilled and become increasingly focused.

"Eight. Seven-five-five-one-zero-seven-nine-one."

He paced to the counter and looked around, seeming to scan the length of it. "It was here before. Where's the box? Nora's keepsake box?"

Andrew met Emily's stare, his eyes narrowing imperceptibly as she felt her mouth fall open, and she nearly dropped her mug.

"Why didn't I remember?" Emily said.

"You had other things on your mind," Andrew replied softly. "Where did you last leave it?"

"In—in our dining room, I think."

They all went pouring out through the doorway and up the stairs into the girls' flat. It was on the fireplace mantle—the vine covered box—right next to Nora.

Emily took it down and placed it on the table, turning the numbers on the lock until they lined up. With a loud click, the latch sprung open.

Slowly opening the lid, she felt the press of everyone huddling next to her. Six heads peered breathlessly inside.

On top lay a stack of letters bundled in red ribbon. Emily took them out, noticing that they looked old but well cared for. Two velvet pouches lay beneath them. Shaking one open, a ring fell into her palm. It was a man's ring, heavy and cool. She held it up; the platinum band reflected the sunlight. It bore the same vine pattern that decorated the box and Nora's ring.

"Is there anything inscribed on the inside?" asked Christian.

Emily squinted, able to decipher the words there etched in a flowing script. She read them aloud. "To Nick, for every lifetime." Her voice caught.

She handed the band to Andrew who took it silently.

"The other pouch," said Zoey. "Open it."

Andrew looked at Emily and picked it up. He palmed it as though it held something heavy. A key slipped out. A single ornate key, decorated with the same vine design.

"Whoa. What do you suppose it's for?" asked Christian.

Andrew found her eyes. "Whatever it's for, I think we need to read these letters."

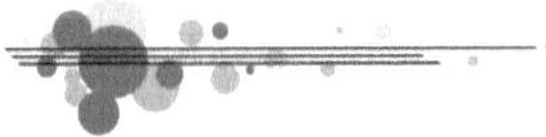

Zoey and Margot sat nestled on either side of Emily on the big overstuffed wicker couch in the attic, letters spread out all over their laps. The men sat on the floor. Andrew's hospital trip appeared temporarily postponed.

Whereas the letters Andrew had found in the trunk had been sent from Nora to Nick, these letters had been sent from Nick to Nora. They covered a period of time much further into their relationship. They read each one aloud to one another too excited to hold the words inside. They spent hours reading. The letters had been urbane and witty. It was impossible not to be charmed by the man, even in memory.

Three letters remained. Andrew began to read them. Emily's fingers curled around the arm of the couch, hanging on his every syllable.

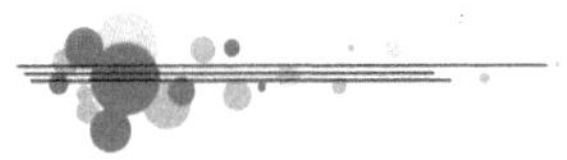

March 25, 1935

Nora,

The case is dragging on a hell of a lot longer than planned, but I should be back soon. Chicago is fine, but the neon sign in the window has got to go.

I've been thinking quite a lot about what you want while sitting here in this flea trap of a hotel room.

We've been through this. I know you want to meet my mother, but I'm telling you, it doesn't matter to me if she never meets you. I don't want you to be exposed to that level of insanity.

Family is not always family. I'd toss out the bunch of them, especially her. Eccentric isn't the word, Nora— deranged and obsessed is closer to the fact.

Honey, I don't want you to get hurt. I'm a sucker that way. Please reconsider. We can do this without anyone's blessing. In fact, I'd rather be cursed.

Yours,

Nick

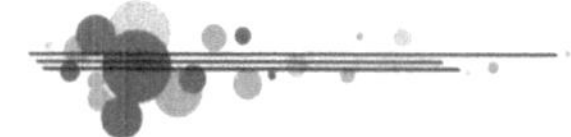

April 29, 1935

Nora,

You really can be a wicked pain when you want to be. You won't take my calls, you won't answer my letters, and you won't let me send you a martini at the Huntington Club.

If it really means that much to you, so be it. I'm warning you. You won't like her, and she definitely won't like you. Don't take it personally. You can charm the devil, lady, but you can't charm a lunatic.

But if you insist. I'm going to marry you one way or the other.

Yours now and always,

Nick

June 25, 1935

Noreen, my love,

I'm truly sorry you had to go through that. I'd like to say I warned you, but that would come up short.

My mother has become fanatical about the supernatural. Ever since she moved into that boarding house in Noyo, she has become obsessed with this lady and all her dire predictions. But that doesn't excuse the vitriol she hurled at you. Wishing you dead. I could have belted her. You shouldn't have stopped me.

Nora, who are you going to believe? A crackpot old woman who hears voices in her head, or me, the man that loves you?

I'm leaving for the coast on Friday as we had planned. I promised you a cottage by the sea. It's the only thing decent from my family, and it's yours — ours — if you want it.

You promised me a honeymoon. You've never broken a promise. It's what I love most about you.

Nick

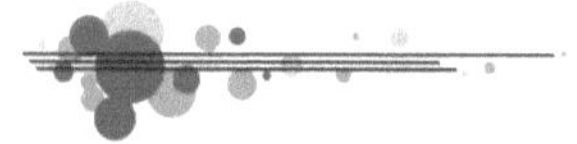

Tears smarted in her eyes as Andrew finished. *June 25th*. The letter was dated June 25th. Nick would be dead in six days' time. And Nora.

Emily wanted to yell at the letter. *No! No, turn back, don't drive up there to that cottage; stay in San Francisco. Stay in this house.* But they didn't. They drove up there despite all the strange and sinister warnings from his addled mother. Closing her eyes, she could picture them, hands intertwined, Nora chatting away as Nick offered some droll insight. And it would all happen in the blink of an eye. The crash, the fall, the ending of so many dreams.

"This lady Nick mentions, the one his mother was obsessed with," Margot said, taking the page from Andrew's hands, "who do you think she was?"

"Maybe she was a medium?" Zoey whispered.

Margot had taken her laptop and entered in the words: *Noyo, California, supernatural.* "Shit," she muttered, clicking ahead.

"What? What?" Emily demanded and poked her face toward the screen.

The words were framed in the Noyo Chamber of Commerce website. Margot read them aloud.

"Sitting above Noyo Harbor since the 1860s lies the haunted Noyo Inn, a bed and breakfast that was once a boarding house. Several ghosts are reported to haunt the site. For years, one such spirit, nicknamed The Lady in White, could be heard in the surrounding forests issuing warnings to travelers and locals alike. Nothing is known of her past, but the Pomo Indians believe she has haunted the grounds long before any white settlers claimed the land. Another ghost, the more infamous 'lady' of the pair, is believed to be the specter of an old woman

who lived in nearby Mendocino, and whose son was killed not far from the site. Mercurial in the extreme, she is alleged to be a violent poltergeist, driving lodgers from their rooms and harrying the staff on multiple occasions. Some reports claim she was responsible for the unsolved disappearance of a young couple that visited the site in the late 1960s. Because of her enraged aura, a violent crimson as opposed to the grayish white of most apparitions, locals refer to her as The Lady in Red."

"We found her," whispered Margot.

"Mrs. Chamberlain, I presume. And here I thought she was called that because her clothes or hair were red," said Christian, amazed.

"The lunatic herself." Andrew's eyes found Emily's.

"Who wants me dead," Emily whispered to herself.

"But why would Nick's mom want Emily to die?" asked Zoey. "What's Emily got to do with any of this?"

"She's a Thomas," Christian said. "Just like Nora."

"But there have to be thousands of Thomases in the world. What's so special about Emily?" said Simon.

"Have your parents called you back?" asked Zoey.

Emily shook her head.

"So what? Nick's mother hates all Thomases because his son wanted to marry one? Seems pretty daft to me. I mean, wouldn't she have a fairly long hit list?" said Simon sarcastically.

"Yeah. I don't know," Emily replied. "Maybe Nora and I are connected somehow? It might be why I'm the only one who can hear her, and why she talks to me and no one else."

"Come to think of it, Paulie, you're the only one who Nick talks to," pondered Simon, taking a look at a very quiet Andrew.

"But what about this part," said Margot, taking up Nick's letters in her hands again as she read. "*Ever since she moved into that boarding house in Noyo, she has become obsessed with this lady and all her dire predictions. But that doesn't excuse the vitriol she hurled at you. Wishing you dead.* And then in this part of the webpage: *Issuing warnings to travelers and locals alike. Nothing is known of her past and Pomo Indians believe she has haunted the grounds long before any white settlers claimed the land.*"

"So this Lady in White must have told Nick's mother some awful prediction. So awful it made her want Nora dead."

"A curse," said Zoey tonelessly. "Dashiell mentioned a curse."

They all stared at one another, not knowing the answers and shaken by the revelations. Nick's mother wanted Nora dead. And she died. Nick's mother wanted Emily dead. And if they didn't figure out why, she might very well end up the same.

"You think that maybe the key in the box might be to this cottage Nick mentioned? Now that would be cool," said Christian, clearly intrigued.

"Well, there's only one way to find out. Road trip," announced Zoey, and she jumped to her feet as though ready to begin packing at that moment.

Emily looked to Andrew, but he didn't say a word. He was too absorbed in twirling Nick's ring between his fingers.

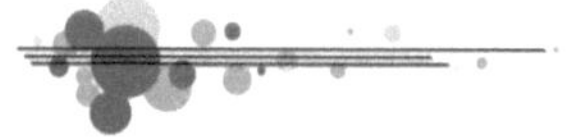

"I'm sorry, did I wake you?" Andrew said gently. He was sitting on the floor strumming his guitar.

Emily rubbed her eyes open, having fallen asleep on the wicker couch while re-reading the letters. Everyone else was gone, probably downstairs, she thought; the sun had set outside, and twilight was falling. She must have been out for hours.

Andrew had a butterfly bandage over his eye and a support dressing strapping his hand.

"You went to the doctor? Thank God. Are you all right? What did they say?"

"Two stitches, bruised ribs, nothing broken, but they warned me if I did anything foolish again with my hand, I could kiss my career goodbye. Although I may have already done that, so it's a moot point, isn't it?"

He played some more, pursing his lip at what must have been the strain in his hand. Then he stopped and placed his fingers over the strings. Curled over his guitar, he held it to his chest until it was silent.

"While I was gone, I was thinking—I think we should stop this search—right now. Just walk away from all this. It's not safe. Since the day I made you take this on you've put yourself in jeopardy. It's my fault. First Vandin, now this. The last thing I want is for you to run off on some wild chase up the coast to some rural little town. It's hard enough to keep you in one piece here."

He began to play again, not wanting to meet her eyes.

"Keep me in one piece? Why do you need to keep me in one piece? I can do that perfectly fine on my own. What do you suppose will happen when you leave to go on tour? I can't walk away—I've seen Nora, spoken with her, and you've spoken with Nick. Either we're all suffering from grand delusions, or what they told us and everything we've learned is the truth."

They had to find Nick's mother, this Lady in Red, who held the answers they needed and the only hope in reuniting Nick and Nora. And somehow Andrew and she were tied up in this in ways they could not imagine. Emily wrapped her arms around her knees, her skirt and sweater suddenly inadequate for the chill that had blanketed the room.

"I can't back out now, and would you even want to? You can't tell me you don't feel responsible for Nick. They'll never be together unless we help."

He began playing again, his fingering becoming more intricate; he was taking his frustration out on the guitar and not her. He couldn't play like he wanted to, and it was galling him. "Let someone else help. It's not safe. Death threats and dire predictions—what more do you need? Wanker professors threatening you? Oh, I forgot, you've already got that one covered." The strumming became more discordant.

"Andrew, what's really wrong?"

He played a while longer, the same phrase over and over. "You're not going up there alone. No way."

"You promised me a holiday. Why don't you come?"

"I believe that might already have been decided. Zoey is running around like a madwoman downstairs arranging the 'Nick and Nora road trip' for six, as she calls it. She's even rung your friends—Dwayne and the lot—claims we need a medium. Christ. Only you would have a business card for a stoner spiritualist on your icebox. You'll be pleased to know, however, that I distinctly put my foot down on driving up in that van of theirs."

She laughed, but he rolled his eyes and strummed a loud chord in response, faking a growl. Then his face grew serious.

"There's something wrong with this whole thing, Emily. I can't describe it, but I feel it. In my gut. Something we've overlooked. Something dangerous. It's there on the edges, but I just can't grasp it."

"Andrew, nothing is going to happen to me or to you. As long as we're together, we'll be safe. Ghosts can't hurt us. Only people."

"That's what I'm afraid of. Do you know what it would do to me if anything ever happened to you? I just found you."

"I'm not walking away from this. I need to know."

Andrew stared at her, unable to respond. Then his hand reached out and cupped her face, his eyes tender and determined all at once. "I love you. But I could kill you sometimes."

He drew closer and held her face more intently, then kissed her, again and again.

The room darkened around them as the night began.

Later that week before their planned trip to Mendocino, Andrew found himself wandering the streets of Pacific Heights alone. Bracing winds whipped along the wide avenues, avenues that in the vivid afternoon sun seemed to rise and fall like rollercoaster tracks under his feet. Narrower streets shot down from the peaks above and dropped their way clear down to the bay. Mansions clung to the hills, some adorned with turrets, gables, and sweeping granite steps, while others fronted modern slabs of concrete and glass. The area reminded him of a grander version of his neighborhood in London, where everything seemed tighter, flatter, and held together in an accepted order.

As the wind kicked up he leaned against a wrought iron fence to shield himself from the gusts and glanced at the slip of paper in his hand which Emily had given him. She had slid it across the table to him at breakfast that morning with an expectant look in her eyes.

"What's this?" he had asked her with a quizzical smile.

"I have my last final this afternoon. It's a graduation gift. You should be happy that I took the effort away from having you choose."

"It's an address. You want me to buy you a house?"

She threw him a look. He'd forgotten that she had little money, while she knew very well that he did. "It's where your mother is staying. You need to talk with her. She loves you. Please."

"Emily—I—I don't know. I don't even know what to say."

"Start with I'm sorry—it usually works wonders."

She walked around to his side of the table, kneeled down in front of him, and kissed him. He couldn't deny her, especially when she kissed him so, or when she drew away and looked at him with such earnestness in her eyes. Eyes that were underscored with dark circles that he knew had little to do with the last of the finals she was taking in a few hours. She'd had nightmares last night, awful ones from the sound of it. She clearly didn't want to talk about them, and he wouldn't have been concerned if this was only the first time, but it was the third nighttime horror in as many days. In the middle of the night she would wake and bolt upright, gasping for air. He would struggle to hold her, to find her frozen lips and kiss them, whisper songs to her, anything to drive the fears away—fear of ghosts, fear of death, fear of losing each other. Whatever they were, she wouldn't speak of them. When he questioned her in the daylight, she would wave her hand dismissively as though they were long forgotten and return to her enthusiastic detective self. It was driving him mad.

But what could he do? He had promised her he would go on this ridiculous road trip to seek out more ghosts, ones who clearly didn't have her best interests at heart. And while he still felt an inexplicable need to help Nick, it wasn't strong enough to risk her life in the process.

When he reached the grand Victorian, he looked up and took a deep breath. He wished he could confide all of this to his mother, but he feared how she would perceive it, given her supernatural leanings. She had always believed in such things, and as a child he had been taken to countless grave-yards and haunted inns about the country. He had a difficult time reconciling this with her profession as a barrister; she seemed so level-headed and wise. If he told her she would fret, or worse yet, want to come along. No, it was better to deal with one clusterfuck at a time.

The etched glass doors of the bed and breakfast opened to reveal a chintz-laden parlor that led to an ornately carved staircase. The entryway was empty, so he followed the gilt framed direction signs up the stairs to suite five. The room was at the end of the hall. He only had to knock once.

His mother stood there, the epitome of style in a black skirt, silk blouse, and endless pearls. She didn't notice his beat up jeans and leather jacket. She looked only at his face, and a moment later her composure dissolved.

"Andrew! What happened to you?"

He had forgotten about his bruises and cuts. He could see the logi-cal and ghastly conclusion she must be coming to, and he quickly replied,

"Some drunken frat boys — I'm fine. The hand's been better, though…" He held up his bandaged fist with a shrug, like a child hoping for sympathy.

The ploy had its desired effect, and with fluttering hands she ushered him into a seat in her small sitting room. A tea set was laid out, scenting the air with bergamot.

"Sorry, I already had mine," he said quietly.

"Since when has that stopped you before? No, you sit down and have a cup of tea. There's coffee there as well. It'll make you feel better. Are you sure you're not hurt? Oh, Andrew…"

He sat down and let her pour while she eyed him as though he might keel over into the china at any moment. He could tell she was thankful for his presence, but an air of nervousness hovered around them as if they had to get used to their bodies being in the same room with each other. As if all the changes and revelations had to find a place to sit, as well.

He plowed on, not wanting to delay. "I said some horrible things, Mum. I was angry, but that doesn't excuse my behavior. I love you. I know you love me, I do — and I want to listen now if you're willing to talk."

He paused, but before he could say another word, she placed her hand tenderly over his and patted his fingers a few times before she tightened her hold. "No, first…first I would like you to tell me about Emily."

"What do you want to know?" he asked. He was still defensive of her, and his tone came across as such. If this was going to descend into another round of judgments, he would be gone.

"What you would have liked to have told me if I had been willing to listen."

So he told her everything about Emily, everything that he could share. He laid bare all his anxiety regarding the future and his fear that when they returned to the road he would lose her. Claudia poured him another cup of tea and sat back. He waited, hoping for guidance.

She stared at him over the rim of her cup and answered his thoughts. "I'm the last person to ask for help, you must know that. I've made a mess of a great deal of my life, and it has taken me a long time to see that." She went to sip her tea but frowned at the cup as though it had become sour and placed it down on the saucer. What she said next surprised him.

"I had another dream the other night. The same one I had in Boston — about the ocean. You were terribly hurt — bleeding." The hair on the back of his neck rose. He remembered the images that had rushed through his head when he found the chest in the passageway: the cliffs, the hotel, the screaming. "What did that man mean the other night about Emily? About someone wanting her dead?"

"It's bullshit, Mum."

"No it isn't, Andrew. Something is obviously bothering you. Tell me."

And so with great reluctance, he explained to her everything they had learned from the ring and the letters and where they were heading off to on Friday morning.

"That's only two days away."

"I know, but part of me wishes it was yesterday — just so we could put this behind us." More than anything, he wanted to end this now. Burn the letters, scatter the ashes, and destroy it all. But he knew he couldn't. No matter how much he wanted it over with, Emily and he could not run from this. It would find them. Because he knew he had seen it all before.

This was his secret — the dreadful secret he could not tell his mum; he couldn't even tell Emily. He was afraid they would think he was losing his mind again. Every detail of this chaos and every step they took seemed eerily familiar, as if he had lived this nightmare over and over. He felt like he was stuck in an endless loop — helpless to change the outcome — lifetime after lifetime after lifetime.

"Well, it doesn't matter," he said, pushing away his fears. "After this weekend we'll have our answers."

"The trip sounds dangerous, Andrew."

He couldn't argue with her. Even Zoey had insisted they invite Dwayne and his fellow stoners to dinner tonight to go over the details of the séance. But what help they could provide seemed tenuous at best.

"Tell me about Neil," he asked brusquely, sick of discussing the bloody mystery.

Taken aback, she placed her hands in her lap, smoothing out the line of her skirt. Always so composed, she transformed before his eyes into a teenager again, gawky and shy.

"I met Neil during his last year at university. It was at a pub in London. He was there for a band — he was always with a band — it was in his nature." She smiled wistfully, as though looking through pages of an old photo album, though her body remained tense. "I loved him the first moment I saw him. I think you may know how that feels. I'm sorry if these words are hard for you to hear. Love can exist in so many different ways. I know you. I know how passionate you are, how driven, how all-consuming love is to you. It was the same for Neil and me. It's just that we, we weren't as brave, you see.

"We were inseparable in those months after we met. He was finishing his final year. Everyone expected him to follow the sensible route. He had so little money, as little as I did. It only made sense that he would pursue a professional future—doctor, barrister…But his true passion, what he loved more than anything, was music. His family's expectations were quite different, as you can imagine. He was never close to them—although he was thankful they had adopted him—but he just felt he was too different, I suppose. So it was me who convinced him to chase his dreams. To rebel."

She took a long breath and looked out into nothing, then back at him.

"I found out I was pregnant with you a month before the end of classes. I cannot begin to explain to you the joy—from the very beginning, Andrew—the pure joy of knowing you would be in this world. Please know that."

He sat very still, knowing what her next words would be before she even spoke them. Yet his heart hammered in his chest as though it was running to reach them.

"So I ended it. I knew what he wanted, and what his dreams were. I couldn't stand in his way."

"Did he know? Did Neil ever know?"

"I did the right thing."

"Mum, did Neil ever know about me?"

His pulse beat so hard he felt it in his fists.

"Yes."

The finality of the word stole away his breath. His hope, a fragile, fledgling thing, died. He was so sure she would say no.

"I know you would like my past to have been some sort of fairy tale. And I wanted that too, Lord did I want it. We were both so young—we had all our lives ahead of us. It would be wonderful to think everything we wanted was possible, because it did seem like that, we were so caught up in each other. Everything mattered, we were going to change the world. But when I told Neil I was pregnant, I knew in an instant by the look in his eyes what he would say before he said it. That he would pay to have it taken care of, that I didn't have to worry. And for the first time I saw what he wanted the most in life, what would always come first for him, what had to come first for him. And it wasn't me.

"I couldn't hate him for it, although I did for a while. It was the hardest time. We barely spoke. He tried to fight for us, or how he wanted us to be, but I was too proud. He never imagined that I would consider keeping the baby. I don't think it entered his mind. So I told him that the baby was gone, and that he should be as well. In the end, we fell apart. He left for the States without even a goodbye. Nothing."

Andrew tried to concentrate on her words, but the room seemed to be spinning around him. She went on tonelessly.

"A few weeks later I went to a party with a friend. I swore that I heard the host say a St. John was there. For one precious moment I hoped against hope that Neil had come back, that he couldn't live without me after all. But it wasn't a St. John. It was a man who just happened to be named John, a man who also had an amazing capacity to love in his own way. Someone who wanted to stay. And it was for the best. Your father adored you, and Neil, well, he went on to achieve everything he ever wanted."

"But did Neil ever know how you felt about…what you wanted?"

"I couldn't do that to him. Oh, Andrew. Regardless of everything else, he was so poor. You can't understand what that's like. The family he lived with could barely feed themselves. I had nothing to offer. I would have only been a burden to him. If he had known about you, he might have stayed and given it all up, and I knew he would come to regret it. Regret me. And—"

"Regret me."

Claudia's beautiful face fell. "He never looked back. It was for the best."

"Did you? Did you look back?"

"Your father was a dear man who loved me more than I deserved. He married me in spite of everything, and we had a fine life together—and he loved you without reserve. It's all over between Lainey and me. It doesn't matter anymore."

"Stop. Why do you call him that? His name is Neil."

"It was his nickname—or my nickname for him. It was a family name, he didn't much care for Claudia either. He always called me C.C." She smiled sadly.

"So what happens now?"

"Now? I'm done telling you what to do, Andrew. I love you, but you're old enough to make your own decisions. I can tell you that my decisions brought me happiness because they brought me you—and your father. Please know I did love him in the best way I knew how."

"But what about Neil?"

Claudia looked lost, caught somewhere between confusion and apprehension. He took her hands in his. "Thank you. I know this was difficult."

"It's too late for Lainey and me, Andrew. Our time is passed."

"Do you want it to be?"

She didn't answer.

He stood up to leave and made it to the door before he turned. "Mum, we're playing tonight at the Elbo Room. It's a small club over on Valencia. It's for Emily—she's graduating and we wanted to surprise her. She thinks it's just dinner—but I would really love for you to be there."

"Oh, Andrew, thank you. Of course I'll be there."

"Nine o'clock, then?"

She nodded.

He wasn't sure it was the right thing to do. He wasn't even sure he wanted to do it, but he knew where he had to go next. He was tired of fate fucking with him.

Andrew paced outside Neil's home for what felt like an eternity. He didn't know how to begin; this was turning out to be much harder than he had expected. All he wanted to do was say his piece and be gone, short and to the point. That was it. In frustration, he sat down on the stone steps and tried to take a few deep breaths, placing his elbows on his knees and his head in his hands. He heard soft footfalls approach and glanced up into the sunshine.

Neil's dark blue suit set off the blond-gray of his hair, and sympathy lined his tired face. "How's your hand?"

"It's been better. How's the chin?"

Neil rubbed it thoughtfully. "No wonder you can play the way you do." Andrew laughed, though he didn't want to. "Want to take a walk?" Neil offered, as though encouraged by the sound. "I was going to grab a bite."

A few blocks down the street they found a taqueria where one could order at the window and sit outside at tables covered by the shade of umbrellas. Outside was good, Andrew reckoned. There would be less chance of a fight with witnesses, and he wouldn't appear the bundle of nerves he was at the moment.

"It must be very hard for you right now," Neil said as they sat down. Andrew couldn't read his eyes; they both wore sunglasses, the afternoon rays blazing down on them.

"I could say the same for you. How much do you...know?"

"Enough, or enough after you came to see me. That kind of clinched the deal. I knew the exact date she sent me away, I found out your birthday. The math was, as they say, elementary."

"So then — you sought us out knowing who I was?"

"No, not then. I had my hunches, but I wanted to see you because of what others had said about your music. I couldn't believe anyone could be that good. But you were, and you were also her son — one look at you told me that. You have her face, her mouth. And so many of her mannerisms."

But I have your drive, Andrew thought.

They drank their beers and watched the people go by. It wasn't until that moment that Andrew realized what all of this might mean to Neil. He was this man's son, as well. Neil had searched him out and had gone to great lengths to keep him close by. Why? Curiosity? Morbid fascination?

"Andrew, I want you to know that I understand, to a small degree, what you're going through right now. I have spent my life loving your mother — and I've tried my best to live without that love. I went on, I found a dear woman, and I lost her to cancer. Up until the moment I saw Claudia the other night, I thought I had found a place for all those memories. But life isn't like that, is it? It's not ordered and organized...it's shocking and messy, and at times we're forced to react instead of act.

"I'm not going to sit here and make excuses for my twenty-one-year-old self or my forty-four-year-old one, either. There is only one thing I need for you to hear and that you must understand. If I had known, if I had realized the situation — no matter what she said to me — I would not have left her. Ever."

"You say that now. It's easy to say that now. But the truth is, you did leave."

"You're right. And it is my biggest regret."

They sat there not knowing what to say to the other. Both of them were trying to hold on to things taken from them and to reclaim lost time.

"How is Emily? That was quite an interesting party the other night," Neil asked, changing the subject.

"That's an understatement."

Their meal arrived, and Andrew spent it telling him what he had learned about Nick and Nora, under the belief that any information he could glean in return would help them, though in reality he didn't want to leave yet. Every minute together seemed to solidify the fact that the situation was real. Neil and he were real.

"That's fascinating," Neil said as a woman cleared the last of their plates.

"May I ask you a question?"

"Of course."

"Could your wife hear them? Nick and Nora?"

This startled Neil, but he shook his head. "No, she could not. Maybe it's because…I don't know." He waved to the waitress for their bill.

"I'm sorry I punched you."

Neil glanced at Andrew, then shook his head as if not wanting to dwell on that subject any longer. "S.J. rang me. She wanted to know why you aren't returning her calls. She says it's urgent regarding the *Rolling Stone* shoot."

"Oh. Well, yeah."

"Andrew, you can do this shoot without any agreements. But a word to the wise. No matter how you feel about her personally, she is incredibly powerful in the industry, and you don't want to make an enemy of her. I work around her to the best of my ability. Jump through the hoops for the shoot and then be done with her if that's what you want, but do not blow her off."

Neil got up to leave, and Andrew realized what he had to do. "Neil," he blurted out.

Neil looked down at him, and Andrew caught the fleeting glimpse of expectation in his eyes. It left him with the feeling of what his face would have looked at the other side of a cricket bat, or the end of a dinner table, or at the edge of a bed behind a book.

"This is a lot for me to take in."

His face softened. "I know."

And looking at him, Andrew knew beyond a shadow of a doubt he did. It made it all the easier to do what he wanted to do.

"We're playing a short set at the Elbo Room tonight, you know — over on Valencia. Emily's graduating, and we wanted to surprise her — and I was wondering, if you were interested, we start at eight — if maybe you might think about — "

"I wouldn't miss it, Andrew."

His throat was too tight to speak. He could only nod his head. They shook hands, and Andrew watched Neil walk away.

With two hours until call, the line out the club was already crazy, making Andrew pace around the risers.

"You need to take a leak or something?" asked Simon, grabbing a swig of water as he kneeled down to adjust the level of his drums.

"Nope, I just want to get started. It's been a while."

Christian and Simon grinned at him, looking how he felt. It was great to be back up on a stage no matter how small, not to mention the stash of new music they were aching to try out. Andrew hadn't told anyone of his plan. He himself didn't want to think of it, but he was still glad he had issued the invitations. Now, it was up to them.

After the sound check, they headed back to the green room and pushed around something that resembled food, but it could have been soylent green for all they cared, as eager as they were to start.

Finally they heard the club owner shout out their name. They pushed open the doors from the back of the club and were hit with an amazing roar, in which Andrew distinctly heard a sharp whistle that he knew to be Zoey's. He peered into the lights and saw her excited, smiling face; next to her sat Emily, who, despite being surrounded by the stoners clad in black robes and matching hats, was grinning like mad. Margot did not look amused. He could not help but laugh at the sight.

While Christian and Simon got situated on stage, he slung his guitar over his shoulders and approached the microphone. "Good evening," he told the crowd.

He had no sooner gotten the words out of his mouth when the screams hit him again, causing him to laugh out loud. God, it was going to be a amazing night; he could feel it. The air was electric.

"Thank you all for coming. Rather thrilled to be here."

"Take off the rest of your clothes!" someone screamed from the back. Andrew ducked his head to hide his grin. It was over one hundred degrees on stage if it was a degree, and they had already stripped down to just their undershirts and jeans during sound check.

Not saying another word, he counted off stridently, and they surged into their first song. He had written it to showcase Simon's talent, a drum solo that set the stage on fire, and Simon did not disappoint. Christian and Andrew took a side stand during the number and let the crowd yell out its praises. Toward the end, Andrew grabbed an extra pair of sticks and played opposite him, causing Simon to grin from ear to ear as they each tried to outdo the other. They ended on one hard note, and the room roared its praises.

They played two more hard rocking numbers. During the middle of the second song he saw Neil slide in and take his seat. He caught his eye and nodded, then set himself to attack a patch of complicated fingering. His hand ached in response to the limits he was pushing by trying to attempt this riff, but he wanted to prove something to himself, or maybe to Neil, but it could be that he just wanted to show off a bit in the process. He felt invincible.

After they finished he leaned toward the microphone, sweaty and out of breath, and smiled. "This next song is in honor of a young woman who finished university today. Who has her whole life ahead of her…" And almost as an aside, he added softly, "Hopefully with me."

The song started sparsely and continued to build as the words tangled over each other in their want to gain freedom. He shut his eyes and pressed his mouth to the microphone as he sang, and his body rocked as the guitar became a part of him. But soon the rush and the power of the song overtook him; the music, his guitar, and the air around him fused. The crush of the song, the very essence of it, coursed through him, and he let it go. For her. Always for her.

As the last chorus tumbled down, his chest heaved from the effort. The applause hit so brutally against him that he flinched. He tried to steady himself and looked to Christian, who leaned over and whispered in his ear. "Fuck! I love you, you asshole. You fucking rule."

Andrew laughed shakily. The screaming was still going on.

"Do your song," he whispered back to him, and Christian gave him a double take. He had been nervous about performing it. "I'll do back up," Andrew promised as he slugged back some water.

Christian came up to the center microphone, and after stalling a bit he spoke, his voice melting into a low baritone laced with cool and charm. "How about the Brit?" The crowd hooted in approval, and he grinned in response. "I'd like to dedicate this song to Zoey, who's sitting out there. Where are you, chere? Hey." His smile widened as he saw her waving a lighter. "I'm going to marry you someday."

Andrew spit out his water, and Simon did a cymbal crash as though he'd fallen off his stool. "Great technique," Andrew told him, trying to cover his shock at his band mate's public confession.

Unfazed, Christian started the familiar melody, playing the tune he had been practicing most days in the flat. Andrew nodded and stood back, content to be in the shadows. *Marriage.* Christ. Had Christian actually said it? Marry Zoey? Whereas he couldn't utter a single definitive word about his future with Emily if his life depended on it, his band mate had laid out the *M* word with no problem. Yes, he had spoken around it: he wanted forever, he wanted never to leave her, he wanted to be only hers, but he could not say the word. Even when he gave her the ring he floundered, grappling onto the vague word "promise" instead.

The only time he could utter the words were when he was pissed, when she couldn't know whether or not it was the booze talking. The suave drunk that he was had no problem unleashing his mouth in that situation. *Marry me now, not later…*

But that would be asking a hell of a lot from her. His mother was right—did he know Emily's dreams? Did he think he could just steamroll over them to get what he wanted? Did she even fancy being married? Did he? They were still so bloody young.

If someone had told him a year ago he would be contemplating marriage, he would have laughed in their face. Andrew Hayes, married? The word seemed almost tyrannical, as though it should be accompanied by a thud of a ball and the dragging of a chain. Live with someone, sure, but lose his freedom, enter into that level of commitment? Yet he had never loved a woman like Emily. Love. It seemed inane for what he felt, for how his life had changed. By day, music raged in him, his hands could not capture it fast enough. And at night, he would shut her bedroom door, and for one quiet moment they would gaze upon each other in tenderness. Then they were lost.

Christian started singing and soon began to geek as only he could. He motioned Andrew toward him, and they dueled with their guitars, forcing Andrew to cast aside his thoughts. When they reached the microphone and sang madly into it, grinning like fools, they were completely in their element—higher than they'd ever been on stage before. They laughed, and all the expectant faces out there couldn't get enough of them. Then all too soon the song came to its resolution and ended in perfect harmony.

Andrew was so over the moon by now that he did something he rarely did: he asked for requests.

A table of students shouted all at once, *"She Kills!"*

He ignored them and asked again. He could sense Christian looking toward him in anticipation. He kept strumming and rocking to a rhythmic chord, while Simon provided the backbone of a steady beat; both were waiting for his choice.

He hadn't played that particular song in a long time, and with good reason. It was the first piece of music he'd written after he returned home from his time with Memphis—a brutal, scathing piece about the hopelessness he had felt. An addict's screed, one reviewer had called it. It was probably the best thing he'd ever written, but it was hell to perform.

The crowd continued to scream for it, for too long and too voraciously; he had to silence them. He could feel Christian's eyes on him as he began to play the opening stanzas. Simon ramped up the blistering drumming that served as the song's heartbeat, and the pulse of Christian's bass joined them.

He wouldn't lose himself this time, he'd stay in control, he told himself as his voice poured out aching and loss. The words and the tune were familiar territory to him, but this time when he played he didn't see the images of his time with Memphis, nor the countless other dives where he had sung this song to nameless crowds. No, the more he played, the more scenes tore through his mind from someone else's lifetime.

Memories came rushing in, and he couldn't stop them: the ocean pounded like Simon's drums; a woman's voice wailed like Christian's guitar. He heard the shriek of gulls and saw jagged rocks, rocks everywhere he turned. And blood. "Nick, stop…no Nick, Niiiiick!"

A scaring pain lanced through his heart, and he bent over his guitar and tried to grab a foothold in reality as his screaming vocals filled the room. He could feel the eyes of everyone in the audience as the world fell apart around him. "No, you're going to win this time," he heard a voice command, a man's voice, rough and impatient. "You've got to win. You're going to live."

With a cry, he threw himself backward and closed his eyes, attacking his guitar. The strings bit into his fingers as he found a lifeline in the melody, and he wailed on it until the final chord when he twisted to the side and nailed the final note.

He fought to remain standing. Through the haze he saw Claudia in the tumultuous crowd. She stood there staring at him, Neil at her side, both faces pale in concern. He had not seen her arrive, and he could tell she saw right through him. And whether she was pleased or not, she was staring at him like she had in the past—as if he were on the edge of madness. She looked up into Neil's face.

Andrew shut his eyes.

After the show, Andrew composed himself enough to sign the obligatory autographs, though he was still shaken from the performance. Thankfully, Claudia and Neil did not stay behind. He didn't have the wherewithal to deal with them or the questions they were sure to ask.

Due to the stoners' special diet, they ended up eating at a holistic bistro next door. Andrew had no sooner walked into the restaurant when he saw Emily's face. She stood up from the table and ran and jumped into his arms. He held her tightly and buried his face into the softness of her hair and breathed in the smell of her, reveling in the warmth of her skin.

"You were amazing. Thank you, it was the best gift ever, ever, ever. But are you all right? You looked—"

He picked her up and swirled her around, ending her speech with a kiss. He didn't want to think of the performance.

"Andrew, did you see your mother and Neil there tonight?"

"Did they look happy?" he asked.

"Yes."

She studied him a bit longer and placed her hand softly against the side of his face. He took her hand and kissed it. Whatever would happen would happen. He didn't care anymore. He was with her. Once at the table, he raised his hand in greeting and received a round of boisterous hellos. Zoey was clad in something feathery and pink and sat in Christian's lap, draping a boa around his neck. Margot, who sat beside Simon, took a moment to offer her compliments on the show before they resumed their debate over the beer list.

Dwayne, Buck, Dinesh, and Egan were already diving into what looked like a bowl of shockingly green hummus.

"Yo, dude," cried Dwayne, the green mixture stuck in his soul patch. "Masterful manipulation of the muse, man."

"Say that five times fast," remarked Christian, reaching across Zoey to grab a breadstick.

They ordered and chatted about the show before Dwayne piped up, glancing at Zoey. "So, the lady here says you need some mediumistic guidance on your trip up to Noyo. Whoa, Noyo — that's some pretty heavy stuff up there."

"You know about it?" asked Emily, talking over him in her interest.

"Everybody knows about it. It's like totally awesome, Muse-lady. It's the freakin' Disneyland of spiritualistic endeavors. They talked about it at our conference last year."

"What conference?"

"The California Astral Liberation Coalition. We gather with the goal of liberating spirits who might be trapped and in need of directions to move on."

"Your mater must be so proud." Simon rolled his eyes.

"It's a gift, man," Dwayne said proudly.

"So do you think you can help us?" Emily asked, trying her best to ignore her supportive friends.

"I've been talking with some colleagues that farm up there — you know, the backyard variety…"

"Where the trees meet the sleaze." Buck whistled.

"They say this Lady in Red is a bitch and a half. Sorry, no offense. I mean I'm all for woman power, but sometimes you just run out of words to quantify the emotion," said Dwayne.

Andrew was starting to wonder when the last time these guys had eaten. Their appetites were bordering on frightening; even Simon seemed impressed. Dinesh spoke up, taking a breather from the dolmas that had just been delivered. "I think we need to bring some neutralizing equipment."

Christian's eyes widened.

"Not a bad idea," seconded Egan, who was blessing a plate of couscous.

Christian could no longer contain himself and slammed his fists down on the table in excitement. "Seriously! You guys pack heat?"

"I wouldn't go that far," intoned Egan, his arms bearing more bangles than Zoey's. "I mean, Buck is still on parole for possession, so we can only carry spiritually licensed neutralizing apparatus."

"Oh man! You mean protein packs and ecto goggles and slime blowers, you got those?!"

Dinesh and Egan did not look amused, although Dwayne did crack a smile.

"Ladies and gentlemen," Emily chided, anticipating a remark any second from Simon about a key-master, "let's not insult our guests. Now Zoey, would you like to give everyone the itinerary for the weekend, please?"

Zoey handed out stapled stacks of paper. Each of their names was written in crayon in the top corner.

Dates, times, and events were listed. Andrew tried to look at his, but images from the show began to slice through his mind. The ocean, the sun blazing on rocks, the touch of a woman's hand on his wrist. He took a deep sip of his wine, but the pictures kept lashing before his eyes.

"Where's the free time? No free time?" Simon asked, getting a chuckle from Margot.

"It's under 'explore at your leisure,'" Zoey told him.

"Hmm. Not quite what he had in mind," Christian remarked into his beer.

"We leave at seven a.m. on Friday and arrive in Mendocino around noon. We'll be stopping at the Dia Vineyards for a wine tasting and lunch."

Nick, let's stop for lunch, I'm parched. And my hair, look at me, where's my hat?

Out of nowhere, the voice rang in Andrew's ears again as it had at the club, too real, too close. Nora's voice. He shook his head roughly, trying to make it go away.

"She doesn't miss a beat, does she?" Christian whispered to Emily, who smiled into her itinerary.

"Then we have a free evening in Mendocino to shop, dine or — well, whatever." Zoey waved the word away with her hand.

Thank God, you packed the gin. Does the house have an icebox? No matter, we'll survive.

Andrew took a deep sip of his wine.

"There, that's what I was looking for, this 'whatever,' not that 'free time,'" Simon said, smiling and gaining a toast from Christian.

Zoey ignored them and continued. "We gather at nine o'clock for breakfast bright and early on Saturday, and then we head off to the Noyo Inn where we've reserved a room for our séance, um…circle."

"Righteous," nodded Dwayne, taking his pile of steamed kale from the waiter.

"After our successful communication with the great beyond, we'll break for lunch and then start our search. Maybe even find the Chamberlains' house if it's still there."

"I feel like I'm going on a fucking supernatural scavenger hunt," Simon huffed, eyeing his tofu burger with consternation.

"I envision we'll find Nick's ashes before happy hour," Zoey said as though they would be looking for the right pair of shoes versus the mortal remains of a man whose belligerent ghost of a mother probably wanted to keep him well hidden. "Next, we've got dinner reservations at Café Beaujolais to celebrate. The rest is a free night, then after breakfast we'll decide where we want to reunite the ashes and head on home. Any questions?"

"When's the making-animals-out-of-hand-towels class?" Margot asked.

"Um, Ms. Zoey, I think you might want to keep lunch optional on that Saturday. These things could take time. Especially if the spirit is, um…" Dwayne struggled for the word.

"A bitch," said Margot.

"Yeah, that. She could make it tough. And there's the small problem that she wants Emily here dead. Them's fighting words. We've got to be careful."

"Andrew, are you okay?" Emily had noticed Andrew leaning back on his chair, sweat on his brow.

"That's the first intelligent thing I've heard the man utter," Andrew told her as she switched his cassoulet with her orange kebab salad, still looking at him strangely.

Nick, you needn't drive so fast, we have plenty of time.

"Dwayne is correct," said Egan, quieting the table. "This isn't some weak poltergeist we're dealing with. She's violent, scary-shit violent, from what they say. If it gets too extreme, I'm going to end it — whether you get your information or not. I don't think it's wise to let her inhabit anyone — best to try to contact her directly. Chances are she'll want to possess someone to get to Emily. We can't let that happen. It would definitely harsh our mellow."

They all stared at each other, not knowing whether to burst into laughter or be terrified to death.

"Now, let's all exchange cell phone numbers so we're all in sync," said Zoey, trying to restore the vacation feel to their plans for the weekend.

"You need to call your boyfriend, Emily," Margot added, munching on some fries. "Tell him you're leaving town."

"Excuse me?" Andrew said to her.

"It's nothing," Emily replied.

"I think Detective Obester has a thing for Emily. He's been calling a lot," Margot told him with a teasing nod.

"He knows I'm worried," Emily insisted. "He's a friend of the family, and there's nothing new to report. Vandin's still out of the country."

"Did you tell this boyfriend of yours you were leaving the city?" Andrew asked flatly. "In case he needs to get a hold of you?"

"Yes. Now will you people please drop it?"

Nick, slow down, please!

He set down his wine glass, afraid it would shatter in his grip.

"Well, here's to our Nick and Nora road trip!" Zoey offered.

NICK, NO, STOP!

They all raised their glasses and drank.

All except Andrew, who had fled from the restaurant and out to the street where he slammed his hands against a car and vomited.

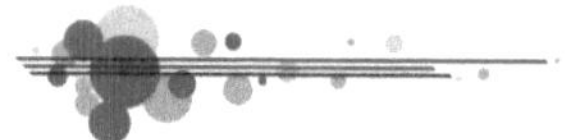

"Andrew, talk to me." Emily stood in his bedroom after having helped to carry him in from the car. The rest of the crowd had reluctantly disbursed once they knew he wasn't going to die on them. They were shaken though, especially Simon, who Andrew had to practically throw out.

Andrew needed time alone to get his head together. Everything was moving too fast for him to control. The visions, this trip, the warnings, everything was crashing down around him.

"I can't help you if you won't talk to me."

"I don't want your help, just leave me alone. I told you, it was something I ate. All I need is sleep."

"No! I'm not going to leave you alone. You almost fainted. You nearly cracked your skull open on the sidewalk."

"Forget it. I'm tired."

"Please tell me this isn't about Detective Obester, because if it is you've gone completely off the deep end, you know that? How can you even think

I would have feelings for anyone other than you? It's insanity. Complete insanity."

"He seems to be pretty attentive for a cop, offering up his personal phone lines."

"He's a friend of the family, you know that, and he has a wife and kids. So what if he gave me his cell? I can get him any time I need him. At least he's accessible. I thought you cared about my safety. Or are you just going to pull the whole protective male brooding crap?"

"I do care about your safety, but forgive me if I point out that you have a pretty piss poor track record when it comes to your judgment in men."

"What is that supposed to mean?"

"Nothing."

"No, nothing, what is that supposed to mean?"

"Well, Vandin, you trusted him."

"Vandin? How can you even bring him into this? You know nothing about the men that have been in my life."

"Men? How many, then?"

"Don't you dare stand there and judge me. How many women have you slept with on the road, Andrew? I've seen the way women throw themselves at you, hang around after your shows, push through the crowd to get to you. At least my relationships had meaning and lasted longer than the time it took to turn in the motel key."

She slammed the door so loudly it nearly fell off its hinges as she marched into the hall. He sat on his bed, his skull on fire. The thought of Emily with other men caused the taste of ocean brine to fill his mouth, the sun to burn his eyes, and screams to tear at his guts. But now they weren't Nora's screams anymore, they were Emily's. His room tilted on its side, and he slid from the bed. The pain in his head was excruciating, and he battled to stand on his feet, overcome with the need to reach her. Lumbering through the flat, he reached the stairway and took the steps three at a time. The conservatory door was open, and he rushed up the stairs.

The moon cast the room in ghostly iridescence. Emily sat on a wicker couch near the windows, beneath the cover of stars. He hovered above her, his heart still racing.

"I'm sorry," he whispered. "I'm so bloody sorry."

"What's wrong? Tell me."

"Nothing, nothing's wrong," he said, his voice thick and unsteady against her hair. "Nothing," he insisted.

"I love you." Emily lifted her hands to his face. "Only you," she whispered. "No one else."

He gazed at her face, her silver eyes, the strong set of her jaw framed by loose curls, and again the roar of the ocean's waves seized him. And the image of Nora gazed at him in return, and he wanted her in that instant, ached in pain for her. So he cast it away and lost himself to pure instinct. He pressed his lips to her ear and whispered all the ways he loved her. Emily. His Emily.

He took her in every way imaginable inside that darkened room that night. In the final act of possession, he clung to her, the wisp of a spirit that enveloped him, floating like vapor as he forced himself into her soul. Emily. His Emily.

Later he wrapped his body around hers and buried his face into her shoulders. They lay there for an immeasurable time, breathing hard, trembling from the unimaginable experience they had shared. Both were shaken not by what they were capable of, but by the desperate and raw emotions it awakened in both of them. They surrendered to it — not wanting to understand, not wanting to fight anymore.

Andrew glanced through his bedroom curtains and watched as swathes of gray fog cast across the sky and forced back the early morning sun that threatened to break through.

Emily lay sleeping upstairs. During the night he had carried her back to her bed, preferring she woke in the morning there in his arms instead of shivering to death on the cold attic floor. Despite being fast asleep when he crawled in beside her, she soon became restless, muttering and tossing and turning until he had hushed her into stillness. Soon after, they fell asleep intertwined, silent lovers with no more nightmares haunting either of them.

At dawn he awoke. It took all his willpower to slip out from under the sheets and steal down the stairs, but he had to; he needed to attend to some unfinished business. His plan was to jog to the ocean and make the call from there in the hopes that the crisp sea air would keep his head straight and his emotions at bay. He also had no desire for Emily to overhear this particular conversation. Business was business; Neil had been right, he could not ignore S.J. any longer.

The air was salty and thick, making the run easy; his muscles were sore yet loosening with every stride. But the salty air only brought back the images from last night. No matter how hard he tried, he could not shake those vile pictures from his mind. It was as though he had been inside Nick, feeling the steering wheel under his clenched hands.

He'd never been what one would call religious. He believed in God, he went that far, but he put his foot down when it came to any of this past life rot. Yet he had spoken to ghosts, ghosts that had warned him repeatedly about death. And Emily, what about her nightmares? Did the same images haunt her? The same cliffs and sea? Did Nora scream in her dreams?

His running shoes smacked harder against the pavement and startled a flock of ravens into flight; their caws echoed madly and sent a jolt to his heart. No. This was absurd. Reality — he needed to focus on reality. Ghosts, warnings, premonitions, nightmares, they were not reality. This was what was real: Emily and he would be together all weekend. They would not take any undue risks. They would have their friends by their side. They wouldn't venture near the edge of any cliffs. They would survive. End of story.

By the time he reached the coffee stand near the beach, his mind and heart were focused. He was Andrew Hayes, there would be no surprises and no nightmares, nothing he couldn't control. He dialed the number.

"Well, if it isn't the invisible man," S.J.'s voice scoffed from the other end. "Now, to stand me up for drinks is one thing, but avoiding me completely? Surely you're not that temperamental, are you?"

From her tone he could tell she was irritated, but not angry. He still retained the upper hand in all this.

"Good morning to you too, S.J. I have to apologize for not returning your call. We had a gig last night that's monopolized our time these last few days. Neil informed me that you rang him regarding the *Rolling Stone* shoot, and he wanted to make sure that I got back to you as soon as possible."

The line hung dead for a few moments. He could almost hear her stubbing out her cigarette. "How many days has it been since I called? Or has it been a week?" Evidently he was wrong. She was angry. She had also put him on speakerphone. "When I call you, I expect the decency of a call in return. If you don't want to do this, I can easily call *Rolling Stone* and let them know. They have a vast pool of talent to choose from. Agreeing to this shoot included making yourself available. Are you available or not?"

"Look S.J., I have apologized. I don't know what else you want me to say, but that's the best I can do. If you want to lecture me on another facet of my reprobate behavior, then by all means, be my guest. I have many, many more faults for you to choose from — take your pick. I'm sure the conversation will be riveting. Otherwise, I'd prefer to discuss the shoot. I believe you would as well."

Silence.

"My, you are a smug British shit, aren't you?"

"Only when I try."

Laughter emanated from the phone. He exhaled, relieved by the sound.

"Well *Rolling Stone* wants access to you ASAP, meaning today and tomorrow. They'd like to do some outside location work, and possibly some shots at your home. Neil told me your house is a wreck with walls falling down or some other mess, and Robert thought it would make for a great backdrop for an up and coming band."

"Did you say today and tomorrow?"

"Yes. That isn't a problem, is it?"

He hesitated. "We're going away for the weekend, and we've already planned on leaving tomorrow morning—"

"Whatever you have planned can't be as important as this. Seriously, Andrew. I don't care what you have to do, cancel it or postpone it, but you jerk around these people anymore and—"

"Emily…" Her name slipped his lips before he could stop it. The air on the other end of the phone crackled.

"Do I need to remind you that this is a once in a lifetime opportunity?"

He paced along the sidewalk as surfers unloaded their boards around him, their gaze searching the sky and out to sea to assess conditions. The rhythmic tapping of her nails was the only sound on the line. S.J. was right—he couldn't fuck up this chance.

"Where do you want us today?"

He could hear her smile through the phone, and the tapping of her nails ceased.

"Meet me at my offices at noon. You and your band mates will need to clear your schedules completely for the next two days. And just to prove to you that I do have a heart, I'll make you a deal. I'll insist that no work takes place over the weekend, how's that? Acceptable?"

"Yes."

"Good, then I'll see you here at noon. You still have my card, right? Or did you toss it away in a fit of rebellion?"

"Yes," he said and hung up, letting her decide which of her questions he had answered.

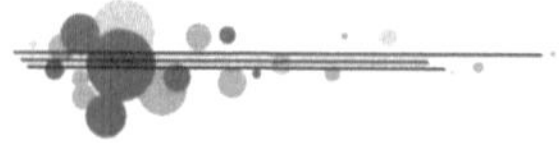

"Hey, I think we should just tell them that we'll leave early on Saturday morning. So we lose a night? It isn't going to kill us," said Simon, driving their truck downtown.

"By the way," Andrew said, glancing over at Christian, "I never got a chance to comment about your proposal last night. Incredibly subtle, that."

"Oh yeah, that."

"Are you serious?"

"Yeah, I am."

"You're certifiable. Marriage. Shit. The option of last resort, is what that is," muttered Simon. "So I suppose we'll be looking for a new bass player next?"

Andrew felt his stomach clench at the thought.

"Never," Christian answered without hesitation. "Lots of people make it work, right? This whole marriage and touring thing, I mean. I've really been thinking about it."

Simon proceeded to systematically shoot down every couple Christian fronted, much to his growing consternation.

"We'll just find a way," Christian said with blind optimism. "Zoey is all for coming on the road this summer — if you guys aren't against it, that is. I figure the bus would be cleaner and we'd eat decently for once."

Andrew's eyes widened in shock. He looked over at Simon, whose face had taken on a kind of strangled quality.

"This summer?" Simon slammed on the brakes. "You're shittin' me? You're moving rather fast, don't you think?"

"Nah. She's was taking the summer off anyway. She said she might want to try it out, and as long as she has a sketch pad, she doesn't care. Called it our 'Bodacious Summer of Love.'"

Simon stared at Andrew across Christian's smiling face. Andrew could feel his heart fall into his gut. How did this happen? How could Christian have gotten so far with his woman while he hadn't even found the courage to open his mouth to Emily? What was he afraid of? Emily saying no? Her hating life on the road so much she'd never want to go again? *Fuck.*

"Now all you gotta do is get Emily to come along and we're set," Christian said, echoing his thoughts and giving him a confident slap on his shoulder. "Nice move with the ring. What's that all about?"

"Nothing," he replied.

"Thank God," said Simon. "But I can tell you right now, you better not sit around the bus and fucking mope for her, cause I'd rather have a white hot soldering iron shoved up my ass."

What supportive mates he had… He knew he couldn't explain the situation to his band mates without incurring more of Simon's hostility. Simon would never accept Emily if he understood she was truly his muse. But the more he thought about her coming on tour, the more sense it made. With Zoey joining them, the whole situation would be better. Emily wouldn't be alone as much, or forced to hang around with three sloppy, juvenile, and periodically inebriated men. His sprits skyrocketed. She could tour with them this summer. It might not be a permanent solution, but it pushed back the time when they would be apart. A reprieve of sorts, but a brilliant one, nonetheless.

By the time they reached S.J.'s office he was totally chuffed, humming and beating his fingers on the dashboard. They could make this work. Everything was going to be stellar. With a valiant sense of purpose, they gazed up through the gathering clouds to the offices on the top floor of a glass and steel high-rise on Sansome, the urban smell of steam and success rising from the streets around them.

"Well gentlemen, prepare for greatness," pronounced Simon, slipping on his sunglasses.

With huge smiles they headed in.

After they exited the elevator onto the fortieth floor, they passed through the imposing smoked-glass doors and into the lobby. An attractive receptionist welcomed them from her mahogany perch. Her accent was distinctly Liverpool, trying hard for Cheshire.

"It's The Lost Boys to see Ms. Gordian, please," Andrew replied with his most proper enunciation and most sincere smile.

She dropped the phone twice trying to dial. Simon rolled his eyes at him and went to scan the magazines.

"Gentlemen, gentlemen!" S.J. strode into the lobby escorted by two men. One he recognized as the photographer who had accompanied her at Diamonds, the other was a blond-haired writer-type who was finishing up a text. When he spotted them, he immediately pocketed away his Blackberry in his well-worn tweed jacket.

"May I introduce Glenn Sommers from *Rolling Stone*, and you already know Robert Bolen."

"Gentlemen, Simon Godden, Christian Wood, and Andrew Hayes of The Lost Boys."

As they shook hands, the inquisitive eyes of the journalist spotted the cut above Andrew's eye and the bruise on his cheek. S.J. was studying him too as she escorted them to a conference room. She whispered in his ear, "Is it just a coincidence that Neil has a matching set?"

He didn't respond.

"I have a little surprise for you, gentlemen," said S.J. as she took her seat at the end of a rich teak table. "KFOG wants you to come into the studio tomorrow and do a live morning show. They specifically requested for you to showcase some of the new material from your latest album. It seems one of their producers was at your little performance the other night, thank you so much for the invite, by the way. She was tremendously impressed."

"Why didn't they contact us directly?" Andrew asked bluntly.

"Word just got around that I was working with you to help arrange this shoot and…you know how these things are."

"No, I don't."

A tense quiet fell over the room. S.J. considered him and smiled. "I apologize if I overstepped my bounds, but I believe you can use all the help you can get."

Andrew could feel the journalist's eyes dart between them. "High strung artist, difficult to manage, temperamental" were all itching to be written down on his notepad. Not wanting to turn this into a soap opera, Andrew smiled and thanked her. It was a great opportunity; he needed to stop being so defensive.

They spent a good deal of the rest of the day traveling around town. Sommers wanted them relaxed and in their element. A young band set loose in a romantic city was his angle. Bolen snapped so many pictures Andrew began to forget he was even there. It was cool, he had to admit, but he knew what both men wanted, craved even; he'd had enough exposure to the press early on to learn his lesson. They lived for that inside scoop, that one word or one photograph that exposes their victim's true nature, laying bare all his hopes and fears. That moment of weakness where you crack wide open and they dive in for the guts and bones. And so it went. A game of cat and mouse while the camera clicked away. They kept digging, and he kept smiling. They weren't going to get anything from him. His guts and bones were his own.

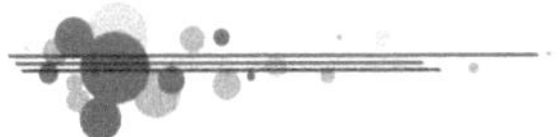

By the time they returned to the office, they were exhausted from being "on" for so long. Andrew wasn't the only one who was forced to be on his best behavior. Both Simon and Christian had appeared downright charming all day, which may not have been a stretch for Christian, but for Simon it represented a minor miracle.

S.J. seemed pleased as they debriefed her about the day, and even more pleased when she informed them to be at the radio station tomorrow morning at six a.m.

The banter in the car ride home was light hearted; they were happy, exhausted, and hurled insults at each other as they came down off their high.

"So who's going to fall on their sword first?" Christian asked as he parked the truck under an old oak.

"Hell, I'd totally forgotten," muttered Andrew.

"Listen, I've got an idea," said Christian. "We tell them all the great stuff, play it up, and then tell them we turned down the radio show to go with them instead. We'll make them come up with the solution of pushing the trip back a day. We escape unscathed."

"I don't know…" Andrew said, looking at the lights in the upper floor.

"It's worth a shot," said Christian. "Women love that stand by your man shit." A second later he started wailing the very song, while holding longingly onto Simon.

Simon looked at Andrew with a pained expression.

"*Stand By Your Man*. Co-written by Tammy Wynette and Billy Sherrill. Recorded by Tammy Wynette and released as a single in September, sixty-eight."

And their plan worked. They were given a heroes' welcome, complete with a dining room table groaning under the weight of a spectacular Italian buffet.

"So, tell the class," Margot said as she headed to the kitchen and reemerged seconds later with a bottle of wine and six glasses tucked between her fingers.

"It was incredible," said Simon, pouring Margot's glass so full it nearly overflowed. "We spent the day with this writer and a photographer who took us all over the city, taking shots of us hanging off a cable car, playing at the Legion of Honor, and this, this was so cool, he had us walk across the Golden Gate bridge like on the cover of *Abbey Road*, which was completely spectacular. I finally felt like a freakin' grown up, like everything we've been working so hard for might just happen, you know? Sometimes, I swear, when we were on the road I thought we'd never break out, and now—I can't even tell you what it's going be like for my mum to see that cover. She'll probably wallpaper the whole bloody living room with it. Jesus."

Andrew's wine glass hung suspended in front of his lips. If he didn't know any better, he'd swear he saw a tear well up in Simon's eyes. There should be an award for this kind of shit.

"Oh," said Margot softly.

They all sat down and tucked in. Emily kept refilling his glass while eyeing him suspiciously. It wasn't until she served the sambuca that he made the fatal error.

"Sommers, he's the *Rolling Stone* writer, was amazed that we handled our own touring and marketing," he boasted, watching the coffee beans sink to the bottom of his glass. "I was telling him about how we poll the fans before shows to get a feel for what the crowd wants on the playlist, and that's how we can mix things around so quickly. So right then and there he rang up KFOG to get an idea of what they want to hear tomorrow, and they shot a list back."

You could hear a pin drop. Actually, you could hear the girl's dessert spoons drop. Each one.

"Tomorrow? Tomorrow? Tomorrow?" Zoey's voice rose with each word, like a pissed off Macbeth. "You made plans for *tomorrow?*"

"About that…" Christian said bravely.

She turned on him. "But we're leaving tomorrow!"

"Listen, honey. They want us to come into KFOG for a live show, and um—*Rolling Stone* still wants some time to interview us. Look, it shouldn't take all day. We could drive up on Saturday morning."

"But we're already packed and ready to go. We have a private room reserved at the winery."

"We can stop on the way home," Christian said soothingly.

"No we can't! I had to call in some serious favors to get a space," she shot back.

"Honey, we have to. I know this is important to you—"

"It's important to Emily! She's the one everyone wants dead."

The mood officially sobered.

"Which is the reason why we will all go. Together. On Saturday morning," Andrew said firmly, putting an end to it.

"No."

He turned. Margot sat there with her arms crossed. "Zoey, we don't have to miss your wine tasting. You all don't seriously think some spooky ghost is going to come and sweep her away on the drive up there, do you? Please. Look, stop, don't say anything, let me finish. The three of us will be together all the time, Andrew. We'll spend the day at Dia and then go to Mendocino. We won't step foot near this inn until you meet us up there."

"No, absolutely not."

"So what are you going to do? Roll her in bubble wrap until you can be by her side? She's a grown woman—she can take care of herself."

"It's too dangerous. She's not going without me."

"She has a name—and is in this room," Emily said. "And she'd appreciate being spoken to like she wasn't a child."

"If you insist on driving up there by yourself then you are a child."

All three women took a collective inhalation of breath as though every molecule of estrogen in the room was combining to make a fist.

"We managed perfectly well before you gentlemen showed up. We don't need anyone to take care of us," said Margot defiantly. "I mean, what is she going to do when I'm gone back East and Zoey is out hanging out with you guys this summer? She's going to have to look after herself then."

Margot's face immediately flushed scarlet, and her teeth clenched together trying to trap the words that had already escaped.

Emily looked to her and then to Zoey with a puzzled expression. "Excuse me?"

"It's nothing," said Margot hurriedly. "What I meant to say is, if these guys think they can just waltz in here and tell us what to—"

"No," said Emily. "What did you say about this summer? You said Zoey's going away with them? Really?"

For the first time ever, Andrew saw Margot flounder, truly flounder for words, but that was nothing compared to the heartbreak on Emily's face.

He wanted to say something right then and there, but he knew it would come off as placating, backpedaling, and utterly insincere. He felt like a complete ass.

When he found Emily in the kitchen, her back was to him and her hands were deep in the sink washing the dishes.

"Force of habit," she said quietly. "We didn't have a dishwasher growing up. I have a hard time digesting food without my hands soaking in scalding hot water."

He tried to approach her but hesitated near the island.

"Emily."

"Andrew, I understand. I really do."

"It's not what you think. I had no idea Christian was going to ask her to come on the road. I just found out today myself. Emily, do you—do you want to come with us?"

Her back remained to him, a glass held motionless in her hands. "I…I can't. I've got my writing seminar…and I have to find a job. These bills won't pay themselves."

"You don't have to worry—I'll take care of them."

The glass slipped from her grip and hit the bottom of the sink.

"No…I mean, no, thank you. But no."

"Emily?"

"I love you," she said into the suds, her voice thin. "But I need to take care of myself. I don't have anything, Andrew. I'm almost broke. My work with Vandin, well, that's gone now. And Myra—I can't expect people to bail me out all the time. I've got to learn to fend for myself."

There was so much he wanted to say to her, so much he wanted her to understand. But how could he tell her he wanted her to come with him and have her believe him now? It would only come off as a cheap way to soothe her hurt feelings.

"I'm really beat. You must be too. I'm going to turn on in. We're going to have to get up early," she said, putting the last of the dishes from the sink on the drain board.

"What?"

"Margot is right. There's no reason why we can't drive up tomorrow. Zoey has her heart set on going to the wine tasting. And I…I'd like to spend some time with them by myself. I haven't had a chance to do that for a while."

"Absolutely not."

"Andrew, I don't want to argue with you."

"Then listen to what you're saying. There is something terribly serious going on, and until we figure out what it is I'm not letting you out of my sight. You have both worlds gunning for you. What else do you need?"

"We're not going to Noyo without you. And Vandin is still out of the country. And when he comes back he might go batshit over me serving as a witness against him, but I doubt he wants me dead."

"He's a sick twisted fuck, Emily."

"Stop! Just stop. I won't be bullied anymore, not by him and not by you."

"Maybe that's the only way you'll see any sense."

"What are you going to do, lock me in my room?"

"If I have to."

"I'm done talking with you. You're acting like an idiot."

"You're doing this for spite, aren't you?"

"What?"

"Because I didn't ask you to go on tour."

"No. You didn't ask me to go on tour because you didn't want me to go on tour. If you had wanted me to, you would have asked long ago. I get it, it's fine. It's your life," she said, her voice strained and hurt. Disappointment overwhelmed her features, and she fled the kitchen without another word.

He turned to run after her when Margot's hand grabbed his arm.

"I think you've done enough damage for one night, Romeo." Zoey was by Margot's side. "We're of the belief that you need a day away from her to get your priorities in order."

Fuck, fuck, and more fuck. Fuck me.

The three men were escorted out of the flat, and the door slammed in their faces.

As they each reached their own empty bedrooms, Christian shouted out, "We're leaving the minute the last fucking photo is taken."

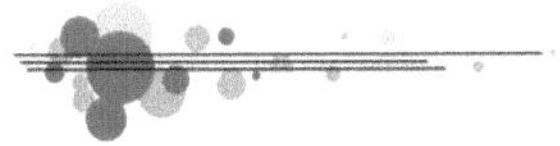

Andrew couldn't sleep. Anxiety bubbled up inside him. He could not leave her; it was wrong. But he knew if he knocked on her door, she would not answer. There was only one way.

The passageway was cold, and the fizzling wall sconces made walking incredibly difficult. The trunk lay off to the side. He paused and held his breath, like a boy whistling past the graveyard. But something drew him to it, as if it were calling him. He had taken to keeping Nick's ring and the key they found in the keepsake box in his pocket, feeling responsible for their safety. The trunk had the same pull.

He reached his hand out and grazed his fingertips along the lid, steeling himself for the shock of pain he knew would follow, but he felt nothing. Tentatively, he sat down on it and put his head in his hands, trying to get his thoughts in order before he spoke to Emily.

How had everything gotten so bollocked up? He knew Emily's insecurities regarding him, but she tried hard not to show them. He felt her eyes on him when she thought he wouldn't notice. She didn't see the man who would love her past his last breath; she saw the lead singer of The Lost Boys, and it scared her. Hell, it scared him as well.

He couldn't fault her for wanting to prove herself by standing on her own two feet; he felt the exact same way about himself. But he needed to make her understand that she could have both, her dreams and them together — he didn't want to take anything away from her; he just wanted her.

No. He couldn't let her go, he couldn't. He needed to protect her from what was out there, from what was plaguing her nightmares. Terror clogged his throat at the thought of them being separated. His fingers rubbed over the worn travel stickers plastered on the top of the trunk, triggering images that flashed like strobe lights before his eyes, but he could only catch the ocean and the cliffs and…the screaming. He beat the side in frustration, his hand cutting against something sharp. Hissing, he pulled his hand to his mouth to stop the bleeding. It stung like hell.

He squinted in the faint light to see what he had cut himself on, certain he'd need a bloody tetanus shot with his luck. He saw a small, uneven brass square with rough edges on the side of the trunk. He squinted down at it, barely able to make out the faint script etched there.

Belden Firm, 1888.

Belden Firm. The words sound so familiar, but he could not remember where he'd seen them. A chill passed down the nape of his neck. A familiar chill.

"Nick?" he said into the darkness. "Is that you? Nick?"

Only silence answered him, and the sound of wind sighing through the eaves.

In that instant he heard Emily cry out. He abandoned the trunk and ran. He reached her wardrobe and pushed his way through her clothes. Her room was dark, she was muttering, and her voice shouted out in strangled cries.

"Andrew, no! Don't! Don't! Let me go!"

He froze in his tracks. He was about to shout her name when he realized she was still asleep. She was having a nightmare, and from the sounds of it, an awful one.

"I don't want you! Stop! Andrew! You're hurting me."

The words made no sense. Why was she screaming for him to go away? No. This was wrong. She couldn't be having a nightmare about him hurting her. No.

He backed up into the passageway. Suddenly, like a violent slap across the face, images lacerated his mind and knocked him to his knees. Emily was screaming. He saw the cliffs and the waves. He stood bleeding before her, and she was screaming at him to stop, her feet inches from the edge. Rage ran through him — deathly rage. He wanted to kill.

"Christ," he said, barely holding himself up. What was happening to him? He stumbled back down the passageway, grasping onto the beams for support. Yet it was not beams he felt. Instead, his hands felt the softness of her neck as his fingers clamped down, choking off the ghastly vibrations of her screams. Her throat constricted under his command…the bones shattered, splintered, her eyes rolled back in her skull, white in terror. He wrested harder until the screams died, and a dull, lifeless weight hung in his grip.

He staggered forward, fighting the bile rushing to his mouth.

He did not sleep that night.

Against all better judgment, he left the house the next morning while it was still dark, with Christian and Simon grumbling in half-awake silence next to him in the truck.

They had found an open coffee shop, but he could only stare at the plastic lid of his cup. His mind kept torturing himself with the horror of his last vision — that the ghost who had haunted his memories and her nightmares was — him. No, he loved her, he had always loved her. He would rather die than hurt her. But the rage he had felt…that unspeakable, consuming rage.

No. He forced it from his mind. No.

The first hint of dawn was breaking across the sky when they entered the building that was already alive and jostling with activity. A program assistant escorted them back to the studios where they could set up and meet with the hosts.

Everyone was bursting with excitement, but it did nothing to ease his sense of dread, knowing that at any minute, miles and miles would begin separating him from Emily. That he would not be able to protect her. That he would no longer be able to keep her safe. That she probably still hated him, as well. But as he tuned his guitar, he bit down on his lip and thought bitterly: *keep her safe from whom?*

Before Andrew knew it, they were on the air.

They chatted and joked with the DJs about touring and life on the road as well as the charity shows they had both supported. The room was full of staff and grew more crowded as the minutes passed. He glanced at the clock. He knew the girls would be on the road themselves by now, and he prayed they had the radio on at least, keeping them joined in some way.

"So what would you like to play for us today? We'll give you the first shot, and then we'll beg for our favorites," said the host.

Andrew smiled, causing the female producer to bobble her coffee cup and drench her white shirt in brown liquid.

"Well," he began, speaking calmly into the microphone, "you see, there are three women out there in some godforsaken minivan heading up the coast that are royally ticked at us right now."

"What did you do?"

"Long story. I'm hoping they haven't snapped off the radio by now. But if not…Emily, luv, if you're out there…"

He thought of everything he could say at that moment: *I'm sorry, I love you, I should have asked you to tour with us long before now, marry me…Run.*

Christian strummed the opening notes, and the song began. A love song, an apology. Andrew sang, the words becoming more and more plaintive, his guitar matching the heartbreak in his voice. When the song at last drifted to a whispered close, the room exploded in cheers.

Christian looked at Andrew with one eyebrow cocked and nodded appreciatively. Simon smiled, equally pleased. They went to a commercial break, and Andrew's cell phone rang. His heart swelled when he saw the caller ID.

"Hey," he whispered, his cheeks hot and his pulse racing.

"I love you!"

"I do too. God, I'm so sorry."

"No, it's all my fault. I shouldn't have run away."

"Listen, luv, we've only got a minute until we're back on the air. I was a fucking prat, a complete fucking prat not to ask you right away. I was so afraid you'd say no. Christ, Emily, I love you, I'm not alive without you. Please come on tour with us."

He could hear nothing but her quick breathing on the other end, and his throat tightened up.

"Please say yes. Emily? Emily, are you there?" He panicked, sure that she would say no.

"Yes! Of course, yes."

The weight of relief smashed into him, and before he knew what he was saying he blurted out, "Marry me."

The room went stone silent. Evidently they were back on the air.

Christian smiled like the cat that had eaten the canary. "Hey, you just made it official. You got witnesses now, dude."

Andrew looked around at the wide-eyed anticipation in the room; the hosts were nearly falling out of their chairs at this once in a lifetime occurrence. Sommers and Bolen had suddenly turned up out of nowhere.

"Emily? Are you still there?"

"Uh huh."

He clutched the phone tightly in his hand and whispered so that only she could hear.

"Marry me now, not later. Now. Tour with me. You can write your book. We'll be together. We'll share the same bed every night. I'll know you're out there. I'll know you're safe. Marry me. Dear God, please say yes."

Anyone tuning in would swear they'd hit dead air. The room balanced on pins and needles awaiting her answer. Andrew could feel the heat of her blush on the other end, the fast rustle of her breath, and the tears glistening on her cheeks.

"Yes."

The space about him erupted in cheers. He could see the DJs high five each other, the staff applaud wildly. He could see Simon's shocked face and the incessant flash of Bolen's camera. But he didn't care. She had said yes.

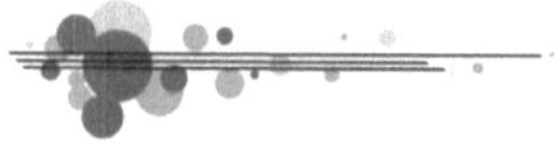

Andrew and Christian were still laughing as they left the studio; Simon remained silent. Evidently the thought of both his band mates married was too much for him to contemplate. Sommers and Bolen were thrilled as well, having gotten a bit of guts and bones for their efforts, so Andrew fought to keep his elation to a dull roar.

In the car he checked his phone; he'd received a text from her:

Love you so! Meeting bodyguards @winery 2 celebrate!

He texted back, rolling his eyes as he did so:

Love you, girl. Bodyguards a +. Don't inhale.

He was still upset that they had gone on ahead, but somehow the terror of what he had felt last night and this morning had subsided slightly. Four men, albeit four stoned men of marginal intelligence, could hold the fort until they got there. Still, he itched to be done with this and get on the road.

Once they arrived back at Neil's house, it took a lot longer than expected to set the lights, since Sid had decided to do some last minute rewiring that caused a plethora of electrical problems. S.J. was micromanaging every detail, which further fueled his irritation. It was already well past noon.

He checked his phone. Nothing.

Why did time seem like it was going backward? A knock came from the door, and Christian trotted over to answer it. Surprisingly, Neil stood there. The last time Andrew had seen him he was in the audience with his mum, looking grave. Now, when he saw Andrew, a wide smile came over his face.

"Congratulations on the happy news," he said. "And you sounded excellent." As they shook hands, he gripped Andrew's shoulder with his other and clamped down hard. "Just so you know, you truly don't need any marketing—you do a fine job without it. Between your music and your charm, the phones were ringing off the hook at the studio."

The click of Bolen's camera fired off.

"Neil St. John, well I'll be." Sommers had materialized out of nowhere, studying their close stance with great interest.

"Mr. Sommers, a pleasure to see you again," Neil said with a consummate balance of sincerity and enthusiasm. "I loved your article about The Who in *The New Yorker*. Kudos on that. It was a fine bit of writing. Is it going to be part of your book?"

Given such an opening, the journalist could not help but expound on the details of the latest chapters to which Neil listened with great interest. Finally, S.J., impatient for things to get going, joined them.

"Fine work with KFOG," Neil commended her. "I had a meeting there this morning, as a matter of fact. Everyone was talking about the show. I've never seen the place like that before. It was utter madness. I don't think they wanted the band to leave."

"No they didn't," S.J. replied. "They were quite a hit. Between the apologies and career-crippling marriage proposals, I honestly lost track of how many songs they played."

"Four."

She looked straight down her nose at him. "I'd love to chat, but if you'd pardon me, we're already behind schedule." She nodded bluntly in farewell and returned to the opposite side of the room with Bolen where she began to move more paint cans around for a particular shot.

"Never knew all this mess would come in handy," Neil remarked to Andrew, who laughed darkly in return.

"You know, it's remarkable," Sommers pointed out. "But you two have the same exact eyes—same color and shape and everything. I don't mean to make you uncomfortable, but the shade is so unique, you don't see it every day."

There was a highly tense moment as those eyes met, and a knowing but guarded expression swept over Neil's face. The reporter was putting two and two together. Andrew's resemblance, living in Neil's house…As if sensing Andrew's inner turmoil, Neil casually smiled and turned to Sommers. "Oh, bloodshot eyes are more common than you think, Glenn. Especially given all the dust while Andrew and his mates have been good enough to live in my property as I destroy it around their heads."

Andrew didn't know what he had expected Neil to say. Neil valued his privacy. Of course he wouldn't announce to God, the world, and *Rolling Stone* that he was his son. Of course not.

"That was quite a stunt you pulled the other night," Neil said to him quietly after Sommers excused himself to take a cigarette break in the back garden.

Andrew didn't reply.

"She was worried about you."

Andrew didn't know what to say, not sure of the implications of Neil's words. But just then the doorbell rang again, signaling the pizza delivery boy dropping off lunch, and Christian and Simon walked over to join them, ending any hope for a conversation. S.J. had exited to the back garden to smoke with Bolen and Sommers, leaving the four of them to huddle around some compound buckets in the living room. They were chatting about the upcoming weekend when Neil cleared his throat.

"I am concerned you gentlemen don't have a manager yet. You need one, desperately. If you didn't before, you definitely do now."

Andrew ran his hands through his hair. "It's an important relationship. We've got to find the right person. You said so yourself."

"What happens if I have the right person?"

"Really?" Simon mouthed, chomping down on a large slice of pepperoni.

"Who?" he asked.

Neil paused. "Me."

Andrew dropped his soda can on the floor.

"Seriously, man?" Simon asked.

"But…you're retired," Christian mumbled, blinking like an owl with cataracts.

"Think about it over the weekend, that's all I'm asking. I can provide references if you require."

"You're truly serious?"

"Andrew, I know how this must look, but please see that I —"

The loud buzz of the newly functioning doorbell interrupted him.

"Damn pizza boy," Simon complained. "He forgot the salads."

The whole crew had wandered back into the living room while Simon got the door. Andrew was about to pull Neil aside when he spotted the man in the entranceway. He definitely was not a delivery boy.

He wore a rumpled jacket, trousers, and a loosened tie that hung over his middle-aged paunch. He peered around the room as he took out something from his pocket to show Simon.

A badge.

"Mr. Andrew Hayes?" the portly man asked, his bald spot shining in the Klieg lights.

Andrew crossed the room in three strides. "Yes, and you would be?"

"Detective Kent from the SFPD. I also need to locate a Miss Emily Thomas. Are you familiar with her?" At the mention of Emily's name, Andrew felt his heart drop.

"Yes, she's my…fiancée. Why, what's the matter?"

"Do you know if she's at home?"

"No, she's on holiday — traveling. What is this in reference to?"

"Is there a place we can discuss this in private?" the detective asked, motioning toward the sea of people behind them. Andrew stepped into the foyer; Christian and Simon were by his side in an instant.

The detective frowned at them.

"No, it's all right. Anything you say to me, you can say to them," Andrew insisted wanting the detective to continue.

"Are you familiar with a Dr. Pavel Vandin?"

"Yes, he's a professor. Emily's professor. What about him?"

"This morning, a Miss Laura Schandler was admitted to San Francisco General. She had been severely beaten and is in intensive care. They're not sure she'll regain consciousness."

"Bloody hell," he muttered.

"Due to her allegations against Dr. Vandin, we acquired a search warrant for his home, and this is what we found."

He handed Andrew the photos. The shots showed a wall papered with photographs of Emily. A depraved shrine, with obscene words scrawled across the pictures — some that had been torn, while others had been mutilated past recognition.

His hands shook so badly that he had to give them to Simon to hold.

"Fuck," Simon groaned.

"We also found extensive information about you as well, Mr. Hayes. Medical records, even. With Miss Schandler's assault, it's imperative that we locate Miss Thomas. She's in extreme danger."

"But she already let you guys know she was heading out of town. She called Detective Obester before she left, she told me. And he told her Vandin was still out of the country."

"Out of the country? From our records, Dr. Vandin never left."

"But Detective Obester told her — "

"Detective Obester?"

"Yes, Anthony Obester. He's handling the rape case against Vandin. He's been taking care of Emily, keeping her apprised of what's going on — she just called him to let him know she was heading to Mendocino. Don't you people talk to each other?"

"Miss Thomas has been calling the San Francisco precinct? Headquarters?"

"Yes, I think so. But he also gave her his cell phone. She may have been using that. He's an acquaintance of Emily's from New York, a friend of the family. He wanted to make sure she was safe."

"Sir, we never give our cell phone numbers to civilians. Ever."

"Then I guess Detective Obester is different."

"Mr. Hayes, I hate to inform you, but the only Detective Obester I know is serving his duty with the National Guard in Iraq. He's been stationed there for the past year. There's no Detective Obester currently active on the force."

"Then who the hell has been calling her all this time? She has to have been talking to someone from the police department."

It was then and only then that he finally understood what had been prowling at the edges of his mind this whole goddamn time. Of course no cop would act like this; of course no cop would give her his cell. Of course no cop would want to know her every move. His shoulders were shaking. He had been blind, stone cold blind.

"Where is Miss Thomas, Mr. Hayes?" the detective demanded.

He fought down the panic rising in his veins. He had announced to the world on the radio show what she was doing and where she was headed. He had offered her up to him single handedly.

His knees buckled. Then he felt it. It wasn't Christian's hand that held his shoulder, or Simon's — but Neil's. He stood behind him, his voice low and urgent, but he couldn't hear or understand.

Sommers was watching everything with rapt attention, and Bolen was firing off shot after shot. Andrew's photograph would be linked to him forever, a black and white masterpiece, an iconic image of the true tortured artist, his guts and bones and heart ripped open.

Click. His voice broke from his throat. *Click.* One word clawed its way free. *Click.*

"Vandin."

“Can't you go any faster?” Christian demanded, his hand wringing the door handle as they raced across the Golden Gate Bridge.

“Why aren't they answering? All three of them? Why the fuck are they not answering?” Andrew sat coiled in the passenger seat, his cell phone fixed to his ear, unable to reach any of the girls.

Simon gunned the engine in response, straining the truck to its limits. Like an invasion of ghosts, the fog swirled across the windows, shrouding their view as they barely missed spinning into the oncoming lane. Only the bridge's orange spires and the churning expanse of water below were visible. Andrew had read long ago what happens to a person who jumps from such heights. The impact fractures nearly all your ribs. The shattered ribs then shred the internal organs and rip the aorta from the heart.

“Don't go there, mate,” said Simon as though reading his mind. He glanced darkly at the look of anguish on his friend's face and back to the highway ahead. “We're going to get there in time. They're going to be fine. The police know to look for them.”

“Yeah, for all the fucking help they're going to be,” shot back Christian. “Fucking useless cops. You heard what the detective said: he'd contact the authorities up there. You don't see him moving his fat ass to help.”

Andrew's memory ratcheted back to when they were still standing in the foyer of their flat. It was barely a half an hour ago, yet it already felt like days. Neil was firing off question after question to Detective Kent while he gripped his cell phone.

The line connected, and he almost cried out in relief. "Emily! Thank God — "

"Hi! This is Emily, please leave a note."

He swallowed down his panic. What could he say to warn her and not terrify her in the process? "Luv, it's me. Call me as soon as you get this message. It's urgent. Please, sweet girl, right away. It's about Vandin. Don't answer any calls from Detective Obester, just don't. Get yourself, Zoey, and Margot to a police station right now. It's vital that you do this. Call me when you get this. Emily…I love you."

He ended the call and immediately. Fuck, bloody hell, why wasn't she answering? He dialed again. Again the message sang to him. He could hear Simon and Christian both curse silently. Evidently they had been thrown into voice mail too.

"We're out of here," Andrew announced sharply.

"Whoa, one minute, Mr. Hayes, we're not done yet. There are still a few more questions I need clarification on."

"Clarification? What the hell have you people done to help Emily? Nothing. How's that for clear? Now if you'll excuse me."

"Sir, I'm going to have to ask you to stay where you are." Detective Kent's voice had lost all its patience; he was done playing good cop. Andrew's eyes sought out Neil.

"I'll take care of everything here, Andrew. Not to worry."

"Mr. Hayes."

Andrew couldn't tell whether the cop was frustrated that the situation with Emily and Vandin had gotten to this horrible point, or enraged that they were running off like vigilantes. Either way, Andrew didn't give a shit. Emily was somewhere out there, prey to a psychopath, with no one to protect her.

Suddenly, S.J. shoved her way between Bolen and Sommers, her eyes narrowing at the sight of the detective.

"What's going on out here?" she asked, annoyed at the delay in the photo shoot.

"We're leaving," Andrew told her and grabbed a hold of his bag that stood waiting by the front door. "Come on guys." He motioned to Simon and Christian who were ready to go. None of them even bothered to cast off their long leather dusters from the shoot.

"What?" cried S.J., clearly having reached the end of her patience. "You said you'd work through the day, and I expect just that. What is this all about? And who the hell is he?" She glared at Detective Kent, who raised his shaggy eyebrows in surprise at the seething woman before him.

"S.J., extenuating matters have come to light in the last several minutes. I think it's wise to let these gentlemen go," Neil explained.

"What extenuating matters? There are no extenuating matters. You get yourselves in here right now and finish what you've committed to."

Sommers and Bolen didn't say a word, although they knew full well all that had just transpired. They were way too thrilled to lap up all the drama. It made good copy.

"We need to leave now! If you have a problem with that—take it up with our manager," Andrew said caustically.

"And who would that be?"

"Neil St. John."

Her eyes darted between them, then zeroed in on Neil as the realization sank in. She started laughing derisively. "Oh my, my, my. You played that perfectly, didn't you? All nobly retired, no desire to step back into that soul-sucking fray, you said. Oh, that's rich. Neil St. John, lost in mourning over his dead wife. Neil St. John, the great philanthropist, the broken-hearted humanitarian who's still in bed with Atlantic after all these years. How much of a cut are you getting, then?"

Neil studied her coldly. "I have no ties to anyone except these men. So you and I, S.J., will step back into that room and arrange the date and times for this session to resume. We will do it with respect and decorum. Do I make myself clear?" His glare then shifted from S.J. onto Sommers and Bolen. "I do not have to remind you why, because all of you know how wildly successful these three men are going to be. If you want to have a prayer in hell of having access to them, or so much as breathe the same air as they do in the future, you will march yourselves right back into my house and not utter another single word. Now, please excuse me while I walk my clients to their car. I will be with you shortly."

Neil waited until they retreated back into the living room and slammed the door. With an about face he took Detective Kent by the arm and escorted him out the door as Christian, Simon, and Andrew raced to the car.

"Mr. Hayes, I have to ask you a few more questions!" the detective shouted after him, breaking away from Neil as Andrew yanked open the car door.

"Mr. Hayes!"

"I need to go!"

"Mr. Hayes, do you want to see your fiancée alive again?"

That froze him dead in his tracks.

"Don't think you can run off and track this Vandin down yourself. It would be a huge mistake on your part. He fits the profile of a violent obsessive. Extremely sadistic, extremely unstable, but also extremely intelligent. He researched her past extensively. He knows her well enough to be able to anticipate her every move. If forensics comes back positive on Miss Schandler, we'll know he isn't afraid to use deadly force to get what he wants. Plus, he had your personal journals, Mr. Hayes. Do you have any idea how he could have obtained them? Have you been robbed recently?"

"No."

"Well, somehow he had them. He also had in his possession certain articles of women's clothing as well. Older style clothes, vintage sweaters, were found in close proximity to the wall that was covered in Miss Thomas's photographs. We don't know if any of those items belonged to her."

"Bloody hell." Andrew closed his eyes to steady himself.

"This is important, Mr. Hayes. You are not dealing with a sane mind here. He is also registered as owning a revolver, which we could not find on the premises."

The car's door handle seemed to bend at the force of Andrew's grip. *He's carrying a gun…*

"We also located a large stash of high-end electronic equipment in his home. That equipment is portable and easy to use on a cell phone, so understand — if he's in a car following her now, he can still convince her he's Detective Obester. If he contacts her before we do, she will be a sitting duck. It's a miracle he never got her alone before now."

"I was a bloody idiot."

"Mr. Hayes, I've seen this type of psychopath before. There's very little you can do to stop him once he has a target. Do you have any idea why he may have this obsession? Did they have a relationship?"

"Never."

"Did she spurn his affections in any way?"

"Yes. And he ridiculed her for it. He nearly assaulted her in his office."

"Well, whatever's happened, someone or something pushed him over the edge. Potentially some emotional shock or traumatic occurrence, there's no way of knowing. Do not attempt to apprehend him on your own. Do I make myself clear? I'll notify the authorities where Emily Thomas and her friends are heading. And we've put out an APB on Vandin."

"Are we done here?"

"I'll need a number to contact you."

Andrew felt Neil's hand on his shoulder. "Don't worry about anything here. I've got it all under control. Go find them."

"I'll be in touch if we learn anything," continued Detective Kent. "Be careful, all of you. You're dealing with a sadistic and possibly armed man who has already committed one violent assault. Find Miss Thomas and her friends and have them call headquarters as soon as possible. We need to question her further."

They shook hands and jumped into the truck. "Go," Neil said, and banged his hand on the roof; Andrew nodded to him, bloody thankful for everything he had done. "Andrew," Neil shouted as they backed up. He quickly rolled down the window.

A crease etched between his eyes. He seemed to be struggling for words. "Just…call when you can."

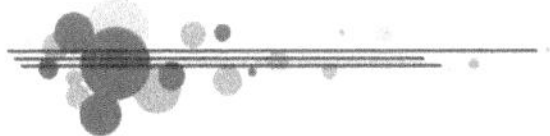

They had contacted the winery, leaving specific instructions for the girls to call them the moment they arrived. More like yelled the instructions. Andrew was sure the proprietors thought he was mad, but short of threatening them with certain death, he made them swear they would lock the girls up in a wine cellar until they got there.

They were a half an hour away now. Andrew's hand brushed against Nick's ring in his pocket. He sought out the key Emily had found in Nora's keepsake box, rubbing it like a rosary.

Suddenly, his coat pocket buzzed. He dropped the key and seized his phone; his eyes riveted on the user ID. He connected the call, nearly shouting in relief into the phone.

"Christ. Emily, thank God! Sweet girl, oh sweet girl. Listen, just listen. You need to go to the closest police station and wait there. Don't go crazy, just let me talk. Detective Anthony Obester is not who you think he is. He's Vandin. Vandin has been impersonating him, faking his voice. You're in real danger, Emily. Please, please, if he calls don't answer. Just get yourself and Margot and Zoey to a police station, wherever you can find one, and we'll meet you there."

He let out a heaving sigh, tears burning his eyes, so fucking glad he had finally reached her. *Thank you God, thank you God. I'll never ask for another thing again in my life. Ever.*

What he heard next made his blood run cold.

"Hello, Andrew."

The words pounded in Andrew's head, his vision clouding in chaos.

"Who is this?"

"You seem to possess a passing intelligence. I thought you would know that."

"Vandin, you sick, twisted mother—where is she? What have you done with her?"

"Do you not know she has the most beautiful eyes when she's frightened? Beautiful, beautiful, beautiful eyes. They are the Thomas eyes, did you know that? So light blue, like silver, like the spray of the ocean. All the Thomas woman have them. She told me. But she doesn't like them, she hates them. Hates them." His voice was disjointed like an addict, raw.

"What the fuck have you done with her?"

"It's your fault, all your fault, all of it. You were supposed to leave—that's what I swore you would do. That's what I told her. Because she wasn't meant for you. She would be wasted on you. Wasted, wasted."

"I'll kill you."

"Did you ever tell Emily you were institutionalized, Andrew? Did they make you bite down on the metal? Shock you? They are cold places, aren't they? You need to lock up your journals better. It makes it too simple to steal them from your desk. It's best not to leave secrets lying around. And all that poetry you wrote to her, did you read it to her in that old brass bed of yours? It smells of her, doesn't it? The sheets, the pillows."

"If you've touched her—if you've laid one bloody hand on her—"

"I felt it inside her when I kissed her. The hesitation, the unknowing. She was afraid and pushed me away. She needed more time. But I'm tired of waiting. So tired. There are too many sounds, too many terrible voices, and it won't stop. She's here all the time now. She screams at me, but she tells me about Emily. She understands, but she won't stop screaming. Do you not understand? The screaming? I've tried to be reasonable, I tried to tell her, but she won't listen to me. Emily is so young. And I love her."

"Where is she? Is she safe? Let me talk to her, damn it. I'll give you whatever you want. Is it money?"

"No! I want you to leave us alone. I won't leave her. I won't leave her to face that monster, because it is going to kill her. She knows! She says it is fate, destiny, and she screams of the cliffs, the rocks, how it will murder her. She's seen the blood, the death. How can I let you near her? You cannot keep her safe from it, you know that!"

"Please, I'll do anything. What do you want me to do?"

He could hear nothing but a dull sobbing and wet, racked gasps as though Vandin were about to begin pleading, then he heard a growl and silence as though he had forgotten the call entirely. The sound of a car door slamming came next, feet on gravel, and Vandin's staggered breaths.

"She's here," he whispered in relief. "She's here. I see her now."

The line went dead. Andrew held the phone, unable to move, unable to breathe. Losing control, he crashed his fist against the dash and howled at the top of his lungs.

24

Zoey drove along a road that was barely visible in the low swirling fog. Oaks snarled together like crooked hands hunched against the harsh wind of the coast. They'd been driving for miles along an obscure country road that was quickly deteriorating into a narrow county road, then barely a road at all. "Where are we?" she asked. Next to her Margot peered at the yellowed map in her lap. "Belden."

In the backseat, Emily pulled her favorite cashmere cardigan from the bag at her feet and wrapped it around her shoulders, pressing her chilly hands against the vents. She missed Andrew. Her phone had no coverage out here in the wilds, and Margot's had died not long after they had left the city. Zoey had left hers behind at the house in a fit of bad humor.

When first she heard the sound of Andrew's voice pour through the speakers that morning, her breath had caught in her throat. For better or for worse, all of the women in the car realized they were involved with "The Next Big Thing," words usually reserved for magazine covers and award shows. Never had she felt so disconnected between who she knew them to be and how the world perceived them. Zoey seemed perfectly at ease with all of it, but she was born to live on a tour bus, dye her hair an even wilder shade of pale, and dance in bangles at the foot of a stage.

Then Andrew had proposed, and the world had changed. She found herself gazing at her hand, at the sweeping lines of life and love, and thought of how there had never been wives there.

"Of course he wants to marry you," she could hear her mother's sermon in her ear. "What kind of future could an academic have with a musician? What happens if he never succeeds? You'll be supporting him your whole life. Have you thought this through?"

No, she hadn't—she didn't want to. Her mother didn't even know about the seminar this summer; how would she ever drop the bombshell of having her only daughter hooking up with a rocker? She rued even opening an e-mail she had received from her right before they left the house. Mercifully, it made no comment about her love life, but it did turn out that her father may have had a distant aunt named Noreen, although she couldn't be a hundred percent sure—it could have been Norma. Still, as she read it, the possibility existed that she shared a history with Noreen Thomas. That Nora's blood ran in her veins.

"I found it!" Zoey screamed, her voice yanking Emily back to the present.

Outside the van's windows, an American Gothic of a town emerged from the fog. The main street was lined with well-worn storefronts and porches, complete with planters of wildflowers and rocking chairs. The fog was so thick it seemed to have a life of its own as it billowed around them. Indistinct shapes swept in and out of it. As Emily stepped out of the minivan, a chill crept up her spine, causing the hair on the back of her neck to slowly stand on end.

Turning around, she scanned the two blocks of small shops from the church to an old inn. No one seemed out of the ordinary—just normal people going about their busy day. She blamed her unease on her firmly entrenched urban roots flailing about in the wide open country. Still, she hurried to catch up with Margot and Zoey.

A restaurant was found in short order—a café with stained glass windows and a preponderance of ferns. Halfway through lunch, Margot looked up from her salad and cursed under her breath. "Look what the cat dragged in."

"Yo! Muse-lady and amigas! Fancy seeing you here! We've been trying to reach you all morning," crowed Dwayne, surrounded by his startled fellow stoners, Dinesh and Buck. They all scrambled forward to meet her, dragging stray chairs in their wake. They grinned goofily as they sat down, their trademark black capes replaced by *Broom Flyers Local 313* T-shirts. Egan swept in through the door last, hooking what looked like car keys on his studded belt, and nodded a cursory greeting.

"Sorry, I didn't get your call. What are you doing here? We didn't think we'd see you until we got to the winery," Emily asked him.

Margot speared her salad. "Remind me to thank you for that," she muttered pointedly to Zoey.

"We've been shopping," Dwayne replied in a tortured tone. "Dinesh's girlfriend, you know, Lucretia, the witch? She wanted him to pick her up something here, or she said she'd turn him into frogspawn…"

Dinesh frowned, a bit put out.

"Here? Why here?" asked Margot, unable to resist.

"Antiques. She wants—"

"No wait," interrupted Margot, "a cauldron, scales, a familiar."

"An engagement ring," Dinesh divulged, a distinct tremor in his voice.

"Oh. She must have heard the radio this morning. My sympathies."

Emily shot her a look. Margot seemed less than impressed by the unorthodox proposal but had the good grace to rise to the mandatory level of celebration.

Dwayne grumbled at the injustice this detour had caused. "We were all set to check out Belden Cemetery for a potential future meeting site of The California Astral Liberation Coalition before we met up with you at the winery. Seriously good ghost juju over there from what we've heard. And they're even supposed to have a lot of slabs for sitting around and dining. It would have been awesome. But nooooo…the witches, man, you can't say no to the witches."

"You have parties in graveyards?" Zoey asked.

"We like to refer to them as meet and glides," Egan corrected her.

"Jesus," Margot muttered.

"We were at Placerville last year," Dwayne informed her. "Then the year before in Georgetown doing karoke with the ghosts, and I'm still hoping to get to Disneyland at some point and get a glimpse of 'Mr. One-Way.' He's this dude who died on Space Mountain back in the seventies. Bummer way to go, though. But we gotta stay focused on the task at hand, right? Dealing with The Lady in Red. That's one gnarly mother. You know there's a rumor that they keep her locked up in a room at the Noyo Inn, right?"

"Like Bertha Mason," said Emily softly.

"I'm thinking more like Linda Blair, personally," Egan reasoned. "But there's been worse."

He proceeded to enlighten them on the goriest episodes of hauntings he had come across in his illustrious career. Near the end of the lunch, he spoke in a hushed voice of Madame Lagree's "torture chamber" in Savannah, an old house plagued by the spirits of twice-dead ghosts—ghosts which were known to have possessed people and driven them to suicide. "Truly the nastiest ghouls on this plane of existence. Ghosts ain't the most happy campers to start with, but these dudes are really twisted, mean mothers. Thought they could get all 'Resident Evil' on folks and pull off high-level human possession. Dumb asses. It tears them apart, like literally. There's only so much of that shit they can take, though." He continued to describe an apparition whose limbs had been chewed away and another who looked like her arms and legs had been broken and set at odd angles, when Margot pushed back her chair in disgust.

"Well, gentlemen, meet you at the winery," Margot told the table, with no regard as to whether Emily or Zoey had finished.

They headed back into the minivan in silence. The lunch, with its talk of malevolent ghosts, had left Emily anxious to call Andrew. But as she hunted for her cell phone in her purse, she couldn't find it anywhere. "Zoey, is my phone up there?" she asked from the backseat.

"Maybe you left it in the restaurant." Margot said.

"No, I had it out when we stopped. What if it fell out of the van? Hell."

Emily rummaged through her purse and around the van, but her phone was nowhere to be found. With a strange sense of unease, she double-checked to see that the vinyl pouch she had transferred Nora into was still packed away safe and sound. She patted it with her hand and pushed it further into her clothes.

The bad luck continued, though; as Zoey started to back up the mini-van, the car began to emit a lug-gug-gugged, lug-gug-gugged noise along the gravel.

"You got a flat," they heard Dwayne shout, standing with his gang next to the sidewalk as they all stared at the useless tire.

"Shit! We're never going to get to the winery now. We're late already." Zoey bashed the steering wheel with her hands.

Dinesh, in a fit of pharmaceutically-enhanced chivalry, offered to stay behind and change the flat, leaving them to take the Wiccan van instead.

Emily didn't know what she was expecting from the Big Doobie, as Zoey had aptly christened it. But whatever it was, the end result was worse. The back of the van had floor-to-ceiling electric-blue, shag carpeting. Peace signs, along with every other conceivable religious talisman, hung around the windows, which were covered in crushed velvet drapes. Of course it had a bar, complete with what looked an awful lot like a hookah pipe, and in the corner stood an incongruous collection of gardening equipment, complete with shovel and pickaxe. The air stunk with the stench of patchouli and pot, and there was nothing to sit on except vinyl bean bag chairs.

"God save us," muttered Margot as they slammed the doors shut on themselves.

"We'll be at the winery in a few minutes," yelled Dwayne from the front. The air conditioning started to fizzle out. At this point Emily realized why they had to stay stoned to travel in this thing, and that she was suddenly hungry again.

They eventually hit the main roads and were soon surrounded by the rolling hills and lush vineyards of the Anderson Valley. She took in a large lungful of air after forcing open a pentagram decorated window, and tasted the faraway hint of salt in the air. They passed into the small town of Philo, and in next to no time turned up the path to Dia Vineyards toward a large timbered house situated on the hill.

Margot was reading from the winery brochure.

"*Renowned for its outstanding pinot gris and gewürztraminers, the family-owned vineyard stores a large amount of their wines in a vast series of underground caves.*

"*The caves were originally built in the eighteen hundreds and are said to be haunted.*" She stopped short and rolled her eyes to heaven dramatically. "Is anything not haunted around here? Maybe your ghosts from the Belden graveyard summer here. What do you think, Dwayne?"

"Righteous!"

Margot snorted and continued. "*The caves' consistent cool temperatures coupled with constantly high humidity and low levels of light offer the perfect spot to produce the perfect wine. Tastings are provided within the vast subterranean serpentine structure. Visitors are required to have an escort, as it is quite easy to become lost along the labyrinthine rows of casks.*"

"Wait, the tasting rooms are in the caves? How far in the caves?" Emily pressed.

"It won't be so bad. We'll hold hands," announced Zoey the moment they pulled up to stop.

Emily attempted to argue but was shoved out the back of the van into the parking lot.

A middle-aged man jumped off the porch and ran to meet them. He looked stricken, evidently having determined that he didn't want that many weirdoes overtaking his tasting room.

"Miss Thomas?"

"Yes," Emily said, surprised that he knew her name.

"A Mr. Hayes called, and he requested for you not to leave here until he meets up with you. He was very insistent."

Margot rolled her eyes. "Can't stand a moment away from you, can he?"

"Did he say when he might get here?"

"He didn't say, but he was—um, very, very insistent."

"Did he want to chain her to the fence?" asked Margot, putting on her sunglasses.

Emily glared at her.

"Why don't we start the tour, and we'll just be a few tastings ahead of them," Zoey decided and rubbed her hands together. Apparently the effects of inhaling pot for ten miles had set in.

"Are these gentlemen in your party?" the proprietor asked in thinly concealed horror.

"Dude, we are the party!" crowed Dwayne. The three of them madly bobbed their heads in agreement.

"Wonderful…So a total of nine, then? Well, um, right this way. My name is Clarence. Welcome to Dia Vineyards."

They followed his stout, tanned frame around the grand house and out into the vineyards. As they walked, they heard thrushes warbling in the trees and inhaled the perfume of the spray of roses against the endless rows of vines, and Emily felt herself relax a fraction. Soon the path narrowed and sloped gradually downhill until it came to rest in front of a large arched wooden door painted bright yellow.

"Like a hobbit hole," Emily said with a smile.

Clarence nodded. "Our ghosts are partial to Tolkien."

"Oh, that's nothing. Ours are totally into Dashiell Hammett," Zoey replied.

He raised his eyebrows, and Emily shrugged her shoulders in response before he heaved open the sizable door to what could only be the entrance to the caves. A blast of cool, damp air enveloped their faces; the beads of sweat on Emily's forehead tingled. She steeled herself against the claustrophobia to come but reminded herself that the door would only be a few yards behind them and focused instead on her surroundings.

Candles would have been more appropriate along the honed, curved walls, she thought; the place appeared so old. Instead, electric sconces were set here and there, shooting columns of light to the ceiling. The hallways seemed endless.

Their footsteps echoed hollowly on the stone floor as Clarence led them along a few twists and turns, eventually guiding them into a long, dimly lit room filled with a refractory table and a credenza covered in wine bottles. From the far wall, the mouths of two darkened tunnels gaped toothlessly at them.

"What's down there?"

"More tunnels—mostly storage now. They're very old—and of course, that's where the ghosts reside," he told her with the relish of a seasoned story teller.

"Do you have a favorite?" Emily asked, intent to play along as she watched him begin to uncork a bottle.

He handed her a wine glass. "Oh, definitely The Lady in White."

The glass nearly slipped from her fingers. "The Lady in White?"

Margot, Zoey, and Emily shared a look.

"She's been here as long as we can remember. Quite famous in these parts, although she doesn't come out as often now—a bit of a recluse, I suppose. But I guess that's a good thing, as she's usually full of warnings and the talk of death. Not the best for business. Although people always want to drink more after she's done with them."

"Wicked," said Buck, lapping up the gewürztraminer. "This is incredible shit, man."

Clarence cringed and poured the rest of the group a glass.

"So she lives in the caves, this ghost?" asked Margot skeptically.

"Haunts," Clarence clarified, and cast a disparaging glance at Buck as he drained his glass and held it out for another round. "More like she inhabits the space between the casks, when she's here at all, that is. She's very mercurial."

"So she has a summer home, as well? Marvelous," Margot muttered.

"One never knows."

Emily's eyes glanced toward the tunnels. The Lady in White—here? She had spoken to Nick's mother—warned her about something that set off the sequence of events leading up to their deaths.

"Are there any other rooms that have entrances to the caves like this, or is this it?" Emily asked, claustrophobia or no, the plan already forming in her mind.

"No, there are several different tasting rooms that open onto the caves. But rest assured, you have the best." He smiled warmly, misinterpreting her question.

"Thank you." By the time they had moved on to the Pinot Noir, Emily had her plan firmly in place. She hadn't flirted in a long time, but Clarence was going to give her a tour and introduce her to the Lady in White whether he liked it or not.

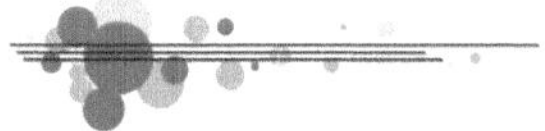

"Oh, sorry Muse-lady, didn't mean to step on your foot. How much longer do you think?" asked Dwayne anxiously from behind Emily.

She didn't answer. Her teeth rattled as she peered at her watch. She regretted having schmoozed Clarence into taking the stoners and herself down here. Zoey and Margot had politely declined, having no desire to trudge through foul, moldy holes in the ground. She had misjudged how intensely her claustrophobia would affect her. They had been creeping through those tunnels for twenty minutes, and she was chilled to the bone, not to mention completely turned around. The tunnels were endless, stretching on and on and looping back around again like some giant earthen maze. She concentrated on her breathing and continued on.

A handful of fluorescent bulbs were scattered across the ceiling like old scratched Christmas lights, casting a fizzling glow down upon the rows of casks. She was thankful that Clarence had handed out a few flashlights or they would be completely blind, but even with them they were constantly bumping into each other. Between the dank earthiness of the caves and the even more pungent earthiness of her friends, her stomach began to turn.

Dusty casks, nearly twelve feet in height, loomed ominously around them and cast massive shadows through which they passed. The farther they walked, the more sporadic the bulbs appeared; it would soon become entirely dark, their flashlights offering only spheres of light in the clammy blackness.

A growing sense of dread washed over her and sharpened her other senses as they passed deeper into the caves. The ground seemed to slope downward as they walked along, adding to Emily's already blinding disorientation.

Several minutes later she heard Dwayne whisper, "Oh, shit." He froze in his tracks, and she slammed into him.

"Why are you whispering?" she choked out.

"See those little dudes over there? Don't want to get them pissed, I can tell you that." He pointed to something in the pitch blackness.

From the darkness a strange sound seeped like hundreds of trembling wings. Peering harder, she saw it. Hanging from the cave walls were a thick line of pulsating blobs.

Bats.

Why hadn't Clarence mentioned anything about bats? The blood rushed to her face and her palms began to sweat.

"We're very deep within the caves now," Clarence told them. "The Lady in White usually likes to hover around the last series of rows up ahead where we store all the old abandoned barrels. That is as far as we can safely go. Mind you, the rows run very long, so we don't go near the far ends. The light is too poor there, and it's too dangerous since we could fall into the other tunnels that lead deeper underground. And don't make any loud noises, you'll annoy the tenants."

"Not a problem," said Emily.

Clarence took the lead, followed by Buck and Egan. They were soon several yards ahead of Emily and Dwayne. She was shining her flashlight into the inky blackness, making sure she could see them, when suddenly a hand grabbed her arm. She jumped out of her skin but quickly realized it was only Dwayne clutching her elbow. His face was beaded in sweat, his pallor a sickening shade of green.

"You must be used to this," she told him through numb lips. "Dealing with ghosts all the time, right?"

"Sure," he squeaked. "Only problem is—I'm claustrophobic."

"Why did you wait till now to tell me that?" she hissed at him. But he looked so much worse than she did that her heart softened at the sight of his trembling facial tattoos. "Don't worry, you'll be fine, just keep taking deep breaths," she tried to reassure him. But with every step they took, the worse off he appeared. Clarence was far ahead now, and they were forced to stumble along, arm-in-arm, their flashlights shaking oval pools of light at their feet.

"Clarence," Emily shouted.

Her voice seemed to vibrate along the walls. With unsteady hands, she shined her flashlight slowly up the back cave wall. It seemed to spire upward, much, much higher on this side than they had seen before. Crags and ledges jutted forth from a monumental sheer face riddled with pock-marked cavities. From those charnel-like holes a fetid wind blew across their faces and a chill of horror shot down her spine. The crags and ledges seemed to be teeming, rippling in a grotesque unearthly way. The sinister pits were alive — they pulsated. They were infested with bats.

Terrified speechless, she staggered back a step, nearly dropping her flashlight. She had never seen so many in one place. They hung in a mis-shapen way, curled upward, their reptilian wings shrouded around their rat-like bodies. A macabre rustle pulsed through the air, and the ammonium stink of guano nearly made her gag.

Suddenly a shape seemed to sweep among them, setting them to stir like an infestation of rats. She frantically grabbed for Dwayne's arm. Except he wasn't there.

"Dwayne?" Emily hissed out, her voice echoing off the walls. The bats twitched, chittering in alarm; the nauseating thrumming from thousands of flesh-covered wings made her blood freeze in her veins. She turned around. Dwayne had passed out dead on the floor.

Fuck! she thought in silent rage, bending down to see if she could shake him awake. "Dwayne?" she whispered as loud as she dared. "Dwayne? Wake up!"

It was then that she heard it. Another set of footsteps. Gratitude rushed through her; someone was here to help.

"Help," she cried softly. "Clarence? Egan?" The bats rustled angrily.

She heard their footfalls coming toward her. Without warning, an icy breeze swept over her body, chilling her down to the marrow of her bones. She spun around. A shape moved in the blackness; she inched backward until she felt a cask pressed against her spine.

"Who's there?" she said sharply. She knew something was out there, standing alone, listening to her voice. It darted from the faint beams of her flashlight.

"A Thomas alone," a chilling voice cooed.

Out of the thick blackness overhead a phantom glided forth. The unearthly apparition of a woman shrouded in a long ivory gown floated before Emily. Her translucent amber eyes blazed beneath a pure white aura of light, holding Emily's gaze in rapt attention. Emily pressed harder against the cask, trembling from head to toe.

"Are you — are you The Lady in White?" she mouthed, her lips barely able to move.

"A Thomas alone," she repeated, the sound of her voice tinkling like broken glass. "No Chamberlain with her?"

The ghost suddenly swept around her, enveloping her body in a chilling embrace. "But there is a Chamberlain. Oh yes, there is a Chamberlain near," her blue-black lips whispered against Emily's goose-pimpled skin.

"Nick — he is a Chamberlain," Emily sputtered out despite her fear. "Is he buried nearby? Can you tell me where he is?"

"Ah, Nick Chamberlain. The young man who did not believe." She drew back, studying her, the temperature plummeting around them. Her glowing eyes hypnotized Emily; her spectral hair billowed in wild ringlets about her narrow face.

"Believe in what?"

"Fate." Her astral shape swirled as the vapors of her face darkened into a caul of blackness.

"Do you know where Nick is laid to rest?"

"He is not at rest."

Emily shut her eyes and tried to summon her courage, her inner Nora. It was easier to speak with her when she didn't have to see those phantasmagorical black lips.

"Please, I need to find Nick Chamberlain's body. I need to know what you told his mother."

"You need much. I don't know where his dust is. And I told his mother the truth, as tragic as it was. But the inescapable truth. The truth he chose to dismiss."

"What truth?"

Suddenly she rose above Emily; her gowned arms flew open wide as though to engulf her.

"Run!" she commanded.

"What?"

"Someone wants to harm you!"

"I don't understand!"

"Miss Thomas!" Clarence shouted as the group of men emerged from the darkness, taking in the twin shocks of the ghost and the prone body of Dwayne on the ground.

The Lady in White twisted in the air, her arms shielding her like a mother would a child. Emily stumbled backward.

"Emily! Emily, please!"

The voice paralyzed every nerve in her body. The horribly familiar voice.

"Who's there?" shouted Clarence. "You shouldn't be down here without an escort."

"Don't hide her from me."

She knew that blunt accent. *Vandin.* How could Vandin be here?

"I don't want to hurt you. I only want her." His voice sounded frayed, unstable. "Emily, please, we have to get out of here, Emily."

Vandin stepped into the ring of flashlights, his clothes disheveled, his hair on end, a gun held in his hands. "I can't…stop her. She's in my mind, Emily. It hurts—she hurts. We have to go. There's no time."

Dwayne had come to and was struggling to his legs. Vandin fired, missing him by inches.

At the sound of the shot, the bats pelted down from the cave walls like an avalanche, shrieking in rage. Emily bolted down the aisle, shouts of distress roaring all around her.

She stopped short. She had reached the end of the row and scrambled under the barrels to hide, dirt choking her throat.

A steady pair of footsteps stalked closer toward her. She pulled herself into a ball, slamming her hand over her mouth to silence her coughs. The footsteps slowed, then stopped directly in front of her. The only sound she could hear was that of labored and hoarse breathing. "Emily," Vandin whispered, kneeling down to peer under the barrel. She whimpered, truly terrified. Her worst fears about this man had been realized. He had lost his mind after seeing Nora; he was insane.

"Come out, Emily. Don't make her mad. You don't want her mad. He's going to kill you. You have to run, you have to come with me, now!"

A flashlight shone into her eyes, blinding her.

Vandin lunged and seized her, dragging her to her feet. She screamed again. His hand slapped hard over her mouth, his fetid breath hot against her ear.

"We need to get out of here. Emily, don't fight me. He'll hear you, he'll break your neck. Do you understand me?"

She shook her head vigorously.

Abruptly, from faraway a clear voice rang out. "Emily!"

"Andrew!" she screamed, wrestling to break free. Vandin slapped her hard across the face and yanked her by her hair.

"Emily!" Andrew hollered. "Emily!"

Vandin hauled her down toward the wall of bats, heading straight to the cave tunnels Clarence had warned them about. One hand was clamped over her mouth and his other pressed the gun into her side.

"Faster! Run faster!"

They were almost at the wall; it was like diving into a swarm of bats. Vandin didn't care. He knew where he was going and where he would take her.

"If you'd only listened. It's all your fault, Emily. All your fault, all your fault. All your fault," he whimpered, his face a twisted mask as he lurched forward.

"Emily!" Andrew screamed. "Christ! Emily!"

Vandin was grunting and growling as they neared a dark fissure in the rock. She knew what would be waiting inside; thousands of bats, and they would swarm them, tear their skin, devour them alive. She fought against him with all her strength.

He slammed her body against a cask and shoved the muzzle of the gun against her breast. "If I shoot him, you'll live. She told me." His black eyes bore into hers, all sanity gone. "You are beautiful, so, so beautiful." He trailed the cold barrel along her cheekbone. She turned away from him, unable to look at the horrible fascination in his eyes. "So, so soft."

She felt his body relax. The gun lowered slowly, and she could feel his eyes find hers. She forced her body to wait. She waited until he moved closer, and closer and closer...

In one fierce move, she thrust her knee as hard as she could into his groin.

He doubled over, writhing in agony. "No!" he spat out. "No!"

She struggled out of his grip and catapulted herself into the darkness, running as fast as her legs could move.

"Emily!" Andrew cried. "Emily!"

"Andrew! Help!" She ran toward his voice. Footsteps thundered behind her. Grappling her hands in the dark like a blind man, she flung herself down another row.

"Emily!" Simon's voice cut through the darkness on her left.

"Simon!" she yelled, praying he could find her, and groped frantically around another corner in the vain hope of reaching someone. She kept yelling Andrew's name as she lumbered ahead, becoming more and more desperate with each step. She clawed at the darkness when suddenly a pair of hands reached out and snatched her. She screamed.

Arms crushed her. A sweating, trembling body clenched her tight. "Oh God, Emily!"

"Andrew!" She clung to him, panting. "Andrew!"

Lips tore at her cheeks, her hair, and back to her lips. Gasping, he plastered her against a barrel and cupped her face in his hands. "Are you okay? Did he hurt you? Sweet girl, oh bloody hell." He pressed his forehead against hers and fought to breathe.

Amidst the mad swirl of passion and desire, the stark cold fear of reality shot through her. "Andrew—Vandin!"

Andrew grasped her by the shoulders so hard that she could feel his pulse hammer inside his fingers. "Stay with me. Don't let go."

With that, he took off into the darkness. They ran hand-in-hand down endless rows. All around people were shouting now, bats swooping down from overhead. Emily stumbled, but Andrew caught her and wrapped his arm around her before he sprinted ahead. They whipped around a corner. A body nearly crashed into them. Andrew threw her behind him.

"It's us!" Simon's voice cried from the darkness. She barely made out the hulking outlines of Simon and Christian, their shoulders heaving in exertion.

"He's here," Andrew hissed at them.

"Was that his gun?" Simon asked.

"Emily, luv, did he…did you see?"

"Yes."

"We've got to get out of here," said Christian. "We can't take him if he has a gun. We need the cops."

"Miss Thomas!" Clarence yelled from behind them. "Are you there?"

The shapes of Clarence and the others materialized from the dark.

"We have her!" said Andrew. "Get out of here now!" They hesitated. "Go!"

Andrew remained. She could feel his eyes on her, his body battling the desires to both protect her and capture Vandin. With a shuddering breath, he pulled her to his side as though he had finally made up his mind. "Come on," he ordered. A tidal wave of relief washed over her, and she clasped Andrew's hand as they raced with Christian and Simon to catch up with the others.

They ran as fast as they could, the giant black masses of casks blurring by them. Unexpectedly Andrew pulled up short. Emily felt Simon and Christian panting around her. Someone was standing directly in front of them.

"Emily?" a voice whispered.

She screamed. With a growl, the three men launched themselves at the sound, descending on the body to tear it apart. Just then the lights flashed on, illuminating the space around them. On the ground, Simon and Christian had a petrified looking Buck in a death grip with Andrew towering over him, his fist raised to pummel his face in.

Simon recognized him instantly and dropped him in a fit of disgust. Buck scuttled away, looking like he might have wet his pants.

"Fuck!" Simon shouted. "Can't we beat him up anyway?"

The rest of the stoners rounded the corner, Clarence bringing up the rear. He looked mortified.

In the faint light, Emily finally saw Andrew. His hair was wild, his sweaty face a study of determination. "We need to get back to the entrance. Now!" He grabbed her hand and laced their fingers tightly together. He barked orders to Simon and Christian, and Emily could only make out every other word, like *police, doors,* and *safe.*

They quickly made it back up to the tasting room and raced out the door. Andrew slammed it shut behind them. Simon launched himself toward the main house yelling for Margot and Zoey, who came flying out to meet them.

Clarence staggered behind them along the path, looking as though he might have a heart attack. "What the hell is going on?"

"Does this door have a lock?" Andrew demanded and pointed to the door.

"Yes," Clarence answered.

"Then lock it the bloody hell up now!" Andrew ordered, and yanked a map from the pocket of the long leather coat he was wearing. "Shit!" he cried. "There are other entrances to the caves."

"Of course," said Clarence, still clearly confused. "There are several. Why the hell is a man with a gun down there?"

Margot and Zoey grabbed Emily in a hug. "The police just arrived," they told Andrew.

"Listen, I don't have time to explain," Andrew told Clarence. "I need you to lock up all the tasting rooms so no one can get out. Get the police to search the caves. That man's a psychopath."

Clarence immediately sobered up and nodded his head vigorously.

"Come on, we don't have any time to lose," yelled Andrew.

They took off for the main house. On the steps of the front porch, Andrew quickly informed the police of what had happened. He turned to Margot, Zoey, and Emily.

"Stay here. And I mean it. Don't move!" He turned to a Dia employee and glanced at his nametag. "Chris, you stay with them and do not let them leave your sight. Do you understand? Sit on top of them if necessary."

"No! We want to come!" the three women cried nearly in unison.

Andrew glared at them, and they backed down. Something in his eyes told them they would never win this argument. He kissed Emily swiftly before joining the others as they went tearing off toward the tasting rooms.

Chris cleared his throat and corralled them back through the doors and into the tasting room. "You ladies want to sit inside at the bar? Given the circumstances, the wine is on the house."

Margot and Zoey deposited Emily between them on a stool. Chris had begun to pour. He politely left the bottle and went to stand guard by the door.

Emily turned to Margot and Zoey. "He was down there. How did he know we were here?" she asked them. They wouldn't look her in the eyes. "What? What is it?"

"It really isn't our news to tell," hedged Zoey.

"Fuck it!" Emily yelled at them. "Tell me."

Margot took Emily's hand in hers and looked her right in the eyes. "This isn't pretty."

She then proceeded to explain how the guys had arrived in a state fit to be tied. How Andrew had told them everything while he paced around the tasting room waiting for her to return. About Detective Kent's findings, about the wall of pictures, her clothes, and the extensive collection of electronic equipment Vandin had used to stalk her. She explained that Vandin had been in their house, her room, in particular; how he knew the most intimate details of her life. How he had called Andrew and tortured him with the belief that he had kidnapped her. And how, when they heard the gunshot from the tunnel entrance, Andrew ordered them to summon the police, and the guys flew down into the caves.

Emily paled. "But how did he trail us?" she asked. "I didn't see anyone."

"He's got a house full of expensive electronic equipment," replied Margot with a large gulp of her wine. "He could have put something in our minivan for all we know. He was probably tracking us every step of the way."

It felt like a frigid hand had swept out and squeezed Emily's heart. Vandin was insane; his crazed mutterings still rang in her ears—the way he spoke of himself in a disembodied third person, and the voices in his mind. *"Don't make her mad. You don't want her mad. He's going to kill you. Don't fight me. He'll hear you. He'll break your neck."* The bottles on the shelves behind the bar seemed to wobble and go out of focus. Zoey's arm steadied her.

"You okay?"

"Does she look okay?" asked Margot sarcastically. "Go ask that Chris person for some food. She needs more than wine in her stomach. And a lot of it."

Food was the last thing Emily wanted, with her mind starting to worry about why the men had been gone so long. A few minutes later, Zoey and Chris returned with a huge tray of bread, cheese, and fruit. She forced a bunch of grapes into Emily's hands. "Eat."

They had no flavor, the tin taste of fear still rife in her mouth. Sitting there, she felt like she was holding up the world on her shoulders, and Margot and Zoey, sensing her imminent collapse, nestled closer to her, their shoulders bearing up hers.

"Eat," commanded Margot, and she shoved another grape into Emily's mouth.

"Where are they? It's been a long time," Emily asked, her voice paper thin.

Just then a flurry of commotion sounded from outside. They raced out the door and rushed toward the three men who were jogging to meet them. Andrew looked at Emily and opened his mouth to say something but thought better. He took her in his arms and pulled her to him.

"Dear God, thank you," he whispered. His hand traced the curve of her cheek, his eyes full of worry and relief. He hugged her fiercely once more.

"Did you find him?" Emily asked, nerves spiked in anticipation of what he would say.

Simon nodded back but didn't say a word. A row of cops were gathered at the door of one of the tasting rooms. From far off she heard another siren.

"Where is he? Did you catch him?"

Still no one replied; Christian and Simon stared at the ground.

"Andrew, tell me what happened," Emily demanded. "Did you find him?"

"Yes."

"Mr. Hayes," shouted the sheriff who had been speaking on his cell phone. The men raced over to him, Margot and Zoey at their heels. Emily walked slowly, not sure she could bear to be near Vandin. She wanted to hurt him, to kill him with her bare hands, but at the same time she was scared to death of him.

The sheriff took Andrew aside. He was built like a Marine, and his voice reflected his demeanor. "Mr. Hayes, I just got off the phone with Detective Kent. He's filled me in on the finer points of Dr. Vandin's recent past. But I'll still need you and your party to remain here for further questioning." Andrew looked up at the sheriff and nodded. "We'll remain here with the body until the coroner arrives. Why don't you take a rest at the main house. I'll be with you shortly."

Emily didn't understand. Vandin was being held behind that door. Had he killed someone? She glanced at the police who seemed subdued, discussing matters among themselves. Andrew turned to face her.

"I want to see the bastard."

"You can't, Emily."

"No, I want to see him now."

"Sweet girl, please."

"Andrew, let me go."

The sheriff and Andrew traded a serious glance. Andrew took Emily by the shoulders and pulled her aside. He took a deep breath and looked her directly in the eyes. "You don't want to see Vandin, Emily. He's dead."

Andrew's cell phone rang. Without so much as a taciturn hello, Detective Kent demanded to speak to Emily. Having done his best to control his temper up to now, Andrew exploded, and he launched into the detective about the hell they had been subjected to in the past hours. "If you people had done your job in the first place," he barked into the phone, "we wouldn't have had to face any of this."

"Andrew. Please, let me talk to him."

It was then that he felt a soft hand pull at his sleeve and looked down to see Emily staring up at him. She kept her voice low while she explained to the detective how Vandin had found her in the caves. "Yes, he had a gun," she answered to a question Andrew could not hear. "Yes, he was acting erratically. He kept muttering — muttering awful things, something about a woman making him do things. No, I don't know who she was."

The longer Emily listened, however, the more still she became, and in time she slipped from Andrew's side and walked toward the far end of the parking lot. He went to follow her, but she gently held up her hand, as if to say "two minutes," leaving him to swelter in the waves of heat rising from the macadam. He watched her turn her back to him and retreat into the house as Margot rushed to catch up with her.

"I don't know about you, mate," Simon remarked, having walked over to his side, his hand fanning his face, "but this is turning out to be one lovely weekend."

Andrew chuckled, albeit despairingly, and moments later Christian appeared. All three made an attempt to talk about anything except how Dr. Vandin had been found, crumbled at the foot of a cask of 1991 cabernet, the splatter of blood and gray matter thick on the dirt floor below his head.

Finally Christian could no longer avoid the subject. "When I heard the gunshot I was positive he'd taken someone down. And when we found him…the way he was lying there…Jesus."

Each man became lost in the memory of how Vandin's body looked almost fetal in death, except for the expression of absolute terror on the remaining pieces of his face.

"But it doesn't make sense. Something doesn't add up," Andrew said. "He was near an exit, he could have easily escaped, and we would never have found him if he hadn't fired the gun."

"He was insane," Simon scoffed. "Who knows what was passing on in that fucked up mind of his. All I know is it would have been Emily if we hadn't gotten to her in time, or anyone else down there if he'd been close enough. A sick, twisted mother is what he was, and he got what he deserved."

"At least they didn't see the body. Christ, all that blood."

Zoey had joined them unaware, her face perspiring and her hair stuck to the sides of her cheeks. "Is he really dead?"

Andrew nodded, wondering how she would react. Zoey was tough as nails, but this was pushing the limit of anyone's tolerance. She blinked as she took in the fact. Her eyes were softer than he remembered, and the sun highlighted the green outline of her irises.

"So you saw the body, then?"

"I'm afraid so, yes."

"Well…" She seemed to be struggling to compose herself. "Well, for what it's worth, death isn't without its benefits," she said dryly and gestured to the complimentary Dia Vineyard water bottles and tray of sandwiches on a nearby table that Dwayne and his crew had already fallen upon. Christian nearly laughed, and she did as well, wiping her brow in exhaustion.

The need to dissect the details of all that had transpired proved too great for them, and they fell into the obsessed rehashing of the information they knew. When at last Zoey began to tell them what Emily had related about her time in the caves with Vandin, Andrew's nerves were near the breaking point. "He kept saying it was her fault, all her fault."

Andrew wrapped his arm around her shoulders and squeezed in an attempt to steady them both. She looked up at him, her eyes now bright. "Don't worry, I'm not going to start bawling…it's just that, well, she's been through hell. Do you think we should turn back and forget all this?"

More than anything, Andrew wanted to say yes. Pack up and never deal with any of this shit again, let Nick and Nora rot for all he cared. But he knew Emily would see this through to the end, with or without him. And after what she had suffered through today, he could not contemplate leaving her.

"Listen," he said, "why don't you take the truck with Christian and Simon and get out of here, and we'll meet up at the hotel. There's no reason for you to stay here any longer."

"What?" cried Simon, "and leave you to enjoy that marvel of automotive engineering all by yourself? Perish the thought. You and Christian head off. I've been dying to ride in the back of that sweet monstrosity forever."

Zoey smiled at both of them, relief flushing her cheeks. "Well, I guess — enjoy the Big Doobie." And with one hand she snagged Christian and hauled him over to the truck.

"The Big Doobie," Simon repeated, peering at the *Lick a Witch* bumper sticker on the back of the van as the afternoon sun beat down on them. "Please tell me they have beer back there."

"I think they have Frank Zappa and Jerry Garcia back there from the looks of it."

Simon snorted, and Andrew paused. "Listen, I just want to say thank you for being there today. I don't know how I would have made it through without you."

Simon followed his friend's gaze to a second story window where they could see Margot pacing while she waited for Emily to finish her call. Simon's face looked more careworn than Andrew had ever seen it, older. "It was nothing," he tossed off, but it didn't hide the ache in his voice.

So it had happened, Andrew thought, glancing at Simon. Of all the women Simon had encountered on the road, from ones who had thrown their bras, much less their contents, at his feet, he chose the one who didn't want him.

"It still doesn't make sense to me," Andrew worried out loud. "Why would he kill himself? Why not try to shoot us, at least?"

"And that's what you wanted?"

"No, it's just that it doesn't add up."

"People do sick shit, Paulie. You have to know, I mean, when you're at the end, when you're in that much pain, there's no other way out. When I was using, when it was at its worst, I could see how—it'd be easy to pull that trigger. He just couldn't stop himself. Whatever monsters were fucking with him, they won."

They stood together and watched Margot, then a few cars full of erstwhile vineyard hoppers that rode up the twisting road and immediately spun around when they spotted the yellow crime-scene tape drabbed across the path. They saw Christian and Zoey drive away in air-conditioned luxury. Zoey waved madly, and Christian smoothly slid on his shades.

"Bet you we get there before they do," Simon said as he lit a cigarette, a smile creasing the side of his mouth. "Gearshift or not—he's going to end up one lucky bastard. Where the hell did I go wrong, is what I want to know."

"But she's a Catholic. She even has a holy card collection. Didn't you swear off them?"

"Holy cards? Never. You fancy a smoke?"

"Hell yes," Andrew cried and took a savoring drag from the offered cigarette, making Simon break into a much needed laugh.

"Those things will kill you, you know."

"What won't?"

From behind them they heard the stoners shifting around and groaning about something and turned to see them perched on the picnic bench, finishing the last of the sandwiches, their faces raised into the blazing sun.

"You gentlemen ready to go?" Andrew asked.

"A few moments more of baking, dude," crooned Dwayne, whose face was framed by a horrid folding, metal tanning tray that he had wrangled from who knows where and positioned for maximum roasting.

"They all look fairly baked to me," Simon quipped. They did appear baked, or at least browner than normal, with the dirt from the caves sticking to their damp faces. "Weren't there four of you?" he asked, counting them off. "Hell, we didn't leave one of you in the caves did we?"

"Naw," answered Dwayne. "Dinesh is back in Belden with the girls' minivan. He offered to change their flat tire. We called him and told him to meet us in Mendocino."

"Where?" Andrew asked, just now realizing the van wasn't there.

"Mendocino."

"I know that! Where was the van and what was the name of the town?"

"Belden. We were scouting out a future meeting site for the California Astral Liberation Coalition when we ran into them. That Belden graveyard rocks, mausoleums and shit—and all those ghosts, man…I bet they love to party. No one popping a cap in anybody's head there, let me tell you."

"Will you let that die?" asked Buck, who was hunched in a ball, evidently not recovered from the episode in the caves as yet.

"Did you say Belden?" Andrew asked again. Why did the name sound so familiar? He had heard it before, he was sure of it. But where? He ran his hand through his hair and was about to start interrogating them further when he looked up and saw Emily standing on the porch. His heart skipped a beat. She was smiling. He beamed back at her like an idiot.

Overcome, he went to kiss her. They missed each other's lips, and then tried again and bashed their noses together.

"Ouch!" she cried and backed up, her hand on her face. She appeared startled and stepped away, looking at him strangely.

"What did the Detective say?"

Anxiety passed across her eyes at his words, then quickly disappeared.

"He needed to ask me some more questions about my time with Vandin. The good news is that Laura is getting better—you remember, the girl…"

"Come here." He grabbed her and hugged as tightly as he dared. "You were so bloody brave."

She didn't say anything, but laid her cheek on his chest. He kissed her sundrenched head and whispered, "Tell me you're all right."

"I will be. The sheriff told me we could leave. He has your number, and he said he'd be in touch if he needed anything. Let's go. I just want to collapse in the truck and get a drink."

"About the truck…"

She peered up at Andrew with a guarded look, blocking her eyes from the sun.

"We pulled the short straw, sweet girl. We're traveling in the van."

She blinked once. Then again. "The Big Doobie?" she mouthed silently.

"Oh, Jesus, Mary and Joseph!" cried Margot, "I am not getting into that thing again."

After much argument, Andrew was the first to jump into the back of the van. He held his hand out to Emily, who met his gaze straight on.

"It's repossessed at midnight by stoners past," he warned her and stole an ardent but quick kiss, then pulled Margot in next as Simon pushed from behind. Dwayne, Egan, and Buck sat in the front, leaving the rest of them to the bizarre and wretchedly un-air-conditioned world of The Big Doobie.

"Fantastic!" cried Simon, immediately rummaging for beer behind a bar decorated with *Dr. Who* and *Teletubbie* merchandise. "What's with the shovel and the pickaxe back here?"

"Um…tools of the trade," Dwayne mumbled back self-consciously before throwing the van into gear.

Andrew settled down into a hot and sticky vinyl bean bag and waited for Emily to finish opening a window before he dragged her onto his lap. Despite the heat, she nuzzled under his chin, her lips near the hollow of his throat, making his heart hammer against hers. Their damp shirts clung together.

"You all right?"

"Fine." He felt her lips twitch against his Adam's apple. "You saw him, didn't you? You saw Vandin."

"Beer?" Simon hovered over them, his hand extended with something dripping wet and brown and cold-looking, which Andrew quickly took so he could avoid the question.

"Hey, look, we hit the coast!" Dwayne cried.

Everyone moved to the windows and pushed aside the crushed velvet curtains; the stunning beauty assaulted their senses, not to mention bringing the first gust of fresh air in miles.

There was something dangerously reminiscent about the white-capped ocean and the grand cliffs to Andrew. The large formations of rocks sprung up like living things from the surf, as if immutable against the ravages of time and tide. The sun was beginning its descent, its rays of orange and vermilion playing against the sinking blue of the sky, and the smell of salt and the burning wood of some distant beach bonfire sailed along the air.

Emily's face was next to his; a few strands of her hair were still glued to her brow, the rest billowing madly about her neck. He forgot everything except her face and the growing unease in his heart until he forced himself to look out the window. They were hugging the coast now. On one side, nothing but a single guardrail protected them from the sheer drop to the rocks below, and straight ahead lay a village perched at the edge of an incredible series of ocean bluffs, a smattering of Victorian mansions nestled in among a series of salt box houses.

"I never got to thank you for the proposal," she told him with a faint smile, her eyes still focused on the coast.

"I improvised."

"You were quite a hit. Was there as much shrieking at the station as there was in our van?"

"I wasn't listening. But I'm glad that—"

Just then an oncoming tractor trailer swerved into their lane. Dwayne slammed on the brakes, and the van spun sickeningly into the cliff barrier. The force sent them flying across the van.

"No!" Andrew screamed, horrified.

He threw his arms out to grab her, but the van pitched hard to the left, pinning him down and sending her crashing into Margot and Simon. They reached to catch her but missed, and she tumbled hard against the back of the van, missing the spiked end of the pickaxe by inches.

In terror he screamed out, praying the door wouldn't blast open. With a grinding lurch they were skidding across the road, bouncing violently along the gravel.

The force launched Emily against the opposite side of the van where she collapsed, gasping. The van righted itself and slowed to a crawl. Margot and Simon lay on the floor, rubbing their elbows and heads. Andrew immediately lunged for Emily and grabbed her in his arms.

"Everybody okay?" cried Dwayne from the front. "Fucking trucks, they haul ass down these roads…" His voice sounded strained, and his hands clutched the wheel.

Andrew looked down at her, white faced. "Are you hurt?" She shook her head, unable to speak. He pulled her into his chest. "We're fine," he hushed her. "We're fine."

But as he did so, he could not shake the belief that they were going to crash over that cliff and that there was nothing he could do to stop it. The scene kept replaying itself in his mind until thankfully, by the time they passed through town and turned onto the main street that abutted the bluffs, her heart had settled to a rhythm that matched his.

He heaved a sigh of relief at the welcoming sight of the hotel with its faded yellow clapboard front and low slung front porch. The sign that hung on the façade announced, *The Mendocino Hotel, established 1878.* Andrew blinked several times, his eyes adjusting to the light as they exited the van, and he found himself reading the words over and over again, fighting off the uncanny sense of déjà vu. Trying to focus on the here and now, he bid Dwayne and company a hasty farewell, and after promising to meet tomorrow morning, he escaped with the others into the hotel's darkened foyer, rich with the cool sweetness of pipe smoke and old wood paneling.

"May I help you?" asked an older woman behind the counter. Her lips seemed to form one solid line as Andrew approached from out of the dim light.

The closer he came, the more startled she appeared. It wasn't until he saw his reflection in the mirror behind the counter that he realized how truly disheveled he was. Surveying his riot of hair, the streaks of crimson and dirt along his face, and his T-shirt sticking with sweat, he knew it was best to turn on the charm. He left the other three behind, stepped gracefully forward, and met the woman's gaze head on.

"I believe the reservations are under the name of Zoey Cohen. I'm Andrew. Andrew Hayes." He extended his hand in greeting. "So sorry, we've had a bad patch of traveling. We normally look a bit less disheveled than we are at the moment." He smiled softly and held her hand.

"Cohen. Zoey." He leaned over the reservation book near her and trailed his finger along, stopping when he reached Zoey's name. "There, I believe." He smiled again and raised his eyes back to hers like a young boy bringing home a stray dog.

She was still blinking when Simon materialized at his shoulder and whispered, "Maybe you should shag her too, while you're at it."

Andrew kicked him under the counter, still beaming at the receptionist.

The woman roused from her stupor, went to the row of cubbies behind the desk, and retrieved a set of keys.

"Mr. Godden?" Simon nodded. "You're in room seven, just up the stairs and at the end of the hall. It's quite lovely and has a charming view of the gardens," she informed him, handing over the key.

"Ms. Larson. Yours is room eight. You have a Jacuzzi tub and a balcony."

"I hope you don't mind, Mr. Hayes." She turned to Andrew as though requesting forgiveness. "There weren't enough rooms left in the main hotel, so we had to move you to the back cottage. It's a space we're sometimes forced to rent out from the town for such emergencies. We haven't had a chance to air it out, however, so it may be a little musty…"

"I take it not many people stay in this cottage?" he asked through set teeth, envisioning a dilapidated shack.

"Well…some people complain that it's haunted, but I assure you our ghosts prefer the hotel."

"Bloody fabulous…Is there anything, anything at all you could do to swap us out?"

"Ummm. I don't think so."

"Sucks to be you," laughed Simon, smirking as he tossed his key in the air. "See you at dinner."

"If you'll excuse me, I'm going to take a bath," Margot announced and tossed her key in the air as well. Simon snatched it from under her nose.

No one said a word. He held it tight in his fist for a moment and stared at her as if asking permission to use it. Then apparently changing his mind, he opened his palm and tossed it back to her with a smile before he walked silently down the hall. Margot watched him go, clearly taken aback.

Andrew did not toss his key but turned with his best expression to face Emily.

"How bad?" she asked.

"I assume there's running water."

Resigned to see what awaited them, they walked back out the doors and along the garden path that led them farther and farther away from the hotel to the edge of the headlands. Outside it was still warm as they hiked through the tall grass. He was so sweaty and dirty he ached for a shower, and he prayed to God this bloody outbuilding at least had a bath so that they wouldn't have to trek back to the hotel and share one with pensioners from New Jersey.

Lost in his thoughts, he didn't realize Emily had walked several yards ahead of him. She moved fluidly as though knowing exactly where she was going, despite the fact that the signs leading the way had become few and far between.

"Wait," Andrew cried, rushing to catch up with her, but she had already turned the corner of a large overgrown garden and disappeared from view. Suddenly, he heard her cry out. He ran, and rounding the corner, he stopped short.

A deserted cottage rose before him. It was old, quiet, and composed with its weathered shingles, sloping gables, and overhanging eaves. There was nothing modern or jarring about it. Time had adorned it with vines of ivy and wild bramble. They overwhelmed its façade as they twined around its mullioned windows, continuing their reach upward. Three blackened chimneys rose from the thick slate roof, which was partly obscured by the ancient pines that encircled the property and edged the roaring ocean beyond.

"It looks like…" Emily's voice trailed off.

A most profound and disturbing sense of nostalgia gnawed at Andrew's heart. He knew what he would find when he opened that door. He knew the shape of the fireplace, how it would take up the whole wall, how the windows would open to the sea, how the wide planked floors would creak under his feet, how the sun would warm a far corner where his chair sat waiting…

Emily took a step toward the door when he stopped her.

"No. This isn't the way it's done…" His mind was tumbling through a whirlwind of déjà vu. Images flashed before his eyes, and he struggled to catch one while an old song unwove its refrain through his memory. But just as quickly as it came, the song was swept away by the roar of the waves. Without another thought, he unlocked the door and took Emily's hand because that is what he had always done. No…no…it was what he wanted to do. Now. Here in the present.

She would smile at him now because that was what she had always done. *Stop.* Stop it. He could not know that. He had never been here before in his life. But then why was the cottage just as he had remembered? Silent and waiting, warm shades of umber and sienna filled the room, from the worn velvet and suede window seat cushions to the faded medieval tapestry print of the drapes. Emily walked about and trailed her hands over the back of the settle that stood in front of the fireplace, dust motes rising in the last rays of the sun. A pendulum clock framed by old black and white photographs sat on the mantle and chimed the hour.

She twirled around and plopped down into the Morris chair in the corner, hoisting her feet up on the matching ottoman and letting out a long, low chuckle. "Sucks to be us."

He wanted to laugh, but he couldn't. What was happening to him? He had to hold her. His hands shook with the need of it. "Come here."

"No. Must check out the rest."

Down a small hall they entered a large bathroom; it was different, newer. It had a wall of showers and a clawfoot tub that stood before a set of French doors which framed the sun setting on the sea beyond. The bedroom lay quietly off to the side—of course it did. There would be an antique four poster bed there, and a sea of pillows…

"Let's never leave this place," she told him.

He wanted to tell her that he never had.

Unable to bear the stifling sensation any longer, his arms enfolded her body. He held her against the granite walls, trying to kiss her — her, the woman he loved, the woman he could feel in his hands. Not a ghost, not a memory. Emily.

In his mind, he believed his desire was driven by the need to escape the hell that they had lived through, to forget death and violence and fear and everything except her, but he knew that wasn't true. There was something more. Refusing to face whatever it was, he hoisted his t-shirt over his head and felt the glorious touch of her fingers, Emily's fingers, encircle his waist. Yes. This was Emily. This was the woman he loved.

Unable to be denied, his hands moved across her body as he undressed her. He kissed her mouth, tasting her, breathing in the smell of salt and sun on her skin. Finally freed of their clothes, he reached for the taps, twisting them on and spinning her to the side as a wall of water poured down. It soon began to steam, creating billows of fog wafting around them. He moved her trembling body into the spray. Her nipples darkened as the water coursed over her, and she tilted her head back and let it wash away the smudges of dirt on her face.

"Christ, you are so unspeakably beautiful…"

The sound of breakers crashing on the rocks far beyond the window filled the room. He lowered his mouth to her lips again, hearing her sighs mix with those of the sea. He could not get enough of her; his hands ached with the need of her skin — to surrender to him, to be his. Emily. Only Emily.

He looked into her eyes and froze. There, reflected deep within those unfathomable spheres, he saw souls of souls, each calling out to him, beckoning him to them, seducing him with their whispers and sighs.

"I love you," he breathed roughly, to her and to them. She leaned forward and rested her forehead on his shoulder. "But how can you do this to me? What are you? What lives inside you that makes me want you every breathing moment? Tell me."

She would not answer, but instead stared into his eyes, a deliberate challenge it seemed to him. Their connection was so intense that he could now feel the souls inside her now, those trembling ghosts that lived within her flushed wet skin as they came closer and closer to the surface. She clenched her arms around his shoulders, her nails biting into the tense muscles of his back, and gripped him tightly. His mouth found hers, and he kissed her with all the love within him. He could barely survive his need for her; it ripped the fabric of his world apart.

"Who are you? Please tell me," he muttered hoarsely, desperate for an answer.

She would not answer.

"Tell me, what are you that makes me so fucking wild?" he demanded and shoved harder into her, over and over, making her scream. "Tell me!"

Enraged, he demanded again and with all his might he drove into her as deeply as he could, sensual waves of lust crashing down his body, arousing the ghosts within him. Each life, past and present, demanding he take this woman as he had for ages.

She clung to him like her very life depended on it, the water beading on her trembling skin. He bowed his head to her neck once more, pressing fierce, feral kisses to her skin. His breathing became shallow as he bit down on the spot just below her ear.

"I love you…but fuck, sweet girl, what are you?" he muttered hoarsely, so on the edge, in trembling, fucking glorious agony. "Tell me!"

Seeking an answer she would not give him, he made love to her mercilessly. There was no longer reason or time. There was only her fevered skin and the pounding water and the ocean far way. He struggled to keep his lips on hers until at last she screamed and wailed, pounding the stone wall with her fist, her body one tight knot of lust as she came and thrashed in mind-numbing spasms, tightening over and over around him, making him cry out in ecstasy.

Yet he still wanted more. *They* wanted more. He slammed into her one last time, screaming against her soaked hair as he forced the rest of himself hot and throbbing, into her, pinning her body to the wall, his heart trying to bash out of his chest beneath her breasts.

Gasping for air, blinded by the water and tears and so bloody reluctant to move, he allowed himself to collapse against her. She was panting his name against his heaving chest, half elation, half sobs. His lips reached hers, and he tasted the salt of her tears and felt the curl of her mouth as he kissed her gently.

He feared she couldn't stand without him, so he gathered her in his arms and shut off the tap, stopping only to grab a towel. She nuzzled into his neck as he carried her in his arms to the bedroom, her heart beating wildly. She searched for his lips as he laid her down and joined her under the thick blankets. Her body was still rippling like waves on the edge of a beach, pulling him to her as the ghosts softly ebbed away. Like the moon to the tide.

He gazed down at her and found her mouth and kissed her, their moist bodies sizzling together.

"Who are you? Please tell me," he whispered, and brushed back the wet strands from her face, amazed at the loving pain rife in his heart.

Her fingers slipped softly around his neck and pulled him down to her. "Yours." And she finally began to cry.

The setting sun had burnished the clouds in gold. Candles flickered on the nightstand, and somewhere far off a piano played, lost in jazz. Emily lay against Andrew's chest as they gazed out of the open bedroom windows from their bed, luxuriating in the sea air.

"Andrew?" she asked.

"Hmmm."

"Does this place—is there anything about this cottage that doesn't seem quite right to you? That seems strange?"

She tilted her head up at him while she spoke. The sky had descended to the mood indigo of dusk, leaving her eyes nearly violet. They shone in the faint light, framed by the waves of her hair that fell to the bare skin of her shoulders.

Strange? Strange didn't cover half of it. He wanted to tell her that for weeks now he couldn't shake this sickening feeling that everything was repeating itself somehow. And that since they had stepped through those doors, it all seemed amplified in his mind. It was as if he was watching himself watch himself, like the past and present were folding in and over on themselves and trapping him in some kind of twisted three-way mirror from which he couldn't escape. Christ, it made no sense and was certainly the release of all this bloody stress—but every time he held her, looked at her, it seemed like he was experiencing it tenfold. It was thrilling, staggering, but he felt as if he was no longer there, like he was a ghost. A ghost haunting all of his lives.

"Yes," he replied, unwilling to say more. How could he explain what he was feeling and not sound mad? It was impossible.

Emily stilled. She was so much like a wisp of ghost herself except for the slow beat of her heart. "It's not the first time I've felt this way, either. When I saw you the in the park, saw you standing there with your guitar, and saw your hands strum those first chords, ever since then, this feeling I have for you…No, it's not a feeling, that's too weak a word—this bond that connects me to you, has only gotten more intense, like it has a life of its own." She looked up at him briefly, her face self-conscious from her confession. "You know when Dwayne told us about all those past lives that day in his shop, when he told us that I was your lover, your concubine…"

"My muse."

"Yes. I wanted to discount it all as craziness, but now—I don't know. I'm haunted, by who I was and who I was to you. And at night, in my dreams—I…"

"Go on, sweet girl?"

She shook her head.

"I know you've been having nightmares, I've heard them."

"No. Oh God, what did I say?"

"What happened? What did you see?"

She hesitated and pulled at the strings on the quilt. "There were cliffs and rocks and we're there, you and I together, but I can't reach you, you're not who I think you are, you've changed somehow, and then…"

"Go on."

"I can't remember. I can never remember the ending."

Just then a chill wind blew in from the window, extinguishing the candles on the nightstands, and a soft chuckle emanated from the dusk of the evening.

"Liars," a voice replied.

The window shutters slammed shut, casting the room in near darkness.

"Damn it, Nick! Cut this shit out!"

"Isssss not Nick, my pretty lad."

The inhuman hiss of a woman's voice sent a jolt of fear down his spine as the temperature around them dropped precipitously. An elaborate phantasm shrouded in an Elizabethan gown swept slowly across the room; she was ghastly beautiful, like dead roses set in a crystal vase.

"Who are you?" he demanded.

"Are? You do insult me with such a word. I have not 'been' in a long, long while."

Emily sat up next to him, her eyes taking in the bone-chilling apparition. He wanted to haul her back to his side, but she kneeled forward, sitting even straighter.

"Andrew, she's The Lady in White," she whispered to him, never taking her eyes from the ghost.

"Ahhhh…behold a Thomas, and she is no longer alone. No, not alone at all. And the lovely lad is naked too. Tsk, tsk." Her sing-song spectral laughter echoed like a wind chime made of glass shards. Her deep green eyes glimmered.

He didn't care for the insinuation behind her words, nor the angle of her sight for that matter, and he pulled the sheet tighter around his hips. She was a formidable old thing, even in death; the very air pulsed with her aura. Emily, however, didn't seem to mind. Oblivious to any danger, she leaned perilously closer to the eerie ringlets of hair that snaked wildly about the specter's face like a spray of asps.

"Thank you for protecting me today. You were extremely brave."

"You saw her — today? Where?" he demanded under his breath.

"The caves," Emily whispered back. "That's why I went down there in the first place."

"Didn't you think this was a bit of information worth sharing?"

"I was preoccupied with trying to stay alive at the time."

The spirit studied him some more, making the hair on the back of his neck stand on end as well as filling him with the strong desire for a robe. Before she turned her attention to Emily, her black lips puckered suggestively at him, and if he didn't know better, he would have sworn she winked. As she turned to stare at Emily, her eyes darkened and narrowed slightly; she rested her hand coquettishly against her transparent cheek.

"I know you didn't have to help," Emily went on in a rushed tone. "I know there are rules about things like that, but I never got a chance to thank you. I'm Emily Thomas, by the way, but I guess you already know that. And this is Andrew Hayes."

The pallid rays emanating from her body rippled with her dissatisfaction as the jeweled dress thrashed the air. She inspected him anew, her head tilting in a perturbed sort of query, as if she was not pleased with what she had heard. Not pleased at all.

"You have pledged yourself to her, pretty boy?"

Andrew tried to grasp the meaning of her words, anchoring them in whatever time she had come from. Had he pledged himself to Emily? Proposed marriage? Is that what she meant?

"Yes."

Suddenly, the air around them dropped another ten degrees. His attention shot back to The Lady in White, whose eyes had narrowed to slits and blackened entirely. "Why? Why did you have to do that to her?" she wailed, her hands clawing at her gown. "Why curse her? Why must it always be that way with you?"

He stared at her in confusion. This was hardly the reaction he was expecting. Wouldn't this have been acceptable behavior during her lifetime? Lying naked with a girl in an unmade bed centuries ago — he better damn well be pledged to her.

"Because I love her."

"If you loved her, you would leave her now, never to see her again. She is far better off without you." Her vapors bled black to match the darkness of her words.

He opened his mouth to protest when Emily moved even closer to her. "Please, please, do you know where Nick Chamberlain's ashes are?"

"You come this close when I am angry. Your heart…I can hear it beating. You are still afraid, I can tell."

"I'm…sorry. I don't mean to be. Do you prefer to be addressed as The Lady in White — or is there another name I can call you? I mean may I call you," Emily stammered.

"No one has spoken my name for centuries," she sighed.

"I'm sorry, it was rather rude of me to ask."

"No — it is simply painful to hear it said aloud. I am not sure I remember how to say it anymore. There are so few of us left. So many of our brethren have passed on. Those who knew our names and those whose voices called for us in the night have long slipped away."

Her melancholy enveloped them like mist.

"But I'd like to know your name—that way you wouldn't be forgotten."

The Lady in White swirled to the window, hesitating, vibrations shaking her image.

"You would—you would do that for me? Something this fearful?"

"Fearful? No, you're beautiful. I've never seen someone like you. I could never forget you."

"Emily…" Andrew warned. Despite his love for Emily, the depth of compassion in her tone bothered him. Two ghosts in one house were bad enough, and he definitely was not bringing this one home.

"What you told me in the caves, what did you mean? What did you mean when you said you told Mrs. Chamberlain the truth?"

"She must tell you. I cannot. But—"

"What truth? What did you tell Mrs. Chamberlain?" Andrew asked sharply, clearly annoyed that there was yet another vital detail that Emily had forgotten to tell him. The Lady in White glared at him.

"Go on, please," Emily pleaded.

The specter fixed her blackened eyes on Emily. "Life is not without hope. You are proof of that. There may be hope for Nick and Nora, but you must be strong, stronger than all the rest. Are you strong, Emily Thomas?" She swept toward her, almost blanketing Emily in her silver glow.

"Yes, I think so."

"Can you live without your heart?"

"Wait!" Andrew cried. "What are you saying? No one is touching this woman. Her heart stays where it is!"

"Please tell me…if we find Nick," Emily asked quickly, "will there be peace for Nick and Nora? Will they be reunited?"

"Peace is a mercurial word. You may only have so much peace in this life. But you have the keys for it. Use them. If you do so, then yes, there will be peace. In its way."

"Keys? What keys?" Emily was nearly nose to nose with the ghost now.

Just then a knocking came from the door. The Lady in White swirled in alarm.

"No, wait! Don't go!" Emily cried.

"Emily Thomas, seek what you want…where the purple-stemmed wild raspberries grow…" And with that she pushed open the shutters and leveled them both with her withering gaze. "But I must warn you. Time is—"

"Fuck no, you're not! You are not going to warn us about time running out. I'm bloody sick of hearing it. No more! Just get the hell out of here."

"Andrew!" cried Emily.

The Lady in White swept toward the ceiling and glared down at him. "Arrogant, smug, overconfident boy—you are all alike. Every time. Only you are so much more so. The worst ever."

"Thank you for your high opinion of men. Now go fucking haunt somewhere else, I've had enough."

"You—you are not scared of me in the least, are you?"

"Not a bit. But I dig the dress."

"Insolent bastard. Breathtaking and stunning you are, with that comely face and eyes of blue, those fine, long, muscles. Yes, you are truly an exquisite specimen. You would make such a superb ghost. Care to try?"

"Shan't happen, not if I have anything to say about it."

She whooshed down from the ceiling until she was inches from the bed, her eyes drinking him in, ravenous, hungry, smoldering…

Bloody hell…he recognized that look—he had seen it a thousand times before—from the stage. He had an undead fan. Christ. There was only one thing he could do.

Cocking a roughish eyebrow at her, he held back his shoulders and leveled her with an equally hungry and ravenous smile.

She froze in midair, stunned. Then the impossible occurred. She seemed to blush. Every one of her silver spectral wisps turned a deep crimson.

"Good night…m'lady," he whispered huskily.

Her ebony lips curled into a trembling, radiant little *O*. The knocking came even louder. She sluiced through the window and was lost to the night.

Emily stared at him in shock. The knocking was quickly escalating into pounding.

"I'll get it," he said, grabbing a towel.

"I'm coming with you!" Emily grabbed another, and they headed for the front door.

"What? Are you expecting others? Was anyone else down there you haven't told me about?"

"I don't think so. But I'll bet you just got yourself another girlfriend," she said, impressed.

"I'd like to take this opportunity to say I'm getting bloody pissed at every damn ghost telling us the end is nigh. It's truly starting to get on my nerves. And I have no desire for another girlfriend. I'm having problems enough trying to keep the one I have under control," he said before yanking open the door.

Simon stood outside, freshly showered and dressed in a pair of navy slacks and crisp white dress shirt, holding their suitcases in his hands.

"You're a bellboy now?" Andrew asked.

"Compliments of the stoner express." Simon dumped the two bags on the threshold, then tried to peer inside the cottage, clearly intrigued.

"Sucks to be you," Andrew retorted, resting his arm against the door jamb and blocking his view of Emily, who stood next to him struggling to keep on her towel.

"My, my, look at this place."

"Trust me, it's not all it's cracked up to be."

"Why is it that you always get all the luck?"

"Because I am a truly exquisite specimen and evidently would make a superb ghost."

"Really?" Simon frowned at him and tried for another look but met with Andrew's shoulder. "Fine. Meet us in the lobby in an hour. Zoey's orders."

"She's back?"

"I was half tempted to throw everything in the boot of the truck and head home, screw waiting around for some sodding ghost. And I still might if I can't get at least one bloody peaceful evening for a change."

"Goodbye, Simon."

Andrew slammed the door in his face.

"Our clothes, thank God," Emily cried.

She grabbed her small bags and headed back to the bedroom, throwing on every light in the cottage in her wake. He could tell from the intensity of her movements that she was in full detective mode, of which he was infinitely grateful. Only Emily could face a phantom and become jazzed. He, for one, was not there yet.

"Hope. She said hope. In all of this—in all this talk of death and terror, there's still a way. It's possible!"

"What's possible?"

"A way to help Nick and Nora. And you know what I think? If we can reunite them, they'll break the cycle of whatever is replaying itself over and over again through us. Because you know that it is, I can tell, no matter what you say. Peace, she said, there could be peace. Now all we have to do is find his ashes."

"Are you forgetting something? She also bitched me out, demanded that I leave you, asked if you could live without your heart, and tried to announce that time was running out. Not my idea of a bloody pep talk. Oh, and she also classified peace as mercurial, so you may not want to hang your hat on that one."

"Where the purple-stemmed wild raspberries grow. Why is that so familiar? Why do I know that from somewhere?"

"Miss Thomas, are you listening to me at all?"

"It's beautiful and sad. The purple-stemmed wild raspberries…"

"Rather cheekily poetic for a ghost, don't you think?"

Her eyes widened. "Yes! It is from a poem. Oh, where have I heard that? It's on the tip of my tongue."

She was pacing. "But we still need keys. She said we had the keys. Are there keys in the poem? Oh bloody fucking hell, why can't I remember?"

"I believe my piss-poor language is beginning to corrupt you. Is there alcohol in here? I need a drink." He began scanning a room for anything with a label.

"A key! But we have a key! The key we found in the keepsake box. Oh crap, it's back at home."

Andrew begrudgingly headed for the bedroom.

"Where are you going?"

His coat lay in a pile of cast off clothing. He nearly sighed at the sight. These bloody ghosts were seriously cutting into his sex life. He thrust his hand into the pocket and felt Nick's ring, then the key.

He held it out to her. It shone like a new penny.

Emily threw herself into his arms, and he twirled her around. Her enthusiasm was contagious. In light of all this terror and horror, she saw the silver lining. And to her, real-life ghosts meant nothing if it meant an end to their nightmares, if it meant peace.

Yes, perhaps they could beat this. The pieces were falling into place. Together they could do anything. His hands brushed her wet hair over her shoulder.

"I love you," he told her. "Right now, in this life. In this very second. And no one is taking that away. Understand, sweet girl?"

"Yes."

"Emily, you aren't—you're not scared of this cottage? Do you want to find another place to sleep tonight? You've been through a ghastly day."

"And you haven't? No, I don't want to leave. We were here first." She said this almost offhand, her eyes now focused on the ocean out their bedroom window, her thoughts lost to him. "We were."

"Yes, we were."

From far off the piano began again. The song caught on the night air, and he hummed it as he watched her slip from his arms.

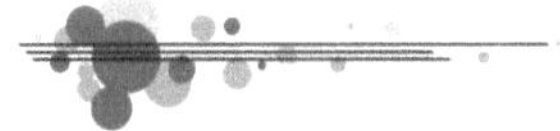

They met the others for a quiet dinner at Café Beaujolais, a small quaint farmhouse half obscured by overflowing gardens and situated within walking distance of the hotel. There they enjoyed a subdued meal, rehashing the day's tumultuous events, waiting until the copious bottles of wine relaxed them enough to feel human again.

Simon ran his finger along the edge of his water glass and looked over the top of his glasses at Andrew. "Paulie, my good man."

"Yes?" Andrew responded archly, preparing himself for a continuation of his bitching from earlier.

"While we were all waiting in the lobby for your bony ass to appear for dinner, I talked to Neil and filled him in on our day. Thought one of us ought to keep our new manager in the loop. He was bloody worried… actually, he sounded frantic. Just so you know, you're seriously falling down in the son department."

Andrew repeated the word in his head. *Son.* It still seemed so strange.

"I had my hands full," Andrew retorted with a shrug.

Emily's heel came down on his foot.

"Hey, did you ever see The Lady in White?" Zoey asked Emily, pouring the fourth bottle of wine.

Emily and Andrew took turns explaining the story, which left them all momentarily speechless, even after the staggering events of the last twenty-four hours.

"So let me get this right. Nick's remains are in some house that you've got the key for. A house with raspberries." It sounded even more absurd when Christian said it. "You know what I think, Mama Chamberlain survived him, didn't she? I bet she kept his corpse locked away in some attic. Like in *Psycho*."

"You know what they say about a boy and his mother," Zoey said sagely.

"Christ, let's hope not," Andrew muttered.

"Chamberlain…" Margot murmured. "The ghost said something to you in the caves, Emily. About a Thomas being alone without a Chamberlain."

Andrew narrowed his eyes at Emily and muttered under his breath. "So that's what she meant back in our bedroom — about you not being alone anymore. Are you forgetting these relevant details for some reason?"

"I had my hands full," she replied *sotto voce*.

"But listen," said Margot, undeterred. "This Lady in White was surprised to see Emily — a Thomas — alone in those caves without a Chamberlain accompanying her. Now this same Lady in White told Andrew he didn't want her near Emily. Maybe Emily is meant to be with a Chamberlain."

"Excuse me?" he sputtered, nearly choking on his wine.

"Yeah, but whatever The Lady in White told Nick's mother about Nora," Christian interjected, "it made her nuts. This 'truth' everyone is talking about — what if it's about Thomases and Chamberlains being together."

"Or not being together. Like Romeo and Juliet," Zoey reasoned aloud. "You know, like doomed star-crossed lovers throughout time. Over and over again," she added melodramatically. "That's what everybody keeps saying — 'it's happening again,' right? First at the séance and now from this Lady in White. Things keep repeating themselves."

Andrew shot Emily a grim look and saw her face had paled.

"Get real," Simon scoffed.

"And talking to ghosts with black lips is real?" Christian cocked his head at Simon.

"Is everyone forgetting a crucial fact? I'm with Emily — she's not with some other man."

"What are you worried about, Paulie? A little competition?" Simon said and leveled a gaze at Andrew over his glass. Andrew couldn't be sure he was teasing anymore. The day had worn away the last pretense of both men's patience.

"Whatever this truth is," said Margot, ignoring them, "Nick's mother is not going to be pleasant to deal with from the sounds of her. If she even shows at all."

"Oh, she'll show. She wants Emily. Dead," Simon concluded with a sip of his wine.

Andrew's hand tightened around the stem of his glass. "Well, she's going to be highly disappointed. Because first, there is no bloody way in hell that Emily is going off with a Chamberlain, and second, if things become even the slightest bit threatening during that séance tomorrow, we bolt. I'm taking Emily and getting the hell out of there." He stared at her. "I still hate the idea of this."

"She can't make me do something I don't want to do."

"We can't be sure of that. And I don't trust Egan to be able to control the situation — he did a wretched job the last time. The moment anything goes sideways, it's over. Understood?"

She nodded, and the rest of the table agreed.

The whole conversation did nothing to abate Andrew's mounting sense of apprehension. If Emily was indeed a victim in this reoccurring tragedy, he did not comprehend where he fit in to it all. And he refused to believe there existed another man who controlled her destiny, who was meant to be with her. But the more he tried to deny it, the more questions rankled up inside him. He remembered his nightmares, the threatening visions of cliffs, and the bone-chilling echo of screams, Emily's screams. If there was a Chamberlain out there, would he be the one who would save her? Save her from Andrew, himself? No. Dammit, there was no other man; there was no need for saving. With that, he laced their hands together and felt her ring press against his palm. It was the palpable reminder of the present and their future. It brought back the memory of the ghost's entreaty:

Have you pledged yourself to her? Yes. From the beginning. Like no man alive. Always.

After dinner the group wandered back into town. Simon, Christian, and Andrew began humming something, making up lyrics and feeling all the better for falling into their familiar camaraderie.

"Andrew, look!" Emily's face lit up and she pulled him along to a small gathering of stores. He followed her to The Raven and the Frost, an old bookshop where a collection of Japanese lanterns glowed in the window next to a sign that read "closed" although the door was wide open.

Capitalizing on her mood, he let the others drift to a shop across the street and waved, agreeing to meet in a little while to walk back to the hotel.

The shop appeared more whimsical attic than bookstore. The Tibetan bells tied to the door chimed richly as they entered. Their eyes blinked, adjusting to the dim light, then their gazes traveled across the first floor, crammed to the ceiling with antique and forgotten tomes. Several small animal skeletons hung suspended from the second story ceiling by thin threads of fishing line and must have forced many a wary customer to duck from the sight on his way down the rickety spiral staircase. Above their heads the gallery appeared to sag under the weight of a massive display case jammed with everything from jade cigarette holders, ivory handled opera glasses, and snuff boxes, to outdated globes and row upon row of cobalt blue bottles in varying shapes and sizes.

The peal of the bells roused a small March Hare of a man from his reverie. He stood on a bookcase ladder, balancing a cumbersome volume of Proust in his hand. The man peered at Emily over the rim of his spectacles as if to say, *Looking for anything in particular?*

"Your poetry section, please?" she asked.

He nodded toward the spiral staircase. She shuddered at the skeletons as she and Andrew navigated their way up the stairs.

"Bet he's a ghost," Andrew murmured in her ear, to which he received a wry glance in return.

Once they reached the gallery, he watched as she pored over the endless volumes stacked around them, all in disarray and shoved in any available space. She tucked her hair behind her ear and smiled up at him sideways. His fingers trailed along her shoulder.

"Help me look," she whispered.

"I am looking."

"Andrew…"

"Kiss me. Just once."

He took her face in his hands, gazing at her, and lowered his mouth to hers, brushing their lips together, back and forth, slowly, exquisitely. There was something so innocent and untouched about her, and every time he kissed her he felt she was offering all of herself to him and him alone. That he would be the only man to taste those lips, and he would be the only man to hear those poetic moans. It was overpowering.

Her hands tangled in his hair as she pressed her lithe body to his and surrendered herself to the kiss. Lost in the haze and stacks of books, he knew where they were, and it would be so easy to take her now, but he needed to kiss her. He needed the clarity that only holding her in his arms could bring. He wanted to show her that he could wash away everything wrong in her world, that he could love her more than she could understand, and that he would never leave her. That he would not hurt her. Ever.

"Why?" he asked her, hoping she knew the answer. *Why, Emily, is every act of love, every touch, haunted by the specter of loss? Why does as if feel as if I've said goodbye to you more than this heart can bear?* Emily's eyes glowed in the dim light, her lips swollen.

Just then they heard the rumbling of a ladder and startled, flew apart; the emotions they had been lost in had been so potent. The old man had pulled his ladder to them. He stood on the rungs and looked at them with his eyebrows arched in question. His skin shimmered faintly in the dusky light, and his stare was so disconcerting that Andrew adjusted his collar and tried not to make eye contact.

"I'm looking…I'm looking for a poem that contains the line, 'purple-stemmed wild raspberries grow.' Do you know who wrote that?" Emily asked, brushing the hair away from her eyes.

He smiled softly and pushed off. The ladder moved faster and much more quietly than Andrew expected, especially with him standing upon it. His hand retrieved a thin black volume from high above. With a whoosh, he glided back to them.

He held it out to Emily with a triumphant look in his eyes.

"Yes! Of course!" she cried.

Andrew angled around to see the spine. *The Voice of the Poet: Robert Frost.*

Emily excitedly pawed through the pages until she stopped short. "That's it! That's it. *The Ghost House.*"

"Why am I not surprised?" Andrew replied wryly.

She began to read aloud.

"I dwell in a lonely house I know
That vanished many a summer ago,
And left no trace but the cellar walls,
And a cellar in which the daylight falls,
And the purple-stemmed wild raspberries grow."

"See? That's it! The purple-stemmed wild raspberries!"

"Go on," he urged her.

"O'er ruined fences the grape-vines shield
The woods come back to the mowing field;
The orchard tree has grown one copse
Of new wood and old where the woodpecker chops;
The footpath down to the graveyard is healed…
I dwell with a strangely aching heart…"

"What do you suppose it means?" Emily asked, still studying the stanzas of the poem.

"That Nick's ashes are in the remains of an old house, or part of an old house, perhaps. But where?"

"A house near a graveyard?"

"Excuse me, sir, do you know if there is a graveyard nearby…"

Emily and he glanced over to the old man. He had vanished.

The bells tinkled, and they peered down at a middle-aged woman walking in the door with a few books under her arms.

"Oh, I'm sorry. Have you been waiting long? I was just next door. May I help you?"

Emily and Andrew shared a knowing glance.

"I told you," he whispered in her ear as he took the book from her hands. "We'll be taking this, thank you."

When they stepped out of the store the others were waiting for them across the street as promised. He stopped and took one last look at the curious shop, the large opal of a moon rising behind it, and turned back to Emily, but she was already crossing the street to join the others, lost in her book.

Unexpectedly a motorcycle zoomed around the corner. Andrew yelled and Emily spun around, her eyes frozen on his. The look on his face must have terrified her, for she swung around, but it was too late. It was gunning directly for her. Christian flew off the steps and grabbed her; the motorcycle skidded out, missing her by inches. The driver barely managed to right himself before he came to a stop and tore off his helmet.

"Jesus! Where did you come from?" he shouted, gasping at Emily.

"Don't drive so bloody fast!" Andrew yelled, getting in his face.

"I'm fine," said Emily, breathless; he felt her hand on his shoulder. "It was an accident."

With a growl he let him get back on his bike, and the driver was off in a flash. Andrew knelt down and retrieved the book from where it lay in the dirt, handing it to Emily.

"Man, that was close. You sure you're okay, Emily?" Christian asked. She nodded.

"Let's head back to the hotel," suggested Simon, motioning toward the end of the street.

"Good idea." Andrew's tone was clipped as he took Emily's hand in his. He gave her a soft kiss on the side of her face. "That's twice in one day."

"Three times," Simon corrected him. And Andrew knew he was right. She'd nearly been killed in the caves, in the van, and now this.

"Three times," Andrew repeated, but Emily slipped her arm around him tightly and continued on.

By the time they neared the hotel, Andrew's nerves had calmed somewhat and he heard faint strains of music coming from the lobby. It was that song again — the song that had haunted him ever since they had arrived at this place. He knew it far better than he should, as though he had sung it countless times. But it was too late to allow guests to be playing the piano in such a manner. Even though the chords were muted, whispered almost, it was nearly midnight.

Upon passing through the front doors Christian swept Zoey away, waving them goodnight, and Simon and Margot followed suit, leaving Emily and him alone in the empty room. Alone, except for a small fire in the fireplace and a lonely lamp glowing on the vacant front desk. Everyone was abed apparently, except the ghosts that undoubtedly lurked in the shadows, enjoying the sultry music.

Whoever was in the adjacent room was quite an accomplished pianist, tossing off a complicated jazz progression with a faint flourish of ragtime. He slinked his arm around Emily's waist and walked her over to a faraway corner where they could stand closer to the fire.

"Dance with me," he said, already taking her in his arms. The music was too fine to say goodnight to quite yet.

He watched the firelight play off the soft auburn waves of her hair. She rested her head against his chest and sighed. Aware for the first time of how very tired he was and how exhausted she must be as well, he laid his cheek on her head and held her closer. It was the end of a hell of a day, and he could do little but sway back and forth and hum softly to her, losing himself to the plaintive piano strains.

He thought about what they would face tomorrow and all that they still had left to do. Surviving Vandin had been one thing, but now they would face a creature that was not of this world and, if she had her way, did not want Emily to remain there either. Why? What had Emily ever done except bear the name of Thomas?

Yet if they found Nick first, they wouldn't have to have this horrible meeting with Nick's mother, this notorious Lady in Red. They were close to finding him, he was sure of it. The answer was right there, just out of reach. An old house near a graveyard — that's where he would be. Near where wild raspberries grew. "I dwell with a strangely aching heart…"

What did that mean?

As he closed his eyes, his thoughts were diffused like a song he had left undone, and he was too weary to wrestle with the problem anymore. He listened as the piano player began to sing.

Andrew's arms tightened around Emily, and he felt sleepy, so sleepy, like he was falling into a waking dream. He yawned and felt his forehead drop to hers. She hummed softly.

He drifted and lost himself in a reverie. In his mind he could see Emily sitting at a bar. Her hair was swept up, and she was wearing a stylish suit, her lips painted a deep burgundy. A row of martinis were lined up in front of her.

"How many of these are yours?" he asked, smiling as he took his seat next to her. His cufflinks reflected in the polished wood of the bar, and his heart was beating uncommonly fast, so thrilled he was to be with her.

"Only one," she announced. "I ordered the same for you."

"But there are four." He laughed, wanting to kiss her but refraining.

"Hmmm. Then you've got your work cut out for you."

"Where are the olives?"

"I ate them. I was hungry and you promised me dinner." She cast him an enchantingly stern look that left him mesmerized.

He motioned to the bartender. "Ray, more olives, and where are the nuts tonight?"

In his vision, Emily raised an eyebrow at him.

Why did he know the bartender's name? How did he know him? He glanced down at Emily's hand. Where was her ring?

He was dreaming. He must have fallen asleep dancing with Emily, and now he was dreaming, but he was too captivated to wake up. He felt different in his skin, more mature, more sophisticated, but no less enthralled with the woman before him.

Emily scanned the room where they were seated; it was an elegant dining room full of people dressed in sharply pressed suits and smart dresses. As she surveyed the crowd, her face held a marvelous vivacity, interested in everyone and everything. He watched her in fascination, feeling jealous that she wasn't gazing at him in the same way.

"So you have no idea why I have these ghosts, I take it?" She returned her attention to him and sipped her martini, her eyes alert and wry.

"I told you to leave traps, but you wanted to go the more humane route."

"I think you're angling to see them yourself, if you ask me. They tend to favor my bedroom. But you knew that, didn't you?"

"Smart ghosts. Sorry to disappoint you, Madam, but I'm not partial to a *ménage à trois*—even the supernatural variety."

"It would be a *ménage a quatre*, I believe. But you look like you could handle it. No, wait—you're right—it would be a *ménage a trois*. You see, my ghosts can't be in the same room for some reason, otherwise I guess I could just vacuum them up or something."

"Didn't peg you as the kind of dame who'd get her hands dirty."

"I wouldn't be so sure." She smiled wickedly and took a long sip of her martini. He watched her lips caress the glass.

"My, sugar, is that an invitation?"

"A disclosure."

"Hmmm."

Then the vision changed. His heart wanted to make it stay. He was flying from the rush of emotion he felt for her.

A phonograph was playing that song. Again.

Now Emily was standing by a darkened window, wearing something sheer that blew in the soft breeze. He stood behind her, his hands on her shoulders. The air smelled sweet, familiar. Her skin was warm.

He turned her around and kissed her. His heart beat. Once. Twice.

"I love you," she whispered at the end of the kiss. He smiled at her smile.

"Why, I believe the little lady does."

"More than I should, if I knew what was good for me."

"I'm good for you."

Nearby, a piano continued to play the song. He kissed her passionately while silent tears slid down his cheeks. He was crying…why the hell was he crying? His hands pressed hard against her skin, craving her warmth. She was crying now too. They kissed madly, fighting to hold onto each other, while his desperate heart felt like it might burst from his chest. Longing and sorrow crushed down on him as he clenched his hands around her shoulders and struggled to keep her in his arms.

"Stay! Please, stay!" she begged in a hopeless prayer.

"I love you so," he said, searing the words into her soul. "I. Love. You. Nora."

"Nicholas!"

The piano playing clattered to a crashing halt. Andrew's body whipped back as though he had been slammed by a fist, the pain was so intense.

Their eyes snapped open. Emily stood shaking, wearing a look of raw shock on her face. They were back in the lobby, while his hands crushed her arms, gasping for air with tears glistening on their faces.

Without pausing for another breath, Andrew clutched her hand in his and ran to the adjoining room, to the piano. The pianist had vanished. A lone martini glass sat on the bench, and sheet music was scattered across the floor. Andrew reached to gather it up.

"Nick! Christ. Nick." The pain was still rife within him. Andrew glanced up at Emily; he knew she felt the same thing, her face looked so haunted.

For the first time since his death, Nick had touched his beloved Nora — touched her through Andrew and Emily. Part of Andrew ached to kiss Nora again, as if Nick's spirit was still within him, still fighting to reach her.

"Nick, God I'm sorry."

It was then that Andrew saw it. There amongst the music was a map. A map of a town. Belden. A water ring left from the martini glass circled a small corner like a bull's eye.

He remembered. He remembered the old steamer trunk hidden in the passageway of their house in San Francisco and cutting his hand against its small metal tag that he thought had read Belden Firm. But it wasn't Belden Firm. It was Belden Farm.

The circle outlined a small property named Belden Farm. A farm near an orchard that sat next to a small cemetery.

"Nick, we've found you."

27

The drizzle had increased to a fierce spatter, and the fog that hung outside the windows of the minivan was broken only by the sight of the trees that twisted like arthritic hands in the wind as they sped by. Inside they were a silent lot, bundled in sweaters and jeans, the scent of coffee warming them. Emily clutched her to-go cup to her chest as the caffeine pumped rapidly through her veins.

Andrew drove, needing to be in control of every facet of their day. He would glance at her occasionally in the rearview mirror, undoubtedly to make sure she hadn't disappeared in a puff of smoke or fallen out the door. She welcomed his glimpses; their breakfast had been punctuated by a series of strained silences. The aggravated expression on his face had made her eat little and speak even less.

"There is no reason why we have to leave here and go to that inn, no reason at all," she remembered him saying to her over his half-eaten scrambled eggs. "We know where Nick is now—I have no doubt he's there. Surely you don't either."

"I have to go. I need to know," she had told him, trying to make him look her in the eye.

"Sweet girl, how can we even be sure?"

"But Nick and Nora, we've seen them—we've felt them. Don't you want to know?"

They had avoided discussing what had transpired in the hotel lobby. And now, it was as if speaking of it would summon all the loss again. The only saving grace was that they both knew they were not crazy—unless they were falling into the same madness together. They were indisputably linked to Nick Chamberlain and Nora Thomas. But how?

"Know what? This 'truth'? This warning every dead thing we meet rails at us about? Do you even hear what you're saying?"

"But it's the same thing over and over. About time running out. It has to be about us. And last night…We can't walk away from whatever this truth is. At least I can't—"

"Stop."

She could tell his willingness to discuss this had hit the end of its endurance. The past twenty-four hours had been the most harrowing of her life, and she could only imagine what it had done to him. She knew she had cajoled and dragged him to this point. This was her ghost story, and because of love or infinite patience, he had trudged along with her, risking his safety and his sanity. Last night had cost him, how much, she couldn't say, but he wore the exhaustion upon his face in the guise of dark circles beneath his eyes.

But how could she make him understand that she had to confront this Lady in Red? In a perverse way, she felt it was like falling down a flight of stairs after missing the first step. She knew it would hurt, but she had to hit the bottom; she couldn't reach out and try to break her fall. And even more than that, she didn't want anyone—ghost or otherwise—holding a sword over their heads. Vandin was dead, but she needed to vanquish this monster, get the truth from her, and be gone. Yet how much more could she push him before he snapped? This was far from what he had originally bargained for.

Simon turned on the radio, returning her to the cold vinyl seat of the minivan. Margot sat next to her. Christian and Zoey huddled in the last row of seats, and by the sounds of it, they were trying in vain to get warm.

"What do you figure this Lady in Red will be like after all?" Simon asked, drumming his fingers to the current song and peering out the passenger side window.

"She won't be wearing blue," Margot retorted.

"At least we're coming armed," Christian said. The sound of his voice left no doubt that he was thrilled with the prospect of the stoners opening up a can of whoop ass on this infamous ghoul.

"Do you honestly think those idiots have actual ghost catching equipment with them?" Margot scoffed. "Can you imagine? It's probably just a bunch of junk they bought off some crazed physics students that saw one too many episodes of *MythBusters*. I bet they have no clue what they're doing—or worse—the stuff will actually work and they'll take out a whole block by pressing the wrong button and inadvertently discovering cold fusion. You know, Andrew, on second thought, you better park the van as far away from the hotel as possible. It's my name on the rental agreement."

"I was thinking of heading to Belden Cemetery, actually."

Emily flashed her gaze up to the rear view mirror.

"Why there?" Zoey asked. Andrew paused and gripped the steering wheel, then proceeded to explain to the group about the map, pointedly leaving out the supernatural possession aspects of their evening.

"If Nick showed you the exact spot, why don't we drive there now? We don't need to see this Lady in Red after all." The relief in Zoey's voice was palpable.

"Thank you, Zoey."

"You promised," Emily warned.

He glanced at her in the rear view mirror. "I've promised a great many things in my sorry sod of a life, Miss Thomas."

"Andrew."

Simon turned up the radio, evidently sensing trouble brewing. Suddenly, the blinding force of Andrew's voice blasted through the speakers.

"Holy hell," Simon gasped, his fingers still frozen on the dial even after the song had ended.

"Well, there you go, folks," announced the DJ. "That's The Lost Boys. They've been touring nonstop this past year, although they seem to be taking a breather lately. But please, I'm begging you, stop with all the requests. I can only play it once an hour. It's total Lost Boys mania over here. Thank God it's for a real band for once. They deserve it."

"You're welcome," murmured Andrew.

He glanced in the rear view mirror once more and met Emily's gaze. Her eyes fell first. There it was, she thought, that look. And she knew what it meant: he wanted to go back on the road. No, he needed to go back on the road. He was getting restless being in one spot for so long. This was not his life.

As the road narrowed on ahead, tree branches began to brush against the sides of the van, a few scraping along as though to hold them back. Soon a bridge rose into view. It spanned a small harbor dotted with fishing boats pulling on their moorings, bobbing hard in the churning whitecaps. The fog made their progress slow, and still the trees scratched against the windows like hopeless creatures in the thick, dank mist. Emily wrapped Andrew's coat around her shoulders. He had draped it around her after noticing her shivering when they left the cottage that morning, her own sweater not warm enough. It made her feel strangely protected as they traversed the bridge and took a switchback of road up to the surrounding bluffs that overlooked the village of Noyo.

But before long, the smell of salty air began to feel heavy, even in the car. She placed her hands on her temples and leaned forward, making Margot turn to her in concern. "Are you all right?"

"Yeah, fine, I'm fine." But she was lying. Vivid snapshots had begun to detonate in her mind, and she was unable to stop them. Cliffs. Screaming. Falling. Falling. Hands clawing a dashboard. Shattered glass. Blood.

"No," she muttered. "No. Stop!"

"Emily?" Margot shook her arm, yanking her back to the present. The visions had stopped, but Andrew's eyes were fixed on her in the rear view mirror.

When they exited the van, the fog and rain were so thick they couldn't see farther than ten feet in front of them. From out of the murkiness the hotel emerged into view, majestic and solitary. It seemed to breathe upon seeing them, to settle a bit, to sigh, as if its expectations were met at long last.

"Christian?" Zoey asked, her voice thin, and she reached out for his hand and held on fast. Endless gables hid under a host of redwoods, and twin trees stood like sentinels around the wraparound porch. Emily glanced up at Andrew's face as they approached. He would not look at her, but only grimly faced the building like he wished he could burn it down.

"We've got you, Emily," Christian told her with a slap on the shoulder, startling her and annoying Andrew. "And look! Reinforcements!"

Out of the mist they marched like warriors, four across, loaded down with large orange gym bags and wearing their black robes like some supernatural SWAT team. Emily's spirits lifted with the sight, and for the first time that morning she felt like smiling.

"Bloody hell," Andrew muttered, looking up to the sky and shaking his head.

"Greetings!" the stoners shouted, waving as they approached.

Buck held something in the air that looked like an oversized cell phone with antennas, shaking it as if he couldn't get coverage. "The readings are phenomenal," he informed them, never taking his eyes from the contraption. "I've never seen such a stew like this. Man, it's amazing the roof is still on this place."

"Lock and load then?" said Christian, beaming.

Egan scowled. "The movie industry has robbed us of our romance."

"Don't worry, we're equipped. We've brought both organic and inorganic methods of dealing with any spectral interference," Dwayne said, patting his bag lovingly.

Margot gazed at them in shock. "Are you guys serious?"

"Deadly," they all said at once.

Andrew made some sort of grunt and hauled Emily to the front doors. "If even one thing goes wrong, I am dragging you out of here, do you understand? We can be back in San Francisco in three hours."

Inside, the hotel resembled an old hunting lodge, heavy with the smell of burning wood and cedar and festooned with mounted animal heads and antlers. At the reception desk stood an old man whose body looked as though it was hinged together with a wire hanger. His eyes narrowed as he saw the odd parade of people pouring through the door.

"The Thomas party?"

"You can call it a party if you'd like," Andrew replied tersely, then a little louder added, "yes, I believe we have a room reserved for…" He couldn't bring himself to say it.

"Oh yes, a séance. Quite a large circle you seem to be having. And you've come prepared, I see." The old man's pained eyes fell to the stoners' bags. "Permit me to introduce myself. I am Hans MacClen, proprietor of the Noyo Inn."

Evidently they had not been the first to journey to this establishment for such purposes, but the tone of the proprietor's voice concerned Andrew, for it was as if he wished they would turn around and run but didn't want to be rude. MacClen cocked his head like an old owl, blinking at Andrew, but just as quickly he returned his attention to the crowd. Without another word, he opened a binder on the counter, took out a series of forms, and handed one to each of them.

"Liability wavers. If any damage occurs to you, we are not responsible. If any damage occurs to the room, you are. Please sign on the dotted line."

"Do you expect there to be damage?" asked Zoey.

"We have had a long and varied history with the ghosts of this establishment. You have decided to try to contact one of them, and this is not a matter to be taken lightly. The Lady in Red has been a resident of this hotel for as long as I have been proprietor here. I must warn you: she does not like to be provoked or antagonized. There have been incidents in the past when people have attempted such things, been cavalier and downright disrespectful—the results were not a sight I would like to witness again. I cannot warn you enough—ask as few questions as necessary and listen only. She is not a charitable being."

He collected the forms. Andrew was the last to hand his back.

"This way, please. Once we reach the room, I'd like to have a few words with you before you enter, for your safety."

Zoey and Emily shared a look. Even Margot, the stalwart cynic in the crowd, had gone slightly pale.

Floor-to-ceiling panels of dark gumwood lined the walls, accented by lantern-esque light fixtures every few yards. There seemed to be few guests in this section of the hotel. Emily tried to peer out the windows to see if she could spot other patrons in the parking lot below, but the windows were stained glass, and what little light the fog allowed in was further obscured by the deep blues and russets in the faceted panes.

After a few more twists and turns they traveled down a remote hallway until they reached an old-fashioned servant's staircase. They began their ascent, climbing three stories of tread-worn stairs that narrowed with each passing flight. The chilly air around them smelled of oiled wood and age, and the floor creaked under their feet from the burden of so much weight.

Once they reached the top landing, Hans paused as if to catch his breath, then turned to them. An amber pool of light raked across his face from the lone lantern in the hallway. He seemed so much older than only a few minutes before, and older still as he cast his eyes upon the far end of the hall to a single door secured by a padlock. Without a word, he took a ring of keys from his pocket.

"You really lock her in?" whispered Christian uneasily.

The old man shook his head. "You cannot keep The Lady in Red contained anywhere. She goes where she desires. This is to keep unsuspecting patrons out. Liability, you know."

Once they reached the door, he paused once more. "You have the room for the next few hours. I sincerely hope you do not require it for that long. If you need me, I will be down in my office."

He opened the door. A gust of cold, stale air blew over the threshold. Emily blinked against it as her eyes fought to adjust to the adjacent darkness. The large room was sparsely furnished, only a dusty sideboard and a few mismatched pieces of worn furniture lined its circumference, as though moved in haste. In the middle of the floor sat an imposing circular wooden table surrounded by haphazardly placed chairs. A lone window was shrouded with a tattered curtain, the gray bleakness of the day bleeding around its frayed edges. Shivering, she buried her hands in the pockets of Andrew's coat and was surprised to find Nick's key and ring at the bottom. She pressed them hard into her hand until she could feel them leave a mark.

"I will leave you to your work," the old man concluded, though he hesitated at the entrance to the room. His eyes settled on Emily, sending one last chill down her spine. "Please remember…there are things in this world we cannot understand, that science cannot explain away, and that the modern day cannot extinguish." Before anyone could respond, he gave a nod and departed. The door sealed shut behind him.

A communal shiver seemed to pass through all of them, and they each looked to one another as how to proceed. Simon muttered, "So, how do we sit? Boy, girl? Meth addict, non-meth addict?"

But Dwayne and Egan were already unpacking their bags, lugging equipment out onto the floor. Anxious, Emily walked over to the window and glanced down at the grounds below.

"You can open the shade," Dwayne told her.

"Won't it interfere with the vapors or something?"

"Believe you me, we want to see this one coming. The really nasty ones like the dark."

"Brilliant," Andrew muttered, staring at both Dwayne and her.

Buck and Dinesh busied themselves assembling their paraphernalia, most of which resembled video cameras on tripods and Klieg lights. Dwayne began to sprinkle a gray powder on the floor.

"What is that?" asked Margot, turning up her nose at the strange odor the dust was emitting.

"Blessed powdered Rowan berries. Wards off evil spirits."

"Isn't that counterproductive?"

"She won't want to stay long."

Next he opened a box and proceeded to hand out leis made of leaves and red berries to everyone present. They smelled the same as the gray powder.

"Is this really necessary?"

"Better to be safe than sorry. Hopefully, they'll be strong enough to keep her out of your body for a bit. You don't want this lady messing around in your mind."

Egan instructed them to take their seats when suddenly cries of *NO, NO, NO!* smashed through Emily's mind. Like a hallway of doors slamming open, the unknown voices wailed at her to flee, to escape. She stood paralyzed on the spot; the closest real door seemed a million miles away and Andrew just as far, though he was merely across the room.

"Emily?" he asked, his brow creased in concern.

She felt as if strings were being cut inside of her and things were falling away, like weights from balloons, and soon she would float away too. She made a fist with her hand to prove to herself that she was alive and real.

"Let us all form a circle," Egan intoned.

She watched Andrew move to the table, his eyes never leaving hers as they sat at the two remaining seats opposite each other. Looking behind him, she gasped. Andrew whirled around. A figure stood across the room — white as a corpse — but it was only her reflection in a mirror that lined the wall. She laid a hand on her chest to calm her heart.

"Emily?" Andrew pressed, offering her one last chance to bolt. She shook her head, took her seat, and closed her eyes upon Egan's command.

Instead of the talk of circles he had fumbled through the last time they had all sat together, Egan began to speak in a language she didn't understand. He chanted for a few moments and quieted, reminding them all to continue to breathe. Next to him, Zoey took a huge gulp of air as though afraid it would be her last.

To Emily's left sat Christian, who reached over and squeezed her hand. After what felt like an eternity, the equipment around them began to buzz and hum and click. An odor, sharp and acrid, filled the air. The closest thing she could liken it to was the smell of burning hair. Margot coughed and seemed to fight down the urge to be ill.

"I, um, we seek an audience with The Lady in Red," Egan mumbled, his control of the situation faltering with the increasingly strained whizzing and wheezing sounds of the apparatus behind him. "Is she here?"

Silence. Deafening silence. Then a sound. A dank, viscous, sucking sound, as if a seeping corpse was willing itself across the floor with one foot still trapped in the grave. Emily held onto Zoey's and Christian's hands even tighter.

The room's temperature plummeted to an icy chill as the low, dull sound came closer. Then a gurgled, choking laughter, a hissing exhalation, froze the blood in Emily's veins. There was nothing alive in this creature, nothing remotely human; it kept no vestige of a heart.

She could hear the sound of Andrew's chair scraping across the floor as if preparing to fight.

"Lady in Red, there is a woman present who would ask you a question. Will you make yourself known?" Egan asked in his most subservient voice.

The wet, evil crawling sound circled them, as if smelling each body. Finally, it came to rest behind Emily. Every hair on the back of her neck stood straight up.

"She's here," a voice rasped. "Again."

Emily's eyes flew open, as did everyone else's. Fear as she had never known overcame her. Reflecting in the mirror behind her, hovered a grotesque vision. Red tatters of a dress licked about her corpse like greedy flames. Putrid abscesses oozing with pus covered her flesh; they sucked in the rags and then blew them free like a foul cancerous wheeze and made the large crucifix that hung around her neck shudder. What was left of her moldering hair hung in sparse clumps around a skull housing a set of hard eyes that were seemingly plucked from a dead trophy animal, except these lifeless orbs were murky, milky white with cataracts. In spite of their hideous film they studied Emily and categorized her every facet in twisted fascination as though preparing her for butchering. Emily's blood ran cold as she remembered the ghost from the night in the Columbarium.

"I want this one."

"No!" Andrew shouted and lunged across the table. Buck and Dinesh grabbed hold of him and struggled to wrestle him back into his seat.

"You'd die for her, wouldn't you?" Her gruesome smile exposed broken, rotting teeth and a tongue the color of rancid meat. She stared in amusement at Andrew as he was fighting to break free. "Always the same."

"Get away from her!"

Finding strength from God knows where, Emily looked into the reflection in the mirror, into those cataclysmic eyes, and made her lips form the words. "Please tell us about the warning you gave your son."

The revulsion in her face was stunning; a festering of jealously and hatred twisted themselves into her words. "What son?"

"Nick — Nicholas Chamberlain."

She hissed and beat her breast repeatedly. "You came here thinking I'd help him? That I'd lift one finger to help that spiteful idiot and that whore? Never. I want them to rot in hell. I want them to suffer forever for what they did to me. I told him, I told her, and they both laughed at me. I gave everything to that boy, sacrificed everything for him — and that was the thanks I got. To be laughed at and insulted. No, I want them in agony. I want them to feel what it's like to be abandoned."

"Emily," Andrew warned, Buck and Dinesh's hands still on him, his breathing uneven.

"Sit back, boy. Don't you know I could kill her right now if I wanted? I could infect her mind and make her crash through that window. Would you like to see that? Her body slashed by those shards of glass and broken on the street? But no, it's so much worse what you'll face."

"What? What is it?" Emily choked out.

The Lady in Red hesitated, staring blackly at Emily, and then two skeletal hands descended on Emily's shoulders while her filthy rags draped down Emily's back and the large crucifix pressed into Emily's neck. Her bones rose to comb through Emily's hair, and she raised a lock to her leprous face and smiled. Emily's stomach roiled.

"You're so beautiful, so alive. Both of you. It's always this way at the end." She closed her eyes and inhaled like she was smelling a baby.

"He cometh forth like a flower, and is cut down: he fleeth also as a shadow, and continueth not." The Lady's putrid breath blew across Emily's cheek, and she closed her eyes, battling the nausea. "When he takes you in bed with him how does it feel? Beyond telling, beyond words, like a million souls are fornicating inside of you?"

Emily's head was throbbing, and the pain felt unbearable, like the ghoul was inside her mind.

"Doesn't it feel that way, boy? Doesn't it feel that way when you're screwing her?"

Andrew shook off Buck and Dinesh and flew from the chair; it crashed behind him.

She smiled, evidently pleased. "You'd never be able to resist her. She's a Thomas. You have to be with her. Can you remember a time you didn't want her? Even as a boy, you dreamed about her, wanted her. But it wasn't normal, was it? It was never normal. You were never normal. Tell me, when they locked you up in those cold, white, piss-scented rooms, didn't you think your mind had snapped? Didn't you wish you were dead?"

"Shut up!" All the color had drained from his face, his fists clenched tight.

"And now, can't you feel it prey on your mind? The need to be with her, to touch her, to feel the skin of this neck?" Her skeletal digits burned along Emily's throat. "Thomases. What a poison they are. That's what the white ghost told me, what I begged Nicholas to understand. Throughout all time, how they destroy Chamberlains' souls. Whores, harlots, adulteresses—they will love you like no other—and seduce you beyond want, beyond sanity."

"Stop it! Just stop it!"

"What do you think happens to that passion when they die, pretty boy? Do you think their need for each other just fades away? Do you think the obsession Nicholas had for his slut perished with their deaths? Of course not. No, it passed on to the next Chamberlain and Thomas cursed enough to find each other. It passed on to you."

"No," Emily whispered. "No."

"But do you know what the truly tragic part is?" she continued, wheezing out the words eagerly. "Each generation builds on the other, becoming more and more violent, and multiplying in each soul. It was awful for Nicholas at the end. I could see it. How are you even alive now? How can you even stand to be near her at this point? How hasn't it killed you?" Her filmy eyes narrowed on Andrew in a sick kind of wonder.

"What the hell are you talking about?" he railed at her.

"Don't you know why Chamberlains and Thomases love more violently than anything ever on this earth? It's because their curse ensures they die the most horrible of deaths—more gruesome than anything imaginable. It's only a matter of time for you now. You see how death has begun to follow you already, how you've barely avoided it. But that specter will find you. You can't run. Especially now, not after you've pledged yourself to her."

Andrew took a step around the table. It would be impossible to say whose face held more hatred at that moment.

"Listen, you fucking piece of death, nothing you say is going to stop me—"

"No Chamberlain who bears the curse has ever married a Thomas. They've all died before they could take the vow. You're no different, boy."

"What the hell do you even know? I'm a Hayes, not a Chamberlain."

She began to laugh, a rheumatic death rattle, her teeth sucking in the flayed flesh of her lips. "Your father's not a Hayes—you're not even a St. John. You're the bastard son of a Chamberlain. It was his birth name. A family name? Remember now, boy?"

A stark pallor fell over Andrew's face. "A family name," he repeated, and stumbled a foot backward as though he had been punched in the gut. Lainey. Lainey, that was the nickname Claudia had called Neil. Lainey…a nickname for Chamberlain.

"Andrew Chamberlain. You suffer a part of that tortured bloodline, just like Nicholas did. It's there in your palm. Even that buffoon could see it." She glared at Dwayne, who cowered under at her stare. "And she, this pitiful thing, holds the curse as well. And it's all happening again."

"What's happening?"

The bones of the phantom's hands bit into Emily's flesh and held her to the chair like she was trying to strangle her, but instead she spoke in a whisper as if she was a small child, though her eyes never left Andrew for one second.

"That man you love who takes your body, he'll murder you. He will kill you. He'll have no choice. The same need that drives him to take you will drive him to destroy you. And if he survives, the image of you dead, bloody, and broken will kill him. He won't be able to live. He'll take his own life. By knife, by gun, or by the rope. Or much, much worse. Nicholas was lucky that he drove them both off that cliff. But they said she still fought to reach him at the end as she drowned in her own blood."

Emily buried her head in her shoulder, to sob, to retch; the ghost yanked it back up by her hair with a hiss.

"Don't you dare show pity for her. Don't you dare! Look at him." She pulled her hair harder, forcing her to witness Andrew's stricken expression. "Look at your killer. I should do it myself if I had any pity. But you're a Thomas, and I prefer to watch you suffer."

Then her mouth, that fetid carcass, pressed itself to Emily's face and kissed her. "You'll make such a wonderfully brokenhearted ghost, Emily, never to see him again. Ever. And you know it's true. Just like Nora. You've dreamt it. You've seen it."

Her words crashed against the walls of Emily's mind, and her stomach contorted with acid. The thousands of souls within her screamed as one.

Without warning, the equipment across the room exploded in a spray of flames. With a shriek, The Lady in Red released her.

At that exact moment, Buck yanked a large silver shotgun from below the table and roared, "Emily! Move!"

She threw herself to the side. Buck aimed and fired.

A blast of light burst from the gun missing Emily by inches. It smashed directly into The Lady in Red's chest, hurling her backward. Howls of rage wailed from her grotesque figure. Emily watched in horror as the apparition crumbled, remnants of her bloody rags floating in the air, air that reeked of seared flesh. Only her crucifix remained for a moment, then disintegrated along with the rags into a black pile of ash.

"Blessed be," muttered Buck as he lowered the gun, shaking.

Andrew raced toward Emily, but she threw one hand up to ward him off. She clenched the other across her mouth to fight back the bile erupting into her throat.

Staggering to her feet, she flew from the room. From behind her she heard Margot chastise Andrew to stay, along with the clatter of chairs and incessant shouting. Sweat poured from her forehead, and her legs barely held her. She ran down the steps and launched herself out the first door she could find, not stopping until she fell behind a giant redwood, and threw up until there was nothing left inside of her.

Hunched over her knees, the abomination's words knifed into her heart. Andrew was a Chamberlain and she was a Thomas. And whatever existed between them was deadly. He would kill her with his own hands.

He would kill her.

She wanted to believe it was a lie; she screamed at herself to believe it was a lie. Andrew would never hurt her. Never. But she knew…in the dark recesses of her heart she had felt that violence within him, and she had seen it in her dreams. And now everything about their past, these last few weeks and the perilous last few days, bore testament to it. They were doomed, cursed.

What could she do? She felt her own sanity ebbing away as visions of cliffs and screaming tortured her. She heard screams that were her own screams, and saw cliffs where Andrew stood, murderous and intent. Then he turned and became Nick, driving recklessly along the coast, staring wildly at her.

Pressing her head against the tree, she closed her eyes and prayed. She whispered to God, begging, pleading. But there was no answer, only the wind and the solitary, numbing drizzle. She began to shake uncontrollably as though she had stepped into an ice cold stream. She opened her eyes and backhanded her tears, then gasped. There stood The Lady in White, far away near the edge of the forest. She hovered above the sodden ground with a face so full sorrow that her very aura seemed restrained as in bereavement.

"Is…is it true?" Emily struggled to say.

"Yes, it is. I wish she could have told you otherwise."

"No. No, it can't be. Please, tell me it can't be, please!"

"You know it is true, Emily. You do. You have always known. He has always been dangerous to you. It is what drew you to him in the beginning. You have chosen not to see it."

"Then there has to be something we can do? A way to escape this? Break this…end this…?"

"No one has ever broken the curse. They have tried, but in the end they have all died, each and every one."

"And Nick and Nora?"

"Yes, they as well. Nora was haunted by the ghosts of another Chamberlain and Thomas fighting to be reunited. That is how she found Nick. He helped her, of course, then he fell in love with her as it has always been throughout time. They had the ashes of those two lost souls in their automobile as they were headed to be married. They wanted to cast them into the sea at the place where the two of them had died. Then Nick…he drove them off the cliff."

"No! I won't believe this. He loved her. He loves her. She knows that. He would never hurt her. He couldn't."

"It cannot be stopped. It has never been stopped. No cursed Chamberlain has ever married a Thomas. Throughout countless lifetimes each one has tried. Once they have pledged themselves, it is only a matter of time until they kill. The murders are horrible, gruesome. And the curse rends the lovers apart in the afterlife. There is no peace."

"There must be something I can do to stop it? I'll do anything. Please."

"Are you strong, Emily Thomas?"

Her past words echoed bitterly back at Emily. "Are you strong, Emily Thomas? Can you live without your heart?"

"Please, please… I'm begging you. Tell me…tell me what I can do." Emily ran toward her, trying to reach out and hold her, but her hands only pawed through icy vapor.

The Lady in White paused and looked out over the redwoods; droplets of water hung on her flowing hair like tears. "Do you love him?"

Emily nodded back, unable to speak.

"Then you must leave him."

No. Anything but that.

"I can't…I can't leave him. I can't. And…and he wouldn't let me go."

"He would if you were dead."

Emily stood there stunned. "No. I won't. I won't."

"You do not have to. He only needs to believe you have."

Emily fell back against the tree. "I couldn't do that to him."

"Pain does not last forever. It fades like all things, until it becomes part of who we are. He will mourn, yes, but he will continue on with his life. He will find a way. He will find things to heal his heart…His family, his friends—"

"His music."

Could she do this? Could she find the strength within her to do this to Andrew? What choice did she have? She couldn't change fate. She couldn't stop believing in ghosts and the horrors of the night—they were real and inescapable.

"Help me," Emily begged her.

She pointed her hand at Emily's coat. "You have the keys."

Her previous words mocked her. The keys to the minivan lay heavy in Andrew's pocket. It was then that a plan, crude and elementary, but a plan nonetheless, began to form in Emily's mind. Before she moved a step, though, she had to know. "Tell me. If I do this, if I leave him, if I never… see him again…can Nick and Nora, can they at least be together?"

The Lady in White didn't answer; she merely continued to look out toward the forest, silent. Her eyes swept back to hers, and they were full of the wistfulness of time. Did she even remember what it was like to yearn, to cry, to say goodbye? Or did she choose to forget? Was it easier?

"Yes."

A calmness, more owing to shock than relief, fell over her. She could do this for Nick and Nora, this one last thing. They would have their happily ever after. As for her, there would be pain, unbearable pain, but what other choice did she have? She was beyond thinking herself sane. *Fate.* Fate was written on her palm, in her life line. Everything was marching steadily to only one conclusion. This supernatural nightmare had only one end unless she changed it.

She needed to run. To run as fast as possible. Once on the road she could think of the next step. Like a ghost with bones, she raced to the minivan. The key slid into the ignition without a sound. The seats were cold, and the smell of coffee lingered. The fog made the descent difficult, but it quickly closed in behind her, obscuring the van from view. She counted her breaths. The only feeling left within her was that of her freezing lips.

"Andrew, just let her puke in peace," said Margot, seizing his arm as he tried to charge the door again. Her face found his, and what she saw there made her drop her hand. "She'll come back when she's ready. Holy Mary, Mother of God, that was awful."

"Awful?" he spat in disbelief. Awful didn't even come close. To stand there and watch that thing, that abomination, spew that garbage and tell her that the man who was supposed to love her until her last breath was going to be responsible for taking it? Fucking no! No! He would not accept this. He recommenced his fevered pacing, raking his hand through his hair, only to glare at the door once more.

Christian stood with his arms around Zoey. Even Simon had slung his arm protectively over Margot's shoulder. Only the stoners carried on as though nothing had happened, putting away their gear while Buck carefully swept up the ashes. *Why, why, why had he let her come here in the first place,* Andrew berated himself. He knew it was wrong. Bloody fucking hell!

He glanced at his watch. She had been gone for almost fifteen minutes. He couldn't take any more; he had to see her. God only knew what she was thinking at this point — Emily, who took everything so seriously. "That's it! I have to talk to her."

"No," said Margot. "Zoey and I will do it. She's probably still a little bit…rattled. It was a lot of information to take in. Just calm the hell down, okay?"

"What information? So what if I'm a Chamberlain? I don't care. For Christ's sake, Neil's a Chamberlain, you don't see him driving off any cliffs. You mean to tell me I'm the one Chamberlain cursed out of thousands? There are no such things as curses. Coincidences, yes — but not curses."

"We'll be back in a minute. Calm, please."

He watched them leave and resumed his pacing, but the more he stalked the room, the more the images assaulted him. His hands around her neck. Her screams. His uncontrollable rage.

"No!" he yelled, frightening the hell out of Egan, who dropped a camera onto the floor.

"Listen, man," said Simon, appearing more troubled by the second. "Let's just get the hell out of here. Find a bar and drink this off."

Andrew scrubbed his face, trying to rid himself of the sense of dread growing within him. Where was she? He had to see her, reason with her, make her understand.

"So do you really think you got her?" Christian asked, staring at the last of the ashes Buck had swept up from the floor.

"There's no way to be sure, man," Dwayne replied. "Neutralizing her psychic makeup is one thing, but to get rid of her for good…? You can suicide with her along for the ride, but if she's strong enough she might get loose, although, face it, she's in a pretty gnarly state as is. You can always try to dry rub her with another ghost's ashes, but good luck getting her to hold still for that."

Andrew ripped the rowan berries off his neck in disgust. Another five minutes passed. By now the stoners had packed up their gear and were about to head out when Margot and Zoey reappeared in the door way. "She's not in any of the ladies' rooms on this floor," Margot told him.

"What?"

"I think she might have gone down to the lobby for more privacy," Margot added quickly. "We're going to look."

He pushed them roughly aside. Together they headed down the stairs, but he outran Zoey and Margot as he rounded the corner of the lobby and sprinted to the nearest restroom.

"Emily?" he hollered, his voice reverberating off the tiles. It was empty, save for a startled cleaning lady huddled near the sink. "Are there any other bathrooms in the hotel?" he demanded.

She crept to the door and pointed a finger at a long corridor. He dashed out the door like a shot and slammed into the girls. Together they searched the next restroom, but it was empty.

"Maybe she didn't make it to a bathroom. She was almost sick before she left the séance. I bet she ran outside, and she's probably under some tree now, getting herself together," Margot said hopefully as they rushed back to the lobby.

The fog was as thick as mud as they raced out of the side doors and into a small park. They broke up, their shouts ricocheted off the trees, but there was no answer; only the cold mist of drizzle hung about them. Andrew kept running, his heart pounding in his chest. He scoured the surrounding acres, from the trees to the rear of the hotel, but could see nothing.

"Emily!" he cried, still hoping he would spot her slouched at the base of some tree. Yet as every second passed, his spirits became more and more fractious. Finally he grabbed the girls, and they ran back into the hotel. Simon and the stoners stood in the lobby, staring at them as they entered like they were insane.

"Where the hell'd you get to?" Simon asked.

"Emily's missing. We can't find her anywhere," Andrew replied bluntly, feverishly scanning the lobby.

Just then Christian dashed in the front doors, his face severe. "Andrew, the minivan. It's gone."

"What? Where'd it go?" Simon cried.

Reality smashed into Andrew. The truth he'd been fighting so hard knocked him blind. Emily believed what that thing had said. She believed he was going to kill her. She was running.

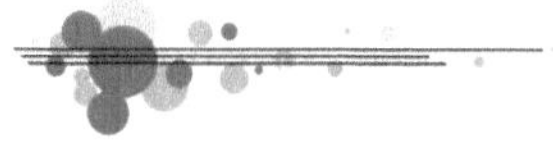

Forward, Emily. You have to leave, run. Now.

As Emily drove the minivan, she estimated how long she could risk at each stop. The hotel was first. She madly combed every inch she could reach, raking clothes, jewelry, and toiletries into her bag. The smell of him was everywhere and overpowering; his very energy bounced off the walls, even in the tousled sheets. Her hand reached out to smooth his crumpled pillow. "Andrew. I'm sorry. So, so, sorry."

No. She needed to run. If she didn't escape soon, she never would. *Forward, Emily*, she screamed at herself. *Forward. You have to leave—run. Don't cry. Don't cry now.*

Two minutes, she had two minutes left. Andrew would know she was gone by now. She could picture him storming out of the inn, tearing across the grounds, and screaming her name. Would he realize the van was gone? Would he know where she was headed?

Shutting the thoughts from her mind, she threw her bag in the back of the van but not before transferring one packet to her satchel. Nora. Her hand patted the cool plastic. *I won't fail you. I promise.*

The fog had socked in the highway, making the sea a silver knife to her right. She reasoned that they would take the stoners' van and go to the hotel first to find her. That left her precious little time. Her hands clenched the wheel as she pushed the van as fast as she dared. Her breathing caught in her chest as she spotted the turn off. It wouldn't be long now. Yet as she stomped on the gas, images of Andrew began to speak to her, fighting to pull her back.

He stood on stage, singing—his eyes closed, his head bent. *"This next song is about a girl. It's always about a girl, isn't it?"* Her hands choked the wheel, and she punched the gas pedal harder. The image changed to him at the foot of their stairway, her shoe held in his hand. *"I believe this is yours."* In anguish, she fumbled on the radio and turned up the volume as loud as it could go. The picture glided to that of him standing in the attic with his hand outstretched to her, wearing an old fashioned dinner jacket, his face beaming. *"Dance with me."*

Her shoulders shook, and she lifted her foot off the accelerator. "I can't do this, I can't do this…" she cried out to the inside of the empty van. And then in one last attempt to reach her, Andrew stood helpless and lost on their front porch, the rain pelting his face. Silent.

She slammed back into the seat at the pain and stomped on the brakes, launching her body into the steering wheel. Shaking, she laid her head on her hands.

No! Not one person had survived this curse, not through lifetimes and lifetimes. And she knew it, she had always known it. The first time he touched her, she knew it. The first time he laid her down on a bed, she knew it. Time was running out. Time had always been running out. That's what they had all meant—Nick, Nora, and all those voices of the dead.

He would hurt, but he would live. He had so much in his life: his music, his family, his band mates. He would survive. Time would pass. The pain would change to a faint, dull ache then slip into wistfulness. He was so strong; she knew he could survive this. He had to survive this. But what about her?

Her foot found the gas pedal, and she drove on. Forward. Away. Cut out any feeling. Survive. Run. She would disappear. She could not fake her own death. She could not do that to her parents—or to Andrew. She would simply disappear.

Belden was easier to find the second time. At a convenience store she bought a local map, not wanting to take the one back at the cottage. The fewer clues she left, the safer she'd be. The clerk behind the counter looked at her oddly, and she tried to smile, but it was like moving her lips through cement. She glanced at her watch; she would have fifteen minutes, tops. An ATM sat in the corner. She drained everything she could from her account.

"Is there an Amtrak station nearby, and do you have a schedule?"

The man produced a pamphlet and handed it to her. The nearest train station was Fort Bragg. She could take the inland roads and then cross over, avoiding the coast. She would call her parents, tell them she was safe and what little else she could. She would find a small town, somewhere, anywhere. She could work, wait tables; she'd clean floors if necessary. Or maybe she could go to Canada, another country. Away. Far, far away.

Clutching the train schedule in her hand, she asked her last question.

"Can I walk to Belden Cemetery from here?"

"Hmmm. You're not one of those crazies are you? We've had enough of that kind around here—we don't want any more trouble."

She thought of Dwayne and his friends; it felt like a lifetime ago. "No, I'm writing a—an article. I need to do some research."

He eyed her strangely and pointed out on the map how to proceed. She could still feel his gaze fixed on her as she rushed out the door.

The sky had darkened with approaching rain clouds, and the wind whipped the trees around her as she climbed up the nearby hills. The branches struck at her face as she struggled over the uneven earth. Drops began to fall, the ground now slick below her feet. A tear hit her cheek—she shouldered it away—then another and another. Freezing and relentless rain began to spatter out of the slate gray sky. It stung her face, and seconds later the sky erupted, sending torrents of rain and sleet crashing to the earth and soaking her jeans to her skin. She ran, clutching her satchel to her chest.

Nora, I'll do this. I will do this one thing. I promise you.

The map melted in her hands, and she squinted to try to see the print. "You're lost, you're going to die," she yelled to herself as she staggered around for what seemed like hours. Then just when she thought all was lost, an orchard came into view, with rows of trees gone wild. She saw a wooden gate in a broken fence.

Belden Farm.

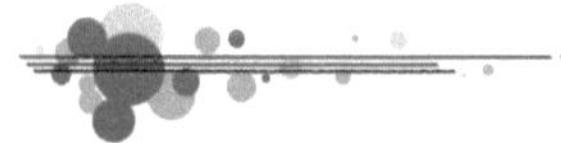

Andrew's fist smashed against the side of the door. Simon's eyes flashed at Andrew from the driver's seat, the road racing past. They had lived this over and over: driving like demons, desperate to find her. Fate. It was playing itself out no matter what they did.

"Easy, Paulie, we'll be needing to return this thing to the inn. It was bad enough when Buck told that old wanker we went medieval on his ghost."

Andrew didn't respond, and Simon drove on.

A second later, Andrew's cell phone vibrated in his pocket. "Yes."

"Andrew, she's not here," said Margot, out of breath. "All her things are gone. The guys are in town trying to find her there. But she didn't even leave a note. Please tell me you've heard something."

"No."

"Wait—hold on, Zoey is on the line with Christian. What? Oh, shit—she hasn't shown up at the inn, either. What are we going to do?"

"Stay there," he ordered her. "Call me if you find out anything. Tell Christian to do the same. Wait—is everything gone? Are Nora's ashes gone as well?"

The line hung dead. "There's nothing here. Andrew, you don't think—?"

"Just stay there! We'll call you if we—when we find her."

He ended the call, his body rocking with fury. What was happening to him? His bones wanted to rip through his skin like knives. The thought of her running from him unleashed an unspeakable wrath—a need to kill. Then from the depths of his hatred came The Lady in Red's voice, rasping in a joyous whisper. "It's starting."

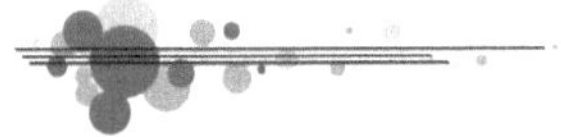

Wrenching the farm gate open, Emily ran. Belden Farm—she had made it. Her satchel crashed into her leg, making her trip, her knees and hands scraping against the rocky ground. The rain blurred her sight, the merciless torrents now bulleting down in sheets. Her clothes were drenched, and her hair stuck to her face. She gulped mouthfuls of air as she spun this way and that.

Through the blinding rain she saw it. Set not far off was the cemetery. Old gravestones jutted from the ground like macabre decorations, bowing in supplication around a central mausoleum. The name "Belden" was chiseled into the cold dead stone. Beyond that stood a farmhouse that had fallen into ruin.

She circled the cemetery, desperate to find a clue. Shoving her hair from her eyes, she attempted to find a wall, or anything that would show her where Nick was buried. Pulling Andrew's coat around her body, she searched and searched for what felt like hours. Nothing, she could find nothing. Nearly hopeless, she thought of clawing at the soil to unearth a hidden grave with her bare hands. *Nick, where are you?*

Yet how much longer could she risk being here? She fell down on her knees in exhaustion and muttered aloud the lines of the poem, the rain lashing in her mouth. "I dwell in a lonely house I know, I dwell in a lonely house I know…in a lonely house."

The house—she had to search inside the house, not look for a grave! Trudging through the downpour, she staggered blindly to the imposing outline of the old farmhouse. She stopped dead. Shouting, she heard shouting. Pure fear, like a white hot strangulation, gripped her. She couldn't move. How, how could he have found her so soon? No! She had to hide. Mired in the grip of viscous mud she struggled to free her feet, looking around wildly in panic, desperate for a place to run. The barn.

Dashing to the faded red door, she shoved it open with her shoulder; it moved silently despite its battered appearance. Inside, the sweet scent of hay hit her. Its warmth enveloped her.

Her breath rose up in wisps in the dim light as she wrenched the door back into place. In the shadowy light she saw the rafters of the barn rise up like a cathedral, the missing slates in the roof sending beams of gray down to the hay-strewn floor. The barn was empty; there was nowhere she could conceal herself where he couldn't find her.

Swallowing down her fear, her gaze whipped up high to the rafters, and there she spotted it—a loft with a window. If she could reach it, she could conceal herself under the hay and then escape out the back. But she had no time—the cries were coming closer by the second.

"Emily!" She knew that sound. Her knees wavered, and she struggled to stand.

"Emily!" Andrew screamed in fury now. The sound unleashed her visions: him hunting her, the earth giving way on the cliffs, his hands gripping her throat.

Trapped in the back corner, she panicked. She had to run. Just then her foot hit against a ring on the barn floor. In one last desperate attempt, her hands swept away the hay and she saw the outlines of a door. She yanked on the ring and the door creaked open. Below was a hole no bigger than a coffin—a storage bin at one time. She didn't have time to think. The shouting had almost reached the barn door.

Dragging her satchel, she shimmied down into the space and lowered the door shut with a resounding click, sealing herself in. The wood was inches away from her face, and the scent of mold and decay permeated the earth around her. Her eyes widened, fighting to adjust to the pitch blackness. The suffocating confines forced her to lie flat on her back, cramped, with her hands clutched over her heart.

Thundering footfalls erupted from above. She could hear the mad dashing of two sets of feet running across the floor. Her throat choked, and her eyes burned from the dirt dislodged around her. She fought back the urge to cough, slamming her hands over her face.

"She's not here," panted Simon, out of breath.

"No! She's here, I know she is. Her footprints—we saw her footprints!" cried Andrew, his own footsteps circling the room. Emily's hands shriveled into fists, and her eyes clenched tight.

"Those could have been anyone's footprints, Andrew. This is where those blokes are going to have their party tomorrow night, yeah? Lots of people come up here."

"No, they're hers. I know—"

"Margot said her stuff wasn't at the cottage. Dwayne and the guys didn't spot her in Mendocino. Maybe she's on her way back to San Francisco.

Maybe this was all too much for her to take? I'll call your mum and send her over to the house to wait for her —"

"No! She's running. She's running from *me*. Don't you see that? She thinks it's all true!"

Andrew's pacing pounded the boards.

"Then why the hell would she come here if she's running? We know she's in the minivan. Let's have the cops track her down. Claim it's a stolen vehicle."

Emily breathed a fraction, thankful that they had not spotted the minivan where she'd hidden it off the road.

"You don't understand!" Andrew shouted back. "She'd come here — to find Nick. She has the key and Nora's ashes. She has everything she needs to reunite them. She doesn't give up on things…Oh bloody hell, I…I could kill her for this!"

"Might want to keep that to yourself," Simon muttered, before he reasoned more loudly, "Hans said we could have his car for a few hours — which personally I think is a miracle after the way you were threatening him with dismemberment — but regardless, let's phone the police, get an APB out on her or whatever they call it, get ourselves another rental, and then sit down and make a plan."

"Listen to me! We have to find her! She's going to disappear, I know it. I can feel it. And Christ, she's alone, and she's probably terrified to death. You know how she is…she believes everything, every bloody thing. If we don't find her now —"

"Calm the hell down."

"You were there; you heard her. You saw Emily's face. Did you see the horror in her eyes? She believed it. Oh God. Fuck. What if it is true…?"

The pacing ceased. Heavy, labored breaths were the only sound. "That ghost knew everything about me. Everything. How the hell could she have known that? I just…I don't trust myself anymore. I'm so fucking angry. I…I can't control it. Control myself…this hatred…There's something wrong with me. That monster was right — there's always been something wrong with me."

"Andrew. You don't believe that shit, do you? I mean really believe it?" Simon asked, his voice suddenly serious. "You're not a killer, man. You're just not. But you need to stay away from Emily. Don't look at me like that, you need to get out. This shit is wrong, don't you see it? The girl's been nothing but a nightmare of trouble since you met her. Get yourself out of here while you still can."

Andrew laughed, bitterness lacing his voice. "Get out while I still can, Simon? I don't know if you've been paying attention or not, but I don't think there's any going back. And you know I can't live without Emily. I've spent my life trying to find her. She's my muse."

"I know."

"Don't you fucking care?"

"I care about you. The rest can go to hell."

Andrew made no response. Emily could picture how he looked standing there, his skin flushed, his lips cold and blue from the freezing rain. Her heart beat so loudly, hammering against her ribs and through to her spine, that she swore he must be able to hear it. Sweat beaded on her face. The air was getting thinner and thinner in the blackness.

"We'll go back to town and call the girls," Simon said, his voice muted but no less uncompromising. "She's not here. We better move. Come on, Paulie, you have to go."

Reluctantly, the weighted footsteps moved away from where Emily lay. They moved to the door, moved to the gravel, moved to the sloping hillside. Moved—away. Silence claimed the space once again, and she listened to the last faraway sounds fade to nothingness. She pressed her hand to the wood above her. Tears streaked silently down her cheeks, burning the sides of her face before falling into her hair.

Was this how the dead felt, left in the earth to hear but never speak? To reach but never touch? Never again would she feel the warmth of his arms, laugh at his smiles, or lose herself to him. In her mind, she could see the door shutting, the end. His hand letting go of her lock of hair, stepping away, disappearing back into the world.

Alone and trembling, she shoved her hands down into her pockets like a small child. Nick's ring brushed her knuckle, and she shoved it on her finger, rubbing it over and over again in an attempt to keep herself from breaking. Then something else in the pocket fell between her fingers. She fumbled for it only to realize what it was: a guitar pick.

She felt the blunt edges of it, and the press of sorrow robbed her of any strength. She lay there silently and closed her eyes, remembering the sound of his fading footsteps, the guitar pick nestled in her palm. She waited a long, long time. Deep in that blackness she counted her breaths, waiting until she was sure of the silence. Her body stilled…she hummed weakly, her breaths slowed.

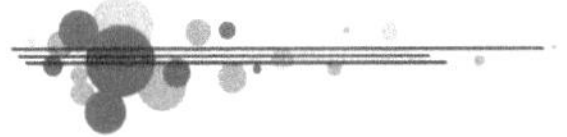

Emily woke with a start, her hands striking against wood, and she cried out in pain. Fear overwhelmed her. Where was she? Then her memories forced her awake and crushed down on her chest like a vice, making breathing impossible. She had fallen asleep for how long? Oh God, how long had she slept?

Desperate to be out of the hole, she pushed at the trap door above her face. It didn't move. She bashed again. The latch rattled, but the door wouldn't budge. She shoved again; the latch held firm. She was locked in.

Oh no. No. This couldn't be happening. Struggling with all her might, she slammed her hands against the wood, her fingers clawed and pried at the sides, and splinters sliced under her nails. She cried out, the cuts throbbing.

"No!" she screamed. "No!" The air was so thick that when she gulped down a mouthful, her lungs felt like shriveled balloons, unable to expand. She shoved until sweat soaked her body.

"Help!" she screamed again, pounding the door with both hands. "Please! Please!" The darkness loomed like a hand over her mouth. In her delirium, she thought she heard the sound of stones being dragged across the floor and a slow wheezing chuckle. Raw panic descended on her.

"Help!" She screamed until her throat was raw.

Time passed. For how long, she didn't know. There was no air left; speckles flashed in the darkness and tears trickled down the side of her face. With one last gasp, she wrenched her knee up and smashed it as hard as she could against the door; it shifted. The pain was excruciating but her heart raced like mad. A waft of fresh air poured into the gap. Gasping, she kicked furiously. Another inch.

"Damn it!" she cried, and jerked her knee into the wood and wailed. The door burst open.

Her body catapulted upward like an animated corpse, and she screamed, her hands pawing at the surrounding earth. She heaved herself out of the dank hole, gulping in mouthfuls of sweet air.

Thank you, God. Thank you, she gasped as she laid her head on her arm and drank in lungful after lungful of air.

Panting like mad, she fought to gain her bearings. With some effort she managed to wrestle her satchel from the ditch, eager to put herself as far from it as possible. The barn stood ominously around her. Night had descended, and the rain continued to beat on the roof. Still, she was grateful for the darkness, as she could pass unnoticed so much more easily. She sat on her knees, rubbing her bloodied fingers against her jeans, and went over her plan. She would abandon the minivan. She couldn't risk the police finding it. So she'd get a cab or hitchhike to Fort Bragg where she could catch a bus or a train. But she needed to find Nick first; she couldn't leave here without him.

Somewhere an owl cooed, and she could hear the scuttling of animals along the rafters. Stumbling to her feet, she made her way to the barn door that swung slightly ajar in the wind. She needed to find a crumbling wall inside the house — that's what the poem had said. Would there be a grave near the crumbling wall?

She had reached the threshold when she heard the sound of a single shuffle, like gravel on dirt. She was not alone. All her senses sprang to life, and she stepped away from the open door, back into the darkness. Someone or something was standing outside — unmoving, waiting. Every hair on her head tingled in complete attention, but her feet felt like lead. Her imagination made pictures in the dark of what stood there: another ghost, an animal, a killer. She stopped dead. Whatever it was had gasped.

She knew that breath.

"You…cannot…believe…her."

Andrew stood there, his breathing ragged as though he had run the entire length of the hillside. Had he heard her cries, or had he waited in the downpour knowing she would return?

"But Christ, you do believe her." It was a statement, not a question, and the menace in his voice was undeniable.

Emily took another step back. She had to run. She dropped her satchel and bolted, racing to the back of the barn. In the dark, her hands flung out in search of a door, a loose board, anything.

"No!" he commanded.

Nightmares of him bore down on her, of the inhuman grip of his hands wrapping around her throat. She stumbled backward.

"Damn it! Stop! So help me, Emily! Stop."

The loft. The window at the back of the loft — if she could reach it, she could jump. With a lunge, she grappled up the ladder and hurled herself into the hay. Struggling through it, she lurched toward the opposite wall. Behind her she heard his feet pounding across the floor and thundering up the ladder. She was inches from the window when he bounded across the planks. She threw her back to the glass.

Andrew's eyes were black, and bruises of crimson stained his cheeks. His pulse hammered in his throat, and his dripping sweater was drenched, plastered to his body.

"I am not letting you go!" he screamed, the cords of the muscles on his neck rigid in anger.

She scrambled away from him, throwing herself into the corner. "Don't hurt me, please, don't hurt me."

If she ever thought he could kill her, it was now. Rage exploded around him, and every muscle was poised to strike. He glared at her, thunderstruck.

"You heard her. You know it's true," Emily implored, playing for time while she tried to figure out a way to escape. "She knows everything. About you and about me. About how I've tortured you your whole life. I can't be near you. It's the only way. You have to let me go."

"I don't care about some bloody curse!"

"Don't you see? It's already started. The van, the motorcycle, Vandin, everything. Then it'll be you—you killing me. I've seen it. We can't stop this. It's always been like this, for all of them."

He still stared at her as though she had lost her mind. "We die, is that it? I murder you with my own hands? Kill you because some curse says I have to?"

"Yes! That's why our palms say what they do. We're part of this curse. For whatever reason, you and I—Nick and Nora, we're the ones. No Chamberlain has ever lived to marry a Thomas   they kill each other before they can—and then…and then they can't even be together in the next life. But I can't…I won't let it happen to us this time. The Lady in White told me that if I left…if I never saw you again—you could be safe, you could live. If you love me, if you ever did, you have to let me go because I can't do this. I can't stand back and watch you die."

Andrew took a step toward her. Her shoulders pressed flat against the wall. She swallowed her fear; the window was only a foot way. She still had one last chance to reach it.

"No Chamberlain has ever lived to marry a Thomas," he said, his voice eerily quiet and at the same time edged with anger as though he had already lost his mind.

She closed her eyes and nodded, praying he would understand, that the last vestige of sanity in him would allow her to escape. But before she could even hope, she felt his body loom over her. Vehemence poured off of him in waves.

"But I can."

His words hung in the air between them. She had no idea what he meant, and her heart crashed through her ribs waiting for what was to come next.

"But I can," he repeated with a strange tilt to his face, a challenging look, as if his own words had taken him unawares. He reached out and seized her shoulders, pulling her to him. His eyes sought hers, fierce and alive.

"If a Chamberlain marries a Thomas, that must change fate. It must. The curse was made to keep them apart, to keep them from marrying. Lifetimes and lifetimes of them came so close. Nick and Nora on the way to their wedding; the couple before them, they wanted to, I know they did. I can feel all of them, but they never made it."

"I…I don't understand."

"Vows declared before each other. It doesn't need to be anything more. Marriages—they were nothing but that for ages and ages. People were sworn to each other, pledged, with nothing apart from an oath and a promise."

He stared at her hand and started tugging off her ring.

"I refuse to lose you. Please, just please, don't run. Just listen. I'm not religious, Emily, I never have been. But if there is a God I'm asking, no, I'm praying, that he's listening right now."

Andrew pulled them both down to the hay and positioned her until they were kneeling face to face. His whole body seemed to shake and stopped only when his grip on her hands tightened. His eyes found hers.

"I, Andrew Hayes Chamberlain—"

"No, Andrew, it won't work, it can't."

He did not release his hold, the pulse in his palm echoed in her own. Inside of her, lifetimes of souls railed at her, their hundreds of hearts began beating as one, wanting, waiting.

"Take thee, Emily Thomas, to be my wedded wife." He kissed her now, and it was not tender; it drove her to the earth, to this place, and to this time. Her fingers shook inside his. "To have and to hold from this day forward."

His lips trembled an inch from hers. Tears slid down along her face. Or were they his? "For better, for worse, for richer, for poorer. In sickness and in health. To love and to cherish."

His mouth kissed her temple and swept down until it reached the flesh below her jaw, and he whispered, "Forsaking all others."

"No, we can't. We can't."

But as she protested, she swayed to him. His lips moved to her shoulder, and he swore, "Till death do us part."

He gazed down on her, in this place, this solitary barn, their church, and placed Nora's ring on her finger.

"Repeat it to me, Emily. You have to—I won't let you leave. We'll stay here forever until you do." He pressed Nick's ring into her palm, kneeling with her, waiting. "Please, sweet girl. Say it."

"No, it's a curse, don't you see?"

"I, Emily Thomas, take thee, Andrew Hayes Chamberlain," he said, his face to hers.

"I...I, Emily Thomas, take thee, Andrew Hayes Chamberlain—oh it won't matter."

"Yes." He kissed her deeply, and tightened his hold on her hands.

"To be my wedded husband."

"To be my wedded husband." She felt his lips move against hers.

"To have and to hold."

"To have and to hold," she repeated.

"From this day forward."

"From this day forward. For better, for worse, for richer, for poorer," she said, unguided. "In sickness and in health. To love and to cherish. Forsaking all others."

His eyes burned into hers, rebellious; all his souls radiated out through him screaming, rejoicing, victorious at what they were only a breath away from.

"Till death do us part." She slid the ring on his finger.

Lifetimes of pain and longing, of searching, of terror and fear and doubt, all were driven from him in that moment. And none of it mattered. Not death, not curses; nothing mattered as long as she was with him. For she understood that she would rather live a second with him and perish, than live a lifetime apart.

He took her and kissed her, and the wind exhaled through the rafters like a blessing.

"You're my wife," Andrew whispered.

"Yes." She gazed into his radiant face.

"And you belong to me." He kissed the side of her mouth. "To love and to cherish."

She swayed, and his arms lowered to encircle her waist. "To love and to cherish."

His nose dusted up her throat and she sighed. "To love and to cherish," he repeated. "I married you." His lips against hers, their breath entwined as he spoke. "I don't care if there are a thousand souls inside you, Emily Thomas. I only want this one."

It seemed right that she could only nod as his hands began to undress her. She was still freezing, her teeth chattering. Concerned, he quickly cast aside her drenched clothes then removed his own. Wasting no time, he turned and reached for her, drawing her closer. The heat of his body enveloped her, and his chest rose and fell quickly with each breath as he lowered her until she was surrounded by the long, lean muscles of his body and the sharp sweetness of the hay beneath her back.

"I love you…" she told him. "You…"

He pressed his hips against hers. He did this slowly, worshipfully, relishing the shuddered moans she made until he paused and found her eyes. She was aware of the stillness around them, the creak of the timbers and the rustle of the trees bending in the night wind. He bowed his head and thrust himself into her. She gasped.

"I, Andrew Hayes Chamberlain," he said, his features rigid, his brow etched in concentration. "Take thee, Emily Thomas. As my wife and lover."

Andrew moved rapturously, as though he couldn't lose himself deeply enough inside her. Emily couldn't stop kissing him; she was so filled with the love of him, so thrilled to be in his arms. She whimpered against his neck as he lifted her body up off the hay and held her to his chest.

His eyes never leaving hers, he whispered the vows again to her, and others even more and more beautiful. With each thrust, with each one of his shuddering cries, he emblazoned the words to her body as he had done to her heart. And somewhere inside of them, all their souls whispered too—smiling, crying, rejoicing.

Deep in the night, drenched in each other's sweat and the wind blowing cool against their skin, he crushed himself to her, and took full possession of her, and her alone. Collapsing in joy against her, he clenched her trembling body in his arms. The souls finally at peace.

Later, when their screams of lust and joy were only echoes in the rafters, he whispered haltingly, "Don't ever leave me again. Please." His body remained hunched over hers, still joined, unwilling to be parted.

"Never," she promised him, her voice breaking. "I'm s-sorry."

He curled his body around hers, spooning them together. His arms wrapped tight across her breasts, not letting her move an inch. "Where were you? Where were you hiding?" he whispered, his face lost in her hair. "I was so scared. I was so fucking scared."

She told him. He didn't move, but clamped his arms harder around her and pressed a heated kiss to her hair.

"It could have been a bloody grave, sweet girl. You could have died."

"I'm so sorry. I was just—I didn't know what to do. I was so lost. After what she said about you dying—I couldn't bear that."

"Shhh, it's all right, now." He kissed her, tightening his hold. "But please, please, please…"

What he was asking, she didn't know. His voice cracked, and he could say no more.

"To have and to hold," she said, linking her arms with his.

"To have and to hold," he whispered back and nestled against her, the hay their only blanket. "It's a wretched wedding night," he sighed. The relief in his voice nearly broke her heart.

Andrew walked out of the barn to where Emily sat on a stone wall. Her face tilted up to watch him approach; a few strands of hay stuck to her hair and the back of his coat, which she now wore tightly wrapped around her. He enjoyed the way it swallowed up her shoulders and dangled from her hands. The absence of it, however, left him in only a hay-strewn fisherman's sweater and a scratchy pair of jeans.

Last night, somewhere amid all that notorious hay, he'd found his cell phone and had the presence of mind to call Simon and inform him that they could call off the search. Andrew didn't offer him any more information other than to say they were safe. He called him again this morning with their location, to which Simon said little, merely asking if he should bring food. Andrew responded with heartfelt thanks.

"How did you know?" Emily asked him quietly, taking his hand in hers as he took his seat next to her. "How did you know where to find me?"

He kissed the inside of her wrist and held it to his lips, wondering how to tell her and not make her feel guilty, or worse, disturbed. Disturbed about feelings that he still didn't understand, and which he wasn't sure he had a grasp on even in the clear air of a new day. She still had a faintly wounded look about her.

"I wanted to run after you the moment you escaped that room, Emily. Your face—you were so, so pale. I'll remember it for the rest of my life,

I swear." She tightened her grip, and it gave him the encouragement he needed to continue.

"By the time we made it to Belden, the rain was nearly unbearable and hiking up to the cemetery was a nightmare, but then the second I spotted a trail of footprints, I couldn't stop. I knew you were here, I knew you were—I could feel you. I can't explain it any other way. Then not to find you, to know in my heart that you were so close and to have to walk away. Christ."

His throat choked up, and he moved closer, sliding his arm around her shoulders, in need of support. "Simon had to drag me the last few yards back down the hill because I wouldn't budge. By the time we reached town, he insisted we take the car back and get a new rental, but I kept arguing that I needed to scour the place to locate anyone who might have seen you. That's when he finally lost his shit. I'm sure he thought me completely gone at that point, standing there screaming in the pouring rain and soaked to the bone. I think his exact words were, 'Fucking call me when you're fucking rational,' or something to that effect. There were a great deal of 'fucks,' as I recall. It took me a while, but I finally found a man who had seen you at his shop, and he told me about your conversation. At that point I was terrified you had bolted to catch a train, so straightaway I phoned Margot and Zoey and sent them to Fort Bragg. I hope you know what trouble you've caused. There were rather many 'fucks' in that conversation, as well."

She hung her head and cringed. She seemed so very small to him at that moment, as if she could fit in the crook of his arm and disappear. He squeezed her tighter.

"Finally I came back here; I had to. I heard you screaming from the edge of the wood, and I couldn't reach you fast enough. But something made me stop short once I reached the barn. Your screams had broken off, and I could see you standing there. I was so furious—I couldn't control myself and I didn't know how to approach you, or even if it was safe to do so. I wanted to hurt you—" He halted abruptly, startled that he had said it aloud. She had stilled but made no other response. He decided to confess everything, she had to know. "After what that ghost had said, I started to doubt what was left of my mind. I had felt that anger, that rage—felt it pound in my blood. I had seen myself hurt you. I knew I was capable of that. But when you ran, I had to stop you in any way I could. I'm sorry if I frightened you, but I had to try to make you understand, even if I couldn't. I would have never stopped looking for you. Ever."

"Do you think that you would have hurt me—do you really believe what she said is true?" she asked in a measured voice.

"Do I believe that we saw a piece of living death yesterday that told me I would murder you? Yes. All those visions came crashing down on me just as powerfully, Emily. I was just as afraid, but even more so because I was the horror in all of this."

He took a rough breath and pressed on. "The only thing I could do was fight back. Break something. Change something, anything. She told me that I could not marry you, and I'd be damned before anyone stood in my way—I had to prove her wrong. I married you last night. *I married you.* I'll take you to a church or a justice of the peace, today if I must, but I did marry you, Emily Thomas."

She nodded, her eyes wide at the force of his voice.

"I did what they all told me couldn't be done. It's what I do best, I'm afraid." He broke off and smiled ruefully, trying to downplay the fury that had coursed through him, and how very close he had come to hurting her. "And see? We're both still very much alive, the sky is blue, and the day is stellar, and I love you. All in all, I think we're beating the odds."

"Andrew, I'm still scared."

He tried to speak as matter-of-factly as possible to mask his own insecurity. "Who wouldn't be? That creature was horrible. I envy Buck that gun of his."

She found his eyes and squeezed his hand. The look on her face was not what he expected—it was so defiant it shocked him. "I know what you're thinking. I'm not afraid of you, do you hear me? That disgusting thing, yes. But not you, not you—ever. I wish I had been as strong as you were. You never gave up. You never did. I heard you when I was lying in that…that place…even when you thought you were a killer you still kept fighting."

He stared at her for a long time. He closed his eyes and imagined himself in that ground, cold and utterly alone.

"If you think I was the only one waging a war against fate, you're wrong. You were bloody brave, sweet girl."

She swallowed and shrugged, making him smile in return, and then she laced her fingers more tightly with his. "I just want to have a life with you. Even if we have ghosts clanking around, I don't care."

"Let's opt for a ghost-free future, shall we?" he said, still flying from his emotions, determined to be able to put an end to this once and for all. "Which means we're falling down on the job. Now come on, we have a body to find. I assume you've looked already."

"Not very well. It was raining and muddy and—"

"You thought I was going to strangle you to death," he muttered.

"Stop." She intertwined her fingers with his as he pulled her off the ledge. She looked him full in the face, stood on her toes, and kissed him thoroughly, much to his surprise, although he did not complain. "No more of that, understand? But I've got one question." He raised an eyebrow at her. "How much longer until they get here?" And she pulled him toward the barn.

"All right, let's see that poem one more time, shall we?"

Casting Andrew a glance, Emily handed him a page from her satchel. They were finally dressed and lying on their stomachs, nestled together at the edge of the hayloft.

"You know, we need to get ourselves one of these," he added as he glanced up at the rafters.

"I bet this one'll come dirt cheap."

"On second thought, I'd rather not. I don't want anything associated with that woman. Horrid sense of fashion and bloody abysmal personal hygiene."

She shuddered. "Andrew? What did that gun do, exactly?"

"Buck's? Who knows, but it made Christian ecstatic."

"It didn't kill her, though, right?" Her brow scrunched up when she said it, the fear still there. He had been a fool to bring it up.

"No, Emily. She's already dead. The worst it did was 'neutralize her psychic make up,' I suppose. Or truly piss her off."

"But you don't think it's the last we'll see of her, do you?"

"It matters not, Mrs. Chamberlain." He stared at her until her frown disappeared. "The curse is broken."

He wrapped his arm around her, his heart pounding steady in his chest. They held their embrace until he kissed her tenderly, staring down at her. The sight of her, with hay in her hair and sunlight in her eyes, caused a strange clenching in his chest and made his throat swell.

"How do you do this to me?"

"Me?"

His finger brushed along her bottom lip. "Yes, you," he said softly, trying to keep his voice from breaking, wondering how he had become so affected by all this. "Now where's that poem?"

He had it memorized, of course, so instead of reading the paper, he proceeded to place kisses from her neck to her collarbone as he spoke the words:

"I dwell in a lonely house I know
That vanished many a summer ago,
And left no trace but the cellar walls,
And a cellar in which the daylight falls,
And the purple-stemmed wild raspberries grow.
O'er ruined fences the grape-vines shield
The woods come back to the mowing field;
The orchard tree has grown one copse
Of new wood and old where the woodpecker chops;
The footpath down to the well is healed.
I dwell with a strangely aching heart."

"It sounds so much better when you say it," she told him.

"I know."

She jostled him off of her, leaving them side by side again. "I think Nick's remains are in the house. I couldn't find anything before when I was looking. Nothing to open that needed a key. Not the mausoleum, not a grave, nothing. But…do you think she simply left his body in the house to rot? That's just too awful."

"Not his body, but his ashes, perhaps. That woman had no love for her son. She probably didn't want him buried properly, but she couldn't cast him aside, either. I mean, he was her child — once. No, I think you're right. Nick is in there somewhere."

"Yo! Where the hell are you two?" Christian's voice boomed up from the barn floor.

Emily and Andrew hung their heads over the edge of the hayloft and smiled. Below stood Simon, Margot, Christian, and Zoey, gaping up at them with incredulous looks on their faces.

Simon, however, stood back near the barn door. He reached for his cigarettes and remarked sourly, "Is it just me, or do you two have a thing about doing it around dead people?"

Emily turned her reddened face into Andrew's shoulder.

"I hope to God you're dressed, because I'm starving and this taskmaster wouldn't let me touch a bite until we were all back together," announced

Margot with a nod toward Zoey, whose arms were filled with a tray of steaming to-go cups.

Andrew bounded down the ladder and jumped the last four rungs.

"Tell me there's tea in there somewhere."

Zoey grinned and handed him a large cup that perfumed the air with bergamot.

"If I didn't tell you before, I adore you." He grabbed her, smiling from ear to ear, and spun her around in a hug, nearly upending her tray.

"I know. I have that effect on people." She burst into a round of chuckles.

Simon, however, was not amused, and as the girls disappeared into the loft and dragged Emily over to the corner, he set his sights on Andrew and then the loft, repeating the movement several times before he asked slowly, "No pitchforks, I take it."

"None that I could find, but the hay is a royal bitch. Sweet Jesus, is that a bagel?"

Simon stared at him as he inhaled it. "So I see you haven't come to your senses."

Andrew shot him a look before he took a long swig of his tea.

"Out with it."

"It's your nightmare, not mine. But if this is what you want, I'm not keen on sticking around to see the end of it. She's bad news, Andrew. This whole thing is bad news."

"So what are you saying? It's her or you? Simon, seriously?"

The stern look on Simon's face spoke volumes. He lit a cigarette and said no more.

"Listen, man," Christian interrupted. "I'm all into blasting skanky ghosts with big ray guns, but I need one fucking day of fucking rest, okay? Do you think that's possible?"

"I'll look into it," Andrew replied curtly, still stung by Simon's remarks.

The rift between the two men seemed palpable, even as they all left the barn and wandered out into the sunshine to set up their breakfast picnic. Just as they were about to sit down, Andrew stopped short. His gaze drifted to the bottom of the hill. Neil and Claudia stood there, her arms waving in greeting, his at his sides. He had never been so glad to see both of them and before he knew what he was doing, he was trotting down the hill; he grabbed his mum in a hug until she pulled back, her eyes shiny with tears.

"Are you all right? Are you hurt?"

"No, Mum."

"We were worried," Neil said, trying to keep his voice light, but failing. "Ever since Simon's call—after we found out about everything with Vandin—we couldn't stay back in San Francisco. So I phoned Simon this morning, and when he told us about that séance, well, here we are."

Andrew could not help but notice the way Neil said *we*, an edge of possessiveness to his voice. He readied himself for the reaction he knew would come but felt only relief. With one hand he shook Neil's and clapped his other one on his shoulder.

"Thank you. I'm glad you're here. It's been a horrendous few days, believe me. Come, come join us." He motioned to their picnic.

Emily and he spent the rest of breakfast filling everyone in on the details. Claudia and Neil seemed the most shocked, but Andrew realized how far they had come when Emily could discuss The Lady in White like she was an eccentric relative and no one seemed the least bit bothered.

"But I don't understand," said Zoey. "Why do you think the curse is broken?"

Emily looked down at her empty cup, her face blushing fiercely. Andrew stared out over at the farmhouse and sipped his tea. "It's broken. Trust me."

Margot sniggered knowingly as she eyed the rings on each of their hands and the hay all over their clothes. She leaned over to Zoey and murmured a few words, then turned to Andrew and spoke so quietly that only he could hear. "My, my, my, so you improvised. Nicely done."

"Pleasure was all mine," he murmured back, his cup inches from his lips when he noticed Simon had lit another cigarette and was beginning to tread toward the house.

"So, what about finding us a dead body?" announced Christian.

Andrew's pulled his fixed gaze from Simon's retreating form and back to the crowd. "We think Nick's remains might be located in the house somewhere. Emily's been throughout the graveyard and hasn't discovered anything that contains a lock for this type of key." He held it up and passed it around so everyone would know what to look for. "I think we should make one more pass about just to be sure, and then we should all split up. Zoey and Christian, would you take the hill behind the barn? Margot, could you go after Simon and see if he'll join you Emily and me in the house? If he's willing. And Mum and Dad, would you—"

His mouth froze. What had he just said? His eyes flashed to Claudia and Neil, who had the good grace not to show the shock he was feeling, although a tremor of a smile hung at the edge of his mother's lips. But this was asinine. He'd had a father his whole life, and for the majority of those years, they loved each other. But now…? Was it wrong to bestow a similar title on another man, a man he barely knew? But no matter how he tried to reconcile the conflicting emotions, the word felt right somehow. Dad… not father. Dad.

The silence was getting uncomfortable when Emily finally spoke. "Yes, would you both mind—I didn't get a chance to search that field behind the house. I'm not sure if there are any graves there, but the farm is so old it's definitely worth a shot."

With no more discussion on the subject, everyone fell in and began their search. Andrew and Emily reached the graveyard. Plots from as far back as the early nineteen hundreds jutted from the ground. Names like Garrett and Mercy, Zachariah and Savannah, all Beldens, were chiseled into the headstones. One stood aside, guarded over by a weathered angel.

VIRGINIA, BELOVED WIFE AND MOTHER

JULY 23, 1860 - MAY 18, 1883

She was twenty-three when she died. Only two years older than Emily. Andrew felt a warm hand take his as he gazed down at the marker.

"The sky is blue and the day is stellar and I love you," she whispered and squeezed his hand, leading him away from the plot. "And you know I'd haunt you if anything ever happened to me. You really don't want that, do you?" She patted the satchel draped across her chest in which Nora's ashes lay. She kissed the inside of his wrist tenderly. "Come on."

They met up with Margot and a clearly unenthusiastic Simon, who were waiting for them in front of the old farmhouse. Unfortunately, it didn't look any less menacing in the daylight, shrouded in three stories of decay and neglect.

"You think it's safe to go inside? It's barely standing," Margot asked as they approached.

"Stay together. If anything gives way, someone will be able to help you."

"So do you suppose this was Nick's mother's home?" Emily asked, her coat catching on a patch of blackberry bramble that had grown up near the front porch.

"Probably. I reckon her maiden name was Belden — it could be a family home. Perhaps he didn't want it. Chances are he didn't pass the most ideal childhood here," Andrew replied.

None of them had appreciated the desolation of the house until they began to navigate the remains of the front porch, which was pockmarked with rot. The structure seemed to suck the clean air from the surrounding trees into its belly to feed the spirits that moved within it. And as the wind blew again, it felt fetid and cold and unshakably dreary, and bore a sound like hissed whispers. The windows glowered at them as they stepped over the threshold.

The inside of the house was devoid of any sign of charm; no white-washed wall or surviving hearth greeted them. The interior had fallen victim to the wind and rain as nature had begun its inexorable reclaiming of the land on which it stood. Vines and bramble smothered every surface. The few rooms still standing were a cacophony of peeling paint, cracked plaster, and water stained floors. They searched each one, every cabinet and shelf, but vandals must have stolen anything that couldn't be nailed down.

Andrew said nothing, prey to what he knew he would feel. He could sense the next turn, the odd step. As though grappling his way through a memory, he found a room that at one time must have served as a kitchen. From there he could hear Margot and Simon on the top floor, their careful footsteps squeaking on the boards above his head.

"You know, I'm not sure, but I think I may have heard her last night," Emily said while opening up what remained of a cupboard.

"Who?"

"You know who. I couldn't tell. It was dark and I was, well, I wasn't thinking straight. But I heard something dragging across the floor when I was in the ground, but I couldn't see anything, I could barely breathe, and when I tried to get out, I couldn't budge the door sealing me in. I thought I was going to be buried alive."

His hand clenched the rotting doorframe. The image of her trapped in that grave while the ghoul stalked the ground above made him punch the wall in frustration. Without warning it crumbled to the ground, and a stream of light poured through the slats between the remaining studs. "Wait, there's something behind here."

He wrenched the rotting wood back, and it fell to pieces in his hands. Emily was at his side in an instant and went at another, but cringed as wet wood slid under her nails, beetles swarming free from inside. He quickly took the scraps out of her hands and cast them aside, then ripped off the rest.

Below them lay the top of a dark flight of stairs. The steps and risers were busted and warped, all of them highly unstable. The sunshine filtering through the gaps in the kitchen floor barely illuminated the space below. But there was a cellar down there. How far it spread, he had no idea; it was too dark to tell.

"Excellent. We'll need rope to get down there," he told her.

"There's some back at the barn. I'll get it."

Margot and Simon had rejoined them as Emily returned with a length of hard coiled rope. Simon appeared dubious about the opportunity of rappelling down into the black hole, Margot even more so. Andrew tied the rope off at the top of the steps and they gingerly lowered themselves one after the other down into the cellar. Andrew was the first to go.

"Floor's dry at least," he shouted back up to them once he had reached the bottom. "Hell, it's pitch black down here."

Simon and Margot were next, followed by Emily.

"You don't suppose there are bats down here?" Emily asked him in a quavering voice as he hoisted her down into the hole.

"They sleep in the daytime. If there were any around they would have been in the barn last night."

She stared up at him, her eyes huge.

"They're more scared of you than you are of them, sweet girl."

"Wanna bet?"

The air hung musty and cold around them. A faint scratching sound filled the murky darkness like hundreds of tiny claws skittering along the foundation. Then it silenced.

"I wish I had a torch," Andrew said, squinting into the gloom.

Hand in hand, Andrew and Emily walked deeper into the cellar with Margot and Simon behind them. The odor of rot permeated the space, and cobwebs hung everywhere like a winter frost. Old wiring above their heads hung low, causing them to stoop and duck as they made their way through the cellar.

The dankness thickened as they crept on. *Please let us not trip over some decomposing corpse,* Andrew thought. He'd welcome the rats if this kept up. A few veins of light bled through the cracks in the foundation, allowing them to walk without tripping over one another. He soon had to breathe through his mouth though, as the rank odor intensified with every step they took.

"Look," said Simon, his voice almost thundering in the claustrophobic space. Up ahead, shelf after shelf lined the walls and were filled with dusty boxes and old rusted tins. "You think Mother Chamberlain dumped her son in a sardine can?" he conjectured, peering at the decomposing larder.

"Hardly. Watch out, there's a nail there." Andrew moved Emily around a loose beam and motioned to Margot and Simon to follow as they went further into the manky depths. He began to worry how structurally sound this cellar was. At any moment, would the ceiling above give way and bury them all alive?

"What else did that poem say?" Andrew asked, hoping to divert Emily's attention from the disturbing surroundings. He pushed aside a particular nasty swatch of cobwebs under which she ducked, a few still clinging to her hair. Behind them, he could hear Margot spit out stray strands in disgust.

Emily recited it again. "'I dwell with a strangely aching heart.' Do you think that's part of the clues?"

"Ugh, by the stench, it wouldn't shock me," muttered Simon. "One ripe ol' juicy rottin' heart, ripped open and oozin'—"

"You're not helping, Simon," Andrew chastised him. "The fact that we're using a twentieth century poet to find the ashes of a dead body is a bit of a leap already, don't you think?" he added dryly.

Margot snorted behind him with another *ptui* at the cobwebs.

"Maybe she knew Robert Frost?" Emily asked Andrew.

"Don't destroy the image of my favorite poet, or I may leave you down here with the rats."

"Rats? You said there weren't any rats."

"I said bats. And I'd suggest you keep walking."

"Guys, over here." Margot stopped in her tracks and pointed. "Holy God. Look at it."

Up against a far wall stood a bookcase filled with what looked to be a collection of old religious statues and dusty votive candles. Dim light from the joists in the ceiling reflected in the jet-black eyes of some saint, making the skin pebble on Andrew's arms.

"It's like yours," Simon said.

She glanced at him with a smirk. "This one's better." Then she approached the make-shift shrine and made the sign of the cross. She flashed him a look before she leaned closer and began to examine the small figurines, her fingers moving them aside like chess pieces. She reached for one and squinted at it in the darkness. "Of course," she whispered.

"Margot?" Emily asked.

"Nick's mother was Catholic. She wore a rosary around her neck and kept beating her breast at the séance. The only people I remember doing that other than my mother and grandmother were the nuns back at Our Lady."

Simon stared at her in disbelief.

"Our Lady of the Immaculate Conception," Margot clarified.

Before anyone knew what was going on, Margot had begun to shove the large figurines from the top of the bookcase. "Look," she whispered.

Hidden behind them a painting hung on the wall. It bore the iconic picture of Jesus with his heart exposed and radiant on the outside of his body. Except that the painting had hinges on one side.

"The Sacred Heart," Margot whispered. "The Sacred Heart of Jesus. The poem. 'I dwell with a strangely aching heart,' it's a clue." Her fingers curled underneath the painting and pulled; it protested on its decayed hinges and swung open. The sound seemed to rattle the rats that swarmed behind the wall, their nails clicking as they rushed away. Behind the door was another metal panel, and in the panel a keyhole.

"Where's the key?" Margot asked.

"I found Nora. Nick's all yours." Emily turned to Andrew and withdrew the key from the pocket of his coat that she was still wearing. He stepped forward and placed it into the lock; it fit perfectly. Anticipation bubbled up inside him, and he smiled at Emily, his heart racing. He turned it, and with a grating click the panel opened.

The rectangular enclosure was about the size of a medicine cabinet. The bottom of it had crumbled away, opening into the space between the walls. Emily hung behind him, holding onto his shoulders and trying to jump up to get a better look.

"Coward," he chided her.

"I'm not going to be the one bitten," said Emily.

"Good point." With a deep breath, he reached out his hand to sweep inside the cavity. "There's something in here! It feels like metal…I think it's a tin. I can just about reach it. Damn it!" he cursed.

"What!"

"There's a tail in there with it. Quick, I need something to nudge it closer."

With a wry look of triumph on her face, Margot handed him a crucifix. He poked it down into the hole until he was sure the space was empty save the small metal tin.

In a flash he reached inside and felt the velvety slime of fur against his hand as he snatched the box out. It resembled an old-fashioned gilded candy box; the face of a Gibson Girl covered in cobwebs and grit smiled back at them. It was heavy for its size, and when Emily took it from him she nearly dropped it. She looked up to Andrew and grinned.

Just then they heard it. A slow, deathly dragging. A rattle of a breath. Wheezing.

"Andrew," Emily whispered, her smile vanishing. "It's her."

"Run!" he ordered and grasped her hand. The four of them tore into the blackness, dashing past the decaying walls, the sound of their footsteps echoing inside the empty cellar.

Suddenly Margot cried out in pain. Andrew wheeled around. She had tripped over a stray pile of wood. She tried to get up but faltered on her leg.

The wet seething stalked the darkness. Margot's eyes froze in terror.

"Give him to me," a phlegm drenched voice gurgled. "He's mine!"

Simon scooped Margot up in his arms. "Move it!" he shouted.

Panting, they reached the stairs. Simon and Andrew heaved Margot up; she groaned in pain but somehow managed to make it to the top of the landing, where she immediately began shouting for help. Emily was next. She shoved the tin into her coat pocket and scurried up the rope, nearly crashing into a shattered beam.

"Drop it to me," Andrew yelled, his heart catching in his throat as she swung near a row of rusty nails.

"No! She wants it!"

"Drop it, Emily," he growled. She couldn't hold on, not with the weight of both the coat and her satchel hung around her body.

"But—"

"Now!"

She shimmied off her satchel instead, and he snatched it. With a final shove she hauled herself up through the hole.

The dragging chill was getting closer. Andrew wrestled the satchel over his shoulder and turned around to glare at Simon. "Get the fuck up there, mate, and don't argue with me."

Simon hoisted himself up and reached the top of the stairs. He whirled around and grabbed hold of the rope.

"Neil! Christian! Quick, we need your help!" he cried, gripping one end of the rope as he latched his hands around the other. "Come here—wait, the stairs aren't stable. Can you hold this rope and help me with Andrew?"

The rustling of rats grew behind Andrew. They were fleeing from something, hell bent on escaping. He knew they would flood the floor below him in seconds. He hoisted himself up the rope just as a swarm of slick bodies collided against his legs. Hand over hand he climbed, but suddenly lost his grip. The rats were jumping up his shins, biting each other in fright. He thrashed against them, his boot hitting the rotten stairs, and the sound sent the rats into hysteria. With a scream of rage, he hauled himself up the rest of the rope and threw himself into the kitchen.

Neil and Christian grappled him up to his feet.

"Andrew, we have to get out of here!" warned Emily. "Nora told me that ghosts can only manifest themselves in places where they've been during their life. We have to get off this farm!"

"The rental car isn't far," Christian cried as they all began running. "Neil, you take Emily and Andrew and Claudia in your car—it's closer—and I'll get everyone else. We need to keep those ashes away from her."

Neil and Andrew reached his Range Rover first. Andrew swung open the passenger side door only to realize that Claudia and Emily had fallen a few yards behind, Claudia's shoe having caught in the mud.

"Get in!" cried Neil. "I'll turn it around and get them."

Andrew slammed the door shut as the Range Rover roared to life. He swung around to make sure that they had cleared a patch of trees. Suddenly, the locks smashed shut.

"Neil, where's the button to unlock the doors?"

He didn't reply.

Andrew repeated his question as the car straightened out, and Neil pounded the gear into drive. The car lurched forward, heading straight for Emily and Claudia.

"Neil!" Andrew hollered. "Watch out!"

Claudia grabbed Emily and threw her out of the way. When she saw Neil she stopped short and covered her mouth in horror. She began shouting his name, and he faltered for a fraction of a second, doubling over the steering wheel as though in intense physical pain.

"Neil, what the bloody hell are you doing!"

Andrew felt a fist connect with his jaw, and he was thrown back against the window. A sharp pain lanced his face, and he felt a trickle of warm blood ooze down his cheek.

Stars and splotches of light filled his vision, then the blurred image of Neil's face and eyes swam to the surface. Except they weren't Neil's eyes. They shone milky and evil and deranged. Another fist connected to his jaw and sent his head crashing against the window as the engine roared and the car careened down the hill.

"Why aren't you dead yet, boy?" the monster inside Neil bellowed.

The Lady in Red, Nick Chamberlain's mother, had possessed Neil and was in control of a massive Range Rover, two and a half tons of steel capable of grinding the bodies of everyone he loved under its tires or smashing at high speed into the surrounding trees, killing them both.

Andrew attempted to move, but his face stung like hell, and his temple throbbed from crashing against the window. Somehow he managed to hoist his body around, desperate to make sure that Emily had escaped unharmed. The pain blurred his vision, but he could make out Emily and Claudia running and screaming in the wake of the car with petrified looks on their faces. The others raced to catch up to them, everyone shouting and waving their arms. Andrew's heart plummeted to the bottom of his chest as they vanished from view; the Range Rover coursed down the hill and peeled out onto the open road.

Don't follow us, Emily. Don't follow us.

Neil's hands clenched the steering wheel, sweat beading across his brow as his breaths came in shallow gasps. The Range Rover veered wildly back and forth across the road, forcing Andrew to brace his hands against the inside door panel as he fought to stay conscious.

"You should have killed her by now! What's wrong with you?" she howled through Neil's lips. "Why is she still alive?"

Despite the vicious screams issuing from Neil's mouth, Andrew saw him fighting The Lady in Red, battling to take back possession of his body. But the harder he fought, the more erratic his driving became.

The ghoul's warning from the séance blazed into Andrew's mind: "*Don't you know I can kill her right now if I wanted? I could infect her mind and make her crash through that window. Would you like to see that? Her body slashed by those shards of glass and broken on the street?*"

She could do the same thing to Neil. She could shred his mind to pieces, or force him to drive this car off the road and smash his body through the windscreen.

"Neil," Andrew whispered, his head swaying as white blotches of light fired around the perimeter of his vision. "Don't do it. Don't fight her. She'll hurt you. Please—don't."

Neil's face contorted in anguish, and his hands clenched the steering wheel as he railed against the monster, every muscle in his body taut in pain.

"Please. Just do what she says. For me. For Mum."

Neil seized as if pain shot through him like an electric shock. It wasn't until that moment that Andrew understood how much Neil cared for both of them and had from the very beginning, even when Andrew hated him for it. Andrew couldn't bear to watch the thing harm him, and he knew she would, in the worst possible way, given the smallest excuse. He was a Chamberlain, after all. They both were.

"What do you want?" Andrew choked out, the pain in his head blinding. "Tell me what you want."

"I want my son back," she spat at him.

"But there are only…ashes. They won't bring him back to you. You must know that, Mrs. Chamberlain."

"Don't you dare call me by that name, boy!"

She backhanded him hard across his face, a ring on Neil's hand gouging his skin, the force slamming his head against the seat. His ears rang with piercing echoes.

"You think you can use your saccharine voice and that pouty face on me? You might charm that whore of yours and all those little girls that fall at your feet, but not me, boy. No, you're just like Nicholas. Stupid, foolish men. Stupid, weak Chamberlains.

"I know what you're planning. You want to join his ashes with hers, so they can be together. So they can spend eternity gallivanting across the earth, hand in hand, without a care. That's what Nicholas wanted when he found the ashes of the ones that haunted her house. To reunite those 'poor lost lovers,' they told me. Thought it was romantic to place them at rest together. Said they felt a need to do it. Need? Of course they felt the need—it was in their blood to help, being a Chamberlain and a Thomas. But did they ever think of my needs? Did they ever worry how they were breaking my heart—no! They never listened to me when I warned them about the curse. They called me a foolish, superstitious old woman. I told them it didn't matter if they combined those ashes—it wouldn't work—the curse was too strong. And it was too strong for them in the end—they couldn't fight it." She paused and glared at him. "What makes you different? Why haven't you killed her yet, why is she still alive? She's a Thomas, she's cursed, she should be dead!"

Andrew pressed his hand against his temple and felt blood trickling through his fingers.

"Nicholas—he promised he'd take care of me after his father left us. We were all we had, Nicky and me. He promised. Promised me that I would never want for anything. And then when that bitch came along—" she pointed Neil's finger at the satchel Andrew had slung across his shoulder "—he left me without a word, despite everything I had done for him, everything I sacrificed for him, despite knowing he would kill her in the end. He came up here with her and called me crazy, a lunatic. Laughed at the truth. Laughed at his mother who loved and slaved and gave him everything! Abandoned me for a tramp he barely knew. A worthless whore!

"And you're no better!" She slammed Neil's fists on the wheel. "Just another Chamberlain! Just like Nicholas's father, just like Nicholas—you barely know that girl—but it doesn't matter, does it? You have to have her. Stupid whoring men, you all are. And fucking whores, those Thomases!"

"Your husband—he didn't—"

"A Thomas. Yes. Twenty-five years of marriage and he left me for one. And do you think anyone would understand? My friends, my priest? There was no one for me. The only one who would listen was the spiritualist. Everyone called her crazy, but she knew, and she could summon the white witch. She held a séance, and that's when I learned about the curse, the evil of the Thomas women. They all should burn in hell. I'll kill you all before I'll let those ashes touch."

Andrew swallowed down his revulsion, the sickening feeling of light-headedness overtaking him. The salty, metallic taste of blood filled his mouth as it slid down the back of his throat. One of his eyes was swollen shut from her beating, making sight nearly impossible.

"What are you going to do?" he asked, not wanting to know the answer.

"I want my son back. He's mine, not hers. Not then, and not now! Do you understand? He was obsessed—just like you. And that Thomas of yours is just as obsessed as his was. She'll do anything for you, won't she? She was willing to leave you forever. I saw the way she buried herself in the ground, how she almost died for you. See, see how she's chasing us? See?" She forced Neil's hand to gesture roughly toward the rearview mirror.

Whipping around, Andrew saw a white sedan gaining on them, close enough now to see Simon at the wheel and Christian next to him screaming into his cell phone. No! No, they had to turn away.

"Your Emily will give me Nicholas's ashes for your life, she will. And if you want to see this man you call 'Dad' alive again, you'll destroy that whore's ashes—you'll throw them into the ocean where they belong."

Despite the fear raging in his mind, something about her words struck a chord. *You'll throw them into the ocean.* She had not said, "I will throw them into the ocean." Could she not touch Nora's ashes for some reason? Was what Dwayne had said true?

There was only one way to find out. Without a sound, he slinked the satchel off his arm. He shoved the bag at Neil's chest. "Here! If you really want to destroy her, take her. She's yours!"

Neil's body plastered itself against the door as if hot coals had been shoved under his skin. His movements, however, caused the car to swerve so violently it careened around the curve on two tires. The Lady in Red hissed and struggled with Neil's body to right the vehicle as it missed an oncoming car by inches.

She couldn't touch the ashes.

Andrew's mind raced with the implications. Even while possessing another body, she could not touch the ashes. Maybe that was why she hadn't taken Nora's ashes before? He shoved the satchel at Neil again, praying it would drive her out of his body.

It was a dreadful mistake. Before the satchel even touched him, Neil's fist connected with his temple, and the force of the blow crashed his mangled face against the window.

"I'll kill both of you, do you understand? Just like I killed that fucking doctor."

Doctor. What doctor? Then the realization hit him. She had killed Vandin. She'd made him pull the trigger and blow his brains out in the caves. She was strong enough to invade his mind, drive him insane, and make him kill himself—what else had she forced him to do? Spy, steal for her? If she could break a man's will like that, they were fucking doomed.

He moaned and saw a haze of blood coating the webbed glass. His head rocked in pain as he tried to focus on the end of the road that was fast approaching—the turnoff to the coast. "The cliffs," he muttered, blood on his lips.

Neil wrenched the wheel around, and they took the curve at a frightening speed. Andrew's hands flailed at the dashboard, attempting to hold himself in place. His pulse hammered in his throat as he tried to focus, tried to concentrate. He had to draw that thing out of Neil, he had to.

Their tires chewed the road, speeding faster as they neared the coast; only a hundred yards ahead was the turnout for the highway. Andrew glanced behind him and gasped. *No!* The white sedan was almost on them, only yards away. Suddenly Neil slammed on the brakes, and the Range Rover screeched and skidded, sending Andrew reeling against the dashboard. The sedan swerved, barely avoiding them at the last second, and headed straight for the ditch on the side of the road.

Andrew's heart hammered against his ribs. They were going to crash. Yet seconds before tumbling into the ditch the sedan righted itself, squealing in the gravel before lurching roughly back onto the road with a roar.

"Yes!" he cried. But his euphoria died instantly as they finally reached the turnout and burst out onto the highway.

The stretch of headlands blurred past them on their left. It was a vast, green length of land that narrowed and ended abruptly with a sheer drop off of perilous cliffs. Neil floored the Range Rover and it rocketed forward, barely avoiding the oncoming traffic.

Neil turned, and Andrew saw the creature's milky eyes narrowing in triumph. Suddenly, Andrew was no longer sure what the demon was going to do. She could wait to get her son's ashes from Emily, or she could drive them both over the cliffs—killing everything she hated and banishing Nora's ashes to the ocean—where they could never be reunited with Nick's.

Andrew's only choice was to try to take control of the car. He fisted his hand as hard as he could, knowing he would have only one chance.

He swung. His fist smashed against Neil's jaw, sending a blinding jolt of pain up Andrew's arm. The car skidded along the divider, metal grinding against metal. The creature roared in anger and flung Neil's fist into Andrew's throat. Andrew's body flew against the window, shattering the glass. A sharp stinging pain sliced the back of his skull, and he felt a thick hot wetness leak down the nape of his neck. Grappling to sit up, Andrew grabbed his scalp and felt blood coating his hand. He reared back and smashed Neil's forehead against the steering wheel.

A blaring horn made Andrew snap his head up, and he fought to jerk the wheel to the right to keep from rear-ending the car in front of them. Curses ripped from their mouths as the Range Rover swerved wildly across the highway. Neil's body convulsed in fury, and his sweat and blood splattered the dash and console. The slickness made their hands slip along the contours of the steering wheel as they battled for control.

Without warning, another horn wailed and they both froze. A dilapidated van crested the top of the hill. He knew that van. *Holy hell!*

The Big Doobie took to the air and hung there as though in slow motion. It smashed down on its tires, and the wheel bed skidded against the ground in a spray of sparks. Its brakes squealed, and the van lurched to a stop, blocking both lanes of traffic. All at once, the doors flew open and bodies dove out and over the divider like rats fleeing the Titanic, as cars careened around it, spinning out of control. One after one, vehicles collided into the van, turning it into a block of distorted metal. Andrew steeled his body for impact, certain they would be crushed on both sides in the pileup of mangled cars.

But the Range Rover skidded to a dead stop instead. Hope rushed through Andrew's heart. He lunged for the door, but a vice-like grip twisted his arm, nearly snapping it in two. He screamed — the pain was beyond excruciating as Neil hauled him out the open door.

"Out!" it bellowed, and dragged Andrew to the side of the road and over the divider.

"Andrew!"

In a white hot panic, he wheeled around to see Christian racing down the road behind him. He could hear Simon shouting as Neil dragged him off onto the headlands.

Then he saw Emily. And she saw him. Their eyes held. He could see the horror in her expression as she took in his battered and bloodied face, his injured arm.

Zoey ran to her side along with Christian and Claudia; Simon overtook them.

"No! Stay back!" Andrew screamed at everyone.

"Neil!" Claudia cried. "Luv! Stop! Neil!"

The Lady in Red within Neil roared in fury and twisted Andrew's arm again. The agony was so severe he nearly blacked out. Claudia cried and rushed forward, but Emily held out her arms, blocking her from going any closer.

Andrew willed her with his eyes not to follow. His nightmare commenced as Neil dragged him toward the cliffs. It had begun, clear, precise — like a movie. This was the end. His body moved without his control. He was a player in a timeless, cursed play.

The monster had him at the edge of the headlands now. Rocks upon rocks jutted cruelly from the ground, the precursor to what lay below. The sea crashed against the cliffs, and the surf churned violently at the base of the outcropping. The wind whipped so hard against his body that he could feel the salt stinging inside his wounds.

He turned and saw Emily standing there, panting for breath.

"Emily, get away from here! Run! Leave the ashes and get away!"

But she didn't. Her eyes never left the monster's as she slowly came closer, like she was approaching a wild animal she thought she could tame.

"Give me the ashes, girl, or I kill him," The Lady in Red demanded, jerking Andrew's arm and making him wail out loud.

"No! Don't listen to her, Emily. Leave! Now!"

"Just give me the ashes and you can have him. All I want is those ashes."

Everyone else drew closer and closer as though empowered by Emily's courage.

"Stop! She'll kill him," Andrew yelled. "Don't you understand? She killed Vandin. She's inside Neil. Get away, all of you! Simon, Christian, for God's sake, take Emily away!"

Emily took another step closer. He turned to face Neil. "Dad, please… Dad, I know you can hear me, please Dad," he pleaded. "Don't hurt her. I'll do anything that monster wants, but please — don't hurt her."

At his words, Neil's body contorted as if he was being burned alive.

"Say any more boy," she hissed, "and I slice his mind to ribbons."

Emily took another step closer.

"No!" Andrew screamed, but it was too late.

In a frenzied rush, the demon threw Andrew to the ground where he landed on his arm, crippling pain slicing down his side. Wrapping his other arm around himself, he grappled against the rocks, fighting to stand, but Neil had descended on Emily and yanked her to the edge of the cliff. His hand went instantly to Emily's neck, the other plundering her coat pocket.

"Where is it? What have you done with him?!" The Lady in Red shrieked. Emily's head whipped around like a ragdoll as the demon shook her, screaming its demands.

"Let her go!" Andrew roared.

Everyone rushed forward, causing the monster to force Emily to the very edge of the cliff. They all froze to a dead stop.

"Why? Why aren't you dead yet? You should be dead!" the abomination screeched at her. Emily's nails clawed over Neil's hands, trying to pry them free.

"I married her. She is my wife!" Andrew screamed.

The words paralyzed Neil's body where it stood, their meaning stabbing their way into the creature's mind.

"There is no more curse. She's mine. Let her go! I'm her husband. We swore our vows to each other. It is enough. You know it is!"

Neil gasped, and his body shuddered, his consciousness breaking free from The Lady in Red and seeking out Andrew. "She knows, Andrew. She knows the curse is broken! Run!"

Emily must have felt his body fail, to falter for a moment; she wheeled around to escape, but the demon was faster and regained control of Neil. She twisted Neil's hands around Emily's throat. With a howl, she smashed Emily to the ground. Her head smacked against the rocks with a hollow thud.

Andrew froze. Everyone around him screamed. Simon and Christian rushed toward Neil, but the monster heaved his body to the edge of the cliff, teetering there, daring them to step forward. Claudia screamed as Neil wobbled. Simon and Christian retreated with their hands held up in surrender.

Andrew ran to Emily. Her hair was the only thing that moved, fluttering around the edges of her face. Her hands lay twisted and lifeless in the dirt, blood under her nails, her wedding ring brilliant in the sunlight.

Why wasn't she moving? Why was she just lying there?

Andrew dropped to his knees and reached out for her. She was just hurt, that was all. Forgetting his own pain, he gathered her to him and rocked her in his arms and hummed, his voice too high and too far gone to be his own. The blood seeping from his face dripped down her cheek like tears. She just wouldn't move. *Someone tell me why she won't move. Please!*

"She will make such a pitiful ghost," the creature said from within Neil, his body perched on the edge the cliffs. Her milky eyes were to the sky, the wind gusting through Neil's hair and whipping his bloodied shirt. "I can feel her already." Then her gaze lowered to the satchel at her feet.

Nora.

The satchel containing Nora's ashes was at her feet. He had cast it aside when he knelt down to hold Emily. With a smile and roar of triumph, she kicked it off the side of the cliff.

No. NO! NO! Rage bellowed its cry inside him. Andrew rose from the ground and charged. "NOOOOOO!"

Andrew's fist smashed into Neil's face. Neil crumpled to his knees at the edge of the cliff with a groan, then he growled as The Lady in Red reared his body back up. He surged forward and crashed into Andrew.

"Where are his ashes, you bastard?" the creature hissed. "Give them to me!"

Neil swung and Andrew dodged the blow, sending the rocks at his feet plummeting down the cliff face. The Lady in Red snatched Andrew's sweater in Neil's hands and hauled Andrew to his feet, locking his arms behind him. The pain in Andrew's arm should have been excruciating, yet he couldn't feel it. He couldn't feel anything anymore. The Lady in Red was forcing him to watch Emily. The worst imaginable sorrow and grief rose up within his soul, ready to devour him. He welcomed it. He craved death.

Then the impossible happened. Emily's finger's twitched. Was it madness, had he already lost his mind? Then she moved again.

"Emily!" he screamed.

She sat up and somehow staggered to her knees. "Please—please stop." Her voice was hoarse, a gash bled on her forehead; her hand rose absently to touch it, but her entire focus was on the creature.

It yanked Andrew's hand into its grip. "Give me his ashes, girl, or I break all these bones. Every single one! You love these hands, don't you? Don't you?" The monster clenched Neil's hands around one of Andrew's fingers and twisted it back to its breaking point. "Your lover made beautiful music, didn't he?"

"No! Not his hands." Her face filled with anguish, and she reached out, pleading. "Neil, please. You can't take his hands. You can't take that from him…please."

The monster yanked his finger back with all its might. Andrew fought everything inside of him not to scream.

Tears blinded Emily's eyes and choked her voice. "Stop!" She pulled the tin of Nick's ashes out from the inside of her jacket.

Andrew felt Neil buckle behind him as though his muscles were breaking apart. The sight of Nick's ashes seemed to have traumatized the monster. Neil's hands shook violently as he fought for control of his body. With a howl of pain he collapsed against Andrew, drenched in sweat, his legs giving way in utter exhaustion.

"Neil? Neil!" Andrew yelled, spinning around and clutching Neil's limp and beaten body in his arms.

"You can't change fate," The Lady in Red hissed from within Neil. "You can't! Give him to me!" Neil dropped to the ground, struggling to breathe.

Emily pleaded with the monster. "Just let go Mrs. Chamberlain, please. Love your son and let him be happy. Only you can give him that. Love him enough to let him go. He has to be with her. I've seen him, I've felt him. He loves her." Her eyes found Andrew's.

Nick did love Nora, just as he loved Emily. Their fate was bound together, inseparable, just like those who had come before them. All of them with the same twisting and intertwining lines on their palms.

"No! She's gone. She doesn't deserve him."

"Yes she does," Emily whispered vehemently as she rose to her feet. "I know she does." For that one moment she was both Nora and Emily and all the Thomases that had gone before her, all headstrong, determined, and bound for eternity to one man and one man alone. With one last fierce look she leaned back and threw the tin of Nick's ashes over the cliff.

Andrew stared at Emily in shock. The ghoul wailed, "Noooo!"

"Nora!" Andrew, Nick, and the countless Chamberlains who had fought and died for these women watched as the tin fell from sight. Andrew's chest constricted, and he felt thick and heavy, as though bound and trapped inside his own body, unable to move as poison flooded through his veins.

Emily stared at him, confused. Andrew looked down at Neil lying on the ground, who now was convulsing and gasping for air, his eyes finally his own. Claudia had run to him, throwing her arms around him, and was hugging him to her chest.

Every bone in Andrew's body began to burn, and he had to fight to breathe. Out of nowhere a rage ignited his blood. The madness and unknown anger of all his years, all the fear of losing his mind, was made manifest and he could do nothing—nothing could fight it. He was in a body that was his, and yet not his. It felt so simple now, so right, the rage and bloodlust. He stepped toward Emily with only one intention—to kill.

Emily staggered back toward the cliffs with the same horror in her eyes that every vision had shown him. But this time she steeled herself—her eyes flashed at something behind him.

Andrew felt a pair of strong arms coil around his shoulders.

"You can't have him." Neil's fierce grip tightened. "You fucking lost your son, but you won't take mine!" Neil spoke rapidly into Andrew's ear. "She can't fight much longer; she's too damaged, too weak. You have to fight her—it's the only way you can beat her. Try! You have to try!"

Emily reached out and grabbed his hand. "Let go. Let us all go. It's time to rest."

Sorrow so profound that Andrew could see its color drowned him. He felt himself scan the sea below; he felt his heart long for a son he had lost and a life he could never have. As the ocean blew across his face, a love he didn't have a name for whispered to him.

His body staggered into Emily's arms. She held him tightly. His head fell to her shoulder as she hushed him tenderly.

"It's all right; everything is going to be all right," she whispered as he felt his body surrender to the call.

Suddenly he seized. *No, boy, you can't. I won't let you,* the creature hissed in his mind. Violence scorched every cell of his body. The force of it overtook his will and destroyed the last of his strength. He burned in hate. Rejoiced in it. Before he knew it, his hands were shaking.

He could hear the creature inside him scream in victory; in a few seconds, it would all be over. Before anyone could react, his hands would be wrapped around Emily's neck, her face would be drained a ghostly white as he choked the life from her body. He knew he would kill her. His eyes met hers. His hands lunged to her throat.

"NO!" he heard himself roar. *No! No!* Emily's breath came in spasms, her eyes pleading. "NO!" he screamed again and steeled his hands to his sides. He wouldn't hurt her — he couldn't hurt her. The demon screeched and tore at every muscle in his body. *Kill!*

He could feel the shards of her ripping apart, like a frayed rag burning in flames. She fought with all her strength not to succumb, and in that split second, when she grappled with her own weakness, he saw it — lying there on an outcropping below was Emily's satchel. And the last part of the vision, the ending he could never see, was made clear — the piece that was missing. It was up to him and him alone now. Nick's words rung like a bell in his head, "Seize life with your hands; it's the only thing that will save you in the end."

They had broken the curse but it was not enough — the last of what remained of The Lady in Red had to be annihilated. He knew that because of the damage done to her from being within Vandin at his death, she could not take another blow and survive.

With a final gut wrenching cry, he stumbled to the edge of the cliff.

Emily's screams pierced the sky.

"ANDREW!"

With his last ounce of strength he hurled his body over the side.

"ANDREW!"

He was falling, twisting, The Lady in Red screeching inside him, believing he had taken his life, her cries lashing through every corner of his mind. Such pain could not exist for her; it was too much for her to suffer. What was left of her soul could not endure another death.

His upper body slammed against the outcropping of rocks. His arms shot out and fought to grab hold of the wet rock where the satchel lay crumpled. With his damaged arm he lunged and grabbed it. Seized it just as Nick had told him. Seized life. Seized love. But the rock was too slick, and he could not hold on. With a final scream he wrenched himself as hard as he could, and his fingers fixed around the soft material and into the ashes within. The Lady in Red shrieked with the contact, her voice fire itself; she could not bear a second more, and the last of her nature, her last ties to this earth, perished. She disintegrated into a final death.

His heart rejoiced at the victory. Then with a sharp pain, reality crashed back into focus. From far atop the cliff he saw Emily's face. His grip slipped to only one hand. She screamed and turned to scramble down.

"No!" he ordered her. "No!"

"Andrew! Hold on!"

He struggled to pull himself up the outcropping, blood seeping down his face as he clung to the jutting rock. The salt spray of the waves soaked his back. His mouth tasted of brine and blood.

She stared down at him imploringly, tears running down her face. He tried to imprint her face in his mind. All the times he had seen that face: in shadows and in light, at dawn and at midnight, huddling at the top of the stairs, peeking at him across an old book, studying a poem. He couldn't hold on anymore.

Without warning, the rocks under him cleaved from the cliff. His body plummeted down the cliff face. *Dear God, please don't let her see me! Not like this.* At that one thought his life flashed before his eyes. A child at a piano writing to his muse, his mother's hands, his father's violin, and all those notes and all those melodies that he would never write or sing. The Lost Boys, the endless miles, the joy and elation, the frenzied life. The crowds and the screaming. Finally, a club and a face with wide eyes. Emily. In everything. His blood, his bones. His whole life. His hands reaching out so hard to find her, reaching, reaching, reaching and only holding her for the space of a breath, the lifetime of a sigh. *Please God, let me find her again.*

Then death smashed into his heart.

Death wasn't gentle. It seized his body in its many hands as he slid down the cliff. Its force made his body quake in excruciating pain as it grabbed and pulled him by his waist, his arms, his legs. It pinned his face and shoulders against the brutally cold rock and forced the breath from his lungs as he hung in its grasp. Death was also screaming. It was screaming a lot. And death had arms, arms that hauled him up to it and into a small cave on the cliff.

He struggled to open his eyes, every bone in his body throbbing. He could hear the distant shouting of joy from far above his head. It was the voices of heaven calling to him.

Since when did angels smell like pot?

"Righteous!" howled a voice in his ear. "Blessed be!" wailed another. Death's arms had bodies which were jumping up and down and screaming again as they all wobbled and smashed back into the rocks.

His eyes fought to focus through his bruised and swollen cheeks. The image of Dwayne grinned back at him, with Egan, Dinesh, and Buck peering down at the sea below.

"We headed over the side when things started looking gnarly, man. Thought we might be able to help," panted Dwayne. "Blessed Mother, you're a lot heavier than you look! We almost lost you there once that rock gave way. Good thing you didn't fall from any higher or we'd all be flatbread right now!"

"Oh, fucking righteous!" Andrew took a huge gulp of air and laid his aching head against the rocks, praying fervently in thanks as he waited for his heart to stop pile-driving out of his chest.

He craned his neck to see the top of the cliff. Emily, his gorgeous, beautiful Emily, stood there, laughing and weeping.

"I love you!" he screamed, battling the roar from the pounding surf.

"Andrew!" she screamed back, too overcome to say anything more.

He waved back madly despite the firebrand of pain shooting down his arm.

"Thank you." He turned back to the guys. "Thank you so bloody much."

Dwayne patted his back. "No problem. But I'll tell you, it helps to work with crystal balls. They build up your catching arm." He nodded to his feet where a metal candy tin sat.

"Oh! Fucking, fucking righteous!" Andrew cried at the sight. He looked up the cliff where the satchel still sat on the ledge above.

Nick and Nora, together. At last.

Between the sweating, the swearing, the laughing, and the crying taking place around him, Andrew didn't know how he was finally hoisted and hauled up the cliffs and back onto solid ground and into the waiting arms of Simon and Christian. They pulled him to safety, careful of his arm.

His mother, equally overjoyed and appalled at his injuries, fell onto him at once. "He needs to go to a hospital," she ordered as she hugged and kissed him.

"You know, I've always wanted to play lead guitar," Christian remarked, panting through a huge smile, though its edges quivered slightly as he inventoried all of Andrew's various cuts and bruises.

"Not on your life. My fingers are still moving."

"Thank God for that," cried Simon, taking a stronger hold as he moved him far from the cliff edge. "Otherwise we'd have to toss you back over the side." His eyes were red and his breath came up short. "Fuck, man. You can't do this shit anymore. I thought we lost you. Do you have any fucking idea?"

"Yes. Yes, I do."

Before Andrew could say more, a swarm of women descended on him. Zoey's large hands flapped about his injuries like a flock of anxious ducks, Margot, her ankle still lame from the fall in the basement, hobbled around him inspecting the damage, and his mother stood guard while Neil held onto her side for support.

Yet he fought to lean around them, this sea of loving hands and ecstatic smiles. Where was she? Where was Emily?

She stood a few feet away, staring at him. His coat hung open on her shoulders, and he could see her chest rise and fall erratically, though her hands lay still at her sides. She took one step, then another, and then there was nothing but her arms, her mouth, her hair, and the warmth of her body in his arms. The smell of her was full of life and tears. There with the wind gusting around them, hands, all those hands joined hers, and held him steady before lowering him gently to his knees. Emily kneeled in front of him, still clutching his hands in hers while she took in his injuries.

Before he could say a word, a cacophony of groans heralded the arrival of Egan and Dwayne, the last of the stoners to make it up the cliff. In their hands they bore the remains of Nick and Nora. Without a word, they placed the tin and the satchel in front of Emily and stepped back. Her eyes widened, and she gasped in shock once she realized their significance.

"It wouldn't have mattered if they hadn't saved them," he said, squeezing her hands. "Nick would have found her."

"We really must get you and Neil to a hospital," his mother repeated. "You need a doctor. Heaven knows what's broken."

"Probably easier to tell what isn't," retorted Simon. "But you know, I think I like it. The boy needed to get roughed up a bit. You were way too pretty before — now you look like a true rocker."

"Is she gone?" Emily asked as she peered into Andrew's face.

He nodded.

"Does it hurt?"

"Only when I breathe."

A half-grin, half-cringe graced her face, and she softly kissed him. "I…I was…I…"

He kissed her in return, holding back a painful grimace at what had to have been a split lip.

But the warmth of her lips worked like a drug, and before he knew what was happening, he couldn't stop kissing her, although the tears that coursed down his face stung like hell.

"Andrew! We really must go. You're still bleeding," his mother insisted.

"No, wait," he said after he removed his lips from those he loved. He wiped the tears and sweat from his face with his good arm. "We have to do this, and we have to do this now."

He touched the tin with Nick's ashes and took it up in his hand. "No time like the present. What do you say, old man?"

"But Andrew, you really should get to a doctor," Neil admonished him as his hand cupped his shoulder. Neil looked over Andrew's beaten face and over to Emily and back again. "I'm so sorry for what I did to you — to both of you. I never wanted…I'm so sorry…"

"There's nothing to forgive. Truly."

What Andrew had wanted to say was, *Thank you for fighting against her to try to save me*, but he was too overcome with emotion by the look on Neil's face.

"He was thinking of all the money he'd lose if you died," Margot said finally, breaking the moment. "Only the royalties kept him fighting, right Neil?"

He chuckled warmly and smiled up into the sky in relief. "Yes. I couldn't allow another manager get a hold of you. They'd totally muck up your licensing."

A siren blared and emergency lights flashed from the direction of the highway. Traffic was backed up as far as the eye could see. They had completely forgotten the wreckage they had left in their wake.

"I've got an idea," said Christian. "Hold tight, everybody." He got to his feet and ran toward the road. A distraught Dwayne and his fellow stoners hurried close behind, evidently off to claim rights on the sardine can that was once the Big Doobie.

With a small chuckle, Neil sat down next to Claudia and placed his arm around her, and Margot and Zoey joined Simon and summarily lowered their heads onto his shoulders. They all took a moment, resting for the first time in what seemed like forever as they gazed out at the horizon. The sea appeared calmer, the whitecaps not as threatening, despite the strong wind.

Emily sat still at Andrew's side, their hands linked.

"I hate her," she whispered bitterly. "I know I shouldn't, I know I should try to feel some sympathy for her, but after what she did — to Nick and Nora, to me — and to you, I just can't find any kindness in my heart for her. I hope she's tortured wherever she is now. I hope she rots in — " Her words caught in her throat, and she paused and stared down at their joined hands, squeezing them harder. "Listen to me. I sound just like her, don't I?"

Andrew studied her face, the bruises that blushed along her neck in a faint line of sickening purple, and the gash on her forehead. How she could try to find goodness in the most irredeemable gave him tremendous hope for their future together.

"It's far easier to hate, sweet girl. Most of the time it takes too much courage to love, to believe. It's easier to lock everything away where we can never be hurt. But you're nothing like her, Emily. I can't imagine anyone as good as you being able to understand what lived in her at all."

"And you do?"

"Yes, more than I'm proud of, I'm afraid. She lived with the loss of love for so long it poisoned her. What was left of her after torturing Vandin and experiencing his death, who knows? But her bitterness consumed the last shreds of her. She hated Nick, and she loved him just as strongly—all she wanted was that love returned…" He faltered for words because he'd known that same emptiness…the same longing for a piece of his soul that would complete him. After stumbling and searching in the darkness for so long, how could he not understand the same anguish that had consumed this ghost?

At the very last moment before he fell, a presence greater than anything he had ever known reached out and engulfed him. Was it God? Redemption? He had no idea, but it had broken his heart with its grace—he could only imagine how it had devastated her. He tried to explain, "I think that she could have been saved—at the end. When she felt what lived…beyond this life, it could have saved her. But she was too far gone. When I saw Nora's ashes I knew that it would destroy her if I touched them. So I took a risk and remembered what Nick had said, to seize life. And I did."

Everyone was staring at him now, riveted by the story. He went on to explain all that The Lady in Red had told him about her husband and her hatred of Nora, and how he discovered she could not touch her ashes. Facing Emily again, his voice was calm but resolute. "I can't forgive her, though. Perhaps that tells you what kind of man I am, but I couldn't let her hurt you ever again."

He feared he had said too much, for Emily leaned against him and buried her face in his shoulder; he shushed her and breathed in a deep lungful of the sea air, so grateful to be alive, so grateful to hold her.

"Why do you think she couldn't touch the ashes?" asked Margot.

"I don't know."

Margot looked away from him to Neil for his response, ever the scientist in need of explanations. "Andrew was right," he said quietly. "She was horrified of them—they represented everything she despised. When she was inside of me, I had only glimpses of consciousness, like I was locked in a black room with mere flashes of clarity. But after Andrew threw Nora's ashes at me, I felt her pain—it was torture for her to be near them. They fueled her hatred and bitterness, and her hatred and bitterness consumed her at the end."

They all stared at the satchel that lay on the ground, innocuous in the sharp midday sun.

Emily's fingers brushed against the remains. "Nora loved Nick so much. A love like that just doesn't disappear. It can't. I know these are only her ashes, but there's something of her still there."

Margot smiled at Emily. "I believe you."

"Got it!" They heard Christian cry and turned to see him jogging across the grass bearing a small shovel. Dwayne and the stoners caught up next to him with despondent and crestfallen looks paining their faces. "Found it in the back of the Big Doobie," Christian told the crowd. "Which, um, is now being dragged away for scrap, unfortunately." The stoners turned their heads to the highway and whimpered at the sight. "We better act quick, though," Christian informed Andrew, "'cause the stretcher is coming for you any second, man. I think they heard your mom from all the way out here."

Andrew took the shovel. "You really want to play lead guitar, don't you, mate? Simon, would you care to do the honors?"

Simon stared at both Andrew and the shovel, and for a brief moment Andrew thought he might walk away, that all of this had forced him to a breaking point. Simon looked between Andrew and Emily and made up his mind. He took hold of the shovel and began to dig a hole. When it was done, he was the one who opened the tin and the bag and each of them in turn took a handful of ashes and laid them to rest in the rich earth. The crowd was silent and respectful; whatever wishes were offered were whispered too quietly for other ears to hear. Finally, it came to Emily and Andrew. She took a handful of Nora's ashes; tears trailed silently down her face and fell into the fine gravel where they disappeared like rain.

"I hope you find him, Nora. I hope you have a forever with him." Her voice broke, and the ashes cascaded from her fingers like diamonds.

There was only one handful left from Nick's tin. Andrew took them and placed them down in the earth upon Nora's. He tried to find the words,

words that would thank Nick for showing him just how damn precious it all was.

"You lucky bastard," he finally offered up. "You'll never have to say goodbye."

Emily replaced the earth in the hole herself and patted it down with her hands until she was satisfied. The whole group gathered to help Andrew to his feet. With his arm slung over Emily's shoulders, they left the lovers to have their moment beneath the cawing gulls and the brilliant sun.

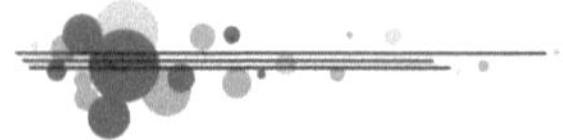

They returned home. The weeks flew by, and before they knew it the day had arrived when they would be leaving San Francisco — Emily to her writer's symposium in Squaw Valley, Andrew to Boston, 2,562 miles apart.

Boston — the first leg of their summer tour. The first official Lost Boys summer tour with their official manager, Neil St. John. Almost overnight their music appeared to be everywhere, which both thrilled and disconcerted them. Neil had engaged a new publicist, which resulted in incredible press. He would be joining them in Boston with Claudia. Apparently the tour would be a family affair, though Neil had the good sense not to subject himself or Claudia to the bus he had chartered for the band.

After Boston, several sold-out venues awaited them in New York City where Emily would join them. Neil had taken the luxury of allowing them to stay there a fortnight, saying they had earned a vacation that didn't involve bodily injury or demonic possession. If they were going to live on the road this summer, they were going to enjoy it.

So it was with mixed emotions that Andrew waited for Emily at the bar in the Huntington Hotel downtown. She had requested this locale, which didn't surprise him — it was old and odd and gorgeous. Dark paneled and intimate, it was the one place where he hadn't been aware of people's eyes on him lately, probably because by walking in the brass-handled doors, he had lowered the median age of the people around him to sixty. The music bore testament to this, as Sinatra was going all *Bewitched, Bothered and Bewildered.*

He ordered them two martinis. After they arrived, he took several minutes to study the rim of the glass before he toasted quietly.

"To you, Nick, wherever you are."

There had been no trace of Nick and Nora since they had returned from Mendocino. Even though Emily took great pains to hide it, he knew she was disappointed. Somehow she thought that the ghosts would make one more appearance, to interrupt dinner or appear at the piano in the attic in the quiet moments when Emily and he lay nestled on the couch, her laptop glowing in the darkness on the floor while his guitar lay discarded nearby after a grueling workout of his arm.

She would repeat her firm belief that Nick and Nora were happy, and weren't they glad to finally have some peace and quiet, or as much peace and quiet cohabitating with Simon, Margot, Zoey, and Christian would allow. Their living quarters had turned into some sort of two-storied commune centering around who would make breakfast and which pantry contained the wine.

Still, he could see her stare out the windows to the roof garden with a distant look on her face, or catch her holding open her closet door longer than necessary, hoping to hear a whisper.

Whispers did rustle the air around him as she entered the bar looking like Ingrid Bergman ready to catch her plane; all that was missing were the letters of transit and a pair of gloves. He stood and waved, rocked by her and the thought that he had only hours left to hold her. She beamed and sailed across the room and kissed him, bringing the fresh warm air in from the street with her.

"You got started without me."

"Not much. I gave you my olives, by the way. Here let me take that… it's blocking your face and makes kissing you a nightmare." She swept off her hat with a chuckle, handing it over. He motioned to the waiter for two more, and they sat down, full of the nervous energy of partings and beginnings.

"Isn't this the best?" she said, sipping her martini, her eyes sweeping across the walnut paneling and old chandeliers. "I bet they came here, you know."

"I bet they did." They toasted, but Emily looked everywhere except at him.

"Zoey is tearing apart the house—be thankful you're here. I'm not sure how much storage you have in the bus, but you might have to rent another one for the art supplies alone. Oh, and Dwayne and his friends stopped by. They wanted to thank Neil for the new van. That was incredibly sweet of him, but I think they miss their old one. It's just the not the same without the blue shag carpeting." She prattled on and on, still not meeting his eyes.

"And Margot, she's going to try to make the shows in New York. She claims she'll be there for work. Simon tried to look duly unimpressed."

"Good for him. So you're driving up to the symposium at noon tomorrow, yes? And you get there at four?"

"And I'll wear my seatbelt and obey the speed limit."

Why was everything so awkward? Perhaps because they'd had barely a minute alone these past weeks. The time they did have had been hampered by his stitches and sling—which he had shed that morning in a fit of manic glee. And now with only a night left, unfettered and deeply in love, he craved two things: time and privacy—one of which he could never control, the other he had every desire to obtain.

With that thought in mind, he reached into the pocket of his jacket to retrieve the room key when the waiter approached their table bearing a bottle of champagne and two elaborate flutes.

Emily looked on in delight as he popped the cork. "Andrew, it's perfect. You shouldn't have done this."

"I didn't."

"Compliments of a friend," the waiter informed them dryly, which immediately piqued their curiosity. "Instructions were left at the bar with this note addressed to you, Mr. Hayes." He handed him an expensive looking envelope.

Andrew nodded and quickly opened it.

A simple but elegant card lay inside, rimmed in gold and engraved with the monogram N.C. Emily leaned over, enrapt, and they read together. The first paragraph was penned in a fast scrawl.

Kid, I always knew you had it in you. Damn proud of you. Hope not to see you soon, but we may visit when in town.

It was signed simply: *Nick*

Underneath that in a distinctly feminine flourish was one word. Emily whispered it out loud:

Live.

It was followed by a beautiful *N*. And a post script:

The flutes are yours. use them—often.

Emily grinned through her tears, reading the card over and over and scanning the room for any signs of the famous couple.

"Andrew, oh Andrew, they found each other…they're together."

They finished the whole bottle, chatting madly now, all hands and smiles and laughter. It was the way they had always been with each other and the way they would always be. It wasn't until he laid the hotel key down on the table that her words ceased and her eyes met his.

Without a sound they walked hand and hand to the elevator.

"For the next twelve hours you're not allowed to leave our bed, do you understand? You're mine. My concubine, my slave, my mistress…my wife."

His body pressed the length of hers against the silk wallpaper as he kissed her hungrily, waiting for the wrought iron doors of the elevator to part. The bell chimed, and he pulled her inside, slamming the button to their floor, his mouth never leaving hers. He had wondered if the madness that he felt for her, that blind need to claim her, would subside now that life lay out ahead of them. Now that they had found peace. He had never been more wrong.

Thankfully, the doors opened to a vacant hallway. Only a few feet more. He fumbled with the key, his hands fisting in her hair, her breaths answering his, when he heard the clearing of a throat from the far end of the hall. It was a tiny, scared, but distinctly male cough.

They swung their heads to the side to see who it was—Emily gasped. There, glowing near a potted palm, hovered a short, wiry looking apparition. He wore a derby, coattails, and baggy pants and rocked back and forth on his spats in distress.

"Are you Andrew and Emily Chamberlain?"

"Pardon?" Andrew answered in disbelief.

"Herschel, Herschel's the name," the ghost replied hastily in a thick Brooklyn accent, his hands wringing together. "You two are famous, don't ya know. Everyone's going on about how you helped Nick and Nora with their little problem, and I was wondering…well, you said you might be heading to New York City soon, and I've got this issue with some ah… former business associates there." His words tumbled over each other as his voice rose to a high neurotic pitch.

"Issue?" Andrew repeated before he realized what he was doing. It was enough to let loose the flood gates.

"They think I took something that's theirs, and they, well, they want it back! I didn't take it, I swear. But they won't listen to me—they're gonna sic their ghouls after me! You have to help."

"But…you're already dead, what's the worst they can do?" Andrew regretted the words the moment they left his lips.

Herschel emitted a great tortured wail. "I didn't do it! I didn't take it." He wrung his coattails in anguish. "You've gotta help me!"

Andrew threw open their hotel room door and grasped Emily by the hand. He'd had enough of ghosts in need to last for several lifetimes.

Emily, however, didn't budge.

"Sweet girl?"

She looked at him with those eyes, those large, trouble-brewing eyes.

"But we'll be in New York soon, Andrew."

He scooped her up in his arms and slammed the door shut with his foot. With a determined stride he carried her past the fireplace and into the bedroom. It was lit only by the city lights, casting her surprised face in shadows. He tossed her down on the bed.

"We'll have two weeks. We could help." She wasn't going to let this lie, he could tell.

He didn't say a word—he merely stared at her.

"You look like her, you know," he finally said, kneeling in front of her so that her back was trapped against the carved mahogany headboard.

"Like who?"

"Nora. Here, at the tip of your chin." His lips kissed there. "And here, at the curl of your smile." His lips kissed there too, as his hands rose to undo her buttons and feel the warmth of her skin.

"So is that a yes? Please, Andrew, we really should help him."

She gasped suddenly as he pushed her down onto her back, her wrists pinioned and her body helpless. Then laughter filled the darkness until his mouth trailed softly down her neck and reached her breast, a breath away from her heart.

They said no more on the subject that night, although hopes and dreams and fantasies were cried and shared between them.

When the morning sun drifted over their naked bodies, and the sound of housekeeping and breakfast trolleys laden with aromas of fresh beginnings lumbered down the hall, it was then, and only then, that he whispered the answer in her ear.

THE END

ACKNOWLEDGMENTS

The Omnific Publishing Team including Elizabeth Harper, CJ Creel, Kimberly Myers and Micha Stone, for their patience, enthusiasm and talent. Lucy O'Dwyer, for her Gaelic know-how and photographic skills. Laura Springer, for her guidance with San Francisco real estate. Steven Kacsmar, for his music expertise. Dave Conroy for his deft hand at swearing. The Muselets who supported this story from the beginning. Mom and Dad, for raising me with love and a love of their era. Peter for doing the heavy lifting, and Matthew and Hannah for sharing their mother's lap with a computer. Finally, to Natalie whose friendship, encouragement and tireless editing skills made this story possible. Thank you all!

*Certain locations mentioned in this book are real,
others imaginary, and still others are a combination of the two.*

A writer and recovering CPA, Sarah M. Glover lives in San Francisco in an old house with a brood of people—some taller, some shorter, all of whom she adores. As a child, she often hid under the blankets with a dog-eared copy of *The Norton Anthology of English Literature*, obsessing over the men in the sepia squares.

Sarah's previous work includes contributions to various anthologies, personal essays for both Public Radio and several national magazines, and musical comedies written to benefit San Francisco charities. *Grave Refrain* is her first novel.

You can follow her at: www.SarahMGlover.com

⟵ ⟶ Romantic Suspense ⟵ ⟶

Whirlwind by Robin DeJarnett

The CONduct Series: With Good Behavior and Bad Behavior by Jennifer Lane

⟵ ⟶ Young Adult ⟵ ⟶

Shades of Atlantis and Ember by Carol Oates

Breaking Point by Jess Bowen

Life, Liberty, and Pursuit by Susan Kaye Quinn

Embrace by Cherie Colyer

Destiny's Fire by Trisha Wolfe

⟵ ⟶ Anthologies ⟵ ⟶

A Valentine Anthology including short stories by Alice Clayton, Jennifer DeLucy, Nicki Elson, Jessica McQuinn, Victoria Michaels, and Alison Oburia

Summer Lovin' Anthology: Summer Breeze including short stories by Hannah Downing, Nicki Elson, Sarah M. Glover, Jennifer Lane, Killian McRae, Carol Oates, and Susan Kaye Quinn

Summer Lovin' Anthology: Heat Wave including short stories by Kasi Alexander, Debra Anastasia, Robin DeJarnett, Jessica McQuinn, Lisa Sanchez, and BJ Thornton

⟵ ⟶ Alternative Romance ⟵ ⟶

Becoming sage by Kasi Alexander